客語及少數族群
語言政策

周錦宏 王保鍵 蔡芬芳 主編

目錄

v 主任委員序
　　客家委員會主任委員　楊長鎮

vii 校長序
　　國立中央大學校長　周景揚

ix 院長序
　　國立中央大學客家學院院長　周錦宏

001 導論　從語言傷痕到語言復振：客語及少數族群語言保障
　　周錦宏、王保鍵、蔡芬芳

■ 2018 臺灣客語及少數族群語言復振國際研討會　經驗實錄

017 【英國威爾斯語 Welsh】
　　威爾斯語言監察使的角色
　　The Role of the Welsh Language Commissioner
　　英國威爾斯語言監察使 Meri Huws 女士
　　Mrs. Meri Huws, Welsh Language Commissioner

045 【德國索勃語 Sorbian】
　　從小開始的雙語教育
　　Being Bilingual from Childhood
　　索勃學校協會主席 Ludmila Budar 女士
　　Ms. Ludmila Budar, Chairperson of the Sorbian School Association

093 【比利時荷蘭語 Dutch】
　　荷蘭語在比利時的政治現況：真實與想像歷史
　　The Real and Imagined History of the Status of the Dutch Language in Belgium
　　國立政治大學語言學研究所 戴智偉副教授兼所長
　　Associate Professor Rik De Busser, Chairperson of Graduate Institute of
　　Linguistics, National Chengchi University

123 【薩米語 Sami】

薩米語言教育之經驗與實踐

Experiences and Practices in Sámi Language Education

挪威薩米大學 Pigga Keskitalo 教授

Associate Professor Pigga Keskitalo, Sámi University, Norway

143 【日本阿伊努語 Ainu】

阿伊努語現況與日本政府的阿伊努族政策

Situation of Ainu Language and the Ainu Policy of Japanese Government

北海道大學阿伊努‧原住民研究中心丹菊逸治副教授

Associate Professor Itsuji Tangiku, Center for Ainu and Indigenous Studies

Arctic Research Center

165 【西班牙加泰隆尼亞語 Catalan】

語言復振：以加泰隆尼亞為例

The Revitalization of Languages: the Catalan Case

加泰隆尼亞區語言使用促進服務負責人 Carles de Rosselló 先生

Mr. Carles de Rosselló, Servei de Foment de l'Ús, Consorci per a la Normalització

Lingüística/ Use Promotion Service of Consortium for Linguistic Normalization

191 【法國布列塔尼語 Breton】

布列塔尼語：從復振到重新本地語化

Breton : From Revitalisation to Revernacularization

法國布列塔尼大區雷恩大學 Stefan Moal 教授

Professor Stefan Moal, University of Rennes, Brittany, France

■ **2021 臺灣客語及少數族群語言政策國際研討會　經驗實錄**

239 【歐洲少數族群語言現代化及語言聲望重建】

歐洲語言平等網絡及區域性語言在歐洲之復振及復甦

ELEN and Territorial Language Revitalisation and Recovery in Europe

歐洲語言平等網絡秘書長 Davyth Hicks 博士

Dr. Davyth Hicks, Secretary-General of European Language Equality Network:

ELEN

271 【紐西蘭毛利語 Maori】

TŌKU REO, TŌKU OHOOH ：**我的語言是我的覺醒；我的語言是我的靈魂之窗**

TŌKU REO, TŌKU OHOOHO: My Language Is My Awakening, My Language Is the Window to My Soul

紐西蘭毛利電視臺首席執行長 Shane Taurima 先生

Mr. Shane Taurima, Chief Executive of Māori Television

289 【英國威爾斯語 Welsh】

威爾斯 2050 計畫與威爾斯語的代間傳遞

Prosiect 2050 and Intergenerational Transmission of Welsh

威爾斯語言部門領導人 Jeremy Evas 博士

Dr. Jeremy Evas, Head of Prosiect 2050

▪ 少數族群語言發展法律條文（中文版）

347 加拿大魁北克法語憲章

367 西班牙加泰隆尼亞語言法

379 威爾斯語 2050 計畫

425 歐洲區域或少數民族語言憲章

薩米語法律

433 ．芬蘭

439 ．挪威

445 ．瑞典

索勃語法律

447 ．勃蘭登堡邦

453 ．薩克森邦

475 日本阿伊努語法律

▪ 附錄　研討會精彩相片錦集

487 2018 臺灣客語及少數族群語言復振國際研討會

491 2021 臺灣客語及少數族群語言政策國際研討會

主任委員序

　　臺灣客家族群先因威權政體統治之迫害，又因居人口之少數而致語言受文化市場之排擠成為棄兒，讓客家族群出現「隱形化」之擔憂；尤其在面對「國語」獨大的母語傷痕，造成客家族群文化活力萎縮、身分認同流失以及參與公共事務式微等危機。儘管前方道路挑戰重重，我們仍不畏險阻，積極推動客語復振相關措施，讓大家尋回對母語的自我認同。本會擬具的《客語發展法》草案，就是為了落實客語為客庄通行語及教學語言之目標，營造客語友善使用環境，讓客語融入日常生活，成為復振客語的基石。

　　2018年適逢「還我母語運動三十周年」，為促進國內外語言推動工作者的廣泛交流，本會補助國立中央大學於12月15、16日召開「客語及少數族群語言復振國際研討會」，邀請國際推動語言復振卓有成效的機構代表來臺分享經驗。嗣於2021年12月4日舉辦「臺灣客語及少數族群語言政策國際研討會」，持續研討客語復振相關措施，拓展客語國際化鏈結網絡，並促成全球語言多樣化的夥伴關係。國立中央大學精心收錄兩屆研討會國外學者專家為復振少數族群語言的心血結晶，除了作為臺灣客語日後政策上的借鏡外，更與國際語言組織建立合作關係之介面。本書同時彙編多國少數族群語言發展的相關法律，可作為各界人士參考的工具書。

　　客語的復興是臺灣轉型正義的一環，本會期望能在目前既有的基礎上，持續推動臺灣客語之回歸與介入主流，並與少數族群語言在國家層次的多向對話交流，一方面展現臺灣多年來復振客語之重要成果，彰顯臺灣捍衛及尊重少數族群語言權利的自由民主作為；另一方面與志同道合的國際夥伴，建構合作網絡的平臺，共同促進與保護少數群體語言的權利、平等及多樣性。

　　讓我們為打造一個多語且互相尊重的新年代，共下打拼。

客家委員會主任委員

楊長鎮

2022.12

校長序

　　語言是社會的根本，承載世代傳承的文化與脈絡。但在變化快速的當代社會中，面對強勢文化的壓迫與同化，語言流失與文化斷層的情形愈發嚴重。客語也在這樣的困境之下，面臨保存與傳承的重大危機。有鑒於推動客語復振工作刻不容緩，本校在 2003 年 8 月創立了全球首創的客家學院，以人文社會科學方法進行客家語言、社會文化、政治經濟等研究，並推廣客家語言文化相關活動，期盼帶動國內外客家學術研究風氣，以及正視推動客家事務的重要性。

　　在此特別感謝客家委員會，在 2018 年、2021 年補助本校客家學院舉辦臺灣客語及國際少數族群語言發展的國際研討會，邀請國內外學者專家就少數族群語言保存與復振的經驗，進行分享與交流，俾利我國政府推動客語政策之參考，實屬獲益良多。尤其是 2018 年研討會後，該次會議專題演講主講人，時任英國威爾斯語委員會主席的 Meri Huws 女士牽線之下，本校客家學院周錦宏院長與王保鍵老師在 2019 年 6 月，陪同客委會楊長鎮主委至加拿大安大略省參加國際語言官署協會（International association of language commissioners）第 6 屆年會，進而促成客家與國際組織建立夥伴網絡，更是難能可貴。

　　這兩次的國際研討會本人皆到場致意，在場所有與會者堅定的神情、與努力不懈的身影，已經深深刻印在我的心中，更想藉著本書出版撰序之機會，對所有學者專家及實務工作者等人士致上我的敬意。國立中央大學所在中壢區是客委會公布的「客家文化重點發展區」，客家語言文化傳承是本校必須承擔的大學社會責任。本校將持續協助客委會推動各項客家事務，扮演客委會的「智庫」角色，匯聚眾人智慧及心力，共同創建美好的客家。

國立中央大學校長

周景揚

院長序

　　當前臺灣語言的政策，在「2030 雙語國家政策」與「國家語言政策」交錯下，出現資源競逐和實作排擠等效應。惟英語習得具有高度的經濟性、工具性，相對於族群母語（國家語言）的復振與傳承，則顯得弱勢化、邊緣化，進而影響族群文化的存續。而客家人和原住民同為臺灣少數族群，更讓客語和原住民族語在語言近用環境上，面臨非常嚴峻的挑戰。

　　國立中央大學客家學院不但承襲長期所積累客語研究的厚實基礎，並在客家社會文化、政治政策、產業經濟和海外客家等領域，有相當不錯的學術表現。然為擴大客家研究視野，中大客院以「客家及其週邊族群」的角度，關懷臺灣客語及其他少數族群語言之發展，期透過國內外少數族群語言政策規劃與實作經驗的交流和討論，讓客語、客家事務、客家學院與世界接軌。

　　為實現上開理念，2018 年年底適逢客家運動 30 週年，我們以「語言復振」為議題，邀請英國威爾斯語、德國索勃語、芬蘭薩米語、西班牙加泰隆尼亞語、法國布列塔尼語、比利時荷蘭語、日本阿伊努語及國內客語、原住民族語、閩南語等語言研究學者和實務專家，來臺灣交流與對話。2021 年年底，因受 COVID-19 疫情的影響，我們則改採視訊和實體會議方式，邀請歐洲語言平等網絡秘書長、2050 威爾斯語計畫主持人、紐西蘭毛利電視臺執行官及國內客語和原住民族語等機構負責人員，一同討論各國「地方通行語政策」推展的情況。而本書蒐錄的內容即這兩次研討會國外學者專家所分享經驗，再加上歐美少數族群語言法律的中譯本，一方面作為客語發展之借鏡，另一方面提供有興趣少數族群語言研究者之參考。

　　本書的出版，要感謝客家委員會前主任委員李永得先生（現任文化部部長）及現任楊長鎮主任委員的大力支持，同時也要感謝兩次研討會參與發表、與談的先進們，才得以讓研討會和專書出版順利完成。又本院王保鍵老師、蔡芬芳老師、湯晏甄老師、蕭宇佳同學、陳郁婷同學辛苦的籌畫與執行，在此一併致上謝忱。

國立中央大學客家學院院長

周錦宏

導論
從語言傷痕到語言復振：客語及少數族群語言保障

周錦宏、王保鍵、蔡芬芳

檢視臺灣語言政策的發展，多會討論到威權統治時期，政府以《教育部國語推行委員會組織條例》、《加強推行國語計畫實施辦法》等所實施的國語（華語）運動，[1] 在學校使用本土語言被處罰的記憶。意即，依 1966 年臺灣省政府頒布「加強推行國語計畫實施辦法」規定，各級學校師生必須隨時隨地使用國語；學生違犯者依獎懲辦法處理（陳美如，2009：304）；學生在學校講方言會被處罰，如罰錢、掛牌子、罰站（陳淑華，2009）。而類似的例子，也曾發生在西方國家，如法國的布列塔尼語（Breton），法國教育部禁止學校使用布列塔尼語，學校張貼「不得隨地吐痰或使用布列塔尼語」（no spitting on the ground or speaking Breton）標示（Hooper，2011）。又如 19 世紀的英國威爾斯，為促使學生使用英語，並禁止學生使用威爾斯語，也實施在學生身上掛上禁說威爾斯語（Welsh Not ／ Welsh Stick）牌子之作法（如下圖）。就此而言，非僅臺灣，各國少數群體語言，都曾遭受過統治者的語言政策之傷害。

---

1 1945 年 6 月 9 日公布《教育部國語推行委員會組織條例》。臺灣省行政長官公署教育廳為推行標準國語（華語），於 1946 年 4 月 2 日訂頒《臺灣省國語推行委員會組織規程》，由國府教育部國語推行委員會常務委員魏建功來臺出任主任委員，並提出「臺灣省國語運動綱領」（黃英哲，2005）。1947 年 4 月 22 日行政院會決議，臺灣省行政長官公署改制為臺灣省政府。1950 年 5 月 27 日臺灣省政府教育廳代電發布「本省非常時期教育綱領實施辦法有關各級學校及各社教機關應行注意遵辦暨應加強推動事項」指示，各級學校及各社教機關應加強推行國語運動。

圖片來源：National Museum Wales（此圖已獲授權使用）

（https://www.bbc.co.uk/ahistoryoftheworld/objects/j35VCjYcS0CC3RGzvkLb-Q）

　　為翻轉少數群體語言的不利地位，各國少數群體語言使用者，嘗試透過社會運動方式，喚醒少數群體語言使用者的自我意識，爭取社會輿論的支持。例如，北歐的薩米原住民族（indigenous Sámi）所推動薩米運動，於 1917 年 2 月 6 日集結了挪威及瑞典的薩米人，在挪威 Trondhjem 召開首次薩米大會（Sámi congress），共同討論薩米族的發展策略（European Digital Treasures，2021），對政府反省過往行政作為，及矯正過往對薩米族的傷害，有著重要貢獻。我國「全國客家日」由「天穿日」改定為「1228 還我母語運動日」，亦參考薩米日（Sámi National Day）的經驗。[2]

　　臺灣少數族群的語言政策之形成與發展，在全球第三波民主化大環境下，1980年代民間社會力解放，發生原住民族運動、客家運動，觸發族群議題進入公共領域。伴隨地方選舉（1994 年臺北市長選舉）、中央選舉（2000 年總統副總統選舉）的競爭性，在族群保障及發展之制度性機制上，逐漸發展出：（1）族群性專責機

2　立法院內政委員會於《客家基本法修正草案》審查完竣時，同時做出一項附帶決議，並於院會三讀時，無異議，通過。附帶決議為：有鑑於天穿日訂為全國客家日爭議未決，等同無法透過全國客家日訂定，以成功凝聚全國客家族群意識，參北歐原住民薩米族係以 1917 年 2 月 6 日，薩米婦女 Elsa Laula Renberg，所召開的全球第一屆「薩米大會」時間作為全球薩米日的訂定，成功凝聚族群與文化意識，並迫使挪威、瑞典等北歐各國重新反省過去對薩米的迫害歷史，積極尋求彌補過去邊緣化與迫害的影響；故主管機關於本基本法通過後，應於六個月內，檢討當前全國客家日推動的爭議，並召開各地公聽會進行重新訂定的社會溝通，並應將 12 月 28 日還我母語運動日、6 月 14 日客委會成立日列入主要討論的選項（立法院公報第 107 卷第 9 期，頁 313）。

關：設置客家委員會、原住民族委員會，分別推動客家人、原住民之族群事務。（2）族群性基本法：以《客家基本法》、《原住民族基本法》，建構客家族群、原住民（族）之權利保障及發展框架。（3）族群性行政區域：以原住民族地區、客家文化重點發展區，作為主要政策推動場域。（4）族群事務公務人員考試：以公務人員特種考試原住民族考試、公務人員高等考試三級考試暨普通考試「客家事務行政」類科，並分發至族群專責機關、族群行政區域內機關、涉及族群事務等機關。（5）國家語言：以《客家基本法》、《原住民族語言發展法》明文規定，客語、原住民族語為國家語言，並為區域通行語（王保鍵，2022：142-143）。以下僅就臺灣語言政策發展、客語及原住民族語言權利，及借鏡國外少數群體語言保障機制的必要性等，進行討論。

壹、臺灣語言政策之發展

　　語言之功能，包含認知、工具、整合、文化等面向（Willyarto et al.，2021：678）；[3] 各個國家，一般以語言政策進行政治社會化，以形塑國民的國家認同感。語言政策及規劃（language policy and planning）關注國家以政策機制介入語言事務，以地位規劃、語型規劃、教學規劃、聲望規劃等手段，發展單一或多種語言。

　　二次世界大戰結束，國民政府治理臺灣，積極推動國語（華語）運動，以建構國族認同，但也對閩南語、客語、原住民族語、馬祖語等各「固有族群」語言造成傷痕，致使各族群母語（本土語言）今日均面臨語言傳承危機。至1970年代中期，發軔於南歐的第三波民主化浪潮，驅動了臺灣民主轉型，在民主進步黨成立（1986年）、解除戒嚴（1987年）、促使第一屆資深中央民意代表退職的司法院第261號解釋（1990年）、廢止《動員戡亂時期臨時條款》（1991年）之民主化進程下，民間社會力解放，臺灣原住民族運動、臺灣客家運動，促使族群事務成為公共政策重要面向，族群母語復振成為重要的政策議題，並驅動國家語言政策的規劃與制定。

　　事實上，臺灣在語言政策及規劃上，早於1983年間，教育部便已開始研擬《語文法（草案）》，當時由於各界反應不一，遂未繼續研訂；嗣後，教育部參酌行政院

3　基本上，語言具有溝通功能、經濟功能（獲得工作與資本的工具）、情感功能、社會表徵功能、歷史與文化功能（文化的載體，反映文化與歷史）、藝術與娛樂功能（以該語言所創作的文學、藝術等豐富的文化資產）、認知與思維功能、個人認同與集體認同功能（想像的共同體）等，是建構社會作為一個共同體的核心要素（臺灣語文學會，2022）。

客家委員會（現為客家委員會）的《語言公平法（草案）》、行政院原住民族委員會（現為原住民族委員會）的《原住民族語言發展法（草案）》、中央研究院語言學研究所籌備處（現為語言學研究所）的《語言文字基本法（草案）》後，擬具《語言平等法（草案）》；惟嗣因考量《語言平等法（草案）》制定事宜，涉及文化保存與傳承事宜，經行政院協調後，於 2003 年 3 月以臺語字第 0920042644 號函，將《語言平等法（草案）》研議及制定等事項，移由行政院文化建設委員會（現為文化部）主責，經該會重新擬具《國家語言發展法（草案）》，報請行政院審議後，於 2007 年 5 月 25 日由行政院以院臺教字第 0960086179 號函送立法院審議，但因未於立法院第 6 屆會期審議完成，再於立法院第 7 屆會期，重新由行政院於 2008 年 2 月 1 日以院臺文字第 0970003868 號函送立法院審議，惟仍未完成立法程序。[4]

　　2000 年《大眾運輸工具播音語言平等保障法》、2017 年《原住民族語言發展法》、2018 年《客家基本法》、2019 年《國家語言發展法》等語言法律，打造了臺灣語言發展的制度性機制，並定「臺灣各固有族群使用之自然語言」為「國家語言」，建構國家語言之平等權，及語言教育、接近使用公共服務等相關語言權利，並可視族群聚集之需求，指定特定國家語言為區域通行語。上開四部語言法律，以及審議中的《客家語言發展法（草案）》，不但增強政府對於語言復振強度與廣度，而且有助於形塑族群集體權、族群成員個人語言權利，是為臺灣語言政策及規劃重要工具。

貳、臺灣少數族群語言權利：原住民族語、客語

　　認識或解讀當代臺灣社會，「族群」為不可或缺的路徑。臺灣歷經明朝鄭成功、清朝、日本、國民政府的治理，各個統治主體以其公權力措施，進行人群分類，政府施行的人群分類標準，透過人口調查及戶籍登記機制，轉化為個人身分確立及權利保障制度，一方面承認既存的族群之分，一方面創設新的族群之別（王保鍵，2018：13）。[5] 當代臺灣社會，普遍接受閩南人、客家人、原住民、外省人等

4　資料來源：文化部 2014 年 2 月 24 日文源字第 1033004215 號函。
5　例如，《原住民身分法》及《客家基本法》對原住民及客家人身分之規範，係以國家法律承認數世紀以來的既存族群真實狀態；惟《原住民身分法》將清領時期的「生番」（日本統治臺灣時期改稱「生蕃」、「高砂族」），劃分為「平地原住民」及「山地原住民」，則係以國家法律創設新的族群分類。而一般所稱的「新住民」（婚姻移民），則因適用《國籍法》及《臺灣地區與大陸地區人民關係條例》之差異，而分成「外籍配偶」與「大陸地區配偶」，在國家法律所創設的人群分類下，賦予不同的權利義務（王保鍵，2018：13）。

四大族群的論述，並試圖將新住民建構為第五大族群。依聯合國對於少數群體的界定，客家人、原住民、外省人為少數族群。[6]

一、原住民族語

就憲法規範架構而言，原住民權利保障有明確的法源，包含：（1）原住民之個人權，如《原住民族工作權保障法》[7]；（2）原住民族之集體權，如《原住民族傳統智慧創作保護條例》。在法律層次，為保障原住民族基本權利，促進原住民族生存發展，建立共存共榮之族群關係，2005 年公布《原住民族基本法》。依《原住民族基本法》第 9 條第 3 項規定，原住民族語言發展，另以法律定之。為實現歷史正義，促進原住民族語言之保存與發展，保障原住民族語言之使用及傳承，依《憲法增修條文》第 10 條第 11 項及《原住民族基本法》第 9 條第 3 項規定，於 2017 年 6 月 14 日公布《原住民族語言發展法》。

為建構原住民族語言為國家語言之制度保障機制，制定《原住民族語言發展法》；有關本法之框架，整理如下表。

表 1：《原住民族語言發展法》架構

構面	主軸	規範
總則性規定	名詞定義	原住民族語言、原住民族文字、原住民族語言能力、原住民族地方通行語。
語言地位	國家語言	原住民族語為國家語言。

6　依聯合國大會 2019 年 7 月 15 日審議少數群體問題特別報告員報告（Report of the Special Rapporteur on Minority Issues）對少數群體（minorities）之定義為：「族群、宗教、語言少數群體（ethnic, religious or linguistic minority），係指在一國全部領土內人數未達總人口一半之任何群體，其成員在文化、宗教、語言等方面具有共同特徵，或此類特徵之任何組合（A/74/160，段 59）。」以上開定義來看，臺灣的閩南人為多數族群，客家人、原住民、外省人等為少數族群。

7　依《原住民族基本法》第 2 條規定，「原住民族」，係指既存於臺灣而為國家管轄內之傳統民族；「原住民」，係指原住民族之個人。《原住民族工作權保障法》之法律名稱雖以「原住民族」為名，但本法第 2 條明定「本法之保障對象為具有原住民身分者」，實屬個人權之保障。

構面	主軸	規範
語言權利	接近使用公共服務	政府機關（構）處理行政、立法事務及司法程序時，原住民得以其原住民族語言陳述意見，各該政府機關（構）應聘請通譯傳譯之。
	嬰幼兒族語學習權利	中央主管機關、中央教育主管機關、中央衛生福利主管機關及直轄市、縣（市）主管機關，應提供原住民嬰幼兒學習原住民族語言之機會。
	學習與教學語言	學校應依十二年國民基本教育本土語文課程綱要規定，提供原住民族語言課程，以因應原住民學生修習需要，並鼓勵以原住民族語言進行教學。
語言推廣	族語推廣人員	直轄市、縣（市）政府、原住民族地區及原住民人口1,500人以上非原住民族地區之鄉（鎮、市、區）公所，設置族語推廣人員，以專職方式協助學校、部落、社區推動族語傳習、保存及推廣工作，全面營造族語生活環境。[8]
	族語推動組織	補助專案人力，並提供辦公處所租賃、辦公設備添置及業務推動經費，協助各族設立族語學習、使用推廣、師資培育、教材編輯及其他具族群特色之族語復振工作等推廣組織。
	公告及設置地方通行語標示	原住民族地區之政府機關（構）、學校及公營事業機構，應設置地方通行語之標示。於原住民族地區內之山川、古蹟、部落、街道及公共設施，政府各該管理機關應設置地方通行語及傳統名稱之標示。
	公文雙語書寫	原住民族地區之政府機關（構）、學校及公營事業機構，得以地方通行語書寫公文書。
	廣播電視節目及課程	政府捐助之原住民族電視及廣播機構，應製作原住民族語言節目及語言學習課程，並出版原住民族語言出版品。

8　族語推廣人員應設置152人，每月薪資3萬6,000元起。

構面	主軸	規範
語言傳習	聘用專職族語老師	發布《高級中等以下學校原住民族語老師資格及聘用辦法》，自 2018 學年度開始，補助各縣市政府聘用專職原住民族語老師（原為教學支援人員），鼓勵更多族人願意投入族語教學工作。
	開辦原住民族語言學習中心	開辦臺北（國立臺灣師範大學）、新竹（國立清華大學）、臺中（國立臺中教育大學）、南投（國立暨南國際大學）、屏東（國立屏東大學）、臺東（國立臺東大學）、花蓮（國立東華大學）等七所原住民族語言學習中心。
	補助大專院校開設族語課程	鼓勵各大專校院開設原住民族語言課程，及設立與原住民族語言相關之院、系、所、科或學位學程，以培育原住民族語言人才。
語言保存	搶救原住民族瀕危語言	推動「原住民族瀕危語言搶救計畫」，採取「師徒制」族語學習，聘請各瀕危語別具族語能力者擔任族語「傳承師傅」，採一對一或一對二方式，與「學習徒弟」。[9]
	語言新詞及語言資料庫	中央主管機關應會商原住民族各族研訂原住民族語言新詞；並應編纂原住民族語言詞典，建置原住民族語言資料庫，積極保存原住民族語料。
語言研究	語言能力及使用狀況之調查	中央主管機關應定期辦理原住民族語言能力及使用狀況之調查，並公布調查結果。
	成立基金會	成立財團法人原住民族語言研究發展基金會。
	獎補助	中央主管機關應補助與獎勵原住民族語言保存及發展研究工作。

資料來源：王保鍵，2022：235-237。

二、客語

　　日本統領臺灣、國民政府治臺初期，客家人的「族群性」尚不明顯。至 1980 年代，《客家風雲雜誌》的發行（1987 年）及「還我母語大遊行」（1988 年），啟動臺灣客家運動，促使客家議題公共化，並於 2001 年設立「行政院客家委員會」（自 2012 年改制為客家委員會）。

9　專職「傳承師」薪資 3 萬 6,000 元及「學習員」薪資 3 萬元。

在憲法層次，《憲法增修條文》並無明文保障規定，係援引《憲法增修條文》第10條第11項前段「國家肯定多元文化」之規定，如《客家基本法》第1條。事實上，2010年制定《客家基本法》，成為當代客家發展的制度性引擎，不但在法律層次定義客語、客家族群（集體）、客家人（個人）等，而且以諸多制度安排，推動客家語言、文化、產業等客家政策。嗣後，2018年修正《客家基本法》，進一步賦予客家族群成員（客家人）個人權，如本法第3條平等權（第1項）、語言學習及使用權（第2項）等。又為落實客語之國家語言地位，保障人民使用客語之權利，客家委員會已依《客家基本法》第3條第3項規定，研擬《客家語言發展法草案》。

表2：《客家基本法》關於客語之規範

構面	主軸	規範
總則性規定	名詞定義	客家人、客家族群、客語、客家人口、客家事務（本法第2條）。
語言地位	國家語言	客語為國家語言之一（本法第3條第1項前段）。
	語言平等	客語與各族群語言平等（本法第3條第1項後段）。
語言權利	學習與教學語言	1. 人民以客語作為學習語言權利（本法第3條第2項）。 2. 政府應輔導客家文化重點發展區之學前與國民基本教育之學校及幼兒園，參酌當地使用國家語言情形，因地制宜實施以客語為教學語言之計畫；並獎勵非客家文化重點發展區之學校、幼兒園與各大專校院推動辦理之（本法第12條第1項）。 3. 客語為通行語實施辦法第9條。 4. 推動客語教學語言獎勵辦法。[10] 5. 客語沉浸式教學推動實施計畫案。[11] 6. 客家委員會推動客語生活學校補助作業要點。[12]

---

10 依《推動客語教學語言獎勵辦法》第2條規定，客語教學語言，係指於公私立各級學校（含國民小學、國民中學、高級中等學校、大專校院及特殊教育學校）及幼兒園以客語為教學及校園生活互動之語言。

11 依《客語沉浸式教學推動實施計畫案》伍之二規定，以客語作為教學語言，試辦國民中、小學以客語進行科目課程、幼兒園 以客語融入教保活動課程，或可使用雙語（華、客語）以漸進方式教學及溝通，整體課程教學語言使用客語比率至少達50%以上。

12 依《客家委員會推動客語生活學校補助作業要點》第5點實施原則為：生活化原則、公共化原則、教學化原則、多元化原則、社區參與原則、現代化原則、同儕化原則等7大原則。

構面	主軸	規範
	接近使用公共服務	1. 人民以客語接近使用公共服務權利（本法第3條第2項）。 2. 服務於客家文化重點發展區之公教人員，應有符合服務機關所在地客家人口之比例通過客語認證；其取得客語認證資格者，應予獎勵，並得列為陞任評分之項目（本法第9條第2項）。[13] 3. 客語為通行語實施辦法第4條至第6條。 4. 客語能力認證辦法。
	傳播資源	1. 人民以客語接近使用傳播資源權利（本法第3條第2項）。 2. 政府對製播客家語言文化節目之廣播電視相關事業，得予獎勵或補助（本法第17條第1項）。 3. 客語為通行語實施辦法第7條。
語言推廣	獎勵客語推行	推行客家語言文化成效優良者，應由各級政府予以獎勵（本法第9條第1項）。
	公告及設置地方通行語標示	客語為通行語實施辦法第10條。
	公文雙語書寫	客語為通行語實施辦法第10條。
語言傳習	培育客語老師	高級中等以下學校及幼兒園客語師資培育資格及聘用辦法。
	進用客語師資	客語為通行語實施辦法第9條。
語言保存	客語資料庫 設立財團法人客家語言研究發展中心	政府應捐助設立財團法人客家語言研究發展中心，辦理客語研究發展、認證與推廣，並建立完善客語資料庫等，積極鼓勵客語復育傳承及人才培育（本法第11條第1項）。

---

13 按「客家基本法修正草案條文對照表」關於本條項說明，係「為營造客語使用環境」；惟慮及本條項規定具有實現人民以客語接近使用公共服務權利之功能，故列於本欄。

構面	主軸	規範
語言環境	支持體系	政府應建立客語與其他國家語言於公共領域共同使用之支持體系，並促進人民學習客語及培植多元文化國民素養之機會（本法第 13 條）。
	客語友善環境	1. 政府機關（構）應提供國民語言溝通必要之公共服務，於公共領域提供客語播音、翻譯服務及其他落實客語友善環境之措施（本法第 14 條第 1 項）。 2. 政府機關（構）應提供國民語言溝通必要之公共服務，於公共領域提供客語播音、翻譯服務及其他落實客語友善環境之措施（本法第 14 條）。 3. 客家委員會提升客語社群活力補助作業要點。[14]
	客語生活化	政府應提供獎勵措施，並結合各級學校、家庭與社區推動客語，發展客語生活化之學習環境（本法第 15 條）。

資料來源：王保鍵，2022：245-247。

按 2010 年《客家基本法》以客家族群集體權益（集體權）為保障核心；惟2018 年修正《客家基本法》導入憲法平等權，建構客家族群成員（客家人）的個人權利。客家人為臺灣少數族群，但客家族群不似原住民族擁有憲法保障依據（《憲法增修條文》第 10 條第 11 項及第 12 項），如欲深化客家人的個人權利，可循司法院釋字第 803 號解釋路徑，[15] 援引國際人權法，參酌國外少數群體語言保障機制。

參、國外少數群體語言保障機制之借鏡

Hamel（1997）從社會語言學視野，整合語言政策、語言規劃、語言立法，提出語言人權的社會語言學架構（sociolinguistic framework for linguistic human rights），並演繹出語言人權的 9 項基本指標（basic/ minimal criteria），其中一項為

---

14 依《客家委員會提升客語社群活力補助作業要點》第 3 點規定所定的補助範圍為：客語社區營造計畫類、客語研習活動類、編撰（製）或出版客語教材（具）類、客語推廣資訊系統類、其他經本會認可有助於推廣客語社群活力之計畫。

15 司法院釋字第 803 號解釋認為「原住民應享有選擇依其傳統文化而生活之權利」，係從《憲法增修條文》第 10 條第 11 項及第 12 項前段規定出發，以《憲法》第 22 條、《公民與政治權利國際公約》第 27 條，及《公約》人權事務委員會第 23 號一般性意見為路徑，加以論證（王保鍵，2022：298）。

國家負有保障及促進少數群體語言的義務（explicit obligations for the state to adopt measures to protect and promote minority languages）。而 Thomas Hill Green 的權利承認理論（the rights recognition thesis）強調權利透過承認而產生（rights are made by recognition），認為權利是一種能力、權利受到社會或他人之承認、權利有助於促進共同的善（common good）；意即，承認既造就亦認可權利（Boucher，2013：108；Gaus，2005）。聯合國的國際人權法，或各別國家的國內法，對於少數群體權利的承認，一方面建構少數群體權利，一方面也形成國家義務。

國際社會關於少數群體語言權利保障，已逐漸形成普世的標準。[16] 聯合國許多國際公約中，規範國家應承擔保障語言少數群體權利者，以《公民與政治權利國際公約》第 27 條及《兒童權利公約》第 30 條最為核心。因應臺灣非聯合國會員國且國際處境特殊，我國發展出「國際公約國內法化」模式，以制定《公民與政治權利國際公約及經濟社會文化權利國際公約施行法》、《兒童權利公約施行法》，賦予國際公約具有國內法效力。

基本上，多數群體擁有人數上優勢，容易以立法方式，獲致該群體所欲的語言

---

16 關於少數群體權利之國際標準，聯合國人權事務高級專員辦事處（Office of the United Nations High Commissioner for Human Rights）指出，包含：（1）聯合國人權條約，聯合國公約所保障的權利，自然亦適用於少數群體，如《公民與政治權利國際公約》（International Covenant on Civil and Political Rights）《經濟、社會及文化權利國際公約》（International Covenant on Economic, Social and Cultural Rights）、《兒童權利公約》（Convention on the Rights of the Child）、《消除一切形式種族歧視國際公約》（International Convention on the Elimination of All Forms of Racial Discrimination）、《消除對婦女一切形式歧視公約》（Convention on the Elimination of All Forms of Discrimination against Women）、《身心障礙者權利公約》（Convention on the Rights of Persons with Disabilities）、《保護所有移徙工人及其家庭成員權利國際公約》（International Convention on the Protection of the Rights of All Migrant Workers and Members of Their Families）、《禁止酷刑和其他殘忍、不人道或有辱人格的待遇或處罰公約》（Convention against Torture and Other Cruel, Inhuman or Degrading Treatment or Punishment）、《保護所有人免遭強迫失蹤國際公約》（International Convention for the Protection of All Persons from Enforced Disappearance）等九部核心人權公約；（2）特定權利宣言，如《在民族、族群、宗教和語言上屬於少數群體者權利宣言》（Declaration on the Rights of Persons Belonging to National or Ethnic, Religious and Linguistic Minorities）；（3）區域人權及少數群體權利標準，如《非洲人權和民族權憲章》（African Charter on Human and Peoples Rights）、《美洲人權公約》（American Convention on Human Rights）、《阿拉伯人權憲章》（Arab Charter on Human Rights）、《歐洲保護少數民族框架公約》（Framework Convention for the Protection of National Minorities）、《歐洲區域或少數民族語言憲章》（European Charter for Regional or Minority Languages）、《歐洲保護人權與基本自由公約》（European Convention on Human Rights and Fundamental Freedoms）、《歐盟種族平等令》（EU Racial Equality Directive）等（OHCHR，2021）。

政策。然而，少數群體因其人數上的劣勢，如欲獲得有利的語言政策，須經過長期的抗爭，並等待政策窗之開啟；且少數群體遭受不利的語言政策傷害時，亦甚難修正或廢止。因而，觀摩歐美國家如何保障少數群體語言權利，及如何以制度性機制保存、復振語言，有助於臺灣學術研究的發展，並提供政府機關於規劃語言政策之參考，藉以提升語言政策與規劃的品質。本書基於上開理念，遂以「客語及少數族群語言政策」為主題，進行編輯。

肆、本書之編輯

本書的形成，來自於「2018臺灣客語與少數族群語言復振國際研討會」的辦理成果。當時本書三位主編在規劃此次研討會時，適逢2018年《客家基本法》修正，意欲引介其他國家少數族群語言保障之實作經驗，作為落實客語為國家語言、客語為通行語等制度性規範的借鏡。本次研討會在客家委員會支持下，邀請了英國威爾斯語、德國索勃語、比利時荷蘭語、芬蘭薩米語、日本阿伊努語、西班牙加泰隆尼亞語、法國布列塔尼語的政府部門官員、學者專家來臺，分享他們在各自國家內語言復振的具體作法、實際成效與未來挑戰。

2019年6月，在Meri Huws女士（曾任英國威爾斯語言監察使）協助下，客家委員會楊長鎮主委（時任副主委）與本書編者周錦宏及王保鍵一同前往加拿大安大略省多倫多市，參加國際語言監察使協會（International Association of Language Commissioners）的第六次年會，對於歐美國家如何復振少數族群語言，如何完善少數族群成員個人語言權利保障，有著深刻的體認。

在新冠肺炎疫情衝擊下，2021年12月以線上搭配實體方式，辦理「2021臺灣客語與少數族群語言政策國際研討會」，此次研討會不僅延續2018年研討會的精神，更擴大範圍，邀請了歐洲語言平等網絡、紐西蘭毛利語、英國威爾斯語等學者專家，與國內學者專家、政府機關官員，進行對話。

本書的編輯，分成三部分：第一部分為「2018臺灣客語與少數族群語言復振國際研討會」實錄，第二部分為「2021臺灣客語與少數族群語言政策國際研討會」實錄，第三部分為歐美國家重要少數族群語言法律、行政措施之中文翻譯。

當前臺灣少數族群語言發展，面對的挑戰，包含：（1）2030雙語國家政策、國家語言政策，兩種語言政策，在政策資源、學校教育之競合；（2）事實上官方語言、多數族群語言之語言使用強度、語言環境，優於少數族群語言；（3）客家原

鄉、原住民原鄉人口流失，都會客家、都市原住民人口快速增加，致使母語流失危機嚴峻。上開少數族群語言傳承的危機，有賴國家積極作為，參照國際人權標準、歐美語言復振實作經驗，以「實質平等」（substantive equality）概念，制定臺灣客語、原住民族語、馬祖語等少數族群語言政策，以促進少數族群語言發展。面對少數族群語言發展的挑戰，本書企圖引介歐美國家對少數族群語言權利保障之制度規範，及歐美國家以語言政策、語言規劃促進語言復振之實作經驗，以借鏡國外語言政策之方式，反思國內在語言法律制定與實施所面對的問題，回饋至臺灣語言政策的規劃，以精進臺灣的國家語言政策。

參考文獻

Boucher, David（著）、許家豪（譯）（2013a）。權利的承認：人權與國際習慣。收錄於曾國祥（編），自由主義與人權，頁 101-128。高雄市：巨流。

王保鍵（2018）。客家發展之基本法制建構。桃園市：國立中央大學出版中心。

王保鍵（2022）。少數群體語言權利：加拿大、英國、臺灣語言政策之比較。臺北市：五南。

陳美如（2009）。臺灣語言教育之回顧與展望（第二版）。高雄市：復文。

陳淑華（2009）。臺灣鄉土語言政策沿革的後殖民特色與展望。教育學誌，21：51-90。

黃英哲（2005）。魏建功與戰後臺灣「國語」運動（1946-1968）。臺灣文學研究學報，1：79-107。

臺灣語文學會（2022）。以「多語臺灣，英語友善」取代「雙語國家」：臺灣語文學會對「2030 雙語國家」政策的立場聲明。http://www.twlls.org.tw/NEWS_20220221.php，檢視日期：2022 年 2 月 26 日。

European Digital Treasures (2021). *The Sámi National Day on February 6*. Retrieved August 17, 2022, from: https://www.digitaltreasures.eu/the-sami-national-day-on-february-6/.

Gaus, Gerald F. (2005). Green's Rights Recognition Thesis and Moral Internalism. *The British Journal of Politics and International Relations*, 7(1): 5-17.

Hamel, Rainer Enrique (1997). Language Conflict and Language Shift: a Sociolinguistic Framework for Linguistic Human Rights. *International Journal of the Sociology of*

Language, 127: 105-134.

Hooper, Simon (2011). Bretons Fight to Save Language from Extinction. CNN. Retrieved October 23, 2021, from: http://edition.cnn.com/2010/WORLD/europe/12/11/brittany. language/index.html.

Office of the High Commissioner for Human Rights [OHCHR] (2021). *International standards*. Retrieved January 13, 2021, from: https://www.ohchr.org/EN/Issues/ Minorities/SRMinorities/Pages/standards.aspx.

Willyarto, Mario Nugroho, Yunus, Ulani and Wahyuningiyas, Bhernadetta Pravita (2021). Foregign Language (English) Learning in Cross-Cultural in Indonesian. In Yilmaz Bayar (ed). *Handbook of Research on Institutional, Economic, and Social Impacts of Globalization and Liberalization.* [pp. 671-684]. Hershey: IGI Global.

2018 臺灣客語及少數族群語言復振國際研討會
經驗實錄

【英國威爾斯語 Welsh】
威爾斯語言監察使的角色
The Role of the Welsh Language Commissioner

英國威爾斯語言監察使 Meri Huws 女士

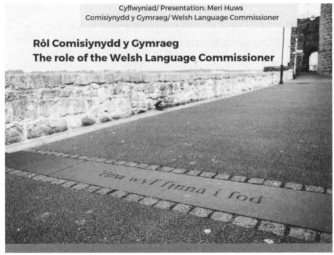

3

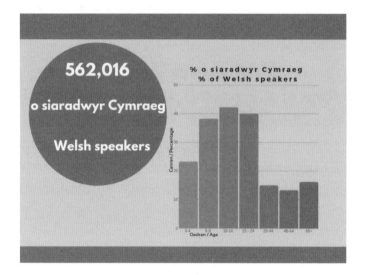

4

Faint o bobl sy'n siarad Cymraeg yng Nghymru?
How many people speak Welsh in Wales?

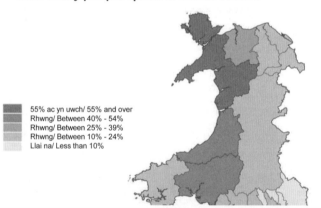

55% ac yn uwch/ 55% and over
Rhwng/ Between 40% - 54%
Rhwng/ Between 25% - 39%
Rhwng/ Between 10% - 24%
Llai na/ Less than 10%

5

DEDDFAU NODEDIG
NOTABLE LEGISLATION

1 DEDDFAU UNO 1536 A 1542-43
ACTS OF UNION 1536 AND 1542-43

2 DEDDF LLYSOEDD CYMRU 1942
WELSH COURTS ACT 1942

3 DEDDF YR IAITH GYMRAEG 1967
WELSH LANGUAGE ACT 1967

4 DEDDF YR IAITH GYMRAEG 1993
WELSH LANGUAGE ACT 1993

5 MESUR Y GYMRAEG (CYMRU) 2011
WELSH LANGUAGE (WALES)
MEASURE 2011

Addysg Gymraeg
Welsh Education

51% o holl siaradwyr Cymraeg wedi dysgu'r iaith yn yr ysgol: 11% yn yr ysgol feithrin, 25% yn yr ysgol gynradd, a 15% yn yr ysgol uwchradd.

80% o siaradwyr Cymraeg 3-15 wedi dysgu'r iaith yn yr ysgol: 22% yn yr ysgol feithrin, 46% yn yr ysgol gynradd, 12% yn yr ysgol uwchradd.

51% of all Welsh speakers learnt the language at school: 11% at nursery school, 25% in primary school, and 15% at secondary school.

80% of Welsh speakers aged 3-15 learnt the language at school: 22% at nursery school, 46% in primary school, 12% in secondary school.

CEFNDIR

- Mesur y Gymraeg (Cymru) 2011
- Statws swyddogol i'r iaith Gymraeg
- Ni ddylid trin y Gymraeg yn llai ffafriol na'r Saesneg yng Nghymru

BACKGROUND

- The Welsh Language (Wales) Measure 2011
- Official status to the Welsh Language
- Welsh should not be treated less favourably than the English language in Wales

Comisiynydd y Gymraeg
Welsh Language Commissioner

Cymru lle gall pobl ddefnyddio'r Gymraeg yn eu bywydau bob dydd

4 swyddfa/ office

A Wales where people can use the Welsh language in their everyday lives

7 mlynedd/ years

9

Hawliau i ddefnyddio'r Gymraeg
Rights to use the Welsh language

Gosod safonau'r Gymraeg

Impose Welsh standards

Rheoleiddio

Regulation

Pwerau i'r Comisiynydd
osod safonau ar
sefydliadau cyhoeddus

Powers to set standards
on public organisations

Cyflwyno
gwasanaethau

Providing
services

Cweithredu
mewnol

Internal
operations

Llunio polisi

Policy making

Hybu

Promote

10

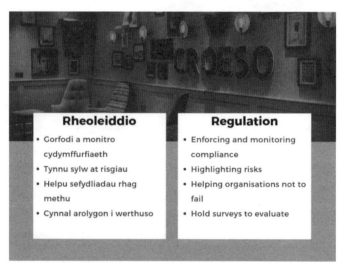

Rheoleiddio

- Gorfodi a monitro
  cydymffurfiaeth
- Tynnu sylw at risgiau
- Helpu sefydliadau rhag
  methu
- Cynnal arolygon i werthuso

Regulation

- Enforcing and monitoring
  compliance
- Highlighting risks
- Helping organisations not to
  fail
- Hold surveys to evaluate

11

Pa sefydliadau sy'n gorfod cydymffurfio â'r safonau?
Which organisations have to comply with the standards?

- Amgueddfeydd/
  Museums
- Heddlu/ Police
- Llyfrgelloedd/
  Libraries
- Cynghorau/
  Councils
- Colegau/
  Colleges
- Prifysgolion /
  Universities
- Llywodraeth/
  Government
- BBC

Hawliau i ddefnyddio'r Gymraeg: Gwneud gwahaniaeth
Rights to use the Welsh language: Making a difference

12

 Roedd opsiynau Cymraeg gan beiriannau awtomatig yn ystod **98%** o'r galwadau lle'u defnyddiwyd

 Automated machines offered options in Welsh in **98%** of calls where that method was used

 Cafwyd ymateb Cymraeg i e-bost Cymraeg mewn **93%** o achosion

 An email in Welsh received a reply in Welsh in **93%** of cases

 100% o beiriannau hunanwasanaeth yn gweithio'n llawn yn Gymraeg

 100% of self service machines worked fully through the medium of Welsh

 Cafwyd cyfarchiad Cymraeg gan y derbynnydd yn ystod **89%** o alwadau ffôn

 A greeting in Welsh was given by the operator in **89%** of telephone calls

13

Gwyliwch fideo am sut y mae'r Gymraeg yn cael ei hybu yn y gweithle:
Watch a video about how the Welsh Language is promoted in the workplace:

Bethan Griffiths
Cydymffurfiaeth gyda Safonau'r Gymraeg
Compliance with the Welsh Language Standards

14

Hybu'r Gymraeg

- Cefnogi busnesau ac elusennau i ddatblygu darpariaeth Gymraeg.
- Cynnig hyfforddiant a chyngor i fusnesau.
- Cynnig gwasanaeth prawfddarllen am ddim.
- Bathodyn/ Cortyn gwddf 'Iaith Gwaith.'

Promoting Welsh

- Support businesses and charities to improve Welsh language service.
- Offer training and advice to businesses.
- Offer free proof reading service.
- 'Iaith Gwaith' (Welsh in Work) Badge/ Lanyard.

Croeso!　Cymraeg

15

Dyma fideo am hybu'r Gymraeg
This is a video about promoting the Welsh language

A new survey shows that 86% of people in Wales feel that the Welsh language is something to be proud of.

16

DYLANWADU
INFLUENCING

Rhoi tystiolaeth lafar
Presenting evidence

Rhoi tystiolaeth ysgrifenedig
Providing written evidence

Cyflwyno argymhellion
Giving recommendations

Cyfarfod â sefydliadau
Meet with organisations

Ymgyrchoedd
Campaigns

Cyfarfod â gwleidyddion
Meet with politicians

17

Sefydlu'r isadeiledd
Establishing the infrastructure

Pam creu rhestr enwau lleoedd safonol?

- Dull cofnodi
- Safoni'r orgraff
- Amlder ffurfiau (safonol ac ansafonol)

Sefyllfa gymhleth

- Enwau Cymraeg yn unig neu Saesneg yn unig
- Enwau gwahanol o darddiad gwahanol
- Amrywiadau safonol o'r un tarddiad
- Amrywiadau ansafonol

Why create standardised list of Welsh place-names?

- Recording method
- Standardisation of the Welsh orthography
- Variation of forms (standard and non-standard)

Complex situation

- Solely Welsh or English place-names
- Different names from different derivations
- Standard variations from the same derivation
- Non-standard variations

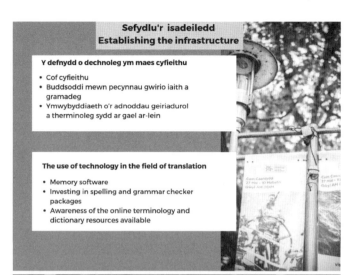

18

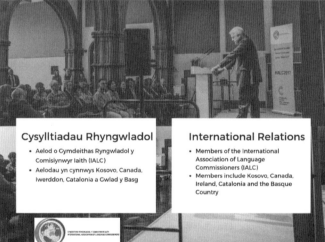

19

20

21

Briefing 1

Thank you for giving me the opportunity in attending this conference. It is a privilege to be here to be part of your discussion.

Two years ago, I met Minister Lee in my office in Wales. He spoke about the Hakka languages and the importance of law. Many people think that legislation and law are the end of a journey. You have a piece of legislation and everything has been achieved. That is not true. Legislation is the beginning of another journey; the law is the beginning of a journey. And you are starting on another part of your journey here in Taiwan. We did something similar seven years ago in Wales. So, I want to talk about that experience—from what we have learned to what we have achieved—during the past seven years, and some of the challenges.

Briefing 2

I can tell you a little bit first about my country, Wales.

Wales is a very small country, right on the edge of the United Kingdom. We are attached to England and have sea right around. We have a population of three million people—the same population as Taipei. Our capital city is Cardiff. We have very good football teams and rugby teams here. We play those games well.

Briefing 3

Of those three million people, 562,000 speak Welsh, 20 percent of our population is 65 years of age plus, and just under 20 percent of the population speak Welsh. But look at the three- to four-year-olds, five- to nine-year-olds,10- to 14-year-olds, and 15- to 24-year-olds.

We have a huge increase in the number of young people learning Welsh. That is a challenge for us.

We have young people learning the Welsh language in our schools. Many of those young people are learning the Welsh language for the first time in their families.

For a century, those young people have gonehome every day to a family which speaks English.They have no one with whom they can communicate after school through the medium of the Welsh language.

And this is a challenge.

We have to create opportunities for our young Welsh learners to use the language.

We have to make it relevant to their lives, and that is part of the challenge I have as commissioner.

So, a small country, in which 20 percent of the population speak the Welsh language. Most of that 20 percent are under 24 years of age, which is a wonderful challenge but a real challenge as well, because many of those children will not speak Welsh after they leave school.

Briefing 4

Where do people speak Welsh in Wales? Most of the Welsh speakers are located on the western seaboard. The sea is right around Wales.

So, most of our Welsh speakers are in the areas along the western coast.

It is a very rural area. Agriculture is the main industry.

They are isolated communities and aging communities.

So, we have the real challenge of the location of our speakers as Welsh education grows, as those young Welsh speakers are coming out of our schools.

That pattern is changing, and we have more Welsh speakers in our cities. And the south of Wales—the old industrial areas, the old coal mining areas of Wales—has a changing demographic in terms of language.

Briefing 5

I would like to talk a little about the legislation and the history of laws relating to the Welsh language in Wales now. This will give you a flavor of why I consider legislation and law to be so important for revitalizing minority languages.

We need legislation and positive action, but legislation is critical, and I must congratulate you in Taiwan for introducing new legislation earlier this year.

That's a very positive step forward.

So, in terms of the Welsh language, and the history of what happened to us in terms of the law:

In 1536, five centuries ago, England took over Wales. Wales was an independent country. It had its own princes; its own legal system. We ran our own country 500 years ago and we spoke our own language—the Welsh language.

The Welsh language had been spoken in other areas of Britain, but by 1536 it was spoken in Wales.

In 1536, we were conquered by the English and we became part of the English parliament.

We were governed by the English monarchy. We were taken over by the English. They took us over politically, and they took us over in terms of our law.

But, in that legislation in 1536, they also told the people of Wales: "You must not use the Welsh language in public life. You can speak the Welsh language in your homes. You can speak the Welsh language when you are in faith if you are using it when you are in the chapel or the church. But you cannot speak the Welsh language when you are in civil life and when you're in public life." This was so for five centuries.

Well, for four centuries, the Welsh language was not used at all in any form of official communication in Wales.

So, it is surprising. It is amazing that the Welsh language survived during those years.

But it survived as a language of the home and religion.

At the beginning of the 20th century, half of the population of Wales still spoke Welsh. So, it had remained a strong community language. However, in 1942, almost 400 years after the Act of Union, a decision was made to pass a piece of legislation, as a consequence of pressure from people in Wales to allow people in the legal system to speak Welsh if they were appearing before a court or if they were charged with an offence.

You were allowed to use the Welsh language in explaining your case and putting forward your case.

So, in 1942,the Welsh Courts Act allowed people to speak Welsh if they could prove they could not speak the English language adequately; they could give their evidence through the medium of Welsh, and that was the beginning of change.

After that, in 1967, the Welsh Language Act gave individuals absolute power to speak Welsh to give evidence in the court system and the legal system. So, slowly the legislation was passed, which gave the Welsh language more legal status in Britain.

It was in 1993 that we had the first piece of really important legislation. What had happened in the sixties, seventies, and eighties? People protested, and I was a protester. I pulled road signs down that were in English only. I protested that we needed a Welsh language television system. I was arrested and taken to court and charged with offences. But it was all part of a protest movement which argued for our right to use our language in our country一not only in our homes but also in our official life.

So, in 1993, we had a piece of legislation passed by the UK government which said that the Welsh language should be treated no less favorably than the English language in Wales. It did not give the language official status. It just said, "Be nice to the Welsh language and treat it well, but if you don't treat it well, we will do nothing." However, it was an important statement. It was the beginning of a journey to the passing of the Welsh language.

Wales measured a piece of legislation in 2011.

That piece of legislation did many important things, but the most important one was to give the Welsh language official status in Wales in public life. So, almost five centuries after 1536, that first piece of legislation gave us a statement that the Welsh language was an official language in our country, and we had the right to use it in public life.

Briefing 6

At the same time, we had legislative changes. At the same time as we had new laws being introduced to give us rights, something else was happening—the growth of Welsh-medium education. I was educated entirely through the medium of English from three years old to today. I have never been taught through the medium of Welsh. However, in the 1970s and the 1980s, the people that were protesting for legal rights, also said we want our children to be taught through the medium of Welsh.

We want them to study from their early years right until their university education through the medium of their language.

And that has grown and grown. Today in Wales, of those young people on the graph who speak Welsh, four out of five of those young people—eighty percent of those young people—have learned the Welsh language in school.

Briefing 7

I learned the Welsh language at home with my family. Today, young people are learning the Welsh language in the school system. So, we have the growth of legal rights and we have a growing young population who can communicate and who have studied through the medium of the Welsh language.

Briefing 8

What I want to do now is just talk a little about my role as Welsh Language Commissioner. What we've achieved in the last seven years through the passing of legislation is the beginning of a journey; it's not the end of a journey. The last seven years in Wales have been amazing. I have been privileged to be part of the change which is happening in Wales; a combination of law and promotion.

So, the Welsh Language Commissioner role was established by the Welsh Language Act of 2011.That legislation gave official status to the language and established the role of the Welsh language commissioner. I am the Welsh Language Commissioner. It's a strange role which is modeled on the language commissioners of Canada, which has had language commissioners since 1969.The first language commissioner was appointed in 1969 as a consequence of the Official Languages Act in Canada. So, the Welsh Language Commissioner is modeled on that role.

Briefing 9

It is a strange role because I am a legal regulator. I'm a legal appointment, and I have legal powers. I also have promotional responsibilities. We decided in Wales to put both those elements—legislative regulatory powers and promotional powers—in the same role. In other countries, those roles are split. I believe that having the two sides of that coin in the same role is important.

It works well. Why do I say it works? Well, I'll describe what's happened in Wales during the past years.

I'm the first Welsh Language Commissioner. I have had a legal mandate for seven years. I started in April 2012. My legal mandate comes to an end on the last day of March 2019. So, this is one of the last conferences I will speak at. I have three months before my legal mandate comes to an end.

Briefing 10

I have an office that is independent of the Welsh government. I'm funded by public money, but I am not a civil servant. I'm independent of the Welsh government, and part of my role is to ensure that the Welsh government complies with the Welsh Language Measure of 2011. I can intervene and actually punish the Welsh government. I can impose a fine on the Welsh government.

But my role is very much not about punishment. It's not about forcing people to comply with the law, although it's quite useful at times to threaten them. But my role is to ensure that people living in Wales can use the Welsh language in everyday life. And I think that is so important, that one word. That is what we are all trying to achieve—that people who speak minority languages have the opportunity to use that language in all aspects of their life. And that has been our challenge during the past years.

How have we done that? I can start by talking about my legal powers. I have a legal duty to require public sector organizations in Wales to comply with standards in relation to the Welsh language standards, which are rules essentially. Public bodies in Wales have to comply with those rules when they are providing services to the public.

So, when I communicate with my local authority, corporations, and the people who provide education and health care, I have the right to use the Welsh language, and they have a duty to respond to my rights. So, when they provide services, they must provide services in both English and Welsh equally. There must be no difference. Organizations must also ensure that people employed within the organization can use the Welsh language as an employee. So, if I was working for a corporation or a health body, I would have the right to use the Welsh language in my work from day to day.

I think again that's important when we create young people who can speak the language—telling them they can have a job, that they will have employment, is such an incentive.

They will want to learn the language and use the language. The organizations, as well those who operate under standards, must also consider the Welsh language as they make policy decisions.

When a corporation nor a local authority decides to build houses in an area, they must ask the question: "What effect will this have on the Welsh language in this area?" So, any policy decisions made have to consider the Welsh language, and public sector organizations have to promote the use of the language. So, these rules are very specific. Most organizations in Wales have 150 rules they must follow in relation to the Welsh language, but it has worked so well, and I'll explain how it has worked well. It has not only changed ways of operating; it has changed the culture of organizations. So, organizations are now thinking and operating in a different way. What I do as a regulator in relation to those standards is to ensure that public sector bodies all follow these rules. This is what we do as an organization.

Briefing 11

What does the Welsh Language Commissioner do?

Well, we test, we monitor, and we undertake secret shopper missions. We phone organizations. We send emails to organizations. We visit organizations and say "I want service in Welsh," and if they can't comply, if they cannot do that, we say "you have to."If they do not comply, I can impose a fine. I can take them to court. I have not imposed fines yet, because I actually believe it is important for organizations to comply because they want to and see the reason for it. However, if an organization or the government was to say no, I can actually say "I will impose a fine on you, and you must pay the money."So, I have that ultimate threat. However, I do believe very strongly that the most important thing is active compliance—that organizations choose to comply—and we seek to help them to do so. We give organizations advice on how to give services bilingually. We give them information. We give them posters to place in their organizations—a poster which says "Use your Welsh whenever you see this sign." We give organizations lanyards for their workers to wear, indicating who can speak Welsh and who is learning Welsh. So, regulation and active encouragement work well together. We undertake investigations into complaints. If a member of the public feels they are not getting the service they should have, we will investigate and intervene to ensure that the situation is resolved.

So, regulation sounds threatening, but we seek to do it in a way which encourages compliance. Organizations in Wales have to comply with standards. The Welsh government, all our local authorities, our local corporations, all our local councils, the police force in Wales—all have to offer a fully bilingual service.

Our universities have to offer a fully bilingual service to their students, including our further education colleges. The BBC in Wales has to offer a fully bilingual service. Libraries, museums—all the places we visit on a daily basis now have to offer a fully bilingual service.

Briefing 12

Do they all succeed? We're talking about the law which has been operating for the past five years. We have been so amazed at the level of compliance and the level of achieving what some organizations thought was impossible. Some of the figures of up from our testing 100% of automated machines. Parking machines in Wales are now 100% fully bilingual. We said "Wow" as well, but it has happened! In98% of public bodies in

Wales, when people answer the phone, they now answer bilingually.

We have seen the standards work so well because they are specific, and organizations know what to do. We help them to achieve these standards. We threaten them a bit if they don't, but they are so proud of what they have achieved, and for me, the greatest indicator is that organizations are no longer saying "Why do we have to do this?" They are now saying "How do we do this? Please help us. We want to achieve. We want to offer a fully bilingual service."I'm now going to show you a brief video from the Welsh government. It's in Welsh and has English subtitles. The first person who is going to speak in this video is the head of our civil service, Ms. Shan Morgan. She's the senior civil servant in Wales. She doesn't speak Welsh, but she has learned this to tell us how proud she is of what the Welsh government has achieved. We made this video to show other organizations and people like you that it is possible for the government in a very brief period of time—in five years—to achieve what we thought was almost impossible.

Briefing 13

That's a brief video that we produced earlier this year to show other organizations what the Welsh government has achieved. When we see the Welsh government providing a bilingual service like that, it is an encouragement for other bodies to follow.

Briefing 14

I've talked about the regulations we have undertaken, but it is also really important that we promote the use of the Welsh language, and we do that alongside our legal duties. Why do we need to promote the use of the Welsh language? As I mentioned, we have many, many young people who are learning Welsh in the schools. We need to encourage them to use the language in all aspects of their life, not only when they are working. So, we work with businesses; we work with voluntary organizations. We work with charities to encourage them to use the language in all aspects of their work. We work very, very actively with the sports council in Wales to make sure that football organizations, rugby organizations, and hockey organizations work in both languages, and that these young people who learn Welsh in school can also use it outside the school setting. We offer services to large businesses to encourage them to use the language in their day-to-day work. We want to create a Wales where the language feels as if it's part of everyday life. We've mentioned, and the video also mentioned, this little sticker that we use very, very actively in all situations to promote the use of the Welsh language and make people proud of being able to speak the language.

So, regulation and promotion really need to sit side by side. I'm going to show you one brief video again, and then we will almost come to the end of the presentation.

This is a video we produced and launched last week. It is a short video in English and Welsh for businesses that are moving into Wales—large businesses, large retailers; the same shops as you have here on your streets in Taipei—to encourage them to use the Welsh language as they develop their shops in Cardiff and throughout Wales.

Briefing 15

Thank you. A very brief video, but very, very powerful in terms of the message. The response we've had from large European businesses has been so positive. It is amazing!

Briefing 16

We regulate, we promote, and we also try to influence. I am particularly interested as language commissioner in talking to the Welsh government—not only about the status of the Welsh language but of the Welsh language in healthcare, in education, in town and country planning, and in all aspects of government life.

There is a great danger when you have one piece of legislation that politicians will think "We've solved the problem. We've got the legislation." But it is so important that politicians and policy makers think of the Welsh language in all situations when we are talking about special educational needs. We need to be talking in Welsh about what we need to do when we're talking about mental health care. We need to be talking in Welsh about what we need to do when we're talking about the care of people living with dementia. We need to be ensuring that those services are available in both languages. So, we regulate, we promote, and we influence, and it is so important to make sure that we think as a bilingual country in all aspects of our work. This is something I'm particularly interested in. I love talking to politicians and policy makers and asking them to think in different ways about how we provide services in Wales.

Briefing 17

We also standardize place names. I have a colleague whose work is to standardize place names in the Welsh language. Why are all our road signs in Wales now bilingual? Think of the person in the 1970s who was pulling those road signs down. We now have bilingual road signs. However, standardizing place names is really important as well in creating a history and identity. Why do these places have these names? Why are they called this in English and Welsh? So, we use our work around place names to ensure that the spelling is correct on road signs. Individuals—young people and older people— realize that we have a bilingual history. So, for the standardization of place names, we have national data and national resources in terms of bilingual place names in Wales.

Briefing 18

We also encourage the use of technology, particularly when it comes to translation. We actively support the use of machine translation. If you're talking about a bilingual country, many organizations have to produce bilingual documents. We encourage the use of technology and the use of memory software to enable that to happen. We are an ancient language but we have to be modern in the way we think, and technology can provide us with so many answers. So, online terminology and online dictionaries are part of the work that we encourage people to develop, and we urge universities largely to develop these types of resources.

Briefing 19

Finally, I've spoken about the work of the Welsh Language Commissioner. As I say, we regulate, we promote, we influence, we enable.

But we also work with our fellow commissioners across the world. We are founding members of an organization called the International Association of Language Commissioners. I would encourage you here in Taiwan to join. You may not have a Language Commissioner, but I do think you should consider becoming members of this organization. I have learned so much from my colleagues in Canada in particular, who are language commissioners. There's a language commissioner in Ireland. There's a language commissioner in Kosovo. There's a language commissioner in Cameroon. Now there is a language commissioner in South Africa. There's a language commissioner in Sri Lanka.

We have an international organization of bodies talking about the same issues in different languages. I've learned so much, and I've had so much support from that organization. We held an international conference in Cardiff years ago in which our first minister—our prime minister—addressed the event. I was chair of the international association for two years. I stepped down in Pristina, Kosovo during Easter in the spring of this year. The organization is now chaired by the Irish Language Commissioner. We all face the same challenges as speakers of minority languages. They're not identical but they are very similar. We can learn so much from each other and not feel alone. There is always the problem when you are a speaker of a minority language that you can feel very lonely. The international association makes sure that you don't feel lonely. So, as I end my presentation, I ask you to consider becoming affiliates of the international association of language commissioners.

Can I encourage you to maintain the link with Wales? I think that we can work with you. We had a very, very good conversation two years ago about similar challenges.

Working internationally as you implement your new legislation is critical. It will enrich the process, so please keep in touch with us as the Welsh Language Commission.

As I end, I see implementing legislation as creating a road map. The legislation itself is the road sign. It tells you which direction you want to travel, but it's the road map behind that legislation which is critical. You are part of creating that road map at this conference today, and again I congratulate you on having a conversation about how you wish to move forward. I would end by saying if you're going to create a road map, and as you plan those roads, the best roads have many, many lanes. It's not just one answer. It's regulation, promotion, enabling, and influencing, all together in one package, and that I think is why we in Wales have seen a very significant shift in the past years.

Briefing 20-21

Thank you for listening.

I hope you have heard something which is of relevance to you. Thank you very much.

簡報 1

感謝讓我有機會參加這次大會。很榮幸能在這裡和各位一起討論。

兩年前我在威爾斯的辦公室見到李主委。他談到客家語言以及法律的重要性。很多人以為立法和法律就是旅程的終點。只要有一項立法，所有問題就都解決了。但事實並非如此。立法是另一個旅程的開始；法律只是旅程的起點。而各位正在臺灣展開旅程的另一部分。我們七年前在威爾斯做過類似的事情。因此，我想談談那段經驗，在這過去的七年裡，我們學到什麼，成就了什麼，以及我們遇到的一些挑戰。

簡報 2

先介紹一下我的故鄉——威爾斯。

威爾斯是一個很小的地區，就在英國的邊緣。我們與英格蘭相鄰，有海洋圍繞。人口三百萬——和臺北差不多。首府在卡地夫。我們有很棒的足球隊和橄欖球隊。這些運動我們很強。

簡報 3

在這三百萬人口中，有 562,000 人講威爾斯語，我們 20% 的人口年齡超過 65 歲，但只有不到 20% 的人講威爾斯語。再看看 3 至 4 歲、5 至 9 歲、10 至 14 歲以及 15 至 24 歲的狀況。

我們學習威爾斯語的年輕人數量大幅增加。這對我們是一大挑戰。

年輕人在學校學威爾斯語。其中許多都是家中第一個學威爾斯語的。

百年來，這些年輕人每天都回到一個說英語的家庭。放學後沒有任何人可以用威爾斯語和他們交談。

這就是一個挑戰。

我們必須為學習威爾斯語的年輕人創造使用威爾斯語的機會。

必須讓語言和生活產生連結，而這就是我身為監察使的部分挑戰。

因此，一個 20% 人口說威爾斯語的小國。這 20% 裡面的大部分人都不到 24 歲，這是一項很好的挑戰，但也是真正的挑戰，因為許多這類兒童在離開校園後就

不再講威爾斯語了。

簡報 4

在威爾斯哪裡有人說威爾斯語？大部分說威爾斯語的人都在西部海岸。威爾斯環海。

所以，大部分說威爾斯語的人都在西部沿岸地區。

那裡很鄉下。以農業為主。

都是些孤立而高齡化的社區。

隨著威爾斯語教育的成長，也隨著講威爾斯語的年輕人離開校園，我們真正的挑戰便是講威爾斯語的人分布的地點。

這樣的模式正在改變，市區開始有愈來愈多講威爾斯語的人，還有南威爾斯（威爾斯的舊工業區、舊煤礦區）在語言方面的人口結構也在改變。

簡報 5

我想談談在威爾斯，目前威爾斯語的立法和法律歷史。這樣可以讓各位知道，為什麼我認為立法和法律對於振興少數民族語言會如此重要。

我們需要立法和積極的行動，但立法是絕對必要的；我必須恭喜各位，臺灣在今年初有了新的立法。

這是向前邁進非常積極的一步。

因此，關於威爾斯語，以及我們關於法律的歷程是這樣的：

於 1536 年，也就是五個世紀之前，英格蘭接管了威爾斯。威爾斯原本是獨立的國家，有自己的王子和自己的法律體系。

500 年前我們治理自己的國家，說我們自己的語言——威爾斯語。

曾經，不列顛其他地區也說威爾斯語，但從 1536 年起，就只有在威爾斯了。

於 1536 年，英國征服我們，而我們也成為英國議會的一部分；

受英國君主統治，被英國接管。他們不但在政治上也在法律上接管我們。

但在 1536 年的立法中，他們也告誡威爾斯人：「不得在公開場合使用威爾斯語。你可以在家說威爾斯語。如果你有信仰，可以在教堂或聖堂裡說威爾斯語。但在社交和公開場合，就不准說威爾斯語。」就這樣過了五個世紀。

其中的四個世紀，在威爾斯的任何形式的官方溝通中，完全聽不到威爾斯語。

所以，讓人驚訝。不可思議的是，威爾斯語竟能在這麼多年之後倖存下來。

但所倖存的也只不過是家裡和宗教的語言。

在 20 世紀初，威爾斯半數人口仍說威爾斯語。因此，威爾斯語仍是強勢社區語言。但於 1942 年，也就是《聯合法》（Act of Union）頒布約 400 年後，在威爾斯人民的壓力下通過了一項立法，允許在出庭或遭指控時可在法律體系中說威爾斯語。

在解釋並提出自己的案件時可以使用威爾斯語。

因此，《威爾斯法院法》（Welsh Courts Act）於 1942 年開始，只要能證明自己無法有效說英語，便可選擇說威爾斯語；亦可透過威爾斯語媒體提出證據，而這就是改變的開始。

之後，於 1967 年，《威爾斯語言法》（Welsh Language Act）對個人賦予在法院體系和法律體系中以威爾斯語提出證據的絕對權利。因此，立法逐漸通過，賦予威爾斯語在英國更多的法律地位。

我們在 1993 年有了第一項真正重要的立法。六零年代、七零年代和八零年代發生了什麼事？有很多人抗議，而我也是當時的抗議人士。我扯下只有英文的路標。我抗議，並主張應該要有威爾斯語的電視體系。我被捕並在法院被控犯罪。但這都只是抗議行動的一部分，我們主張有權在自己的國家使用自己的語言，不僅僅在家，而是在正式的生活中。

因此，英國政府於 1993 年通過一項立法，明定威爾斯語在威爾斯所受的待遇不得低於英語。這並未賦予威爾斯語官方語言的地位，而只是規定「請尊重並善待威爾斯語，但如果不尊重、不善待，也不會怎樣。」但這依舊是一項重要的聲明。這是威爾斯語傳承之旅的開始。

威爾斯於 2011 年衡量了一項立法。

該項立法有很多重要貢獻，但最重要的便是賦予威爾斯語在公共生活中的官方語言地位。因此，在 1536 年大約五個世紀之後，這第一項立法對我們宣告，威爾斯語是我們國家的官方語言，而我們有權在公共生活中使用。

簡報 6

於此同時，我們進行立法改革。就在引進新法律並賦予我們權利的同時，也發生了一些其他事——以威爾斯語為媒體的教育開始成長。我從三歲起到現在一直是透過英語接受教育，我從未透過威爾斯語受教育。但在 1970 和 1980 年代，爭取法

律權利的抗議人士也表示，希望自己的子女透過威爾斯語接受教育。

　　我們希望子女們從小一直到大學教育階段，都能透過自己的語言接受教育。而這個現象不斷擴大。目前在威爾斯，如圖表所示，每五個說威爾斯語的年輕人之中就有四個（80%）曾在學校學習威爾斯語。

簡報 7

　　我是在家裡跟家人學威爾斯語的。而現在，年輕人在學校體系中學習威爾斯語。所以，我們有愈來愈多的合法權利，我們有愈來愈多可以透過威爾斯語溝通和學習的年輕人口。

簡報 8

　　我現在只想談談自己身為威爾斯語言監察使的角色。我們過去七年來透過立法取得的成就只是旅程的起點；而不是終點。過去七年的威爾斯真的令人讚嘆。我有幸參與了威爾斯正在發生的改變；法律和宣傳的結合。

　　因此，2011 年《威爾斯語言法》（Welsh Language Act）確立了威爾斯語言監察使的角色。該立法賦予了威爾斯語官方語言的地位，並確立了威爾斯語言監察使的角色。我是威爾斯語言監察使。這是模仿加拿大語言監察使的一個奇怪角色，加拿大自 1969 年以來一直就設有語言監察使。第一位語言監察使係於 1969 年依加拿大《官方語言法》（Official Languages Act）任命。因此，威爾斯語言監察使就是模仿那個角色。

簡報 9

　　那是一個奇怪的角色，因為我是一名法律監管人員。我是法定任命人員，擁有法律權力。我也有推廣職責。我們在威爾斯決定將這兩個要素——立法監管權和推廣權——放在同一個角色裡。在其他國家，這些角色是分開的。我認為讓硬幣兩面發揮相同的作用很重要。

　　這樣運作得很好。為什麼我會說這樣很好呢？讓我描述一下威爾斯過去幾年發生了什麼事。

　　我是第一位威爾斯語言監察使。我的法定任期是七年，從 2012 年 4 月份開始，我的法定任期於 2019 年 3 月底結束。所以，這是我最後一次致詞的大會。在我的法定任期結束前，我還有三個月的時間。

簡報 10

　　我有一個獨立於威爾斯政府的辦公室。我接受公費資助，但我不是公務員。我獨立於威爾斯政府，而我的部分角色是確保威爾斯政府遵守 2011 年《威爾斯語言法》（Welsh Language Measure）。我可以干預並實際處罰威爾斯政府，我可以對威爾斯政府處以罰款。

　　但我的角色可不僅僅是處罰。重點不在於強迫他人守法，雖然有時候威嚇他們一下也很管用。但我的角色是確保生活在威爾斯的人於日常生活中可以說威爾斯語。而我覺得這一點非常重要。這是我們想要達成的目標——說少數民族語言的人有機會在生活的所有層面說自己的語言。而這也就是我們過去數年來的挑戰。

　　我們做得如何？我可以從我們的法定權力說起。我在法律上有義務要求威爾斯的公部門組織遵守關於威爾斯語的標準，實際上就是一些規則。威爾斯的公務機構為大眾提供服務時，都必須遵守這些規則。

　　因此，當我與提供教育和醫療的地方當局、企業和人員溝通時，我有權使用威爾斯語，而對方則有義務回應我的權利。因此，他們必須公平地以英語和威爾斯語提供服務，不得有差別待遇。各組織也必須確保，其僱用之人員即使身為員工也可以使用威爾斯語。因此，如果我受僱於一家企業或健康機構，便有權在日常工作中使用威爾斯語。

　　我也認為這一點很重要，當我們培養說威爾斯語的年輕人時，如果告訴他們將會有一份工作，將受到僱用，這會非常有激勵性。

　　他們會想要學習並使用威爾斯語。在標準下經營之各組織和人員擬定政策時，也必須考慮威爾斯語。

　　企業或地方當局決定在某區域蓋房子時，必須問這個問題：「這會對該地區的威爾斯語產生什麼影響？」因此，所做的任何政策決定都必須考慮威爾斯語，且公部門組織必須促進使用威爾斯語。因此，這些規則非常具體。在威爾斯的大部分組織必須遵守 150 條關於威爾斯語的規則，但這一直運作得不錯，讓我說明一下。這不僅僅改變了組織經營的方法，也改變了它的文化。因此，各組織現在以不同的方法思考及經營。我身為監管人員就這些標準所做的，就是確保公部門機構都遵循這些規則。這是我們身為一個組織所做的。

簡報 11

威爾斯語言監察使做哪些事？

我們測試、監督並執行神祕顧客任務。我們會打電話給各組織，對各組織寄發電子郵件，我們會前往各組織並說「我想要以威爾斯語接受服務，」而如果他們無法照做，如果做不到，我們便會說「你必須這麼做。」如果他們不照做，我可以處以罰款。我可以把他們告進法院。我未曾對任何人處以罰款，因為我實際上認為組織會遵守，因為他們想要而且知道原因。但若某組織或政府拒絕，我真的可以說「我會對你處以罰款，而你就必須付錢。」所以，我有最後的威脅。但我強烈相信，最重要的是主動遵守──各組織選擇遵守──而我們則嘗試協助他們遵守。我們會就如何提供雙語服務對各組織提出建議。我們會為他們提供資訊。我們會給他們可以放在組織內部的海報──上面會寫說「看到此標誌請使用您的威爾斯語。」我們為組織的工作人員提供掛牌，顯示誰會說威爾斯語，而誰正在學習威爾斯語。因此，監督加上積極鼓勵可以得到很好的效果。我們會對投訴展開調查。如果民眾覺得自己沒有得到應有的服務，我們便會調查並干預，確保解決問題。

因此，規定聽起來有點可怕，但我們嘗試運用鼓勵的方法。威爾斯的所有組織都必須遵守標準。威爾斯政府、所有地方當局、當地企業、所有地方議會、警察──都必須提供完整的雙語服務。

我們的大學必須為學生提供全面雙語服務，包括進階教育學院。威爾斯的BBC必須提供全面雙語服務。圖書館、博物館──我們每天去的所有地方，現在都必須提供全面雙語服務。

簡報 12

他們都成功嗎？我們談的是過去五年一直在運作的法律。我們對於遵守和實踐的水準感到非常驚訝，因為某些組織認為這是不可能的。從我們對 100% 自動化機器的測試可以看到一些上升的數字。威爾斯的停車繳費機現在已經 100% 全面雙語。我們也會說「哇！」，但真的做到了！在威爾斯 98% 的公家機構，現在接聽電話時都會以雙語回答。

我們已經看到這個標準運作良好，因為很具體，且各組織都知道如何做。我們協助他們達成這些標準。如果他們不做，我們會威脅他們一下，但他們對所取得的成就感到自豪，就我而言，最大的指標便是各組織不再說「為什麼我們必須提供

雙語服務？」他們現在會說「我們該怎麼做？請協助我們。我們想要達成。我們想要提供全面雙語服務。」現在給各位看一段在威爾斯政府拍的短片。說的是威爾斯語，但有英文字幕。短片中第一位說話的是我們的公務員主管 Ms. Shan Morgan。她是威爾斯高階公務員。她不會說威爾斯語，但她知道這一點，並告訴我們她為威爾斯政府取得的成就感到多麼自豪。我們製作這部短片是為了對像你們這樣的其他組織和人員證明，政府的確有可能在很短的期間（五年）內實現我們認為幾乎不可能實現的目標。

簡報 13

這部短片是我們今年稍早製作的，可以向其他組織顯示威爾斯政府取得的成就。看到威爾斯政府提供這樣的雙語服務時，可以鼓勵其他機構效法。

簡報 14

我已談過我們採用的規定，但我們推廣使用威爾斯語也很重要，我們在履行法律義務的同時做這件事。為什麼要推廣使用威爾斯語？正如我前面說的，有很多年輕人在學校學習威爾斯語。我們需要鼓勵他們在生活的所有層面使用威爾斯語，而不僅僅是在工作的時候使用。所以，我們與企業合作；也與志願組織合作。我們與慈善機構合作，鼓勵他們在工作的所有層面使用威爾斯語。我們非常、非常積極地與威爾斯體育委員會合作，確保足球組織、橄欖球組織和曲棍球組織以雙語運作，讓在學校學習威爾斯語的年輕人也可以在校外環境使用威爾斯語。我們為大型企業提供服務，鼓勵他們在日常工作中使用威爾斯語。我們希望創造一個感覺威爾斯語就是日常生活一部分的威爾斯。我們曾提到，影片中也提到，我們在所有狀況中非常積極使用這種小貼紙，以促進使用威爾斯語，並讓人們因為會說威爾斯語而感到自豪。

所以，規定和推廣真的需要攜手並進。我再給各位看一部短片，然後就差不多可以結束這段簡報了。

這是我們上週製作並發布的影片。這是一部使用英語和威爾斯語，為遷至威爾斯之企業（一家和各位在臺北街上看到的大型零售企業一樣）製作的短片，以鼓勵他們在卡地夫和威爾斯全面展店時使用威爾斯語。

簡報 15

　　謝謝大家。一部很短的影片，但訊息強而有力。我們從歐洲大型企業得到的回應非常正面。很棒！

簡報 16

　　我們監督、推廣也試圖影響。身為語言監察使，我對與威爾斯政府交涉特別感興趣——不僅僅是關於威爾斯語的地位，也包括威爾斯語在醫療保健、教育、城鎮和國家規劃以及政府生活等所有層面。

　　有了立法之後可能會出現很大的危險，政客們會認為「問題已經解決了，已經立法了。」但在我們談論特殊教育需求時，政治家和政策制定者在所有狀況下必須想到威爾斯語，這一點非常重要。談到心理健康照護時，我們需要以威爾斯語討論我們需要做的事。談到照護失智者時，我們需要以威爾斯語討論我們需要做的事。我們必須確保以雙語提供這些服務。因此，我們監督、促進並影響，而最重要的是確保我們以雙語國家思考工作的所有層面。這是我特別感興趣的事。我喜歡與政治家和政策制定者交涉，並要求他們以不同的方式思考如何在威爾斯提供服務。

簡報 17

　　我們也將地名標準化。我有一位同事的工作就是以威爾斯語將地名標準化。為什麼現在威爾斯的所有路標都使用雙語？想想 1970 年代扯下這些路標的人。我們現在有雙語路標了。但地名標準化對於創造歷史和身分也非常重要。為什麼這些地方有這些名字？為什麼以英語和威爾斯語稱呼這些地方？所以，我們利用圍繞地名的工作確保路標上的拼字正確。個人——年輕人和老年人——意識到我們有雙語歷史。因此，對於地名標準化，我們在威爾斯雙語地名方面擁有國家資料和國家資源。

簡報 18

　　我們也鼓勵運用技術，尤其在翻譯方面。我們積極支持使用機器翻譯。談到雙語國家，許多組織都必須製作雙語文件。我們鼓勵使用技術和記憶軟體執行翻譯工作。我們使用古老的語言，但思維方式必須現代化，而技術可以為我們解決許多問題。因此，線上術語和線上詞典是我們鼓勵人們發展之工作的一部分，我們敦促各大學大量開發這些類型的資源。

簡報 19

最後，我談到過威爾斯語言監察使的工作。正如我所說，我們監督、促進、影響並賦予能力。

但我們也與世界各地的夥伴專員合作。我們是一個名為國際語言監察使協會的組織的創始會員。我鼓勵臺灣也加入。你們可能沒有語言監察使，但我真的認為你們應該考慮成為這個組織的成員。我從在加拿大擔任語言監察使的同事那裡學到很多。愛爾蘭有一位語言監察使，科索夫有一位語言監察使。喀麥隆有一位語言監察使。現在，南非也有一位語言監察使，斯里蘭卡有一位語言監察使。

我們有一個由多個機構組成的國際組織，討論不同語言面臨的相同問題。我學到很多，也得到該組織的許多支持。幾年前我們在卡地夫舉行了一次國際會議，我們的第一任部長——我們的總理——在該活動中致詞。我擔任了兩年該國際協會的主席。今年春天復活節期間，我在科索沃普里斯提納卸任。該組織現在由愛爾蘭語言監察使擔任主席。我們都面臨講少數民族語言者相同的挑戰。這些挑戰並不完全相同，但非常類似。我們可以互相學習很多東西，而不會感到孤單。講少數民族語言的人一定會有感覺很孤單的問題。該國際協會可以確保你不會感到孤單。因此，在結束我的簡報時，邀請您考慮成為國際語言監察使協會的會員。

可以鼓勵各位與威爾斯保持聯繫嗎？我覺得我們可以與您合作。兩年前，我們就類似的挑戰，進行過很有意義的對話。

實施新立法時與國際合作非常重要。這將使過程變得豐富，因此，請與我們威爾斯語言委員會保持聯絡。

最後，我將實施立法比喻為繪製路徑圖。立法本身是路標。可以指出您想要去的方向，但關鍵仍在於立法背後的路徑圖。在今天的大會中，你也參與了繪製這份路徑圖，再次恭喜您已就希望如何邁進展開對話。最後我想說，如果想要繪製路徑圖，在規劃這些道路時，最好的道路應該有很多車道。重點不僅僅是一個答案。還包括監督、促進、支持和影響，所有這些都整合在一起，而我認為，這就是我們過去幾年看到威爾斯有重大轉變的原因。

簡報 20-21

感謝聆聽。

希望各位聽到了一些自己感興趣的內容。非常感謝。

【德國索勃語 Sorbian】
從小開始的雙語教育
Being Bilingual from Childhood

索勃學校協會主席 Ludmila Budar 女士

Dear Ladies and Gentlemen:

My name is Ludmila Budar (or 璐德彌拉・布達 in Mandarin). I am also known by my Sorbian name Budarjowa. I come from Bautzen of Germany, which is close to Dresden and is some 9,000 kilometers from Taiwan. The Sorbs are a native people of Germany, having existed for 1500 years and having developed their own language and culture. In Brandenburg, the Sorbs are also known as Wenden. Lusatia is a Sorb-inhabited area. Located in eastern Germany, it is under the jurisdiction of Saxony and Brandenburg. There are also German people living in Lusatia, an area that is 100 kilometers long and 40 kilometers wide. 100 years ago, there were about 100,000 Sorbs in Lusatia, now there are about 60,000, including 20,000 native speakers of Upper Sorbian language, and 7,000 native speakers of Lower Sorbian language. However, it is not possible to know the exact number of Sorbs, because based on the first article on Sorbian affairs in the Constitution of Saxony, and the second article on Sorbian (Wendish) affairs in the Constitution of Brandenburg, it is against the law to make inquiries about a person's ethnic identity. Such laws were enacted to protect the Sorbs from unfair treatments. Possibly half of the inhabitants of Lusatia are of Sorbian/Wendish lineage. Upper Sorbian language and Lower Sorbian language are two types of Slavic scripts with different grammatical rules. The European Charter for Regional or Minority Languages recognizes Upper Sorbian and Lower Sorbian as endangered languages. The Sorbs do not have a country of their own. They are a native ethnic minority of Germany. Collectively they constitute a unique feature of Lusatia, a unique feature which is not found in other parts of Germany.

Legal Basis

Article Three of the Basic Law for the Federal Republic of Germany safeguards the personal rights, not the collective rights, of the Sorbs.

Article Three of the Basic Law for the Federal Republic of Germany

No person shall be favoured or disfavoured because of sex, parentage, race, language, homeland and origin, faith, or religious or political opinions.

Article Six of the Constitution of the State of Saxony

Sorbian inhabitants of Saxony are citizens entitled to equal rights. The identity and rights of Sorbian people are protected and safeguarded in the free state of Saxony, especially the right of the Sorbian people to preserve and promote their language and cultural heritages through primary and secondary schools, kindergartens, and other cultural facilities.

Article Twenty-Five of the Constitution of Brandenburg

The Sorbian people are entitled to the right of preserving and promoting Sorbian language and culture through public initiatives, and of passing down knowledge related to Sorbian language and culture in primary schools, secondary schools, and kindergartens.

The aforementioned rights did not automatically take effect. It was only after the Sorbs/Wendish kept pushing for them on the political front that they finally took effect.

Personally, I care deeply about the preservation and continued growth of Sorbian language, culture, and identity. I was born into a large Sorb family, and many in my family are teachers. My grandfather happens to be one of the first teachers trained by a Sorbian teachers college. My grandparents have a total of 13 children. My father and four of his brothers are all teachers. I have 10 siblings, including three teachers.

For nearly 30 years, I have been working as the Chairperson of the Sorbian Schools Association, while also working other jobs. The mission of Sorbian Schools Association is to represent the rights of the Sorbs to language education, including bilingual preschool education, and bilingual or multilingual education from kindergarten, primary school, secondary school, gymnasium, to college.

According to studies by the Sorbian Institute and the Sorbian Schools Association, the Sorbs have been suffering rapidly growing pressure of assimilation since the last century. In the state of Brandenburg, the number of native Sorbian speakers has been falling for two generations. In the state of Saxony, the number of first-grade to twelfth-grade students who study Sorbian language as a native language suffered a 50% decrease for the past 25 years to about 740 today. At present, about 2000 students are learning Sorbian/Wendish at Brandenburg, including 350 students under the Witaj project. In Saxony, about 2700 students are currently learning Sorbian language, including 740 with native speaker proficiency.

We at the Sorbian Schools Association were determine to reverse the plight, so we turned our focus on language revitalization and early language learning support measures for European children. The DIWAN model adopted by Brittany, France inspired us to formulate an immersion-based Sorbian language education approach. We introduced Witaj , an immersion education project in the 1990s. Witaj makes possible the learning of two languages at the same time, including German, the first language or the majority language, and Sorbian, the second language or the minority language. Our goal is to create new users of Sorbian language to push for preservation, revitalization, and systematic growth of Sorbian language. In 1998, the Sorbian Schools Association introduced Witaj to a kindergarten in Cottbus to pursue the cause of Sorbian language revitalization. It laid a solid foundation for the future development of a comprehensive language learning plan which stretches from kindergarten to college in Saxony and Brandenburg. Witaj is a registered trademark protected by law, and also a symbol of quality assurance given by the Sorbian Schools Association.

I. Kindergartens

What is Witaj ®?

- Witaj ® means "welcome" in Sorbian language. We welcome children with or without previous knowledge of Sorbian language.
- Witaj ® also means a second language learned in an institutional environment and condition.

What does Witaj ® teach?

- Witaj® uses (full or partial) immersion education which has been proven to be effective in a number of countries.
- Immersion takes place in a Sorbian language-using environment.
- It works under the theory of "one language to one person." In other words, the choice of language between two people would remain largely unchanged. For example, a child who speaks German with his father all the time will use no other language but German in future interactions with his father. A child who is used to speaking Sorbian with his mother will continue speaking Sorbian with his mother. Children are likely to associate a certain language with a certain person. As such, children can easily tell one language from another, and have no difficulty switching between languages.

What are the advantages of Witaj®?

- Witaj® fosters development of socializing, interactive, and cognitive abilities in children.
- Witaj® gives children a head start in the learning of other languages, because children have developed the ability to describe an item in two or more languages. In other words, the children are able to interact with speakers of different languages.
- Witaj® fosters learning of a second language at early childhood, since the

children's neural network had already been developed by the time they learned their first language.

- Witaj® students are familiar with both Sorbian and German alphabetical systems, so they will be able to understand Sorbian and German texts once they begin elementary School.
- Witaj® fosters greater acceptance and tolerance for other languages and cultures.
- Witaj® is a rather economical option for parents.

What are the differences between Witaj® daycare and Witaj® groups?

- Witaj® daycare: Full immersion education; students are divided into daycare (ages 1-3), kindergarten (ages 3-6), and afterschool care (ages 6-10).
  - ➢ All students are taught Sorbian language, and Sorbian is used as the only medium for instruction.
  - ➢ All the teachers at Witaj® possess native or near native command of Sorbian language.
  - ➢ Witaj® is under the jurisdiction of the Sorbian Schools Association. Witaj® comprises of 7 daycares/kindergartens with an enrollment of 600 children. 5 out of the 7 daycares/kindergartens are located in the free state of Saxony, and 2 are located in Brandenburg.
- Witaj® groups practice partial immersion education:
  - ➢ Not all of the children learn the Sorbian language.
  - ➢ Only a small number of teachers have various levels of command of Sorbian language.
  - ➢ Witaj® groups are under the jurisdiction of various government agencies, but mostly are under the supervision of Sorbian affairs-related government agencies.

In Saxony and Brandenburg, around 650 children are currently learning Sorbian language through full immersion, around 320 children are learning Sorbian language through partial immersion, and around 250 children either only learn Sorbian language in their spare time, or merely practice Sorbian songs and poetry. When Sorbian teachers call in sick or ask for a leave, the children are often left in the care of teachers who are not fluent users of Sorbian language, which could seriously compromise the children's learning outcome.

What comes after Witaj®?

- **Witaj**® builds up a solid foundation for the networks of Sorbian language and German language schools.
- **Witaj**® provides the best blue print for school-based language education development in Saxony and Brandenburg.
- Preschool education at **Witaj**® is a guarantee of a successful language learning process. The parents of **Witaj**® students are fully informed as to how Sorbian language is taught at **Witaj**®.

The Immersion

As stated above, for children, immersion as a way of learning Sorbian language invokes human's inherent ability to learn language. However, there are fears that immersion would bring extra burden to the learner. Such a fear hardly makes sense. A crucial factor of immersion education is that teaching must be structural and consistent from beginning to end, and must be enhanced with facial expressions and gestures from the instructor. Children are born with the prerequisites of language learning, such as ability to understand and language ability.

Translating Sorbian language into German is hardly a good way to teach Sorbian language to children, because this renders the children unable to make any meaningful progress in the learning of a new language. Besides, teaching Sorbian language by translating it to German might lead children to mistakenly believe that German is the more important language of the two, since they frequently come into contact with German as a mainstream language in class. In addition, learning the meaning of Sorbian language in German could be confusing to children and counter-effective to their learning, as young children might have difficulty at times telling Sorbian from German, and as a result might mix up the two languages and end up formulating a language hybrid in their brain.

In other words, their brain would not be able to construct a logical flow of language.

What happens inside the brain?

Neurological specialists have demonstrated that children's brain develops only one set of neural network from learning two languages since birth. In other words, children are able to learn two languages at the same time without difficulty since birth. Children might have difficulty learning a second language if they wait until they begin school to learn a second language, because by the time they begin school, their brain would have already developed a second set of neural network. By the time they reach the age of three, children are able to store more languages in theirbrain. As such, their brain works more productively in language learning, capable of absorbing a large number of information like sponge. Over a longer period of time, young children are able to remember more types of language in their brain. This is the reason why the Sorbian Schools Association has introduced immersion education at preschool level.

Based on the theory of imitation, children can learn different languages well without difficulty. This causes some to believe that young children can actually learn many first languages.

Generally speaking, in the course of their development, children would not suffer negatively from multilingual learning, provided that the languages are taught to them clearly, structurally, and systematically. Bilingual or multilingual learning could make children more attentive because they are able to discern immediately which are the mother language expressions they are familiar with, and which are new or strange expressions. As a result, they are likely to listen to their teachers more attentively in class, and afterwards would be able to tackle more logically complex and more creative tasks, and wield a wider vocabulary to describe events or issues. According to an important study from Brandenburg,[1] children are likely to do better in mathematics and music in

---

1 http://neu.sielow-cottbus.de/index.php/unserortsteil/kultur/sorgeninsielow/14-ortsteil/informationen8/1 77-irena-goetze and "10 lĕtmodelowyprojektWitaj/10 Jahre ModellprojketWitaj, (1998–2008). Jubiläumsausgabe, Bautzen: SorbischerSchulverein e. V. 2008, S. 34-35.

primary education if they begin bilingual education at an early stage of their childhood. There are other interesting discoveries from studies from neuroscience perspectives.

In conducting immersion education, it is important that teachers repeat their messages to students over and over again. Repeating the same words over and over when describing a situation to children would help the children formulate new usages from a new language on their own. They become increasingly aware of these new usages and capable of using them on their own. This development process requires a lot of patience and compliments, rather than correction and reproach, from teachers.

Recent studies on the subject of memory loss shows that the brains of bilingualor multilingual seniors actually perform more productively. Multilingualism requires a more advanced level of thinking, and those who spend their entire life switching to and from different languages can slow down memory loss and facilitate brain functions.

What kind of role do parents play?

Parents are the most important partners of teachers, because they are closest to their children and often wield decisive influence over language learning of their children. When parents display an interest in learning a new language, and even learn with or from their children, their children can take pride in this and even feel understood. Some preschools give parents a list of the most commonly used words, phrases, expressions, proverbs, and greetings in Sorbian language. The Sorbian Schools Association writes a bilingual letter to the parents of students every season. Family days[2] and festival celebrations are regularly held in Witaj kindergartens (e.g., the Witaj's 20th anniversary celebrations). Language learning can be effective with the right conditions. As our slogan goes, "Monolingualism is the mother of nonlingualism!" or "Monolingualism can be saved!" These are reasons that many parents, grandparents, and their friends opt for children to begin multilingual education early on in childhood.

---

2 Each year, the Sorbian Schools Association invites parents and grandparents of students to visit the kindergarten, watch the shows presented by students, and chat over afternoon tea.

How does the learning process work?

Language learning is an intrinsically active and constructive process. For a language learning process to work smoothly, <u>the key is to teach intensively, coherently, and consistently.</u>

Acceptance: The signs of resistance displayed by children in the early stages of language learning are often frustrating to grownups. Yet these are common and perfectly normal. Through parallel learning of Sorbian language, parents can help children overcome such resistance. After the phase of silent resistance, children would gradually move on to the phase of understanding.

Passive withdrawal from language learning and confusing one language and another would have little effect on children's language learning. In the stage ofacceptance, learners show acceptance of a new language, and start to store elements of this language in their brain. Children begin to have an understanding that people might describe an item in different words. Some children need to spend more time on the first phase than others. Besides, children will experience the first phase over and over, because they never stop learning new things.

Then comes the hearing phase, in which language learning plays the role of decoding, as is evident from the behaviors of infants. Children encounter in kindergarten on a daily basis the repetitive use of languages as well as words associated with the use of languages. In the early stage of childhood, children might quickly move from this stage to the stage of understanding. The duration of this stage also varies from child to child.

Output stage: The beginning of the stage in which children start to use Sorbian vocabulary varies from child to child. External factors also play a role. The intensive, coherent, and structural use of Sorbian language mentioned above has a major influence on language acquisition. In addition, language acquisition is also affected by how much time children spend in preschool/kindergarten, and by the percentage of students who are native Sorbian speakers. The positive motivation which arises from demonstration effect and keen interactions with Sorbian as a second language also has a decisive impact. After making simple replies with simple sentences, children start to try a new language and move beyond the output stage and start to make intensive comparisons of their mother language and second language. They (suddenly) begin to use the target language, not out of coercion. However, this stage is often invisible. Children at this stage are able to learn by singing or reading picture books. After moving past the stage of output, children are able to talk to their teachers in Sorbian language.

Encourage children to speak the language

Children need natural motives and familiar surroundings to be able to speak up. They need to learn from reference models a natural way to speak a language as accurately as possible. The importance of emotional factors in language learning should not be underestimated. Children will find in a language they love comforting and soothing qualities, which would cause them to have confidence in, and closeness with, this language. Videos and audio books can never replace spoken words in real life interactions. When children learn two or more languages at the same time, they encounter a slight hiatus in language development at a certain stage, because language learning is not a linear process. A study that I conducted on preschool children[3] (ages 3-6) (Budar 2009) demonstrates that bilingual children who begin school at the age of six display good language skills in learning German language, even outperforming monolingual (German) children.

Language support outside preschool/ kindergarten and school

More importantly is the use of additional Sorbian language environments. Indispensable learning aids include songs, children's songs, riddles, stories, picture books, plays, movies, and new media. For this purpose, the Sorbian Schools Association set up a constantly upgraded new website (www.dyrdomdej.de), which provides instructional materials for teachers and parents with an interest in Sorbian language. At

---

3 Ludmila Budarjowa/Jana Šołćina: Serbšćinuwuknyć a wučić – ewaluacijaWitaj a 2plus (= Sorbischlernen und lehren), in: Witaj a 2plus wužadanje za přichod / Witaj und 2plus – eineHerausforderungfür die Zukunft, Bautzen: SorbischerSchulvereine.V. 2009, s. 60–75 (pages 66-75 are writen by Ludmila Budar) .

present the website provides Upper Sorbian language-related materials only, with Lower Sorbian language-related materials coming up in 2019. The website is called "dyrdomdej" because learning Sorbian language is like an adventure! As part of the Sorbian Schools Association's Witaj® project, the website is designed to facilitate intensive language learning, with cartoon characters by the name of Majka, Le ka, Korla, and Little Flori (a puppy) helping children learn the language. The website begins by introducing Sorbian vocabulary to users. The important thing is that there are teaching activities such as DIY, sports sessions, Guess What, activities for general and specific purposes, experiments, memory power exercise, basic math drills, songs, culinary recipes, and observations with illustrations and texts to help students learn in an interactive and communicative way. The aim is to use games as an immersion learning aid for children to learn Sorbian language. The website is constantly updated. The first learning activities on the website were about fruits. Later on games about colors and other topics were added.

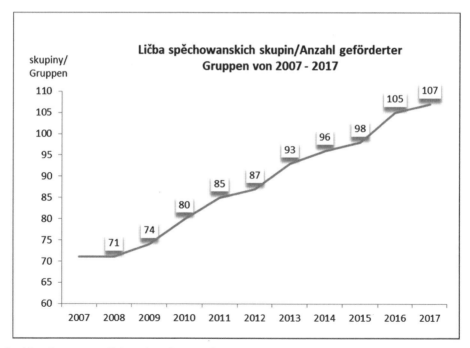

Sorbian Language Education Groups funded by the Free State of Saxony, 2007-2017

© *Ludmila Budar/Budarjowa 2017, žórło/Quelle: KrajnoradnyzarjadBudyšin/Landratsamt Bautzen a SMK*

At present, 107 Sorbian language education groups are being funded by the free state of Saxony, including 32 run by the Sorbian Schools Association, which adopt full immersion. Most of the rest teach Sorbian language occasionally, using partial immersion.

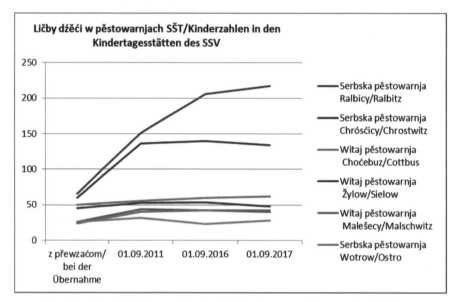

The Number of Students Enrolled in Kindergartens Run by the Sorbian SchoolsAssociation (The Sorbian Schools Association introduced immersion educational approach to the kindergartens it took over in 2011, 2016, and 2017 respectively.)

© *Ludmila Budarjowa 2017, žórło/Quelle: Serbskešulsketowarstwo z.t./SorbischerSchulvereine.V.*

For the past 20 years, parents flocked to enroll their children in kindergartens run by the Sorbian Schools Association, sometimes even before their children were born, because they opted for immersion education for their children. However, the kindergartens do not have enough space for more students.

II. Primary and Secondary Schools

All the schools that use Sorbian language as the medium for instruction, and those that use Sorbian and German languages as the medium for instruction, are public schools mostly under the jurisdiction of regional or municipal authorities. To date, there is not yet any private Sorbian school or Sorbian higher education institution.

As stated above, Witaj can get students ready for schools where Sorbian and German languages are used as a medium for instruction. Children enrolled in Witaj kindergartens, especially those who learn through full immersion, will have little difficulty to excel in 2plus programs[4] offered by bilingual schools (Sorbian and German) in Saxony and bilingual courses offered in Brandenburg.[5] In other words, Witaj enables students to move further in the overall language learning process and makes possible multilingual education at school level.

What is 2plus?

- **2plus** was officially introduced in the free state of Saxony in the 2013/14 academic year.
- **2plus** students learn the two languages of German and Sorbian, plus another language (e.g., English, French, Czech, Spanish, Russia) at school.
- **2plus** is opened to all students of Sorbian schools.
- Other schools (usually the ones that used German as the major medium for instruction, with only a portion of students learning Sorbian language) adopt 2plus-style single-class or single-group teaching.
- Students are divided in three groups for Sorbian language education, depending on their different levels of Sorbian language proficiency:
  - ➤ **Language Group I:** The children have learned Sorbian language, and are able to use it in everyday life and school like a native language.
  - ➤ **Language Group II:** The children have learned Sorbian language, and are able to use it in everyday life and school as a second language.
  - ➤ **Language Group III:** A group of students who want to be able to at least use Sorbian language as a second language.
- As a discipline, Sorbian language is both a medium for instruction and also an

---

4　weitereInformationenunter www.abc.brandenburg.de.
5　weitereInformationenunter www.abc.brandenburg.de.

objective for learning.

- Sorbian language can be used as a full or partial medium for instruction in other disciplines. (Primary schools may choose which of the three disciplines should use Sorbian language as a medium for instruction, such as mathematics or physical education. Secondary schools can decide for themselves which of the five disciplines, including history, geography, biology, physical education, music, or art, should use Sorbian language as a medium for instruction.) Teachers can work in groups (two teachers working together) to teach these disciplines.
- Other disciplines are taught bilingually.
- Students who join a class after the beginning of semester may choose a class in which two languages are used as medium for instruction. Additional Sorbian language courses might enable them to attain Language Group III proficiency.
- The learning objectives and curriculum of public schools in Saxony are applicable and binding on local bilingual (German and Sorbian) students, who are to be conferred diploma of equivalent education level.
- Class lectures are delivered by teachers in Sorbian and German languages.
- Each school has a school coordinator6 who takes part in language teaching.

Unfortunately, due to a shortage of Sorbian language teachers, 2plus-style teaching cannot be practiced by every school.

Sorbian language as a foreign language

In addition to 2plus, there are also cases in which Sorbian is taught as a foreign language. In such cases, Sorbian language is treated as a not-so-important discipline, and is often given strange or not-so-ideal class hours, which could compromise learning outcome. In areas of Saxony and Brandenburg where no Witaj® kindergarten exists,

---

6 Each school has a school coordinator. School coordinators teach at bilingual schools (Sorbian and German), and have a good command of Sorbian language. They teach bilingually and support the concept of 2plus, and see to it that 2plus principles are being properly practiced in schools. School coordinators work in close collaboration with school management (Landesamtfür Schule und Bildung 2017, https://www.schule.sachsen.de/download/download_bildung/18_10_18_2plus_Konzept_Stand_Septem ber_2018.pdf).

Sorbian language education is conducted in this way.

Continuing education and college education

Adults can study at colleges or higher-level educational institutions in Bautzen. Wendish language courses are offered at the Cottbus Lower Sorbian Language and Culture School. Teacher training is found in the Sorbian College of Social Education in Bautzen and also in Cottbus Center for Higher Education. Leipzig University's Institute of Sorbian Studies offers diploma and degree programs in Sorbian language and Wendish language studies. These educational institutions are not under the jurisdiction of Sorbian authorities, but the government of Germany. Recent years saw the rise of e-learning of Sorbian language. Basically speaking, compared to other European minority languages, Sorbian language needs more public exposure, more multimedia-enabled teaching using radio, television, modern media, and especially digital media, as well as real breakthroughs as part of bilingualism and mother language, second language, and foreign language education at schools. As such, continued developments in teacher training and pedagogy are much needed, and teachers with native speaker proficiency are especially needed, to fuel the process of Sorbian language revitalization.

Länder	1994/95	2009/10	2014/15	2015/16	2016/17
Sakska/ Sachsen	3.683	2.232 (1083 rěčnaskupina/ Sprach- gruppe 1)	2.476 (654 rěčnaskupina/ Sprach- gruppe 1)	2.674 (652 rěčnaskupina/ Sprach- gruppe 1)	2.628 (744 rěčnaskupina/ Sprach- gruppe 1)
Brani-borska/ Brandenburg	1.051	1.824 (234 Witaj-šulerjow/ Schüler)	1.522	1.468 (301 Witaj-šuler/ Schüler)	2.010 (349 Witaj-šulerjow/ Schüler)
cyłkownje/ Gesamt	4.734	4.056	3.998	4.142	4.638

Comparison of the number of students in Saxony and Brandenburg

© Ludmila Budar/Budarjowa, 2017, Quellen/žórła: SBAB, ABC, MBJS

The number of students studying Sorbian language and the number of students treating Sorbian as a foreign language in Saxony

© *Ludmila Budar/Budarjowa, 2017, Sakska/Sachsen, žórło/Quelle: SBAB*

Children who have reached native speaker level (Language Group I) only account for 28% of children ages 6-12 studying Sorbian language at school. The aim of Sorbian Schools Association is that children who reach Language II status by the time they graduate from Witaj® preschools/kindergartens will be able to reach native speaker proficiency towards the end of primary school education.

Conclusion

The Witaj® project introduced by Sorbian Schools Association not only creates a new language theory, but also demonstrates with real actions that the same pattern can be successfully applied to all languages under certain conditions. The first condition is emotional and financial support from the majority ethnic group and Germany, Saxony, and Brandenburg (states where Upper and Lower Sorbian peoples inhabit). In addition, native speakers of Sorbian language need to fight for preservation, continued development, and revitalization of their mother language on a legal basis. It is also necessary that

Sorbian publications and existing Sorbian instructional materials are accessible in digital format (because Sorbian is not merely a language used at home or in the court of law. It is a language on equal status with other modern European languages!) That is why the DYRDOMDEJ website is so important to us! A similar website may be constructed to help children learn Hakka language.

After 20 years of development, the Witaj® project not only caused German and Sorbian parents to be increasingly interested in bilingual and multilingual education, intellectuals from around the world, including Taiwan, also show an interest in learning more about bilingual and multilingual education. Language is the most important trait of identity. Culture is spread through language, and relationship bonds are also forged through language. Parents and family members play an important role, acting as examples for children and planning a good path of learning for children, and being able or willing to support children. For parents, what is so important is that Witaj® offers **a comprehensive language learning plan** lasting from kindergarten to college, though this plan needs further expansion and adjustment.

It is possible to revitalize, sustain, and strengthen a language and thereby enhances cultural identity of the users of this language. The prerequisites of successful language revitalization are the collective will of the people and the political will to preserve language and culture heritages. Such a complicated and challenging task requires the joint efforts of people who share the same aspirations.

Works Cited

Budar, Ludmila (Hrsg. und Mitautorin): 20 lět Jahre Witaj®, Witaj k nam! Herzlichwillkommen! Serbskešulsketowarstwo/SorbischerSchulverein, Bautzen, 2018, 222 S.

Budar, Ludmila (Hrsg. und Mitautorin): Wo přiswojenjuserbšćiny a němčiny, 25 lětSerbskešulsketowarstwo z.t. Zumsorbisch-deutschenSpracherwerb, 25 Jahre SorbischerSchulvereine.V., Serbskešulsketowarstwo/SorbischerSchulverein, Bautzen, 2016, 82 S.

Budar, Ludmila, Maćeršćinuzaměrnišosp chować; Witaj a 2 plus słušatej k najmodernišimkonceptam za zažnenawuknjenjerěčow w Europje (Mutterspracheziel gerichteterfördern; Witaj und 2plus gehörenzu den modernstenKonzeptenfür den fr hkindlichenSpracherwerb) in: Serbskašula 1-20015, S.19-28.

Ludmila Budarjowa: LE SORABE L'ÉCOLE: LES SIGLES WITAJ ET 2PLUS,Revue des études Slaves, Institutd'études Slaves, UMBR 8224, Paris-Sorbonne, 2014.

Ludmila Budar und Jana Šołćina, Wuwićeserbsko-němskejedwurěčnosćepolapředšulsk ichdźěći-metodypřepytowanja a přěnjewuslědki. / Die Entwicklung der sorbisch-deutschenZweisprachigkeitbeiVorschulkindern-Untersuchungsmethoden und ersteErgebnisse. In: Rozhlad 55, 9/10, S. 349-359.

Budar, Ludmila (Hrsg. und Mitautorin):Witaj und 2plus eineHerausforderungfür die Zukunft, Serbskešulsketowarstwo z.t./SorbischerSchulvereine.V., Bautzen, 2010, 219 S.

Budar, Ludmila, Zumsorbischen Schulwesen, in: Wiater, Werner &Videsott, Gerda (Hrsg.), Schule in mehrsprachigen Regionen Europas. School Models in Multilingual Regions of Europe, s. 315-334, Frankfurt a. Main/Berlin/Bern/Bruxelles/New York/ Oxford/Wien et al.: Peter Lang 2005.

Bärbel Brash, Andrea Pfeil: DLL 09: Unterrichten mit digitalen Medien: Fort- und Weiterbildung weltweit, Ernst KlettSprachen GmbH, 2017.

GundaHeyder: Das WITAJ*-Projekt in Kindertagesstätten der Niederlausitz http://www. mbjs.brandenburg.de/media_fast/4113/

Jana Schulz, Bilingualer Spracherwerb im Witaj-Projekt, Bautzen 2015, Broschur 232 Seiten, Domowina Verlag.

Kramer, Katharina: Wie werde ich einSprachgenie? In: Gehirn und Geist, Spektrum Akademischer Verlag, Heidelberg 2/2003, S. 48-50.

Ratajczak, Cordula: Der Überlebensdiskurs der sorbischenSprachealsinnersorbischer Dialog. Bedingungen, Probleme und neuereEntwicklungen. In: Dietrich Scholze (Hg.): Im Wettstreit der Werte. SorbischeSprache, Kultur und Identität auf dem Weg ins 21. Jahrhundert (Spisy Serbskehoinstituta = Schriften des SorbischenInstituts 33).

Bautzen 2003, S. 303-313.

Chilla Solveig, Niebuhr-Siebert, Sandra: Mehrsprachigkeit in der KiTa: Grundlagen – Konzepte-Bildung, Taschenbuch-11, Kohlhammer, 2017.

Schneider, Stefan, Bilingualer Spracherwerb. München, 2015, UTB Reinhardt.

Walde, Martin: Wie man seine Sprachehassenlernt. Bautzen, 2010, Domowina-Verlag.

Landtag Brandenburg Drucksache 6/7529, 6. Wahlperiode, Nr. 2988 Landtag Brandenburg, 6. Wahlperiode, Drucksache 6/6246, Antwort der.

Landesregierung auf die KleineAnfrage 2469, der Abgeordneten Kathrin Dannenberg und Anke Schwarzenberg der Fraktion DIE LINKE, Drucksache 6/6024 Schulverwaltungssoftware SaxSVS, Kerstin Wittig, Sächsische Staatsministerium für Kultus.

Statistisches Landesamt des Freistaates Sachsen, Kamenz 2017 Statistische Ämter des Bundes und der Länder, 2014 Landratsamt Bautzen/Budyskikrajnoradnyzarjad.

SächsischeBildungsagentur, Regionalstelle Bautzen.

Internetseiten

https://20 lětSerbskešulsketowarstwo z.t.: 20 Jahre SorbischerSchulvereine.V. https://www.sorbischer-schulverein.de

https://www.kindergartenpaedagogik.de/

https://de.wikipedia.org/wiki/Bilingualismus

https://de.wikipedia.org/wiki/Mehrsprachigkeit

https://de.wikipedia.org/wiki/Spracherwerb

http://www.zweisprachigkeit.net/Verein fürfrüheMehrsprachigkeit an Kindertageseinrichtungen und Schulen, FMKS e.V.:

https://www.fmks-online.de/

譯者：蔡芬芳

親愛的女士與先生：

我是 Ludmila Budar（中文為璐德彌拉・布達），索勃語為 Budarjowa。我來自德國包岑（Bautzen），在德勒斯登（Dresden）附近，距離臺灣大約有 9,000 公里。索勃人（the Sorbs/ die Sorben），在勃蘭登堡邦亦稱溫德人（Wenden），為德國原生民族，已有 1,500 年歷史，並有自己的語言與文化。勞席茨地區是索勃民族聚集區，該區位於德國東部，分屬薩克森自由邦與勃蘭登堡邦。該區亦有德意志民族居住，約為 100 公里長，40 公里寬。在 100 年前，此地區索勃民族人數尚有 100,000 人，今日為 60,000 人，其中以上索勃語為母語者共計 20,000 人，以下索勃語為母語者則約 7,000 人。然而無法提供有關索勃民族的正確人數，因為根據薩克森邦憲法中的索勃條文之第 1 條以及勃蘭登堡邦憲法中之索勃（溫德）條文第 2 條，不得調查個人身分，以避免索勃民族遭受不當對待。勞席茨地區約有一半居民的祖先可說是索勃人／溫德人。上索勃語及下索勃語是兩種各自有著不同文法的斯拉夫書寫語言。上索勃語及下索勃語在《歐洲區域及少數語言憲章》（Europäischen Charta der Regional-und Minderheitensprachen / European Charter for Regional or Minority Languages）中被承認為受威脅的語言。索勃民族沒有屬於自己的國家，而是德國原生少數民族。與其他地區相比，索勃／溫德是勞席茨地區的獨特標誌，凸顯的是此地區的獨特之處。

法律基礎

德意志聯邦共和國基本法在第 3 條中賦予索勃民族個人權利，非群體權利：

德意志聯邦共和國基本法第 3 條

無人因其性別、血緣、種族、家鄉與祖先來源、信仰、宗教或是政治觀點受到歧視或優惠。

薩克森邦邦憲法第 6 條

本邦內居住屬索勃民族之公民為享有平等權益之國民。本邦確保及保護對索勃民族之認同及其維護之權利，尤其是透過中小學、幼兒園及各項文化設施以保存及發展該民族語言、文化及傳承。

勃蘭登堡邦邦憲法第 25 條

索勃人有權就公共事務中維護及促進索勃語言及文化，於中小學及幼兒園教授索勃語言及文化的相關知識。

　　上述權利並非自動生效，必須由索勃人／溫德人持續不斷地在政治上提出新的要求才能達成。

　　我個人相當關心於索勃語言、文化與認同的保存與發展。我來自家中孩子眾多的索勃家庭，可說是老師世家。我的祖父是索勃師範體系培育的第一位教師，祖父與祖母一共生了 13 個孩子。我父親與他的四個兄弟亦皆為教師。我有 10 個兄弟姊妹，其中三人也是教師。

　　幾乎近 30 年的時間，除了我自己本身的工作之外，本人始終擔任索勃學校協會主席。該協會旨在代表索勃民族的語言教育權利，包括學前雙語教育以及囊括從幼兒園、小學、中學、文理中學與大學之雙語或多語教育。

　　索勃研究所的學術研究與索勃學校協會之分析已經顯示，索勃民族所遭受的同化過程自上個世紀以來急遽地進行。在勃蘭登堡邦，已有兩個世代的索勃母語者人數下降，在薩克森邦，以母語程度學習索勃語且分布在 1 到 12 年級的中小學生，在過去的 25 年以來，人數減半，至今約餘 740 名母語程度學生。目前在勃蘭登堡邦約 2,000 名學生學習索勃語／溫德語，其中 350 名為參加 Witaj 計畫的學生。在薩克森邦，約有 2,700 名學生學習索勃語，其中 740 名為母語程度者。

　　做為索勃學校協會，我們要阻止上述的發展，所以我們學習歐洲孩童早期的語言支持學習與語言復興。法國布列塔尼 DIWAN 概念激發了我們以沉浸式學習推動索勃語的學習。我們在 1990 年代開始以沉浸式學習概念發展出 Witaj® 計畫。以此，兩種語言皆可顧及，亦即作為多數群體的第一語言——德語，少數族群的第二語言之索勃語。我們的目標在於，帶出新的語言使用者，以讓索勃語得以維持、復振，以及有目標地繼續發展。1998 年，索勃學校協會開始在寇特布斯（Cottbus）幼兒園以 Witaj® 計畫進行索勃語之復振過程，同時，此舉則為薩克森邦與勃蘭登堡邦從托兒所到大學之整體語言學習計畫立下基石。Witaj ® 是受到法律保護的專有名詞，而且是索勃學校協會之品質標章。

I. 幼兒園

何謂 Witaj ® ？

- Witaj ® 為索勃語，意為「歡迎」。無論孩童是否具有索勃語先備知識，我們都竭誠歡迎。
- Witaj ® 意謂在機構環境與條件下所學習的第二語言。

Witaj ® 在教什麼？

- Witaj® 運用國際經驗已證實的（完全或部分）沉浸式教學。
- 沉浸於索勃語環境中。
- 原則為「一個人一個語言」，亦即語言與人連結，例如與父親只用德語溝通，孩子就始終維持以德語和父親溝通，若和母親用索勃語溝通，則維持與母親僅用索勃語溝通。孩子看到某人，就與某個特定語言連結，如此能夠讓孩子容易分辨語言，同時容易在不同語言之間進行轉換。

Witaj ® 有何優點？

- Witaj® 促進孩子額外的社會、互動與認知能力。
- Witaj® 孩子在學習其他語言時具有優勢，因為孩子已經學會，對於同樣一個物件，用兩種或多種語言描述，而且文法亦不相同。而且，孩子會有能力與操持不同語言的人互動。
- Witaj® 促進孩童早期第二語言的學習，因為在學習第一語言時神經元網絡已經存在。
- Witaj® 孩童可以在進入小學時，可以同時閱讀索勃語及德文讀物。
- Witaj® 有助於促進對於其他語言及文化的包容度與接受度。
- Witaj® 對家長來說，並不會造成額外的經濟負擔。

Witaj ® 托兒所與 Witaj ® 團體差別何在？

- Witaj® 托兒所：採完全沉浸式教學，分為三組，托兒所（1-3 歲孩童）、幼兒園（3-6 歲孩童）與課後照顧（6-10 歲學童）。

> 所有孩童學習索勃語，且完全以索勃語作為使用與互動語言。
> 所有老師的索勃語程度皆達母語人士標準。
> 索勃學校協會為其主管單位，總共是 7 個托兒所／幼兒園內 600 個孩童，其中 5 個在薩克森邦，2 個在勃蘭登堡邦。
- Witaj® 團體以採部分沉浸式教學：
> 幼兒園中部分孩童學習索勃語。
> 僅有少數的老師會索勃語。
> Witaj® 團體的主管機關不一，但大部分仍是由與索勃相關機關負責。

在薩克森邦與勃蘭登堡邦約有 650 個孩童以完全沉浸式學習索勃語，約 320 個孩童採部分沉浸式。另外 250 個孩童僅在某些時間內學習索勃語，或只是練習索勃歌謠或詩歌，假若當索勃老師生病或請假時，則由不會索勃語的老師代替照顧孩童，因此如此學習索勃語的效果大打折扣。

Witaj® 帶來的效果為何？

- **Witaj®** 為索勃語及德語學校網絡創造堅實的基礎。
- **Witaj®** 對於薩克森邦與勃蘭登堡邦後續推行的學校語言教育概念奠定最佳的前提。
- 學齡前 **Witaj®** 教育對於成功的整體語言學習過程是一項保證。父母會獲得充分的資訊，了解學校如何教授索勃語。

沉浸式方法

如前所述，孩童以此方式沉浸於索勃語世界之中。如此語言學習方式符合自然的人類學習語言的能力，然而卻引發質疑的聲音，擔心沉浸式學習增加學習者的負擔，如此的恐懼是不合理的。實行沉浸式學習時相當具有決定性的要素在於，以始終如一、結構化的教學並且以臉部表情與手勢強化學習。孩子與生俱來具備不同的學習語言的前提要件，例如理解能力與語言天分。

在教導孩子時，應避免將索勃語翻譯成德文，因為會使得學習新語言停滯，無法向前邁進。若翻譯為德文，孩童可能因此透過頻繁使用主流語言德語，而間接地被教導，德語是比較重要的語言。再者，常常混雜索勃語與德語之字句，反而造成學習上的反效果。年幼孩童無法將成人的表達辨別出並歸納為是德語或是索勃語。

如此產生一個危險，孩子會創造出混雜語言。如此一來，在孩童腦神經的發展上，無法建構出有規則可循的語言系統。

大腦發生了什麼事？

神經內科專家已經證實，從出生學習兩種語言，孩子大腦為雙語僅發展出唯一神經元網絡。因此孩子以玩耍方式，並且毫無困難地可以同時學習另一種語言。若孩童到學校才學第二種語言，大腦建構了第二套神經元網絡，學習另一種語言將會顯得吃力而且困難。直到三歲時，孩子大腦可以儲存更多種語言。如此，大腦在面對語言學習時更有效率。孩子可以像海綿般吸收所有資訊。年幼孩子在較長的時間內，其大腦中儲存更多種語言。因此索勃學校協會已在托兒所採沉浸式方式教學。

依照模仿原則，孩童可以輕而易舉地將更多語言學習得很好。因此學者認為，年幼小孩可以學習多個第一語言。

一般說來，孩子在其發展過程中，並不會因為多語而產生負面影響，前提要件是在學習語言時，必須要有一個明確學習對象，清楚地以結構化方式且有系統地傳遞語言。雙語及多語有助於促進注意力提升，因為孩童可以立即判斷，什麼是自己所熟悉的母語表達，什麼又是新的或陌生的表達。孩童會更加專心聆聽，而且之後可以解決較抽象的、較具邏輯性的，以及更具創意的任務。在語言的使用上，具有更多詞彙來描述事務或議題。根據勃蘭登堡邦的重要研究顯示[7]，孩子從小受雙語教育，在小學中的數學與音樂有較好的表現。在腦部的研究發展亦有些其他有趣的結果發現。

教師在進行沉浸式教學時特別強調重複。在和孩童對話時，碰到相同情形時，始終用同樣的句子強調如此，孩子自己可以在新的語言中發展出新的用法，逐漸地會加以注意，之後則可以自行運用。這需要許多的耐心，並非一直糾正與責備，而是多加稱讚。

最新關於記憶衰退的研究顯示，雙語或多語年長者腦部較能有效運作。透過多語能力證明較佳的思考能力。終身在多種語言之間轉換，減緩記憶衰退並且具有腦

7　http://neu.sielow-cottbus.de/index.php/unserortsteil/kultur/sorgeninsielow/14-ortsteil/informationen8/177-irena-goetze 以及 "10 lět modelowy projekt Witaj/10 Jahre Modellprojket Witaj, (1998–2008). Jubiläumsausgabe, Bautzen: Sorbischer Schulverein e. V. 2008, S. 34-35.

部訓練的功能。

父母扮演何種角色？

　　父母是老師最重要的夥伴，因為他們與孩子有最緊密的關係以及對於語言學習具有決定性的影響。孩子可因此引以為傲，而且會感受到被同理，當父母對新的語言感到興趣，而且甚至與孩子一起學習，或是向孩子學習。有些托兒所會給予父母索勃語一張清單，上有重要的索勃字詞、句子、成語以及問候語。每一季，索勃學校協會會寫一封雙語信件給父母。在托兒所／幼兒園持續舉行家庭慶祝活動[8]以及重要的節慶（例如慶祝 Witaj 二十週年紀念）。若一切配合得當，語言學習將會發生其效用。我們的標語是「跟隨單語而來的是無語！」或是「單語是可以補救的！」這些標語讓父母、祖父母與周遭朋友們接受從小學習多語的教育。

學習過程如何進行？

　　語言學習是一個本質上活躍與建構的過程。語言學習過程是流暢地進行的。成功的關鍵在於密集地、始終如一、持續與耐心教授語言。

　　接受階段：孩子在一剛開始拒絕，是會讓大人感到沮喪的。如此的行為是常見的，而且不需過度擔心。透過平行學習索勃語，父母可以幫助孩子克服這個階段。在沉默階段之後，孩子逐漸開始進入理解階段。

　　孩子被動退縮或是混淆語言，在語言學習上並不會產生作用。在接受階段，學習者接受新的語言而且在大腦儲存這些語言成分。孩子開始去理解，每個人以不同的字彙描述同樣的物件。第一階段每個人情形所需時間不一，而且從未結束，因孩子持續在學習新的東西。

　　聆聽階段對於語言學習扮演解碼的角色，這是可以在嬰兒的身上可以觀察到。透過重複的語言使用，與語言使用連結的字彙，是孩子每天在幼兒園所經歷的，這個階段在孩童早期可以快速地達到理解階段。這個階段同樣也是依每個小孩發展階段不同而定。

　　產出階段：孩子何時開始自己使用索勃字彙，依孩子個別能力而定。外在條件亦具有影響力。之前所提到的密集、始終如一與結構化的運用索勃語對於語言習

8　每一年索勃學校協會皆會邀請家長與祖父母，參觀幼兒園，並且大家共同欣賞孩子表演節目，共享下午茶，且大家互相交流。

得具有重大影響力，此外，在托兒所或幼兒園時間長短，以及在學生之中索勃母語學生人數比例，對語言習得亦有影響。因自示範效果以及與第二語言索勃語的敏銳互動而產生的積極動機亦具有決定性作用。在簡單的回答與字句的運用之後，孩子開始嘗試新的語言並越過產出階段。開始密集比較母語及第二語言異同。並非受到強迫，開始（突然）會使用目標語言，但這個階段常常是隱而不見的。可以藉由唱歌或閱讀繪本學習。直到達到產出階段之後，教師與孩子之間可以開始以索勃語交談。

鼓勵開口說

孩童需要自然的動機與熟悉的環境，開口表達。參考對象的語言應該是以自然的方式與盡可能精準的使用。學習語言的情感因素應不能低估，因為如果語言是孩子喜愛的，可以有安慰作用的，也可以安撫情緒的，那麼孩子會對這個語言產生信任感且是親近的。影片與有聲書無法取代互動中所經歷的開口說話。當孩子同時學習兩種或更多種語言時，在一個特定階段中，語言發展會短暫停滯，因為學習語言並非直線過程。我個人針對學齡前兒童（3-6 歲）的研究[9]（Budar, 2009）顯示，六歲進入學校的雙語孩童在學習德語時同樣擁有優良的語言能力，甚至其表現優於以德語單語學習的孩童。

在幼托兒所／幼兒園語學校之外的語言支持

重要的是額外索勃語言空間的使用。不可或缺的輔助工具，例如歌曲、童謠、猜謎、故事、繪本、戲劇、電影與新媒體。為達到這些目的，索勃學校協會架設新的網站（www.dyrdomdej.de），內容持續更新與擴充。網站內提供教材給予教師與對索勃語有興趣的父母，目前只有上索勃語，2019 年將有下索勃語的教材。學習索勃語如同冒險，即此網站 dyrdomdej 之意！該網站透過本協會的 Witaj ® 計畫促進密集的語言學習。以卡通人物 Majka、Le ka、Korla 以及小 Flori（小狗）引導孩童學習。首先，網站的內容首先在介紹索勃詞彙。重要的是，透過互動與溝

---

9 Ludmila Budarjowa/Jana Šołćina: Serbšćinu wuknyć a wučić – ewaluacija Witaj a 2plus (= Sorbisch lernen und lehren), in: Witaj a 2plus wužadanje za přichod / Witaj und 2plus – eine Herausforderung für die Zukunft, Bautzen: Sorbischer Schulverein e.V. 2009, s. 60–75 (66-75 頁作者為 Ludmila Budar)。

通，藉由具有不同教導活動的插畫與文字幫助孩童學習，例如動手做、運動、猜猜看、大略與精細的活動、實驗、記憶訓練、基本數學、歌曲、食譜與觀察。主要的目標在於透過沉浸以遊戲方式學習索勃語。該網站持續更新，網站最初之際以水果作為主題開始，後來逐漸加入顏色等。以此方式發展，逐漸擴充網站內容。

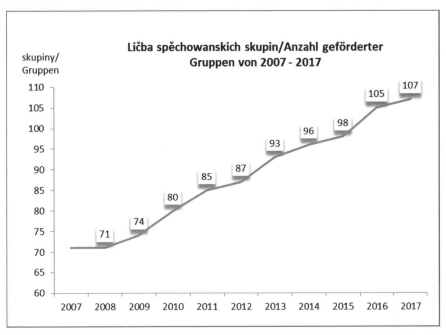

2007-2017 薩克森邦所資助之索勃語教學群體

© Ludmila Budar/Budarjowa 2017, žórło/Quelle: Krajnoradny zarjad Budyšin/Landratsamt Bautzen a SMK

　　由薩克森自由邦所資助的群體有107個，其中32個是由索勃學校協會所負責，皆採完全沉浸式教學。在其他受資助的群體中，索勃語採部分沉浸式進行教學，大部分則是偶爾教授。

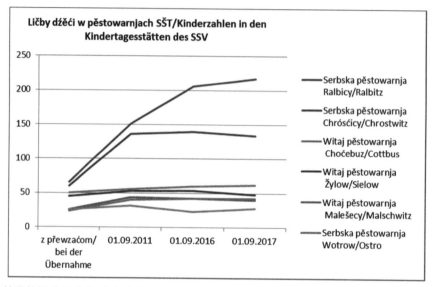

索勃學校協會幼兒園孩童人數（時間點為索勃學校協會接收了幼兒園，並實施沉浸式
教學，分別為 2011、2016、2017）

© *Ludmila Budarjowa 2017, žórło/Quelle: Serbske šulske towarstwo z.t./Sorbischer Schulverein e.V.*

　　自 20 年來，家長在孩子尚未出生之前就已經向索勃學校協會登記，以讓孩子
可以進入以沉浸式方法進行教學的幼兒園。然而因為幼兒園空間容納的問題，無法
招收更多的學生。

II. 中小學

　　所有使用索勃語教學的學校與使用索勃語與德語的學校皆為公立學校，大部分
的主管機關為地區或城市。至今並無任何私立的索勃學校或高等教育機構。

　　如前所述，Witaj 為使用索勃語及德語教學的學校已經奠定良好穩固的基礎。
進入 Witaj 幼兒園就讀的孩童，特別是完全沉浸式教學方式學習的孩童，擁有最
好的條件選擇薩克森邦索勃語及德語雙語學校之 2plus[10]，以及勃蘭登堡邦的雙語課
程[11]。整體語言學習過程之路可以向前再跨一步。多語則可提升為學校課程。

---

10 請參閱 www.abc.brandenburg.de。
11 請參閱 www.abc.brandenburg.de。

何謂 **2plus**？

- **2plus** 於 2013 ／ 14 學年度正式在薩克森自由邦開始執行。
- **2plus** 意謂<u>在校修習德語及索勃語，再加上另一個語言</u>（如英語、法語、捷克語、西班牙語、俄語等）。
- **2plus** 課程對象是<u>索勃學校的所有學生。</u>
- 其他學校（通常是以德語為主要教授語言的學校，僅有部分學生學習索勃語）則是以單一班級或團體以 2plus 概念教學。
- 將索勃語視為授課科目是依據學生不同的語言程度，分為三個群體教授：
  - ➢ **語言群體一**：孩童已學習索勃語，在日常生活與在校學習已達母語程度。
  - ➢ **語言群體二**：孩童已學習索勃語，在日常生活與學校學習之索勃語程度為第二語言。
  - ➢ **語言群體三**：至少以將索勃語學習達到第二語言為目標的群體。
- 將索勃語當成一個授課科目，<u>其既是課程使用語言亦是課程學習目標。</u>
- 在其他科目中使用索勃語，可以是完全或是部分的課程使用語言（小學為三個學科，由學校自行決定，例如數學或體育；中學則為五個學科，亦由學校自行決定，例如歷史、地理、生物、體育、音樂或藝術）。在這些科目中，老師可以在班級以<u>團體教學</u>（兩位老師共同教學）方式進行。
- 其他學科的學習內容將以雙語進行。
- 對於<u>中途加入學生</u>，可選擇以雙語進行教學的班級，透過參加額外提供的索勃語課程，學生在學習後可達語言群體三之語言程度。
- 所有薩克森邦公立學校之學習目標與課綱皆適用於索勃語及德語雙語學生，且具有效力。畢業後獲得等值文憑。
- 在班上，由雙語（索勃語及德語）教師授課。
- 每一個學校內，學校協調員（<u>Schulkoordinatoren</u>）[12] 參與語言教學過程。

可惜目前無法全面以 2plus 概念進行教學，因為索勃語師資缺乏。

---

12 每個學校指派一名學校協調員，他們任教於索勃語暨德語雙語學校，本身通曉索勃語，以雙語進行教學，認同 2plus 教學概念目標，且負責在校正確執行 2plus 教學。學校協調員與學校高層緊密合作（Landesamt für Schule und Bildung 2017, https://www.schule.sachsen.de/download/download_bildung/18_10_18_2plus_Konzept_Stand_September_2018.pdf）。

作為外語的索勃語

除了 2plus 概念之外，索勃語被當作外語來教授。索勃語被當作額外科目，而且上課時段常被安排在不好的時間，語言教學無法達到良好效果。在薩克森邦與勃蘭登堡邦境內沒有 Witaj® 幼兒園的區域皆以如此方式進行索勃語教學。

進修與大學教育

成年人可在包岑專科以上學校學習。溫德語則在寇特布斯下索勃語及文化學校教授。師資則由位於包岑的索勃社會教育專業學校以及寇特布斯之高階中心培育。萊比錫大學的索勃研究所提供學習及研究索勃語及溫德語的課程與學位。這些機構的主管單位並非為索勃民族自身，而是德國政府。學習索勃語的網路教學在近幾年來開始架設並運作。和其他歐洲少數民族比較起來，基本上來說，索勃民族需要的是更多的公共語言空間，並且透過廣播、電視、現代媒體，特別是數位來輔助索勃語的教學與學習。為了雙語概念以及在學校少數民族的語言可作為母語、第二語言或是外語教學的發展與實踐，師資培育與進修的方法與教學法是相當必要的。特別是具有母語能力的專業人才，以能夠積極支持語言復振計畫。

Länder	1994/95	2009/10	2014/15	2015/16	2016/17
Sakska/ Sachsen 薩克森邦	3.683	2.232 (1083 rěčna skupina/ Sprach- gruppe 1)	2.476 (654 rěčna skupina/ Sprach- gruppe 1)	2.674 (652 rěčna skupina/ Sprach- gruppe 1)	2.628 (744 rěčna skupina/ Sprach- gruppe 1)
Brani-borska/ Brandenburg 勃蘭登堡邦	1.051	1.824 (234 Witaj- šulerjow/ Schüler)	1.522	1.468 (301 Witaj- šuler/Schüler)	2.010 (349 Witaj- šulerjow/ Schüler)
cyłkownje/ Gesamt 總數	4.734	4.056	3.998	4.142	4.638

薩克森邦與勃蘭登堡邦學生人數比較

© Ludmila Budar/Budarjowa, 2017, Quellen/žórła: SBAB, ABC, MBJS

薩克森邦學習索勃與學生人數／將索勃語視為外國語言

© *Ludmila Budar/Budarjowa, 2017, Sakska/Sachsen, žórło/Quelle: SBAB*

　　達到母語程度的孩童（語言群體一）僅占所有 6 到 12 歲在學校學習索勃語言孩童的 28%。索勃學校協會希望，從 Witaj® 托兒所／幼兒園畢業，在讀小學時到語言群體二（第二語言者）的小孩在更高年級時可以達到母語程度。

結論

　　索勃學校協會所提出的 Witaj® 計畫不僅發展出語言概念，而是在實作上證明，對於世界上的所有語言來說，可在其對應的條件之下是可以運用的，而且可以成功。一般條件是必須，首先是政治上，亦即多數群體與德國政府、薩克森與勃蘭登堡邦（上、下索勃民族所在之行政區域）在精神上與財政上的支持。此外，索勃母語人士自己亦須投入心力。法律上能夠使得索勃語保存下來、繼續發展以及復振。重要的是，索勃書籍、符合當前情況的教材（需進行數位化，因為索勃語並非家庭或法庭語言，而是一個現代的歐洲平等的語言！）同時也是必要的，因此 DYRDOMDEJ 網站對於我們來說是極具重要性的！這個網站也可以提供客家孩童學習客語作為參考，並應用之。

在 Witaj® 計畫實行 20 年之後，不僅是德意志與索勃家長對於雙語及多語教育的興趣逐漸攀升，對於全球學者來說，包括臺灣，亦有興趣了解。語言是最重要的認同特徵。文化透過語言傳遞，同時與語言建立情感連結。父母與家庭成員扮演重要角色，他們是模範，而且為他們的孩子決定了一條有益的學習之路，同時可以或是願意支持孩子。對父母來說特別重要的是，Witaj® 在實作上，提供囊括幼兒園到大學的整體語言學習計畫，當然這個計畫必須持續擴張與調整。

復振、維持與強化語言是有可能的，且以此強化文化認同。語言復振成功的前提是人民的集體意識，以及保存傳承語言及文化的政治意圖。這個複雜困難的過程應由有志之士齊力完成。

◎講者之德文原稿

Sehr geehrte Damen und Herren,

mein Name ist Ludmila Budar, sorbisch Budarjowa. Ich komme aus Bautzen inDeutschland, nahe der Stadt Dresden (PowerPoint/Karte!), ca. 9.000 km entfernt von Taiwan. Die Sorben, in Brandenburg auch Wenden genannt, verweisen als autochthones Volk auf eine 1.500-jährige Geschichte, eine eigene Sprache und Kultur. Das Siedlungsgebiet der Sorben　die Lausitz　liegt im Osten Deutschlands im Freistaat Sachsen und im Land Brandenburg. Das deutsch-sorbische Siedlungsgebiet ist etwa 100 Kilometer lang und 40 Kilometer breit. Hier lebten vor 100 Jahren noch 100.000 Sorben, heute sind es 60.000: ca. 20.000 Obersorben und ca. 7.000 Niedersorben oder Wenden.

Genaue Zahlen liegen nicht vor, da zum sorbischen Volk gehört, wer sich zu ihm bekennt. Nach § 1 des Sächsischen Sorbengesetzes und § 2 des Brandenburgischen Sorben (Wenden)-Gesetzes darf das Bekenntnis nicht überprüft werden, damit den Sorben keine Nachteile erwachsen könnten. Etwa die Hälfte in der Lausitz lebender Bürger hat sorbische/wendische Vorfahren. Die ober- und niedersorbische Sprache sind zwei eigenständige slawische Schriftsprachen mit jeweils unterschiedlicher Grammatik.Die Sprachen der Ober- und Niedersorben sind in der Europäischen Charta der Regional- und Minderheitensprachen als bedrohte Sprachen anerkannt. https://rm.coe.int/168007c089

Die Sorben haben keinen eigenen Staat, sie sind eine autochthone Minderheit in Deutschland. Das Sorbische/Wendische ist das Alleinstellungsmerkmal der Lausitz gegenüber anderen Regionen und hebt die besondere Spezifik dieses Siedlungsgebietes hervor.

Gesetzliche Grundlagen

Das Grundgesetz der Bundesrepublik Deutschland gewährt den Sorben im § 3 nur das Individualrecht, kein Gruppenrecht:

Grundgesetz für die Bundesrepublik Deutschland Art 3

(3) Niemand darf wegen seines Geschlechtes, seiner Abstammung, seiner Rasse, seiner Sprache, seiner Heimat und Herkunft, seines Glaubens, seiner religiösen oder

politischen Anschauungen benachteiligt oder bevorzugt werden.

Artikel 6 Verfassung des Freistaates Sachsen

(1) Die im Land lebenden Bürger sorbischer Volkszugehörigkeit sind gleichberechtigter Teil des Staatsvolkes. Das Land gewährleistet und schützt das Recht auf Bewahrung ihrer Identität sowie auf Pflege und Entwicklung ihrer angestammten Sprache, Kultur und Überlieferung, insbesondere durch Schulen, vorschulische und kulturelle Einrichtungen.

Art. 25 Verf. – (Rechte der Sorben/Wenden in der Verfassung des Landes Brandenburg)

(3) Die Sorben/Wenden haben das Recht auf Bewahrung und Förderung der sorbischen/wendischen Sprache und Kultur im öffentlichen Leben und ihre Vermittlung in Schulen und Kindertagesstätten.

Dieses Recht wirkt nicht automatisch, es muss ständig von den Sorben/Wenden politisch neu eingefordert werden.

Die Sorge um die Bewahrung und Weiterentwicklung der sorbischen Sprache, Kultur und Identität ist mir in die Wiege gelegt worden. Ich stamme aus einer kinderreichen sorbischen Lehrerfamilie. Mein Großvater war der erste Leiter des Sorbischen Lehrerbildungsinstituts und hatte 13 Kinder. Mein Vater und vier Onkel waren Lehrer. Ich habe noch zehn Geschwister, von denen drei Lehrer sind.

Seit nunmehr fast 30 Jahre bin ich neben meiner beruflichen Tätigkeit ehrenamtliche Vorsitzende des Sorbischen Schulvereins e.V. (SSV). Dieser vertritt die Interessen der Sorben auf dem Gebiet der zweisprachigen Vorschulerziehung und des zwei- und mehrsprachigen Bildungswesens von den Kindertagesstätten und Grundschulen über Oberschulen und Gymnasien bis zur universitären Ausbildung.

Wissenschaftliche Untersuchungen des Sorbischen Instituts und Analysen des Sorbischen Schulvereins haben bekräftigt, dass der Assimilierungsprozess der sorbischsprachigen Bevölkerung seit dem vergangenen Jahrhundert dramatisch voranschreitet. In Brandenburg fehlen bereits zwei Generationen muttersprachlicher

Sorben und die Anzahl der Kinder, die in den Schulklassen 1 bis 12 in Sachsen Sorbisch in muttersprachlicher Qualität Sorbisch lernen, haben sich in den vergangenen 25 Jahren auf nur noch ca. 740 Schüler halbiert. Zurzeit lernen in Brandenburg ca. 2 000 Schüler Sorbisch/Wendisch, davon 350 Witaj-Schüler. In Sachsen lernen ca. 2 700 Schüler Sorbisch, davon nur 740 in muttersprachlicher Qualität.

Wir als Sorbischer Schulverein e.V. wollen diese Entwicklung stoppen und haben uns über Konzepte zur Sprachförderung und Sprachrevitalisierung bereits im frühen Kindesalter In Europa informiert. Bei den Bretonen in Frankreich begeisterte uns dasDIWAN-Konzept. Wir haben die Idee des immersiven Lernens in den 1990er-Jahren aufgegriffen und das Modellprojekt Witaj® entwickelt.Dabei wurde der Status der beiden Sprachen, Deutsch als dominante Erstsprache der Majorität und Sorbisch als Zweitsprache der Minorität berücksichtigt. Unser Ziel ist es, neue SprecherInnen - newspeakers – hervorzubringen, damit die sorbische Sprache erhalten, wiederbelebt und gezielt weiterentwickelt werden kann. Im Jahre 1998 startete der Sorbische Schulverein mit dem Modellprojekt Witaj® in der Kindertagesstätte in Cottbus den Revitalisierungsprozess der sorbischen Sprache und legte damit den Grundstein für ein ganzheitliches Spracherwerbsprogramm von der Kinderkrippe bis zur Universität in Sachsen und Brandenburg. Witaj® ist als Eigenname rechtlich geschützt und wurde zum Qualitätssiegel des Sorbischen Schulvereins e.V.

I. Kindertagesstätten

Was ist Witaj®?

- **Witaj**®ist ein sorbisches[13] Wort und heißt <u>Willkommen</u>. Alle Kinder, egal ob mit oder ohne sorbische Vorkenntnisse, sind herzlich willkommen.
- Witaj bedeutet Zweitspracherwerb <u>unter institutionellen Bedingungen.</u>

---

13 sorbisch wird in der Niederlausitz auch wendisch genannt.

Wie wird Witaj® vermittelt?

- Witaj® bedeutet Anwendung der international bewährten Immersionsmethode (vollständig oder partiell).
- Eintauchen in ein sorbisches <u>Sprachbad</u>, Kinder tauchen in eine Welt ein, in der alles in einer anderen Sprache passiert.
- Prinzip<u>eine Person – eine Sprache</u> (Sprache ist an Personen gebunden)*Die Zuordnung von Person und Sprache erleichtert den Kindern die Abgrenzung zwischen den Sprachen und damit das Umschalten zwischen ihnen erheblich.*

Welche Vorteile bringt Witaj®?

- **Witaj®** fördert zusätzlich <u>soziale, interaktive und kognitive Fähigkeiten</u> der Kinder
- **Witaj®**-Kinder haben einen <u>Wissensvorsprung</u> beim Erwerb von weiteren Sprachen
- **Witaj®**<u>fördert</u> den <u>frühen Zweitspracherwerb</u>, da bereits auf bestehende neuronale Vernetzungen des Erstspracherwerbs zurückgegriffen wird
- **Witaj®**-Kinder können beim Eintritt in die Grundschule mit der <u>sorbischen und der deutschen Fibel gleichzeitig</u> alphabetisiert werden
- **Witaj®** fördert <u>Toleranz und Aufgeschlossenheit</u> gegenüber anderen Sprachen und Kulturen
- **Witaj®** bedeutet für die Eltern <u>keinen finanziellen Mehraufwand</u> bei der Betreuung ihrer Kinder

Welcher Unterschied besteht zwischen Witaj®-Kindertagesstättenund Witaj®-Gruppen?

- Witaj®-Kindertagesstätten – dazu gehören in der Regel: Kinderkrippe (Alter1 bis 3 Jahre), Kindergarten (3 bis 6 Jahre) und Hort (Schulkinder im Alter von 6 bis 10 Jahren) –wenden die vollständige Immersion an:
  - ➢ alle Kinder lernen sorbisch und die Umgangssprache ist nahezu zu 100%

sorbisch.

➢ alle Erzieherinnen beherrschen die sorbische Sprache in muttersprachlicher Qualität.

➢ Witaj®-Kindertagesstätten befinden sich in Trägerschaft des Sorbischen Schulvereins (SSV[14]), insgesamt werden ca. 600 Kinder in 7 Kitas betreut, in Sachsen 5 und in Brandenburg 2 Kindertagesstätten.

• Witaj®-Gruppen wenden die partielle Immersion an:

➢ nur in ausgewählten Gruppen der Kitas lernen die Kinder sorbisch.

➢ nur einige Erzieherinnen beherrschen die sorbische Sprache.

➢ Witaj-Gruppen befinden sich in unterschiedlicher, meist in nicht sorbischer Trägerschaft.

In Sachsen und Brandenburg lernen ca. 650 Kinder durch vollständige Immersion, ca. 320 Kinder durch partielle Immersion und ca. 250 Kinder nur punktuell sorbisch.

Was kommt nach Witaj®?

• **Witaj**® schafft ein solides Fundament für ein sorbisch-deutsches Schulnetz.

• **Witaj**® ist die beste Voraussetzung zur Teilnahme an weiterführenden sprachpädagogischen Schulkonzepten in Sachsen und Brandenburg.

• **Witaj**®in der Vorschule ist die Garantie für einen erfolgreichen ganzheitlichen Spracherwerbsprozess. Eltern werden umfangreich informiert, wie das Erlernen der sorbischen Sprache in der Schule weiter geführt wird.

Zur Immersionsmethode

Wie bereits erwähnt, tauchen Kinder bei dieser Methode in eine Welt ein, in der alles in sorbischer Sprache passiert. Da dieser Spracherwerb am besten der natürlichen menschlichen Sprachlernfähigkeit entspricht, ist die Angst, immersives Sprachenlernen würde die Lernenden überfordern, unberechtigt. Bei der Immersion ist entscheidend, dass die neue Sprache Sorbisch konsequent und strukturiert gelehrt und mit Mimik und Gestik

---

14 SSV = Sorbische Schulverein e.V., weitere Informationen unter www.sorbischer-schulverein. de.

verstärkt wird. Kinder besitzen von Geburt an unterschiedliche Voraussetzungen für das Erlernen von Sprachen, wie Auffassungsgabe und Sprachbegabung.Deshalb wird eine der Situation angepasste Kommunikation angestrebt.

Vom Übersetzen ins Deutsche sollte Abstand genommen werden, da das Erlernen der neuen Sprache auf einem niedrigen Niveau stagnieren könnte. Dem Kind könnte durch die häufige Verwendung der Majoritätssprache Deutsch indirekt vermittelt werden, dass Deutsch die wichtigere Sprache ist. Auch das häufige Mischen sorbischer und deutscher Wörter bzw. Sätze ist kontraproduktiv. Kleinkinder können die Äußerungen Erwachsener weder der deutschen noch der sorbischen Sprache zuordnen. Es besteht die Gefahr, dass von den Kindern eine Misch-Sprache (Sprachmix) kreiert wird. Dadurch können sich im kindlichen Gehirn keine geordneten Sprachsysteme bilden.

Was passiert im Gehirn?

Neurologen haben festgestellt, dass bei einem Kind, welches von Geburt an zwei Sprachen lernt, nur <u>ein einziges neuronales Netz</u> für beide Sprachen gebildet wird. Deshalb erlernt das Kind spielend und ohne Schwierigkeiten parallel auch weitere Sprachen. Wenn es aber erst in der Schule die zweite Sprache erlernt, bildet sich im Gehirn <u>ein zweites neuronales Netz</u>und das Erlernen weiterer Sprachen ist bedeutend mühsamer und schwieriger. Bis zum dritten Lebensjahr werden bei Kindern mehrere Sprachen gespeichert. Dabei arbeitet ihr Gehirn beim Spracherwerb besonders effektiv. Es saugt alle Informationen wie ein Schwamm auf. Das Kleinkind kann auch mehrere Sprachen längere Zeit im Gehirn speichern. Deshalb hat der Sorbische Schulverein e.V. in seinen Einrichtungen den immersiven Spracherwerbsprozess bereits in die Kinderkrippe vorverlegt.

Beruhend auf dem Prinzip der Nachahmung lernen Kinder mehrere Sprachen genauso gut und sicher, wie nur eine Einzige. Deshalb sprechen Wissenschaftler bei Kleinkindern auch vom mehrfachen Erstsprachenerwerb.

Generell sind Kinder in ihrer Entwicklung durch Mehrsprachigkeit keinesfalls gefährdet, nur Sprachen müssen von den Bezugspersonen geordnet, klar strukturiert und systematisch vermittelt werden. Zwei- und Mehrsprachigkeit fördert sogar die Aufmerksamkeit, denn Kinder unterscheiden sofort, was sind vertraute Äußerungen der

Muttersprache und welche sind neu oder fremd. Sie hören konzentrierter zu und können später abstrakter, logischer und kreativer unterschiedlichste Aufgaben lösen.Sie haben in ihrem Sprachgebrauch immer mehrere Wörter für die gleichen Gegenstände oder Sachverhalte parat. Die neuronalen Voraussetzungen dafür sind im Kleinkindalter optimal ausgebildet. Zentrale Untersuchungen im Land Brandenburg haben ergeben, dass Kinder, die von Anfang an zweisprachig aufgewachsen sind, in der Grundschule über bessere Leistungen sogar in Mathematik und Musik verfügten. Dazu gibt es auch sehr interessante weitere Ergebnisse aus der Gehirnforschung.

Die Erzieherinnen setzen im Rahmen der Immersion sehr stark auf Wiederholung. Im Gespräch mit den Kindern werden ständig wiederkehrende Situationen mit den immer gleichen Sätzen untermalt. Dadurch können sich die Kinder die Redewendungen in der neuen Sprache selbstständig erschließen, nach und nach auch merken und später selbst anwenden. Dabei ist viel Geduld notwendig, ohne ständige Korrektur und Tadel, sondern mit viel Lob.

In neuesten Studienergebnissen zum Gedächtnisabbau im Alter wurde sogar festgestellt, dass zwei-oder mehrsprachige Senioren ihr Gehirn effektiver einsetzen. Durch ihre mehrsprachigen Fähigkeiten wurde eine bessere Denkleistung nachgewiesen. Das lebenslange Umschalten zwischen mehreren Sprachen verlangsamt den Gedächtnisabbau und fungiert als eine Art Gehirntraining.

Welche Rolle spielen Eltern?

Die Eltern sind die wichtigsten Partner der Erzieherinnen, da sie die engste Bindung zu ihrem Kind haben und somit auch entscheidenden Einfluss auf dessen Spracherwerb haben. Die Kinder sind sehr stolz und empfinden die Empathie, wenn sich auch ihre Eltern für die neue Sprache interessieren und eventuell sogar mit oder von den Kindern lernen. In manchen Kindertagesstätten werden den Eltern die wichtigsten sorbischen Wörter, Sätze, Redewendungen und Begrüßungsformeln auf einer Listeüberreicht. Quartalsweise gibt der Sorbische Schulverein einen zweisprachigen Elternbrief heraus. Es finden kontinuierlich Familienfeste in den Kindertagesstätten aber auch zentrale Feste statt. Sprachförderung gelingt, wenn alle an einem Strang ziehen. Auch unsere Slogans wie „Nach Einsprachigkeit kommt Sprachlosigkeit!" oder „Einsprachigkeit ist heilbar!" haben dazu beigetragen, die Eltern, Großeltern und Freunde vom Weg zur frühen Mehrsprachigkeit zu überzeugen.

Wie verlaufen die Lernphasen?

Spracherwerb ist ein eigenaktiver und konstruktiver Prozess. Die Phasen der Sprachaneignung verlaufen fließend. Entscheidend für den Erfolg sind die <u>Intensität, Konsequenz, Kontinuität und Dauer der Sprachvermittlung.</u>

Rezeptive Phase: Die anfängliche Ablehnung durch das Kind kann für die Erwachsenen frustrierend sein. Solches Verhalten ist nicht ungewöhnlich und auch kein Grund zur Sorge. Durch paralleles Mitlernen der sorbischen Sprache können Eltern helfen, diesen Schritt zu überwinden. Nach einer Phase des Schweigens beginnt nach und nach die Phase des Verstehens.

Ein passives Zurückhalten oder eventuelles Mischen der Sprachen seitens des Kindes hat auf den Spracherwerb keine Auswirkung. In der rezeptiven Phase nimmt der Lernende die neue Sprache auf und speichert Bestandteile dieser in seinem Gehirn. Es beginnt zu begreifen, dass verschiedene Menschen gleiche Gegenstände mit verschiedenen Wörtern bezeichnen. Diese erste Phase ist unterschiedlich lang und niemals abgeschlossen, da ständig Neues vom Kind aufgenommen wird.

Die Zuhörphase dient der Entschlüsselung der Sprache, wie es bereits beim Säugling zu beobachten ist. Durch den wiederholten Gebrauch der Sprache, deren Wortschatz in direkter Verbindung mit dem steht, was das Kind täglich im Kindergarten erlebt, kann die Stufe des Verstehens im frühen Kindesalterschnell erlangt werden.Diese Phase ist ebenfalls abhängig von dem jeweiligen Entwicklungsstadium jedes einzelnen Kindes.

Produktive Phase: Wann das Kind beginnt, sorbische Wörter selbst zu verwenden, ist von den individuellen Fähigkeiten des Kindesabhängig. Auch äußere Bedingungen spielen eine Rolle.

Erheblichen Einfluss auf die Sprachaneignung haben bereits die erwähnte intensive, konsequente und strukturierte Anwendung der sorbischen Sprache, die Dauer des Verweilens in der Kindertagesstätte und der Anteil der Kinder mit sorbischer

Muttersprache in der Gruppe. Auch die positive Motivation, die daraus resultierende Beispielwirkung sowie der sensible Umgang mit der Zweitsprache Sorbisch sind entscheidend. Nach zunächst einfachen Antworten und Redewendungen beginnt das Kind, sich in der neuen Sprache zu erproben und geht in die produktive Phase über. Esbeginnt die Mutter- und die Zweitsprache auf Unterschiede und Gemeinsamkeiten intensiver zu zu vergleichen.Ohne Zwang beginnt esdann (plötzlich) die Zielsprache anzuwenden, oft auch versteckt. Das kann beim Singen von Liedern oder beim Anschauen von Bilderbüchern sein.

Erst nach dem die produktive Stufe erreicht ist, kann der Austausch zwischen Erzieherinnen und dem Kind in sorbischer Sprache erfolgen.

Anregungen zum Sprechen

Das Kind braucht natürliche Anlässe und vertrautes Umfeld, um sich zu äußern. Die Sprache der Bezugspersonen sollte auf natürliche Weise und nach Möglichkeit exakt angewandt werden. Die emotionale Komponente beim Spracherwerb sollte nicht unterschätzt werden, denn die Sprache in der das Kind geliebt, getröstet und beruhigt wird, ist ihm vertraut und lieb. Filme und Hörbücher können erlebtes Sprechen in der Interaktion nicht ersetzen. Wenn Kinder zwei oder mehrere Sprachen gleichzeitig lernen, kann die Sprachentwicklung in einer bestimmten Phase kurzfristig stagnieren, da der Spracherwerb kein linearer Prozess ist. Meine wissenschaftlichen Untersuchungen im Vorschulalter haben gezeigt, dass beim Schuleintritt mit sechs Jahren die zweisprachigen Kinder auch in der Majoritätssprache Deutsch eine gleich gute Sprachkompetenz besitzen, sehr oft ist diese sogar besser als bei einsprachig deutschen Kindern. Anhand verschiedener Tests bei Kindern von drei bis sechs Jahren habe ich den Lernfortschritt des Sprachförderkonzepts in drei sorbischen Kindertagesstätten dokumentiert.

Sprachförderung außerhalb der Kindertagesstätte und der Schule

Wichtig ist die Nutzung von zusätzlichen sorbischen Sprachräumen. Zu den unverzichtbaren Hilfsmitteln dienen unter anderem Lieder und Reime, Rätsel, Geschichten, Bilderbücher, Theatervorstellungen, Filme und neue Medien. Zu diesem

Zweck hat der Sorbische Schulverein eine neue Web-Seite erarbeitet, die ständig ergänzt und erweitert wird. www.dyrdomdej.de(PowerPoint)Es ist Lehrmaterial für die Erziehrinnen und interessierte Eltern (nur obersorbisch, es wird 2019 in die niedersorbische Sprache übertragen.). Gemeinsam Sorbisch lernen ist wie ein Abenteuer – dyrdomdej!Diese Web-Seite ist ein Beitrag zur immersiven Sprachförderung durch unser Modellprojekt Witaj®. Sie begleiten die Figuren Majka, Le ka, Korla und der kleine Flori (Hund).Es geht in erster Linie um Vermittlung der sorbischen Lexik. Wichtig ist dabei: Interaktion, Kommunikation (anhand der Illustrationen und Texte in unterschiedlichen didaktischen Funktionen wie): Basteln, Bewegung, Raten, grobe und feine Motorik, Experimente, Gedächtnistraining, mathematische Vorkenntnisse, Lieder, Rezepte zum Essen, Wahrnehmung → Ziel ist das spielerische Erlernen der sorbischen Sprache durch Immersion.Diese Seite wird ständig ergänzt und weiterentwickelt. Der Beginn war das Thema Obst. Schon bald stellen wir im Internet Texte und Illustrationen zu den Farben ein und so wird diese Seite ständig erweitert.

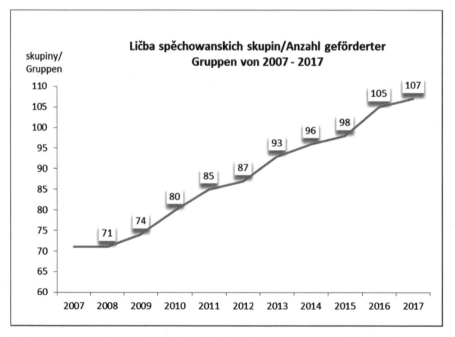

© *Ludmila Budar/Budarjowa 2017, žórło/Quelle: Krajnoradny zarjad Budyšin/Landratsamt Bautzen a SMK*

Von den 107 vom Freistaat Sachsen finanziell geförderten Gruppen sind 32 in Trägerschaft des Sorbischen Schulvereins, in denen die vollständige Immersion angewandt wird. In den weiteren geförderten Einrichtungen wird die sorbische Sprache teilweisedurch Immersion, in den meisten Einrichtungen jedoch nur gelegentlich vermittelt.

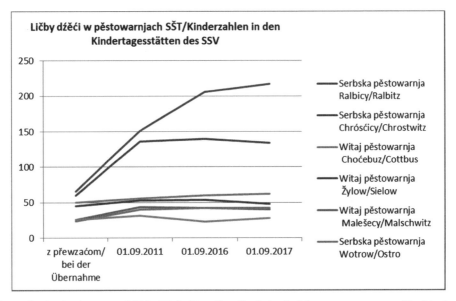

© *Ludmila Budarjowa 2017, žórło/Quelle: Serbske šulske towarstwo z.t./Sorbischer Schulverein e.V.*

Seit fast 20 Jahren führt der Sorbische Schulverein e.V. Wartelisten für die Eltern, die ihre Kinder oft bereits vor der Geburt an diesen Einrichtungen anmelden. Die Eltern wünschen die Anwendung der vollständigen Immersion. Aus Kapazitätsgründen (Gebäudesind zu klein) können leider nicht mehr Kinder aufgenommen werden.

II. Schulen

Alle sorbischen und sorbisch-deutschen Schulen sind staatliche Schulen, meist in Trägerschaft der Kommune oder der Städte. Private sorbische Schulen oder

Hochschuleinrichtungen wurden bisher nicht geschaffen.

Wie bereits erwähnt, schafft Witaj ein solides Fundament für ein sorbisch-deutsches Schulnetz. Den Witaj-Kindern, insbesondere mit der Anwendung der vollständigen Immersion, ist die beste Voraussetzung zur Teilnahme am schulartübergreifenden Konzept für zweisprachige sorbisch-deutsche Schulen „2plus"[15]in Sachsen und am bilingualen Unterricht[16] in Brandenburg geschaffen worden. Es kann nun der Weg des ganzheitlichen Spracherwerbsprozesses weiter beschritten werden. Mehrsprachigkeit wird zum Schulprogramm erhoben.

Was bedeutet 2plus?

- **2plus** wurde ab dem Schuljahr 2013/14 offiziell im Freistaat Sachsen eingeführt.
- **2plus** bedeutetDeutsch und Sorbisch plus weitere Sprachen mit den dafür notwendigen Rahmenbedingungen werden an Schulen weiter vermittelt.
- 2plus wird bei allen Schülern an sorbischen Schulenangewandt.
- Aneinigenweiteren Schulen wird in einzelnen Klassen oder Gruppen nach dem Schulkonzept 2plus unterrichtet.
- Das Fach Sorbisch wird je nach Sprachstand der Schüler **in drei Sprachgruppen** unterrichtet.
  - ➢ **Sprachgruppe 1** Kinder haben insoweit Sorbisch erlernt, dass ihr Sprachniveau bei Alltags- und Bildungssprache dem eines Muttersprachlers entspricht.
  - ➢ **Sprachgruppe 2** Kinder haben insoweit Sorbisch erlernt, dass ihr Sprachniveau dem einer Zweitsprache in Alltags- und schulischen Bildungskontexten entspricht.
  - ➢ **Sprachgruppe 3** Kinder erlernen Sorbisch mindestens mit dem Zielniveau einer Zweitsprache.
- Im Fach Sorbisch ist die sorbische Sprache sowohl Unterrichtssprache als auch Unterrichtsgegenstand.
- Sorbisch ist in anderen Fächern (drei Unterrichtsfächer in der Grundschule und

---

15 weitere Informationen unter www.abc.brandenburg.de.
16 weitere Informationen unter www.abc.brandenburg.de.

fünf in der Oberschule und am Sorbischen Gymnasium) vollständig oder teilweise Unterrichtssprache. In diesen Fächern können zwei Lehrer in der Klasse – Team-Teachingunterrichten.

- Die Lerninhalte der anderen Sachfächer werden bilingualgelehrt.
- Für Quereinsteiger ist der Zugang zu den zweisprachigen Klassen gewährleistet, in dem sie durch zusätzlichen Sorbisch-Unterricht an das Sprachniveau der Sprachgruppe 3 herangeführt werden.
- Alle Lernziele und Lehrplaninhalte für sächsische öffentliche Schulen sind für zweisprachige sorbisch-deutsche Schulen gültig und verbindlich. Es werden gleichwertige Abschlüsse vergeben.
- In den Klassen unterrichten zweisprachige(sorbisch-deutsche) Lehrkräfte.
- An jeder Schule begleiten Schulkoordinatoren die Sprachbildungsprozesse.

Leider wird gegenwärtig das 2plus-Konzept nicht vollumfänglich umgesetzt, da sorbischsprachige Lehrer fehlen.

Sorbisch als Fremdsprachenunterricht

Außer dem 2plus Konzept wird Sorbisch als Fremdsprache gelehrt. In Form eines zusätzlichen Schulfaches und oft in Randstunden kann letztendlich diese Sprachvermittlung kaum zu einer ausreichenden Beherrschung der sorbischen Sprache führen. Diese Spracherwerbsmethode wird in jenen Gebieten Sachsens und Brandenburgs angewandt, in denen (noch) keine Witaj®-Gruppen existieren.

Weiterbildung und Studium

Die sorbische Sprache können Erwachsene an der Kreishochschule Bautzen lernen. Die wendische Sprache wird an der Schule für Niedersorbische Sprache und Kultur in Cottbus gelehrt. Erzieherausbildung findet an der Sorbischen Fachschule für Sozialpädagogik in Bautzen und im Oberstufenzentrum Cottbus statt. Am Institut für Sorabistik an der Universität Leipzig können die sorbische und die wendische Sprache studiert werden. Diese Einrichtungen sind entweder in deutscher Trägerschaft oder Bestandteil deutscher staatlicher Einrichtungen. Eine Reihe von sorbischen Online

Portalen zum Erlernen der Sprache sind in den letzten Jahren entstanden. Im Vergleich zu einigen anderen nationalen Minderheiten in Europa benötigen wir generell mehr öffentliche Sprachräume, auch mithilfe von Rundfunk, Fernsehen, moderner Medien, besonders durch die Erweiterung von digitalen Angeboten.Für die Entwicklung und Realisierung bilingualer Konzepte und für das Unterrichten in der Minderheitensprache als Mutter-, Zweit- oder Fremdsprache in den Schulen, ist eine spezielle Methodik und Didaktik in der Aus- und Weiterbildung der Lehrkräfte notwendig. Das setzt nicht zuletzt die Bereitschaft vom muttersprachlichenFachpersonal voraus, das Revitalisierungsprogramm aktiv zu unterstützen.

Länder	1994/95	2009/10	2014/15	2015/16	2016/17
Sakska/ Sachsen	3.683	2.232 (1083 rěčnaskupina/ Sprach- gruppe 1)	2.476 (654 rěčnaskupina/ Sprach- gruppe 1)	2.674 (652 rěčnaskupina/ Sprach- gruppe 1)	2.628 (744 rěčnaskupina/ Sprach- gruppe 1)
Brani-borska/ Brandenburg	1.051	1.824 (234 Witaj-šulerjow/ Schüler)	1.522	1.468 (301 Witaj-šuler/ Schüler)	2.010 (349 Witaj-šulerjow/ Schüler)
cyłkownje/ Gesamt	4.734	4.056	3.998	4.142	4.638

© Ludmila Budar/Budarjowa, 2017, Quellen/žórła: SBAB, ABC, MBJS

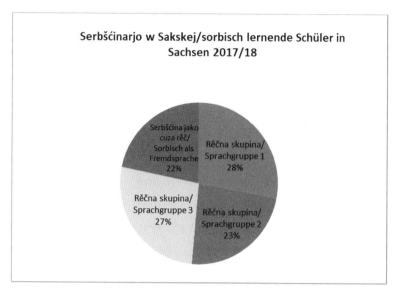

Serbšćinarjo w Sakskej/sorbisch lernende Schüler in Sachsen 2017/18

© Ludmila Budar/Budarjowa, 2017, Sakska/Sachsen, žórło/Quelle: SBAB

Kinder, die Sorbisch auf muttersprachlichem Niveau beherrschen (Sprachgruppe 1), betragen nur 28 % aller, die die sorbische Sprache in der Schule von 6 bis 12 Jahren lernen. Der SSV hegt berechtigte Hoffnungen, dass die Kinder, die aus den Witaj®-Kindertagesstätten kommen und in der Sprachgruppe 2 sind, in den höheren Schulklassen die sorbische Sprache in nahezu muttersprachlicher Qualität beherrschen werden.

Fazit

Der Sorbische Schulverein hat mit dem Modellprojekt Witaj® nicht nur ein Sprachkonzept entwickelt, sondern auch in der Praxis bewiesen, dass es für alle Sprachen der Welt bei entsprechenden Rahmenbedingungen anwendbar und erfolgreich sein kann. Das istin erster Linie eine politische Aufgabe: moralische und finanzielle Förderung von Witaj® von der Mehrheitsbevölkerung,und dem deutschen Staat und den Ländern Sachsen und Brandenburg, zusätzliches muttersprachliches sorbisches Personal (auch deren Ausbildung!), gesetzliche Garantien, das die sorbische Sprache erhalten, weiterentwickelt und revitalisiert wird. Wichtig sind auch sorbische Bücher, Lehrmaterialien auf dem aktuellsten Stand (Digitalisierung, Sorbisch ist nicht eine Haus-

und Hofsprache, sondern eine moderne europäische gleichberechtigte Sprache!), deshalb ist DYRDOMDEJ Web-Seite für uns sehr wichtig. Diese Web-Seite könnte theoretisch auch für Hakka-Kinder angewandt werden.

Nach 20 Jahren hat das Modellprojekt Witaj® eine regionale, landesweite und europäische Dimension erlangt. Das Interesse für Zwei- und Mehrsprachigkeit nimmt nicht nur unter den deutschen und sorbischen Eltern zu, sondern auch bei Wissenschaftlern auf der ganzen Welt, auch hier in Taiwan. Die Sprache ist das wichtigste Identitätsmerkmal. Mit ihr wird die Kultur vermittelt und zugleich eine emotionale Bindung zu ihr aufgebaut. Eine herausragende Rolle spielen dabei die Eltern und Familienangehörigen. Sie sind das Vorbild und entscheiden, welcher Bildungsweg für ihr Kind vorteilhaft ist und wie weit sie es unterstützen können und wollen. Insbesondere für die Eltern ist es wichtig, dassein in der Praxis bewährtes**ganzheitliches Spracherwerbsprogramm** von der Kinderkrippe bis zur Universität vorliegt. Natürlich muss es ständig erweitert oder auch nachjustiert werden.

Es ist also möglich, Sprachen zu revitalisieren, zu erhalten und zu festigen und damit auch die kulturelle Identität zu stärken. Dies hat eine Sonderstellung der Region zur Folge, und wer möchte denn nicht eine Soderstellung einnehmen?Voraussetzung für den Erfolg des Revitalisierungsprogramms ist ein entsprechendes kollektives Bewusstsein der Bevölkerung und der politische Wille der Sprache und Kultur (auch einer Minderheit) einen besonderen Wert beizumessen. Diesen abspruchsvollen Prozess sollten charismatische,engagierte und anerkannte Persönlichkeiten steuern.

【比利時荷蘭語 Dutch】

荷蘭語在比利時的政治現況：真實與想像歷史
The Real and Imagined History of the Status of the Dutch Language in Belgium

國立政治大學語言學研究所　戴智偉副教授兼所長

3

比利時

- 成立於1831年
- 人口：11,570,762
- 30,278平方公里（≈台灣：35,980平方公里）
- 西歐的十字路口
- 布魯塞爾
  - 比利時的首都
  - 歐盟的首都
- 多語國家

(CIA World Factbook 2018)

4

DE TAALGRENS

比利時語言邊界

黃：荷蘭語
紅：法語
綠：德語

5

比利時

- 聯邦制（federalism）

國家	聯邦政府		
大區 Regions	法蘭德斯 Vlaanderen	布魯塞爾首都 Brussel/ Bruxelles	瓦隆 Wallonie
社群 Communities	法蘭德斯語社群 Vlaamse Gemeenschap	法語社群 Communauté française	德語社群 Deutschsprachige Gemeinschaft
官方語言	荷蘭語（60%）	法語（40%）	德語（<1%）

6

比利時的語言邊界

- De Taalgrens (荷蘭語) / Frontière linguistique (法語)
- 法蘭德斯 ⇔ 瓦隆
  - 有爭議的地區：布魯塞爾
  - 德語社群現代變雙語區 (德法語)

- 不同的

	法蘭德斯	瓦隆
語言	荷蘭語	法語
媒體 (電視)	VRT, VTM, VIER, VIJF, ZES	RTBF (法), BRF (德)
政黨	N-VA, CD&V, Open VLD, ...	PS, MR, cdH, ...
政治偏好	偏右 (社會民族主義，自由主義)	偏左 (社會主義)
文化、...		

7

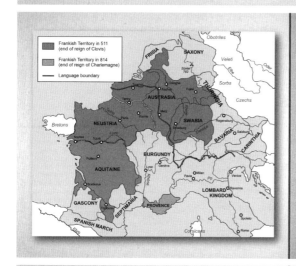

FRANKISH EMPIRE
法蘭克帝國

Based on Raskin (2012, p. 24)

8

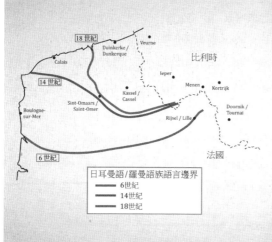

語言邊界的移動

Based on Raskin (2012, p. 94)

9

法蘭德斯語

- 12世紀：法蘭德斯縣的日耳曼語的方言
- 18世紀末之後：比利時北部的荷蘭語
  - 區語（regiolect）
- ≠ 分開的語言
- 方言的多元化相當大

- 到第19世紀末：比利時的荷蘭語是**低級語言**，大部分的時間**不當國家官方語言**
  - （除了

10

法蘭德斯語

"Maer de Nederduysche tael is hier wel mishandelt by ons, en vooral in Brussel: zy is in deze stadt niet alleen veronachtzaemt, maer ook veracht: men spreek er schier niet als de straettael; nouwelyks eenen geleerde die ze middelmatig weet; 't gemeyn meynt dat ze gebrekkig is, en veracht ze zonder kennen ..."

「但是比利時荷蘭語被虐待，尤其在布魯塞爾：市民不只看不起但是也鄙視荷語，連不願意把它當成街頭語言。學者都不會使用荷蘭。貧民認為荷語是一個缺陷的語言；他們雖然不了解自己的語言，仍然看不起它。」

Jan Baptist Verlooy, 1788, *Verhandeling om d'onacht der moederlycke tael in de Nederlanden*

oordeele best te zyn, het oud te houden , tot dat-er eens eene doorflaende betering beraemt zy.

Maer de Nederduytfche tael is hier wel

der moederlyke Tael. 39
anders mishandelt by ons , en voor ul in Bruffel: zy is in deze ftad niet alleen veron-achtzaemt, maer ook veracht: men fpreek-er fchier niet als de ftraet-tael : nouwelyks eenen geleerden die-ze middelmatig weet : 't gemeyn meynt dat-ze gebrekkig is en ver-acht-ze zonder kennen : geenen Bruffeler oft hy zal beleyden , dat hy nooit fermoon kan ichoon vinden in 't vlaems , maer dat dit moet in 't frans en van eenen Fransman

11

兩個交織的故事

- 想像歷史
  - 法蘭德斯的英雄
  - 從羅馬時代開始連續反抗外來的入侵者
  - 為了保護法蘭德斯的文化與語言
- 真實歷史
  - 比利時北部的公民
  - 因為19世紀的社會與經濟的變化
  - 得到了語言的全力

12

故事1：法蘭德斯的英雄

- 羅馬時代以來，法蘭德斯人不斷地鬥爭：
  - 為得到政治獨立
  - 為獲得文化、語言認可
  - 為反抗外來的侵略者

13

故事1：法蘭德斯的英雄

主角

- 有道德的國王、騎士、高貴的貧民、等等
- 勇敢的貧民或農民
- 反抗對於法蘭德斯人的不公正
- 自我犧牲

- 出生地：法蘭德斯（或德國南部）
- 母語：荷蘭語

對手

- 羅馬帝國
- 法國的國王
- 殘忍的貴族
- 貪婪的統治階級與經濟精英

- 出生地：國外
- 母語（或通用語）：法語（、拉丁語、德語、等）

14

故事1：法蘭德斯的英雄

"Gallia est omnis divisa in partes tres, quarum unam incolunt Belgae, aliam Aquitani, tertiam qui ipsorum lingua Celtae, nostra Galli appellantur ... Horum omnium fortissimi sunt Belgae, ..."

Julius Caesar, *Commentarii de Bello Gallico*, 58-49 BC

「全高盧分為三部分，貝爾蓋人居住第一步，阿基坦人居住另外一部，第三區域的人自稱凱爾特人，被我們命名為高盧人。」

尤利烏斯‧凱撒‧『高盧戰記』

15

DE SLAG DER GULDEN SPOREN

金馬刺戰役

Nicaise de Keyser
1836

16

故事1：法蘭德斯的英雄

- De Brugse Metten
  - 布魯日，1302年5月18日
  - 為保護與英格蘭的羊毛貿易
  - 屠殺法國來的雇用兵
  - **"Scild en vriend"**（盾與朋友）

17

故事1：法蘭德斯的英雄

英雄

- Jan Breydel
  - 屠戶
- Pieter de Coninck
  - 織工

銅像
布魯日廣場

敵人

- 腓力四世
  - 法國的國王

- 說法語的雇傭兵

18

故事1：法蘭德斯的英雄

- De Guldensporenslag（金馬剌戰役）
  - 科特賴克，1302年7月11日
  - 法蘭德斯城邦的民兵打敗國王軍隊

- Hendrik Conscience, 1838, *De Leeuw van Vlaenderen of de Slag der Gulden Sporen* (法蘭德斯的獅子或金馬剌戰役)

- 法蘭德斯的國慶日

Hendrik Conscience

19

"Ik ben maar een arme boer en al heb ik veel miserie gehad, toch is het boerenleven het schoonste leven dat er bestaat. Ik wil nog met geenen koning verwisselen.

God, ik dank U dat Gij van mij een boer hebt gemaakt!"

我只是個貧窮的農夫。雖然我的生活充滿了困難，我還是確信農夫的生活是世界最美好的生活。我仍不想當國王。

主啊！感謝祢把我做成一個農夫！

FELIX TIMMERMANS

BOERENPSALM
農夫詩篇

Van Kampen
Amsterdam, 1935

20

兩個交織的故事

- 以上的故事屬於歷史嗎？
  - 事實發生了
  - 理想化

"Vlaanderen [is] een term die in zijn huidige betekenis pas in de jaren [achtien] veertig in zwang begon te komen"

「法蘭德斯現代的含意是1840年代在產生的」

(Reynebeau 2009, p. 96)

21

法蘭德斯的範圍

16世紀中 哈布斯堡時代

22

故事2：比利時19世紀平民

- 1831: 比利時被建立
- 王室與權力精英：
  - 法語
  - 投票權
- 中產階級：
  - 荷蘭語
  - 沒有投票權到1893
- 貧民
  - 荷蘭語
  - 經濟狀況不好、沒有政治全力

23

故事2：比利時19世紀平民

- 社會不平等很大
- 社會流動性低
- 一般公民沒有投票權
- 法蘭德斯語不是官方語言

24

故事2：比利時19世紀平民

- Vlaamse Beweging (法蘭德斯獨立運動)
  - 法蘭德斯中產階級（與全公民）的政治權力
  - 法蘭德斯語的語言全力
    - 教育語言的保障
    - 官方語言
  - （法蘭德斯獨立）
- 法蘭德斯語的文學
  - 歷史小說
  - 田園小說
  - 中世紀文學
  - 產生法蘭德斯的自我認同

25

結論

- 語言、文化、民族認同
- 一個語言需要它的故事
  - 事實歷史 / 理想性的歷史
  - 語言、文化、民族的象徵
- 語言的歷史需要文學、藝術

- 歷史的變幻莫測

26

參考書目

- Raskin, Brigitte. 2012. *De taalgrens* [語言邊界]. Leuven: Davidsfonds.

- Reynebeau, Marc. 2009. *Een geschiedenis van Belgie: Nieuwe en geactualiseerde editie* [比利時現代史：更新版]. Tielt: Lannoo.

Briefing 1

I discovered that the PPT I prepared had some Belgian names that were difficult to translate into Chinese. It would be better to use the original text, especially if I was discussing Belgium's history. So I occasionally use Dutch.

My original expertise wasn't Dutch or Belgian; I was just teaching linguistics in Taiwan. But I'm Belgian, and we've all had to learn this stuff previously, and we're pretty opinionated about our language. Before I started researching, I found that something about my understanding of my native language was wrong. So I started reading history books. I don't know why I've always had an inclination for the past 30 years like there seems to be a little problem. It's intimately related to language development, as we will see later. That's why my title is "Real and Imaginary History." All countries have both kinds of history because it comprises the facts and the many stories you hear. Come to think of it, are the stories you heard at home or the history you learned at school really true? Are all politicians excellent people? Haven't they done anything wrong? The same goes for Belgian history.

Briefing 2-3

Belgium is the red part. It is a small country. Our population is almost half of that of Taiwan. Belgium was established in 1831 and is a very young country. This also has something to do with our story. The size of our nation is the same as Taiwan, approximately 35,000 square kilometers. These are the basic information you can find from the CIA World Factbook. But you don't need to go too deep into this part if you want to understand the language.

In the past, the CIA World Factbook would call Belgium the "Crossroads of Western Europe," which has its advantages and disadvantages. The area was very rich in the Middle Ages, and Belgium did not exist back then. This land is where rich people lived. But many wars have passed through Belgium, which is a very troublesome problem. Our capital is Brussels. It is important, but not so important to our story today. The capital of Belgium is actually the capital of the European Union. We are a multilingual country; otherwise, I would not be here to tell my story.

Briefing 4

The Belgian feature that is historically, linguistically, and politically important is that we have "De Taalgrens." We all know from childhood that if you ask a Belgian what a "De Taalgrens" is, the people in northern Belgium, like Vlamingen, would know what it is. We have a linguistic border between us in Belgium. The Dutch-speaking areas are above the border, the French-speaking areas are below the border, and some people speak German in the green part in the east. if you mention the history of the Belgian language, people usually forget them because most don't discuss them, so we probably won't talk about them very much today. Yellow speaks Dutch, red speaks French, and the one in the middle that speaks two languages is Brussels. Brussels was originally a bilingual area, but most people there speak French. I forgot the percentage, but I think it should be over 70%.

Moreover, these areas are semi-independent polities. So there is Flanders at the north and Wallonia at the south, and their regional flags are next to them. You can see that our system is quite complicated. Of course, our country has a federal government, and the politicians from Flanders and Wallonia will come together.

Briefing 5

There are two divisions below, the first being the "Regions" of Flanders, Brussels, and Wallonia. Their language styles are not the same. The Brussels we just mentioned speaks French and Dutch, so it's a bilingual area. Regions are more concerned with politics. The "communities" part is more concerned about language and culture. There is the "Flemish community (Vlaamse Gemeenschap)," which is the Dutch community; the "French community (Communauté française);" and the "German community (Deutschsprachige Gemeinschaft)." You can see that the German-speaking regions are smaller, accounting for just under 1%. The French-speaking community accounts for about 40% of our population, and the Dutch-speaking community is 60%.

Briefing 6

But if we mention language, people generally think about Flanders and Wallonia. So the average person cannot distinguish very clearly. Brussels is inherently a contentious community because people have argued about who it belongs to for centuries. As we have mentioned, "De Taalgrens (Dutch) / Frontière linguistique (French)" generally marks the boundary between Flanders and Wallonia.

So, We linguists call it "De Taalgrens, the Linguistic Boundary," or the so-called cultural boundary. If you see my table over there, it is not that Flanders and Wallonia do not support different languages. For example, their media TV stations are different. Flanders has VRT, VTM, VIER, VIJF, ZES; French has RTBF; and German has BRF.

The political parties are also different, and our parties are completely separate. Flanders is N-VA, CD&V, Open VLD; and the largest ones in Wallonia are PS, MR, cdH. If you compare the other things, you'll also find differences. We only have two things that are the same, beer and chocolate. That's about it. As you can see in other cultures, our literature is different. The general people also like different music as French-speaking and Dutch-speaking pop music is different. But it doesn't mean that the average Flemish doesn't care about the southern culture at all, it's just not our own culture.

Briefing 7

Another thing we need to understand is that this language boundary has been around for a long time. From the sixth to the ninth century, the Frankish Empire already had a boundary between the Romance language family and the Germanic language family, which is almost the same as the boundary between the Dutch-speaking and French-speaking areas today. So it has an extremely long history.

Briefing 8

But it will gradually move throughout history. The red part is the border between Belgium and France. But if you look at the yellow part of the language border that was probably here in the 6th century, it gradually moved upward during the 14th century. This is because France was not a country at that time. The king of France was the king of Paris, and he wanted to invade and plunder the land of Belgium. Then the people from the French-speaking areas slowly migrated north, and our language boundary was almost reached here by the 18th century. The current language boundary is further up.

Briefing 9

I was talking about the northerners. So it is difficult to explain what my native language is. I just said the northerners speak Dutch, right? But if you ask the general people what language they speak, they'll answer "Flemish." Since childhood, I have always thought Flemish is not a language but a Dutch dialect. But I have several linguists here asking me whether "the Flemish language is actually a separate language" every year. I would say no. Someone else would ask, "You Belgians have two languages, Flemish and French, right?" I would say no. It's not Flemish. It's Dutch. It is quite complicated. If you look at history, Flanders is not a thing. It's a historical name, but it describes different things. For example, 12th-century Flanders is basically the language of the Flemish gods, not modern Flanders. We'll take a look at a map later. But is the northern part of Belgium considered modern Flanders? The current East and West Flanders are not all of Flanders, and it is the westernmost part of modern Flanders.

After the 18th century, Flemish became a language for entire northern Belgium, not a dialect. There are several different dialects in northern Flanders. Depending on how you want to divide it, linguists think there are maybe five or six different Dutch dialects. If you go to different villages in Flanders, you will find that each village's dialect or local language is a little different. The dialects in the west and the east are extremely different. We almost came from the same area, the city of Antwerp. For example, my mother is from the east, and her dialect is entirely different from mine. My father didn't understand it before and still can't understand my mother's dialect now. So we all have to speak standard Dutch at home. Otherwise, we can't communicate.

So I have just said that it is not a separate language, but the diversity of dialects is very large. We're talking about a minority language today. To be honest, I'm a little embarrassed because modern Flemish is in pretty good shape. We're the biggest language in Belgium, but it wasn't always the case. It wasn't until the end of the 19th century. I think that's a bit conservative. It should be the middle of the 20th century that Flemish was not a very important language in Belgium. If you want to be a teacher or a politician, you must learn French, no matter what kind of good job you want. In fact, all primary education provides French and Dutch education. But starting in junior high school, only

French education is available. All universities also use French. So the Flemish language used to be discriminated against and was spoken by farmers and workers at the time. But you would not use this language to communicate with others if you have received any education at all. It is not the official language of Belgium.

Briefing 10

But it wasn't the same five to six centuries ago. But that's beyond the scope of our discussion today. Let me take an example. When Belgium belonged to France In 1788, a local scholar wrote the book "Verhandeling om d'onacht der moederlycke tael in de Nederlanden," and its contents mentioned that:

> Maer de Nederduysche tael is hier wel mishandelt by ons, en vooral in Brussel: zy is in deze stadt niet alleen veronachtzaemt, maer ook veracht: men spreek er schier niet als de straettael; nouwelyks eenen geleerde die ze middelmatig weet; 't gemeyn meynt dat ze gebrekkig is, en veracht ze zonder kennen ⋯⋯
>
> — Jan Baptist Verlooy, 1788, *Verhandeling om d'onacht der moederlycke tael*
> *in de Nederlanden*

It means that the Dutch language in Belgium at the time was abused, according to my own translation. So the general public, especially in Brussels, both supports and hates it. They felt it was a language that shouldn't exist and were reluctant to consider it a street language, so no one speaks Dutch on the streets. Scholars don't speak Dutch, and ordinary people think Dutch is a "flawed" language. They don't know the language yet still look down on it. This situation should be about the same if you go back to Belgium in the 19th century or about a hundred years later.

Briefing 11

If you want to understand the status and changes of the Dutch language in Belgium, you should start by researching its history. But the history of Belgium we learned in primary and secondary schools seems to be different from the facts. So let me explain two stories first, and then I'll discuss where they are wrong.

The first one is "Imagined History." In fact, it should be called the "Imagined

History" of northern Belgium because if you study Belgian history in Flanders, we must explore the situation of Flanders in Belgium. The southern part is not that important, and I'm not sure what the southern part studies because I never went to Wallonia to study. The other side should be the opposite because they'll say, "Wallonia has a great history." That's basically the way it is.

Briefing 12

If you ask children what they know about Flanders' history, they will tell you a story about the heroes of Flanders: "There are people in the history of Flanders who, since a very long time ago, have protected their language and the Flemish culture." This story is not accurate according to history. In this story, the current status of Flanders is like this, "some heroes have been working hard for our language since 800 years ago." But if you study the data from modern historians, you'd find that the language status in Belgium developed due to the politics of the 19th century. Something that happened so long ago is not so relevant to our current language. The first story involves the heroes of Flanders protecting our language. This is interesting because in Flemish popular culture in general, many people think that we Belgians are Flemish and rebelled against those who spoke French since the Roman times. The Romans spoke Latin then, but it was still almost the same. They declared independence for Belgium and Flanders to achieve political independence. The difference cannot be clarified in our story. To protect our culture, our language, and resist foreign invaders, it was the bad guys who came into our country to steal our land and destroy our culture.

Briefing 13

The protagonists in such stories are almost the same. Their status in society sometimes changes. Sometimes they're kings, which I won't discuss today, but some were quite interesting. Their mother tongue is not Dutch, but they often become Dutch heroes. They were often some knights, brave commoners, or ordinary people with a hard life. But they're smart, and yes, they love their country very much. So they usually rebel against foreign regimes, kings, or governments; the protagonist may be Napoleon or whatever. But their enemies generally have one thing in common, they all speak French most of the time. Some speak Dutch and German, but most of their enemies speak French or Latin in Roman times. These heroes were all raised and born in Flanders or southern Germany because these were Dutch-speaking areas at the time. In fact, Dutch and German were not separate languages back then. If we go back about 800 years, the native language was Dutch or Germanic.

Briefing 14

As I've said, the first example started in Roman times, right?

Gallia est omnis divisa in partes tres, quarum unam incolunt Belgae, aliam Aquitani, tertiam qui ipsorum lingua Celtae, nostra Galli appellantur ... Horum omnium fortissimi sunt Belgae, ...

— Julius Caesar, *Commentarii de Bello Gallico*, 58-49 BC

So Gaul. Gaul, right? The entire Gaul is divided into 3 parts, "Belgae." It's the first step to life. It continued to say, "Horum omnium fortissimi sunt Belgae." So the bravest of those different tribes are Gauls, which are Belgians. In Belgium, especially the Flemish people's heads, these Belgians are Flemish because they rebelled against a Latin empire. I put these two cartoons in because I don't know if you've seen "The Adventures of Asterix" (Astérix le Gaulois in French). They are cartoon versions of Belgian heroes that little kids want to see.

Briefing 15

Second, if you asked a Belgian kid, especially a Flemish kid, what the "De slag der gulden sporen" (Battle of the Golden Spurs) was in history, the kid would answer: "Yes, yes, I know, I know!" They don't know much about this history, but they know some very brave Flemish people fought against the king of France at the Battle of the Golden Spurs. That's it.

Let's explain the original history first. It's a fourteenth-century incident. Modern Flemish people still know it. We may not know much about the 14th century, but every Belgian or anyone in northern Belgium knows about the Battle of the Golden Spurs.

Briefing 16

That history has two parts. The first is the "De Brugse Metten". It has no official translation in Chinese, so Chinese is not included. But let me explain. On May 18, 1302, trade with England in Bruges was very prosperous, especially the wool trade. So the Flanders was famous for their fabrics back then. But the kings of France restricted trade with Britain due to conflicts, which was a huge problem for Flemish politics. This was especially true for Burges, which was the largest port in Western Europe at that time. It was Britain's biggest business, so its citizens rebelled against France and decided to protest. On May 18th, they massacred the French troops in Bruges.

The language was involved during their battles because they used it to classify allies and foes. They asked everyone to say the sentence "Scild en vriend (Shield and friend)," which made no sense, right? But French speakers pronounce it differently. So everybody knows the person is French and would get rid of him. That's how the story goes. Did that really happen? I'm not sure. But every kid knows the phrase "Scild en vriend (Shield & Friend)."

Briefing 17

So there are two "De Brugse Metten" heroes and they are in Bruges. If you have a chance to visit Bruges, you should see their bronze statues on the square. "Jan Breydel (the butcher) and Pieter de Coninck (the weaver)" were civilians who grew up in Bruges. They claimed that the king of France devastated these two industries, and they were the leaders of this battle.

I've mentioned the king of France and the French-speaking army. So we know that the king of the city-state of Flanders and the king of France had some conflicts during the 9th century. There were often conflicts, so the king or emperor at that time usually brought mercenaries into Belgium.

Briefing 18

The king of France did not care about the 2nd part, of course. So when he sent a big army to Belgium, Bruges and other Flemish cities to cooperated and joined forces with a big militia army to defeat the king of France on July 11th during an incident called "De

Guldensporenslag (Battle of the Golden Spurs)." I mentioned that you definitely would have learned this history if you were a Flemish child. Why? Because Belgium was just established in the 19th century, French was the main language in Belgium back then. French was the mother tongue of important people. It wasn't until the 19th century to mid-19th century did some people in Belgium started to contemplate how our Dutch language, or the Belgian Dutch language, could improve. Mr. Hendrik Conscience wrote a novel "De Leeuw van Vlaenderen of de Slag der Gulden Sporen" (Flanders - the Lion of Sri Lanka or the Battle of the Golden Spurs) in 1838.

I'm an English and Germanic graduate, so I have taken Dutch literature courses, but I honestly never read this novel because it seemed boring. But it's extremely popular. We have a copy at home, and Flemish people usually keep a copy at home. He described a story of the Battle of the Golden Spurs. Another important influence is that July 11th became the National Day of Flanders. It is critical for the self-recognition of our race.

All these things did happen, right? Are these events that important in our history? I am not sure. Would we be without Belgium now if the Battle of the Golden Spurs hadn't happened? Would there be any Flanders? I'm not sure.

Briefing 19

I mentioned that our hero stories often touted ordinary people for becoming heroes, right? Another type of literature began to develop from about the same period as the book discussed above. That is, the "Peasant Psalm." The Chinese translation seems to be "Pastoral Literature." So some authors started to write the story of the farmer's plights. A farmer had worked very hard in his fields since he was a child, etc. Another famous author is Felix Timmerman. He wrote, "Boerenpsalm" (Farmer's Psalm). Here are the first two or three sentences:

Ik ben maar een arme boer en al heb ik veel miserie gehad, toch is het boerenleven het schoonste leven dat er bestaat. Ik wil nog met geenen koning verwisselen.

God, ik dank U dat Gij van mij een boer hebt gemaakt!

— Hendrik Conscience, *De Leeuw van Vlaenderen of de Slag der Gulden Sporen*, 1935

I am just a poor farmer. Although my life is full of plights, I am convinced that a farmer's life is the best in the world. I still don't want to be a king.

God! Thank you for making me a farmer!

It's also very interesting and important that their religion is Catholic. One point is that these authors don't seem to need to be farmers themselves because no life is so picture-perfect.

Briefing 20

So is the story above historically accurate? These things did happen, but they were somewhat idealized. When I was preparing this article, I read a book that said something that gave me some ideas and changed a thing. It said "Vlaanderen [is] een term die in zijn huidige betekenis pas in de jaren [achtien] veertig in zwang begon te komen." (The modern connotation of Flanders was created in the 1840s.) It said that our modern concept of Flanders only began to emerge in the 1840s, and the former Flanders is the Flanders in the west of Belgium we just mentioned.

Briefing 21

There were 3 pictures on this page, and the 3 pictures are merged.

So now Flanders is this piece, as we just saw in that same map, a similar map. But if you looked at the United Kingdom of the Netherlands in 1790, Flanders is this little piece. It wasn't the same region, country, or area. Flanders was this little piece during the 16th century. So the Flanders now has nothing to do with the Flanders back then. I just explained to you that the battle of Golden Horses has nothing to do with Belgium.

Briefing 22-24

The second story is related to these authors who wrote about the history of Belgium.

Here are the historical facts. Belgium was established in 1830. Back then, all important people, such as the nobles or kings, were native French speakers. The Flemish people were uneducated, and their conditions were very bad, similar to the indigenous people in Taiwan 30 years ago. But middle-class people start to make money. The uneducated people speak Dutch but still make progress in life. So they began to gradually push the Flemish language movement called "Vlaamse Beweging (Flemish Independence Movement)." It is now translated as the Flemish Independence Movement. But people at that time did not necessarily want Flemish independence. They just wanted equal rights. What they really wanted was equal rights, especially language equality and education. There was nothing to educate at that time, and they just wanted Flanders to be the official language of Belgium. The two authors I showed you belonged to this movement. So they started writing historical novels, pastoral novels, medieval literature, and restoring medieval literature.

Briefing 25

That's about it. Why did I tell you this story? Because you cannot see the real history if you read the stories from Flanders or Belgium or their history. That's not to say they're all deceitful or worthless because our race, our Flemish race, is related to these historical stories. Regardless of true or false, if you want a language to exist, that language must have a history and some stories. You must be able to say, "Actually, that's where my language came from, and it's important." If you want to develop the history of a language, you'd need literature or art, popular art, or advanced art. You must understand that history is not a fixed thing. History is woven together by stories, some of which are real, and some may be imagined.

簡報 1

我發現我準備的 PPT 有一些比利時的名稱很難翻成中文，特別是如果要討論比利時的歷史的話，使用原文會更好，所以我偶而會使用荷蘭語。

我本來的專長不是荷蘭語或比利時的語言，我只是在臺灣教語言學，但是我是比利時人，我們以前都要學這種東西，而且我們對自己的語言也很有意見。我開始研究之前，我發現到我對自己母語的了解有一些是不對的，所以我開始看歷史的書籍。我不知道為什麼我過往 30 年一直有的想法，好像有一點問題，這和語言的發展非常有關係，我們等一下會看到。所以這就是為什麼我的標題是「真實與想像的歷史」，其實所有的國家都有這兩種歷史，因為歷史不是只有事實而已，很多的是你聽到的故事。在家裡聽到的故事，或你在學校學到的歷史，要好好想一想那些都是真的嗎？這些政治家都是那麼優秀的人嗎？都沒有做錯事嗎？比利時的歷史也是

這樣子。

簡報 2-3

比利時是紅色那一塊，是一個小小的國家，我們的人口是差不多只有臺灣的一半，我們是一個很年輕的國家，在 1831 年才建立，這跟我們的故事也有關係。然後我們的面積和臺灣一樣大，差不多 3 萬 5 千平方公里，這些是基本資料可以去 CIA World Factbook 查詢，但如果你要了解語言的話不需要太深入這部分。

以前 CIA World Factbook 會說比利時是「西歐的十字路口」，這有好處也有缺點。因為中世紀時這個區域很有錢，那時候還沒有比利時這個國家，但這片土地是有錢人居住的地區，很多戰爭也是經過比利時，所以這是一個很麻煩的問題。我們首都是布魯塞爾，它很重要，但對我們今天的故事不是那麼的重要。比利時的首都事實上也是歐盟的首都，我們是一個多語的國家，不然我就不會在這邊講我的故事了。

簡報 4

那我們在歷史上、語言上、還有政治上比較重要的比利時特色是我們有「De Taalgrens」。從小我們都了解，如果你問一個比利時人「De Taalgrens」是什麼，在比利時北部的人，像弗拉芒人（Vlamingen）都知道是什麼。我們比利時中間有這一條線，是我們的語言邊界。邊界以上都是用荷蘭語的地區，以下都是法語地區，還有東部那個綠色的那一塊，有些人說德語，但是事實上如果你討論比利時語言的歷史，你通常會忘記他們，一般人不會討論他們，所以我們今天可能不太會談到他們。黃色荷蘭語、紅色法語，然後中間的那一塊有兩個語言就是布魯塞爾。布魯塞爾本來是雙語地區，但是事實上大部分的布魯塞爾他們都說法語，我忘記百分比了，應該是 70% 以上。

還有這些地區他們都是他們半獨立的政體，所以北部是法蘭德斯，南部是瓦隆，旁邊是他們的區旗，你看我們的體系是真的蠻複雜的。當然我們國家有一個聯邦政府，法蘭德斯跟瓦隆的政治家他們會集合在一起。

簡報 5

那以下有兩個分隔，第一個是「大區（Regions）」法蘭德斯、布魯塞爾，還有瓦隆。事實上他們的語言風格不太一樣，我們剛剛說的布魯塞爾有法語、

有荷蘭語，所以是雙語地區。大區他們比較管政治的部分；那我們看到語言還有文化相關它們是屬於「社群（Communities）」的部分。有「法蘭德斯語社群（Vlaamse Gemeenschap）」就是荷蘭語社區，然後你有「法語社群（Communauté française）」、以及「德語社群（Deutschsprachige Gemeinschaft）」。你已經看到德語地區不太重要，僅有 1% 以下，法語社區大概 40%，我們的人口的 40%；荷蘭語社區是 60%。

簡報 6

但是如果我們討論語言，一般人都會討論法蘭德斯還有瓦隆，所以一般人不太會分得那麼清楚。因為布魯塞爾本來就是一個有爭議的社群，已經好幾百年都在吵該歸屬哪一方。所以我們剛剛說的「De Taalgrens（荷蘭語）／ Frontière linguistique（法語）」，一般就是法蘭德斯與瓦隆的分界。

那我們語言學家稱作「De Taalgrens，語言邊界」，或者我們應該要說它是一個文化的邊界。因為如果你看到我那邊那個表，這兩個地區，法蘭德斯、瓦隆他們並不是不支持有不同的語言。如果你看到他們的媒體，比如說他們的媒體電視臺也是不一樣，法蘭德斯是有 VRT、VTM、VIER、VIJF、ZES；法語區有 RTBF、和德語的 BRF。

政黨也是不一樣，我們的政黨是完全分開的。法蘭德斯地區是 N-VA、CD&V、Open VLD；瓦隆現在最大的是 PS、MR、cdH。如果你比較其他的東西，你也會發現不同的地方，我們只有兩個東西是一樣的，是啤酒還有巧克力，差不多是這樣子。其他文化方面你也可以看到，我們的文學不一樣；我們一般人喜歡的音樂也不一樣；法語區和荷蘭語區的流行音樂不一樣。但這不代表一般人法蘭德斯人完全不會理南部的文化，只不過這不是我們本體的文化。

簡報 7

我們還要了解另外一件事，這個語言邊界已經存在很久了。法蘭克帝國 6 到 9 世紀已經有羅曼語系跟日耳曼語系的一個界線，就差不多跟我們現在的荷蘭語區還有法語區的界線一樣，所以它有一個非常非常久的歷史。

簡報 8

但是它在歷史上會慢慢移動，比說這是紅色的部分是比利時跟法國的邊界，但

是如果你看到語言邊界大概 6 世紀大概才在這邊的黃色的那一部分，14 世紀才往上面移動。這是因為法國，特別是那時候法國不是一個國家，法國的國王是巴黎的國王一直想侵入掠取比利時的土地，然後法語區的人慢慢遷移到北部，第 18 世紀我們的語言邊界大概差不多到這裡，那現在的狀況語言邊界更往上一些。

簡報 9

我剛才說我是北部人，所以我的母語是什麼，這是很難解釋的一個東西，我剛剛說北部的人他們說荷蘭語對不對？但是如果你問一般的人你講的語言是什麼，他們會說「Flemish」（法蘭德斯語），那我以為是從小對我來說法蘭德斯是一個，就不是語言，就是一個荷蘭語的方言，但是我來這邊每年有幾個語言學家，應該要了解語言的人問我「其實你們法蘭德斯語是一個分開的語言嗎？」我說沒有。下次有另外一個人問「你們比利時有兩個語言，法蘭德斯語還有法語對嗎？」我說沒有，這不是法蘭德斯語這是荷蘭語。這很複雜，如果你看到的歷史，法蘭德斯不是一個東西，歷史上他是一個名稱，但是它是描寫不同的東西，比如說 12 世紀法蘭德斯基本上是法蘭德斯神的語言，而不是現代的法蘭德斯，我們等一下會看到一個地圖，但是不是現代的法蘭德斯，那個比利時北部的那一塊，但是就是現代的東法蘭德斯跟西法蘭德斯，這不是法蘭德斯的全部，這是現代法蘭德斯的最西部的那一塊。

從 18 世紀開始，法蘭德斯語才成為那個比利時北部全部的一個語言，而不是一個方言。因為法蘭德斯北部有好幾個不同的方言，要看你要怎麼區分，語言學家認為荷蘭語有大概五、六個不同的方言，但是如果你去法蘭德斯，去不同的村莊你會發現每一個村莊的方言或是地方的語言都有一點不一樣，西部跟東部的方言非常非常不一樣，我們是幾乎從一樣的地區來的，安特衛普這個城市。但是比如說，我媽媽是從東部來的，他的方言跟我的方言完全不一樣，我爸爸以前聽不懂，現在還是聽不懂我媽媽的方言，所以我們在家裡都要說標準的荷蘭語，不然沒辦法溝通。

所以我剛才已經說了不是分開的語言，方言的多樣化非常大。我們今天討論的是少數語言，老實說我有點不好意思，因為現代的法蘭德斯語的狀況還蠻不錯的，我們是比利時最大的語言，但不是一直以來都是如此的一件事。大概到 19 世紀末期，其實我那一邊有一點保守，應該是從 20 世紀中法蘭德斯語不算是一個非常重要的語言在比利時裡面，如果你要當一個老師、政治家，不管你要什麼好的工作，

你一定要學法語，所有的教育，其實小學的教育有法語的教育、和荷蘭語的教育，但是中學開始你只能用法語，所有的大學也是用法語的，所以它是一個以前說被歧視的語言，法蘭德斯語那時候是一個農人還有工人說的語言，但是你有一點教育你不應該要用這種語言跟別人溝通，它也不是當一個國家的官方語言，比利時的官方語言。

簡報 10

如果你回去 500 年、600 年狀況不太一樣，但是我們今天沒有辦法討論。我拿一個例子，比如說 1788 年那時候比利時屬於法國，有一個當地學者寫一本書 *Verhandeling om d'onacht der moederlycke tael in de Nederlanden* 內容說到：

Maer de Nederduysche tael is hier wel mishandelt by ons, en vooral in Brussel: zy is in deze stadt niet alleen veronachtzaemt, maer ook veracht: men spreek er schier niet als de straettael; nouwelyks eenen geleerde die ze middelmatig weet; 't gemeyn meynt dat ze gebrekkig is, en veracht ze zonder kennen ......

— Jan Baptist Verlooy, 1788, *Verhandeling om d'onacht der moederlycke tael*
in de Nederlanden

意思是說當時在比利時的荷蘭語是被虐待的，這是我自己的翻譯，所以尤其在布魯塞爾一般市民不僅是支持、更還討厭它們，他們覺得這是一個不應該存在的語言，也不願意把它當成一個街頭語言，所以路上沒有人會說荷蘭語。學者都不會用荷蘭語，還有一般平民他們認為荷蘭語是一個「有缺陷」的語言，還有他們不了解這個語言，他們還是看不起它。這個狀況應該如果你回去比利時大概是 19 世紀應該還是差不多一樣，約一百年之後還是差不多。

簡報 11

如果你要了解荷蘭語在比利時的狀況和變化，你要開始研究它的歷史，還有我們小學、中學學的比利時的歷史跟事實好像不太一樣。所以我先解釋這兩個故事，然後我討論一下它們哪裡有錯誤。

第一個是「想像的歷史」。其實該說是比利時北部的「想像的歷史」，因為如果你在法蘭德斯學比利時的歷史，我們就來討論法蘭德斯在比利時的狀況，南部的部分不是那麼非常的重要，同時也是因為南部我不太確定，因為我從來沒有去瓦隆讀

書過，所以我不太確定他們學什麼，但是應該也是相反的，他們會說「我們瓦隆的歷史是多麼的厲害。」基本上就是這個樣子。

簡報 12

但是如果你問小朋友，一般人他們對法蘭德斯歷史的了解，他們會告訴你一個關於法蘭德斯英雄的故事：「法蘭德斯歷史上有一些人，從很久很久以前，他們就在保護他們的語言；保護法蘭德斯的文化。」事實上這個歷史是不太一樣，在這個故事裡面法蘭德斯的現況現在是這樣子，「有些英雄大概從八百年以前一直為了我們的語言努力」但是你如果真正的看到比如說歷史學家，現代的歷史學家，你發現到他們會覺得其實比利時的語言狀況還是從大概 19 世紀的政治開始發展，那麼久以前的時間，其實跟我們現在的語言比較沒有什麼關係。第一個故事，所以這是法蘭德斯的英雄他們保護我們的語言，這個很有趣，因為在法蘭德斯的一般流行文化上，很多人認為我們比利時的人是算是法蘭德斯人，他們從大概羅馬時代開始反抗那些說法語的人，那時候是羅馬人說拉丁語的，但是還是差不多一樣，為了政治獨立，所以他們要獨立比利時、法蘭德斯，在我們的故事裡說不清楚這個差別。為了保護我們的文化、我們的語言，為了反抗外來的侵略者，都是壞人他們進來我們的國家偷我們的土地、破壞我們的文化。

簡報 13

在這種故事裡面我們的主角都是差不多一樣的人，所以其實他在社會上的地位有時候會改變，有時候是一個國王，我今天不會討論這個問題，雖然很有意思，有時候他們是國王，但事實上母語不是荷蘭語，但是他都變成荷蘭語的英雄，或是一些騎士，類似這種東西，或是常常也是勇敢的平民，那些生活很苦的一般的人，但是他們很聰明，還有他們對他們的國家很有愛，所以他們通常反抗外國的政體、國王或是政府，或是拿破崙或是我不知道是誰，但是他們這些敵人通常有一個東西，他們有一個共通特質，大部分的時候他們都是說法語，有一些說荷蘭語、有一些說德語，但是在羅馬時代，大部分的敵人都是說法語或是拉丁語。這些英雄都是在法蘭德斯長大的、出生的，或是在德國南部，因為那時候也是荷蘭語地區，其實荷蘭語跟德語那時候還不是分開的語言，如果回去大概 800 年前，他的母語是荷蘭語或是日耳曼語。

簡報 14

第一個例子我剛剛是說從羅馬時代開始。

Gallia est omnis divisa in partes tres, quarum unam incolunt Belgae, aliam
Aquitani, tertiam qui ipsorum lingua Celtae, nostra Galli appellantur … Horum
omnium fortissimi sunt Belgae, ...

— Julius Caesar, *Commentarii de Bello Gallico*, 58-49 BC

所以，全高盧分為三部分，「Belgae（貝爾蓋人）」是高盧人中的先鋒，還有他
繼續說「Horum omnium fortissimi sunt Belgae」，所以高盧人中最勇敢的是比利時
人，在比利時的，特別是在法蘭德斯人的腦袋裡面，這些比利時人就是法蘭德斯
人，因為他們反抗一個拉丁語的帝國，我放進去這兩個卡通是因為我不知道你們有
沒有看過《阿斯泰利克斯歷險記》（法文為 Astérix le Gaulois），他們就是那些比利
時人將他們卡通化，變成一種小孩子想要看的東西。

簡報 15

第二個，歷史上如果你問一個比利時的小朋友，其實特別是法蘭德斯的小朋友
「De slag der gulden sporen（金馬刺戰役）」這是什麼東西，他一定回答：「對對對，
我知道、我知道！」他們不太了解這個歷史，但是他們知道在金馬刺戰役有一些很
勇敢的法蘭德斯人反抗法國的國王，就是這樣子。

我先解釋一下原始的歷史，這是 14 世紀的一件事，現在的法蘭德斯人都還知
道這件事，我們完全不了解 14 世紀，但是金馬刺戰役是每一個比利時的人，比利
時北部的人都知道。

簡報 16

那個歷史的過程有兩部分，第一段是「De Brugse Metten」這個詞中文裡沒有
正式的翻譯，所以沒有放上中文。但是我解釋一下。1302 年的 5 月 18 號，在布魯
日這個城市，那時代跟英國的貿易往來非常繁榮，特別是羊毛貿易，所以那時法蘭
德斯很有名的一個是他們的布料，但是法國的國王跟英國有衝突，所以他們限制跟
英國的貿易，這對法蘭德斯的政治是非常大的一個問題，特別是對布魯日，布魯日
那時候是西歐最大的港口，英國是他們最大的做生意對象，所以他們的市民反抗法
國，決定要抗議，而他們在 5 月 18 號時，屠殺布魯日裡面的法國軍隊。

特別的是，他們的戰鬥和語言有關係，因為他們用此分類誰是朋友、誰是敵人，他們讓大家都說出來一句話「Scild en vriend（盾與朋友）」，沒有意思對不對？但是說法語的人發音不同，所以大家都知道這是法國人，那就把他趕走，故事是這樣子。這是真的發生的嗎？我不太確定，但是每個小朋友知道「Scild en vriend（盾與朋友）」。

簡報 17

所以「De Brugse Metten」的英雄就是有兩個，而他們在布魯日，如果你有機會去布魯日看他們的廣場上面還有他們的銅像，「Jan Breydel（屠戶）和 Pieter de Coninck（織工）」這兩位是在布魯日長大的平民，他們就說這兩個行業被法國的國王影響了，所以他們當這個戰鬥的領導。

那敵人我已經說過是法國的國王還有說法語的軍隊，所以那時候國王因為法蘭德斯的城邦，從大概第 9 世紀開始，我們知道的是從第 9 世紀開始一直跟他們的國王有一點衝突，常常有衝突，所以那時候的國王或皇帝他們通常把一些雇傭兵帶進來比利時。

簡報 18

那第二段法國的國王當然不管了，所以他送一些很大的軍隊到比利時去，那布魯日還有其他的法蘭德斯的城市和他們合作，他們跟一個大的民兵的軍隊打敗法國的國王，這是在 7 月 11 號，這一個事件叫「De Guldensporenslag（金馬刺戰役）」。我剛剛說如果你是一個法蘭德斯小朋友，你一定會學到這一塊歷史，為什麼呢？因為第 19 世紀中比利時剛剛被建立，在當代的比利時以法語為主，重要的人、主要的語言的母語言都是法語，大概以 19 世紀中到 19 世紀末有一些比利時人開始發展或是開始想像我們荷蘭語要如何進步，我們荷蘭語，比利時荷蘭語的狀況。這一位亨德里克・康西安斯（Hendrik Conscience）於 1838 年寫了一本小說《De Leeuw van Vlaenderen of de Slag der Gulden Sporen》（法蘭德斯之獅，或稱金馬刺戰役）。

老實說我是英文和日耳曼語系畢業，所以我們本來有荷蘭的文學，但我從來沒有看到這本小說，因為好像很無聊。但是它非常的、非常的流行，我們家有一本，法蘭德斯人的家裡通常會有。他描寫金馬刺戰役的一個故事，有另外一個重要的影響是 7 月 11 號之後變成法蘭德斯的國慶日，所以對我們的自我人種是非常的、非常的重要。

這些東西都發生過對不對？這是他們在我們的歷史上那麼的重要嗎？我不太確定，如果金馬刺戰役沒有發生，我們現在會沒有比利時嗎？沒有法蘭德斯嗎？我不太確定。

簡報 19

我剛剛也說在我們這個英雄的故事裡面，常常也有一些一般人平民當成英雄對不對？從大概跟剛剛那本書同一時期，也有另外一種文學開始發展，就是「農夫詩篇」，中文翻譯好像是「田園文學」。有一些作者開始寫農夫痛苦的故事，像是農夫從小一直在農田裡很辛苦的工作。還有一個很有名的作者是菲利克斯・蒂默曼斯（Felix Timmerman）他寫了《Boerenpsalm》（農夫詩篇），以下是最前面的兩、三句話：

Ik ben maar een arme boer en al heb ik veel miserie gehad, toch is het boerenleven het schoonste leven dat er bestaat. Ik wil nog met geenen koning verwisselen.

God, ik dank U dat Gij van mij een boer hebt gemaakt!

　　— Hendrik Conscience, De Leeuw van Vlaenderen of de Slag der Gulden
Sporen, 1935

我只是個貧窮的農夫。雖然我的生活充滿了困難，我還是確信農夫的生活是世界最美好的生活。我仍不想當國王。
主啊！感謝祢把我做成一個農夫！

也是很有趣，因為你就看的出來有另外一個很重要的東西——天主教是他們的宗教。真的有一點，當然這些作者好像不用自己當農夫，因為應該沒有那麼的漂亮的一個生活。

簡報 20

所以以上的故事屬於歷史嗎？其實這些事情真正發生過，但是他們有一點理想化。其實我準備這篇文章，我在看一本書，那個桌子裡面寫了一句話，我那時候我看到了，我突然頭腦裡面有了一個想法，改變了一件事，他說「Vlaanderen [is] een term die in zijn huidige betekenis pas in de jaren [achtien] veertig in zwang begon te komen」（法蘭德斯現代的含意是 1840 年代產生的）所以他說法蘭德斯這個概念，我們現代的法蘭德斯的概念，是 1840 年代才開始產生，以前的法蘭德斯就是我們剛剛說的比利時西部的法蘭德斯。

簡報 21

有三張圖片在此頁面，之後三張圖一併放上。

所以現在的法蘭德斯是這一塊，我們剛剛看到那個一樣的地圖、類似的地圖，但是如果你看到比說 1790 年荷蘭聯合王國的時代，法蘭德斯是這一塊而已，它不是一樣的區域，它不是一樣的國家、它不是一樣的地區，第 16 世紀法蘭德斯是這一塊，所以我們現在的法蘭德斯跟那些法蘭德斯完全沒有關係，但是我剛剛跟你解釋的那個金馬刺戰役跟比利時沒有什麼關係。

簡報 22-24

第二個故事是我們剛才看到這些作者他們開始寫跟比利時的歷史有關係的東西。

所以事實的歷史就是這樣子，1830 年比利時被成立了，那時候我剛剛說貴族國王所有重要的人母語都是法語，法蘭德斯人都是沒有受到教育的人，他們的狀況非常的不好，像現在的或是大概 30 年以前的原住民，就是臺灣的原住民差不多，但是中產階級的人他們開始賺錢，他們沒有受到教育的人他們說荷蘭語，但是他們生活上還是要進步，所以他們開始慢慢推動法蘭德斯語的運動，「Vlaamse Beweging（法蘭德斯獨立運動）」，現在翻成法蘭德斯獨立運動，但那時候的人不一定要法蘭德斯獨立，他們只是要平等的權利，所以他們要什麼平等的權利，其實特別是語言的平等權，特別是教育上，那時候沒有什麼可以教育，光他們要法蘭德斯當一個比利時的官方語言，我跟他說剛剛給你看的兩個作者他們都是屬於這個運動，所以他們開始寫歷史小說、田園小說、中世紀的文學，開始恢復中世紀的文學。

簡報 25

我們談到這裡，所以我為什麼告訴你這個故事，其實如果你看到法蘭德斯在比利時的故事或是歷史，你就看不出來真正的歷史，你看到一個故事而已，那這不是說他們都是騙人的或者是沒有價值的，因為我們的自我人種，我們法蘭德斯自我

人種跟這些歷史的故事都有關係，不管是真的或是假的，所以如果一個語言，你要一個語言存在，他需要他的歷史，他需要一些故事，你需要可以說「其實我的語言有這一個是從這邊來的，有這個重要性。」如果你要發展一個語言的歷史，你需要文學或是藝術，流行藝術或是高級藝術都可以，你都要了解歷史不是一個固定的東西，歷史就是一些故事而已，有一些是真實的、有一些可能是想像的。

【薩米語 Sami】

薩米語言教育之經驗與實踐
Experiences and Practices in Sámi Language Education

挪威薩米大學 Pigga Keskitalo 教授

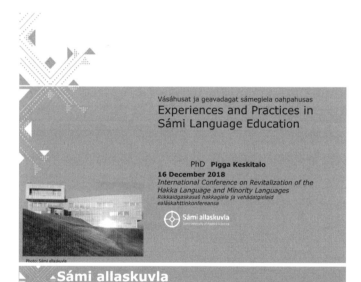

1

Vásáhusat ja geavadagat sámegiela oahpahusas
Experiences and Practices in Sámi Language Education

PhD **Pigga Keskitalo**
16 December 2018
International Conference on Revitalization of the Hakka Language and Minority Languages
Riikkaidgaskasaš hakkagiela ja vehádatgielaid ealáskahttinkonfereansa

Sámi allaskuvla
Sámi University of Applied Sciences

Photo: Sámi allaskuvla

2

Sámi allaskuvla
Sámi University of Applied Sciences
Norway, Guovdageaidnu

- Established in 1989
- Funded by Norwegian government, Finland and Sweden give funding for research
- 350 students, 45 teaching personnel, 30 administration
- Departments: Sámi language, duodji, reindeer herding and social sciences, Sámi teacher education and indigenous journalism

- Sámi language beginning courses, bachelor, master and PhD in Sámi
- Indigenous journalism master (in English)- Sámi journalism bachelor
- Sámi handicraft master and bachelor (in Sámi) DUODJI
- Reindeer herding bachelor (in Sámi)
- Sámi teacher education master grades 1-7 and 5-10 (in Sámi)
- Practical pedagogical education (in Sámi)
- Other courses about Sámi culture and bilingualism

3

Sámi area and languages

public domain image: http://en.wikipedia.org/wiki/File:Sami_languages_large.png

- 9 (10) different Sámi languages, as different grammar and spelling,
- North Sámi is the biggest (dialects: east and west, coastal and others), we do not make a big deal with those, rather think this is a diversity and richness,
- 100 000 people, 35 000 approx. speak Sámi languages.
- In Finland 10 000: Aanar Sámi (550), North Sámi (1300) and Skolt Sámi (350-500)
- Sweden 15 000. less than 6000
- Norway 50 000. less than 20 000
- Russia 3000. less than 1000
- Not accurate statistics about ethnicities and language speakers.
- Seriously threatened languages
- Finno-Ugric language family (Hungary, Finnish...) Proto Sámi and early Finnish-Sámi
- Sámi peoples' genetic connection to Siberia

4

Suoma sámediggi
Finnish Sámi Parliament
www.samediggi.fi

Minister of Justice, Sámi Parliament Law. Sámi parliament takes care of cultural aunomy, funded by Finland

Culture board, education board, law board, and livelihood board.
Sámi parliament and government are led by President and plenary meetings

Photos: Sámi Parliament Photo Bank

5

Sámegiellalágat - Sámi language laws

Map: Sámi Parliament in Finland

Map: regjeringen.no

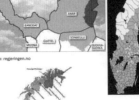

Map: Wikimedia Commons Map of official miniority languages in the municipalities of Sweden

- **Finland** Sámi language law since 1992 (using Sámi within authorities in Sámi administrative areas)
- **Norway** 1987
- **Sweden** 1992
- Indigenous Peoples are protected under Article 69 of the Russian Constitution (still highly endangered Arctic Indigenous people and minorities)

6

Aanaar Sámi language vitality

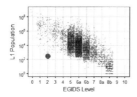

Ethnologue
https://www.ethno
logue.com/cloud/s
mn

The language is
used in education,
work, mass media,
and government
within major
administrative
subdivisions of a
nation.

700 Aanaar Sámis
550 speakers (different
backgrounds)

7

Early childhood education

Sámi allaskuvla

- Early childhood education law **in Finland**> right connected to **mother tongue** in whole Finland (Aanaar, North and Skolt Sámi)
- Early childhood education law **in Norway**> right connected to ethnicity in Sámi administration areas. In other areas of Norway, communities need to secure the language and culture of Sámi children (North, Julev, and South Sámi)
- Practically **private kindergartens** take care of language revitalization: Sámi language kindergartens conduct "compound of language nests and kindergarten" in Norway in cities and funding of language nests for the communal and private sector in Finland in Sámi administrative areas and outside that
- 23 kindergartens in Finland, 13 of them are language nests
- 37 Sámi language kindergartens in Norway (communal and private) 37 sámi mánáidgárddit. North Sámi 752 children, 27 children in Julevsámi kindergarten, and 10 children in South Sámi kindergartens.
- Sámi kindergarten (national minorities and minority languages) in 18 municipalities of Sweden.

8

Language programs Finland (bilingualism)

Sámi allaskuvla

- Finland: mothertongue 7 hours per week (classes 1-2), 9 hours (classes 3-6), 5 hours (classes 7-9, Finnish or Swedish) and in Sámi areas (Sámi (Skolt, Aanaar or North) or Finnish or Swedish.
- A1 language (normally English, could be other languages also) 4-5 hours per week
- B1 language (Swedish or Finnish depending where) 1 hour (classes 1-6), 2 hours (classes 7-9). (you can choose Swedish if you learn Sámi as mother tongue, then Finnish is your B1 language)
- Voluntary A2 language (6 hours) or B2 (2 hours) added to primary school hour distribution. (Sámi in Sámi areas)
- Outside the Sámi areas (minority and Sámi added to your hour distribution as voluntary language 2 hours).>negative pedagogy (outside the curriculum)

9

Primary school law in Finland ⊕ Sámi allaskuvla

- In Finland in Sámi Home area if pupil can speak Sámi language, the teaching should be organized mainly in Sámi (practically between 51-100%). most of the children—75%—live outside the core area.The thread of language shift as they can learn only voluntary Sámi 2 hours per week. Law changes needed immediately (critical question the future of Sámi language)
- Most of the Sámi speaking elders living in Sámi core areas (90 %).
- Demographic changes happened since 1960, still going on.

10

In Sweden ⊕ Sámi allaskuvla

- Sámi school system classes 1-6 (six schools in core areas) and Sámi curriculum conducted in Sámi language for Sámi speaking children (critical question: who can speak enough and who is choosing?)
- Classes 7-9 at communal schools, couple of hours Sámi (critical question the development of mothertongue
- Most of the Sámi children going to communal schools classes 1-9 (critical question the maintenance of Sámi languages)
- No regulations on which students should belong to which level > ingen reglering för vilka elever som ska tillhöra vilken nivå

11

Primary school in Norway ⊕ Sámi allaskuvla

- 2336 children learning Sámi in Norway. (mothertongue 964, the second language 547, the third language 647)
- If Sámi language as the first language, then Norwegian is the second, the third is English.
- 4 hours of Sámi and 3 hours of Norwegian, and English two hours (classes 1-7)
- Other hours for upper classes
- If over 10 pupils are demanding it, the communities will organize it.

Vocational education and junior high
 Sámi allaskuvla

12

- Compound high and vocational school in Norway mothertongue 217 (190 North Sámi)
- Less in Sweden and Finland *no more than 10 per year
- Studies at vocational schools (Sámi, handicrafts, traditional knowledge, tourism, digitalisation)
- University studies in Umeå, Tromsø, Bodø, Helsinki, Oulu, Rovaniemi, Alta and Kautokeino

Different school histories under nationalism 1800's-1950– different assimilation policies
Sámi allaskuvla

13

Photo: Sami Museum Siida / Máret Nummela photos (Saamva 082_024)

The period of missionaries 1600-1850,

Nationalism 1850-1960: Norwegianization

Sweden: exclusion (nomad schools)

Finland: Finnishness and Finnish language (not attention to minorities)

Russia: not allowed during1941-1980 (18 teachers were sent to Siberia (Kotljarchuk 2019)

Research
 Sámi allaskuvla

14

- Keskitalo 2010 PhD: Culture sensitive Sámi school. Sámi allaskuvla.
- Keskitalo, Määttä & Uusiautti 2013 "Sámi education". Peter Lang.
- Keskitalo, Lehtola & Paksuniemi (Eds.) 2014 Sámi school history in Finland. Migration Institute.
- Edited volyme. 2019 All-Sámi and Indigenous school histories. Palgrave.
- Paksuniemi & Keskitalo (Eds.) 2019. Finnish education system. Brill.
- Virtanen, Keskitalo & Olsen (Eds.) 2019. Indigenous Methodologies.
- Hoven, Trimmer & Keskitalo (Eds.) 2019. Indigenous Postgraduate Students' Experiences.

Sámi Education

15

Thank You! Giitu!

pigga.keskitalo@samiskhs.no

pigga.keskitalo@samiskhs.no

Briefing 1

My name is Pigga Keskitalo. I come from the Sámi allaskuvla [Sámi University of Applied Sciences], Kautokeino, Norway. I also hold the title of Docent (Adjunct Professor) at the University of Helsinki and was promoted to Professor in Education, in Arctic issues, on 1 August 2022 at the University of Lapland, Finland.

Thank you for inviting me. It has been wonderful to be here and get to know your education and linguistic practices. I'm going to share with you the experiences and practices of Sami education and the Sámi University of Applied Sciences, from the perspectives of language revitalization and Sami teacher education. The University is located in Northern Norway, a Sami-speaking community.

I live in north-west Finland, in the village of Peltovuoma, which is part of the Enontekiö municipality in the border area of Samiland in the Sami homeland area. This area is covered by the Sami Parliament Act in Finland and consists of the Inari, Enontekiö, Utsjoki, and Sodankylä (north area) municipalities. I was born in Nuorgam, a very small village in the northernmost part of Finland. The Sami homeland area has changed a lot since the 1970s. A lot of people have moved to the towns from little villages, and huge demographic and societal changes have taken place. I think we share this kind of experience with indigenous communities around the world, so what I'm going to tell you about is our Sami teacher education programs and how we conduct primary school education and early childhood education, as well as some experiences within adult education. These educational actions are part of language planning, which reveals act-based practices implemented in educational practices and practices shared by people.

Briefing 2

The Sámi University of Applied Sciences was established in 1989 to ensure that Sami communities can develop the Sami culture and language education in higher education. It is fully funded by the Norwegian government. Finland and Sweden have also given funding for the institution to conduct research. It's a small institute, with about 350 students, 45 teaching personnel, and 30 persons working in administration. What is unique about the Sámi University of Applied Sciences is that all the work can be carried out in the Sami language, both teaching and administration. How is this success possible?

Importantly, it is because language policy and language ideology have been consciously put into practice, and support for that possibility has been offered. It also requires economic support and flexibility as some permanent personnel may be on study leave while studying. Hence, it has been a premise of the Sámi University of Applied Sciences that its working and teaching language is Sami. Even though many Sami-speaking personnel have been employed, there are obviously challenges finding competent teaching personnel who are fluent in the Sami language and personnel who are able to use Sami in their daily work in both its oral and written forms.

Different kinds of policies have been created as the basis for this kind of emphasis on competency. If you want to work at the Sami University of Applied Sciences, you must be not only trained to meet the general competency demands of your job, but your Sami language skills must also be at a certain level if you are teaching personnel; otherwise, you can prove your language competency in other professions or that you are willing to study Sami within a certain period. The Sámi University of Applied Sciences has, from the outset, offered courses in the Sami language department from the basics through PhD level so it is possible for staff and students to refresh their Sami skills or learn them.

Stipendiaries and staff have also been supported to study and build their competency in other areas, for example preparing for their master and doctorate theses.

Other places where you can study Sami in the Nordic countries include the University of Oulu, the University of Helsinki, and the University of Lapland in Finland, Umeå University in Sweden, Nord University in Norway, and the Arctic University of Norway in Norway. There are also vocational education and adult education courses in Sami, for example summer courses organised by third-sector associations or summer universities or a company which specialises in education and learning materials.

When I was an employee of the Sámi University of Applied Sciences, I worked in the Sami teacher education section, mostly in primary school teacher education programs. A kindergarten teacher education program is also run. Teacher education belongs to the same department as an indigenous journalism master's program which is conducted in English and bachelor programs conducted in Sami. It is called the Journalism and Sami Teacher Education Goahti (Hut). Philosophically, the North Sámi word goahti, 'hut', means applying Indigenous thinking and scholarly and educational work in higher education institutions brought together to function as a department. What is also unique at the Sámi University of Applied Sciences is that we have a Sami handicraft master's program and a reindeer herding bachelor's program conducted in Sami. There are also different kinds of courses about Sami culture, bilingualism, and traditional knowledge.

Briefing 3

The Sami area is very large, stretching from mid-Norway and Sweden to the Russian Federation, and different kinds of languages are in use. A language policy decision was made to consider the ten Sami languages (North, Inari, Skolt, Akkala, Ter, Kildin, South, Pite, Ume, and Lule) separately on the grounds that, as their spelling and grammar differ so much, they are different languages rather than dialects.

I represent the Northern Sami speakers, and I can easily understand the neighbouring Sami languages and, to some extent, all Sami languages, partly because I studied South Sami, Lule Sami, and Inari Sami while studying Sami at tertiary education level.

Within these language groups, there are dialects. Yesterday, there was some talk about dialects and how we have come to work with them. For example, in the largest language, Northern Sami, the main dialects are east and west dialects, as well as coastal dialects and other local dialects. Dialects show diversity and richness. They affect pronunciation, and there may be an effect on spelling.

In the Sami areas of the four countries in which Sami people live, there are about 100,000 Sami people. Today, about 30% of them speak (at least) one of the Sami languages.

The church has been in the Sami areas and more or less active for nearly 1000 years. The church started strong attempts to educate young Sami males, and later women, to work as priests and clergy in the 1600s, and nationalism policies until the 1960s made assimilation so powerful that many Sami have lost, at least in part, their ability to use and speak their own language.

In Finland, there are about 10,000 Sami people. I wish more efforts could be made to create learning materials and help children do well in their own language and feel comfortable at school. The Education Act safeguarding Sami language teaching, including outside the Sami core areas, is important, as competency in a heritage language is an essential part of children's wellbeing and identity building.

In Norway, where there are more Sami people than in other countries with Sami population, maybe fewer than 30,000 can speak Sami. In Russia, the situation is even worse: maybe fewer than 1,000 people can speak Sami languages there. In Sweden, it is estimated that less than one third of 15,000-20,000 Samis can speak it.

We do not have accurate statistics about ethnicities and language speakers, so these are only estimated numbers. And, of course, because there are not many speakers, these are endangered languages according to the UNESCO criteria.

Sami belongs to the Finno-Ugric language families, which also include Hungarian and Finnish. So, these languages are related. There have also been a proto-Sami and an early Finnish Sami language. Quite recently, the University of Helsinki published research about Sami people's genetic connection to some Siberian peoples.

Briefing 4

The Finnish Sami Parliament works with cultural determination issues and, for example, Sami languages and teaching materials, and it also advises the national parliament about cultural self-determination issues. It's funded by Finland. There are also Sami parliaments in Norway and Sweden, and there is joint Nordic cooperation with the Sami parliaments. There is no Sami parliament in the Russian Federation, but the Nordic Sami parliament, as a non-governmental association, works in Russia as well.

Briefing 5

We have had language laws in Finland in place for many years concerning the Sami languages spoken in Finland. The four communities in Finland where the language law is enforced are the municipalities of Inari, Utsjoki, Enontekiö, and Sodankylä, and it is enforced by authorities both in- and outside this region. In Sweden, 18 municipalities are involved in enforcing minority language laws. In Norway, there are 16 municipalities. Russia has Article 69 of the Russian constitution, but it is not broadly implemented in the Kola Peninsula Murmansk oblast. The situation is still highly dangerous for Arctic indigenous peoples and minorities living in Russia.

Briefing 6

Here is a table from *Ethnologue* which shows the vitality of the Inari Sami language. It's interesting because 700 Sami people live in the village of Inari. Around our lake, there are 550 speakers, and they have different backgrounds. There are also many non-Sami speakers now because they have had an effective recent language revitalization program with inclusive thinking. This means that the language is used in education, work, mass media, and government, the major administrative subdivisions of the nation.

Briefing 7

Next, I will talk about early childhood education.

It has been conducted differently in the Sami context. For example, in Finland, the rights are connected to the mother tongue competency. That can be very challenging for those who don't have mother-tongue Sami language ability. Do they have the ability to take part in early childhood education conducted in Sami? The way this has been solved is that private associations started language revitalization efforts by running Sami language 'nests' to immerse children in the Sami language because it was not possible for everybody to do this.

In Norway, the right to ethnicity in the Sami administration areas is connected to the 16 Sami language administrative areas, outside which communities need to secure the language and culture. What does that mean? It means that if parents come to demand early childhood education, communities must, in one way or another, apply for funding from the Sami Parliament of Norway and start this activity for families.

In Sweden, Sami early childhood education has been conducted in 18 municipalities. In practice, however, only a few are doing what they should in this area because there are some problems putting the Act into action. There are not enough teachers or there are not enough children, and maybe other resource challenges remain.

There are 23 kindergartens in Finland teaching in Sami, 13 of which are language nests. It is a unique solution in a Nordic context to have this kind of functioning language nest system organised by communities, communes, or associations.

Norway has 37 Sami-language kindergartens, with 752 children attending Northern Sami kindergartens, 27 in Julevsámi, and 10 in South Sami, which is a severely endangered language.

Briefing 8

In Finland, if you live in an official Sami area, you get seven hours per week of Sami language education. It then changes, but these are the first classes, grades one to two.

The A1 language, which is normally English but might be another language, is taught for 4.5 hours per week. Then, you can choose the B1 language, which is Swedish or Finnish, depending on where you live in Finland. That means, for Sami children, one-hour Finnish classes in grades one to six and two hours in grades seven to nine. Then they can choose a voluntary A2 language, which can also be Sami.

Briefing 9

Outside the Sami areas, the situation is challenging because Sami language education is voluntary and most of the children—75 percent—live outside the core area. So, there are questions about the future of the Sami language in Finland. This provision is provided as an extracurricular activity, two hours per week outside regular school hours. It is challenging for both the education providers and the children and families.

Briefing 10

In Sweden, the situation is a little different. There are six schools in Sami school areas that conduct Sami language education. After grades one to seven, this situation stops, and children move to communal schools, so Sami-language education is not so effective anymore. In reality, most Sami children go to communal schools in Sweden, so the fact that there are no regulations about Sami teaching is a challenge.

Briefing 11

In Norway, over 2,000 children receive Sami-language education. Under 1,000 are learning it as their mother tongue, 547 are learning it as a second language, and 647 are learning it as a third language.

You can see how many children are attending education and that Sami is the first language, Norwegian is the second, and the third is English. They get four hours of Sami, three of Norwegian, and two of English. This is for grades one to seven, as other hours apply for the upper classes. Outside the core areas, communities need to organise Sami language education. If over 10 pupils request it, the communities will organise it. For example, in Oslo, because there are more children now, a Sami class is functioning. You can see that the situation is best in Norway, as there is a separate curriculum, Sami school system, and Sami teacher education. But practically, how they conduct that varies on a day-to-day basis. For example, some Sami schools use Sami as a main teaching language.

Briefing 12

Now let's talk about vocational education and junior high.

There are about 200 young people attending compound high and vocational school education in Norway, 190 from north Sami, and fewer in Sweden. There are no more than 10 per year in Finland, so most Sami children do not go to junior high schools. They go to different kinds of educational institutions. But you can study Sami at vocational schools when learning Sami handicrafts, traditional knowledge, tourism, or digitalisation in the Sami Education Institution in Inari, Finland. You can also take university studies, as I mentioned, in these places in Nordic countries.

Briefing 13

In Russia, the situation is very worrying. They get two hours of Sami teaching in the largest language in the village of Lovozero. From World War II until 1980, it was forbidden to teach Sami languages so children did not receive an education at all in Sami. For example, 18 Sami-speaking teachers were sent to Siberia in 1943, according to Andrej Kotljarchuk. That had a big impact on the situation in Russia. I have already talked a little about assimilation processes, and these have varied a lot across different countries with a Sami population.

In Norway, there was a written national policy, and in Sweden, the policy was segregation. They started nomadic schools for reindeer herders in Sweden, and other children were sent to Swedish-speaking municipality schools. This kind of history caused some problems to do with ethnicities and who is who. In Finland, for historical reasons, Finnishness and the Finnish language were highlighted. No attention was paid to minorities, and that caused assimilation as no support for your own heritage language was given by the education system.

There was no written policy about minorities in Finland, but education was conducted differently, by highlighting the mainstream language and culture, Finnish. This process partly induced minorities to get rid of cultural features, including languages.

Briefing 14

Here is some research that I have been doing. I did my Ph.D. in the Sami curriculum. In Norway, there is a special Sami school system. It's equal to a national Norwegian school, and there is also an equal curriculum. I researched how this Sami school and the Sami curriculum work and what kind of challenges and good practices there are. This is quite a familiar story to all indigenous people, as it is a challenge to organise your schools so that children can learn traditional knowledge, know how to take care of their ancestors' language, and be indigenous people in a modern world. Our teacher education institution has been working a lot with these kinds of issues, such as how to organise culturally-aware education for everybody. I think we also need to be quite inclusive and remember that everyone is ultimately welcome to learn similar things in context, for example where Samis live in Nordic areas. I have also been taking part in Sami and indigenous school history research, and a new book about this was published in 2019.

When you conduct indigenous research, part of the research ethics and thinking about your motivation is positioning yourself and writing about your motivation. My father decided to take teacher education, so he travelled 1,000 kilometres about 60 years ago to South Finland to study it. I also decided to become a teacher and dedicate myself to Sami language education issues.

We are part of the globalised world nowadays, so these issues are not so familiar to people anymore. When teaching kids, we also have to transform this kind of knowledge for future generations, as not every parent can do that anymore. So, when we teach our student teachers, we make a lot of effort to give that traditional knowledge. They are also good traditional knowledge bearers.

Thank you, everybody.

Giitu!

簡報 1

我名叫 Pigga Keskitalo 。來自挪威凱於圖凱努的 Sámi allaskuvla（薩米應用科學大學），同時擁有赫爾辛基大學的講師（兼任教授）頭銜（於 2022 年 8 月 1 日晉升為北極問題教育教授）。

感謝邀請我來。很高興來這裡認識你們的教育和語言實務。我將分享薩米語教育和薩米應用科學大學的經驗和實務，包括語言復興及薩米語教師教育等觀點。薩米位於挪威北部，是一個講薩米語的村莊。

我住在芬蘭西北部佩爾托沃馬村的埃農泰基厄市，位於薩米蘭邊境地區的薩米原住民地區。該地區受芬蘭《薩米議會法》（Sami Parliament Act）保護，由伊納里、埃農泰基厄、烏茨約基和索丹屈萊（北部地區）自治市組成。我出生在芬蘭最北部的一個小村莊努奧爾加姆。自 1970 年代以來，薩米原住民地區已經改變很

多。如今，很多人從小村莊搬到了城鎮，人口和社會都發生了巨大的改變。我猜想我們與世界各地的原住民社區都有這種經驗，所以我要向各位報告的是我們的薩米語教師教育計畫，以及我們如何進行小學教育和幼兒教育，以及一些成人教育的經驗。這些教育行動是語言規劃的一部分，顯露出教育實務中體現的行為基礎實務，以及人們共享的實務。

簡報 2

薩米應用科學大學成立於 1989 年，旨在確保薩米社區有能力在高等教育中發展薩米文化和語言教育，經費由挪威政府全額資助，芬蘭和瑞典也為該機構進行的研究提供資金。它是一所普通小型機構，大約有 350 名學生、45 名教學人員和 30 名行政人員。薩米應用科學大學的特色在於以薩米語完成教學和行政方面的全部工作。這怎麼可能？

最重要的原因是，刻意將語言政策和語言意識形態付諸實踐，並為此創造出支持和可能性。這也需要經濟影響力和彈性，因為有些人可能在學習期間休學。所以提薩米應用科學大學的前提是，工作和教學語言都是薩米語。雖然可以找到許多說薩米語的人，但顯然，原住民語言可能面臨的挑戰是，哪裡可以找到具薩米語能力的合格教學人員，以及能在日常工作中以口頭或書面形式使用薩米語的人。已經有各種不同政策為這種訴求打基礎。如果想在薩米應用科學大學工作，除了一般工作能力要求之外，教學人員還必須接受過一定程度的薩米語教育，或能證明其他職業中的語言能力，或願意在一定期限內學習薩米語。薩米應用科技大學自一開始便開設了語言課程，從基礎到更高階的都有，因而使振興薩米語及／或讓教職員和學生學習薩米語變得可能。學校也設有獎學金，並支持教職員學習及培養自己其他方面的能力，例如準備碩士論文和博士學位。而該校薩米語學系開設了一些薩米語教學課程，從最基礎的課程一直到博士研究。因此，想要振興其語言或接受教育的人都可以在該校進行。北歐國家也有可以學習薩米語的其他地方，例如芬蘭的奧盧大學、赫爾辛基大學和拉普蘭大學，瑞典的于默奧大學和挪威的挪威北極大學。還有以薩米語進行的成人職業教育課程，例如由第三部門協會或暑期大學或專門從事教育和學習資料事務之公司開設的暑期課程。

受僱於薩米應用科學大學期間，我在薩米語教師教育部門工作，主要從事小學教師教育課程。那裡也有幼兒園教師教育課程。教師教育屬於一個學系，於其中

開設以英語進行的原住民新聞碩士課程和以薩米語進行的新聞和薩米語教師教育Goahti（小屋）學士學位課程。北薩米語中的 goahti「小屋」一詞從哲學上來看係指在集中於某一學系的高等教育機構中應用原住民思維、學者和教育工作。薩米應用科學大學的另一個特色是，我們有以薩米語進行的薩米手工藝碩士課程和馴鹿放牧學士課程，還有多種關於薩米文化、雙語和傳統知識的各類課程。

簡報 3

薩米地區很廣大，從挪威中部和瑞典到俄羅斯聯邦，使用多種不同語言。將North、Inari、Skolt、Akkala、Ter、Kildin、South、Pite、Ume 和 Lule Sami 等十種薩米語分別視為單獨的語言是一種語言政策選擇，因為這些語言彼此之間的拼寫和文法差異頗大，因而認定這些是不同語言，而非方言。

我代表說北方薩米語的人，我可以輕易理解鄰近的薩米語，且在相當程度上可以理解所有薩米語；部分原因是我過去幾年在學習薩米語的高等教育階段學過南方薩米語、盧勒薩米語和伊納里薩米語，在這些語言群中還有很多方言。昨天有一些關於方言以及我們如何與其合作的討論。例如在最大的語言北薩米語中，主要方言就包括東、西方言以及沿海方言和其他地方方言。但實際上我們對此並不在意，因為這顯示出多樣性和豐富性。方言會影響發音，進而可能影響拼寫。

在隸屬於四個國家的薩米地區大約有 100,000 個薩米人，其中約 30% 會說當今的某一種薩米語。

教會已在薩米地區存在了大約 1,000 年，它更積極地展開教育年輕薩米男性（之後也包括女性）擔任牧師和神職人員，而 1950 年代之後的民族主義政策更增強了這種同化作用，使得許多薩米人至少已部分喪失了使用以及說自己語言的能力。

芬蘭大約有 10,000 個薩米人。我希望加緊致力於及時製作學習教材，協助孩童學習自己的語言，並在學校感覺自在。語言問題非常重要。

挪威的薩米人比較多，但會說薩米語的可能不到 30,000 人。而俄羅斯的狀況更糟，會說薩米語的可能只有不到 1,000 人。瑞典的 15,000 至 20,000 薩米人中，會說薩米語的估計不到三分之一。

我們並沒有關於種族和語言使用者的精確統計資料，所以這些都只是估計數字。當然，由於沒有大量使用者，根據聯合國教科文組織的標準，這些都是不同程度的瀕危語言。

薩米語屬於芬蘭—烏戈爾語族，包括例如匈牙利語和芬蘭語，過去曾有原始薩米語和早期的芬蘭薩米語，因此，這些是相關語言。赫爾辛基大學最近發表了關於薩米人與部分西伯利亞人血緣關係的研究。

簡報 4

芬蘭薩米議會致力於決定薩米語及教材等文化議題，並就文化自決議題對議會提供建議。薩米議會由芬蘭資助。挪威和瑞典也有薩米議會，還有北歐與薩米議會的合作。俄羅斯聯邦沒有薩米議會，但北歐薩米議會以非政府組織身分在俄羅斯運作。

簡報 5

芬蘭訂有在芬蘭使用之薩米語的相關語言法，已經實施多年。在芬蘭有四個社區執行語言法，即伊納里、烏茨約基、埃農泰基厄和索丹屈萊自治市，且在此區域內外有多個當局。瑞典有多達 18 個自治市執行少數民族語言法律，例如取決於各自治市的薩米語、梅安語和芬蘭語。挪威有 16 個自治市。俄羅斯雖有俄羅斯憲法第 69 條，但並未於摩爾曼斯克州科拉半島實施。我們看到那裡的情況，對北極原住民和居住在俄羅斯的少數民族仍存在高危險。

簡報 6

這裡有一張來自《民族語言網》（Ethnologue）的表格，展示了伊納里薩米語的薩米語活力。這很有趣，因為伊納里村住有 700 名薩米人。在我們的湖的周圍，有 550 個說薩米語的人，而他們都有不同背景。現在還有很多不講薩米語的人，因為他們最近已推出了具包容性思維的有效語言振興計畫。這表示薩米語已用於該國主要行政區的教育、工作、大眾媒體和政府。講薩米語的人還是很少，但成效不錯。始終存在的一個關鍵問題是，如何評估語言及相關事物在瀕危語言和少數民族語言環境中的影響力。

簡報 7

接下來我想談談幼兒教育，其執行方式各不相同。例如在芬蘭，權利與母語相關，但最近已有所改變。以前的法律並沒有這麼規定，但現在規定整個芬蘭以母語教育。對於沒有薩米語能力的人而言這或許非常具有挑戰性。他們有能力參加以薩米語進行的幼兒教育嗎？解決這個問題的方法是，第一個私人協會已展開語言振興

工作，透過舉辦薩米語巢沉浸於薩米語，因為不可能每個人都參與這種可能性。

在挪威，薩米行政區的種族權利與這 16 個地區相關，於此之外，社區需要確保語言和文化。這是什麼意思？這表示，若父母要求提供幼兒教育，則社區需向挪威薩米議會申請資助，並開始為家庭提供這類教育。

瑞典已有 18 個城市開始實施薩米語幼兒教育。但實際上，只有少數可以做到應有的水準，因為執行該法案還有一些問題。沒有足夠的師資或沒有足夠的兒童，且或許還有其他資源挑戰。

芬蘭有 23 所幼兒園以薩米語教學，其中 13 所是語言巢。這是北歐情境下的特殊解決方案，設置這種由社區、公社或協會組成的官方語言巢。

挪威有 37 所幼兒園的 752 名兒童參加北薩米語幼兒園，有 27 所 Julevsámi 幼兒園以及 10 所南薩米語幼兒園，這些都是真正瀕危的語言。

簡報 8

關於小學課程──我想介紹這個確保將語言納入規劃語言行動水準的學校體制。

在芬蘭，若居住於官方薩米語地區，每週可接受七小時的薩米語教育和一小時的芬蘭語教育。之後就會改變，但這些是初級、一年級到二年級；三到六年級有九小時。

A1 語言通常是英文，但也可以是其他語言，每週 4.5 小時。然後你可以根據自己居住的地方選擇以瑞典語或芬蘭語為 B1 語言。這表示薩米兒童一至六年級有一小時的芬蘭語課程，七到九年級則有兩小時。然後他們可以選擇自願的 A2 語言，也可能是薩米語。

簡報 9

薩米地區以外的狀況真的很有挑戰性，因為薩米語教育是自願性的，而大部分兒童（75%）都生活在核心區域之外。因此，薩米語在芬蘭的未來令人憂慮。這項規定在正常上課時間之外每週提供兩小時課外活動，這對教育提供者以及兒童和家庭都很有挑戰性。

簡報 10

瑞典的狀況略有不同。薩米學區有六所提供薩米語教育的學校。一至七年級之

後，這個狀況就停止了，孩童將升上公立學校，而薩米語教育也不再那麼有效了。

　　事實上，大多數薩米兒童就讀於瑞典的公立學校，面臨的挑戰是沒有規定哪些學生該屬於哪個級別。

簡報 11

　　挪威有 2,000 多名兒童接受薩米語教育。不到 1,000 人將其作為母語學習，547人將其作為第二語言學習，而有 647 人將其作為第三語言學習。

　　所以，你可以看到有多少兒童所受的教育第一語言是薩米語，第二語言是挪威語，第三語言是英語。他們有四個小時的薩米語課程，三小時的挪威語課程和兩小時的英語課程。這是一年級到七年級。還有其他時數適用於更高年級。核心區域之外的社區需組織薩米語教育。如有超過 10 個學生要求，社區便會組織起來。例如在奧斯陸，由於現在有較多兒童，各位可以看到挪威的狀況最好。但實務上，出現了很多關於他們每天如何進行的問題。

簡報 12

　　現在讓我們談談職業教育和初中。

　　挪威約有 200 位青年參加綜合高中和職業學校教育。其中北薩米人有 190位，而瑞典人較少。而且每年不超過 10 人，所以大多數兒童不上初中。他們會就讀於不同類型的教育機構。但若在伊納里中心學習薩米手工藝、傳統知識、旅遊或數位化，便可在職業學校學習薩米語。正如我提到的，你也可在北歐國家這些地方讀大學。

簡報 13

　　俄羅斯的狀況非常嚴苛。他們在洛沃澤羅村接受兩個小時最大語言的教育。自二戰以來直到 1980 年，完全不允許以這些語言接受教育，根據 Andrej Kotljarchuk 的說法，1943 年有 18 位說薩米語的教師被發配到西伯利亞。這對俄羅斯的狀況而言意義重大。我曾提到關於同化的一些問題，而這已經有很大的改變了。

　　挪威有書面的國家政策，而瑞典的政策是各別分開的。瑞典為馴鹿牧民開辦了游牧學校，其他兒童則送到講瑞典語的學校。所以，這樣的歷史造成了一些種族和身分的問題。在芬蘭，由於歷史因素，芬蘭人和芬蘭語受到重視。沒有關注到少數民族，導致那裡的同化。

芬蘭並沒有針對少數民族的書面政策，但透過強調芬蘭語的主流語言和文化採取不同措施。這個過程使得少數民族部分遺失了自己的文化特徵。

簡報 14

這是我一直在做的一些研究。我在薩米語課程中取得了博士學位。挪威有一個特殊的薩米語學制，相當於國立挪威語學校，也有對等的課程。我研究了這所薩米語學校和薩米語課程的運作方式，以及有哪些挑戰和好的作法。對每個原住民來說，這是非常熟悉的故事，因為這是一項挑戰，如何組織學校讓兒童可以學習傳統知識，知道如何延續祖先的語言，並做個現代世界的原住民。所以，我們的教師教育機構一直致力於諸多此類事務，包括如何為每個人組織文化認知教育。我認為我們還需要更具包容性，切記畢竟我們歡迎每個人學習環境中類似的事情，例如居住在北歐地區的薩米人。我也曾參與薩米語和原住民學校的歷史研究，並於 2019 年出版了這方面的新書。

最後，進行原住民研究時，研究倫理和動機思維是確定自己的立場並寫下自己的動機。我的父親他決定接受教師教育，所以大概在 60 年前走了 1,000 公里到南芬蘭學習教師教育。我也決定成為一名教師，並關心薩米語教育問題。

我們現在是全球化世界的一部分，所以這些問題已經不是每個人都那麼熟悉了。教小孩的時候，我們也必須為後代轉化這種知識，因為並不是每個父母都還能做到。所以，在教導我們的學員老師時，我們付出了很多努力傳授傳統知識。他們也是優秀的傳統知識持有者；有時更勝於我們！

以上就是我的故事。非常感謝。真的很高興來這裡。

謝謝各位。

Giitu!

【日本阿伊努語 Ainu】
阿伊努語現況與日本政府的阿伊努族政策
Situation of Ainu Language and the Ainu Policy of Japanese Government

北海道大學阿伊努‧原住民研究中心丹菊逸治副教授

1

Ainu language revitalization based on individual activities

Situation of Ainu language and the Ainu policy of Japanese government

Hokkaido University
Center for Ainu and Indigenous Studies
Tangiku Ituji

1

2

IRANKARAPTE ITAK

Nispautar
katkematutar
irankarapte itak
kuye rusuy pe ne na.

Kuani kurehe
Tangiku Itsuji
sekor an pe ne wa,
Sisam kune yakka

Aynu itak
aenepakasnu wa
itak komoyokur
kune akorka

ponno patek ne yakka
Aynu itak
kuye easkay pe
kune ruwe tapan.

Itak komoyokur
kune korka
iteki iruskano
nu wa enkore yan.

Tanan to tasi,
nispautar or wa
aentak wa
kani sinta kuo wa

tuyma repun
kukari wa tane
tan pirka mosir
kukosirepa

oripak tura neyakka
nispautar eun
tane Aynu itak
nekona an ka,

husko or wa
tane pakno
nekon iki wa
onumposo ka

pon oruspe ne
kukar wa kuye
inure kusu ne
ruwe tapan na

ponno patek
nu wa enkore
yanani.
onkamian na!

2

3 Greeting words (translation)

- Ladies and gentlemen, I would like to tell greeting words for you. My name is Tangiku Itsuji, a Japanese and not an Ainu descendant, only I learned Ainu language. I am not a fluent speaker but please don't get angry. This day, people invited me and so I came here crossing the sea, in order to tell you about the situation of Ainu language, the struggle of Ainu people for conserving their heritage language. It takes you some time but please listen to me.

3

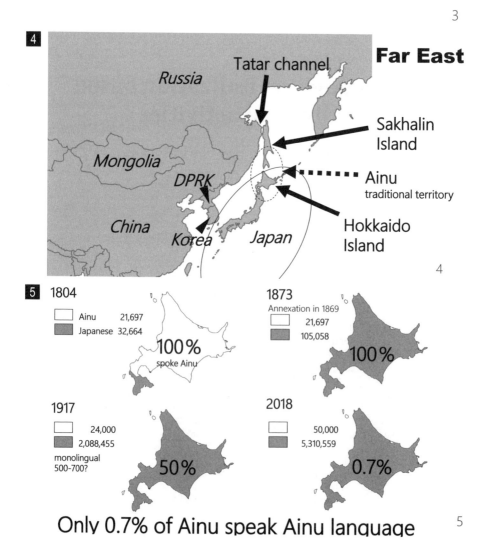

4

Far East

Russia

Tatar channel

Sakhalin Island

Mongolia

DPRK

Ainu
traditional territory

China

Korea

Japan

Hokkaido Island

4

5 1804

| | Ainu | 21,697 |
| | Japanese | 32,664 |

100%
spoke Ainu

1873
Annexation in 1869
21,697
105,058

100%

1917

24,000
2,088,455
monolingual
500-700?

50%

2018

50,000
5,310,559

0.7%

Only 0.7% of Ainu speak Ainu language

5

- 1551   Border demarcation between Ainu land and Japanese land   **6**

- 1869   Annexation of Ainu land (migration started)
- 1917   Ainu **monolingual speakers 500-700?**
- 1930's Ainu parents stopped using Ainu at home
- 1980's **Very few fluent speakers, and all over 60-70 years old**

- 2018   10-15 "native" speakers over 80 years old
          L2 speakers 20 ?
          50-100 understand some words and phrases

6

- **1980's** Private Ainu language courses started   **7**

- **1997 Ainu culture promotion act.**
- **FRPAC** (Foundation for Research and Promotion of Ainu culture) established.
- Official <u>Ainu language courses</u> started (14 places in 2003)

- **2007 DRIP** (UN Declaration on the Rights of Indigenous peoples)
- **2008 Japanese Diet declaired Ainu indigenous**
- 2009 **UNESCO 3rd report** on endangered languages
- 2013 <u>Ainu language archive project</u> by Japanese government started
- 2015 "1st Endangered Languages Summit"

- 2018 FRPAC reformed into "Foundation of Ainu Culture"
- **2020** "**National Ainu Museum & Park**" (The Symbolic Space for Ethnic Harmony) will be opened.

7

FRPAC programs based on Ainu culture promotion act 1997   **8**

- **Ainu language courses** : once or twice a month in some local areas.
- **Ainu language text books** : entry, basic and advanced courses in 8 dialects.
- **Ainu language Radio program**.

Language text books
by FRPAC

8

9 Ainu language and culture courses in schools.

- Nibutani elementary school has Ainu language entry course. (1 hour/month)
- Ainu children

- Chitose-Suehiro elementary school has been doing Ainu culture courses for children. (20 hour/year)
- Japanese children

9

10 Problems of Ainu language policy in Japan

- **Ainu language courses**
- No effect. Nobody became "speakers".

- **School education**
- The government insists that it is difficult to make Ainu language courses in schools, as it is against the equality of education.
- There is no Ainu Schools and it is impossible to have Ainu language immersion space.

- **Motivation of learners**
- Ainu language is regarded to be the "symbolic language" of their indigenousness, not for daily use.

10

11 You can learn from elders!

- "*Ainu : Human being*"(2018) documentary film about 4 Ainu elders in Biratori.

- Some elders were nursed and learned language and traditional culture by grandparents in childhood.

- Younger generation can learn language, traditional culture, and history, not in schools but from elders!

11

"1 to 1" or "Master and Apprentice" method **12**

- "How to Keep Your Language Alive: A Commonsense Approach to One-on-One Language Learning"
- Leanne Hinton (2002)

- Some Ainu elders trained younger generation by almost the same method

12

Individual activities **13**

traditional alter

13

In the future? **14**

- Ainu language courses

- Ainu language archive project

- Individual activities

15

Iyairaykere
Thank you very much

Nispautar

katkematutar

irankarapteitak

kuyerusuy pe ne na.

Kuanikurehe

TangikuItsuji

sekor an pe ne wa,

Sisam kune yakka

Aynuitak

aenepakasnuwa

itakkomoyokur

kune akorka

ponnopatek ne yakka

Aynuitak

kuyeeaskay pe
kune ruwetapan.

Itakkomoyokur
kune korka
itekiiruskano
nu waenkoreyan.

Tanan to tasi,
nispautar or wa
aentakwa
kanisintakuowa

tuymarepun
kukariwatane
tan pirkamosir
kukosirepa

oripakturaneyakka
nispautareun
taneAynuitak
nekonaan ka,

husko or wa
tanepakno
nekonikiwa
onumposo ka

ponoruspe ne
kukarwakuye

inure kusu ne

ruwetapanna

ponnopatek

nu waenkore

yanhani.

onkamianna!

Ladies and gentlemen, I would like to tell greeting words for you. My name is Tangikultsuji, a Japanese and not an Ainu descendant, only I learned Ainu language. I am not a fluent speaker but please don't get angry. This day, people invited me and so I came here crossing the sea, in order to tell you about the situation of Ainu language, the struggle of Ainu people for conserving their heritage language. It takes you some time but please listen to me.

So, this is the way ofthe traditional greetings thatthe Ainu people did. Maybe a little bit different from that in theprinted version, butevery timeAinu people didthe greetings, they made this kind of song. This was the traditional way, and of course, nowadays there are only a few people who can do this. I am not a very good singer, but I learned this language from the elders so I tried to like this.

Briefing 4

The Ainu people live in the northern part of the Japanese islands, here is Hokkaido island, and the Japanese island is here. And we are here now.

Ainu people's traditional area is mainly HokkaidoIsland. They lived on Sakhalin island too, but their population was very relatively small, and they moved to Hokkaido after World War II. They also lived on theKurilIslands and in Kamchatka, on the southern part of the Kamchatka peninsula. They are alsoa diaspora. Some of them moved to Kamchatka,and most of them moved to Hokkaido.

They were suppressed people, and their population has been relatively small.They mainly live in Hokkaido now.

Briefing 5

I will show you abrief history of this language.

1804 was a pre-modern-age period. Before the modernization of Japan, there was a border between the Japanese people's area and the Ainu people's area. This border was madein the middle of the 16th century, and for several hundred years the border was kept, until the end of the 19th century. At that time, the population of the Ainu people was about 21,000, and the number of Japanese people in Hokkaido was 32,000. Not a verylarge population of Japanese people was there at that time, of course. 100% of the Ainu people spoke inthe Ainu language. It was exclusively their language.

In 1869, the Japanese government started modernization, andthey decided to erase the border.

They started large-scale migration from Japanese areas to Hokkaido. Japan annexed this Island in 1869. In 1873, about four years after the annexation, the Ainu people were already a minority group. The number of Japanese people in Hokkaido was 100,000.

At that time, all the Ainu people spoke the Ainu language. We have statistics about the speakers of the Ainu language. Several decades after, in 1917, the Japanese population in Hokkaido was already two million, and the Ainu people became a one percent minority in Hokkaido. But at that time, still half ofthe Ainu people spoke the Ainu language. But for monolingual Ainu language speakers, we estimate there werejust several hundred people, from 500 to 700,and that's all.

Now (2018), we estimate the ethnic Ainu population to be about 50,000. The total population of Hokkaido, including the Ainu people, is now five million.

So, the speaker's ratio isunder one percent;we estimate about0.7 percent. Only 0.7 percent of the Ainu ethnic population can speak the Ainu language. They don't use the Ainu language in ordinary life.

Briefing 6

Now, for the so-called native speakers of the Ainu language, we estimate there are from 10 to 15 persons, and all of them are over 80 years old. But some learners can speak the Ainu language as a second language. The number of them may not be more than 20.

And some relatively young elders can understand words or phrases from their ancestors or in language schools; their number may be from 50 to 100. They don't speak the Ainu language, but they understand some words and phrases. So, from modernization until now, it took only 150 years, and the Ainu language almost disappeared.

Briefing 7

But of course, there have been some revitalization efforts.

The first large-scale effort started in the 1980s. At that time, some people began private Ainu language courses. There was also the first Ainu member of the Japanese National Diet; his name was 萱野茂 / かやのしげる Kayano Shigeru, and he started the private revitalization program.

And there are some other people. In 1997, the Japanese government made a new law about Ainu culture, called the Ainu Culture Promotion Act. The Foundation for the Research and Promotion of Ainu Culture was established based on the Act in the same year. The Ainu Foundation started offering official Ainu language courses, and the number of places already increased to 14 in 2003.

The Ainu people were divided into many communities in local areas, and they lost their exclusive territory. They are now minorities everywhere in their homeland, Hokkaido. So, the Foundation had to provide these language courses in local areas.

In 2007, the UN created the Declaration on the Rights of Indigenous Peoples. After the Declaration, the Japanese Diet declared the Ainu people as indigenous people. It was the first recognition of their indigenousness. In 2009, UNESCO presented the third edition of Report on Endangered Languages. It stated there were eight endangered languages in Japan. Based on this report, the Japanese government started a new project. The Ainu Language Archive Project was one of them.

The government started a festival of endangered languages. They named it "Endangered Languages Summit." It was very significant that the Japanese government held this kind of event. It was a symbolic festival of recognition of the endangered languages in Japan. Before then, the Japanese government always said they were dialects, but UNESCO's report expressed that they are languages. The Japanese government now thinks that they are not dialects but independent languages.

This year (2018), the FRPAC reformed into the Foundation of Ainu Culture. It became an organization for Ainu culture rather than for the research. In 2020, the government will prepare the National Ainu Museum and the Park. It is to be called "Symbolic Space for Ethnic harmony." It's a Japanese expression. These are the recent topics on the Ainu language.

Briefing 8

The Japanese government has done revitalization programs of the Ainu language based on the promotion act until now. And by the programs, FRPAC published language textbooks and organized Ainu language courses and radio programs. There are eight dialect textbooks. There are few differences among these dialects; people can understand each other without any translation, but they prefer to make their textbooks for their dialects.

Briefing 9

And there are some activities in schools, including Ainu language and culture courses in elementary schools, but there arevery few examples.

The most important examples are maybe these two.

In NibutaniElementary School, there are Ainu language entry courses. Nibutani is a district where many Ainu people live. It is maybe the only elementary school where Ainu children are the majority.

Of course, the target of this program is Ainu children, but it's only one hour per month. Every month, only one hour. It is hard to acquire language by this, of course.

The second example is in Chitose-Suehiro Elementary School, where there have been new cultural courses for Japanese children. This course is 20 hours per year. It's relatively better than Nibutani elementary school, but it is not a language course. It's a general traditional culture course, and the target is Japanese children.

Briefing 10

Of course, it's difficult to say that the revitalization program is sufficient in Japan.

Ainu language courses are very old-fashioned ones, and the main parts of the courses are Ainu language grammar and learning the lexicon. They sometimes practice singing songs and learning old oral stories or legends by heart. There is little practice in conversations.

And so, the fact is that the programs are not effective. You cannot become a speaker through those programs and school education. No school has real Ainu language course. The Japanese government insists that it is impossible to present Ainu language courses in schools because it is against the equality policy of education. Ainu children have right to know their language, but the Japanese government insists that they cannot distinguish Ainu children and Japanese children. As there is no Ainu school, it is impossible to have Ainu language immersion spaces. There are no language nests or immersion schools.

And not only that, honestly speaking, there are problems with motivations on the learners' side. They regard Ainu language the symbolic language of their indigenousness. They think their heritage language assures their indigenousness, but they think they don't need to speak it in daily use.

Briefing 11

I have talked about the negative aspects of these policies.

Now I want to talk about the positive things. The Ainu people themselves have made an effort for revitalization. For example, this is a documentary film about four Ainu elders in Biratori, or you can say Nibutani, as they are the same place. They are over 80 years old. Some elders were nursed and learned the language and traditional culture from their grandparents in childhood. It means that there were several hundred monolingual speakers around 1917. At that time, these monolingual speakers nursed their children and grandchildren. They spoke to their grandchildren in the Ainu language because they did not know other languages.

Around the 1930s, local authorities prohibited to use Ainu language in schools. So, Ainu parents stopped themselves from speaking in the Ainu language, even at home. After the 1930s, nobody could learn their heritage language, even at home.

But until then, there were some monolingual speakers, and their grandchildren could speak and learn from them. The grandchildren are now the age of 80, and younger generations can learn the language and traditional culture from them. If schools don't present language courses, Ainu youngers can learn from the elders.

Briefing 12

Some Ainu people used a one-to-one approach—In other words, the master and apprentice approach.

This is a textbook of this approach, which was published in 2002. It was written in English, so the Ainu people didn't know this. They invented almost the same method themselves around the 1980-1990s.

The one-to-one approach is like this, if the elder knows how to teach language, the elder asks the apprentice some questions and teaches how to answer at the same time— question and answer. The elders themselves teach the question and the answer to their students in a one-to-one circumstance.

What if the elder does not know how to teach? Of course, most of the elders are not professional teachers. If the elder does not know how to teach, the apprentice has to have the initiative. The apprentice should ask questions to the elder, and learn how to question and answer in the Ainu language.

This way is like what linguists do in the field, almost the same method. As the apprentices remember the questions and the answers, they can use these expressions the next time. The important thing is to prepare structured questions and answers. It seemed they invented it themselves.

Briefing 13

Some Ainu people have tried to conserve their language and culture using the one-to-one approach. It is important that they are individual and local activities. Traditional Ainu culture depends on local communities. There are about 200 Ainu communities. Each community has about 200 members. The 200 members are independent of each other. An Ainu can decide everything on their own. Japanese researchers and other outsiders sometimes think Ainu individualism is too radical, but it is essential to Ainu society.

The one-to-one approach may not be the best way to increase the number of speakers. But they succeeded in conserving the language on an individual scale. Ainu language revitalization activities are not limited to language itself. Traditional ceremonies often accompany them.

This photo shows a traditional altar. Ainu traditional Alters are not very complicated. You have to make offering wood items called "inaw" on various occasions. Traditionally every individual had to have this altar at home. Today these individual altars are rarely made, but some activists make ones personally. They are trying to revitalize both Ainu language and Ainu culture at the same time. They practice traditional ceremonies in the Ainu language. They pray for the gods in the Ainu language and have conversations in Ainu language. They dedicate songs, traditional stories, and dances to the gods in the Ainu language. They sometimes use Ainu language on SNS, but it's rather demonstrations.

Briefing 14

So, as I have said, there are official Ainu language courses and Ainu language archive projects. Unfortunately, I have to say that the Ainu language courses have had no effect until now, but maybe it's possible to redesign them. As for the archive projects, we are waiting for the results. We now know that the individual activities of the Ainu people are very effective. Will the official language courses become more effective if influenced by one-to-one activities?

At present, the situation is very complicated. The individual activities and the official language courses are divided and separated. They are thinking about how to do better separately. That is the situation.

Thank you very much.

簡報 1-3

Nispautar

katkematutar

irankarapte itak

kuye rusuy pe ne na.

Kuani kurehe

Tangiku Itsuji
sekor an pe ne wa,
Sisam kune yakka

Aynu itak
aenepakasnu wa
itak komoyokur
kune akorka

ponno patek ne yakka
Aynu itak
kuye easkay pe
kune ruwe tapan.

Itak komoyokur
kune korka
iteki iruska no
nu wa enkore yan.

Tanan to tasi,
nispautar or wa
aentak wa
kani sinta kuo wa

tuyma repun
kukari wa tane
tan pirka mosir
kukosirepa

oripak tura neyakka

nispautar eun
tane Aynu itak
nekona an ka,

husko or wa
tane pakno
nekon iki wa
onumposo ka

pon oruspe ne
kukar wa kuye
inure kusu ne
ruwe tapan na

ponno patek
nu wa enkore
yan hani.
onkamian na!

　　各位女士、先生，我想為大家說幾句問候語。我的名字是 Tangiku Itsuji，日本人，不是阿伊努人的後裔，只是學過阿伊努語。我講得不流利，請見諒。今天，受到主辦單位邀請，所以我就跨海來到這裡，告訴各位阿伊努語的狀況，以及阿伊努人為維護自己祖傳語言所做的奮鬥。這需要花點時間，但請聽我說。

　　所以，這就是阿伊努人傳統的問候方式。可能和印刷版有點不同，但阿伊努人每次問候都會唱這種歌。這是傳統的方式，當然，現在能這麼做的人已經很少了。我唱得不好，但我從前輩學到這種語言，所以我試著喜歡它。

簡報 4

　　阿伊努人生活在日本列島北部，這裡是北海道島，日本島在這裡。而我們現在在這裡。

阿伊努人的傳統地區主要在北海道島。他們也生活在薩哈林島，但人口相對較少，二戰後移居北海道。他們也生活在千島群島和堪察加半島南部堪察加。他們也都是離鄉背井的族群。他們有一部分遷徙到堪察加，而大多數則遷徙到了北海道。

他們是受打壓的一群人，他們的人口一直相對較少。他們現在主要住在北海道。

簡報 5

先請大家看看這個語言的簡短歷史。

1804 年是前現代化時期。在日本現代化之前，日本人地區和阿伊努人地區之間有一條邊界。這條邊界劃設於 16 世紀中葉，數百年來一直保存到 19 世紀末。當時，阿伊努人的人口數約為 21,000 人，而北海道的日本人則為 32,000 人。當然，當時日本人的人口並不多。100% 的阿伊努人說阿伊努語，那是他們特有的語言。

1869 年，日本政府開始現代化，於是決定撤除邊界。

他們開始從日本地區大規模向北海道遷移。日本於 1869 年吞併了這個島。於 1873 年，也就是大約在吞併四年後，阿伊努人已經是少數民族了。在北海道的日本人有 100,000 人。

當時，所有阿伊努人都說阿伊努語。我們有阿伊努語使用者的相關統計資料。幾十年後，到了 1917 年，北海道的日本人口已經達到 200 萬，而阿伊努人在北海道成了百分之一的少數民族。但當時，仍然有一半的阿伊努人會說阿伊努語。但我們估計，只會說阿伊努語一種語言的人大約只有數百人，500 到 700，僅此而已。

現在（2018 年），我們估計阿伊努族人口約為 50,000 人。北海道包括阿伊努人的總人口現在是 500 萬。

因此，說阿伊努語的人比例不到百分之一；我們估計大約為 0.7%。只有 0.7% 的阿伊努族人會說阿伊努語。他們在日常生活中不會使用阿伊努語。

簡報 6

現在，我們估計所謂以阿伊努語為母語的人只有 10 到 15 人，而且都已超過 80 歲。但有些學習者能以第二語言說阿伊努語，這些人可能也不超過 20 個。一些相對較年輕的老人可以聽懂他們祖先或語言學校的單詞或短語；這些人的數量可能在 50 到 100 人之間。他們不會說阿伊努語，但可以聽懂一些單詞和短語。所以，

從現代化到現在，阿伊努語在短短 150 年內便幾乎消失了。

簡報 7

當然也有一些振興工作。

第一次大規模工作始於 1980 年代。當時有人開設了私人的阿伊努語課程。還有日本國會第一位阿伊努議員；他的名字是萱野 茂／かやの しげる Kayano Shigeru，他展開了私人的振興計畫。

還有一些其他人。日本政府於 1997 年制定關於阿伊努文化的新法律，稱為《阿伊努文化促進法》（Ainu Culture Promotion Act）。同年依該法成立了阿伊努文化研究促進基金會。阿伊努基金會開始提供正式的阿伊努語課程，地點數已於 2003 年增至 14 個。

阿伊努人在當地被劃分到許多社區，失去了自己的專屬地區。他們現在在自己的家鄉北海道各地也都是少數民族。因此，該基金會不得不在當地提供這些語言課程。

聯合國於 2007 年制定了《原住民權利宣言》（Declaration on the Rights of Indigenous Peoples）。該《宣言》之後，日本國會宣布阿伊努人為原住民。這是第一次承認他們的原住民身分。聯合國教科文組織於 2009 年提出第三版瀕危語言報告。指出日本有八種瀕危語言。根據這份報告，日本政府啟動了一項新的專案。阿伊努語言建檔專案便是其中之一。

政府舉辦了瀕危語言節，命名為「瀕危語言高峰會」。日本政府舉辦這類活動的意義非凡，是日本承認瀕危語言的象徵性節日。在那之前，日本政府一直堅稱該語言是方言，但聯合國教科文組織的報告卻表示那是一種語言。日本政府現在也承認那不是方言，而是獨立的語言。

FRPAC 於今年（2018 年）改組為阿伊努文化基金會。它成為阿伊努文化組織，而不再是研究組織。政府準備將於 2020 年興建國家阿伊努博物館和公園，將其稱為「民族共生象徵空間」。這是日語詞彙。這些是最近關於阿伊努語的話題。

簡報 8

日本政府迄今已根據該促進法展開多項阿伊努語振興計畫。FRPAC 透過該計畫出版阿伊努語教科書，並組織阿伊努語課程和廣播節目。有八種方言教科書。這些方言之間差異不大，無需任何翻譯便可相互理解，但他們比較希望為自己的方言

製作教科書。

簡報 9

學校也有一些活動，包括小學的阿伊努語言和文化課程，但案例並不多，最重要的案例可能是這兩個。

二風谷小學有阿伊努語入學課程，許多阿伊努人居住在二風谷地區，可能是唯一阿伊努兒童占多數的小學。

當然，該課程的對象是阿伊努兒童，但每個月只有一小時。每個月只有一小時。當然，這樣很難學會一種語言。

第二個案例是千歲末廣小學，他們有針對日本兒童的新文化課程。該課程每年20個小時，該課程相對優於二風谷小學的課程，但並不是語言課程，那是一般的傳統文化課程，對象是日本兒童。

簡報 10

當然，很難說日本的振興計畫足夠。

阿伊努語課程是很過時的課程，主要部分是阿伊努語文法和學習詞彙，有時會練習唱歌，或背誦古老的口述故事或傳說，很少有會話練習。

因此，這些計畫實際並沒有什麼效果。沒有人可以透過這些計畫和學校教育成為說阿伊努語的人，沒有任何學校有真正的阿伊努語課程。日本政府堅持不可能在學校開設阿伊努語課程，因為那樣會違反教育平等政策。阿伊努兒童有權知道自己的語言，但日本政府堅持不能區分阿伊努兒童和日本兒童。由於沒有阿伊努語學校，就不可能有阿伊努語沉浸式空間，沒有語言巢或沉浸式學校。

不僅如此，老實說，學習者的動機方面也有問題。他們將阿伊努語視為其原住民身分的象徵性語言。他們認為自己的傳統語言確保了自己的原住民身分，但認為日常生活中並不需要說阿伊努語。

簡報 11

我已經說了這些政策的消極面，現在我想談談積極的事。阿伊努人自己也為語言振興做出了努力。例如，這是一部關於平取（也可以說是二風谷，因為在同一個地方）四位阿伊努老人的紀錄片。他們都 80 多歲了。一些老人從小就由祖父母照顧，並從祖父母學習語言和傳統文化。這表示 1917 年左右有幾百人只會說一種語

言。當時，這些只會說一種語言的人照顧自己的孩子和孫子。因為他們不會其他語言，所以對孫子孫女說阿伊努語。

大約在 1930 年代，地方當局禁止在學校使用阿伊努語。因此，阿伊努父母甚至在家也不再說阿伊努語。1930 年代之後，即使在家裡也沒有人可以學習自己的傳統語言。

但在那之前，有一些只會說一種語言的人，他們的孫子女可以跟他們說並向他們學習阿伊努語。那些孫子女現在已經 80 歲了，而年輕一代可以向他們學習語言和傳統文化。如果學校不開設語言課程，阿伊努年輕人可以跟長輩學習。

簡報 12

一些阿伊努人會用一對一的方法——也就是師徒法。

這是這種方法的教科書，出版於 2002 年。這是用英文寫的，所以阿伊努人不一定知道這一點。他們在 1980-1990 年代左右自己也發明了幾乎相同的方法。

一對一法大概是這樣的，如果長輩會教語言，便可問徒弟一些問題，同時教他們如何回答——問與答。長輩在一對一的環境下自己教導學生問題和答案。

長輩不會教怎麼辦？當然大部分長輩並不是專業老師。如果長輩不會教，徒弟就得採取主動。徒弟應向長輩提問，並學習如何用阿伊努語提問和回答。

這種方法就像語言學家在該領域所做的一樣，幾乎是相同的方法。徒弟記住問題和答案後，下次就可以實用這些表達方式了。重點是準備結構化的問題和答案。看起來好像是他們自己發明的。

簡報 13

有些阿伊努人曾試圖透過一對一法保存自己的語言和文化。重點在於這些都只是個人和地方性的活動，傳統的阿伊努文化依賴當地社區。大約有 200 個阿伊努社區，每個社區大約有 200 名成員，這 200 名成員彼此獨立。阿伊努人可以自己決定一切，日本研究人員和其他局外人有時認為阿伊努個人主義過於激進，但這對阿伊努社會非常重要。

一對一法可能並不是增加說阿伊努語人數的最好方法，但成功地在個人層次上保存了阿伊努語。阿伊努語振興活動並不以語言本身為限，經常也伴隨著傳統儀式。

這張照片是一個傳統祭壇。阿伊努傳統祭壇並不複雜。不同場合必須提供稱為

「inaw」的木製品。傳統上每個人在家裡都必須有這樣的祭壇。現在已經很少製造這些單獨的祭壇了，但某些行動主義者會自己做。他們試圖同時振興阿伊努語和阿伊努文化。他們會以阿伊努語舉行傳統儀式。他們用阿伊努語拜神，用阿伊努語交談。他們以阿伊努語對神奉獻歌曲、傳統故事和舞蹈。他們有時會在社群媒體使用阿伊努語，但這只能算是炫耀。

簡報 14

　　所以就像我說的，雖然有官方的阿伊努語課程和阿伊努語建檔專案。很遺憾我必須說，阿伊努語課程迄今並無實效，但也許可以重新設計。關於建檔專案，我們正在期待結果。我們現在知道，阿伊努人的個人活動成效卓著。如果受到一對一活動的影響，官方語言課程是否會變得更有效？

　　目前狀況很複雜。個人活動和官方語言課程各管各的。他們個別都在思考如何可以做得更好。狀況就是這樣。

　　非常感謝。

【西班牙加泰隆尼亞語 Catalan】
語言復振：以加泰隆尼亞為例
The Revitalization of Languages: the Catalan Case

加泰隆尼亞區語言使用促進服務負責人 Carles de Rosselló 先生

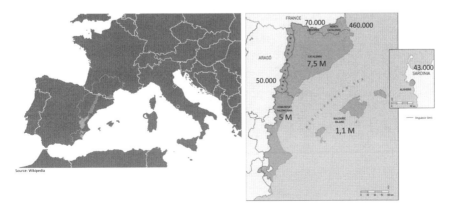

1

THE REVITALIZATION OF LANGUAGES:
THE CATALAN CASE

TAIPEI 15-16TH DECEMBER 2018

Generalitat de Catalunya
Departament de Cultura

2

Europe and the Catalan-speaking regions

3

Knowledge of Catalan (1975)

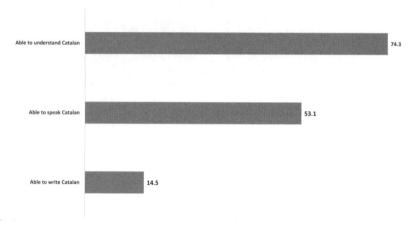

4

Demographic context

Most of the **foreign population** are within the **most productive age** groups

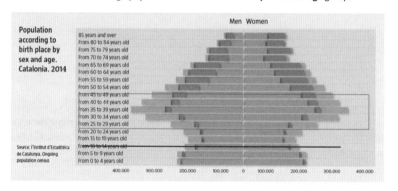

5

Knowledge of Catalan: 2003 – 2008 – 2013

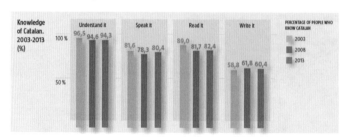

Knowledge of Catalan 2003 – 2013. Absolute numbers

	2003	2008	2013
Understand it	5,423,600	5,832,200	5,899,418
Speak it	4,583,500	4,823,400	5,027,165
Read it	4,999,500	5,034,400	5,152,416
Write it	3,303,800	3,807,300	3,776,266

First language and language of identification

Almost 3 million people for whom Catalan is not their first language can speak it today

Difference between those who can speak it (5,027,200) and those who have it as a first language, alone or combined with Spanish (2,092,700)

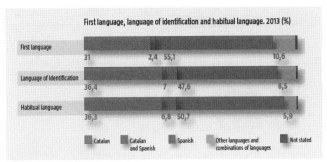

First language, language of identification and habitual language. 2013 (%)

	Catalan	Catalan and Spanish	Spanish	Other languages and combinations of languages	Not stated
First language	31	2,4	55,1		10,6
Language of identification	36,4	7	47,6		8,5
Habitual language	36,3	6,8	50,7		5,9

Source: Directorate General for Language Policy and Statistical Institute of Catalonia.
Survey on Language Use of the Population of Catalonia 2013. People of 15 years and over.

Article 3.1

Castilian is the official Spanish language of the State. All Spaniards have the duty to know it and the right to use it.

Article 3.2

The other Spanish languages shall also be official in the respective Self-governing Communities in accordance with their Statutes.

Priority areas to attract new speakers

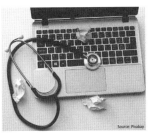

social cohesion   work   health

9

Countries of origin of students born abroad

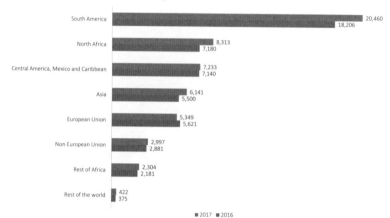

Country	2017	2016
South America	20,460	18,206
North Africa	8,313	7,180
Central America, Mexico and Caribbean	7,233	7,140
Asia	6,141	5,500
European Union	5,349	5,621
Non European Union	2,997	2,881
Rest of Africa	2,304	2,181
Rest of the world	422	375

■ 2017   ■ 2016

10

11

"Check the pulse of the Catalan language"

(brochure edited by the Health Department – Government of Catalonia)

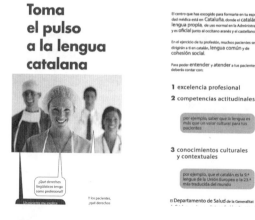

Four challenges ahead

12

| Extension of knowledge | Extension of use | (Re)define the position of languages | Increase the presence of Catalan |

MOLTES GRÀCIES
THANK YOU
SHIN-MUNG NGI

13

THE REVITALIZATION OF LANGUAGES: THE CATALAN CASE

TAIPEI 15-16TH DECEMBER 2018

Generalitat de Catalunya
Departament de Cultura

Briefing 1

Thank you very much for your presentation and for the invitation. Also, for such a well-organized congress.

I'm very pleased to be here with you. I'm going to read my speech. I will speak firstly about the Catalan sociolinguistic situation and the legal framework. Secondly, I will deal with some of the measures that the government of Catalonia carries out to promote the knowledge and use of Catalan among the adult population. And finally, I will refer to the linguistic challenges ahead we face as a society.

Briefing 2

Let me start by sketching briefly some basic data about the Catalan language in order to help you understand its current situation.

Catalan is a language spoken in four European states: Spain, Andorra, France, and Italy, Spain being by large the country where most of its speakers live. It is estimated that around 14 million citizens live in the area where Catalan is spoken. Ten million of them are capable of speaking it, and between seven and eight million use it in different degrees on a daily basis. Given these figures, Catalan is a language similar to that of Finnish, Croatian, and Danish, and therefore more than a minority language, it should be considered a medium-sized language in the European multilingual context.

In other words, relatively speaking there have never been so many native and secondary speakers of Catalan in history. Reaching this point has not been easy.

The 20th century left as an inheritance a military dictatorship that prohibited the public use of Catalan and its teaching in schools for almost 40 years, from 1939 to 1975. The consequences of this policy resulted in a whole generation—the generation of my parents—having many difficulties in reading and writing the language.

Apart from this, already important enough in itself, we must add the fact that from the mid-20th century, and for a period of 25 years, about 1.5 million people from the rest of Spain and without previous knowledge of Catalan came to Catalonia–a reasonably prosperous economic region at that time– in search of a better future.

Briefing 3

The first linguistic data available is from 1975. This data didn't reflect what happened to the whole of Catalonia but to its most populous area; that is, the city of Barcelona and its surrounding towns, where most of the Catalan population is concentrated.

The knowledge of Catalan, at the end of the dictatorship, showed figures in which the capacity for understanding was quite high (74 percent; we mustn't forget that Catalan and Spanish are related languages, so it follows that knowing one grants easy access to the other, at least in terms of comprehension skills).However, the ability to speak it was reduced to half of the population, and only 14 percent stated that they could write it.

In a period of just 40 years, Catalonia had moved from being, essentially, a monolingual to a bilingual country ruled by an asymmetric bilingualism: while all Catalan speakers were fully competent in Spanish, newcomers had much more trouble accessing Catalan. They were usually skilled enough to comprehend Catalan but remained far from being active users of the language.

Despite these adverse conditions, the Catalan cultural, editorial and the literary world remained strong during periods of oppression and enforced exile. And as the regime was getting older, the voices that demanded freedom, democracy, and the restitution of the role of Catalan in our society, especially in the education system, galvanized.

In some way, Catalan had maintained its prestige. People continued to consider it a useful language which connected us with our past and simultaneously projected us into the future. And this prestige wasn't concentrated only among the people who already spoke it but also among many of the newcomers, who were the first to demand schools in Catalan so that their children could have access to this linguistic capital, which they couldn't access because of the political circumstances at the time.

The advent of democracy in 1978entailed the restitution of the Catalan government, which gradually built an institutional structure to protect and revitalize Catalan by formulating three cornerstone measures:

One, by promoting Catalan as the main language of tuition in education; second, by establishing public mass media where Catalan was the primary language; and third, by setting Catalan as the language of normal use in the Catalan administration.

Briefing 4

After 40 years of democracy, Catalan speakers and Spanish speakers were by far the two largest linguistic groups in Catalonia. But the scenario has changed dramatically, especially from the beginning of the 21st century until 2012.

In little over ten years, the population has increased from 6.3 million inhabitants to 7.5 million, the vast majority of whom come from outside Spain. It is important to have this demographic aspect in mind to understand the evolution of the Catalan language, which in 2003 was in a relatively balanced situation regarding Spanish. However, in 2008 Catalan suffered a clear setback. For the period between 2008 and 2013, no short drops were detected anymore. So right now, we are in a period of stability. At present, people born in Catalonia make up 65 percent of the Catalan population, while people born in the rest of Spain and abroad represent the other 35 percent—17.5 percent for each group.

The nature of these two last collectives vary sharply in several ways, age being one of the most prominent, as those born in Spain are getting older whereas those born abroad are fully active in labor terms.

Briefing 5

Regarding language abilities, the knowledge of Catalan has substantially increased since the 1980s, reaching relatively stable figures:

About 94 percent can understand Catalan.

About 80 percent are capable of speaking it.

About 82 percent can read it.

And, about 60 percent can write it.

The knowledge of Spanish in these four abilities verges on 100 percent in all areas. In other words, only eight percent of the survey respondents stated they had little or no knowledge of Spanish related to disabilities. This is not the case for Catalan, since 19 percent declared having problems in understanding the language; another 19 percent stated they couldn't speak it at all; 30 percent cannot read it (or they can but with difficulties); and 32 percent are not capable of writing it. In other words, the knowledge of the Catalan language is still far from being at the same level as that of Spanish.

Briefing 6

Another key point that must be observed is the first language and the language of identification.

In 2013, Spanish was the first language of the majority of the population (55 percent), followed by Catalan (31 percent) and other languages (10.6percent). However, as a language of identification, Catalan scored better than as a first language, at 36.4 percent, and Spanish scored a little worse, at about 47 percent. This pattern has remained constant since 2003.

One of the most salient features of Catalan as a language of identification is its appeal; that is, almost 750,000 people state that Catalan is their language, despite the fact they have other linguistic origins. Where do these people come from?

Basically, from those whose language is Spanish and at the same time are born either in Catalonia or in the rest of Spain. By contrast, Spanish demonstrates its strength among foreign language speakers.

On intergenerational language transmission, Catalan is the language spoken to children among the population whose first language is also Catalan. This fact has remained unchanged since 2003. It is noteworthy that 27 percent of those born in Catalonia, but whose parents were born outside of Catalonia and hence their first language is likely to be Spanish, use Catalan with their children as well.

One of the main concerns the Catalan language has to face is its use on a daily basis. In the last decade, the use of Catalan has decreased in several public domains. Hence, by 2003, the use of Catalan and Spanish was fairly balanced, at 48 percent. Yet, ten years later, the mean of use of Catalan was 41 percent and that of Spanish was 53 percent. The patterns with regard to language use are also interesting to observe. Catalan is the language most used among people born in Catalonia, but there are still 500,000 of those who use it less than ten percent daily. On the contrary, Spanish is used consistently by all the linguistic groups present in the country. Moreover, Catalan-language speakers have more bilingual practices than Spanish-language speakers; while among the Spanish language speakers, the exclusive use of Spanish is very consistent.

So, in accordance with the data presented so far, Spanish is used more than Catalan throughout the day. If we try to group the population based on their linguistic practices, we can see that around 33 percent use Catalan predominantly, 20 percent could switch between Catalan and Spanish, and finally, a little less than 50 percent use little or no Catalan at all.

This imbalance is largely due to the population of foreign origin, who, if they haven't attended school in Catalan, has many more difficulties incorporating Catalan in its various dimensions: as a language of identification, as a habitual language or acquiring abilities like writing and speaking. The new immigration, therefore, integrates linguistically into Catalan society through Spanish, and this seems to be enough. It remains far from my desire to put the blame on these people for their linguistic behavior. I limit myself to state a fact.

One other factor must be considered to understand the current situation: the reproduction over and over again of the rule of using Spanish with newcomers (or people who, apparently, cannot speak Catalan for the same strange reasons: because they are Black, Asian, or have a blonde hair). The endurance of this fact has intensified the use of Spanish in many social domains.

The picture depicted so far is not complete if we don't look also at the schooling system, which is probably the cornerstone of the Catalan language policy. In Catalonia, we have opted for a model of conjunction, which favors social cohesion since it doesn't discriminate against children depending on any linguistic reason, geographical origin, or any other characteristic. And with a clear linguistic objective: finishing the compulsory schooling with a full competence in both Catalan and Spanish languages, as is evident from the studies conducted so far.

Briefing 7

The overview presented so far wouldn't be complete without making a reference to the legal framework.

Previously we talked about the situation of bilingualism in Catalonia, which favored an imbalance towards Spanish. The legal framework is also characterized by a disequilibrium that favors the use of Spanish over the other languages spoken in Spain. What is this disequilibrium? That which comes from Article 3 of the Spanish constitution: On one hand, Spanish is the official language of the entire state, while the rest of the languages are official only in their own regions. On the other hand, the knowledge of Spanish is a duty for each Spanish citizen and they are not able to assert lack of knowledge for the language, while knowing other languages is not an obligation but only a right.

Thus, the state favors the presence of one language over the others. For example, of the 40 television channels currently available in Catalonia, 32 are Spanish-speaking media and only eight are in Catalan.

Or, in the case of the justice system, Catalan is also grossly underused. In a nutshell, these and other domains regulated by the Spanish state leave Catalan in a clearly subordinate position.

The Catalan legislation, depending on the Spanish, states that Catalan and Spanish, along with Aranese Occitan, are the official languages of Catalonia.

Moreover, Catalan is considered the native language of Catalonia –together with Aranese Occitan in its respective territory. For this reason, Catalan is consistently used within the public bodies and Catalan public media. The Catalan legislation points out that no citizen can be discriminated against for the use of either Catalan or Spanish.

At this point, I would like to explain some of the measures in which the government of Catalonia works to attract new speakers and to extend the presence of Catalan in those areas where it exhibits symptoms of weakness.

These actions are carried out by the Directorate General for Language Policy, attached to the Ministry of Culture, and by the Consortium for Language Normalization—the organization where I work—which is organically dependent on the Directorate. Our target population is those over 18 years old, so education is not the responsibility of the Directorate and therefore is not one of the priority areas in which we work to attract new speakers.

Briefing 8

The priority areas we are working on are three: social cohesion, the world of work and the field of health.

Social cohesion is a fundamental value. In a context of a large migratory movements, with a significant mix of cultures, different ways of perceiving the world,with dispute over jobs and also in public resources, language policy must help to reduce the differences between citizens. The creation of two or more differentiated communities within the same society must be avoided. Catalonia wants to be a cohesive, welcoming, and open country in a multilingual framework.

One of the ways in which language policy can achieve these goals is to provide people with full competencies in the language or languages present in a territory because this guarantees equal opportunities for all citizens. To put it in another way, the linguistic project promoted by the Catalan government is an additive rather than a substitutive one. This project is also what the great majority of the Catalan population prefer.

The second area is the workplace. This is one of the fields where it has been detected that Catalan still has a long way to go, especially in the private sector. In post-graduate or executive environments such as science parks or universities, favorable dynamics are generated for the use of Catalan. On the other hand, in other basic occupations on the professional scale (such as elementary occupations, installation operators, manufacturing, and construction), the lowest rates of knowledge of Catalan continue to show, particularly where the old Spanish-speaking immigration and the new multilingual one are combined.

In short, while the knowledge of Catalan increases among the most qualified occupations, it decreases among the least qualified.

The third area where I want to focus my attention is health. I would like to tell a personal anecdote to illustrate this area better. My son is now six years old. When he was two and a half, he decided to check the elasticity of his parents' mattress, so he started jumping on the mattress. The result, as you can imagine, was a strong blow to the teeth that forced us to hurry to the hospital.

There, a young surgeon born abroad treated him very kindly. But, when he said "Let's see, open your mouth, I want to see your teeth" in Spanish, my son didn't do what he was told; not because he was disobedient but simply because he didn't understand it: at the age of three, many children in Catalonia are still monolingual.

Because the doctor couldn't speak Catalan, my partner and I ended up becoming improvised translators. The labor and social insertion process of a population born outside Catalonia has, for example, led to the fact that in the period of 2008-2013, there were 400,000 fewer patients speaking only Catalan with doctors.

To develop each of these three areas from the Consortium for Language Normalization various activities are carried out. Let me highlight some.

Briefing 9

The first one is our main activity, courses of Catalan. We organize courses for all the levels established by the Common European Framework of Reference for Languages as well as specific courses to meet specific needs of professional groups such as companies or hospital centers. Currently, the Consortium catalog is made up of more than 50 courses, and in 2017 we had more than 76,000 registrations.

Most of our students are enrolled in the first level of language—those that we call linguistic reception courses—that is, those that allow them to carry out everyday activities with ease. As you can observe, our students come from all continents. Those born in Central and South America represent more than 52 percent. The total number of foreigners enrolled in the Consortium courses last year was slightly above 53,000.

One of the main problems that we have in the courses, and more specifically in the reception courses, is the continuity of the students on the course; the low number of people that enroll in the following trimester. This means that many people only take a course in the Consortium, that lasts 45 hours. If it turns out that this course is just the Initial or the Basic one, this means that the impact on their linguistic capacity is naturally minimal—sufficient to have an acceptable understanding of Catalan but with very little or no ability to speak or write the language.

Briefing 10

The second program I want to highlight is the Volunteering for Language program, the VxL (Voluntariat per la llengua).

This program aims to promote the use of Catalan in personal relationships. How? In the most basic way, the VxL matches a person who usually speaks Catalan, called the volunteer, with another with basic knowledge, the learner.

This linguistic pair meets for a minimum of ten hours in a relaxed atmosphere, with the aim of incorporating the Catalan language into natural daily activities, fostering the learner's work or social relationships.

The program has evolved over time. It was launched 15 years ago and its success has been steadily increasing. The number of language pairs has stayed above 10,000 annually in the last eight years, and since the beginning of the program, 130,000 pairs have been created. This has led to a progressive rolling out of the program, and currently, there are even pairs in areas as diverse as companies, prisons, or religious centers. It is especially satisfying to observe how people who started being learners finally become volunteers.

Briefing 11

The third and final action I want to comment on is the social linguistics awareness sessions. I will do it with another personal anecdote. Because my level of English is at most so-so, a teacher helped me in writing this speech. Normally we met in my office, but one day we made an appointment in a café. When I asked for a drink, I did it in Catalan, and the waitress answered me in Spanish instead. When my teacher, with a clear British accent, asked for a coffee in Spanish, the waitress replied to him in English. That the waitress would take advantage of any occasion to practice her English seems to me perfect–I would do the same, since the Catalans of my generation have an inferiority complex with our level of English–, but as a client I felt disappointed and annoyed when I saw that my linguistic choice was not corresponded to, and even more so when the waitress made an effort to adapt to the native language of an English-speaking person. In gastronomic terms, I felt as though my dish had been served cold.

To avoid situations of this kind, the Consortium carries out guided sessions on sociolinguistics awareness. These sessions have a short duration, usually between two and four hours, and are aimed at different groups—medical staff, public facing workers, sports monitors, and so on. Regardless of the group, the message we try to transmit is always the same: to be better professionals, and to better serve the client or the user, it is important that you respect their linguistic choice and therefore speak in the language that has been addressed to you.

Briefing 12

Finally, I would like to close my speech by addressing the challenges we have in the near future.

The first is, as we already doing, the extension of knowledge among newly arrived adults. This sector of the population doesn't go through the Catalan school and therefore accesses the labor market with fewer options than the native speaking population because its linguistic capital is lower in terms of knowledge of local languages, especially the Catalan language. However, here we have an important difficulty: focusing on the language skills of this group is very difficult because the system "takes you" –as seen before– for a maximum of 45 hours and from then on it already depends on the will of the person to deepen their knowledge of the language. If we add that Spanish has become the language for relationships between autochthonous people and immigrants and also between immigrants, it is expected that the knowledge of Catalan between this group will continue to be low during the next decades.

The adult immigrant population occupies several places in the labor market: many are concentrated in small neighborhood stores usually associated with food or local corner shops, but they're also in companies, and there are others in the health sector. An obvious challenge then is that all those people who work towards the public must have at least linguistic availability in Catalan and Spanish.

The second challenge is to reverse the rule of convergence towards Spanish. Let me illustrate with the third and final anecdote from my personal life, which I hope you will find amusing.

I have a friend who's from Japan and with whom I studied my PhD courses in Barcelona. At that time, she was proficient in Catalan and not particularly fluent in Spanish. She's now fully competent in both languages. Once, she invited me to try some delicious Japanese cuisine. First, we stopped off at a bakery to buy some desserts. There a strange thing occurred: a young immigrant Japanese girl was speaking in Catalan while being responded to in Spanish by the local Barcelona shopkeeper. Despite the fact that she continued to converse in Catalan because that was the language she was most comfortable speaking, the only language the shopkeeper chose to reply in was Spanish.

I was there watching the scene unfold and noting the clear Catalan accent of the shopkeeper, which led me to conclude that she was almost certainly a Catalan speaker. So, I decided to intervene in the conversation by communicating with the shopkeeper in Catalan. What was her reaction? She spoke back to me in Catalan. Historically, the Catalan government, through institutional campaigns, has promoted the idea of not changing the language over an interlocutor who understands Catalan but doesn't speak it. This linguistic behavior exists in Catalan society but is minority, and the prevailing behavior is linguistic convergence, especially towards Spanish when immigrants are involved in the conversation. Since this strategy hasn't worked, I think that there is a need to focus on the still quite unexplored idea of using Catalan by default. In doing so, the person can present himself as linguistically available, since the knowledge of Spanish in Catalonia is universal, and the number of interactions in Catalan could grow substantially, making it possible for immigrants to increase their chances of speaking Catalan and integrating better into our society.

The third challenge is redefining or defining the position of languages in multilingual societies. As mentioned previously, in Catalonia, there are two historical languages—Catalan and Aranese Occitan—which, at this time, occupy a subordinate position with respect to Spanish. The efforts of the government of Catalonia have focused on balancing the situation, with the ultimate goal of making Catalan the preferred language in Catalonia. However, this must be done by guaranteeing—as has been done so far—the full formal knowledge of the Spanish language (the informal one is guaranteed with current linguistic conditions).

Spanish is a very valuable linguistic resource for the Catalan population:

it is the most widely-known language; it is a widely-used language in Catalonia itself; and it's the language that allows us to communicate with more than 500 million speakers around the world. For all this, groups who advocate "stopping learning Spanish" are currently a very small minority in Catalonia. However, the strength of Spanish is so powerful that it's necessary to define the language roles to avoid Spanish from taking its toll on Catalan or Aranese Occitan.

The fourth and last challenge would be to revitalize the use of Catalan in those areas where it is still in the minority. For example, only 48 percent of employees at bars and restaurants in Barcelona can speak Catalan; or, for example, television, given that the number of channels available in Catalan is below 20 percent; or, for example, Justice Administration, where court rulings in Catalan don't even arrive at nine percent.

Briefing 13

Thank you very much for your attention.

承蒙您！(Shin-mung ngi!)

Moltesgràcies!

簡報 1

非常感謝您的介紹和邀請。也感謝如此籌備完善的大會。

很榮幸和大家齊聚一堂。我將開始我的演說。我會先談談加泰隆語的社會語言狀況和法律框架。其次，我將介紹加泰隆尼亞政府為在成年人之間促進加泰隆語的知識和使用，所採取的一些措施。最後，我將提到我們社會所面臨的語言挑戰。

簡報 2

先讓我簡單描述一下關於加泰隆語的一些基本數據，以協助各位了解其現狀。

加泰隆語是在四個歐洲國家使用的語言：西班牙、安道爾、法國和義大利，而加泰隆語使用者大部分都住在西班牙。估計大約有 1,400 萬公民生活在說加泰隆語的地區，其中 1,000 萬人會說加泰隆語，700 萬到 800 萬人每天以不同的程度使用加泰隆語。根據這些數字，加泰隆語是一種類似芬蘭語、克羅地亞語和丹麥語的語言，因此超過少數民族語言，應視為歐洲多語環境中的一種中等規模語言。

換句話說，相對而言，歷史上從未有過如此之多以加泰隆語為母語和第二語言的人，達到這一點並不容易。

20 世紀留下一個軍事獨裁政權，從 1939 年到 1975 年的近 40 年期間內，禁止公開使用也禁止在學校教導加泰隆語。這項政策導致整整一代人——我父母那一代——在閱讀和書寫加泰隆語上有許多困難。

除此之外，雖然這本身就足夠重要了，但我們還必須補充一個事實，從 20 世紀中葉起的 25 年期間，大約有 150 萬原先不懂加泰隆語的人從西班牙其他地區來到加泰隆尼亞（當時是一個相當繁榮的經濟區）尋求更美好的未來。

簡報 3

第一個能取得的語言數據來自 1975 年。這些數據並未反映發生於整個加泰隆尼亞的狀況，而只反映了其人口最多的地區；也就是大部分加泰隆尼亞人聚集的巴塞隆納市及其周邊城鎮。

獨裁統治結束時，對加泰隆語的了解顯示出，理解能力的數據相當高（74%；別忘了加泰隆語和西班牙語是相關語言，因此，只要會其中一種就很容易學會另一種，至少在理解能力方面）。但說加泰隆語的能力降到只有一半人口，且只有 14% 的人表示他們可以寫加泰隆語。

就在短短 40 年期間內，加泰隆尼亞已經從實質單語國家轉變成由不對稱雙語統治的雙語國家：雖然所有加泰隆語使用者都能充分掌握西班牙語，但新移民在使用加泰隆語方面便困難得多了。他們通常都能了解加泰隆語，但還遠遠稱不上是加泰隆語的積極使用者。

雖然有這些不利條件，但加泰隆尼亞文化、社論和文學界在受壓迫和強制流放期間仍然很強大。隨著政權老化，有愈來愈多聲音要求自由、民主以及恢復加泰隆語在我們社會（尤其是教育體系）中的角色。

以某種方式，加泰隆語維持了它的威望。人們仍然認為加泰隆語是一種很有用的語言，將我們連結到過去，同時也將我們投射於未來。這種威望不僅集中於已經會說加泰隆語的人之間，也集中於許多新移民之間，他們首先需要加泰隆語學校，才能讓自己的子女取得這種因當時政治環境原本無法取得的語言資本。

1978 年民主的出現迫使加泰隆尼亞政府回歸，透過制定三項基本措施逐步建立起保護並振興加泰隆語的制度性結構：

第一，促進以加泰隆語作為教育的主要教學語言；第二，建立以加泰隆語為主要語言的公共大眾媒體；第三，將加泰隆語定為加泰隆尼亞政府的正常使用語言。

簡報 4

經過 40 年的民主，加泰隆語和西班牙語成為目前加泰隆尼亞最大的兩個語言群體。但情境有了重大改變，尤其是從 21 世紀初到 2012 年。

短短十年多內，人口從 630 萬居民增加到 750 萬，而其中絕大部分來自西班牙以外地區。請記住這項人口因素，才能了解加泰隆語的演進，加泰隆語在 2003 年還處於和西班牙語相對平衡的狀態。但在 2008 年，加泰隆語遭受明顯挫敗。於 2008 年至 2013 年之間，已沒有再看到瞬間的滑落。所以現在，我們正處於一個穩定期。目前，在加泰隆尼亞出生的人占加泰隆尼亞人口的 65%，而在西班牙其他地區及國外出生的人則占另外 35%——每一群體各 17.5%。

最後這兩個全體在性質上有多方面的重大差異，年齡是最明顯的，因為在西班

牙出生的人正在變老，而在國外出生的人正活躍於勞動市場。

簡報 5

語言能力方面，對加泰隆語的認識自 1980 年代以來大幅增加，達到相對穩定的數字：

大約 94% 的人能了解加泰隆語。

大約 80% 的人能說加泰隆語。

大約 82% 的人能讀加泰隆語。

而大約 60% 的人能寫加泰隆語。

西班牙語在這四種能力方面的知識於所有領域都趨近 100%。換句話說，只有 8% 的調查受訪者表示，關於語言文字障礙，他們不太懂或完全不懂西班牙語。加泰隆語的狀況就不同了，因為有 19% 表示在理解加泰隆語方面有困難；另有 19% 表示根本不會說；30% 無法閱讀（或雖然可以但有困難）；32% 不會寫。也就是說，對加泰隆語的了解程度遠不及西班牙語。

簡報 6

另一個必須觀察的重點是第一語言和認同語言。

於 2013 年，西班牙語是大多數人口（55%）的第一語言，其次是加泰隆語（31%）和其他語言（10.6%）。但就識別語言來看，加泰隆語的得分高於作為第一語言，為 36.4%，而西班牙語的得分略降，約為 47%。這種模式自 2003 年以來一直沒變。

以加泰隆語作為識別語言最顯著的特點之一就是其感染力；也就是說，幾乎有 750,000 人表示加泰隆語是他們的語言，即使事實上他們有其他語言血統。這些人是誰的後代？

基本上，他們祖先的語言是西班牙語，但他們出生於加泰隆尼亞或西班牙其他地區。相反的，西班牙語的實力展現於外語使用者之間。

在代際語言傳播中，加泰隆語是第一語言也是說加泰隆語的人之間對子女說的語言，這個事實自 2003 年以來一直沒變。值得注意的是，出生於加泰隆尼亞但其父母出生於其他地區且因此其第一語言很可能是西班牙語的人之中，有 27% 也和他們的子女使用加泰隆語。

加泰隆語必須面對的主要問題之一是其日常使用率。過去十年中，加泰隆語在

幾個公領域的使用率已減少。因此，截至 2003 年，加泰隆語和西班牙語的使用率相當平衡，有 48% 使用加泰隆語。但十年後，加泰隆語的平均使用率為 41%，西班牙語為 53%。語言使用模式也很值得觀察。出生於加泰隆尼亞的人最常使用加泰隆語，但仍有 500,000 人每天使用加泰隆語的比率低於 10%。相反的，該國所有語言群體使用西班牙語的頻率都很一致。此外，加泰隆語使用者使用雙語的比例高於西班牙語使用者；而在西班牙語使用者之中，只使用西班牙語的比率很一致。

因此，根據目前看到的數據，全天使用西班牙語的比例高於使用加泰隆語。如果我們試著依語言習慣將人口分類，就可以看到大約 33% 的人主要使用加泰隆語，20% 的人可以在加泰隆語和西班牙語之間切換，最後，略低於 50% 的人很少或完全不使用加泰隆語。

這種不平衡主要是因為外國血統人口，這些人如果沒有就讀過加泰隆語學校，便難以將加泰隆語融入其不同層面：作為識別語言、作為習慣語言或取得寫和說的能力。因此，新移民在語言上透過西班牙語融入加泰隆尼亞社會，而這樣似乎就足夠了。我真的無意苛責這些人的語言行為，我規範自己陳述一個事實。

為了解現況，還必須考慮另一個因素：新移民（或因同樣奇怪的原因而似乎不會說加泰隆語的人：因為他們是黑人、亞洲人或有金頭髮）使用西班牙語的規則一再複製。此事實的長久存在強化了西班牙語在許多社交場合的使用率。

如果不探究學校教育體系，目前描繪的畫面便不完整，學校教育體系可能是加泰隆尼亞語言政策的基石。在加泰隆尼亞，我們選擇了一種有利於社會凝聚的結合模式，因為兒童不會因任何語言原因、地理血統或任何其他特徵而受歧視。同時有明確的語言目標：完成義務教育，取得加泰隆語和西班牙語的完整能力，這可以從截至目前進行的研究中證明。

簡報 7

如果不參考法律框架，截至目前提出的概要便不完整。

之前我們提到過加泰隆尼亞的雙語狀況，有利於西班牙語的不平衡，法律框架也明顯不平衡，有利於使用西班牙語而不利於在西班牙說的其他語言。這種不平衡是什麼？這源自西班牙憲法第 3 條：一方面，西班牙語是整個國家的官方語言，而其他語言則僅在其自己的區域為官方語言。另一方面，了解西班牙語是每個西班牙市民的義務，任何人不得主張自己不懂西班牙語，而了解其他語言並不是義務，只

是一種權利。

因此，國家傾向於使用某一種語言而不使用其他語言。例如，在加泰隆尼亞目前的 40 個電視頻道中，32 個是西班牙語的媒體，只有 8 個加泰隆語媒體。

或就司法體制而言，明顯較少使用加泰隆語。簡單說，西班牙國家轄下的這些和其他領域，都使得加泰隆語處於明顯的下級地位。

加泰隆尼亞立法（取決於西班牙語）規定，加泰隆語、西班牙語，以及阿蘭奧克西唐語都是加泰隆尼亞官方語言。

此外，加泰隆語被認為是加泰隆尼亞的本土語言──連同其各別地區的阿蘭奧克西唐語。因此，公家機關和加泰隆尼亞公共媒體一直在使用加泰隆語。加泰隆尼亞立法指出，不得因任何公民使用加泰隆語或西班牙語而對其有所歧視。

此刻我想說明加泰隆尼亞政府的一些措施，亦即為吸引新的加泰隆語使用者，並在加泰隆語不受重視的地區擴大使用加泰隆語而採取的措施。

這些行動係由隸屬於文化部的語言政策總局和語言規範化聯盟（我任職的組織，機能上依附於該政策總局）執行。我們的目標族群是年滿 18 歲的人，所以教育並不是該政策總局的責任，也不是我們吸引新的加泰隆語使用者的重點工作。

簡報 8

我們有三大重點工作領域：社會凝聚、工作場所和健康領域。

社會凝聚是一項基本價值觀。在大規模移民運動的背景下，有大量的文化融合，對世界的感知方式不同，對工作和公共資源存有爭議，而語言政策則必須有助於降低公民之間的差異。必須避免在同一個社會中創造兩個或更多分化的社區。加泰隆尼亞希望能在多語框架中成為一個有凝聚力、包容而開放的國家。

透過語言政策實現這些目標的方法之一，便是讓人們具備使用該地區出現之語言的充分能力，因為這樣便可保證所有公民的公平機會。換句話說，加泰隆尼亞政府推動的語言專案是一項補充專案，而非替代專案。該專案也是絕大多數加泰隆尼亞人接受的專案。

第二個領域是工作場所。這是已知加泰隆語仍路途遙遠的領域，尤其是在私營部門。在研究生或高階主管環境中，例如科學園區或大學，應創造使用加泰隆語的有利動力。另一方面，在專業規模的其他基本職業（如初階職業、安裝作業員、製造和建築）中，持續出現對加泰隆語最低的認知率，尤其是在講西班牙語的舊移民

和多語種新移民混合的地方。

簡單說，雖然對加泰隆語的知識在條件要求最高的職業中有所增加，但在條件要求最低的職業中卻降低了。

我要關注的第三個領域是健康。我想講一個個人的故事更清楚地說明這一方面。我兒子現在六歲。在他兩歲半的時候，想要確定父母床墊的彈力，就開始在床墊上蹦跳。結果，你可以想見，大力撞到牙齒，逼得我們趕快送醫。

在那裡，一位在國外出生的年輕醫生很親切地治療他。但是，當他用西班牙語說「讓我看看，嘴巴張開，我要看看你的牙齒」時，我兒子並沒有照做；不是因為他不聽話，而只是因為他聽不懂：加泰隆尼亞許多小孩在三歲的時候還只會說一種語言。

因為醫生不會說加泰隆語，伴侶和我只好充當臨時翻譯。舉例而言，出生於加泰隆尼亞以外地方的人，在勞動和社會融合過程中造成了這樣的事實，於 2008 年到 2013 年期間內，與醫生只說加泰隆語的病患人數減少了 400,000 人。

為了能從語言規範化聯盟發展這三個領域，已展開各種活動。讓我講講其中的一些。

簡報 9

第一就是我們的主要活動，加泰隆語課程。我們規劃《歐洲共同語言參考標準》（Common European Framework of Reference for Languages）建立之所有級別課程，以及為滿足公司或醫院中心等專業團體特定需求的特定課程。目前，聯盟目錄中有 50 多門課程，而於 2017 年註冊人數超過 76,000 人。

大部分學生都參加第一級語言——我們稱之為語言學習課程——也就是讓他們可以輕鬆進行日常活動的課程。你可以看到，我們的學生來自各大洲，出生於中南美洲的占 52% 以上，去年參加聯盟課程的外國人總數略高於 53,000 人。

課程中（更具體的說是接待課程中）遇到的主要問題之一，是學生的課程繼續率；下一學期的參加人數很少。這表示許多人只參加持續 45 小時的聯盟課程。如果事實證明這只是初級或基礎課程，自然就表示對他們語言能力的影響非常微小——足以了解加泰隆語達可接受的水準，但說或寫加泰隆語的能力很低或完全沒有。

簡報 10

　　我要強調的第二項計畫是志願語言計畫，即 VxL（Voluntariat per la llengua）。

　　該計畫旨在促進於人際關係中使用加泰隆語。如何做？在最基本的方法中，VxL 將通常說加泰隆語的人（志願者）與另一位具基本知識的人（學習者）媒合。

　　這組語言夥伴將在輕鬆的氣氛下至少見面十個小時，旨在將加泰隆語融入自然日常活動，並促進學習者的工作或社交關係。

　　該計畫已隨著時間而發展。該計畫於 15 年前開始實施，其成功案例一直穩定增加。過去八年，語言夥伴的數量每年都維持於 10,000 組以上，自該計畫開始以來，已建立 130,000 組。這引領此類計畫逐步推出，目前，甚至在公司、監獄或宗教中心等不同領域都有媒合。觀察最初的學習者最後如何成為志願者尤其令人欣慰。

簡報 11

　　我要說的第三個也是最後一個行動是社會語言認知課程。我會用另一個親身經驗做例子。因為我的英文水準充其量也只是普普，有一位老師協助我寫這篇講稿。通常我們會在我的辦公室碰面，但有一天我們約在咖啡廳。我點飲料時用的是加泰隆語，但女服務生以西班牙語回答。而我的老師以明顯英國口音的西班牙語點咖啡時，女服務生卻以英文回答。我覺得女服務生把握每個機會練習英文真的很好——我也會這麼做，因為我這一代的加泰隆尼亞人對自己的英文水準有點自卑——但身為客人，如果我的語言選擇沒有得到回應，我會感到失望且不悅，而當女服務生努力適應說英語者的母語時，就會更加失望且不悅了。以美食術語來說，我會覺得好像菜送上來的時候都已經涼掉了。

　　為避免這類狀況，聯盟開設了社會語言認知指導課程。這類課程為期很短，通常只有兩到四小時，針對不同族群——醫療人員、接觸一般大眾的工作人員、運動監控員等。不論哪個族群，我們試圖傳達的訊息一直沒變：成為更好的專業人員，更適當地服務客人或使用者，尊重對方的語言選擇很重要，因此要使用對方對你說的語言。

簡報 12

　　最後，我想談談我們最近將面臨的挑戰。

　　第一個是我們正在做的，增加新進成年移民的語言知識。這部分人沒有上過加

泰隆語學校，因此進入勞動市場的選擇比母語人士少，因為其當地語言（尤其是加泰隆語）知識方面的能力較低。但我們有一個很大的困難：聚焦於這個族群的語言技能很難，因為系統最多「帶你」（如前述）45 小時，之後便只能取決於個人深化自己語言知識的意願了。再加上西班牙語已成為本地人和移民間以及移民彼此間之關係的語言，預期這一族群間的加泰隆語知識在未來數十年仍將很低。

成年移民人口占據勞動市場的幾個地方：許多人集中於通常與食物相關的小型社區商店或當地街角商店，但他們也出現於公司中，還有其他在衛生部門。另一個明顯的挑戰是，工作中面對一般大眾的所有人必須至少具備加泰隆語和西班牙語的能力。

第二個挑戰是逆轉趨同西班牙語的規則。讓我用個人生活中第三個也是最後一個實例說明，我希望各位會覺得很有趣。

我有一位來自日本的朋友，我們一起在巴塞隆納攻讀博士。當時她的加泰隆語很好，但西班牙語不太流利。她現在兩種語言都完全沒問題。有一次，她邀請我品嘗些美味的日本料理。我們先在一家麵包店買了些點心。發生了件奇怪的事情：一位年輕日本移民女孩用加泰隆語說話，而巴塞隆納當地的店員卻用西班牙語回答。即使她繼續用加泰隆語交談，因為那是她最自在的語言，但店員選擇回應的語言一直只有西班牙語。

我眼看著劇情的展開，並注意到店員明顯的加泰隆語口音，讓我幾乎可以斷定她會說加泰隆語。因此我決定打斷他們的談話，並以加泰隆語和店員溝通。她有什麼反應呢？她以加泰隆語回我。在歷史上，加泰隆尼亞政府透過制度運動，提倡不改變懂加泰隆語但不會說加泰隆語的人的語言。這種語言行為存在於加泰隆尼亞社會但僅少數，普遍的行為則是語言趨同，尤其是有移民參與對話時，趨同於西班牙語。由於此策略並未成功，我認為有必要聚焦於尚未探索的預設使用加泰隆語的構想。在這麼做的時候，該人可以表示自己在語言上可以配合，因為在加泰隆尼亞普遍都懂西班牙語，且以加泰隆語互動的數量可能大幅成長，因此移民能有更多機會說加泰隆語，並更容易融入我們的社會。

第三個挑戰是重新定義或定義語言在多語社會中的地位。如前所述，加泰隆尼亞有兩種歷史語言——加泰隆語和阿蘭奧克西唐語——目前相對於西班牙語處於下級地位。加泰隆尼亞政府一直致力於平衡局面，最終目標是讓加泰隆語成為加泰隆尼亞的偏好語言。但這必須透過保證（正如目前所做的）西班牙語的完整正式知識

（非正式的知識以現行語言條件保證）。

對加泰隆尼亞人而言，西班牙語是一種非常珍貴的語言資源：

西班牙語是最廣為人知的語言；是在加泰隆尼亞本身廣泛使用的語言；是讓我們能與全球超過 5 億說西班牙語的人進行交流的語言。主張「停止學習西班牙語」的族群目前在加泰隆尼亞僅為極少數。但西班牙語的力量非常強大，因此有必要定義語言角色，以避免西班牙語對加泰隆語或阿蘭奧克西唐語造成影響。

第四個也是最後一個挑戰是在加泰隆語仍屬少數人語言的地區重振使用加泰隆語。例如，巴塞隆納的酒吧和餐廳中只有 48% 的員工會說加泰隆語；或例如電視，加泰隆語的可用頻道數量低於 20%；或例如司法行政，以加泰隆語書寫法院裁決的甚至不到 9%。

簡報 13

非常感謝您的聆聽。

承蒙您！（Shin-mung ngi!）

Moltes gràcies ！

【法國布列塔尼語 Breton】

布列塔尼語：從復振到重新本地語化
Breton : From Revitalisation to Revernacularization

法國布列塔尼大區雷恩大學 Stefan Moal 教授

客語及少數族群語言復振國際研討會
**International Conference on Revitalization of the Hakka Language
and Minority Languages, Taipei, 16 December 2018**
會議議程

1

Breton : from revitalisation
to revernacularization

Stefan Moal, university of Rennes, Brittany

2

Minority ? A highly relative term

French is a **majority** language in France and in Québec **but** it is a **minority** language in north-western Italy (Val d'Aoste), in the USA (Louisiana, New-England) and in Canada, with various degrees of legal protection.

It even happens to English to be a **minority** language : for example in Québec and in Cameroon.

Most Catalan speakers would reject the term '**minority** language' when applied to their situation : they may be a linguistic minority within the borders of the Kingdom of Spain but they consider themselves to be the **language majority in Catalonia**.

Breton however is definitely a **minority** – or rather **minoritized** – language, both in France at large and within the territory of Brittany.

3

French speaking minorities in the US

English speaking minority in Cameroon

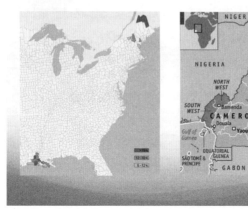

4

Language policy : the choice of terms does matter

Heritage language ? Ethnic ? Autochtonous ? Indigenous ? Aboriginal ? Vernacular ?
Minority ? Minoritized ? National ? Regional ? Local ? Languages of France ? Languages of Taiwan ?

Language attrition ? Death ? Documentation ? Reclamation ? Revival ? Maintenance ?
Revitalization ? Revernacularization ? Reversing language shift ? Normalization ?

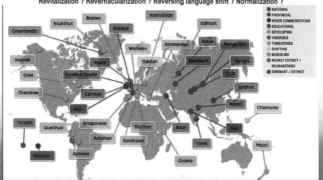

5

Language revitalization : Latin *vīta* ("life").
An attempt to halt or reverse the decline of a language (or to revive an extinct one). It may involve linguists, cultural or community groups, local authorities or governments.

Language revernacularization : Latin *vernāculus*
("domestic, indigenous") from *verna* ("native, home-born").
An attempt to make a language become again the everyday speech or dialect, including colloquialisms, as opposed to just a heritage, cultural, literary or liturgical language.

Brittany and Breton within the French territory and linguistic landscape

- 34 000 km2 (Taiwan 36 000 km2)
- 4,6 M inhabitants (Taiwan 23,6 M)

Germanic languages, romance languages, Basque + Breton, the only continental celtic language

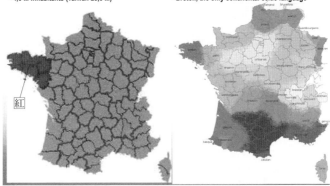

Breton: a language without an official status

- 'The language of the Republic is French' : the first alinea was added on June 25th, 1992, to Article 2 of the Constitution of 1958, to counter the hegemony of English. The Minister for Justice certified before the Chamber of Deputies and the Senate that this would not be detrimental to the regional languages, but it has been, on many occasions.

- The Council of Europe's **European Charter for Regional or Minority Languages was signed by France on May 7th, 1999, but it has not been ratified**. The Constitutional Council declared on June 15th, 1999, that ratifying the Charter would contravene the constitutional principles of indivisibility of the Republic, equality before the law, unicity of the French people and official usage of the French language. The Council of State confirmed this judgement in 2013, and pronounced again a negative advice to ratification on July 30th, 2015.

- Meanwhile, Article 75-1, added in 2008, acknowledges that **regional languages belong to France's heritage**. This does not give them any kind of official status however. The only official language, including in overseas territories, is still French.

- In 2004, **the Regional Council of Brittany** voted unanimously to declare that Breton and Gallo were « **languages of Brittany** » but France is a centralized state, not a federation of regions, so this regional declaration is merely symbolic and does not carry any official value.

The European Charter for Regional or Minority Languages

Signed and ratified: dark green. Signed but not ratified: light green.
Neither signed nor ratified: white. Non-member states: grey.

9

Breton :
a Celtic language

10

**The six Celtic
countries today**

深綠

Scotland

Wales

Ireland

The Isle of Man
(located between Ireland,
Scotland, Wales and
northern England)

Cornwall
(far south-western
corner of England)

Brittany
(far western
corner of France)

11

Celtic expansion, the classic (and still prevailing) view:

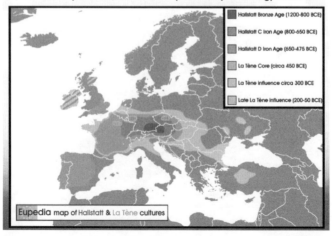

12

Celtic expansion, a newer alternative theory :

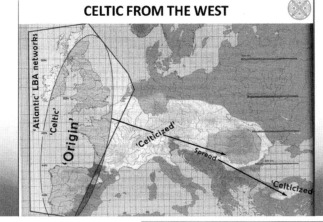

13

Migrations from Britain to Armorica (former name of Brittany)

3rd - 6th century AD

14

Breton amidst the other Celtic languages

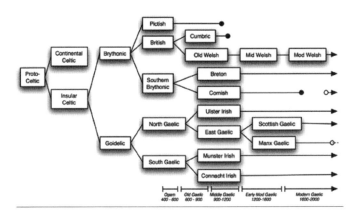

15

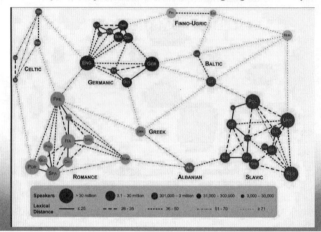

Lexical proximity / distance between languages of Europe

16

The Celtic Family					
	Welsh	**Cornish**	**Breton**	**Irish**	**Gaelic**	**Manx**
Family	Teulu	Teylu	Familh	Teaghlach	Teaghlach	Mooinjer
Father	Tad	Tas	Tad	Athair	Athair	Ayr
Mother	Mam	Mamm	Mamm	Máthair	Màthair	Moir
Parents	Rhieni	Kerens	Kerent	Tuisti	Pàrantan	Ayr as Moir
Son	Mab	Mab	Mab	Mac	Mac	Mac
Daughter	Merch	Myrgh	Merc'h	Iníon	Nighean	Inneen
Children	Plant	Flehes	Bugale	Páisti	Clann	Cloan
Brother	Brawd	Broder	Breur	Deartháir	Bràthair	Braar
Sister	Chwaer	Hwor	C'hoar	Deirfiúr	Piuthar	Shuyr
Husband	Gwr	Gour	Pried	Fear Céile	Feas Pòsda	Dooinney
Wife	Gwraig	Gwreg	Gwreg	Bean (Chéile)	Bean Phósda	Ben
Grandfather	Taid / Tad-cu	Tas Gwynn	Tad-kozh	Seanathair	Seanair	Shaner
Grandmother	Nain / Mam-gu	Mamm Wynn	Mamm-gozh	Seanmháthair	Seanmhair	Shenn Voir

17

Speakers of Celtic languages today

STATUS OF THE CELTIC LANGUAGES IN THE 21ST CENTURY

Speakers of a Celtic Language
- > 10%
- > 15%
- > 20%
- > 25%
- > 30%
- > 40%
- > 50%

Scottish Gaelic (2011)
57,000 speakers
1.1% of Scotland's Population

Manx (2011)
Extinct ~1975, 2nd language revival; 1,650 speakers*
1.9% of Isle of Man's Population

Irish Gaelic (2011)
94,000 speakers*
1.5% of Ireland (inc. NI)'s Population

Welsh (2011)
562,000 speakers
19.0% of Wales' Population

Cornish
Extinct ~1800, 2nd language revival; possibly 100s
<1% of Cornwall's Population

Breton (2007)
210,000
6.7% of Brittany's Population

*Only regular speakers, does not include those who use it solely in education system

Gaelic :
Ireland *vs* Scotland.
Language policy
does matter...

...but
knowing
the language
does not mean
speaking
the language.

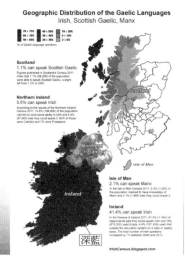

Geographic Distribution of the Gaelic Languages
Irish, Scottish Gaelic, Manx

% of Gaelic language speakers

Scotland
1.1% can speak Scottish Gaelic
Figures published in Scotland's Census 2011 show that 1.1% (58,000) of the population were able to speak Scottish Gaelic, a slight fall from 1.2% in 2001.

Northern Ireland
5.6% can speak Irish
According to the results of the Northern Ireland Census 2011, 10.6% (184,900) of the population claimed to have some ability in Irish and 5.6% (97,600) said they could speak it. 90% of those were Catholic and 7% were Protestant.

Isle of Man
2.1% can speak Manx
In the Isle of Man Census 2011, 2.3% (1,650) of the population claimed to have knowledge of Manx and 2.1% (1,660) said they could speak it.

Ireland
41.4% can speak Irish
In the Census of Ireland 2011, 41.4% (1.78m) of respondents said they could speak Irish and 14% (613,000) used it daily. 4.4% (187,600) used Irish outside the education system on a daily or weekly basis. The total number of Irish speakers increased by 7% between 2006 and 2011.

IrishCensus.blogspot.com

深藍

Other aspects of Breton culture, music, dance, wrestling : maintenance / revival have been more successful than language related efforts.

Breton dancing : from tradition to folklore and public performance

21

From near extinction in the 1930s
to reappropriation since the 1970s.
From rural to urban :
the fest-noz,
a popular traditional dance event
(added by UNESCO in 2012 to the
Representative List of the Intangible
Cultural Heritage of Humanity).

Festoù-noz can be enormous : 8000 dancers
in Rennes at Yaouank (« young ») every year…

… or local and small (here in my hometown).

There is even a cyber fest-noz
for the Breton diaspora !

22

Main areas of traditional Breton dance styles (simplified)

■ Gavotte
■ An-dro
■ Tour, pilé-menu
■ Dañs Leon
■ Dañs Treger
■ Dañs plin
■ Rond
　Avant-deux (dominant)

23

The Goadeg sisters in the late 1960s

The Goadeg sisters and Alan Stivell

The transmission and evolution of traditional dance singing

Manu Kerjean & Erik Marchand

Erik Marchand & Krismenn

Krismenn & Alem

The biniou + bombarde
(bagpipes + oboe) traditional duo :
moribund in the 1930s…

…but utterly reappropriated
and popular today.

Traditional use of musical instruments in Brittany

Gouren :
the folk
wrestling
of Brittany

intergenerational and popular…

… also
interceltic /
international

27

The Breton language : background

28

Lower Brittany (west) traditionally Breton-speaking
Upper Brittany (east) traditionally Romance-speaking

29

Evolution of the diglossic situation
in Lower-Brittany, 1864-1997

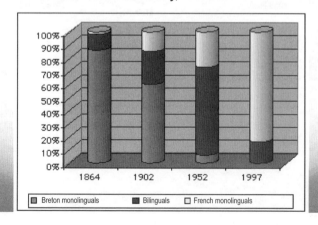

Languages received at home, by age group, in the three *départements* of Western Brittany

(source: INSEE National Statistics Institute, 1999)

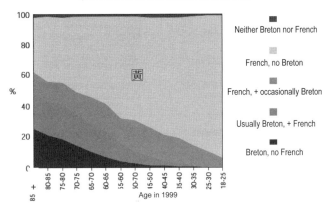

- Neither Breton nor French
- French, no Breton
- French, + occasionally Breton
- Usually Breton, + French
- Breton, no French

% / Age in 1999

Declining community of Breton speakers / growing general population in Brittany

(sources: 1886 Sébillot estimation, 1928 Hemon estimation, 1952 Gourvil estimation, 1983 RBO survey, 1991 TMO survey, 1997 TMO survey, 2018 TMO / Region survey)

	Estimated population of Breton speakers	Total population of Brittany
1886	1 982 300	3 137 000
1928	1 158 000	3 063 000
1952	700 000	3 072 000
1983	604 000	3 703 000
1991	250 000	3 848 000
1997	240 000	4 037 000
2018	207 000	4 660 000

- Written Breton can be traced back to the 8th or 9th century AD, but we don't have extensive ancient texts as compared to Irish or Welsh. A rich oral literature prevailed until the late 19th century, with the exception of texts for Catholic edification.

- Two written standards (Northwestern + Southern dialects) from the 17th to early 20th century. Unified written standard nowadays, taking all dialects into account as best as possible.

- Up to the end of the 19th century, virtually everybody spoke Breton in Lower-Brittany. Rural and maritime populations were monolingual Breton speakers. The clergy and the bourgeoisie were bilingual by necessity, so was the local gentry.

- From the school laws (1881-83) to World War II : everybody gradually became bilingual. Breton was banned from schools (ban included punishment) and strictly kept to private use, except for Catholic preaching.

- World War I and its social consequences had a great impact. The economic interest of knowing French became more obvious : civil service, emigration to Paris.

- It became desirable, fashionable to speak French, especially for young women. Self-deprecation – if not self-hatred in some cases – got internalized.

- During the post-World War II decade, family transmission of Breton litterally collapsed. Until then, Breton was, of all six Celtic languages, the most commonly spoken on a daily basis.

33

Languages spoken in France: rate of father to child transmission within a generation

Percentage of fathers who have not *usually* spoken to their 5 year old children the language that their own father had *usually* spoken to them at that age

Breton: the second worse case

(source: INSEE National Statistics Institute, 1999)

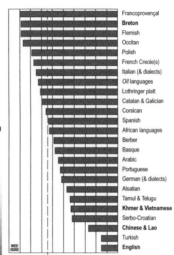

34

Today's situation and prospects

35

Can you speak Breton ? (very well / quite well)
(source : TMO / Regional Council of Brittany sociolinguistic survey, 2018)

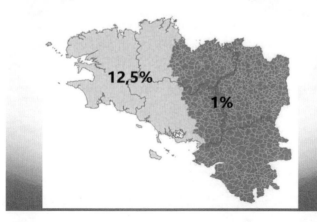

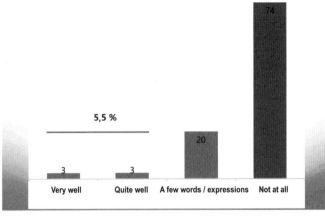

Can you speak Breton ? Estimation : 207 000 speakers 36
(source : TMO / Regional Council of Brittany sociolinguistic survey, 2018)

Can you speak Breton ? 37
(very well + quite well)

Rate of speakers :

-by municipal population

-in the three big cities :
Rennes, Nantes, Brest

-by type of area : urban, suburban, rural

(source : TMO / Regional Council of Brittany sociolinguistic
survey, 2018)

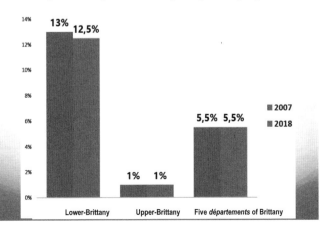

Can you speak Breton ? (very well / quite well) 2007 / 2018 38
(source : TMO / Regional Council of Brittany sociolinguistic survey, 2018)

39

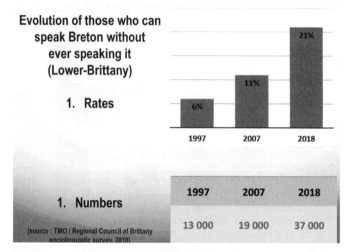

Evolution of those who can speak Breton without ever speaking it (Lower-Brittany)

1. Rates

	1997	2007	2018
			21%
		11%	
	6%		

	1997	**2007**	**2018**
1. Numbers	13 000	19 000	37 000

(source : TMO / Regional Council of Brittany sociolinguistic survey, 2018)

40

Frequency of use by age group
(source : TMO / Regional Council of Brittany sociolinguistic survey, 2018)

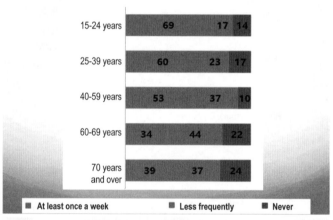

	At least once a week	Less frequently	Never
15-24 years	69	17	14
25-39 years	60	23	17
40-59 years	53	37	10
60-69 years	34	44	22
70 years and over	39	37	24

■ At least once a week　■ Less frequently　■ Never

41

No other choice but to count on schools

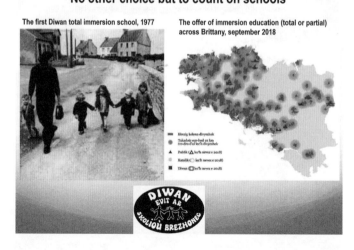

The first Diwan total immersion school, 1977

The offer of immersion education (total or partial) across Brittany, september 2018

42

Evolution of the number of pupils
in Breton-French bilingual education
(Source : Breton Language Public Office, 2018)

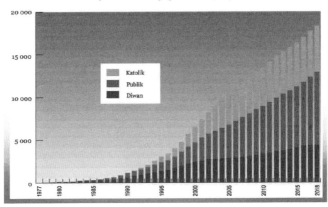

43

Main mode of acquisition
by age group
(source : TMO / Regional Council of Brittany sociolinguistic survey, 2018)

- Family transmission
- Formal education
- Self-taught

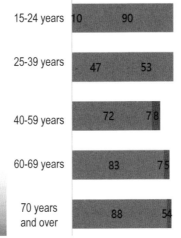

44

Age pyramid of all Breton speakers
(source : TMO / Regional Council of Brittany sociolinguistic survey, 2018)

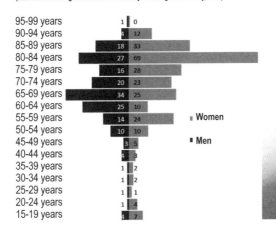

45

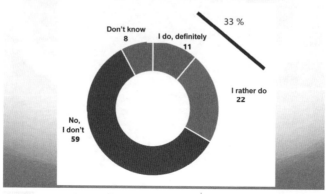

Scope for much greater development of Breton education :

Do you wish your children knew / would have known Breton ?

Basis : all parents with children over two years and whose children can't speak Breton.
(source : TMO / Regional Council of Brittany sociolinguistic survey, 2018)

33 %

Don't know
8

I do, definitely
11

I rather do
22

No,
I don't
59

46

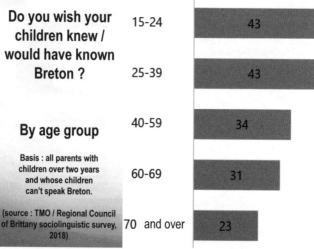

Do you wish your children knew / would have known Breton ?

By age group

Basis : all parents with children over two years and whose children can't speak Breton.

(source : TMO / Regional Council of Brittany sociolinguistic survey, 2018)

15-24 · 43
25-39 · 43
40-59 · 34
60-69 · 31
70 and over · 23

47

Do you wish your children knew / would have known Breton ?
Results by origin : Brittany / outside Brittany

Basis : all parents with children over two years and whose children can't speak Breton.
(source : TMO / Regional Council of Brittany sociolinguistic survey, 2018)

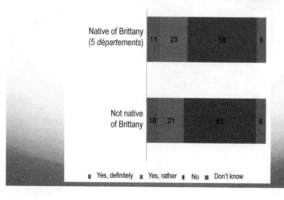

Native of Brittany
(5 départements) · 11 · 23 · 58 · 8

Not native
of Brittany · 10 · 21 · 61 · 8

■ Yes, definitely ■ Yes, rather ■ No ■ Don't know

Breton language education : some facts and issues

48

- Diwan created in 1977 modelled on the Basque ikastola and Irish gaelsoileanna.

- Followed by State schools 1984, Catholic schools 1990 : partial immersion, 50%-50%.

- Need to develop pre-kindergarten care : creches in Breton now developing.

- New terminology had to be created for all school subjects, especially in secondary education. Grassroot operation, by secondary schooll teachers on their free time.

- Teacher recruitment and training still a major issue : structural shortage.

- Continuation into secondary education is problematic : loss of students.

- Figures are still very low in percentage of the total school population : about 3%.

- Effective use of the Breton by the youth, between themselves, outside the education system is not as common as it could, even when they are attached to the language.

Do you wish you knew / would have known Breton yourself ?

49

Basis : non-speakers.
(source : TMO / Regional Council of Brittany sociolinguistic survey, 2018)

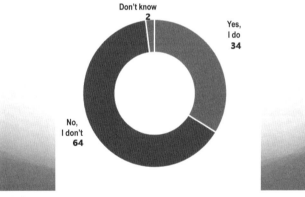

Don't know
2

Yes,
I do
34

No,
I don't
64

Adult learners : over 5000.

50

Most of them attend weekly night classes : 3200 registered.

Over 500 persons have attended a week-long course.

900 a one-day or week-end course.

Intensive training sessions of 6 to 9 months : 380 people, the majority of them job-seekers. Courses taken in charge financially by the Regional Council of Brittany.

Professionnal language trainers for adults : 80 (60 full-time jobs).

Pour une société bilingue à la fin du XXIe siècle

Deskiñ d'An Oadourien   DAO

Objective within the next 15 years : manage to train 5000 adult speakers yearly.

51

Wish there was « more Breton » ? Are you in favour of :
(source : TMO / Regional Council of Brittany sociolinguistic survey, 2018)

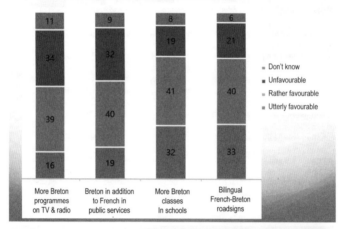

- Don't know
- Unfavourable
- Rather favourable
- Utterly favourable

More Breton programmes on TV & radio	Breton in addition to French in public services	More Breton classes In schools	Bilingual French-Breton roadsigns
11	9	8	6
34	32	19	21
39	40	41	40
16	19	32	33

52

Ongoing roadsign campaign since the mid-1980s

53

The Breton Language Public Office
Ofis Publik ar Brezhoneg is a public organization created in 2010, mostly financed by the Regional Council of Brittany.

Staff is limited : 25 full-time positions. However it is the strongest of all offices of the kind in France, together with the Basque language office.

Prior to this the Breton Language Office existed as an association / fundation.

OFIS PUBLIK
AR BREZHONEG

OFFICE PUBLIC
**DE LA LANGUE
BRETONNE**

emglev an 21vet kantved
Ya
d'ar brezhoneg

Ya d'ar brezhoneg / Yes to Breton.
A Language Office initiative. Designed for local companies and firms, sport associations, cultural fundations, municipalities, etc.

They sign a charter stipulating a series of practical commitments in favour of the use of Breton.

Since several levels of charters are offered, each organization can decide to sign again later for another series of more demanding commitments once their initial goals have been achieved.

54

Ar Redadeg
(Run together)

• An idea borrowed initially from the Basques...
...and now being imitated across western Europe.

• A 10-day, round the clock, relay race operation,
every second year, with lots of Breton language
events along the way.

• An inclusive, festive, popular way of celebrating
the language even for non-speakers while raising
funds for various Breton related projects (each
kilometer is "bought" individually or collectively)

• Towns now compete to be chosen as the arrival
locality. A festival is organised. On this occasion,
the message hidden inside the relay stick is
disclosed and read to the audience.

55

Identity / sense of belonging
Would you say you feel you are :
(source : TMO / Regional Council of Brittany sociolinguistic survey, 2018)

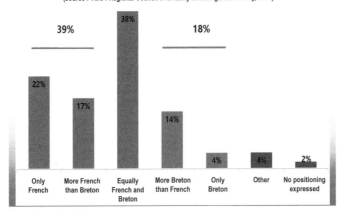

56

Identity / sense of belonging and languages
Would you say you feel you are :
(source : TMO / Regional Council of Brittany sociolinguistic survey, 2018)

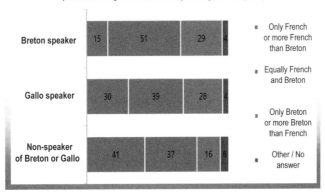

Pathways for future language policy measures

- The support for more Breton in the media, education, public services and roadsigns ranges from 55% to 73% : legitimacy.
  ➢ these policies should be reinforced.

- The wish one's children knew Breton is widespread across Brittany.
  ➢one can not be happy with 3% of Breton-medium education.

- A resumption of family transmission is essential, but still uncertain.
  ➢it should be openly encouraged and promoted by Regional authorities.

- The language / identity link proves relatively strong.
  ➢the Regional Council of Brittany should build on this.

- Regular sociolinguistic surveys are needed in Brittany.
  ➢if only in order to monitor the effects of language policy efforts.

- Breton will have to operate its "digital ascension" (Apps, interfaces, social media, etc) before long : costly, time-consuming and depending on the GAFAs.
  ➢the threat of "digital death" is looming, as is the case for many languages.

Trugarez !

Briefing 1

Thank you very much. I want to thank the organization for such a perfect conference. From way back when I was first contacted, everything has been really perfect and the welcome has been warm.

I realize that it's a formidable challenge to be the last speaker on this floor on a Sunday afternoon, when everybody's probably thinking of doing other things. So, I'm going to try to entertain you while informing you about the Breton situation, which is very different from the Catalan situation, unfortunately.

Briefing 2

As we were just told now, a minority can be a whole lot of different things. Even the French language can be a minority language, as it is in Louisiana or in Italy. Even English can be a minority language. You've probably heard about Cameroon, for example, where English is a minoritized language.

Most Catalan speakers, but I'm not going to repeat that after a Catalan, would not consider themselves a minority anymore, if ever they have, because they are the language majority of Catalonia. It may be different in Valencia, in the northern part of Catalonia on French territory. But certainly, in the main part of Catalonia around Barcelona, that's the case.

Breton, however, I must say, is definitely a minority, or rather minoritized, language—because words are important. Minoritized both in France at large but also within its own territory.

Briefing 3

This is the map. The one on the left is not very good. It's very white, but just a map of Cameroon to show you that English, even English can be a minority language.

Briefing 4

Now, words matter. Mr. Carles de Rosselló mentioned the word "normalization", and I wish we could use it in Brittany.

It's far too early yet to talk about normalization. Normalization on the other side of the Pyrenees in the Iberian Peninsula means a normal use of your language in everyday situations, which is very different from normativization or whatever you call it, which means making a standard for the language and written standards and everything.

But words do matter, and this is why the title to my paper today is "re-vernacularization", which means really making your language again the language of every task and every feeling on an everyday basis, because revitalization is not enough, as you will see in the Breton case.

This morning, for example, when we heard the Ainu presentation, we could see that it was more like documentation than proper revitalization or re-vernacularization. But for example, look at the words at the top here, you know, are you prepared to call your language a minority language or a minoritized language?

The French government likes to speak about the languages of France, and there was a heated debate earlier on about what the languages of Taiwan are. But I'm not going to go into that.

Briefing 5

So, what's the difference between revitalization and re-vernacularization?

Revitalization is an attempt to halt or reverse the decline of a language or to revive an extinct language, like in the Cornish case. It may involve linguists, cultural or community groups, local authorities, or governments.

But re-vernacularization of a vernacular, domestic, indigenous, native language is to make a language become again the everyday speech or dialect, including colloquialisms, as opposed to just a heritage cultural literary or even liturgical language.

Briefing 6

Now, France. I've skipped the map of Europe because Carles showed it to us earlier on.

You have Brittany here in red, on the very western tip of Franceinto the Atlantic Ocean.

The size of Brittany is roughly that of Taiwan, but of course, the population is much smaller—about a fifth of your own population.

And on the right-hand side, you've got a map of France as you probably never saw it until now, because France likes to think about itself as a monolingual country. They wish it was, and they certainly have done everything for it to happen. But to this day, there are languages of very differentIndo-European families, and even one non-Indo-European language, namely, Basque, that are spoken on the French continent and territories and Corsica, and this is without mentioning of course the overseas territories that France still has all over the world—in the Americas and in the Pacific Ocean, where of course lots of local aboriginal languages are spoken.

Now you have Breton at the very west of Brittany, but you have also Germanic languages, Flemish, dialects of German; you have Catalan, and you have Occitan of course, and Corsican, which is very close to Italian.

Briefing 7

Now, as you have probably heard, there is no status whatsoever for any language in France apart from the French language.

That's just the long and the short of it; there's not much to be said about it anymore.

"The language of the Republic is French" was added to Article Two of the Constitution.

So, it just shows you how high in the Constitution it is, and that was to counter the hegemony of English.

But of course, it hasn't served very much for this; however, it has served in the courts repeatedly, to the detriment of so-called regional languages.

Briefing 8

France hasn't ratified the European charter for regional languages. They had signed it but the Council of State repeatedly on two occasions in 2013 and 2015 decided that was against the Constitution.

So, all we have is a little ridiculous article that acknowledges regional languages as a part of France's heritage. I personally don't care very much about heritage when it comes to languages; I care a lot more about use.

This doesn't give us any official status. The only official language, including in overseas territories, is still French. Now we have the Regional Council of Brittany.

I was talking to Meri this morning—Meri Huws from Wales—and telling her that the budget of our Regional Council of Brittany is not even 1/20th of the budget of the Welsh Assembly.

So, it gives you an idea of how much they can do and not do because France is an extremely centralized country.

Briefing 9

They declared Breton, the Celtic language, and Gallo, which is a romance language in the east of Brittany, to be the languages of Brittany.

But this is merely symbolic. It doesn't give us any official value in court or in legislation.

Briefing 10

This is a map of the countries that have signed and ratified the European Charter for Minority Languages.

You have the ratifying states in dark green and France, which signed but didn't ratify.

Breton is a Celtic language. You have six countries today, from Scotlandin the north to Brittany in the south. Scotland for example is not completely Celtic at this stage. It was way back in the Middle Ages, but it's not at the moment.

A lot of Scottish people wouldn't describe themselves as Celts, but in Ireland for example and Wales they certainly would, and many Bretons would also recognize themselves as part of the Celtic world. Now the other two languages, Manx on the Isle of Man and Cornwall, have disappeared from everyday use, but they've been revived during the late 20th century and are still in the process of being revived.

Briefing 11

Now I'll just give you a quick glimpse at what we think the Celtic expansion could have been.

This is the classic view, that in the bronze age after the Indo-Europeans arrived in Europe, there was a sort of cultural nest in Central Europe—in Bavaria, Austria, and Bohemia—and that from there the Celtic influence then moved west and east as far away as the Iberian Peninsula and even today's Turkey.

Briefing 12

But there's also a new alternative theory that Celticmoved from the west. It's still a theory, but maybe the origin would have been on the Atlantic seaboard, including the northwest of Spain, for example—today's Spain, and the expansion would have gone eastwards instead of westward.

Now the origin of this theory is the fact that there's a language that has been discovered on gravestones in the south of Portugal and Andalusia. It looks like it is a Celtic language. It hasn't been proved 100 percent, but it's older than what was found in central Europe, and it looks like it is Celtic.

Briefing 13

The Breton language in Brittany is the result of the recent celticization, so to speak, of a part of the continent by migrations at the very end of antiquity or the very beginning of the Middle Ages, between the third and sixth century.

Part of our ancestors came from what is now Wales, Cornwall, Devon, and the north of England, or else Cumbria, and they came to establish themselves especially in the west of Brittany.

Briefing 14

Breton, therefore, is one of the Celtic languages. Breton is here.

It's very close to Welsh, which we heard about yesterday, modern Welsh and Cornish. It's a cousin language of Gaelic here, and Irish as well.

Briefing 15

You can see the distance and proximity between the languages of Europe. You've got clusters here—the Germanic cluster, the Roman cluster, the Slavic cluster, and way to the northeast of my map, so to speak, you've got the Celtic languages together, but they are quite remote from each other really, in terms of the lexicon, much more remote from each other than, for example, the romance languages together.

These words show you the two Celtic branches: a branch on the left-hand side with Welsh, Cornish, and Breton, and the Gaelic branch on the right-hand side.

Words to say various things like son, mab, and mac show that they're from the same family.

Briefing 17

Now, the state of the Celtic languages in the 21st century.

You can see here that the concentration of speakers is really stronger in Wales than in any other part of the Celtic world.

In Scotland, it's in the northwest islands of the Outer Hebrides and the north western part of the highlands. In Ireland, when you talk about the everyday use of course, it's only the Gaeltacht—the small pockets of Irish-speaking populations in the west.

Briefing 18

I'll show you maps of Brittany later on in detail.

When we look at Gaelic in Ireland, versus Scotland, you see that language policy does matter because if Ireland is so blue it means that a lot of people declare that they can speak Irish. But as we know, knowing a language doesn't mean speaking the language.

Briefing 19

Other aspects of Breton culture.

We saw some aspects of aboriginal culture yesterday, like dance and music, which have somehow proved much easier to maintain or to revive. Music, dance, wrestling :the efforts to revive or maintain those parts of our culture have been much more successful.

Briefing 20

For example, Breton dancing. If you ever come to Brittany you'll see that it moves from tradition to folklore and public performance, but then again it moves back into the people's lives, and you have enormous festivals where people dance traditional dances.

Briefing 21

And they're very young, and very with it, and very in. You know, it's not something that is old-fashioned or anything like that. As many as eight thousand dancers dancing together sometimes. The photograph here is in my own hometown.

I live in a small fishing harbor in the west of Brittany, so there's only about 200 to 300 of us dancing together.

There's even a cyber fest noz, or dance festival, for the Breton diasporathat happens once a year in cyberspace.

Briefing 22

These are just to show you the diversity of dances in Brittany.

Briefing 23

Singing is the same.

At the bottom of this slide, you can see that the singer with the cap on learned from an older singer, and then he taught a younger singer. The younger singer is now singing with a rapper from Lyon actually, near the French Alps. It's still danceable singing music to which you can also dance traditional dances.

Briefing 24-26

The same with the bagpipes and oboe, this style was nearly extinct in the 1930s, but now, it's been completely reappropriated and is popular today. Everybody learns it, and a lot of young people learn it and listen to it.

Wrestling is the same. Wrestling is quite popular as well, and it's even gone into the Celtic internationals, and there are championships for backhold and Breton wrestling.

Briefing 27-28

But the language is a different story, sadly.

Here's the map of Brittany. We have dialects, much more so than the Welsh language has.

We have four historical dialects, so to speak, but the situation is of course more complicated than that. You know that there are isoglosses, but you don't usually jump over a river and it's a different dialect. That's not the way it happens; it's very gradual.

And in the east of Brittany, you have mostly French speakers, and the two big cities of Rennes and Nantes are outside of the historical Breton language heartland.

Briefing 29

This is the evolution of the diglossic situation in lower Brittany.

Lower Brittany is the west of Brittany, where historically the language was spoken, because in the east it was mostly Gallo or French that was spoken.

As you can see, in the 19th century, practically everybody was monolingual—Breton speaking—in the west of Brittany, and the situation hasn't changed much since 1997.

It shows you that it's the reverse situation that prevails today.

French monolinguals are the vast majority and everybody else is at least bilingual, if not trilingual.

Briefing 30

This is what happened with the language received at home by age groups in western Brittany.

You can see that French and not Breton, which is the yellow part, has gradually become the norm.

French plus occasional Breton has nearly disappeared, and the use of Breton and a little bit of French has basically disappeared.

It's only picking up again now.

And Breton without any French? That hasn't happened since maybe 50 or 60 years ago.

Briefing 31

Which gives you the figure, at the bottom of this slide, of an estimated 200,000 speakers today, out of 4.6 million people in Brittany.

So, when I was telling you that we are a minority within the minority, it's exactly this.

Briefing 32

The traces of written Breton are quite old.

The Breton language was written way back in the eighth or ninth century, but writing wasn't used very much.

We certainly don't have for example a biblical tradition like the Welsh have.

It was mostly a rich oral literature that prevailed.

As far as written standards are concerned, there used to be two, but now, since the mid-20th century, the two written standards have been brought together to form one written standard that is used in schools and the media.

Up to the 19th century, everybody spoke Breton in Lower Brittany, especially the rural and maritime populations. Even the clergy and the bourgeoisie were bilingual by necessity, and so was the local gentry.

It's really after the school laws and between the school laws and World War II that everybody gradually became bilingual, like we've heard so many times in your own situation in Taiwan and nearly everywhere. It was not as bad, I suppose, as in Spain during Franco times, but Breton was subtly banned from schools, and that included punishment. It was strictly kept to private use, except for Catholic preaching.

But what happened most of the time during the second half of the 20th century is that it became desirable and fashionable to speak French, especially for young women and young mothers. Self-deprecation and in some cases self-hatred became internalized, so the government didn't even have to do anything anymore because it had become internal. You were ashamed of your language and everything that had to do with your language.

And, during the post-World War II decade, family transmission practically collapsed in less than ten years.

Until then, Breton was, of all six languages in the Celtic world, the most commonly spoken by far, but it's not anymore.

Briefing 33

If you look at the top of this list of languages here, these are the languages spoken in France and the rate of father-to-child transmission within a generation.

It was done in 1999, so it's nearly 20 years ago, but I think it's still valid today.

You can see that Breton is the second-worst case of not being transmitted down to the next generation, whereas if you look at Chinese, for example, the Chinese in France or the Lao in France are not as good as the Turks and the English speakers, but they certainly try to pass down their language a lot better than what happened with Breton, Occitan, and Franco-Provençal.

Briefing 34-35

This is the newest regional survey, which was carried out in June of this year (2018). It was some event for us in Brittany because for the first time, the regional council of Brittany put money into having a proper survey done about the use of languages in Brittany, with a sample of over 8,500 people composed of all generations, professions, and genders, in a very scientific way.

This showed that in the west of Brittany, only 12 percent of the population speak Breton.

Briefing 36

When you look at that on five departments, it's six percent, but technically they had to put 5.5.This is the way statisticians count. Only three percent consider that they speak very well, and 74 percent don't speak Breton at all.

Briefing 37

It's mostly a small town or village language—a rural area language more than that used in urban areas.

Briefing 38

The stability between 2007 and 2018 surprised us somehow because we thought that because so many speakers die every day, it would have gone down, but apparently, it did not.

But the thing is, the evolution shows that those who can speak Breton without ever speaking it has grown.

Briefing 39

And it has grown steadily since, for the past 20 years.

This means that people know Breton, but because they're isolated, maybe in a big city or because their friends have died or maybe their spouse has died, they don't use the language anymore. It's only in their heads and nowhere else to be found.

Briefing 40

Now, a good result.

The good thing about this survey is that it showed us that among all generations, the ones who do have Breton and use it most are the younger generation, and this is very good.

As you can see, for the people who are from 60 to 69 years old and speak it at least once a week, only one person out of three speaks it once a week, whereas it's two people out of three that speak it once a week at least in the younger generation.

So that's good news for us. We have to concentrate on the good news because there isn't that much.

Briefing 41

You can understand that since the collapse was nearly complete in the 1950s, we have had no other choice but to count on the schools.

It's certainly not the best situation, but it was that or nothing else.

You have a photograph here, I find there's something really tender about the whole thing.

This is a school teacher with his fiddle in his hand who is going to school or maybe, I don't know, going to the sea or something like that, with the very first five children to attend a total immersion school in 1977.

As you can see, the sticker for those schools at the bottom of my slide here was not copied but was inspired by the photograph.

And on the right-hand side, you've got the offer of immersion education, either total or partial, across Brittany as of September18, 2019.

Back in 1977, a lot of politicians thought that these parents who asked for a school for their children totally through the medium of Breton were completely crazy, and that this would just disappear after a while when they'd come back to their senses, but actually, that's not what happened.

Breton-medium education has grown ever since.

Briefing 42

This is the growth since 1977.

As you can see, Catholic schools opened as well, and public schools did, too.

But sadly, these figures hide the fact that only three percent of the school population in Brittany are in those schools, which means that 97 percent are not in Breton-medium schools.

Briefing 43

The main mode of acquisition by age group. As you can see at the top of my slide here, when you're aged between 15 and 24 years, it's formal education that gives you Breton, more than any family transmission or self-teaching.

Briefing 44

This is the age pyramid, but look at the bottom. The bottom is small, of course. It's a small base, but it could be the beginning of something—picking up again from the younger generation.

Briefing 45

Now there is scope for much greater development for Breton.

Because, when you ask "Do you wish your children knew or could have known Breton?" you have 33 percent of people who say they would like or would have liked their children to know Breton, as compared to three percent in the schools, so there is plenty of scope normally for development.

Briefing 46

And the younger parents are more in favor of their children knowing Breton, so this is also comforting.

Briefing 47

Also, whether people were native of Brittany or not native of Brittany didn't make any difference in the wish for their children to know Breton.

This is a bit like the Catalan situation, whereby people come from outside of Brittany but still have no problem with their own children speaking Breton and learning Breton.

Briefing 48

Adults are very important as well. One adult in three wishes they would have known Breton themselves.

Briefing 49

So, what do we do?

Because children aren't enough, there are also adult learners, and over 5000 learners are learning the language at the moment. We have an organization.

As you can see in the middle here, intensive training sessions of six to nine months are taken in charge financially by the regional council of Brittany for job seekers, for example.

So this is very hopeful as well.

Briefing 51-52

The people in Brittany wish there was more Breton on TV, on the radio, in the public services, in schools, and on road signs as well.

You have a majority of people who are in favor of Breton, including in the non-Breton-speaking part of Brittany.

This is the road sign campaign, which has been going on since the mid-1980s.

It included having to blacken signs at night, which is an occupation that I must say I did myself as well when I was a student.

Briefing 54

Another example that can bring people together and bring support to the language is the run for the Breton language.

You have a map here that shows you the route of the ten-day around-the-clock relay race held every second year, with lots of Breton-language events all the way.

It's a very inclusive, festive, and popular way of celebrating the language, for non-speakers as well as speakers.

You buy a kilometer, and the money goes into organizing or fulfilling various

Breton-language-related projects.

Briefing 55

Now, identity. These will be my last two slides.

Identity in Brittany is felt in very different ways than it is in the rest of the Celtic countries.

Only about four percent of people consider themselves to be only Breton; fourteen percent feel they are more Breton than French, and thirty-eight percent feel they are equally French and Breton.

But then you have a lot of people who consider themselves to be only French—nearly one-quarter of the population.

Interestingly though, Breton speakers are much more likely to think of themselves as being either only Breton or equally French and Breton or more Breton than French.

The more you speak one of the two native languages of Brittany, the more you feel that you are equally Breton and French or more Breton than French.

Briefing 57

This is my conclusion. There must be pathways for future language policy measures because the support is so strong.

I think that the Regional Council of Brittany should reinforce all these policies for education, the media, and public services.

The fact that the wish children knew Breton is so widespread means one cannot be happy with three percent of Breton-medium education.

I just dropped some of the other things that you can read for yourself, but the last line I think is very important.

You know, in our situation today of digital civilization, Breton will have to operate digitally through apps, interfaces, social media, etc. before long.

It's costly and time consuming, and it depends a lot on the GAFAMs as well, but the threat of digital death is looming, as is the case for many languages.

Thank you very much.

Trugarez!

簡報 1

非常感謝。感謝貴單位舉辦如此完美的會議。從第一次有人接觸我開始，一切都很完美，也受到熱情歡迎。

我知道擔任星期天下午最後一位講者會是一大挑戰，每個人可能都在想著做其他事。因此我會試著娛樂大家，同時向大家介紹布列塔尼語的狀況，不幸的是，這與加泰隆語的狀況非常不同。

簡報 2

正如我們剛剛聽到的，少數民族可以是許多不同的事情。即使是法語也可能是少數民族語言，例如在路易斯安那州或義大利。甚至英語也可以是少數民族語言，例如你可能聽說過，英語在喀麥隆是一種少數民族語言。

我不打算在加泰隆尼亞人之後重複這一點，但大部分說加泰隆語的人已不再（即使曾經有過）認為自己是少數，因為在加泰隆尼亞他們所使用的是主要語言。法國領土上之加泰隆尼亞北部瓦倫西亞可能有所不同，但加泰隆尼亞在巴塞隆納附近的主要部分，狀況就是如此。

但我必須說，布列塔尼語絕對是一種少數族群語言，或更確切地說是遭受少數化的語言——因為文字很重要。不論是在整個法國，還是在其自己的領土內，都被少數化了。

簡報 3

這是地圖。左邊那個不太好，很白，不過只是一張喀麥隆的地圖，顯示出英語（即使是英語）也可能是少數民族語言。

簡報 4

現在，文字很重要。Mr. Carles de Rosselló 提到「正常化」一詞，我希望我們可以在布列塔尼用這個詞。

現在談正常化還太早。正常化在伊比利亞半島庇里牛斯山脈另一邊的意思是於日常生活中正常使用自己的語言，這與規範化（或您用來稱呼它的任何術語）截然不同，這表示對於語言和書面標準以及所有一切制定標準。

但是文字真的很重要，這就是為什麼我今天的論文標題是「重新本土化」，意思是讓自己的語言真正再次成為每天每一項任務和每一種感覺的語言，因為正如布

列塔尼語案例中看到的,只有振興還不足夠。

例如今天早上我們聽到阿伊努的簡報時,我們可以看到它比較像是文件紀錄而不是適當的振興或重新本土化。但例如,請看最上面的文字,您是否已準備好將自己的語言稱為少數民族語言或遭少數化的語言?

法國政府喜歡談法國的語言,而之前關於臺灣有哪些語言也曾激烈辯論。但我不打算深究。

簡報 5

那麼,振興和重新本土化究竟有什麼區別?

振興是嘗試停止或扭轉一種語言的衰落,或恢復一種已滅絕的語言,就像康瓦爾語的案例。可能涉及語言學家、文化或社區團體、地方當局或政府。

但方言、當地語言、原住民語言、本國語言的重新本土化則係指,讓一種語言再次成為日常語言或方言,包括口語,而不僅僅是一種傳統文化文學甚或禮儀語言。

簡報 6

現在看看法國。我跳過了歐洲地圖,因為 Carles 稍早之前已對我們展示過了。紅色的部分是布列塔尼,位於法國最西端深入大西洋。

布列塔尼的面積與臺灣差不多,但人口少很多——大約是臺灣人口的五分之一。

右邊是一張您可能從未見過的法國地圖,因為法國喜歡將自己視為單語國家。他們希望如此,而且當然已為此做了一切努力。但截至目前,在法國內陸和領土以及科西嘉島,一直都有非常不同的印歐語系語言,甚至還有一種非印歐語系語言(即巴斯克語),還有一點當然不用說,法國在世界各地仍有海外領土(美洲和太平洋),當然有許多當地原住民語言。

布列塔尼西部有布列塔尼語,但也有日耳曼語族、佛拉蒙語、德國方言;有加泰隆語,當然還有奧克西唐語和非常接近義大利語的科西嘉語。

簡報 7

現在,您可能已經聽說過,除了法語之外,法國的所有語言都沒有任何地位。總而言之,這方面沒什麼好說的。

憲法第二條增訂了「共和國的語言是法語」。

所以，這顯示了法語在憲法中的地位，其目的在於對抗英語的霸權。

但是，當然，在這方面並沒有太多助益；而只有一再於法庭發揮作用，犧牲了所謂的區域語言。

簡報 8

法國尚未批准歐洲區域語言憲章。他們已簽署該憲章，但國務委員會於 2013 年和 2015 年兩次裁定其違反憲法。

所以，我們所擁有的，只是一小段荒謬的條文，承認地方語言是法國遺產的一部分。就語言而論，我個人並不太關心遺產，而更關心使用。

這並沒有給我們任何官方地位。唯一的官方語言，包括在海外領土，仍然是法語。現在我們有布列塔尼區域委員會。

今天早上我與來自威爾斯的 Meri Huws 交談，並告訴她我們布列塔尼區域委員會的預算甚至還不到威爾斯議會預算的二十分之一。

因此，您可以大概知道他們能做什麼和不能做什麼，因為法國是一個非常集權的國家。

簡報 9

他們宣告布列塔尼語、凱爾特語以及高盧語（布列塔尼東部的羅曼語）為布列塔尼的語言。

但這只是象徵性的，在法庭或立法中並沒有任何官方價值。

簡報 10

這是已簽署並批准《歐洲少數民族語言憲章》的國家地圖。

深綠色代表已批准的國家，還有已簽署但未批准的法國。

布列塔尼語是一種凱爾特語。今天有六個國家，從北部的蘇格蘭到南部的布列塔尼。例如蘇格蘭現階段並未完全使用凱爾特語，可以追溯到中世紀，但目前不是。

很多蘇格蘭人不會說自己是凱爾特人，但在愛爾蘭和威爾斯就一定會，且許多布列塔尼人也會承認自己是凱爾特世界的一部分。現在其他兩種語言（曼島上的曼島語及康瓦爾語）已從日常使用中消失，但在 20 世紀後期已經恢復，且仍在繼續

振興。

簡報 11

現在向各位簡單介紹一下我們認為凱爾特語可以如何擴張。

這是很經典的觀點，在印歐人進入歐洲後的青銅器時代，中歐（巴伐利亞、奧地利和波希米亞）有一種文化巢，凱爾特語的影響從那裡向西和向東擴展到伊比利亞半島甚至到今天的土耳其。

簡報 12

但還有一個新的替代理論，認為凱爾特人是從西方遷移過來的。這還只是理論，但可能源自大西洋沿岸，包括例如西班牙西北部（今天的西班牙），且為向東擴張而非向西。

這個理論源自於在葡萄牙和安達盧西亞南部的墓碑上發現一種語言，看起來像是一種凱爾特語，雖然尚未 100% 證明，但比在中歐發現的更古老，看起來像是凱爾特文。

簡報 13

布列塔尼的布列塔尼語可以說是古代末期或中世紀初期（3 世紀至 6 世紀間）由移民造成部分大陸凱爾特化的結果。

我們的部分祖先來自現在的威爾斯、康瓦爾郡、德文郡和英格蘭北部或坎布里亞郡，他們大多在布列塔尼西部建立了自己的家園。

簡報 14

因此，布列塔尼語是一種凱爾特語。布列塔尼在這裡。

非常接近我們昨天提到的威爾斯語，現代威爾斯語和康瓦爾語。這是蓋爾語的表親語言，也是愛爾蘭語。

簡報 15

你可以看到歐洲語言之間的距離和接近程度。這裡有好幾個集群——日耳曼語集群、羅馬語集群、斯拉夫語集群，以及通往我地圖東北部的路，可以這麼說，我們將凱爾特語放在一起，但實際上它們彼此相距甚遠，就語彙而言，它們彼此之間的距離比羅曼語族還遠。

這些語詞對您展示了兩個凱爾特語分支：左側分支包括威爾斯語、康瓦爾語和布列塔尼語，右側是蓋爾語。

表示「兒子」、「mab」和「mac」等各種事物的語詞顯示他們來自相同語系。

簡報 17

這是凱爾特語在 21 世紀的狀態。

你可以從這裡看到，凱爾特語使用者在威爾斯的集中度確實比凱爾特語世界任何其他地方更強。

在蘇格蘭集中於外赫布里底群島的西北島嶼和高地的西北部。在愛爾蘭談論日常使用時，當然只有愛爾蘭語地區——西部一小部分說愛爾蘭語的人口。

簡報 18

稍後我會展示詳細的布列塔尼地圖。

比較愛爾蘭和蘇格蘭的蓋爾語時，您會發現語言政策確實很重要，因為如果愛爾蘭這麼藍，就表示很多人宣稱自己可以說愛爾蘭語。但正如我們所知，了解一種語言並不表示說那種語言。

簡報 19

布列塔尼文化的其他方面。

我們昨天看到了原住民文化的某些層面，例如舞蹈和音樂，已透過某種方式證明這些比較容易維護或振興。音樂、舞蹈、摔跤：振興或維護文化的這些部分努力已遠遠更為成功。

簡報 20

例如布列塔尼舞蹈。如果來布列塔尼，你會發現它從傳統轉向民俗和公共表演，但之後又回到人們的生活中，你會看到很多跳傳統舞蹈的節日。

簡報 21

他們非常年輕，非常和諧，非常投入。你知道，這並不是已經過時或類似的東西。有時會有八千名舞者一起跳舞。這是我家鄉的照片。

我住在布列塔尼西部的一個小漁港，所以我們只有大約200到300人一起跳舞。

每年甚至在網路空間為布列塔尼僑民舉辦網絡狂歡節或舞蹈節。

簡報 22

這些只是讓大家看看布列塔尼舞蹈的多樣性。

簡報 23

歌唱也一樣。

在這張投影片下方，可以看到戴帽子的歌手向一位年長歌手學習，然後再教導一位年輕歌手。這位年輕歌手現在正在和來自里昂的繞舌歌手一起唱歌，實際上是在法國阿爾卑斯山附近。這是可以跳舞的歌唱音樂，也可以跳傳統舞蹈。

簡報 24-26

風笛和雙簧管也一樣，這種風格於 1930 年代幾乎絕跡，但現在已被徹底重新採用而且非常流行。每個人都學，很多年輕人也學也聽。

摔跤也一樣，摔跤也很流行，甚至進入了凱爾特人的國手，還有扣摔和布列塔尼摔跤的冠軍。

簡報 27-28

但可惜，語言是另一回事。

這是布列塔尼的地圖。我們有方言，比威爾斯語還多。

可以說我們有四種歷史方言，但情況當然比這複雜得多。你知道有許多等語線，但你通常不會跳過一條河然發現是不同的方言。事情不是這樣發生的；而是非常漸進的。

布列塔尼東部主要是講法語的人，而雷恩和南特這兩個大城市位於歷史悠久的布列塔尼語中心地帶之外。

簡報 29

這是下布列塔尼雙層語言狀況的演變。

下布列塔尼指的是布列塔尼西部，歷史上講布列塔尼語，因為東部主要講高盧語或法語。

各位可以看到，於 19 世紀，布列塔尼西部幾乎每個人只會說布列塔尼語，而這種狀況自 1997 年以來都沒有太大改變。

這顯示出，現在的狀況已經不同了。

只講法語的人占絕大多數，其他人至少會講兩種甚或三種語言。

簡報 30

這是布列塔尼西部不同年齡組在家中接收的語言的狀況。

可以看到黃色部分（法語而不是布列塔尼語）已逐漸成為基準。

法語加上偶爾的布列塔尼語幾乎已經消失了，使用布列塔尼語和一點法語基本上已經消失了。

現在又開始回升。

而沒有法語的布列塔尼呢？可能 50 或 60 年前就沒有發生過了。

簡報 31

這張簡報最下面的數字顯示，在布列塔尼的 460 萬人中，目前估計有 200,000 名布列塔尼語使用者。

所以，當我跟大家說我們是少數中的少數時，就是這樣。

簡報 32

書面布列塔尼語的痕跡非常古老，早在 8 世紀或 9 世紀就已經有書面的布列塔尼語了，但書寫的使用並不多。

例如我們當然沒有像威爾斯人的聖經傳統。

主要都是豐富的口頭文學。

曾經有兩個書面標準，但自 20 世紀中葉以來，這兩個書面標準已經結合成一個用於學校和媒體的書面標準。

截至 19 世紀，下布列塔尼的每個人都說布列塔尼語，尤其是農村和海上居民。即使神職人員和中產階級也一定會說雙語，當地仕紳也一樣。

真的是在學校法之後，以及學校法和二戰之間，每個人都逐漸變成了雙語人士，就像我們多次在臺灣和幾乎所有地方聽到的狀況一樣。我認為並沒有像西班牙佛朗哥時代那麼嚴重，但布列塔尼語被巧妙地排出學校，而且還有懲罰。除天主教布道之外，嚴格限於私人使用。

但 20 世紀下半葉大部分時間發生的事，就是說法語變成一種渴望和流行，尤其是年輕女性和年輕媽媽。自暴自棄以及有時候自我仇恨已經內化了，因此政府甚至不必再有任何作為，因為已經內化了。你對自己的語言以及相關的一切感到羞恥。

二戰後的十年內，家庭傳承實際上在不到十年的時間內就崩潰了。

在那之前，布列塔尼語是凱爾特語世界全部六種語言中最常用的語言，但現在已經不是了。

簡報 33

請看這份語言清單的最上面，這些是法國使用的語言以及一個世代之內父子之間的傳承率。

這是 1999 年完成的，也就是將近 20 年前，但我認為到今天仍然有效。

各位可以看到，布列塔尼語沒有傳承給下一代，這是第二糟的案例，而如果你看中國人，例如在法國的中國人或在法國的寮國人，雖然比不上土耳其人和英文使用者，但他們一定會嘗試傳承自己的語言，遠勝於傳承布列塔尼語、奧克西唐語和法蘭克—普羅旺斯語。

簡報 34-35

這是今年（2018 年）6 月進行的最新區域調查。這在布列塔尼算是一件大事，因為布列塔尼區域委員會第一次花錢對布列塔尼的語言使用狀況進行適當調查，以非常科學的方法納入包括所有世代、職業和性別並有超過 8,500 人的樣本。

結果顯示，布列塔尼西部只有 12% 的人口說布列塔尼語。

簡報 36

如果細看這五個部門，這是 6%，但技術上應該是 5.5%。這是統計學家的計算方式。只有 3% 的人認為自己布列塔尼語說得很好，而 74% 完全不會說。

簡報 37

這主要是一種小鎮或鄉村語言——農村地區用得比城市地區多的語言。

簡報 38

2007 年至 2018 年之間的穩定性讓人感到驚訝，因為我們認為，某種語言的使用者每天都會死一些人，因此人數應該會下降，但顯然卻沒有。

但演進的結果顯示，會說布列塔尼語而從來不說的人數成長了。

簡報 39

且過去 20 年來一直穩定成長。

這表示他們雖然會布列塔尼語，但可能在大城市，或因為親友、配偶過世而不

再使用這種語言。這個語言只存在於他們的腦海中，其他地方找不到。

簡報 40

現在有很好的結果。

這次調查可喜的部分是，顯示出在所有世代中，真正懂得並最常使用布列塔尼語的是年輕一代，這非常好。

我們可以看到，在 60 至 69 歲且每週至少說一次布列塔尼語的人之中，只有三分之一的人每週說一次，而年輕一代卻有三分之二的人每週至少說一次。

所以這對我們來說是好消息。我們必須專注於好消息，因為好消息真的不多。

簡報 41

請理解，由於 1950 年代幾乎完全崩潰，我們別無選擇，只能依賴學校。

這當然不是最好的狀況，但也只能如此或什麼都不做。

這裡有張照片，我發現整件事有些東西真的很體貼。

這是一位學校老師，手裡拿著小提琴，正要去學校，或不知道是不是要去海邊之類的地方，於 1977 年帶著最初的五個小孩上全浸式學校。

各位可以看到，我簡報下方的學校貼紙並不是複製的，而是受到照片的啟發。

在右邊，您可以看到截至 2019 年 9 月 18 日在布列塔尼提供的全部或部分沉浸式教育。

回到 1977 年，許多政治人物認為，要求完全透過布列塔尼語的媒介教育子女的父母簡直是瘋了，等他們回過神來，這種想法就會消失，但實際並非如此。

從那時起，以布列塔尼語為媒介的教育就一直在成長。

簡報 42

這是 1977 年以來的成長狀況。

各位可以看到，天主教學校也開放了，公立學校也開學了。

但很可惜，這些數字隱藏了一個事實，事實上布列塔尼只有 3% 的學生人口在這些學校就讀，也就是說 97% 的人並未在以布列塔尼語為媒介的學校就讀。

簡報 43

依年齡群組劃分的主要學習模式。各位在簡報最上面可以看到，15 到 24 歲之間透過正規教育接受布列塔尼語教育，超過任何家庭傳承或自學。

簡報 44

這是年齡金字塔，請看最下面。當然，底部很小。這是一個很小的基礎，但可能是某些事情的開端——從年輕一代重新趕上。

簡報 45

現在布列塔尼語還有更大的發展範圍。

因為，被問到「您是否希望自己的小孩學習或有機會學習布列塔尼語？」時，有 33% 的人表示希望或原本希望自己的小孩了解布列塔尼語，而實際在學校學習的只有 3%，因此有很大的正常發展空間。

簡報 46

而年輕父母更傾向於讓孩子學會布列塔尼語，所以這也頗令人欣慰。

簡報 47

此外，無論是否出生於布列塔尼，都不影響其希望自己子女學習布列塔尼語的願望。

這有點像加泰隆語的狀況，來自布列塔尼以外的人也都希望自己子女說布列塔尼語及學習布列塔尼語。

簡報 48

成年人也很重要。每三個成年人中就有一個希望自己會布列塔尼語。

簡報 49-50

所以該怎麼辦？

因為兒童不夠，所以也有成年人學習，目前學習此語言的共有超過 5,000 人。我們有一個組織。

各位可以在中間看到，例如布列塔尼區域委員會花錢為求職者提供為期六到九個月的密集訓練課程。

所以這也非常值得期待。

簡報 51-52

在布列塔尼的人希望電視、廣播、公共服務、學校和路標也能有更多布列塔尼語。

多數人都支持布列塔尼語，包括在布列塔尼但不會說布列塔尼語的人。

這是 1980 年代中期以來一直在進行的路標運動，包括必須趁夜間把標誌塗黑，我必須說，這是我在學生時代也做過的工作。

簡報 54

另一個可以聚集人群以支持該語言的範例是「為布列塔尼語而跑」。

這張地圖顯示的是每兩年舉行一次為期十天的全天候接力賽路線，沿路會有許多布列塔尼語活動。

對於布列塔尼語的非使用者及使用者而言，這都是一種非常有包容性、喜慶且受歡迎的語言慶祝方式。

你每買一公里，那筆錢便可用於組織或完成布列塔尼語的各種相關專案。

簡報 55

現在談到身分認同。這是我最後兩張簡報。

布列塔尼人的身分認同感與其他凱爾特語國家大不相同。

只有大約 4% 的人認為自己只是布列塔尼人；14% 的人認為自己是布列塔尼人的成分比法國人的成分多一點，而 38% 的人認為自己既是法國人也是布列塔尼人。

但有很多人認為自己只是法國人——幾乎占人口的四分之一。

但有趣的是，講布列塔尼語的人比較更有可能認為自己只是布列塔尼人，或既是法國人也是布列塔尼人，或布列塔尼人的成分比法國人的成分多一點。

愈常說布列塔尼兩種母語中的任一種，就愈有可能覺得自己既是布列塔尼人也是法國人，或布列塔尼人的成分比法國人的成分多一點。

簡報 57

以下是我的結論。必須有未來語言政策措施的途徑，因為支持力量如此龐大。

我認為布列塔尼區域委員會應強化所有此類教育、媒體和公共服務政策。

如此普遍希望子女懂得布列塔尼語的事實顯示，對於只有 3% 以布列塔尼語為媒體的教育不可能感到滿意。

我省略了一些各位可以自行閱讀的其他內容，但我覺得最後一行很重要。

各位知道，在現今數位文明的狀況下，布列塔尼不久之內就必須透過應用程式、介面、社群媒體等進行數位化操作。

　　這會是既昂貴又耗時的工程，且大多也取決於 GAFAM，但就像許多語言一樣，數位死亡的威脅正在逼近。

　　非常感謝。

　　Trugarez!

2021 臺灣客語及少數族群語言政策國際研討會
經驗實錄

【歐洲少數族群語言現代化及語言聲望重建】
歐洲語言平等網絡及區域性語言在歐洲之復振及復甦
ELEN and Territorial Language Revitalisation and Recovery in Europe

歐洲語言平等網絡秘書長 Davyth Hicks 博士

ELEN | EUROPEAN LANGUAGE EQUALITY NETWORK

International Conference on Policies of the Hakka Language and Minority Languages

ELEN and Territorial Language Revitalisation and Recovery in Europe.

Dr. Davyth Hicks
ELEN Secretary-General

ELEN | EUROPEAN LANGUAGE EQUALITY NETWORK

- European Language Equality Network (ELEN) and its work.
- Essential ingredients for language recovery.
- Building the language recovery infrastructure.
- Family, community, civil society.
- Education
- Language legislation
- Challenges, the best of times/ worst of times?
- Recent developments in Europe for context: Molac Law, Irish Language Act, Catalan immersion model.
- Benefits of revitalisation.
- Success stories
- Recommendations
- Conclusions.

3

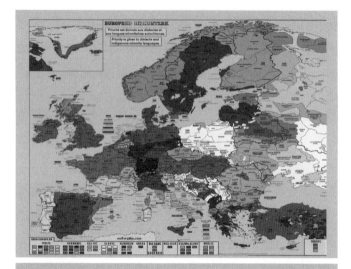

4

Overview

•There are around 60 territorial, regional or minoritised languages in Europe (CoE ECRML figure).

•Around **55 million people**, **10%,** in the European Union speak a minoritised language.

•Territorial/ regional, minoritised, endangered languages (RMLs) are spoken in all European countries, except for Iceland.

5

ELEN

• Set up in 2012 replacing EBLUL.

• ELEN members represent **47 languages with 168 member organisations in 23 European states.**

• ELEN members comprise most of Europe's civil society territorial language organisations.

• ELEN provides a direct connection between grass-roots organisations and the European and international institutions.

6

ELEN EUROPEAN LANGUAGE EQUALITY NETWORK

ELEN Membership

Examples of member organisations are:

- The award winning **Diwan** Breton-medium schools organisation in Brittany, parent organisations such as Comann nam Parant (Scotland).
- Umbrella organisations such as Kevre Breizh (Brittany), Kontseilua (Basque Country), Mudiadau Dathlu'r Gymraeg (Wales), and Uralic (Estonia).
- Large cultural organisations such as Accio Cultural Pais Valencia (Valencia), and Plataforma per la Llengua and Omnium Cultural (Catalonia).
- Academic institutions such as the Consiglio Nazionale Ricerche (Italy) and the University of Mainz (Germany).

7

ELEN EUROPEAN LANGUAGE EQUALITY NETWORK

8

ELEN EUROPEAN LANGUAGE EQUALITY NETWORK

ELEN's work comprises two main pillars:

1) **Advocacy** work for the protection, promotion and well-being of our languages with a focus on linguistic rights. With the Council of Europe, EU, UN, OSCE and UNESCO, States, autonomous governments and locally.

2) **Project work** where ELEN works with member organisations on EU funded language projects that act to develop and revitalise our languages. Digital Language Diversity Project, LISTEN Project, ELE project, TITLE project.

9

ELEN | EUROPEAN LANGUAGE EQUALITY NETWORK

Three pillars of language maintenance:
* Family, community, civil society
* Educational system
* The local state

When one or more of these supporting pillars is weak it can threaten the long-term vitality of the language.

10

ELEN | EUROPEAN LANGUAGE EQUALITY NETWORK

For the language recovery process there are four essential ingredients:

•Adequate binding language legislation
•Holistic language planning
•Adequate economic resources
•Public interest and support.

Aim: to be able to fully live our lives in our language.

11

ELEN | EUROPEAN LANGUAGE EQUALITY NETWORK

1. Family, community, civil society

•Language recovery will only work if it's a grass-roots driven process.
•Top-down measures on their own will not work.
•Start with micro-level, family, community.
•Civil society organisations act as the drivers for change.
•Civil society pressure results in education and language legislation.

12

ELEN EUROPEAN LANGUAGE EQUALITY NETWORK

2. Education

•Need to build the education infrastructure for effective recovery.
•Pre-school, primary, secondary, college, university and teacher-training and pedagogical materials.
•Immersion education most effective: Diwan, Basque Model D.
•State support for immersion education ideally.
•Private schools.

13

ELEN EUROPEAN LANGUAGE EQUALITY NETWORK

3. Language Legislation
•Legislation acts to **underpin** and empower the language recovery effort across different language domains.
•It gives a legal base for educational development, the provision of public services, the provision of media, and the right to use the language in various contexts.
*Overarching aim is to **normalize** language whereby the speakers are easily able to live every aspect of their lives in their language.*

14

ELEN EUROPEAN LANGUAGE EQUALITY NETWORK

Domestic language legislation
Welsh, Gaelic, Catalan Language Acts.

International treaties
• Europe's Charter for Regional or Minority Languages
• Framework Convention for National Minorities.

The new standard-setting tool, the Donostia Protocol to Ensure Language Rights.

15

ELEN EUROPEAN LANGUAGE EQUALITY NETWORK

- Catalan, Basque, Galician, and Frisian language legislation has acted to aid regeneration, and ensure language use.
- Legislation underpins their different educational models.
- Note that for languages without legislation (Breton, Occitan) their language recovery effort is constantly under threat.
- Underlines importance if all three pillars being in place.

16

ELEN EUROPEAN LANGUAGE EQUALITY NETWORK

Challenges.

- Civil society underfunded. Lack of support for RML families and communities.
- Education, bilingual or immersion, problems of states redefining immersion.
- Language legislation, divorced from sociolinguistic reality, not helping language recovery effort.
- Rise in discrimination, hate-speech against RML speakers and languages.
- Lack of clear, unambiguous legislation for the protection of rights.
- Optimism of 1990s but disillusion of 2020s.

17

ELEN EUROPEAN LANGUAGE EQUALITY NETWORK

Challenges

•**No clear, unambiguous, territorial language rights** in Europe.

•Blocking of the modest proposals in an ECI by the EU marks a 20 year failure of any meaningful progress by the EU in national and linguistic minority rights.

•Lack of even the most basic health information in most RMLs during the COVID-19 pandemic.

•Our challenge now is to get territorial language rights and their well being back on the agenda and for the EU to act with the same vigour as it has against racism and other forms of discrimination and enact clear national and linguistic minority protection measures.

18

Recent developments in Europe: France

- Molac Law for regional languages fully supported in National Assembly.
- Allows for public schools to use immersion.
- Blanquer: Censure of the Molac Law for regional languages, immersion "unconstitutional".
- ELEN appeal to UN.
- Impacts on RML immersion education, unconstitutional.
- Impacts children's rights, use of RML in school.

19

20

Recent developments in Europe: Irish

- Irish Language Act for north of Ireland
- Promised 15 years ago, St Andrews Agreement.
- Needed to underpin successful recovery.
- Long-running campaign by civil society.
- Language recovery infrastructure in place
- Successful Irish-medium schools
- Reintroduced intergenerational transmission
- Urban context.

21

Recent developments in Europe. Irish

22

Recent developments in Europe: Catalan

- Catalan immersion model under threat
- Spanish Court rules that 25% of lessons must be in Spanish.
- Catalan model supported by vast majority of Catalan society for over 40 years.
- Model brings social cohesion, inclusion and equal opportunity.
- Ruling, if implemented, undermines immersion model and social cohesion.

23

24

Benefits and added-value from language revitalization

- Cognitive benefits of bilingual education.
- Bilingual schoolchildren have higher grades, lower drop-out rates.
- Well-being and health benefits.
- Improved career prospects.
- Territorial/ minoritised languages are a unique selling point and act to boost the local economy.

25

Language Rights are Human Rights

•Language legislation addresses the language equality deficit, it acts to bring meaningful respect and rights to lesser-used language speakers and helps to normalize its usage;

•Language rights are human rights. Language discrimination is a form of both direct and indirect racism. Language legislation acts to uphold our fundamental human rights.

•Language legislation enhances social cohesion and helps to build bridges between communities on a shared culture and history.

26

Success stories

Basque

•Some indicators show increase of number of speakers and of usage.

Cymraeg

•Innovative measures, language impact assessments.
•Number of young speakers steadily increasing.
•Target of one million speakers by 2050.
•Supportive government, new co-operation agreement.

27

Success stories
Irish in north of Ireland
•Successful language recovery in urban environment
•Irish-medium education fastest growing sector
•Contribution to the peace process.
•Remarkable achievement in an English language setting.

28

ELEN Recommendations

1)Endangered Languages EU Directive/ Regulation, to ensure that all Member States act to promote and protect their territorial languages. If the EU can protect fish and trees - why not European endangered languages?
2)European Languages Commissioner and linguistic observatory. (CoE)
3)Lack of implementation/ violation of **ECRML/FCNM to trigger EU infringement procedure.**

29

Conclusions
•Optimism of the 1990s but disillusion of 2020s.
•The language recovery boosts the local economy.
•Language recovery good for well-being + cognitive benefits
•Language legislation addresses the equality deficit and enhances social cohesion.
•Language rights are human rights.
•Some successes but a work in progress.

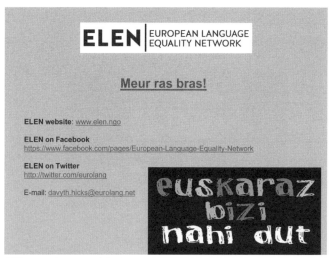

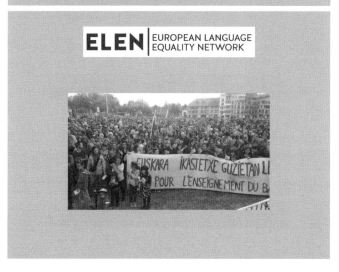

33

The Donostia Protocol to ensure linguistic rights launched in December 2016, http://protokoloa.eus/

24

35

Briefing 1

Hello, Madames and Monsieurs, Ladies and Gentlemen.My name is Davyth Hicks, Secretary-General of the European Language Equality Network (ELEN).

I'm delighted to have been invited to speak to you today about territorial language revitalization and recovery in Europe, especially in the interesting context of policies for the Hakka language and minority languages in Taiwan.

Briefing 2

These are the main headings that I will be addressing. First of all, a bit about us—the European Language Equality Network and our work. What we see as the essential ingredients for language recovery—building the language recovery infrastructure, the family community, civil society, education, and language legislation. And then we will look at some of the challenges—the best of times, and the worst of times, comparing the 1990s to the 2020s.

And then we will look at recent developments in Europe for some context—the MolacLaw in France, the Irish Language Act in the north of Ireland, the current attack on the Catalan immersion model, the benefits of revitalization, some success stories and recommendations, and then we willdraw some conclusions, after which hopefully we can have some discussion.

Now we'll be going through the PowerPoint. So.

Briefing 3

This is a map of Europe and shows its language diversity. I have always quite liked this map because it shows how languages don't necessarily obey state borders, and that they're quite an organic.

Briefing 4

There are around 60 territorial, regional, or minoritized languages in Europe. This is a Council of Europe figure.

Around 55 million people, 10% of the population in the European Union, speak a minoritized languagenow, with territorial, regional,minoritised and endangered languages spoken in all European countries, except for Iceland.

Briefing 5

RegardingELEN, we were established in 2012 to replace the European Bureau for Lesser-Used Languages (EBLUL). Currently, we represent 50 languages, with 174 member organizations in 24 European states. ELEN members comprise most of Europe's civil society territorial language organizations, and ELEN provides a direct connection between grass-roots organizations and European and international institutions.

Briefing 6

Regarding ELEN membership, some examples of our member organizations are the award-winning Diwan Breton-medium school organization in Brittany and parent organizations such as ComannnamParant in Scotland.

Umbrella organizations, such as KevreBreizh in Brittany, Kontseilua in the Basque Country, MudiadauDathlu'rGymraeg in Wales, and Uralic in Estonia.

Large cultural organizations, such as Accio Cultural Pais Valencia in Valencia, and Plataforma per la Llengua and Omnium Cultural in Catalonia.

And then, also academic institutions, such as the Consiglio Nazionale Ricerche in Italy and the University of Mainz in Germany.

Briefing 7

Here is a picture of us at our most recent General Assembly in Galicia. There should have been more of us, obviously because of COVID 19 restrictions, but everybody who could travel came. We had a very successful meeting, and there arereports about iton our website. Let's turn to our work.

Briefing 8

ELEN's work comprises two main pillars.

Firstly, advocacy work for the protection, promotion, and well-being of our languages, with a focus on linguistic rights.

This work mostly takes us to the Council of Europe inStrasbourg and the EU in Brussels, where I'm based,the UN inGeneva, the OSCE in The Hague, and UNESCO in

Paris.

We also work with member states of the EU and other states, as well as with autonomous governments and local governments.

The other pillar of our work is project work, where ELEN works with our member organizations on EU-funded language projects, often with Erasmus+ or Horizon, to develop and revitalize our languages.

For example, we've got the Digital Language Diversity Project, the LISTEN Project, and the ELE project about digital development for our languages,and the TITLE Project, which is about teacher training.

You can find more details about these on our website now.

Briefing 9

Turning to langage maintenance, I'd like to give you anoverall theoretical framework about what we do. There are three pillars of language maintenance. Firstly, family, community, and civil society. Secondly, the educational system, and thirdly, the local state. When more and more of these supporting pillars areweak, it can threaten the long-term vitality of the language. This framework was developed by Prof. Colin Williams.

Briefing 10

Referring to the language recovery process, we see that there are four essential ingredients: binding language legislation, holistic language planning, adequate economic resources, and public interest and support,with the overarching aim of being able to fully live our lives in our language.

Briefing 11

Looking at the family, community, and civil society.In our experience, language recovery will only work if it's a grass-rootsdriven process led by civil society organizations.

Top-down measures on their own will not work, and recent experience shows us that we have to look at the micro level—family language planning, the community, the village, the town, and the social spaces where you use the language. For us, civil society organizations act as the drivers for change.

Civil society pressure will, for example, result in educational development, the provision of immersioneducation, and language legislation.

Briefing 12

Turning to the second pillar, education, for effective language recovery an educational infrastructure has to be in place. This meanspre-schools/kindergartens, primary schools,the secondary college level, and universities, as well as teacher-training courses and pedagogical materials that go with that.

What we havefound is that immersion education is the most effective, and when we say immersion, we mean where the school is 100 percent using the minoritised language. For example, the Diwan schools in Brittany, and the Basque Model Dikastolasare seeing a lot of success. We expect state support for immersion education, but this is not always the casein Europe.

When you don't have the state's support, some organsiations have had to take the route of establishing private schools. The Diwan Breton medium schools are actually private and work on funding raised by parents and by special events.

Briefing 13

The third pillar of language maintenance is language legislation.

Legislation acts to underpin and empower the language recovery effort across the different sociolinguistic domains. It gives a legal basis for educational development, the provision of public services, the provision of media, and the right to use the language in various contexts.

The overarching aim is to normalize language, whereby the speakers are easily able to live every aspect of their lives in the language.

Briefing 14

Domestic language legislation is easily and by far the best and most useful. For example, the Welsh, Gaelic, Catalan and Basque Language Acts. There are also the international treaties from the Council of Europewhich give support. For example, the

European Charter for Regional or Minority Languages (ECRML) and the Framework Convention for National Minorities (FCNM).

We were also involved in draftingthe Donostia Protocol to ensure language rights. This is now seen as a new standard-setting tool, designed in 2016 by civil society organisations, to show what we expect to have in termsof adequate language rights, language development, and language recovery.

Briefing 15

We can see that Catalan, Basque,and Galician legislation has acted to aid regeneration; it helps to ensure language use, and legislation underpins their different educational models.

Furthermore, we can see that for languages without legislation, like Breton or Occitan in France, their language recovery effort is constantly under threat because it has no legal base. This underlines the importance of having all three pillars in place for successful revitalization.

Briefing 16

Turning to theoverarching challenges, a recurring problems is that civil society organisationsare often underfunded, and there's a lack of support for lesserusedlanguage-speaking families and their communities.

There's a problem a lot of the time with education, about choosing between bilingual or immersion, and there's a newly emerging problem of states trying to redefine what immersion is, suggesting that this could be less than 100 percent.

Referring to language legislation, increasingly we need to reviewthe legislation and ensure that it is helping with the language recovery effort. Can it be better? Is it divorced from the sociolinguistic reality?

We would like to see impact assessments of language legislation. Is it working? Can it be improved?

Another major challenge is the rise in discrimination and hate-speech against all of our languages, especially on social media.

Many speakers of our languages experience hostility on an everyday basis, not just in Europe, but globally.

An overarching theme is that of the optimism of the 1990s: we had the Charter, the Framework Convnetion, and domestic language legislation, andwe could see some progress. But now in the 2020sthere's been no progress, we're in a regressive situation, and people are becoming increasingly disillusioned.

So, to continue with the challenges.

Briefing 17

One of the big problems is that there are still no clear, unambiguous territorial language rights in Europe. Even the very modest proposals in a recent European Citizens' Initiative was blocked by the EU. Itmarks a 20-year failure of any meaningful progress by the EU in national and linguistic minority rights. I think one of the most disgraceful thingsthat havehappened recently is this lack of even the most basic health information in our languages during the COVID-19 pandemic. To be honest, it's disgraceful. There are a lot of old people in some areas; for example, Hungarian speakers in Romania, who simply do not speak the state language very well.

For them not to receive any health information in their own language was potentially life threatening. It's something we were shocked about, as well as the Council of Europe and OSCE.

Whether we willsee any changes regarding health information is uncertain. Our challenge now is to get territorial and language rights back on the agenda and for the EU to act with the same vigour as it has against racism and other forms of discrimination and enact clear national and linguistic minority protection measures.

Briefing 18

I wanted to add some colour and talk about recent developments in Europe. In France, in April of this year, the Molac Law for regional languages was fully supported in the National Assembly.

This allowed public schools to use immersion education andwas a step forward considering that for something like 70 years there wasno progress at all for regional languages. However, one month later, Blanquer, the education minister, decided to gather a few other deputies and managed to get the Molac Law censured, which means it blocked parts of it on the basis that immersion education could be seen as unconstitutional. This raises huge amounts of problems because if immersion education becomes unconstitutional, it doesn't just affect the public schools where they were trying to have full immersion, but it starts to have an impact on the private schools where there is immersion, such as at the Diwan schools.

There's also an implication in the censure that children cannot use Breton or Alsatian in the school normally, or in the playground, or while they're in the corridor.There's an insistence in the censurethat French is used. For us, this impacts children's rights as well as undermining immersion education. It meant that ELEN along with our members in the French state, appealed to the UN in July. It is acompletely unacceptable situation and highlights how the French state is one of the worst states in Europe for protecting its languages.

Briefing 19

Here's a picture from one of the many demonstrations that happened after the censure. This one is from Brittany with some of the schoolchildren there, but there were big demonstrations as well in the Basque Country,and in the Alsace and in Corsica. Its an issue that's not going away, and it's something we're very busy working on at the moment.

Briefing 20

Another major issue we've been working on is campaigning for an Irish Language Act in the north of Ireland. Irish language legislation was promised 15 years ago in the St Andrews Agreement and forms part of the overall Good Friday Agreement, which, as you know, is part of the peace process going on between the UK and Ireland.

It's been delayed repeatedly. The UK promised to pass it in Westminster, yet they failed to meet their own deadline. That last deadline was in October. We want to see this legislation becauseit underpins the successful recovery that's been going on in the North.

What is amazing to see in the north of Ireland is that there has beena long-running campaign by civil society, by our memberorganisations,to ensure that the language recovery infrastructure is in place, especially in education. We see successful Irish-medium schools. They've managed to reintroduce intergenerational transmission. This has been done in an urban context, but things are being held back because they still don't have this legislation. So we're continuing to push for the overdue legislation and we're going to be talking about itthis weekat the UN,at the Forum forMinority Issues.

Briefing 21

Here's a picture of schoolchildren demonstrating in Belfast from a couple of years ago. They've been really, really active in pushing for this. And we hope there's going to be some turnaround soon.

Briefing 22

Referring to recent developments with Catalan and the Catalan immersion model. Currently, when you go to school in Cataloniaall of your education is in Catalan. The objective is that you become proficient in Catalan and proficient in Spanish so that you leave schoolas a proficient bilingual.

That method has worked for 40 years. It's very successful, and it's hugely supported by the public. Yet, the Spanish court ruled last week that 25 percent of lessons must be in Spanish.

This isgoing completely againstCatalan public opinion and against its elected representatives. The Catalan model brings social cohesion, inclusion, and equal opportunity. If this ruling is implemented (and Catalan NGOs are talking about civil disobedience so as not to implement it) it will undermine the immersion model and social cohesion. It's another exampleof the Spanish judiciary being a kind of leftover from the past when there was a dictatorship in the Spanish state.It doesn't really modernize itself, but instead, it wants to punish Catalansfor the independence campaignby attacking the language. The ruling is symptomatic of that attitude. ELEN ishelping its members in their campaign against the ruling and we will take it up with the international institutions. Its worth noting that the Catalan immersion model has been praised by the EU institutions.

It will be hard for Spain to try to get this implemented, and hopefully, we can get the ruling overturned before campaigners have to turn to civil disobedience.

Briefing 23

Here are some newspaper headlinesfrom the ELEN General Assembly, where we talked about the 25% ruling and the problems facing Galician.

Briefing 24

What are the benefits and added value from the language revitalization, what do they bring to us? What are the reasonsforourwork? Well, first of all, there are the cognitive benefits of bilingual education. Bilingual schoolchildren have higher grades and lower dropout rates.

There are thewell-being and health benefits as well. It's an area that we know we should focus on more in Europe. The indigenous language communities are very good at discussing the spiritual benefits, for example, of revitalizing their indigenous languages. We should focus more on the well-being and health benefits of using our languages.The topic is being more widely discussed, but the concept ofwell-being issomething that needs to feed into language policy. Also, there are improved career prospects from being able to speak your language.

Referring to economic benefits, territorial or minoritized languages are a unique selling point and act to boost the local economy. A thriving language leads to a thriving local economy. Welsh, Catalan, Basque, and Irish-medium schools, for example, are economic hubs. Radio stations and TV stations create prestigious jobs.

These all create very good and attractive work for lesser-used language speakers.

Briefing 25

There are the legal benefits and language legislation benefits under the broader heading of language rights that arepart of the overall human rights framework. Language legislation addresses the language equality deficit. It acts to bring meaningful respect and rights to lesser-used language speakers and helps to normalize their usage. Language rights arehuman rights.

The Council of Europe has discussed language discrimination as a form of both direct and indirect racism. Language legislation acts to uphold our fundamental human rights and legislation, enhances social cohesion, and helps to build bridges between communities on a shared culture and history.

Briefing 26

There are some success stories, such as with the increase in Basque speakers, and we're seeing some indicators that show an increase in the number of Welsh speakers. Its good to see innovative measures like Welsh language impact assessmentsand something thatcould be copied by other language communities. We see the number of young Welsh speakers steadily increasing. There's a target of one million speakers by 2050. We have a very supportive government in Wales, with a new cooperation agreement between Welsh Labour and Plaid Cymruwhich will take further measures to help develop the language.

Briefing 27

So, watch this space. Turning back to Irish in the north of Ireland, it needs to be emphasized that this is a fantastic success story. We're seeing successful language recovery in an urban, English-speaking environment. Irish-medium education is the fastest growing sector in education in the north of Ireland. We see its contribution to the peace process. Its a remarkable achievement to see the growth of the Irish language despite living withthe biggest, most dominant global language in the world. So, a fantastic achievement.

Briefing 28

And then, turning to the ELEN recommendationswhich aim to address some of the overarching problems facing our languages today.

We are working for an EU directive or preferably, a regulation, to ensure that all member states act to promote and protect their endangered languages. If the EU can protect endangered fish and trees, we ask, why can't Europe protect its own endangered languages?

We'd also like to see a European languages commissioner—Canada has a language commissioner, and other countries as well—and a linguistic observatory to back that up, which would monitor the health and well-being of the lesser-used languages, especially. Maybe this is something that the Council of Europe could do. The language commissioner will be there to monitor and enforce language rights, and would be given themandate to do that.

Next we would like to see that when you have alack of implementation or a violation of the Charter (ECRML) or the Framework Convention (FCNM), that this would trigger EU infringement proceedings. Currently, those two treaties of the Council of Europeare hampered in their usefulness as they have no teeth, and states can ignore them with impunity. We need to see some change in that. Our proposal is to tie them to the EU infringement procedureso as to ensure better implementation.

Briefing 29

So, some conclusions. I'd like to turn back again to the theme of the optimism of the 1990s and disillusion of the 2020s. It describes how many activists are feeling. The failure of the Minority SafepackECI, with the Commission stating that they were going to carry on as normal,just shows how difficult it is to try to get the member states to change. This needs to change. France, for example, refuses to move on its control of regional language policy. We need to see that change sowe can get Europe to celebrate its linguistic diversity.

The EU keeps talking about that, but not really making any progress on it.

The positive factors are that we cansee that language recovery boosts the local economy.

It's a fact that language recovery is good for people'swell-being and has cognitive benefits.

We see how language legislation addresses the equality deficit and enhances social cohesion, and that language rights are human rights and need to be properly included in the broader human rights framework.

Overall, we can say there have been some successes, but its a work in progress. Language policy, language planning, and language development are still a relatively young science. We're still learning as wego along. In the 1980s and 1990s, when there was a lot of optimism, with high expectationson language recovery, manythought we could achieve language recovery in 20 years.

However, the realization is that it will take50, 70, or even one hundred years before you start to see things really improving at a meaningful level, in particular at the community level. So everything is a work in progress. We have everything to work for. I'm sure that we're going to get through the period of being disillusioned andstart to be positive againbecause we see some successes now, but with the caveat that we can also see that substantive language recovery will take a few generations.

I would like to thank you very much. Meurras bras as we say in Kernewek (Cornish). I very much welcome any questions or discussions that you have. You can follow our activities on social media and on our website. Thank you again, ladies and gentlemen, for inviting me to speak at your conference.

簡報 1

各位先生女士好。我的名字是 Davyth Hicks，是歐洲語言平等網路（ELEN）的秘書長。

我很高興今天能受邀，到這裡發表關於歐洲的地區性語言振興與復原，尤其是在臺灣客語及少數語言政策的有趣背景下。

簡報 2

這是我今天著重的題目。首先，請容我稍微介紹我們歐洲語言平等網路和我們的工作。我們認為的語言復原要素，有建立語言復原基建、家族社群、公民社會、教育、語言立法。接著我們要觀察一些挑戰，最佳時機、最差時機，比較 1990 年代與 2020 年代。

然後我們要觀察最近的歐洲語言發展，獲取一些脈絡，如法國的 Molac 法律、北愛爾蘭的愛爾蘭語法案，目前對加泰隆尼亞語沉浸模式的攻擊，復振的益處，以及一些成功故事和建議，再來就是結論，希望之後我們還可以有些許討論。

現在我們就來看看簡報。好的。

簡報 3

這是歐洲地圖，顯示語言的不同。我一直都很喜歡這張地圖，因為這呈現了語言不一定遵守國境線，而且它們是有組織的。

簡報 4

歐洲大約有 60 種地域性、區域性、少數語言。這是歐洲議會的圖。

約 5,500 萬人中，也就是歐盟人口的 10%，目前使用少數語言，加上所有歐洲

國家使用的地域性、區域性、少數、瀕危語言，冰島除外。

簡報 5

至於 ELEN，我們在 2012 年成立，取代了歐洲少數使用語言局（EBLUL）。目前，我們代表 50 種語言，在 24 個歐洲國家有 174 個組織。ELEN 會員包括大部分歐洲公民社會地域性語言組織，且 ELEN 提供基層組織與歐洲、國際機構間的直接聯繫。

簡報 6

關於 ELEN 的會員資格，舉例來說，部分會員組織是有位於布列塔尼，獲獎的 Diwan Breton 語授課學校組織，以及蘇格蘭 Comann nam Parant 的總會組織。

傘狀組織，例如布列塔尼的 Kevre Breizh，巴斯克的 Kontseilua，威爾斯的 Mudiadau Dathlu'r Gymraeg，以及愛沙尼亞的 Uralic 。

大型文化組織，例如瓦倫西亞的 Accio Cultural Pais Valencia 和加泰隆尼亞的 Plataforma per la Llengua、Omnium Cultural 。

還有學術性組織，例如義大利的 Consiglio Nazionale Ricerche 和德國的梅因斯大學。

簡報 7

這是我們最近一次在加利西亞舉辦大會的合照。我們應該有更多人參加，但顯然受到新冠疫情限制，不過能來的都來了。我們的會議非常成功，我們的網站上有報導。再回到我們的工作。

簡報 8

ELEN 的工作包括兩大主軸。

首先是語言的保護、促進、福祉倡議工作，集中在語言權利上。

這項工作讓我們進入了位於斯特拉斯堡的歐洲議會，布魯塞爾的歐盟，也是我目前工作的地點，日內瓦的聯合國，海牙的歐洲安全暨合作組織（OSCE），以及巴黎的聯合國教科文組織（UNESCO）。

我們也和歐盟會員國及其他國家、自治政府、地方政府合作。

我們工作的另一項主軸是專案工作，這些工作是和我們的會員組織合作歐盟資助的語言專案，通常是發展與復振語言的伊拉斯謨計畫（Erasmus+）或地平線計畫

（Horizon）。

例如，我們有一個數位語言多元化專案 LISTEN，還有 ELE 關於語言數位發展的專案，教師訓練的 TITLE 專案。

這些都可以在我們的網站上找到更多詳情。

簡報 9

回到語言的維護，我想先告訴大家我們工作的整體理論架構。語言維護有三大主軸。首先是家庭、社群、公民社會。其次是教育系統，第三則是當地國家。如果愈來愈多的支持性主軸趨於虛弱，就可能威脅到語言的長期生存。這個架構是由 Colin Williams 教授所開發的。

簡報 10

說到語言復原過程，我們看到這裡有四個要素：約束性的語言法律、整體性的語言規劃、適當的經濟資源，以及公共利益與支持，再加上能夠完全以我們的語言過生活的整體大目標。

簡報 11

看看家庭、社群、公民社會。在我們的經驗中，語言復原只有在公民社會組織領導下，從基層推動的流程，才會成功。

他們自身由上往下的方法不會成功，最近的經驗也告訴我們，我們必須從微觀著眼，家庭語言規劃、社群、村莊、城鎮，還有使用語言的社會空間。對我們而言，公民社會組織扮演了改變的動力。

例如公民社會壓力會導致教育發展，提供沉浸式教育，以及語言法律。

簡報 12

回到第二個主軸，教育，要能有效復原語言，就必須有教育基礎建設。這表示在學前／幼兒園、小學、中學、大學，還有教師訓練課程與教學法教材都要配合。

我們發現，沉浸式教育是最有效的，我們說的沉浸式，是學校百分之百使用少數語言。例如布列塔尼的 Diwan 學校，以及巴斯克的 Model D ikastolas 都卓有成效。我們期待國家能支持沉浸式教育，但在歐洲，情況並非一直如此。

如果沒有國家支援，有些組織必須得走上開辦私立學校這條路。Diwan Breton 中學實際上是私立的，且由家長和特殊活動來集資。

簡報 13

第三個語言維護的主軸是語言法律。

法律是橫跨不同社會語言場域各種語言復原努力的基石，也賦予其力量。這是教育發展、提供公共服務、提供媒體、在各種背景下使用語言的法律基礎。

整體大目標，是將語言正常化，讓使用者可以輕鬆地在生活各個層面使用這種語言。

簡報 14

國內語言立法簡單，到目前也是最棒、最有用的。例如威爾斯語、蓋爾語、加泰隆尼亞語和巴斯克語法案。還有一些歐洲議會的國際協約給予支持。例如歐洲區域或少數民族語言憲章（ECRML），以及國際少數民族架構條約（FCNM）。

我們也參與了草擬保障語言權利的 Donostia 協定。這目前被視為是新的標準設定工具，於 2016 年由公民社會組織所設計，展現了我們對適當語言權利、語言發展、語言復原的期望。

簡報 15

我們可以看到，加泰隆尼亞語、巴斯克語和加利西亞語法律已經實施，協助這些語言重生；這有助於確保語言使用，且法律支持其不同的教育模式。

此外，我們可以看到沒有法律的語言，例如法國的布列塔尼語和奧克語，這些語言因為沒有法律基礎，語言復原的工作一直處於威脅之下。這彰顯了成功復振必須具備三大主軸的重要性。

簡報 16

回到整體挑戰上，反覆不斷的問題之一，是公民社會組織通常經費不足，使用少數語言的家庭和社群缺乏支持。

很多時候選擇雙語學校或沉浸式教學是個問題，另一個想重新定義沉浸式的國家也出現新問題，表示這可能不是百分之百。

說到語言法律，愈來愈多時候，我們必須檢視法律，確保法律有助於語言復原的工作。可以更加改善嗎？這是否與社會語言的現實撕裂？

我們想看到更多語言法律的影響力評估。這是否有效？可以改善嗎？

另一個重大挑戰，是針對我們所有語言的歧視和仇恨言論的興起，尤其是在社

群媒體上。

許多使用我們這些語言的人，每天都在體驗敵意，不只在歐洲，而是全球各地。

一項整體主題是 1990 年代的樂觀主義：我們有了憲章，有了架構協約，還有國內語言法律，我們可以看到有所進展。但現在到了 2020 年代，絲毫沒有進展，我們反而是在退步，大家愈來愈幻滅。

所以說回挑戰。

簡報 17

一個大問題是歐洲仍舊沒有清楚不曖昧的地域性語言權利。即使目前歐洲公民倡議最謙遜的提案，也被歐盟阻攔。這表示歐洲在國家與語言少數權利上，在 20 年內毫無任何實質性的進展。我認為最近發生最丟臉的事情之一，是在新冠疫情期間，甚至連最基本的健康資訊也沒有我們的語言版本。坦白說，這很丟臉。部分地區有很多老人，例如羅馬尼亞說匈牙利語的人，他們無法流暢使用該國國語。

他們無法用自己的母語接受健康資訊，基本上威脅到生命。這件事令我們和歐洲理事會、OSCE 都震驚了。

不確定我們是否會看到健康資訊有所改變。我們現在有一項挑戰，是讓地域性和語言權利回到議程中，讓歐盟用對抗種族主義和其他形式歧視的同樣熱情，採取行動，實施清晰的國家及語言少數保護措施。

簡報 18

我想增添點花絮，聊一聊最近歐洲的發展。今年 4 月在法國，針對區域語言的 Molac 法受到國家議會全體支持。

這使得公立學校可以使用沉浸式教育，對於約 70 年間毫無進展的所有區域性語言而言，是前進了一步。但是一個月後，法國教育部長布朗凱決定集結其他幾個副部長，想辦法譴責 Molac 法，這表示該法律有一部分，因為基於沉浸式教育可能被視為違憲的理由而遭到阻攔。這導致許多問題，因為如果沉浸式教育為限，不只想實施完全沉浸式教育的公立學校受影響，還會開始影響已經實施沉浸式教育的私立學校，例如 Diwan 學校。

這項禁令也意味著孩子不能正常在學校、遊戲場、走廊上使用布列塔尼語或阿爾薩斯語。在譴責中，有人堅持應該使用法語。對我們來說，這影響到孩子的權

利，並破壞沉浸式教育。這也表示 ELEN 和我們在法國的會員，在 7 月向聯合國提出訴願。這個情況完全不能接受，也凸顯了在歐洲，法國是自身語言保護做得最差的國家之一。

簡報 19

這是譴責後的許多示威中，一次示威的照片。這場示威是在布列塔尼，有些學童參加，但是在巴斯克、阿爾薩斯、科西嘉也有大型示威。這個問題並沒有解決，也是我們目前忙於處理的事務。

簡報 20

另一個我們正在努力的重大問題，是北愛爾蘭的愛爾蘭語法案。愛爾蘭語言法律在 15 年前的聖安德魯協議中已經許下承諾，並構成整體耶穌受難日協議的一部分，如各位所知，這是英國和愛爾蘭間和平進展的一部分。

但這份法案反覆延宕。英國承諾在西敏寺通過這項法案，但卻沒有配合自己的時限。最後一次的時限是 10 月。我們希望看到這項法律，因為這支持了北愛爾蘭持續已久的語言成功復原。

在北愛爾蘭，令人訝異的是能看到由我們成員組織的公民社會，所長期運作的活動，保證語言復原基建的存在，特別是教育方面。我們看到成功的愛爾蘭語授課學校。他們想辦法重新引進世代間的交接。這是在城市背景下完成的，但因為仍舊缺乏這套法律，很多事情都裹足不前。所以我們繼續推動這套過期的法律，本週將在聯合國的少數人士議題論壇上討論。

簡報 21

這是幾年前，貝爾法斯特的學童示威照片。他們對於推進這件事真的非常非常積極。我們希望情勢很快就會逆轉。

簡報 22

說到最近加泰隆尼亞語和加泰隆尼亞語沉浸模式的發展。目前，如果在加泰隆尼亞上學，所有教育均以加泰隆尼亞語授課。其目標是大家能流利使用加泰隆尼亞語和西班牙語，離開學校的時候成為雙語流利人士。

這個方法已經發揮效果達 40 年。這個方法非常成功，也受到廣大群眾支持。但西班牙法院上週判決，有 25% 的課程必須以西語授課。

這完全違背加泰隆尼亞的民意，也違反當地選出代表的意見。加泰隆尼亞語模式帶來了社會共存、包容、平等的機會。若此項判決付諸實行（加泰隆尼亞的非政府組織正在討論公民抗命，以免實行），將會破壞沉浸模式與社會共存。西班牙司法仍有過往遺留的另一個例子，是西班牙的獨裁政權。西班牙政權本身並未真正現代化，而是想要用攻擊語言，懲罰加泰隆尼亞的獨立運動。這項判決正是與這種態度為盟。ELEN 正在幫助會員們對抗該項判決的運動，我們將會把這件事帶到國際機構上。值得一提的是，加泰隆尼亞語沉浸模式曾受歐盟機構讚揚。

西班牙要付諸實現有所困難，希望我們能在運動變成公民抗命前推翻判決。

簡報 23

這裡是一些 ELEN 大會的報紙標題，我們在會議中討論了 25% 的判決和加利西亞語面臨的問題。

簡報 24

語言復振有何益處和附加價值，又對我們帶來什麼影響？我們工作的理由是什麼？首先，雙語教育有認知上的益處。雙語學童的成績較佳，輟學率較低。

這也有福祉和健康上的益處。這是我們知道應該要在歐洲多加著重的領域。原住民語言社群非常善於討論精神益處，例如復振他們的原住民語言。我們應該更集中於使用我們母語所帶來的福祉和健康益處。這個主題正受到更廣泛的討論，但福祉的概念，必須灌入語言政策。而且，能夠說母語，也能改善就業前景。

說到經濟益處，地域性或少數語言，是獨特的賣點，也能振興地方經濟。繁榮的語言，會帶來繁榮的地方經濟。例如威爾斯語、加泰隆尼亞語、巴斯克語和愛爾蘭語授課學校，都是經濟樞紐。廣播電臺和電視臺創造頂級職位。

這都會為使用少數語言的人，創造非常吸引人的好工作。

簡報 25

在語言權利的更大範圍內，還有法定益處與語言法律益處，是整體人權架構的一部分。語言法律著重於語言平等的缺陷。這會為少數語言使用者帶來意義與權利，幫助語言使用正常化。語言權利是人權。

歐洲議會討論過語言歧視，是一種直接兼間接的種族主義。語言法律堅守我們的基本人權與法律，強化社會共存，有助於建立社群間共享文化與歷史的橋樑。

簡報 26

這不是沒有成功先例，例如巴斯克語使用者增加，我們看到更多指標，顯示威爾斯語使用者人數增加。看到像威爾斯語影響力評估等創新措施，還有能更讓其他語言社群仿效之舉，是一件好事。我們看到年輕的威爾斯語使用者持續增加。目標是 2050 年前達到 100 萬名使用者。威爾斯政府非常支持，且威爾斯勞工黨和威爾斯黨的新合作協議，將會採取進一步措施，幫助發展威爾斯語。

簡報 27

所以可以關注這方面。回到北愛爾蘭的愛爾蘭語，必須強調這是一個美妙的成功故事。我們看到城市的英語環境中，成功地復原了愛爾蘭語。愛爾蘭語授課教育是北愛爾蘭成長最快的教育部門。我們看到這對和平進展的貢獻。看到愛爾蘭語在世界上最龐大的主宰性語言環境中，還能有所成長，是了不起的成就。所以是個夢幻般的成就。

回到 ELEN 的建議……

簡報 28

……其目標是強調我們母語現今面臨的部分整體問題。

我們正致力於歐盟指令，或最好是法規，保證所有會員國都能採取行動，促進與保護他們的瀕危語言。若歐盟可以保護瀕危的魚類和樹木，我們要問，為何歐洲不能保護自己瀕危的語言？

我們也希望看到有歐洲語言監察使——加拿大和其他國家都有語言監察使，還有支援語言監察使的語言學觀測站，特別是監測少數語言的健康與福祉。也許這是歐洲議會可以做的事情之一。語言監察使會獲得委任，監測與執行語言權利。

接著我們想看到的是，若沒有實行，或違反憲章（ECRML）或架構協約（FCNM），就會觸發歐盟侵權程序。目前這兩項歐洲議會的協約，都因為不具懲罰效力而窒礙難行，有罪而不罰，使得國家可以對其視而不見。我們必須有所改變。我們的提案是將其與歐洲侵權程序綁定，保證能夠實施得更徹底。

簡報 29

所以，說說結論。我要再次回到 1990 年代的樂觀主義，和 2020 年代幻想破滅的主題。這說明了多少運動人士的感受。少數安保協議歐洲公民倡議（ECI）的失

敗，加上歐盟執委會聲明他們會繼續如常運作，只是顯示嘗試讓會員國改變有多困難。這也必須改變。例如法國，拒絕變動區域性語言政策的控制。我們必須看到這項改變，才能讓歐洲讚頌其語言多元化。

歐盟一直在討論這件事，但沒有實際進展。

我們看到的正面因素，是語言復原會振興地方經濟。

語言復原對於民眾福祉，有認知益處，也是事實。

我們看到語言法律如何強調平等缺失，強化社會共存，語言權利是人權，必須妥善地納入更廣泛的人權架構中。

整體而言，我們可以說，已經有部分成功，但同志仍須努力。語言政策、語言規劃、語言發展，仍就是相對新興的科學。我們一路走來，仍在摸索學習。在1980年代與1990年代，當時樂觀氣氛高漲，非常期待語言復原，許多人認為我們可以在20年後達到語言復原。

但是現實是，要花上50年、70年，甚至100年，才會開始看到事情真正大有改善，特別是在社群層級。所以一切都還在努力中。我們有所有必須努力實現的心願。我確定，我們會經歷破滅的時間，然後開始又恢復信心，因為我們現在看到了部分成功，但是要維持警覺，我們要看到實質性的語言復原，需要好幾代的時間。

我要向各位致上深刻謝意。Meur ras bras as we say in Kernewek（康沃爾語）。我非常歡迎各位的任何問題或討論。各位可以在社群媒體或我們官網上追蹤我們的活動。再次謝謝各位先生女士，邀請我在會議上演說。

【紐西蘭毛利語 Maori 】
TŌKU REO, TŌKU OHOOH ：我的語言是我的覺醒；我的語言是我的靈魂之窗
TŌKU REO, TŌKU OHOOHO: My Language Is My Awakening, My Language Is the Window to My Soul

紐西蘭毛利電視臺首席執行長 Shane Taurima 先生

Mr. Shane Taurima, Chief Executive of Māori Television

I acknowledge the esteemed leaders gathered here today - greetings to you all. The karanga or call is the first sound you hear when you visit our *marae* or our traditional places of gathering. The *karanga* acknowledges our ancestors – your ancestors and mine. It acknowledges those that have gone before us. Although we are meeting online, we call on our *tīpuna* or ancestors to gather. We acknowledge them, grieve for them, and bid them farewell. The *karanga* also acknowledges the living and the *mana* or prestige that we collectively bring to this gathering.

I acknowledge the Hakka Affairs Council and the College of Hakka Studies of the National Central University. It is a pleasure to join you at the International Conference on Policies of the Hakka Languages and Minority Languages. I acknowledge the work you are doing to revitalise the Hakka language – the language of your ancestors. My name is Shane Taurima. I am Māori – the indigenous people of Aotearoa New Zealand. Aotearoa New Zealand is located in the south-western Pacific Ocean. It is made up of two large islands – TeIka a Māui (North Island), and Te Waka a Māui (South Island). I am from the East Coast of the North Island and from the tribes of Ngāti Kahungunu and Rongomaiwahine.

I'm privileged to be the Chief Executive of Māori Television. Two years ago, I had the privilege of visiting your beautiful country as part of a New Zealand delegation. We were invited by the Taiwan Subcommittee on the Reconciliation of Taiwan. We were hosted by Professor Jolan HSIEH and the National University of Donghua. We also met Mr. PasuyaPoiconx, who I note is one of the esteemed speakers at this conference.

In February 2020, we hosted Professor Jolan HSIEH and her delegation at Māori Television. I'm a journalist and have spent more than twenty five years working in Māori and mainstream media. Mainstream media has had a big impact onthe Māori language. They were up until recently the storytellers of our Māoristories. Our language was often mispronounced, used incorrectly, and Māori as a people were often portrayed negatively.

Video 03:21

Māori media began in the early nineteen eighties through tribal radio and had a very small presence on mainstream television. Through Māori media we have reclaimed our narrative and tell our stories in our language and in our ways. It's an expression of tino rangatiratanga. Our fight for self-determination. The ability for us to make our own decisions and determine our own futures.

Our history talks of the great Polynesian navigator Kupe, who sailed from Hawaiiki and discovered Aotearoa. His wife, Kuramarotini named the country Aotearoa, the land of the Long White Cloud.

In 1642, the Dutch explorer Abel Tasman became the first European to find the country, which he then named New Zealand after the region of Zealand in his home country of the Netherlands. The country was colonised in the 19th century. In 1840,Māori chiefs signed TeTiriti o Waitangi, a treaty between Māori and the British Crown. In 1841, the country became a colony within the British Empire and gained full statutory independence in 1947.

Video 04:41

We have a population of 5.1 million. Māori make up 16% of the total population. European make up the majority, followed by Asian and Pasifika. Today, only one in sixMāori can speak the Māorilanguage and only 3% can speak the language in the entire Aotearoa population. TeReoMāori is described by UNESCO as vulnerable.

My presentation will attempt to answer three questions. 1. How did this happen? 2.

What are we doing about it? 3. What does the future look like?

Video 05:20

I'm not an expert in language revitalisation. I'm an advocate and a foot soldier of the language revitalisation movement that we have here in Aotearoa. It's a passion. It's a duty. It is a responsibility that is left to us by our ancestors to ensure that our language, culture and identity is never lost, but continues to thrive today and tomorrow. But before we look ahead, we must look back.

Video 06:02

Each year, over one and a half million people tune into TeMatatini. A Māori erforming arts extravaganza that celebrates our language and culture. It is the biggest platform for the Māori language to be heard worldwide.

Video 06:25

Prior to European settlement, Māori were thriving and the Māori language was dominant in New Zealand. Colonisation decimated the Māori population, crippling the ability to pass the Māori language on to future generations. The 1867 Native Schools Act punished children who dared to speak Māori.

Video 06:55

Our grandmother's generation wasn't encouraged to speak Māori. They would be strapped for speaking Māori.

Video 07:27

In the 1970s, Māori fought back through protests, through petitions and to the steps of Parliament. In 1987, the Māori Language Commission was set up and the Māorilanguage was declared an official language of Aotearoa New Zealand. It was an era which saw the birth of Māori language preschools, schools, universities and radio stations, all dedicated to language survival. Broadcasting is perhaps the most powerful media of communication that we have.

Video 08:15

In 2004, Aotearoa New Zealand's first indigenous television network aired without apology. Today, Māori Television's digital strategy connects our families, our audiences and our language to the Māori world. It is excited and feel like the video is relevant to their world. Then we are winning. The content we create influences how our future generations see themselves and how the world sees them.

Video 08:56

Māori is giving birth to our voice to be heard. It is a digital footprint. We will imprint forever

Video 09:15

At the turn of the 20th century, Māori communities mainly spoke Māori, but the education system had undermined the use of tereoas the main language of communication. Generations of Māori that grew up being punished for speaking their language at school then became parents and didn't speak tereoto their children in fear of disadvantaging them or exposing them to punishment. It was these children that grew up speaking only English and the intergenerational transfer of language was lost in many families.

Video 10:10

From the nineteen forties, Māori and big numbers moved from their traditional rural settings to live in urban centres. This is known as the urban migration. This further contributed to language loss. In Māori communities, even those where English had made inroads. TeReoMāori was still the predominant means of communication. But in cities and large towns, English was the dominant language, and Māori, who moved to these environments, had little choice but to communicate in the language of thePākehā. The mass media was also exclusively in English. It was during this period that tereoMāori declined even more sharply.

Video 10:50

In 1973, we began on a nationwide survey that interviewed over thirty three thousand people from nearly six and a half thousand families. The survey findings were grim. And confirmed what we knew anecdotally. The language was in a perilous state, with only 18% of Māori, mainly elderly, were fluent speakers.

Video 11:13

The education system, the location where Māori language had been so damaged became a battleground where Māori began to fight back. The TeKōhangaReo Movement, which started in 1982, became the basis for a new generation of Māori speakers. Kura Kaupapa for Primary school, Wharekura for high school, and Wānanga for university students.

Video 11:44

Dr. HinurewaPoutū, Director of Reo, Māori Television

I am a graduate of KōhangaReo, Kaupapa Māori and Wharekura. Which is Māori medium education. And I started on my very first birthday. My parents didn't grow up as speakers of tereoMāori. Instead, they learned in their early twenties and they felt a really strong sense of what we call *mamae* and tereoMāori and Māori, which is a strong sense of pain and hurt. Having grown up not knowing our language and they didn't want their children to feel that way. And that's one reason why I grew up through KōhangaReo and could and so did my brother. I felt very much like a family and a whānau. We were surrounded with tereoMāori and everything was done entirely in tereoMāori.

I learned to read and write and sing and perform and dance, and even complete many of my senior high school examinations in tereoMāori. If I think about my mum and dad who didn't have that opportunity and in fact, some parts of school weren't very positive in terms of Māori identity and even my grandfather was punished at school for speaking Māori. So that's really changed the experience of our family and to one of being really positive about our language and our culture.

As a former teacher, having spent a lot of time teaching at Māori medium schools, one of the benefits for Māori children through the Māori language education system is that firstly it was founded on Māori values in a Māori world view.So that's really the foundation of how the schools operate. And whānau or families are actively involved in the decision making. So it's not something that's been imposed externally. It's a very empowering process to be involved in.

Video 13:43

Historically, in Aotearoa New Zealand, the education system has really disadvantaged and discriminated against Māori. And the evidence is showing that Māori language education is benefiting Māori children. They're doing very well academically, culturally and holistically, even in terms of national assessments. Māori children tend to do better through Māori medium education compared to mainstream schools, in which English is the main language of instruction.

Video 14:18

Māori Television launched in 2004. For more than 20 years, we had been able to speak and hear our language on radio, but this was the first time that we could speak here and see ourselves on our own channel. It was the first time that we could tell our own stories in our own ways, in our own language.

Video 14:54

Today, we celebrate the start of the MāoriTelevision channel, a new era in broadcasting.

Video 16:28

It's storytelling. Family history.

Video 16:35

(Teaching our tamariki)

Video 16:44

(Relating to our rangatahi)

Video 16:55

(making us laugh)

Video 17:04

(Tautoko our teams)

Video 17:15

The good thing about being Māori is we adapt quite easily to adversity.

Video 17:18

There are a lot of things that makes us unique. We live, breathe and practice and speaktereoMāori There is so much potential to just keep developing. This is Māori. It's a really great place to work.

Video 17:42

Five years ago, the Māori Language Act 1987, which made TeReoMāorian official language was updated. Te Ture mōTeReo Māori 2016 includes a Crown acknowledgement for the harm it inflicted on tereoMāori and a commitment to its revitalisation.

Video 18:25

Professor Rawinia Higgins was the Chair of the panel, set up to develop the Act and is the Chair of the MāoriLanguage Commission.

Prof. Rawinia Higgins, Chairperson of Māori Language Commission

The purpose of Te Ture mōteReo Māori, the Māori Language Act, is to give greater effect to the status of TeReoMāori or the Māori language and Aotearoa New Zealandby namely acknowledging that TeReoMāori is the indigenous language of Aotearoa New Zealand, that it is an official language of this country. But also, to give greater effect to Māori and communities to be able to lead in language revitalisation, more specifically. And so part of the Act was around creating a framework that allows greater effect of our Treaty of Waitangi relationship,but more importantly, to focus on language revitalisation for Māori. The Act also puts a strong emphasis on the importance and need for language planning to support language revitalisation.

TeWhare o teReoMauriorais the concept that we chose in the development of this Act. More specifically, a traditional Māori House which has two sides to the house and one side is a narrow side and another side is a larger side in terms of the design of the house. The narrow side is there primarily for the hosts of that. And so we are pushing that side to Māori. And then the larger side of the house is to the Crown or government agencies. The purpose for this is to give the analogy and structure to be able to support micro language planning, as well as macro language planning.

The two sides of the houseare designed to enable Māori to lead on the areas of the strategy that is related to them in terms of intergenerational language transmission and also the larger side of the house or macro language planning the side of the Crown and government agencies on how they set better conditions for our society to enable and enhance body language revitalisation across the board.

So, the house has two strategies one for Māori and one for the Crown. At the top of the house, we have a shared vision to ensure that our language is the living language in a governance sense.

The Ministers and TeMātāwai, or the entity that looks after and leads our modern language strategy are able to have shared conversations and strategy. Then you have Te Papa Kōrerowhere the strategy is enabled and acted upon by the Chief Executive Officers of both TeMātāwaiand the Crown entities.

It's important to consider language revitalisation planning, and policy as part of revitalisationbecause it allows us to focus on the areas that should be driven by the right people. So, for example, TeMātāwai looks at the focus on families and intergenerational language transmission and to be able to focus in that space on what we need in the homes because language in the homes is important. But this is not the role of the Crown or government entities.

But the Crown has to take responsibility in terms of providing and setting conditions for society to enable the language to be seen and heard in a way that it gives it value, that it gives it purpose, and also that we can see that our language in this country is being given greater effect as an official language of this country.

The future for the language looks bright. There are dedicated Māori strategies and initiatives that are seeing the language flourish in some communities. We have never heard so much tereoMāori or Māori being spoken in mainstream media and workplaces and out on our streets. The numbers of people wanting to learn the language has skyrocketed in recent years. But sadly our biggest challenge is encouraging Māori themselves to learn and use the language. The future of our language lies in the hands of our rangatahi, our young people. We must ensure there are opportunities for rangatahi to learn and use the language and the ways that are relevant to them. Here at Māori Television, we do that by enabling them to make their own decisions in creating their own opportunities.

Video 24:00

Prof. Rawinia Higgins, Chairperson of Māori Language Commission

For me, I'm optimistic about the future of tereoMāori. We have many initiatives that have focused on language revitalisation and the home, particularly within communities, but also we've seen a huge uptake by society for our language.

The Māori Language Commission has done a lot to attract wider New Zealand to become part of the movement and there has been a significant uplift in the numbers - with over a million people signing up to be part of that movement. I am hugely optimistic that we will achieve that.

But of course, language revitalisation is an intergenerational kaupapaand so it takes three generations to restore a language. And so we will still have to wait until my grandchildren come to see how far we've managed to progress.

Video 24:54

Dr. HinurewaPoutū, Director of Reo, Māori Television

The future of tereoMāori looks very bright and promising. Working here at MāoriTelevision, we're telling and showcasing so many amazing stories across platforms that even people of my grandfather's generation could never have imagined. When television was first launched here in Aotearoa, tereoMāori didn't even feature. And in fact, when I was growing up in the 1980s and 1990s, we only had five minutes worth of news in tereoMāori.

And now there are an array of opportunities, not only in terms of the media, but in terms of creative fields in education. I have nieces and nephews who are growing up overseas and they are speakers of tereoMāoriand so they're still living their lives and tereoMāori across the vast ocean. And I'm confident that they will continue to carry on our language onto future generationswhich is ultimately our key goal. And for me, that's what I hope, and I'm confident that will be the case.

Video 25:57

Mr. Shane Taurima, Chief Executive of Māori Television

I want to thank the other speakers that you have seen today.Professor Rawinia Higgins and Dr. HinurewaPoutū.

I also want to acknowledge the many people that have been, continue to be, and will be part of the Māori language revitalisation movement.My strength is not the strength of one. My strength is the strength of many.

毛利電視臺臺長 Shane Taurima 先生

感謝在場所有先進，大家好。大家造訪我們傳統聚會所時，首先會聽到 *Karanga* 呼喚。以呼喚感謝我們的祖先，你們與我們的祖先，感謝所有已離開我們的人。雖然我們今天在線上會面，仍要呼喚祖先來聚首。我們感謝祖先，為失去他們感到悲傷，並向他們道別。*Karanga* 也感謝所有活著的人，以及 *mana* 也就是我們共同為聚會帶來的影響力。

我要感謝客家委員會與國立中央大學客家學院。很榮幸能獲邀參與臺灣客語及少數族群語言政策國際研討會。感謝各位為復振客語所做的努力——你們祖先的語言。我是 Shane Taurima，我是毛利人，是紐西蘭原住民。紐西蘭位於太平洋西南方。主要由兩大島嶼構成，北島與南島。我來自北島東岸的 Ngāti Kahungunu 與 Rongomaiwahine 部落。

我很榮幸擔任毛利電視臺的執行長。兩年前，我很榮幸有機會與紐西蘭代表團一起造訪你們美麗的國家。當時受到臺灣和解小組的邀請，主辦方謝若蘭教授與東華大學熱情款待，當時也見到同樣為今天研討會主講貴賓的浦忠成先生。

2020 年 2 月，我們接待造訪毛利電視臺的謝若蘭教授與代表團。記者出身的我，在毛利電視臺與主流媒體工作 25 年。主流媒體對毛利語有相當大的影響。直到近年來都是訴說毛利故事的主流聲音。我們的語言經常有發音錯誤、使用錯誤的問題，毛利人的形象也經常以負面呈現。

影片 03:21

毛利媒體在 1980 年代初期開始發展，先是部落廣播電臺以及比主流電視臺出現的頻率低很多。透過毛利媒體，我們找回自己的敘述，用我們的語言、用自己的

方式來說我們的故事。這就是我們爭取自決的方式，爭取為自己做決定。並決定我們自己未來的能力。

　　我們的歷史可回溯到偉大的玻里尼西亞航海家庫佩，他從原鄉啟航後發現紐西蘭。他的妻子 Kuramarotini 將這個國家命名為 Aotearoa，有著長長白雲之地。1642年，荷蘭探索家亞伯・塔斯曼成為首位發現這個國度的歐洲人。他將這裡命名為紐西蘭，跟著他在荷蘭家鄉的地名而命名。我國在 19 世紀時曾被殖民。1840 年時毛利人首領與英國政府簽訂《懷唐伊條約》。1841 年，我國成為大英帝國的殖民地，又在 1947 年依法獲得獨立。

影片 04:41

　　我們人口共 510 萬人。毛利人占總人口 16%，歐洲人占大多數，接著是亞洲人與太平洋人。現在六位毛利人只有一位會說毛利語，總人口中只有 3% 會毛利語。聯合國教科文組織將毛利語定義為脆弱等級。

　　我的簡報將嘗試回答以下三個問題：1. 毛利語如何到今天的境況？2. 我們該怎麼辦？3. 未來將何去何從？

影片 05:20

　　我不是語言復振專家，我是倡議者，是紐西蘭語言復振運動的戰士。這是我的熱忱與責任。我們有這個責任，繼承祖先的遺志，以確保我們的語言、文化與身分永遠不會消失，而是持續蓬勃發展到未來。但在展望之前，我們必須先回顧。

影片 05:53（字卡）

　　毛利語為毛利人的生命動力。

影片 06:02

　　每年有 150 萬人收看毛利表演藝術大會，讚頌我們語言與文化的活動。這是最大的平臺，讓全世界聽見毛利語言。

影片 06:25

　　在歐洲人移居之前，毛利文化蓬勃發展、毛利語是紐西蘭主要語言。殖民大量殺害毛利人、破壞我們將毛利語傳承給未來世代的能力。1867 年的原住民學校法會處罰敢講毛利語的人。

影片 06:50（字卡）

1913 年有 90% 毛利學童會講母語。

影片 06:55

我們祖母的世代不鼓勵講毛利語，講了會被打。

影片 07:03（字卡）

1953 年只有 26% 毛利學童會講母語。

影片 07:09（字卡）

1970 年代只有 5% 毛利學童會講母語。

影片 07:27

到了 1970 年代，毛利人透過抗爭、請願與到國會抗議。1987 年成立了毛利語委員會，宣布毛利語為紐西蘭官方語言。這個世代見證了毛利語幼兒園、學校、大學、廣播電臺的設立，都是為了語言存續。廣播或許是我們所擁有最強大的溝通工具。

影片 08:10（字卡）

2004 年毛利電視臺開播。

影片 08:15

2004 年，紐西蘭第一家原住民電視臺盛大開播。今天，毛利電視臺的數位策略將我們的家庭、觀眾及語言，與毛利世界緊緊相連。讓人興奮又振奮，感覺身歷其境，那我們就贏了。我們創造的內容會影響未來世代如何看待自己，以及世界如何看待他們。

影片 08:56

毛利語讓我們自己的聲音被聽見。這是我們將永恆烙下的數位腳印。

影片 09:15

在 20 世紀初，毛利部落裡主要使用毛利語，但教育系統讓我們無法再使用毛利語為主要溝通語言。世世代代的毛利人成長過程中，講自己的語言在學校會被處罰，於是成為不敢對小孩講毛利語的父母，害怕讓小孩失去優勢或害他們受罰。這

些孩子成長過程中只會講英文，世代間的語言傳承就此在許多家庭中消失。

影片 09:48

「我們在學校講毛利語會被處罰。父母認為我們必須學習歐洲人的語言及生活方式。」

影片 10:10

從 1940 年開始，毛利人大批從鄉下搬到都市生活，又稱為都市移民。因此進一步造成語言流失。在毛利部落即使已經有英文出現，多數主要還是使用毛利語。但是在城市與大的鄉鎮裡，英文是主要語言，搬到這些環境的毛利人沒有選擇，只能以歐洲人的語言來溝通。大眾媒體也主要使用英語。就在這個時期，毛利語又更加急遽衰落。

影片 10:50

1973 年，全國針對 33,000 人、來自 6,500 個家庭進行調查。調查結果令人沮喪，證實了一直以來的觀察，語言狀態相當危險，只有 18% 的毛利人能夠流利使用毛利語，多數是年長者。

影片 11:13

教育制度中甚少使用毛利語，因此成了主要戰場，毛利人開始反擊。語言巢於 1982 年展開，成為培養新世代毛利語使用者的基礎。然後是國小、國高中以及大學的毛利語學習制度。

影片 11:44

毛利電視臺語言及文化部主任 HinurewaPoutū 博士

我畢業於毛利語言巢、全毛利語小學、毛利語高中。我從一歲就開始學毛利語。我的父母親成長過程沒有學毛利語，他們到了 20 歲初才開始學。因此他們一直感到一股強烈的 mamae 感，毛利語的意思是一種強烈的傷痛。因為他們成長過程中不會講毛利語。他們不希望自己的小孩也有同樣的感受，所以我和我的哥哥從小就透過語言巢的方式學習毛利語。這感覺就像一個大家庭，我們完全沉浸在毛利語的環境。

我學習用毛利語聽、說、讀、寫、唱歌跳舞，我的高中專業考試很多也甚至是

用毛利語完成的。想到我自己的爸媽，他們並沒有這樣的機會。甚至以前學校也並不贊同毛利意識，我的爺爺在學校講毛利語甚至會被懲罰。所以我的毛利語學習過程其實也完全翻轉了過去我們家人對自己的語言和文化的觀感，變成一個正面的體驗。

我過去曾在毛利語授課學校教書，全毛利語授課教育體制其實對毛利孩童非常有利，因為這樣的教育體制是建立在毛利價值與毛利世界觀上。學校運作的基礎正是這樣的共同價值觀，而且毛利家庭也積極參與決策過程。也就是說這樣的體制並不是從外部施加的，反而是一個能夠賦予參與者極大權力的制度。

影片 13:43

紐西蘭的教育體制過去長期不利於毛利人，甚至有所歧視。而現在證據顯示毛利語授課的教育體制有利於毛利孩童的發展，他們不管在學術、文化、整體面都發展非常好，國家考試上的表現也很優異。毛利孩童在毛利語授課教育體系的表現比起使用英文授課的主流教育體系還要好。

影片 14:18

毛利電視臺成立於 2004 年，過去 20 多年來，我們雖然能夠在電臺上使用並聽見毛利語，但電視臺成立後，我們第一次可以在自己的頻道上看見毛利人使用毛利語。我們第一次可以用自己的方式和語言去述說自己的故事。

影片 14:42（毛利語字卡）

我的語言，我的靈感。

影片 14:45（毛利語字卡）

我的語言，我的珍寶。

影片 14:53（字卡）

旅途開始。

影片 14:54

我們今天在此歡慶毛利電視臺的開播，電視臺的成立開啟了廣播業的新篇章。

影片 15:03（字卡）

旅途持續。

影片 15:17（字卡）

分享我們的故事。

影片 15:31（字卡）

向祖先致敬。

影片 15:45（字卡）

實現夢想。

影片 15:56（字卡）

使我們思考。

影片 16:01（英文字幕）

「你自己說要用毛利人方式處理的。」

影片 16:04（字卡）

述說歷史。

影片 16:16（字卡）

這天已經到來。

一起上街遊行。

影片 16:23（英文字幕）

我們必須維持與陸地和海洋的連結。

影片 16:28

我們在講故事。家庭的歷史。

影片 16:33（英文字幕）

我們沒有忘記你。

影片 16:35

（字卡：Teaching our tamariki）
教導我們的孩子。

影片 16:44

（字卡：Relating to our rangatahi）
連結我們的青年。

影片 16:55

（字卡：making us laugh）
娛樂大眾。

影片 17:04

（字卡：Tautoko our teams）
支持我們的團隊。

影片 17:15

毛利人的優勢在於我們的適應能力很強。

影片 17:18

毛利電視臺的工作讓我們保持獨特性。我們遵循毛利習俗，講毛利語。有非常多的可能，只要我們繼續發展下去。毛利電視臺的工作環境非常棒。

影片 17:42

1987 年毛利語言法確立了毛利語的地位，承認是正式語言。五年前紐西蘭更新了這條法。新的 2016 年毛利語言法包含了政府承認過去對毛利語的迫害，並承諾將協助毛利語的復振。

「……紐西蘭政府承認過去政策及作為的迫害性，且在過去的世代並沒有積極保護並提倡毛利語，也未善盡責任鼓勵毛利部族與毛利人使用毛利語。政府在此表示願意與毛利人一起合作，持續積極地為未來世代保護並且提倡毛利語。」

影片 18:25

Higgins 教授是 2016 年毛利語言法起草委員會的主席，也是現任毛利語語言監

察使。

毛利語委員會主席 Rawinia Higgins 教授

　　2016 年的毛利語言法的主要目的是更進一步提升毛利語的地位，透過承認毛利語是紐西蘭原住民語言，也是國家的官方語言。同時也讓毛利人與毛利社群更能夠主導毛利語的復振。更準確地說，新法案同時也創建了一個更好的框架去發揮《懷唐伊條約》所確立的關係。以及更重要的是專注在毛利語言的復振。新的法案也更強調了語言規劃對於支持語言復振的重要性與必要性。

　　「活語言之屋」這個概念是我們用來起草新法案的參考。這個概念中的屋子是一個傳統毛利屋，分兩邊，一邊比較狹窄一邊比較寬長。較狹窄的那邊通常是由主人使用，那一半邊代表毛利人，另外較寬敞的一邊代表政府單位。我們用屋子的比喻來把宏觀及微觀語言計畫之間的關係視覺化。

　　屋子分兩邊，一邊是毛利人，和毛利人較相關的領域像是跨世代語言傳播方面，由毛利人主導。屋子的另一邊則代表宏觀的語言規劃，屬於政府單位的權責範圍，由他們來營造更好的社會條件，提倡全面的毛利語言復振。

　　所以這個屋子涵蓋兩個策略，一個是毛利一個是政府。屋子上方的屋頂代表的則是雙方共享的願景，也就是確保語言的存活。

　　在這樣的概念下，政府的部長與 TeMatawai，也就是負責主導毛利語言策略的單位在同一個屋簷下交流，擬定策略。屋內的地板 te papa korero 代表的則是實際執行面，由雙方毛利及政府執行官實際去執行。

　　語言規劃和政策也是語言復振重要的一環。因為它讓我們可以確保此事是由合適的人來推動。舉例來說 TeMatawai 這個單位注重的是家庭與語言的代間傳遞，以及家庭內所需要的條件，因為家庭當中的語言使用非常重要，但這不是政府單位該扮演的角色。

　　政府單位的責任是建立有利於有效使用語言的大環境，讓毛利語能夠被看見以及被聽見，讓毛利語的使用是有價值且有目標的。讓毛利語作為國家官方語言，發揮更大的作用。

　　毛利語的未來非常光明。我們推出了專門的毛利語政策和計畫讓毛利語在某些社群蓬勃發展。在主流媒體、工作場域、或一般日常生活中使用毛利語的人非常多。近年來，想學毛利語的人數也大幅上升。可惜的是我們目前最大的挑戰反而在鼓勵我們自己毛利人學習並使用毛利語。毛利語的未來掌握在年輕人手上，我們必

須確保年輕人有機會用自己的方式去學習並使用毛利語。在毛利電視臺我們致力於提供年輕人管道可以自己做決定並自己創造機會。

影片 24:00

毛利語委員會主席 Rawinia Higgins 教授

我個人對於毛利語的未來非常樂觀。我們現在有許多計畫聚焦於語言復振，特別是在毛利部族家庭內的語言復振，我們同時也看到社會對毛利語的接受度也提高了。

最近，毛利語委員會努力吸引了紐西蘭廣大的社會參與毛利語的復振，參加人數大幅上升。我們看到超過一百萬人報名參加這個運動。我也非常樂觀我們可以達到目標。

當然，語言復振是跨世代的，需要經歷三個世代才能成功復振語言。所以必須等到我的孫兒出生才能回頭檢視我們的進展。

影片 24:54

毛利電視臺語言及文化部主任 HinurewaPoutū 博士

毛利語的未來非常明亮且充滿希望。在毛利電視臺工作，我們述說並傳達的故事透過各式各樣的平臺播送，這是我爺爺那一輩無法想像的。紐西蘭剛開始有電視的時候，根本不可能在電視上聽到毛利語。我的成長過程中，1980 年、1990 年代時電視上新聞頂多只有五分鐘是用毛利語播報。

現在有各式各樣的毛利語媒體，橫跨媒體、創意教育領域。我的侄子侄女雖然住在國外，他們同樣會講毛利語。雖然隔著海洋，毛利語仍是他們生活的一部分。我也有信心他們會繼續將毛利語傳給下一代，這也是我們最終的目標。我有希望，也有信心我們做得到。

影片 25:57

毛利電視臺臺長 Shane Taurima 先生

在此我想要感謝這段影片中的另外兩位講者，Rawinia Higgins 教授與 HinurewaPoutū 博士。

同時我也要感謝過去、現在、與未來參與毛利語復振運動的所有人。我的力量並不是一己之力，我的力量是眾人集結的力量。

【英國威爾斯語 Welsh】
威爾斯 2050 計畫與威爾斯語的代間傳遞
Prosiect 2050 and Intergenerational Transmission of Welsh

威爾斯語言部門領導人 Jeremy Evas 博士

1

01　WELSH IN FIGURES AND WORDS

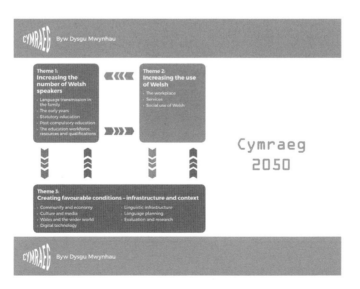

2

3

Cymraeg 2050

- Increase the number of speakers to 1,000,000
- Double daily use from 10% to 20%

4

Trajectory by 2050

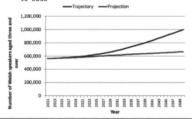

- Projection and trajectory of the number of Welsh speakers aged three and over, 2011 to 2050

5

Language Surveys

- Welsh Social Survey 1992: 21.5% (590,800) are Welsh speakers 13% (370,000) are fluent in Welsh

- Language use surveys 2004-06 20.5% (588,000) are Welsh speakers 12% (317,000) are fluent in Welsh

- Language use surveys 2013-15 24% (677,800) are Welsh speakers 11% (318,800) are fluent in Welsh

Fluency levels by where people had learnt to speak Welsh
(Source: *Welsh Language Use in Wales, 2013-2015*)

6

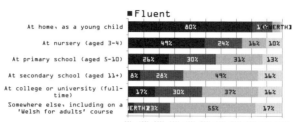

■Fluent

At home, as a young child	80%		10%	[GWERTH]
At nursery (aged 3-4)	49%	24%	16%	10%
At primary school (aged 5-10)	26%	30%	31%	13%
At secondary school (aged 11+)	8%	28%	49%	16%
At college or university (full-time)	17%	30%	37%	16%
Somewhere else, including on a 'Welsh for adults' course	[GWERTH] 23%	55%		17%

0% 10% 20% 30% 40% 50% 60% 70% 80% 90% 100%

Percentage of children aged three to four able to speak Welsh by household composition
(Source: Census 2011 and Census 2001)

7

■2001 ■2011

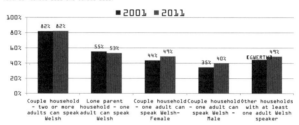

	Couple household – two or more adults can speak Welsh	Lone parent household – one adult can speak Welsh	Couple household – one adult can speak Welsh-Female	Couple household – one adult can speak Welsh – Male	Other households with at least one adult Welsh speaker
2001	82%	55%	44%	35%	[GWERTH]
2011	82%	53%	49%	40%	49%

Number of children aged three to four able to speak Welsh by household composition
(Source: Census 2011 and Census 2001)

8

■2001 ■2011

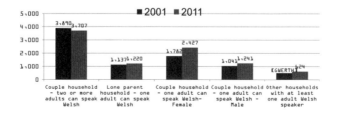

	Couple household – two or more adults can speak Welsh	Lone parent household – one adult can speak Welsh	Couple household – one adult can speak Welsh-Female	Couple household – one adult can speak Welsh – Male	Other households with at least one adult Welsh speaker
2001	3,890	1,137	1,782	1,041	[GWERTH]
2011	3,707	1,220	2,427	1,241	124

9

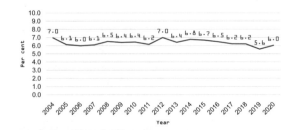

Percentage of five-year-old children
(at the start of the academic year) who
speak Welsh fluently at home
(Source: Pupil-Level Annual School Census)

10

Fishman

Graded intergenerational
disruption scale (GIDS)

- 【to attempt to revive language】 via stylish efforts to control the language of education, the workplace, the mass media and governmental services, without having safeguarded 【intergenerational language transfer】 is equivalent to constantly blowing air into a tire that still has a puncture.

11

- Mudiad Meithrin
- Welsh early years specialists

Mudiad Meithrin is the main
provider and facilitator of
Welsh medium early years
childcare and education in
the voluntary sector.

Mudiad Meithrin is the
umbrella organisation for
the following early years
provisions:

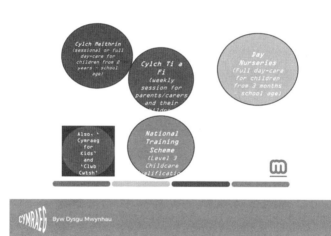

Cymraeg for Kids
· Encouraging and supporting
  families to use Welsh

15

02 THE BACKGROUND
RESEARCH

CYMRAEG Byw Dysgu Mwynhau

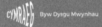

16

**The influence of social and social
psychological factors on the
intergenerational transmission of Welsh**

Jeremy Evas, Jonathan Morris & Lorraine
Whitmarsh
Cardiff University

CYMRAEG Byw Dysgu Mwynhau

17

Project Overview

- Project commissioned by the
  Welsh Government and
  published in line with
  Government Social Research
  publication protocols (June
  2017).

- The views expressed in this
  paper are those of the
  researchers and not
  necessarily those of the
  Welsh Government.

- In collaboration with
  Statiaith and Arad Research.

- Full report:
  http://gov.wales/statistics-
  and-research/?skip=1&lang=en

Llywodraeth Cymru
Welsh Government

Dadansoddi ar gyfer Polisi

YMCHWIL GYMDEITHASOL
Y LLYWODRAETH
GSR
GOVERNMENT SOCIAL RESEARCH

Analysis for Policy

CYMRAEG Byw Dysgu Mwynhau

Project Aims

- The project aimed to:
  - Examine the patterns of Welsh language transmission and use in families with children between 0 and 4 years old across Wales; and to
  - increase our understanding of the factors influencing these trends.

- Welsh-language policy context:
  - *A Living Language: a Language for Living* (Welsh Government 2012).
  - *Moving Forward* (Welsh Government 2014).
  - *Consultation on a Welsh Government Draft Strategy: A Million Welsh Speakers by 2050* (Welsh Government 2016).

Research Context: Previous studies of the transmission of Welsh

- 'Bilingual mothers rear monolingual English children because the encouragement, even pressures, for that language generally are stronger and more widespread than the corresponding support and facilities fostering bilingualism in Wales' (Harrison et al. 1981, p. 61).

- Lack of confidence in Welsh among some parents (Harrison et al. 1981; Bellin 1994).

- Tensions over the use of Welsh in some linguistically exogamous families (Harrison et al. 1981; Bellin 1994; Lyon 1996; Bellin & Thomas 1996).

Research Context: Previous studies of the transmission of Welsh

- Intergenerational language donation rather than transmission (Lyon 1996; Evas 1999).

- The role of the Welsh-speaking caregiver on early language socialisation (Jones & Morris 2005, 2007).

- Transmission of Welsh tends to be an unconscious decision for couples who are both from primarily Welsh-speaking backgrounds (Gathercole et al. 2007).

21

Research Questions

1. What are the conditions that facilitate Welsh language transmission within families, and the conditions that make Welsh language transmission less likely?

2. What are the conditions that influence patterns of Welsh language use within families with children in the 0-4 age group?

CYMRAEG Byw Dysgu Mwynhau

22

Methodology: Overview

- Mixed-methods approach comprising:
  - Quantitative analysis of questionnaire data, incorporating social psychological approaches (*Theory of Planned Behaviour*, e.g. Ajzen 1991).
  - Qualitative thematic analysis of semi-structured interview data.

- 60 main caregivers of children aged 0-4 from north west and south east Wales (note that the study does not present an areal comparison of these areas).

- 32 questionnaires returned by partners (where applicable).

- Recruitment through schools and National Survey of Wales respondents.

CYMRAEG Byw Dysgu Mwynhau

23

Methodology: Sample

- Majority of main respondents were women (*n*=51).

- Respondents aged 20-45.

- All of the main respondents reported being able to speak Welsh; 47% acquired Welsh through family transmission.

Map data ©2017 Google

- 75% of partners reported ability in Welsh; 38% of these acquired Welsh through family transmission.

CYMRAEG Byw Dysgu Mwynhau

Methodology: Data coding and analysis

24

- Intention to act is preceded by:
  - attitude towards the behaviour
  - subjective (or social) norms
  - perceived behavioural control (PBC).

- Adapted TPB measures presented as seven-point Likert items.

Theory of Planned Behaviour (Ajzen 199

- Stepwise regression in SPSS.

CYMRAEG　Byw Dysgu Mwynhau

Methodology: Data coding and analysis

25

- Coding of qualitative data:
  - The respondent's language use and attitudes towards Welsh in childhood.
  - The respondent's current language use with extended family, and in their social networks and wider community.
  - The family's current linguistic behaviour in the home.
  - Discussions with partner, extended family, and/or external agencies regarding language use in the home prior to the birth of the child and during early childhood (if applicable).

- Thematic analysis based on these codes.

CYMRAEG　Byw Dysgu Mwynhau

Results: Quantitative Analysis

26

- Almost always speaking Welsh with children:
  - 42 per cent of main respondents ($n=25$).
  - 33 per cent of partners ($n=11$).

- Strong correlation between Welsh language background and transmission:
  - $r=0.70$ ($p<0.01$) for main respondents.
  - $r=0.76$ ($p<0.01$) for partners.

CYMRAEG　Byw Dysgu Mwynhau

27

Results: Qualitative Analysis

- The transmission of Welsh to children as
  an unconscious behaviour by respondents:

'Mae bob dim yn fy mywyd i wedi bod drwy'r
Gymraeg—mae fy addysg i wedi bod trwy'r
Gymraeg, ac wedyn mae fy ngwaith i wedi bod
trwy'r Gymraeg, ac mae fy ngŵr i'n Gymraeg, mae
fy mhlant i'n Gymraeg felly dydi hi ddim yn
rhywbeth dwi wedi gwneud yn 'conscious' er mwyn
cael gwaith… mae jyst wastad wedi bod yna'.

*'Everything in my life has been through Welsh—
my education has been through Welsh, and then
my work has been through Welsh and my husband
is Welsh-speaking so it isn't something I've
done consciously in order to get work…it's just
always been there'.*

—Mother, Gwynedd.

28

Results: Qualitative Analysis

- Increasing the use of English in a Welsh-
  speaking home:

'Dwi'n meddwl fod o'n bwysig bo' nhw'n
siarad Saesneg hefyd achos mae'r gymdeithas
fel mae hi yn ddwyieithog so yr unig
anfantais dwi'n teimlo bo' fi di gael ydi bo
fi ddim yn *confident* yn siarad Saesneg'.

*'I think it's important that they also speak
English because society as it is bilingual
so the only disadvantage I feel that I've
had is that I don't feel confident speaking
English'.*

—Mother, Anglesey.

29

Results: Qualitative Analysis

- Discussions about transmission in a
  linguistically exogamous family:

'I gychwyn roedd o'n meddwl ei fod o'n syniad
bendigedig bod yn siarad Cymraeg ac wedyn…doedd o
ddim yn hoffi'r syniad bod ei [blentyn] o a fi a'i
[sibling] yn mynd i fod yn siarad mewn iaith na
fasa fo ddim yn deall...oedd o'n hoffi'r syniad
ond fel oedd y gwirionedd yn dod yn agosach doedd
o ddim yn hoff iawn o'r syniad o gwbl'.

*'To start with he thought it was a great idea
speaking Welsh and then…he wasn't keen on the idea
that his [child] and me and his [sibling] are going to be
speaking in a language he didn't understand…he liked the idea but
when it came to it he didn't like the idea at all'.*

—Mother, Gwynedd.

Results: Qualitative Analysis

30

- The transmission of English as an
  unconscious behaviour:

'If you don't speak Welsh at home, which we
didn't, when you have a child, it tends to
be that you don't even think about the
language…'. When they start school, then you
make a decision. If you're not used to
speaking [Welsh], English is the default
setting'.

—Father, Rhondda Cynon Taf.

Results: Qualitative Analysis

31

- Intergenerational language donation:

'Even before I was pregnant I've always said
that I wanted my children to go to a Welsh
school and my partner has always known
that'.

—Mother, Caerphilly.

'My ex-partner did not want the children to
go to a Welsh school whatsoever. Completely
and utterly against it. So obviously, that's
a massive barrier to begin with...'.

—Mother, Rhondda Cynon Taf.

Results: Qualitative Analysis

32

- Increasing the use of Welsh in the home
  when the child goes to a Welsh-medium
  school:

'[My] confidence in Welsh is building. I
really enjoy it, it's all still in there. I
use more Welsh with them'.

—Father, Anglesey.

'[Language use] is probably 90% English.
I'll ask her of a morning if she wants *dŵr*
(water) or *llaeth* (milk)'.

—Mother, Caerphilly.

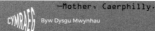

33

- Lack of confidence in Welsh (often linked
  to lack of opportunity for use) and
  perceived negative experiences:

'I probably get a bit flustered [speaking
Welsh], I think if I used it a lot more it
would come more natural again but I think
[daughter] tests me when she's asking me
constantly 'what's this in Welsh?' and for
the life of me, I'm thinking, eh?'

—Mother, Caerphilly.

'When you speak to them they look at you as
if to say, you're not even speaking proper
Welsh'.

—Father, Rhondda Cynon Taf.

34

Discussion & Conclusions: Transmission

- Intergenerational language transmission
  tended to be an unconscious behaviour
  except in couples where one respondent
  spoke Welsh (and came from a Welsh-
  speaking family) and their partner did
  not.

- Intergenerational language *donation* was
  considered both prior to birth and/or
  during early years by most of the
  respondents who had acquired Welsh through
  Welsh-medium education.

- Social factors (e.g. linguistic
  background) seem to be more influential
  than psychological factors (e.g. attitudes
  towards Welsh).

35

Discussion & Conclusions: Use

- Respondents tended to label language use
  as either Welsh or/English, though some
  respondents did note using both (possible
  limitation in research design).

- Formulaic Welsh used by many respondents
  who had acquired Welsh through Welsh-
  medium education once their child had
  started school.

- Barriers to using more Welsh with their
  children include:
  - Lack of confidence in Welsh or
    perceived negative experiences
  - Perceived lack of opportunity to use
    Welsh since leaving school.

Discussion & Conclusions: Further Work

- Observational research of language use among both parents and children in the home.

- Longitudinal studies of Welsh speakers, especially after leaving Welsh-medium education (cf. linguistic *mudes*, Pujolar and Gonzàlez 2013).

- Application of Theory of Planned Behaviour measures to both transmission and other aspects of linguistic behaviour using a larger sample.

03　BEHAVIOURAL
　　SCIENCE

MINDSPACE
Influencing behaviour through public policy

39

Messenger	we are heavily influenced by who communicates information
Incentives	our responses to incentives are shaped by predictable mental shortcuts such as strongly avoiding losses
Norms	we are strongly influenced by what others do
Defaults	we 'go with the flow' of pre-set options
Salience	our attention is drawn to what is novel and seems relevant to us
Priming	our acts are often influenced by sub-conscious cues
Affect	our emotional associations can powerfully shape our actions
Commitments	we seek to be consistent with our public promises, and reciprocate acts
Ego	we act in ways that make us feel better about ourselves

40

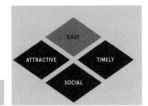

EAST
Four simple ways to
apply behavioural insights

41

TWO DIMENSIONAL MODEL OF BEHAVIOUR CHANGE

REASONABLE HUMAN BEING

INFORMATION TO MAKE
INFORMED DECISIONS

INCENTIVES AND
DISINCENTIVES
TO ENCOURAGE A BEHAVIOUR
'IN HIS/HER OWN
INTERESTS"

THREE DIMENSIONAL MODEL OF BEHAVIOUR CHANGE

`42`

THE 14 MOTIVATORS THAT WILL PERSUADE US TO ACT
[TO SPEAK WELSH TO OUR KIDS?]

`43`

COM-B Behaviour Change Framework

`44`

Capability	Opportunity	Motivation
Does your target audience:	**Does your target audience:**	**Does your target audience:**
Have the right knowledge and skills?	Have the resources to undertake the behaviour?	Want to carry out the behaviour?
Have the physical and mental ability to carry out the behaviour?	Have the right systems, processes and environment around them?	Believe that they should?
Know how to do it?	Have people around them who will help or hinder them to carry it out?	Have the right habits in place to do so?

45

04 THE POLICY AIMS

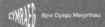

46

National policy on Welsh
language transmission
and use in families

Main aims…
Inspire today's generation of
children and young people to
speak Welsh to their children in
the future.

Reignite the Welsh language
skills of those who may not have
used Welsh since their school
days, or who aren't confident in
their language skills, to speak
Welsh with their own children.

Support and encourage use of
Welsh within families where not
everybody speaks Welsh.

Support Welsh-speaking families
to speak Welsh with their
children.

47

05 THE POLICY'S
PRINCIPLES

Principles

48

Children are individuals and have their own sense of agency.

Children may express language preferences themselves regarding what language they use

Messaging is an important element of any intervention in any field, but it's not necessarily the intervention itself.

Family types are more diverse, e.g. many children in one parent families and/or in families where parents/carers belong to LGBTQI groups.

The balance between the influence of the home, the wider family, community and external social influences.

Principles

49

We'll plan in advance using theories of change to better understand how to get from where we are to where we want to be.

This will help everyone know in advance what success looks like. And if what we do doesn't work, we'll change it or find a better way of helping families use more Welsh.

All interventions developed through this Policy will be based upon behavioural science and other relevant methodologies.

Principles

50

All interventions will use an iterative approach whereby we'll aim to quickly find out what's successful and what's not, where we expect things to fail, learn lessons from those failures and document how to strengthen future work.

We'll focus on ensuring children gain positive Welsh language experiences with the aim of those experiences spilling over to their use of Welsh outside of school and their linguistic behaviour in later life.

51

06 THE POLICY
ACTIONS

52

- To manage the work we'll do as part of this Policy, we'll establish a **programme board**, the members of which will have a range of perspectives of family support interventions. We'll include other stakeholders on this board to advise, assist, and provide challenge. We'll use this board not only to regularly review what we're doing, but to also what we're achieving. And if we aren't achieving, we'll make sure we learn from this and adapt what we do accordingly.

- Welsh Government programmes reach thousands of families of all types across many sectors. We'll analyse the opportunities these touchpoints offer to support the aims of this Policy.

53

- We'll analyse interventions in the field of language transmission and look at how lessons learnt **elsewhere in the world** can be applied to our situation in Wales. In doing this we'll work with the Network to Promote Linguistic Diversity (NPLD), the indigenous, minority and lesser-used languages group of the British-Irish Council and any other relevant networks.

- We'll look at work done with families in **other fields** and, if appropriate, adapt that work to help families to use more Welsh with their children.

- We'll **analyse how we communicate with families** and their extended members (beyond the immediate caregivers) about their use of Welsh with the aim of sustaining and increasing the intergenerational transmission of Welsh. This could involve looking at which channels we use, the way we use them as well as which individuals these channels target.

- We'll **provide practical advice and/or techniques to families where not everybody speaks Welsh** on how to increase their use of Welsh in all sorts of family situations.

- We'll **create new initiatives building on our existing work** to support Welsh language transmission and use in families. They'll use the latest techniques to change behaviours. Amongst others, they'll support people who may not have used their Welsh language skills since their school days to speak Welsh with their children. These may be built around the needs of specific geographical areas, target audiences and/or the social networks of parents/carers (whether face to face or virtual) and will take into account the demographics of these areas.

- We'll **make advice available to parents/carers** on what they could do when their children lack confidence in using Welsh or may be reticent to use it for other reasons. This could include targeted interventions via the health, childcare, education, or other sectors, and may be delivered at a particular times of transition or 'mudes' as we note above.

- For those parents who haven't used their Welsh language skills in some time, we'll trial a **language use pledge programme.** This may build on the successes of a Basque language initiative called *Euskaraldia*. We'll start on a small scale with parents/carers of different family language backgrounds.

- We'll explore opportunities for **peer-to-peer support** amongst parents/carers so they can help each other increase the amount of Welsh they use within their families.

57

- We'll **create projects to use parent/carer networks** around schools to help families use more Welsh with their children.

- We'll give professionals the skills and learning resources to help them **positively encourage** children to speak Welsh with one another. These will aim to help children become confident speakers of Welsh in later life, empowered to use their Welsh language skills, whatever their family language background.

58

- We'll use all the possibilities **the workplace offers to increase individuals' use of Welsh** and explore what potential there is for this to 'spill over' into families. We'll consider how this work needs to be tailored to meet the needs of various demographic groups.

- We'll ensure that **Welsh for Adults courses reinforce the aims of this Policy**, and look at ways of developing the specific skill set needed for using the Welsh language with a child. This will be particularly relevant to parents who were educated through the medium of Welsh, but were themselves raised in non-Welsh-speaking homes.

59

- We'll look at techniques used in other countries to **develop people's assertiveness and confidence in using languages** and, where we these have been proven to work, we'll implement them in our work with families.

- We'll **develop an online presence** to assist parents/carers who could, but for whatever reason, don't speak Welsh with their children. This may involve helping parents who have no personal experience of raising a child in a home where more than one language is spoken (e.g. helping them learn child-directed speech in Welsh).

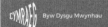

- We will explore the opportunities **gaming, other technologies and physical play** offer to help children use more Welsh and how that in turn can provide opportunities to help more use of Welsh in the household.

- We'll put specific actions in place for **disabled people and those who have additional needs, impairments or health conditions** to help them use more Welsh with their family. We'll also make sure that these people and their families are at the centre of all our work.

60

- We'll **review our existing work and examine past interventions** on language transmission in families and make sure that we base what we do on evidence from behavioural science and on a sound theory of change. We'll feed what we learn from this review into pilot interventions. We'll learn from those pilots and if they don't work, then we'll change them or find a better way of helping families use more Welsh.

61

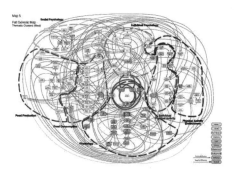

62

Briefing 1

Good afternoon. I'm Jeremy Evas from the Welsh Government, and I am head of Prosiect 2050, anointer disciplinary and multidisciplinary unit that helps people use more Welsh. More about that later.

I am here today to talk to you about the intergenerational transmission of our language. When parents can speak your language, and many of them do, that's how languages survive; when some of them don't, that's how languages don't survive. I'd like to talk to you about the work we're doing in the field of the intergenerational transmission of Welsh and what we're going to be doing over the next 10 years. I hope your conference goes very well, and I look forward to receiving your questions. So, before we get on to the details of the intergenerational transmission of Welsh, I'd like to talk to you about the Welsh language. Wales is in the United Kingdom, and we have the Welsh language there, which is a member of the P-Celtic branch of the Indo-European family of languages.

Let's get onto the figures.

Briefing 2

I'm also strategizingaboutwhat's happening in Wales to promote and increase the use of our language. There are three themes to our government strategy, published back in 2017, called Cymraeg 2050. Cymraeg is the Welsh word for "Welsh language", so by 2050, we have a bold vision. We want more people speaking Welsh, more people using Welsh, more people knowing Welsh, and more Welsh language services in the infrastructures around them. Let's have a look at these strategic themes.

Theme one of the three is about increasing the number of people who can speak Welsh, and that's done in many ways—through language transmission in the family, through the early-years provision of playgroups and childcare, through statutory education systems, and all types of education to provide adult and vocational and qualifications in the workplace.

But that's only so much. There are more things to do than merely creating people who can speak Welsh. The challenge is how to help them use the Welsh that they have, and again, I'll be talking about that today. What situations do we have where people can use their Welsh in an unfettered and uninterrupted way and where they know they can speak Welsh to other people?

The plain fact of the matter is that in lots of minority language contexts, those situations are not as numerous as we'd like them to be. We are looking at how we can create more situations, like in the workplaces, for people to use Welsh with each other. Now of course, the workplace has changed over the last year and a half. What are the implications for future workplaces in-person or online, after the COVID pandemic has passed? What does technology have to offer to that?

And, the social use of Welsh. People use Welsh when they socialize with each other. In order for all these things to happen, we needinfrastructure, we need supporting infrastructure, whether it's inthe community or the economy, and whether you know what we have in terms of culture and media content in Welsh to consume, bearing in mind that the vast majority of Welsh speakers can also speak English.

Therefore, we are able to access the enormous amount of content that is available in the English language. What canwe do to enable content, to create content which is original and attractive for people who are bilingual in one of the world's biggest languages to use?

Digital technology, as I've already mentioned. What's that going to look like post-pandemic? How arewe going to be using it? How can it enable technology? Microsoft Teams will shortly have a simultaneous interpretation facility, so I could, for example, speak in Welsh in the future to you. And there could be a human interpreter interpreting that into your language, so that's something to look forward to as well, and that won't just work for Welsh. It willwork for all languages in the world.

And then, the linguistic infrastructure. What are the technological components? What arethe corpus planning, the status planning,the terminology dictionaries, lexicons, and technological components that other people can incorporate in their products? Of course, all this has to be done on a research basis. We've got big ambitions for our language and we've got big plans to implement them. What we want to do is to increase the number of Welsh speakers from around 562,000 to one million by 2050.

Briefing 3

It's a bold ambition, but as I said, there's a difference between knowing a language and using that language, and we want to ensure that our language is more used as well. At the moment, according to surveys,the Welsh language is used by 10% of the population of Wales every day. We want to double that to 20% by 2050, so those are the two top level targets of our Cymraeg 2050 strategy一one million Welsh speakers, and doubling the daily use.

This is the trajectory. You can see where we're at in 2011. We need to make sure that the factory一the education system, the intergenerational transmission system一produces more Welsh speakers. Historically, the number of Welsh speakers has declined since the census was first taken in 1891, and this is what we need to do. All this is published in our Cymraeg 2050 strategy, which will be available to you as attendees at the conference.

Briefing 4

So that's the number of people who can, and who are projected, to speak it. We need thenumber of speakers to get to one million. This is about language use surveys, which will be coming up as well. Back in 1992, 21.5% of the population of Wales said they were able to speak Welsh, and 13% in the same survey said they were fluent in Welsh.

Briefing 5

Now, what does fluent mean? Well, it's a self-declaration. It's not a scientific definition; it's self-reporting. In areas where people speak minority languages or regional minority languages, we have two languages to choose from.The dominant language, in the situation of diglossia, is often rated by individuals as their confidence beinghigher in that language than in the minority language. Back in 1992, 13% said they were fluent, whatever fluent means.

OK, 12 years later, or maybe 12 to 14 years later, 20.5%, or 2000 fewer people, said they were Welsh speakers, and 12%, that's quite a drop there, said they're fluent. This is not a 100% sample; this is a representative sample.

Then later again, we're up to 24% stating they are Welsh speakers; 677,800. That's quite the increase there, but 11%, or 318,000, are fluent in Welsh.

Briefing 6

Let's now get a bit closer to the intergenerational transmission and see the fluency level according to where people learned Welsh.

So, of people who are fluent in Welsh, 80% of fluency levels are due tolearning at home as a young child. Let's just look at this. This proves how important the intergenerational transmission of a language is, because what our research shows us is that the earlier you learn a language, the more you are likely to use it later on in life.

So,the nursery is responsible for 49% of those people who learned it fluently at home.

The home is an extremely important nexus, as Joshua Fishman has said. If you're not familiar with the work of Joshua Fishman, I would really recommend you read: Reversing language shift, published by him back in around 1991 or1992, I think. Let's have a look at this.

Fluent and can speak a fair amount, so you've got 93% there at home as a young child. The statistics are clear—the home is extremely important.

Briefing 7

But what of it?What do we do with it? Let's have a look at this by household composition. This is just in the home. There are two censuses—the 2001 census and the 2011 census here. Let's have a look at it.

This is a household where there are two parents, and bothof those parents can speak Welsh. Where two parents are Welsh speakers and there are children aged three to four, 82% of those children can speak Welsh in both censuses.

So, there's a loss of about 20% of child language capacity in two-parent Welsh-speaking families with children who are three or four years of age. Now, that's not to say that they won't learn Welsh later in life through the education system; they haven't got Welsh language skills at that time, and we infer from these statistics their language use. These are not language use statistics, they're language knowledge statistics. It is an inferential statement about transmission there.

There are households where both people in a couple speak Welsh, but what about in single-parent families, where one adult can speak Welsh? In single-parent families where that single parent is Welsh-speaking, the transmission rate is much lower. We don't know exactly why, but again, we have inferred that itmay be due to childcare issues when the parent goes out to work and the child is looked after somewhere else.

OK, we're back to households where there are two adults. In the 2001 census, in households where the female was aWelsh speaker and the male was not,44% of the children spoke Welsh, which means that 56% of the children in two-parent households where the female parent was Welsh-speaking did not speak Welsh. And, 49% could speak Welsh in the 2011 census. Let's look at the corresponding figures for both censusesfor males.

In 2001, in couple households where the male adult was Welsh-speaking, 65% of the kids did not speak Welsh between ages zero to four, and this was 60% in 2011.

Another household composition coming up there. That's some quite stark statistics there.

Briefing 8

Let's have a look at something else.

These are the numbers we're talking about, the exact same numbers that I just mentioned in percentage terms.

There's not an enormous amount of difference between them. There's quite a lot of geographical variation in the transmission rates bycounty, but as you can see, the number of people in bilingual families, where both parents are present and only one of them can speak Welsh, is increasing.

Briefing 9

Now let's have a look at a different source. We've been talking about language and surveys. We've talked about the census, and now we're going on to the Pupil Level Annual School Census, which is a different one again. Let's go back to 2004. We can see the percentage of five-year-old children—up to now we've been dealing with children zero to four years of age. These are the percentages of five-year-old children at the start of the academic year who speak Welsh fluently at home. It has been hovering between 6%

and 7% over the last 16 years.

Briefing 10

I talked about Joshua Fishman, and how seminal and important his work is, for the intergenerational transmission of all languages. He has created theGraded Intergenerational Disruption Scale which if you don't know, you might want to take a look at.It's quite simple and quite interesting.

Maybehe's revising it now in thisnew world, as it's over 20 years old. What he said was: "to attempt to revive language via stylish efforts to control the language of education, the workplace, the mass media, and governmental services, without having safeguarded intergenerational transfer or transmission, is equivalent to constantly blowing air into a tire that still has a puncture."

Maybe we'll come back to that atthe end.

Briefing 11

So, what's going on in Wales? There are a whole host of interventions; there are lots of provisions. MudiadMeithrin, formerlyMudiadYsgolionMeithrin, is an enormous organization which looks after children of preschool age. They are the Welsh early year's specialists. They are the main provider.

Briefing 12

They're the umbrella organization for lots of sub-brands

Briefing 13

Who give the Welsh language to a lot of families who don't have it.We haveCylchMeithrin, which provides full day care or sessional day care for children from two years old,CylchTi a Fi, a weekly session for parents, and there are carers and their children, as well as day nurseries. Thereis all manner of things going on there.

Briefing 14

We have the Cymraeg for Kids program,which isalso running in substantial part by MudiadYsgolionMeithrin, remembering of course that Cymraeg is the Welsh word for

"Welsh language". We have done work in the past with the health sector and midwives, those medical staff who help mothers give birth and provideclasses before and after giving birth, to see how we canget messages to parents to use the Welsh language or to send their children to Welsh-medium school. Every parent in Wales will get a birth card, and there are messages about the Welsh language on that.

And we've got booklets and information. These are all informational things. Maybe we'll get into more behaviorally-drivenapproaches later.

Briefing 15

I'm here to talk about our policy on the intergenerational transmission of Welsh. This policy is based on research and by way of a declaration of interest.

Briefing 16

I used to work at Cardiff University, where I lead a team that included Jonathan Morris and Lorraine Whitmarsh, who did this research. This research is called "The influence of social and social psychological factors on the intergenerational transmission of Welsh."

Briefing 17

It was commissioned by the Welsh government where I now work, so I'm talking in my current job about the work I did in my previous job.

Briefing 18

What did wetry to do? Well, welooked at patterns of the language used and transmission in families with children aged zero to four, the same category as I talked about earlier in the census, and we wanted to increase our understanding of what went on there. And the strategic fit, as I've already talked about, the current strategic fit isCymraeg 2050. Our ambition is to have a million Welsh speakers and to double the daily use of Welsh by 2050. This was published just before that strategy was published.

Briefing 19

Now, there was a lot of work done on Welsh language policy in the past in Wales.

It's really, really, really interesting because I think the discourse around transmission has changed. Back in 1981, there was astudycalled "Bilingual mothers in Wales and the language of their children", and as much as I'd like to talk in length about it, the time doesn't allow it. Let's just look at a quote from the study:"Bilingual mothers bring up monolingual English children because the encouragement and even pressure for that language are generally stronger and more widespread than the corresponding support and facilities fostering bilingualism in Wales."

So, remembering that report, people, confidence levels, and maybe perceptions of these social-economic values of Welsh, the prevailing discourse around the Welsh language at the time created a situation where parents thought: "Let's decide not to speak Welsh to our child because that's not the way forward." And you do hear lots of stories about that in the past. Let's have a look at what's happened since.

In 1994, 13 years later, by some of the same team, Harrison and Bellin—Bellin was also part of the first team—found a lack of confidence in Welsh among some parents. They didn't speak Welsh to their childrenbecause they weren't confident in their own Welsh language skills. Then again, some of the same people, in 1991 and 1994, or Jean Lyon in 1996, found the theme of tension over the use of Welsh in some linguistically exogamous families. "Exogamous" is a sort of posh word for couple households where the couple is not bilingual but linguisticallyexogamous—one parent speaks Welsh, one parent doesn't—and this research showed that there can be tensions in such situations.

Briefing 20

Let's move on.Intergenerational language donation rather than transmission, as discussed by Jean Lyon in 1996 and myself in 1999. We'll revisit this later because what we found was that some parents who could speak Welsh didn't necessarily speak Welsh with their children for whatever reason, but would make sure that their children could speak Welsh via the education system. They donated the language to their children rather than actively spoke it to them. And then, Katherine Jones looked more atthe role of Welsh-speaking caregiversin the early language socialization process. Coming closer to the present day, 2007, before we get onto the research that I led, Virginia Gathercole led a team of researchers for the Welsh Language Board, who came to the conclusion that the transmission of Welsh isnot a conscious decision. Maybe it had been in times gone by, but it tends to be an unconscious decision for couples who are both from primarily Welsh-speaking backgrounds. If everyone speaks Welsh, everyone speaks Welsh to the children, then it's not an issue.

Briefing 21

On to the current research. These are the two research questions:

What are the conditions that facilitate Welsh language transmission within families, and what are the conditions that make Welsh language transmission less likely?

The second research question is: What are the conditions that influence patterns of Welsh language use within families with children in this zero to four age group? The reason we talked about the zero to four age group is that we believed people in that age group will be far less touched by the formal education system. We were trying to disaggregate it to get rid of the possible influence of education there and really find or make inferences about what happens in the family.

Briefing 22

We used a mixed-method approach. We did some quantitative analysis; we did some social psychological theory-planned behavior approaches; we did some qualitative interviews.

This sample wasreasonably small, 60 caregivers, and it wasnot an entire geographical spread all over the whole of Walesdone in the broadest terms; it was done in North West Wales and South East Wales, and these were all parents aged 20 to 45.

Briefing 23

All of these parents at some point had facilities in the Welsh language; all of these parents could, at one point, speak Welsh.

Briefing 24

Okay. Some of this presentation is going to be about behavioral theory. Someof the methodologies we used in the report werethetheory of planned behavior and thetheory of rational action. That's all aboutsomething that will come intothe COM-B model later in the presentation; the intention to act in the context of this research is the attitude that the person has towards the Welsh language—the subjective or social norms. So, what do people think about the Welsh language around here? How did people behave about the Welsh language? And, perceived behavioral control. How much control do you think you have over it? Can I use Welsh? Is my Welsh good enough?

Briefing 25

And so, we adapted that theory and evaluated it on a 7-pointscale,and we did lots of statistical analyses of them.

In terms of the qualitative data—the interview data, we examined the people who responded and their attitudes towards Welsh. We examined their use of Welsh in their childhood, their current languages with their own extended family, their social networks, their linguistic behaviorsat home, and any discussions that had happened with their partners, their extended family, or external agencies, regarding the language to be used prior to birth.

What was theinformation in these people's heads? Or, did they just carry out their language behaviorbecause that's how it hadalways been done for them? Let's have a look.

Briefing 26

There is a strong correlation between the Welsh language background aperson has and how likely they are to transfer the Welsh they have to their own children.

The more Welsh language you have in your own background, the more likely you are to speak Welshwith your children.

Briefing 27

It's an unconscious behavior, according to areport that replicates the report ofGathercole in 2007.

The transmission of Welsh children was listed as an unconscious behavior by the respondents. You can read English on the slide. I think it's probably time you heard some ofthe Welsh language, so I'll read this slide out in Welsh.

Mae bob dim ynfymywydiwedi bod drwy'rGymraeg-mare fyaddysgiwedi bod trwy'rGymraeg, ac wedynmaefyngwaithiwedi bod trwy'rGymraeg felly dydi hi ddimynrhywbethdwiwedigwneudyn 'conscious' ermwyncaelgwaith... maejystwastadwedi bod yna.

So, if everything is Welsh, everything is Welsh, and it's always there.

Briefing 28

It's an unconscious thing.It just happens.

In Anglesey, in Northwest Wales, we have a story of a mother who saidthat she thinks it's important that her children also speak English because the society is bilingual.

Well, she doesn't feel that confident speaking English herself, so she wants her children to speak English as well.

as their Welsh.

Briefing 29

There are discussions about transmission in a linguistically exogamous family. That word again refersto a two-parent family where one of the parents doesn't speak Welsh.

I'll read it out in Welsh again, and we can pause on this:

I gychwynroeddo'nmeddwleifodo'nsyniadbendigedig bod o'nsiaradCymraeg ac wedyn... doedd o ddimynhoffi'rsyniad bod ei [blentyn] o a fi a'i [sibling] ynmy ndifodynsiaradmewniaithnafasafoddimyndeall... oeddo'nhoffi'rsyniadondfeloedd y gwirioneddynagosachdoedd o ddimynhoffiawno'rsyniad o gwbl.

So to start with, this father thought it was a great idea that his partner would speak Welsh to their child. But then he realized that he wouldn't understand what mother and child one and child two were going to be saying to each other. He liked the idea at first, but when it came to it, he didn't like the idea at all. That was quite a strong theme.

Briefing 30

The transmission of English. We've had a transmission of Welsh as an unconscious behavior. Now, we have transmission of English. "If you don't speak Welsh at home, which we didn't, when you have a child, it tends to be that you don't even think about the language. When they start school, then you make a decision. If you're not used to speaking Welsh, English is the default setting." We will be hearing more about default settings later, as we talk about behavioral theory.

Briefing 31

"Even before I was pregnant, I've always said I wanted my child to go to Welsh-medium school, and my partner has always known that."This mother in South East Wales, which has a lower percentage of Welsh speakers, has told her partner that their child will go to a Welsh-medium school, and the partner is okaywith that.But another mother said: "My ex-partner didn't want ourchildren to go to Welsh school whatsoever. He was completely and utterly against it. Obviously, that's a massive barrier." Now you've got two parents disagreeing about the education the child is going to have.

Briefing 32-33

Lack of confidence—I've mentioned this already and often linked it to the lack of opportunity for use, and maybe the perceived negative experiences of using the Welsh language in the past: "I probably geta bit flustered speaking Welsh, a bit of confused or anxious, maybe? I think if I used it a lot more, it would come more natural again, but I think my daughter tests me when she's asking me constantly 'What's this in Welsh', and for the life of me, I'm thinking, eh?"

Briefing 34

As we come to the conclusions of this primary research, what we need to reiterate is that the intergenerational language transmission behavior this research showed tended to be unconscious, except in those exogamous couples and couples where one parent spoke Welsh and came from a Welsh-speaking family buttheir partner did not.

Intergenerational language donation was considered both prior to birth and/or during the early years by most of the respondents who had acquired Welsh through Welsh-medium education. These people tended not to have spoken Welsh in their own families when they were children but went to the Welsh-medium education system, wanted their own children to be able to speak Welsh, and wanted to send them to the same Welsh-medium education system that they attended themselves as children, but they didn't necessarily speak Welsh with those Welsh-speaking children, although they could speak Welsh. They didn't do that for many reasons.

Social factors and background factors seem to be more influential in the transmission of Welsh than psychological factors; i.e., attitudes, because they were very, very positive attitude stroke. The whole sample here moved towards the Welsh language, but the transmission rate wasn't 100%.

Briefing 37-38

Ok, let's move on to behavioral science for a bit. That's the background research; the strategic concepts, the strategic context. What are we going to do about it? Well, what we've said is we're going to base our policy work in the intergenerational transmission of Welsh on behavioral theory. Mindspace is a behavior change model, created by the United Kingdom Cabinet Office many years ago and it's a mnemonic.

Briefing 39

So, messenger, incentives, norms, defaults, salience, priming, affect, commitments, and ego—that's quite complex, isn't it?

We are heavily influenced by people who communicate information.

Briefing 40

A few years later, this was boiled down to a simpler concept for behavior change known as EAST, meaning: Is it easy? Is it attractive? Is it social? Is it timely?

If it's not easy, people are not going to do it. If it's not attractive, you know, it's really quite self-evident. It's not easy for someone to speak Welsh to their child ifthey are lacking confidence because they've not had an opportunity for a while, so they arerusty. Or, if they didn'thave the language as a child, then they're not going to do it.

Briefing 41

In the past, I think we applied lots of rational thinking to behavioral work, and maybe that's a bit too two-dimensional. We think of people, according to the rational 'man' theory, whereby if we give that person information, they will process that information in a way that best suits their future quality of life, and will change their behavior to accord with that.

That's just not how human behavior works.

Briefing 42

That's the two-dimensional model of behavior change, whereas life is actually more like this, you know: we've got time, what's going on, the habits, what other people around me do—"My friends don't speak Welsh to the kids, but they can, so I'm not going to speak about that"—that kind of thing. Behavior change is messy, behavior change is very complex, and behavior change is irrational.

Briefing 43

We as human beings are predictably irrational, which is the title of one volume on behavior change.

What do we need? Do we need good reasons? Emotion? What do we feel about the Welsh language? What are our principles? What do I get out of it? Do I have control? What is my perceived behavioral control? Do I have the language in Welsh to speak to a baby, asI didn't actually speak Welsh until I was five years of age when I was at school?

All these kinds of questions go through people's heads in an absolute nanosecond, and again, boils down to something quite good: COM-B, which I mentioned at the start.

Briefing 44

COM-B:capability, opportunity, and motivation equal behaviors. Does it? Okay, let's have a look at the capability for the intergenerational transmission of Welsh.

Our target audience is parents who have facilities in Welsh and who obviously have children because they are parents. Do they have the right knowledge and skills?

How do they practice their Welsh? Have they used their Welsh since leaving school?

Do they have child language? Do they have the physical and mental ability to carry out while they do? Do they know how to do it? Well, maybe not. Part of the capability is there, and when there is only part of it, how do we reinforce the part that's not there?

So,opportunity. Does your target audience have the resource to undertake the behavior? Do they know what to do if they haven't spoken Welsh for five years? Is it reasonable to expect them to do that with their own child when they don't have child language?

They have people around them who will help or hinder them to carry it out. Is it a mother tongue or is it an extended family tongue? Virginia Gathercole and her research team found, back in 2007, that it is a constellation of social networks rather than just mother tongue that helps transmission or hinders transmission andmotivations.

So, COM-B: capability, opportunity, and motivation. Do they want to do it? Do theybelieve that they should? Have they ever seen anyone else do it? Do theyhave the right habits in place to do so? And that, or not, will lead to the desired level of behavior.

Briefing 45-46

That's what our policy is about. We published our policy on the Intergenerational Transmission of Welsh in February 2020. Its main aims are to inspire today's generation of children and young people to speak Welsh to their own children in the future, to reignite the Welsh language skills of people who may not have used Welsh since their school days or who aren't confident in their Welsh language skills, to speak Welsh with their own children, and to support and encourage the use of Welsh within families where not everyone speaks Welsh.

So, we've taken the research, we've taken the statistics, we've taken the recommendations, and we've written the policy based on that. And we've talked to a lot of people who are interested in the field of intergenerational language transmission and child development, and early years and the Welsh language.

Briefing 47-48

There are a new set of principles forthis. I think we need to spend a bit of time looking at these. As I cometo the last quarter of the presentation, children, we should remember, are individuals.They have their own sense of agency, and they can engage in what is called upward transmission. They can say, "Speak Welsh to me, mum, or "Don't speak Welsh to me, mum."

They may tell their parents what language they want to speak with them.

Again, I talked about messaging earlier on.

Messaging in and of itself is not an intervention. It may be a part of it, but it's not the intervention itself. Family types are more diverse than back in 1981, when Godfrey Harrison's research was published about bilingual mothers in Wales and the language of their children. And we have more one-parent families. We have more two-parent families where both parents don't speak Welsh. We have more parents in LGBTQI groups— lesbian, gay, bisexual, trans or transgender, queer, and intersex groups. The family unit is not what it was, and it's far more diverse. What does that mean for our policy work?

Briefing 49

Principles. Theories have changed. We need to know exactly what changes we want to see before we engage in an intervention. We need to use behavior change, but we need to, plain and simple, document what change we want to see and how that will be, and then challenge each other on what we think will get us there. We want to know what success looks like before we do anything. We also know that not everything we do will work, and if it doesn't work, we just need to be honest about that. We need to tell people and change it.

Briefing 50

We will fail at some things. We will change them. We will learn and will do that quickly.

And also, we look at behavioralspillover, which is a concept I haven't yet mentioned, and which focuses on children getting positive Welsh language experiences, with the aim of those experiences spilling over to their behavior outside school.

Briefing 51-52

So those are the principles. What are the actions?

Okay. We believe in a respectful and intelligent and critical challenge. We have formed a board of people who can challenge what we're doing, and if you have any challenges for us, I'd be happy to take them as well. Also, throughout the Welsh Government, we have policies which reach many thousands of families that are not specifically about the Welsh language, but we need to get our messaging or our interventions in those as well.

Briefing 53

In order to do that, what we're going to look at is work that has been done elsewhere all over the world, so we're going toanalyze interventions in the field of language transmission and see what worked elsewhere or what didn't.We work with a lot of international partners, so if you have any research or lessons to share with us, please dothat. Also, and we're doing this at the moment, we're carrying out a review of behavior change work, or scientifically informed behavior work, that's being done with families in other fields that have nothing to do with language, and we're seeing what we can do to adapt that work toward using more Welsh with children. We're trying. We've caught it in statistics, we've caught it in research, and now we're catching it in behavioral science.

Briefing 54

We really, really, really want to get a scientific approach behind this. We look at how we communicate with families and their extended members, as I said, because it's not just a mother tongue; it's a network tongue.

And that couldnot necessarily be paper-based, leaflet based, or informational based. We'll see what we can do about that.

Briefing 55

Also, we need to look at the different types of Welsh speakers that are out there, so we're going to create new initiatives to build on what we already do to support this goal of transmission. As I said, wewill be using behavioral science to support people who speak Welshevery daybut whose partners are non-Welsh-speaking, people who didn't speak Welsh as children, those who went to a Welsh-medium school but don't speak Welsh anymore, or those who feel they can't speak Welsh anymore, to speak Welsh to their children.

This is not a one-size-fits-all approach. It's not an approach which will work all over Wales. We can target audiences indifferent social networks and different parents or carers,either face to face or virtually. And we can take demographics into account as we do that. Also, we will make advice available to parents or carers on what they cando when their own children lack confidence in using the Welsh that they have butmay not want to use for other reasons.

Briefing 56

Also, we'recoming to the really interesting stuff, which we've been talking about to the Basque—the government of the Basque Autonomous Community. What we're looking at doing is, for parents who haven't used their Welsh language skills in some time, we're going to trial a language use pledge program. Pledges or promises are quite powerful tools in behavioral science. This could be something based on the Basque language program known as*Euskaraldia*, where people promise to understand Basque but respond in Spanish. Maybe the power of bilingual conversations is something we need to harness a bit more.

And, we also explore opportunities for peer-to-peer support so that well-speaking parents can help other parents who may be not so confident in Welsh to speak Welsh to their children.

Briefing 57

Also, we need to look at, and we will be looking at, what we can do to bridge the school and the wider community out there. What can we do to engage parents more in the life of a Welsh-medium school so they can reignite their Welsh language skills?

Briefing 58

Again, we look at the workplace to see this behavioralspillover. What can we spillover from people who use Welsh in the workplace to help them or give them the tools, confidence, or whatever they need to use Welsh in their home with their children?

Briefing 59

We will look at techniques used in other countries to develop people's assertiveness. Assertiveness means they can assert their language identity or their language skills. Lots of work is being done in Valencia by Professor Ferran Suay and others on that, and there are lots to learn from that. We will develop an online presence. This doesn't mean Twitter. This doesn't necessarily mean a website, but what it could mean is some sort of tool on a pre-existing platform to help parents use their Welsh to have a bit more child language. Maybe something could popup on your phone at feeding time with some specific words you can use with your child and in the Welsh child language.

Briefing 60

And we will look at what we can do with gaming, technologies, and physical playso that people use more Welsh with their children. Also, disabled people and those who have additional needs, impairments, or health conditions. What can we do? Well, we can do quite a lot to help them use more Welsh with their families. And we'll involve them in our work as well.

Briefing 61

Also, we need to look at ourselves. We need to learn hardlessons from what we've done in the past, and we need to make sure that what we've done in the past is based on behavioral science and a sound theory of change. We'll create some pilot interventions, and if they don't work, we'll learn from them or find a better way.

Briefing 62

I've often said that intergenerational transmission is a bit like anobesity map. This is the obesity map. There are so many calls; it is hard to identify a single one, a single silver bullet we could use. But I think that if we do engage all the scientific background, all the research that we've found and we've used, and if we do adopt a humble approach, knowing that we don't know everything, and promising at the start that we're going to **stop** things, I think we can achieve our aims. So *diolchynfawr am wrandoheddiw*, thank you very much for listening today. I hope the rest of the conference goes well.

簡報 1

午安。我是威爾斯政府的 Jeremy Evas，也是 Prosiect 2050 的負責人，這是一個幫助民眾更常使用威爾斯語的跨學科、多學科單位。我們稍後會談到更多。

我今天是要告訴各位，關於我們母語的世代間交接。如果家長會說母語，而

且很多人會說，那麼語言就會存活；如果有人不說，語言就無法存活。我想告訴各位，我們在威爾斯語世代間交接的工作，以及我們在未來 10 年的工作計畫。我希望這場會議順利，並期待收到各位的提問。所以在我們討論威爾斯語世代間交接的細節前，我想先跟各位聊聊威爾斯語。威爾斯屬於聯合王國，我們有威爾斯語，是印歐語系的 P 凱爾特語分支。

接下來我們來看看數據。

簡報 2

我正在規劃威爾斯的活動策略，促進並增加我們母語的使用。我們在 2017 年發布的政府策略《Cymraeg 2050》有三個主題。*Cymraeg* 是威爾斯語中，「威爾斯語」的意思，所以在 2050 年前，我們有個大膽的願景。我們希望更多人說威爾斯語，更多人使用威爾斯語，更多人懂威爾斯語，身邊的基建提供更多威爾斯語言服務。先來看看這些策略主題。

三大主題中的第一個，是關於提高會說威爾斯語的人數，這有很多方法執行，透過家庭中的語言交接，透過早期共學與托兒的提供，透過法定教育系統，以及各類型教育，提供給成人、職業以及職場資格。

但只有這麼多。除了僅僅創造會說威爾斯語的人之外，還有更多事情要做。挑戰在於如何幫助他們活用已經學會的威爾斯語，再說一次，我今天會講到這件事。我們有哪些狀況，是大家可以無拘無束，不受阻撓地使用威爾斯語，而且他們知道自己可以跟別人說威爾斯語的？

現實說穿了，就是在許多少數語言的脈絡下，這些狀況遠少於我們的希望。我們正在觀察如何創造更多狀況，例如在職場上，讓大家能夠彼此使用威爾斯語。當然，過去一年半期間內，職場已經變了。經歷過新冠病毒疫情後，這對未來線上與線下職場有什麼意涵？科技必須對此提供什麼？

還有威爾斯語的社交使用。大家彼此社交時使用威爾斯語。為了讓這些事情發生，我們需要基礎建設，需要支持性的基礎建設，無論是在社群或是經濟，且無論各位是否知道我們在威爾斯語文化與媒體內容上有什麼，都要記得，絕大部分的威爾斯語使用者也都會說英語。

因此，我們可以獲得大量以英語提供的內容。我們能夠做些什麼，為使用世界最大宗語言之一的雙語人口，啟動並且創造既原創又吸引人的內容，讓他們使用？

正如我已經提到的數位科技。疫情後，看起來會是什麼樣子？我們要怎麼利用？這會怎麼發揚科技？微軟團隊很快就會有同步口譯設備，舉例來說，我以後就能對各位說威爾斯語。會有人類的口譯員翻譯成各位的語言，這也是期待的目標之一，不只是用在威爾斯語上。全世界的語言都能利用。

接著是語言基建。這有什麼科技要素？其他人可以在他們的產品中，加入哪些語料庫規劃、狀態規劃、術語字典、詞典、技術元件？當然，這些都要在研究的基礎上進行。我們對自己的母語有遠大雄心，我們也有大規模的計畫加以實踐。我們想做的，是將威爾斯語的使用者人數，在 2050 年前，從大約 56.2 萬人提高到 100 萬人。

簡報 3

這個雄心偉大，但正如我所言，知道一個語言，和使用那個語言是不一樣的，我們想要確保我們的母語更常被使用。根據調查，現在每天使用威爾斯語的威爾斯人口為 10%。我們希望在 2050 年前，將這個比例翻倍達到 20%，所以我們的《Cymraeg 2050》策略有兩個最高層目標，就是 100 萬個使用威爾斯語的人口，以及日常使用翻倍。

這是我們的方向。各位可以看看 2011 年的樣子。我們必須確保，工廠，也就是教育系統、世代間交接系統，能產生更多威爾斯語使用者。過去，威爾斯語使用者人數從 1891 年開始普查以來一直下降，這就是我們必須做的事。這都發表在我們的《Cymraeg 2050》策略，這項策略會提供本次會議的與會者。

簡報 4

所以這就是可以說，還有預定會說威爾斯語的人數。我們要讓說威爾斯語的人數達到 100 萬。這是關於語言使用調查的事，很快就會舉辦。回到 1992 年，當時有 21.5% 的威爾斯人口說自己會說威爾斯語，而同樣調查中，有 13% 的人說自己能說流利的威爾斯語。

簡報 5

現在，「流利」是什麼意思？這是自我宣稱。這沒有科學定義，都是自稱的。在民眾說少數語言或區域性少數語言的地方，我們有兩種語言可以選。主導語言，在雙語情況中，通常會被個人評定為他們比少數語言更有信心的語言。回到 1992

年，13% 的人說自己威爾斯語流利，不管流利的定義是什麼。

好，12 年後，或也許 12-14 年後，20.5%、或減少了 2,000 人，說自己會說威爾斯語，其中 12% 的人說自己威爾斯語流利，減少了非常多。這不是 100% 的樣本，這只是代表性樣本。

之後，我們又回到有 24% 的人說自己會說威爾斯語，共 677,800 人，增加了不少人。但只有 11%，或 318,000 人會說流利的威爾斯語。

簡報 6

現在根據民眾學習威爾斯語的地點，更仔細觀察世代間交接與流利程度。

所以在會說流利威爾斯語的人中，八成的流利程度是因為小時候在家裡學會。讓我們就觀察這一點。這證明語言的世代交接有多重要，因為我們的研究顯示，愈早學習一種語言，就愈可能日後在生活中使用。

所以托兒所要為 49% 在家中學會流利威爾斯語的人負責。

正如 Joshua Fishman 所言，家裡是非常重要的節點。若各位不熟悉 Joshua Fishman 的工作，我非常推薦各位閱讀：他在 1991 年或 1992 年發表的作品，《逆轉語言變化》。讓我們來看看。

流利和能說大量語言，這樣就有 93% 的人是小時候在家裡學的。這個統計數據很明確，家庭非常之重要。

簡報 7

但這又如何？我們要怎麼利用？讓我們透過家庭組成來觀察。這只是在家。這裡有兩項普查，2001 年和 2011 年的普查。讓我們來看看。

這是一個雙親家庭，雙親都說威爾斯語。在雙親均說威爾斯語，孩子年紀在三、四歲的情況下，82% 的孩子在兩項普查中都會說威爾斯語。

所以雙親均說威爾斯語，孩子年紀在三、四歲的情況下，兒童語言能力的流失大約為 20%。現在，這不是說他們日後不會在教育系統中學到威爾斯語，他們當時沒有獲得威爾斯語技能，我們是從他們語言使用的統計數據推斷的。這些不是語言使用統計數據，這是語言知識統計數據。這是關於交接的推斷性陳述。

這是雙親都說威爾斯語的家庭，那如果是單親家庭，只有一名家長說威爾斯語呢？只有一名家長說威爾斯語的單親家庭中，交接率低了很多。我們不知道確切原因為何，但話說回來，我們推斷，是因為家長外出上班，孩子托兒在其他地方的育

兒問題所導致。

好，回到有兩名成人的家庭。在 2001 年的普查中，若女性說威爾斯語，男性不說，有 44% 的孩子會說威爾斯語，意指母親說威爾斯語的雙親家庭中，有 56% 的孩子不會說威爾斯語。而 2011 年的普查中有 49% 的孩子會說威爾斯語。讓我們看看兩項普查中，男性的對應數據。

在 2001 年，男性成人說威爾斯語的雙親家庭中，有 65% 零至四歲的孩子不會說威爾斯語，在 2011 年比例則為 60%。

另一個家庭組成出現在這裡。這裡有些非常明確的統計數據。

簡報 8

讓我們看看別的。

這是我們討論的數字，是我剛剛說到百分比的實際人數。

兩者之間相去不遠。以各郡而言，交接率的地理變化很大，但正如各位所見，雙親家庭，僅一名家長會說威爾斯語的雙語家庭中，人數正在增加。

簡報 9

讓我們看看差異的來源。我們講過語言和調查。我們講過普查，現在我們要討論小學生程度的年度學校普查，這又是不同的普查。讓我們回到 2004 年。我們可以看到，五歲孩童的百分比，剛剛都是在講零到四歲的孩童。這些是在學年開始，能流利使用威爾斯語的五歲孩童百分比。過去 16 年間一直徘徊在 6% 到 7%。

簡報 10

我剛剛提過 Joshua Fishman，還有他的工作在所有語言的世代交接上，多麼具有開創性與重要性。他建立了世代失調分級表，如果各位不知道這個量表，或許會想瞧一瞧。這非常簡單，也非常有趣。

或許他在這個新世界有所修改，因為這已經有超過 20 年的歷史。他說過：「嘗試透過風格努力復振語言，以控制語言教育、職場、大眾媒體、政府服務，而不捍衛世代轉移或交接，等於在輪胎有洞的狀況下一直打氣。

也許我們最後會回到這一點。

簡報 11

所以威爾斯的情況如何呢？這裡有整套干預；有很多規定。以前稱為 *Mudiad*

Ysgolion Meithrin 的 *Mudiad Meithrin*，是一個照顧學齡前兒童的龐大組織。這是威爾斯的早教專家。他們是主要提供者。

簡報 12

他們是擁有很多子品牌的傘狀組織，

簡報 13

向許多不會說威爾斯語的家庭提供威爾斯語。我們有 *Cylch Meithrin*，提供兩歲以上兒童全日托兒或區段日間托兒，還有每週家長課程 *Cylch Ti a Fi*，有照顧者、兒童，以及日間托嬰。這都是現在威爾斯的狀況。

簡報 14

我們有兒童威爾斯語計畫，這很大一部分是由 *Mudiad Ysgolion Meithrin* 運作，別忘了 Cymraeg 是威爾斯語裡，「威爾斯語」的意思。我們過去在健康和產婦方面做了工作，這些助產，以及提供產前產後課程的醫療人員，看看我們是否能向家長傳遞訊息，使用威爾斯語或讓他們的孩子去上威爾斯語授課的學校。威爾斯每一位家長，都會取得出生卡，上面都有關於威爾斯語的訊息。

我們還有手冊和資訊。這都是資訊方面的事。也許我們稍後要更深入行為驅動的方式。

簡報 15

我來這裡討論我們對於威爾斯語世代交接的政策。這項政策是基於研究，並以宣告利益的方式進行。

簡報 16

我曾經在卡地夫大學工作，領導一個團隊，成員包括做了這項研究的 Jonathan Morris 和 Lorraine Whitmarsh。這項研究名為「社會與社會心理因素對威爾斯語世代交接之影響」。

簡報 17

這項研究由我目前任職的威爾斯政府委託，所以我是在現職上討論我前職的工作。

簡報 18

我們想做什麼？我們觀察語言使用的模式，以及家庭中對零至四歲兒童的交接，也就是我先前提到的普查中同一種類，我們想提高對於現況的了解。這項策略如我所言，目前貼切的策略是《Cymraeg 2050》策略。我們的企圖心是在 2050 年前獲得百萬名威爾斯語使用者，並使日常使用比例翻倍。這剛好在策略公布前公布。

簡報 19

過去在威爾斯，為了威爾斯語言政策做了很多工作。這真的非常非常有趣，因為我認為以交接為中心的論述已經變了。回到 1981 年，有一項稱為《威爾斯雙語母親與其兒女語言》的研究，雖然我很想長篇大論，但時間不允許。讓我們看看引述自研究的一段話：「雙語母親養大只會說英語的兒女，因為英語的鼓勵，甚至壓力，通常比在威爾斯培養雙語的對應支持與設施而言，更加強大、廣為擴散。」

所以要記得，報告、人、信心水準，也許對威爾斯人的社經價值觀感，當時圍繞著威爾斯語的主導論述，創造了一個狀況，家長會認為：「我們就決定別跟孩子說威爾斯語啦，因為以後不流行這一套。」以前一定聽過很多人講這方面的事。現在來看看後來發生的事。

13 年後的 1994 年，同一團隊的幾個人，Harrison 和 Bellin，Bellin 也參與了第一次研究，發現部分家長缺乏說威爾斯語的信心。他們不跟孩子說威爾斯語，是因為他們對自己的威爾斯語技能沒有信心。而同一批人中，又有一部分在 1991 年和 1994 年，還有 Jean Lyon 於 1996 年，發現部分不同語系通婚的家庭中，使用威爾斯語的緊張主題。「異族通婚」是對於夫妻不是雙語，但來自不同語系的家庭來說，算是時髦的用語，也就是一個家長說威爾斯語，一個不說。而研究顯示，這種狀況可能會出現緊張。

簡報 20

讓我們接下去。如 Jean Lyon 於 1996 年，以及我本人在 1999 年討論過的，世代間的語言捐贈而非交接。我們稍後再回來討論，因為我們的發現是部分會說威爾斯語的父母，因為各種理由不一定跟孩子說威爾斯語，但會確保孩子透過教育系統學會說威爾斯語。他們對兒女貢獻語言，而非積極地跟他們說這種語言。接著 Katherine Jones 更深入觀察了在早期語言社會化過程中，說威爾斯語的照顧者角色

更接近當下的 2007 年，在我們著手我領導的研究前，Virginia Gathercole 替威爾斯語委員會，帶領一組研究員，得到的結論是威爾斯語的交接並非有意識的決定。或許時間已經過去了，但對於主要都出身於威爾斯語背景的夫婦而言，這往往是一個無意識的決定。如果大家都說威爾斯語，每個人都對孩子說威爾斯語，那就不是問題。

簡報 21

說到目前的研究。現在有兩個研究問題：

什麼條件會在家庭中輔助威爾斯語的交接，什麼條件會導致不太可能有威爾斯語的交接？

第二個研究問題是：什麼樣的條件影響家庭中對零到四歲幼童族群使用威爾斯語的模式？我們說零到四歲幼童族群的理由，是因為我們相信，這個年齡層的人很少接觸到正式教育系統。我們嘗試將其分解，擺脫教育可能的影響，真正找到，或推論出家庭發生的狀況。

簡報 22

我們使用混合法。我們做了一些量化分析；我們採用一些社會心理理論計畫的行為方法；我們也做了質性訪談。

此一樣本數合理地少，為 60 位照顧者，地理分布而言，並非以最大範圍可能擴及到的整個威爾斯地區，而是在威爾斯的西北部與東南部進行，所有的家長年齡在 20-45 歲之間。

簡報 23

所有這些家長都曾在某個時間點掌握過威爾斯語，所有這些家長都曾一度會說威爾斯語。

簡報 24

好的。這項陳述有一部分是關於行為理論的。我們在報告中使用的部分方法，是計畫行為理論，以及理性行動理論。這都是為了出現在簡報中稍後會提到的 COM-B 模式的一件事；在此研究背景下的行為意圖，是一個人對於威爾斯語的態度，主觀或社會常態。所以大家對威爾斯語有什麼想法？大家對威爾斯語有何種行為？還有感受到的行為控制？你覺得自己對這件事有多少控制能力？我能使用威爾

斯語嗎？我的威爾斯語夠好嗎？

簡報 25

所以我們配合該理論，以七分量表加以評估，做了很多統計分析。

就質性數據而言，也就是訪談資料，我們檢驗了回應者和他們對威爾斯語的態度。我們檢驗了他們在童年時期的威爾斯語使用，他們目前和自己延伸家庭使用的語言、社交網路、在家的語言行為，以及在孩子出生前，任何和伴侶、延伸家庭、外部機構間，發生過所使用語言的討論。

這些人腦中有什麼資訊？或者，他們只是因為他們一直都是這樣處理，就延續了同樣的語言行為？讓我們來看看。

簡報 26

一個人的威爾斯語背景，和他們將自己會的威爾斯語轉移給兒女的可能性有強烈相關性。

自身背景中的威爾斯語愈多，就愈可能跟兒女說威爾斯語。

簡報 27

根據重複 Gathercole 在 **2007** 年報告的報告，這是無意識的行為。

威爾斯語兒童的交接，被回應者列為是無意識的行為。各位可以看簡報上的英文。我認為現在可能是時候讓各位聽聽威爾斯語，所以我會用威爾斯語來讀簡報。

Mae bob dim yn fy mywyd i wedi bod drwy'r Gymraeg-mare fy addysg i wedi bod trwy'r Gymraeg, ac wedyn mae fy ngwaith i wedi bod trwy'r Gymraeg felly dydi hi ddim yn rhywbeth dwi wedi gwneud yn 'conscious' er mwyn cael gwaith... mae jyst wastad wedi bod yna.

所以如果一切都是威爾斯語，那全部都是威爾斯語，也一直都會在那裡。

簡報 28

這是無意識的。就這樣發生了。

在威爾斯西北部的 Anglesey，有個故事是某位母親說她認為孩子也會說英文很重要，因為這是個雙語社會。

好吧，她自己沒有信心說英文，所以她也想要自己的孩子會說英文。

還有威爾斯語。

簡報 29

有討論是關於不同語系通婚的家庭中的交接。再說一次，這個字是雙親家庭中，一位家長不會說威爾斯語。

我會再次用威爾斯語朗讀，可以暫停在這裡。

I gychwyn roedd o'n meddwl ei fod o'n syniad bendigedig bod o'n siarad Cymraeg ac wedyn... doedd o ddim yn hoffi'r syniad bod ei [blentyn] o a fi a'i [sibling] yn mynd i fod yn siarad mewn iaith na fasa fo ddim yn deall... oedd o'n hoffi'r syniad ond fel oedd y gwirionedd yn agosach doedd o ddim yn hoff iawn o'r syniad o gwbl.

所以一開始，這位父親認為伴侶對小孩說威爾斯語是很棒的想法。但他發現，他聽不懂媽媽跟兩個孩子間在說什麼。他一開始喜歡這個想法，實現以後就根本不喜歡了。這是一個很強大的主題。

簡報 30

英文的交接。我們的威爾斯語交接是無意識行為。現在我們有英語的交接。「如果在家不說威爾斯語，我們先前沒有，等到有了小孩，那就根本不會想到這個語言。他們開始上學以後，你會做出決定。如果你不習慣講威爾斯語，英文就是預設語言。」我們稍後討論行為理論時，會聽到更多關於預設語言的事。

簡報 31

「即使在我懷孕前，我就一直說我想讓孩子去上威爾斯語授課的學校，我父母已經知道這件事。」這位母親來自威爾斯語使用者人數比例偏低的威爾斯東南部，告訴她的伴侶，他們的孩子會去上威爾斯語授課的學校，而伴侶也同意了。但另一個媽媽說：「我的前伴侶不想要小孩上任何威爾斯語學校。他完全徹底地反對這個想法。顯然這是個巨大的障礙。」現在有兩個家長對於小孩要受的教育意見相左。

簡報 32-33

缺乏信心，我已經說過這件事，而這通常和缺乏使用機會有關，或許還有以前使用威爾斯語所感受到的負面體驗：「我可能對於說威爾斯語有點慌張，有點困惑或焦慮，也許吧？」我覺得如果我能夠多用，就會恢復自然，可是我覺得我女兒一直問我『這個用威爾斯語怎麼說』的時候，是在考我，我想這輩子就這樣了，對吧？」

簡報 34

我們來到這個初步研究的結論，我們要重申的是，該研究顯示的世代語言交接行為通常是無意識的，除了那些不同語系通婚的夫妻，以及一人來自於說威爾斯語家庭，也會說威爾斯語，但伴侶不說的夫妻。

大多數透過威爾斯語授課教育，學會威爾斯語的受訪者，在產前或是孩子幼年時期，考慮過世代間語言捐贈。在幼年時代，通常在家裡不說威爾斯語，但去上威爾斯語授課教育系統的人，想要自己的孩子會說威爾斯語，也想把孩子送進和自己童年時期，同樣用威爾斯語授課的教育系統，但他們雖然會說威爾斯語，不一定和說威爾斯語的孩子說威爾斯語。他們不這麼做有很多理由。

社會因素與背景因素似乎在威爾斯語的交接方面，比心理因素更有影響力；亦即態度，因為他們的態度是非常非常積極的。這裡全部的樣本都朝向威爾斯語，但交接率並非百分之百。

簡報 37-38

好，讓我們稍微聊聊行為科學。這有個背景研究、策略概念、策略脈絡。我們要拿這些怎麼辦？我們說過，我們要將行為理論，作為威爾斯語世代交接的政策工作基礎。思維空間是一種行為改變模式，多年前由聯合王國內閣辦公室創造，現在是個記憶輔助法。

簡報 39

所以，信差、誘因、常態、預設、顯著性、啟動、影響、承諾、自我，好複雜，對不對？

我們受到溝通資訊者的嚴重影響。

簡報 40

幾年後，這簡化為一個更簡單，稱之為 EAST 的行為變化概念，意指：這簡單嗎？這吸引人嗎？這有社交性嗎？這及時嗎？

如果不簡單，大家就不會去做。如果不吸引人，那就不用說了。如果某個人因為他們一段時間沒有機會跟孩子說威爾斯語，變得很生疏，所以缺乏信心，那對他們而言就不容易。或如果他們幼時沒有學會，那也就不會這麼做。

簡報 41

以前，我認為我們在行為工作上運用了很多理性思考，也許有點太平面了。根據理性「人」理論，我們要思考到人，如果我給那個人資訊，他們會以最適合他們日後生活品質的方式處理該項資訊，並據此改變行為。

這不是人類行為的運作方式。

簡報 42

這是行為改變的平面思考，人生實際上更像是：我們有時間、發生什麼事、習慣、周邊的人怎麼做——「我朋友不跟小孩說威爾斯語，但他們可以，所以我不會對此表示意見」這樣子。行為改變非常麻煩，行為改變非常複雜，行為改變並不理性。

簡報 43

我們身為人類，可想而知並不理性，這是行為改變中的一冊主題。

我們需要什麼？我們需要好理由嗎？情感嗎？我們對威爾斯語有什麼感覺？我們有什麼原則？我們從中得到什麼？我能控制嗎？我感受到的行為控制是什麼？如果我到五歲上學前，都沒真正說過威爾斯語，我有威爾斯語可以跟嬰兒說嗎？

這些問題會瞬間掃過人的大腦，然後簡化成一件很棒的事：COM-B 模型：我一開始說過的。

簡報 44

COM-B ：能力、機會、動機等同於行為。是嗎？好，讓我們看看威爾斯語世代交接的能力。

我們的目標受眾是具備威爾斯語設施家長，他們因為是家長，那當然有小孩。他們有正確的知識與技能嗎？

他們怎麼練習威爾斯語？他們離開學校以後還使用過威爾斯語嗎？

他們有兒童語言嗎？他們在做的時候，有身心方面的能力去執行嗎？他們知道怎麼做嗎？可能不知道。能力有一部分就在那裡，如果只有一部分，我們要怎麼強化不在那裡的部分？

所以就是機會。你的目標受眾有資源承擔行為嗎？如果五年沒說過威爾斯語，他們知道要怎麼辦嗎？期待他們沒有兒童語言時，還對自己的小孩這麼做，是

合理的嗎？

他們周邊有人會幫助或阻礙他們執行嗎？這是母語，還是延伸家族的語言？Virginia Gathercole 和她的研究團隊在 2007 年時發現，社交網路的人才聚集，比起母語，更有助於或阻礙交接與動機。

所以，COM-B：能力、機會、動機。他們想要這麼做嗎？他們相信應該這麼做嗎？他們看過別人這麼做嗎？他們已有這麼做的正確習慣嗎？有或沒有，會導致希望的行為水準。

簡報 45-46

這就是我們的政策內容。我們在 2020 年 2 月，公布了對於威爾斯語世代交接的政策。其主要目的，是啟發現在的兒童與年輕世代，日後跟自己的孩子說威爾斯語，讓離開學校後沒說過威爾斯語的人，或是對自己的威爾斯語沒信心的人重燃威爾斯語技能，跟自己的孩子說威爾斯語，並支持、鼓勵在不是人人說威爾斯語的家庭中，使用威爾斯語。

所以我們做了研究，我們統計了數據，我們接納建議，並據此擬定了政策。我們和很多對於世代語言交接、兒童發展、早教和威爾斯語有興趣的人討論過。

簡報 47-48

這有一套新的原則。我想我們要花點時間來看看。在我講到簡報最後的四分之一，我們要記得，兒童也是個體。他們有自己的自主感，可以參與所謂的向上交接。他們可以說「媽，跟我說威爾斯語，」或「媽，別跟我說威爾斯語。」

他們可能會告訴家長，要跟他們說什麼語言。

話說回來，我先前講過傳遞訊息。

傳遞訊息，與訊息本身不是干預。這可能是一部分，但不是干預本身。家庭類型比 1981 年更加多元化，當時 Godfrey Harrison 曾經發表過關於威爾斯雙語母親與其兒女語言方面的研究。我們現在單親家庭更多了。我們有雙親都不說威爾斯語的雙親家庭。我們有更多女同、男同、雙性戀、跨性別、酷兒、雙性人（LGBTQI）群體的家長。家庭單位和過去不同，更加多元化。這對我們的政策發揮效果有什麼意義？

簡報 49

原則。理論已經變了。我們必須確實知道我們想要什麼改變，才能投入干預。我們必須使用行為變化，但直白地說，我們也必須記錄我們想要看到什麼改變，將會是什麼樣的改變，然後挑戰彼此想法，讓我們達成目標。我們想知道成功的模樣，才著手行動。我們也知道我們所做的事情不會樣樣成功，如果不成功，我們只需誠實面對。我們必須告訴大家，並加以改變。

簡報 50

有些事情我們會失敗。我們會改變。我們會學習，會很快著手。

同時，我們也觀察行為的擴散，這是我還沒提到的概念，這針對於孩子獲得正面威爾斯語體驗，旨在讓體驗擴散到他們校外的體驗。

簡報 51-52

這些都是原則。那麼有什麼行動呢？

好的。我們相信尊重、智慧、關鍵的挑戰。我們已經組成委員會，由會挑戰我們的人組成，如果各位想挑戰我們，我樂於迎接。而且，在威爾斯政府上下，我們有不是針對威爾斯語的政策，觸及數以千計的家庭，但我們也必須透過這些政策傳達訊息或干預。

簡報 53

為了這麼做，我們要觀察的，是世界其他地方完成的任務，這樣我們可以在語言交接的領域中分析干預，並觀察其他地方成功或不成功的案例。我們和許多國際性夥伴合作，如果各位有研究或課程可以和我們分享，請不吝提供。還有，我們當下正在進行的工作，是對行為改變的檢視工作，或科學性知情行為的工作，這是和其他和語言無關的領域中的家庭合作，我們正在觀察我們能做些什麼，調整這些工作，朝向兒童使用更多威爾斯語的方向進行。我們正在努力。我們已經有了統計數據，有了研究，現在要從行為科學下手。

簡報 54

我們真的，真的，真的很想找到這背後的科學方法。我們觀察我們如何和家庭與其延伸成員溝通，如我所言，因為這不只是母語，這是**網路**語言。

這不必然是基於紙張，基於傳單，或基於資訊。我們要看看我們能對此做些什

麼。

簡報 55

還有，我們必須觀察現在不同種類的威爾斯語使用者，所以我們會基於我們已經在做的工作，建立新的倡議，以支持這個交接的目標，如我所言，我們將會使用行為科學，支持每天都說威爾斯語的人，但那些不會說威爾斯語的夥伴，孩童時期不說威爾斯語的人，上過威爾斯語學校但不再說威爾斯語的人，或者覺得他們再也不會說威爾斯語的人，會對他們的孩子說威爾斯語。

這不是一體通用的方法。這不是我們在整個威爾斯採取的方法。我們可以針對不同社群網路上的受眾，不同的家長或照顧者，無論是面對面或虛擬接觸。我們這麼做的時候可以考量人口分布。而且，我們會針對家長或照顧者在孩子沒有信心使用已學會的威爾斯語，但因為其他原因不願意使用的時候，提供建議。

簡報 56

還有，我們會遇到真的很有意思的事情，這就是我們談到巴斯克時說的，巴斯克自治區的政府。我們想要對有段時間沒使用威爾斯語技能的家長所做的事，是試驗語言使用承諾計畫。承諾或保證在行為科學上是很有力的工具。這可以是用巴斯克語言計畫，也就是 Euskaraldia 為基礎，在該計畫中，民眾承諾了解巴斯克語，但用西班牙語回答。也許雙語對話的威力，是我們必須更加以掌握的。

而且，我們也探索同儕間支援的機會，讓擅長威爾斯語的父母，可以幫助其他比較沒自信跟孩子說威爾斯語的父母。

簡報 57

還有，我們必須觀察，也會觀察，我們能做什麼去橋接學校與外面更廣大的社群。我們能做什麼，讓更多父母參與威爾斯語學校的生活，以便他們重燃威爾斯語技能？

簡報 58

再說一次，我們觀察職場的行為擴散。我們能夠從職場中使用威爾斯語的人擴散出什麼，幫助他們或給予他們工具、信心，或他們需要的一切，在家裡和孩子說威爾斯語？

簡報 59

我們將會觀察其他國家發展民眾自信所使用的技巧。自信表示他們可以相信自己的語言身分，或他們的語言技能。Ferran Suay 教授及其他人，在瓦倫西亞對此做了不少工作，有很多值得借鏡之處。我們會開發線上呈現。這不表示是推特這不一定是網站，但可能是某種已存在平臺上的工具，幫助家長使用威爾斯語當作更多和孩子溝通的語言。也許餵食的時候，電話上會迸出什麼，說特定的字彙，讓大家可以用在孩子身上，還有在威爾斯兒童語言中使用。

簡報 60

我們會觀察能夠在遊戲、科技、實體遊戲中做些什麼，讓大家能夠多對孩子使用威爾斯語。此外，身心障礙人士以及有其他需求、損傷、健康狀況的人士。我們能做些什麼？我們可以做很多事情幫助他們多和家人使用威爾斯語。我們也會讓他們參與我們的工作。

簡報 61

還有，我們必須觀察自身。我們必須從過往經驗中努力學習，我們必須保證我們過去做的，是基於行為科學，且有穩固的改變理論。我們會建立一些前導干預，如果不成功，我們會從中學習，或找到更好的方法。

簡報 62

我常常說世代間交接有點像肥胖地圖。這就是肥胖地圖。這有很多呼籲，難以找出單單一顆我們能使用的銀子彈。但我認為，如果我們確實投入所有科學背景，所有我們已經發現和使用的研究，且如果我們採用謙遜的態度，知道我們並非無所不知，一開始就承諾我們會停止事物，我想我們會達到目標的。So diolch yn fawr am wrando heddiw，非常感謝各位今天的聆聽。祝其餘的會議順利成功。

少數族群語言發展法律條文（中文版）

Minority Language Acts（English Edition）：

Québec ✠

更新至 2021 年 12 月 1 日
本文件具有官方地位。

第 C-11 章

法語憲章

前言

有鑑於法語是一個法語居住地人們所使用之獨特語言，是該民族表達自身身分的工具；

有鑑於魁北克國民議會承認魁北克人盼見法語素質及影響力有所保障，故決意使法語成為政府及法律之語言，與工作、教育、通訊、商務及業務之標準日常語言；

有鑑於國民議會欲以公平開放之精神追求此一目標，尊重魁北克英語社群的機構、尊重少數族群，他們對魁北克之發展的貢獻卓著，為議會承認；

有鑑於魁北克國民議會承認魁北克本地最早居民美洲印地安人與因紐特人保存並發展其原生語言及文化之權利；

有鑑於上述觀察及意圖符合對世界各地民族文化價值之新認識，以及每個民族以自身特有方式為國際社會作出貢獻之義務；

故此，女王陛下於魁北克國民議會建議及同意下，頒布如下：

第一編

法語地位

第一章

魁北克官方語言

1. 法語為魁北克之官方語言。

第二章

基本語言權利

2. 人人均有權要求民政機關、衛生服務與社會服務、公用事業企業、專業協會、員工協會及一切於魁北克開展業務之企業以法語與其溝通。

3. 人人均有權於議事會中以法語發言。

4. 勞工有權以法語進行活動。

5. 商品與服務之消費者有權接受法語之資訊及服務。

6. 有資格於魁北克受教育者均有權以法語受教育。

第三章

立法機關及法院之語言

7. 法語為魁北克立法機關及法院之語言，並須遵守以下規定：

(1) 立法法令於印刷、出版、通過及批准時應使用法語和英語，且法規於印刷、出版時應使用該二種語言；

(2) 適用 1867 年《憲法》第 133 條之法規及其他類似之法令制定、通過或公布，以及印刷、出版時，應使用法語和英語；

(3) 第 1 項和第 2 項所指文件之法語和英語版本具有同等權威；

(4) 任何人於魁北克任何法院或在其中任何書狀或程序中均得使用法語或英語。

8. 如不適用 1867 年《憲法》第 133 條之法規或其他類似之法令有英語版本，在有差異時，應以法語版本為準。

9. 法院做成之各項判決及履行準司法職能之機關做成之各項決定，因一方當事人之請求，應翻譯為法語或英語，視情況由負責承擔該法院或機關運行費用之民政機關為之。

10. （刪除）。

11. （刪除）。

12. （刪除）。

13. （刪除）。

第四章

民政機關之語言

14. 政府、政府部門、其他民政機關及其服務應僅使用其法語名稱為稱謂。

15. 民政機關應以官方語言書寫並發布其文本及文件。

    本條規定不適用於與魁北克外之人間之關係、新聞媒體以法語外之語言所發表宣傳及公報，或民政機關與自然人間之信函（如後者使用法語外之語言）。

16. 民政機關於與其他政府及於魁北克設立法人之書面通訊中應使用官方語言。

17. 政府、政府部門、其他民政機關間之書面通訊僅得使用官方語言。

18. 法語為政府、政府部門、其他民政機關之內部書面通訊語言。

19. 民政機關各議事會之會議通知、議程及會議紀錄，均應以官方語言製作之。

20. 任命、調任或升遷至民政機關之職位者，須掌握與所申請職位相應之官方語言。

    於前項申請，各民政機關應訂定認證標準及程序，並交魁北克法語辦事處核定之，如否，辦事處得自行訂定。如辦事處認為標準及程序不如人意，得要求相關單位為修正或自行訂定之。

    於第 29.1 條所承認，實行辦事處依第 23 條第 3 項核定之措施之機關或機構，本條規定不適用之。

21. 民政機關訂立之契約，包含相關分包契約，應以官方語言製作。民政機關與魁北克外之一方訂立契約時，前述契約及相關文件得以他種語言作成之。

22. 民政機關之標誌及海報中，除因健康或公共安全而須一併使用他種語言外，僅得使用法語。

    對於交通標誌，法語文字得以符號或象形文字為補充或替代，如無符合健康或公共安全要求之符號或象形文字，得使用他種語言。

    但政府得依法規決定民政機關得於標誌及海報中使用法語和他種語言之案例、條件或情形。

    22.1. 於自治市之領土內，如用詞經用法認可或因其文化或歷史利益令該用詞具無可置疑之優點，法語外之特定用詞得結合使用通用法語用詞以命名通道。

23. 第 29.1 條承認之機關及機構須確保向公眾提供官方語言之服務。

    其針對公眾之通知、通訊及印刷品須以官方語言製作之。

    其須規定向公眾提供官方語言服務之必要措施，並規定驗證官方語言知識之標準及程序，以適用本條規定。前述措施、標準及程序須經辦事處核定。

24. 第 29.1 條承認之機關機構得以法語與他種語言豎立標誌及海報，以法語文字為主。

25. （廢止）。

26. 第 29.1 條承認之機關機構得於其名稱、內部通訊與相互通訊中使用官方語言及他種語言。

    承認之機關機構中，兩人得於彼此書面通訊中使用其選擇之語言。但因履行職責過程中須查詢該通訊之人請求，機關或機構應準備其法語版本。

27. 於衛生服務及社會服務中，臨床紀錄之文件應依製作人認為合適者，以法語或英語作成。但各衛生服務或社會服務得要求該類文件僅以法語作成。臨床紀錄之簡歷須依要求以法語供給任何獲授權取得之人。

28. 雖有第 23 條和第 26 條規定，第 29.1 條承認之學校機構仍得於教學相關之溝通中使用教學語言，不必同時使用官方語言。

29. （廢止）。

29.1 英語語言學校服務中心及濱海學校服務中心為承認之學校機構。

因市政府、機關或機構之請求，辦事處應承認：

(1) 自治市過半數居民以英語為母語者；

(2) 機關受一或數自治市管轄，參與對其領土管理，且所屬各自治市均為承認之自治市者或

(3) 附表所列之衛生及社會服務機構，其為多數使用法語以外語言者提供服務者。

政府因不再符合獲辦事處承認條件之機關或機構之請求，得於認為情形適當且會商辦事處後撤銷該承認。前述請求應向辦事處提出，辦事處應將之連同紀錄副本移交政府。政府應將其決定通知辦事處及機關或機構。

第五章

半公共機構之語言

30. 公用事業企業、專業協會及專業協會成員須安排以官方語言提供服務。

其須以官方語言製作針對公眾之通知、通訊及印刷品，包含公共交通票證。

30.1 專業協會成員須因其服務之人請求，提供其作成而有關該人之任何通知、意見、報告、專業知識或其他文件之法語副本，而無須支付翻譯費用。請求得隨時提出之。

31. 公用事業企業及專業協會於其與民政機關及法人為書面通訊時，應使用官方語言。

32. 專業協會於其與普通會員為書面通訊時，應使用官方語言。

但其得於與個別成員通訊時，以該成員語言為回覆。

33. 針對以法語外之其他語言發布之新聞媒體公報或宣傳，不適用第 30 條及第 31 條規定。

34. 專業協會應僅使用其法語名稱為稱謂。

35. 專業協會，除向官方語言知識適合其專業實務之人員外，不得核發許可證。

具有適當知識之人員應：

(1) 曾接受以法語進行，不少於三年之全日制中學或中學後教育；

(2) 曾以法語為第一語言通過中學四年級或五年級考試；

(3) 於 1985-86 學年及之後，於魁北克獲得中學證書。

其他一切情形下，個人須取得魁北克法語辦事處核發之證書，或持有政府規定之同等證書。

政府得以法規決定辦事處核發證書之程序及條件、訂立辦事處組成審查委員會之組成規則、規定該委員會之運作模式，並規定評估法語知識是否適合某種或某類專業實務之標準，及評估該類知識之模式。

36. 取得許可進行實務之合格文憑前最後二年內，於核發該文憑之教育機構註冊者，均得證明其官方語言知識符合第 35 條規定。

37. 專業協會得向來自魁北克外已獲資格從事其專業但官方語言知識不符合第 35 條規定者，核發效期不超過一年之臨時許可證。

38. 第 37 條所設之許可僅得於公共利益需要下，經魁北克法語辦事處授權後延期三次。每次延期時，有關人員須依政府規定參加考試。

辦事處於其年度活動報告中，應說明其依本條規定授權延期許可證之數量。

39. 於魁北克取得第 36 條所規定文憑者，於 1980 年底前，得適用第 37 條及第 38 條規定。

40. 於符合公共利益之情形下，專業協會獲魁北克法語辦事處事先授權後，得向經他省或他國法律授權從事其專業者核發限制性許可證。該限制性許可證授權其持有人為單一雇主之專屬賬戶從事其專業，其職位不涉及與公眾交流。

於本條所定情形下，亦得向配偶核發許可證。

第六章

勞動關係之語言

41. 雇主均應以官方語言製作其與員工之書面通訊。其應以法語製作及發布僱用或升遷通知。

42. 工作邀請如涉民政機關、半公共機構或企業之僱用，而其須設法語化委員會、具實施法語化計畫之證明或持法語化證書時，依情形而定，雇主如於以法語外語言出版之日報上發表該工作邀請，須同時於以法語出版之日報上發表，並至少具有同等展示效果。

43. 集體協議及其附表須以官方語言製作，包含須依《勞動法》（第 C-27 章）第 72 條提交之協議。

44. 對集體協議談判、延期或審查之申訴或爭議為仲裁後作成之仲裁裁定，應因一方當事人之請求翻譯為法語或英語，由當事人交付費用與否依情形而定。

45. 雇主不得僅因員工僅使用法語或對法語外之特定語言了解不足，或因其要求尊重本章所規定之權利，而解僱、資遣、降級或調動之。

不受集體協議限制之員工，如認為自己因第 1 項禁止之行為而受損害，得向行政勞工法庭行使救濟措施。有關僱員行使《勞動法》（第 C-27 章）所生權利之救濟措施之適用規定，得經必要修正後適用之。

受集體協議限制之員工，如認為自己受有該損害，而代表該員工之協會未能提出申訴，得將申訴提交仲裁。申訴仲裁適用經必要修正後之《勞動法》第 17 條規定。

46. 雇主不得因官方語言外之語言知識或特定知識程度給予工作或職位，但職責性質須該類知識者不在此限。

任何人，無論是否與雇主具勞僱關係，如認為自己因違反第 1 項規定而受損害，且不受集體協議限制，得向行政勞工法庭行使救濟措施。有關僱員行使《勞動法》所生權利之救濟措施之適用規定，得經必要修正後適用之。

受集體協議限制者，如認為自己受有該損害，而代表其之協會未能提出申訴，得將申訴提交仲裁。

應於雇主告知申訴人工作或職位語言要求之日後，或於支持雇主違反本條第 1 項規定之指控最近一次行為後 30 日內向法庭提出救濟措施。

雇主應負責向法庭或仲裁員證明執行工作需要法語外之語言知識或特定知識程度。

如法庭或仲裁員認定申訴正當，法庭或仲裁員得發布法庭或仲裁員認為該情形下公平合理之任何命令，特別是停止所申訴行為、執行如延期該工作或職位人員配備流程之行為，或向申訴人支付賠償或懲罰性賠償金之命令。

47. 認為自己因違反第 46 條第 1 項而受損害者，得於行使該條規定之救濟措施前，以書面形式向魁北克法語辦事處申請向調解員提交該事宜，允許當事人與雇主交換意見，並經書面協議促進迅速解決問題

當事各方應參加調解員召開之一切會議；調解員和當事各方得以電話或其他通訊設備聽取彼此言論。申訴人可由申訴人所屬員工協會代表。

調解不得延展超過申請日後之 30 日。如調解員認為其介入於當時情形下不適宜或不合宜，得於該時間前終止調解。調解員應書面通知當事各方。

調解期間停止計算向行政勞工法庭或仲裁員提出訴訟之時間。於申訴人收受終止調解通知後或於申

請調解後 30 日內重新開始計算該時間。

47.1. 除當事各方同意外，調解過程中所說或所寫之任何內容均不得為法院或行使裁決職能之行政部門個人或機關採納為證據。

47.2. 不得強迫調解員揭露於履行職責時向其透露或其獲悉之任何資訊，或向法院或行使裁決職能之行政部門個人或機關出示該履行過程中準備或取得之文件。

雖有《公共機構持有文件暨個人資訊保護法》（第 A-2.1 章）第 9 條規定，任何人仍均不得接觸調解紀錄所含文件。

48. 除有關員工及其協會之既得權利者以外，不符本章規定之法律行為、決定及其他文件均為無效。使用本章規定外之語言不得視為《勞動法》（第 C-27 章）第 151 條含義內之形式缺陷。

49. 員工協會均應使用官方語言與其成員為書面通訊。其得於與個別成員之通訊中使用其語言。

50. 本法第 41 條至第 49 條視同一切集體協議之組成部分。協議中與本法任何規定相牴觸之任何條款均為絕對無效。

第七章

商務及業務之語言

51. 產品、其容器或包裝，或隨附文件或物品上之文字，包含使用說明及保證書，均須以法語製作。菜單及酒單亦適用之。

法語文字得附一種或數種翻譯，但他種語言文字不得較法語文字為突出。

52. 目錄、小冊子、文件夾、商業目錄及任何類似出版品，須以法語製作。

52.1. 一切電腦軟體，包含遊戲軟體及作業系統，無論其為安裝或解除安裝，均須提供法語版，但未有法語版者不在此限。

軟體亦得以法語外之其他語言提供，但其法語版本除反映較高生產或發行成本之價格外，其取得應同等容易，且具有至少同等之技術特性。

53. （廢止）。

54. 玩具及遊戲，除第 52.1 條規定者外，其操作用詞非為法語者，不得於魁北克市場銷售之，但該玩具或遊戲之法語版本於魁北克市場銷售之待遇不低於原版者，不在此限。

54.1. 政府得以法規及規定之條件，規定適用第 51 條至第 54 條規定之例外情形。

55. 由一方預立之契約、包含印刷標準條款之契約及相關文件，須以法語製作。亦得依當事各方明確意願以他種語言製作之。

56. 如任何法令、樞密令或政府法規要求提供第 51 條規定之文件，其得不受該條規定限制，但製作該文件所用語言應為聯邦與省、省際或國際協議之主體。

57. 工作申請表、訂單、發票、收據及離職申請，應以法文製作。

58. 公共標誌、海報及商業廣告，須使用法語。

如法語顯為主要，亦得同時使用法語及他種語言。但政府得以法規規定公共標誌、海報及商業廣告須僅使用法語，無須以法語為主，或該標誌、海報及廣告僅使用他種語言之場所、案例、條件或情形。

58.1. （刪除）。

58.2. （刪除）。

59. 第 58 條不適用於以法語外之語言刊登之新聞媒體廣告，或非出於盈利動機，具有宗教、政治、意識形態或人道主義性質之資訊。

60. （廢止）。

61. （廢止）。

62. （廢止）。

63. 企業名稱須為法語。

64. 取得法人資格須有法語名稱。

65. 非法語之名稱須於 1980 年 12 月 31 日前完成變更，但該企業登記法不允許者，不在此限。

66. 於以聲明方式登記於《企業法定公開法》（第 P-44.1 章）第 2 章所稱名冊之名稱，第 63 條、第 64 條及第 65 條亦適用之。

67. 姓氏、地名、由字母、音節或數字人為組合形成之詞句，及取自其他語言之詞句，依其他法令和政府法規，得於企業名稱中出現以指稱之。

68. 企業名稱得附法語外之他種語言版本，但使用時，應至少以該名稱之法語版本為主。

　　但於公共標誌、海報及商業廣告中，名稱得使用法語外之語言版本，但限於依第 58 條及依該條規定制定之法規，於該種標誌、海報或該種廣告中使用他種語言之範圍。

　　此外，於僅以法語外之他種語言製作之文本或文件中，名稱得僅以其他語言出現。

69. （廢止）。

70. 1977 年 8 月 26 日前採用法語以外語言名稱之衛生服務及社會服務，得繼續使用該名稱，惟其應增加法語版本之名稱。

71. 專門致力於文化發展或維護特定族群特殊利益之非營利組織，得採用該族群語言之名稱，惟其應增加法語版本之名稱。

第八章

教學之語言

72. 幼兒園及中小學之教學應使用法語，但本章另有規定者，不在此限。

　　附表定義內之學校機構，及依《私立教育法》（第 E-9.1 章）獲得補助認證之私立教育機構，於認證涵蓋之教育服務中，適用本規則。

　　本條任何內容均不得排除遵循政府依《教育法》（第 I-13.3 章）第 447 條規定訂定之基本學校法規所定手續及條件，目的為促進學習之英語教學。

73. 因父母之一方要求，下列兒童得接受英語教學：

　　(1) 其父或母為加拿大公民且於加拿大受英語初等教育之兒童，但以該教育構成其父或母於加拿大所受初等教育之主要內容者為限；

　　(2) 其父或母為加拿大公民，且其於加拿大曾或現受英語初等或中等教育之兒童，以及該兒童之兄弟姐妹，但以該教育構成其於加拿大所受初等或中等教育之主要內容者為限；

　　(3)（該項廢止）；

　　(4)（該項廢止）；

　　(5)（該項廢止）。

73.1. 政府得以法規規定依第 75 條指定之人員評估所受教育主要內容時須使用之分析架構，用於支持依第 73 條規定之資格請求。該分析架構除其他事項外，得訂定規則、評估標準、權重系統、決斷或及格分數及詮釋原則。

　　該法規得具體規定兒童推定或視為符合第 73 條所定接受英語教學為主要內容要求之情形及條件。

　　該法規由政府依教育暨休閒運動部長及主管本法執行之部長聯合建議通過。

74. 得提出本章所定請求之父母須為親權持有人。但如親權持有人不反對，未持有親權之兒童實際監護人亦得提出該請求。

　　如父母另一方以書面反對受考量之請求，部長指定人員得暫時中止考量父母一方所提請求。

75.　教育暨休閒運動部長得授權該指定人員依第 73 條、第 81 條、第 85 條或第 86.1 條規定核實及決定兒童接受英語教學之資格。

　　除法規所定文件資訊外，部長指定人員得要求個人於規定時間內，將有關依本章規定提出請求之文件或資訊交付指定人員。指定人員亦得要求文件或資訊附有其真實性之宣誓書。

76.　教育暨休閒運動部長依第 75 條規定指定之人員得核實兒童接受英語教學之資格，縱其已在或即將接受法語教學者亦同。

　　該人員亦得宣布父或母於 1977 年 8 月 26 日後就學之兒童有資格接受英語教學，且未曾接受此類教學，亦有資格依第 73 條規定接受此類教學。但如其父或母於 1982 年 4 月 17 日前就學，則應依該日期前之第 73 條規定決定其資格，於該條第 a 項及第 b 項後加上「但以該教學構成其於魁北克所受初等教育之主要內容者為限」。

　　76.1. 依第 73 條、第 76 條或第 86.1 條規定獲宣布有資格接受英語教學者，視為以第 73 條為目的，已接受或正接受英語教學。

77.　以詐欺或虛偽陳述方式取得之資格證書，絕對無效。

78.　教育暨休閒運動部長得撤銷誤發之資格證書。

　　78.1.　任何人均不得允許或容忍不符資格之兒童接受英語教學。

　　78.2.　任何人不得設立或經營私立教育機構，或變更教學之組織、定價或分發方式，以規避第 72 條或本章有關接受英語教學資格之其他規定。

　　私立教育機構，對於兒童不為英語學校服務中心之學校或依《私立教育法》（第 E-9.1 章）獲補助認證之私立英語教育機構錄取者，尤不得以予之英語教學資格為目的經營。

79.　學校機構未於校內為英語教學者，無須為之，未經教育暨休閒運動部長事先明確授權者，不得為之。

　　但學校機構均應於必要時，依《教育法》（第 I-13.3 章）第 213 條規定，安排由此獲資格之兒童接受英語教學。

　　如教育暨休閒運動部長認為，學校機構管轄範圍內有資格接受本章所定英語教學之學生人數有保證，應予以第 1 項所定授權。

80.　政府得以法規訂定依第 73 條或第 86.1 條規定提出資格申請之程序。

　　該法規得包含下列有關措施：

　　(1) 學校機構於提出申請之作用；

　　(2) 學校機構或部長分別為遞交申請或審查申請而得收取之費用；

　　(3) 提出申請之時間；及

　　(4) 申請須附之資訊及文件。

　　法規條款得因申請性質及就讀教育機構之特性而異。

81.　有嚴重學習障礙之兒童得因父母一方之請求，於需要時接受英語教學以促進學習過程。因而免於適用第 72 條第 1 項規定之兒童，其兄弟姐妹亦得豁免。

　　政府得以法規定義前項所定之兒童類別，並訂定取得該豁免所應遵循之程序。

82.　（廢止）。

83.　（廢止）。

　　83.1.　任何人均不得對部長或指定人員為虛偽或誤導陳述，或拒絕向其提供其有權獲得之資訊或文件。

　　83.2.　（廢止）。

　　83.3.　（廢止）。

83.4. （廢止）。

83.5. 依第 73 條、第 76 條、第 81 條、第 85 條或第 86.1 條規定所為，兒童接受英語教學資格之任何決定，得於決定通知後 60 日內向魁北克行政法庭提出異議。依第 77 條或第 78 條規定所為之任何決定亦同。

84. 不具教育暨休閒運動部課程要求之法語口語和寫作知識之學生，不得核發中學畢業證書。

85. 臨時居住魁北克之兒童，因父母一方之請求，得免適用第 72 條第 1 項規定，於政府法規規定情況或情形及條件下接受英語教學。該法規亦應規定得授予此豁免之期限及取得或延長豁免所應遵循之程序。

85.1. 如有嚴重家庭或人道情形之理由，教育暨休閒運動部長得因合理請求並依審查委員會建議，宣布部長指定人員曾宣布資格不符之兒童有資格接受英語教學。

該請求須於不利決定通知後 30 日內提出。

該請求應送交由部長指定成員三人組成之審查委員會。委員會應將其意見及建議報告部長。

部長應於《教育暨休閒運動部法》（第 M-15 章）第 4 條所定報告中具體說明依本條規定宣布有資格接受英語教學之兒童人數，及其獲資格之理由。

86. 政府得訂定法規，延展第 73 條之範圍，以將魁北克政府可能與他省訂定之任何互惠協議中可能考量之人員包含在內。

86.1. 除第 73 條規定情形外，政府得因父母一方請求頒布命令，授權一般下列兒童接受英語教學：

(a) 兒童之父或母，於加拿大他地以英語接受其大部分基本教育，並在於魁北克設定住所前，居住於其命令指定之省或地區，且其認定該地向法語使用者提供之法語教學服務與魁北克向英語使用者提供之英語服務相應；

(b) 兒童之父或母於魁北克設定住所，且兒童於其最近一學年中或自本學年始，於命令指定之省或地區以英語初等或中等教育；

(c) 第 a 項及第 b 項所定兒童之弟妹。

第 76 條至第 79 條規定，於本條規定人員適用之。

87. 本法規定均不禁止使用美洲印地安語向美洲印地安人提供教學，或以因紐特語向因紐特人提供教學。

88. 雖有第 72 條至第 86 條規定，於克里學校董事會或卡特 克學校董事會下轄學校中，依《克里、因紐特及納斯卡皮原住民教育法》（第 I-14 章），教學語言應分別為克里語與因紐特語，及魁北克之克里與因紐特社區於協議簽訂日當時使用之其他教學語言，協議即《詹姆斯灣及北魁北克相關協議核定法》（第 C-67 章）第 1 條所稱協議，該日期即 1975 年 11 月 11 日。

克里學校董事會及卡特 克學校董事會應追求使用法語為教學語言之目標，使其學校畢業之學生未來如有意願，能於魁北克他地之法語學校、學院或大學繼續其學習。

克里委員會與學校委員會協商後，及因紐特委員會與家長委員會協商後，委員應決定以法語及英語為教學語言之引進比例。

於教育暨休閒運動部協助下，克里學校董事會及卡特維克學校董事會應採取必要措施，使第 72 條至第 86 條規定適用於父母非屬克里或因紐特族群之兒童。就第 79 條第 2 項之目的，所稱之《教育法》為《克里、因紐特及納斯卡皮原住民教育法》第 450 條。

本條規定經必要修正，於謝弗維爾之納斯卡皮族群適用之。

第八章之一

學院或大學等級機構之法語使用及素質相關政策

88.1. 提供學院教育之機構，除未獲補貼目的認證之私立機構外，於 2004 年 10 月 1 日前，須採取學院等級教育適用之法語使用及素質相關政策。《大學等級教育機構法》（第 E-14.1 章）第 1 條第 1

項至第 11 項所列大學等級機構亦適用之。

適用第 1 項，於 2002 年 10 月 1 日後成立或獲認證之機構，須於其成立或獲認證後二年內採取此類政策。

88.2.　向多數學生以法語提供學院或大學教育之機構，其語言政策須有關：

(1) 教學語言，包含手冊與其他教學工具之語言，及學習評估工具之語言；

(2) 該機構行政部門於其正式文本與文件及任何其他形式通訊中使用之通訊語言；

(3) 學生、教職員（尤其於招聘時）與其他員工之法語素質及對法語之掌握；

(4) 工作語言；及

(5) 政策之實施及對其應用之監督。

向多數學生以英語提供學院或大學教育之機構，其語言政策須有關以法語為第二語言之教學、該機構行政部門與於魁北克所設民政機關及法人間之書面通訊所用語言，與政策之實施及對其應用之監督。

88.3.　教育機構語言政策於訂定後須立即送交高等教育、研究、科學暨技術部長。政策之修正亦適用之。經要求，教育機構須向部長提出其政策實施情形之報告。

第九章

其他

89.　如非本法規定僅得使用官方語言之情形，官方語言及他種語言得併用之。

90.　依第 7 條規定，依魁北克法令或英國國會法令於省級管轄範圍內適用於魁北克之規定，或依法規或樞密令之規定，須以法語及英語公布者，得僅以法語公布之。

依法令、法規或樞密令之規定，須刊登於法語報紙及英語報紙者，亦得僅刊登於法語報紙。

91.　如本法授權以法語及一種或數種其他語言製作文本或文件，法語版本之展示須至少與其他語言同等明顯。

92.　於政府所指定國際組織或國際慣例所需情形之語言使用，不禁止其減損本法。

93.　除本法所定其他法規制定權外，政府得制定法規促進本法實行，包含定義本法用詞及表述或定義其範圍之法規。

94.　（廢止）。

95.　下列人員、機構有權使用克里語及因紐特語，且除第 87 條、第 88 條及第 96 條外，不適用本法：

(a) 依《詹姆斯灣及北魁北克相關協議核定法》（第 C-67 章）第 1 條所稱協議，於協議所定領土內，有資格受益之人員；

(b) 依該協議於協議所定領土內設立之機構；

(c) 於該協議所定領土內，成員過半數為第 a 項所稱人員之機構。

本條規定經必要修正，於謝弗維爾之納斯卡皮族群適用之。

96.　第 95 條規定之機構須將法語使用引入其行政管理，與魁北克他地及其管理下該條第 a 項規定未涵蓋者以法語溝通，及以法語服務之。

政府得會商有關人員決定過渡期間，該期間內民政機關與第 95 條所定機構之通訊，不適用本法第 16 條及第 17 條規定。

本條規定經必要修正，於謝弗維爾之納斯卡皮族群適用之。

97.　印地安保留區不受本法之限制。

政府應以法規規定，於何種案例、條件或情形下，授權附表所定機關或機構，於現居或一直居住於保留區、原住民社群所居聚落，或《詹姆斯灣及新魁北克地區土地制度法》（第 R-13.1 章）所稱 I 類

及 I-N 類土地者，排除其適用本法一項或數項規定。

98.　本法所稱各民政機關、衛生服務與社會服務、公用事業企業及專業協會，於附表列之。

第二編

語言官方化、地名、法語化

第一章

廢止，2002, c. 28, s. 12.

99.　（*廢止*）。

第二章

語言官方化

100.　（*廢止*）。

101.　（*廢止*）。

102.　（*廢止*）。

103.　（*廢止*）。

104.　（*廢止*）。

105.　（*廢止*）。

106.　（*廢止*）。

　106.1.　（*廢止*）。

107.　（*廢止*）。

108.　（*廢止*）。

109.　（*廢止*）。

110.　（*廢止*）。

111.　（*廢止*）。

112.　（*廢止*）。

113.　（*廢止*）。

114.　（*廢止*）。

115.　（*廢止*）。

116.　民政部門機關得設語言委員會，規定其組成及運作。

　　委員會應辨識其指定領域中之用詞缺陷與問題用詞及表述。其應將偏好用詞及表述送交官方語言委員會。委員會得再將之送交魁北克法語辦事處為標準化或推薦之。

　　如部門機關未設語言委員會，辦事處得依語言官方化委員會提案，正式請求其為之。

　116.1. 魁北克法語辦事處得依語言官方化委員會提案，推薦或標準化用詞及表述。辦事處應傳播標準化之用詞及表述，尤應於《魁北克政府公報》公布之。

117.　（*刪除*）。

118.　辦事處標準化用詞及表述於《魁北克政府公報》公布後，民政機關之文本、文件、標誌與海報及其為一方之契約，及於魁北克以法語出版，經教育暨休閒運動部長核定之教學手冊與教育及研究作品，均應使用之。

　188.1.（*廢止*）。

188.2.（*廢止*）。

188.3.（*廢止*）。

188.4.（*廢止*）。

188.5.（*廢止*）。

119.　（*廢止*）。

120.　（*廢止*）。

121.　（*廢止*）。

第三章

地名委員會

122.　地名委員會設於魁北克法語辦事處，因行政目的歸入之。

123.　委員會置成員七人，包含主席，由政府任命，任期不超過五年。
政府應規定委員會成員之薪酬與附加福利及其他雇用條件。

123.1.　委員會成員縱任期屆滿，亦繼續任職至重新任命或撤換。

124.　委員會有權向政府提出一切地名之選擇標準及拼寫規則，對尚未命名之地名為最終決定，及核定任何地名變更。
政府得以法規規定地名之選擇標準、地名相關事宜之拼寫規則，與地名選擇及核定取得之方法。

125.　委員會應：
(a) 向政府提出地名應遵循之拼寫標準及規則；
(b) 編目及保存地名；
(c) 與辦事處合作建立及標準化地理術語；
(d) 使地名正式化；
(e) 宣傳魁北克之正式地理命名；
(f) 就政府送交委員會之任何地名相關問題向政府提供建議。

126.　委員會得：
(a) 就任何地名相關問題向政府及其他民政機關提供建議；
(b)（該項廢止）；
(c) 於非建制領土上，命名地理地點或變更其名稱；
(d) 經對地名有共同管轄權之民政機關同意，決定或變更地方市轄地區內之地名。

127.　委員會於當年核定之名稱須於《魁北克政府公報》每年至少公布一次。

128.　委員會選擇或核定之名稱於《魁北克政府公報》公布後，民政機關與半公共機構之文本及文件，交通標誌、公共標誌與海報，及於魁北克出版，經教育暨休閒運動部長核定之教學手冊與教育及研究作品，均應使用之。

第四章

民政機關法語化

129.　須時間遵循本法特定規定或保證其領域內普遍使用法語之各民政機關，須盡速於辦事處管轄與協助下採取法語化計畫。

130.　法語化計畫須考量臨近退休或長期於民政機關服務者之情形。

131.　各民政機關須於其展開活動後 180 日內向辦事處提出報告，報告應分析該機關之語言情況，並說明對其已採取措施及為遵循本法而擬採取之措施。
辦事處應規定此類報告之形式及其須提供之資訊。

132.　如辦事處認為所採取或設想之措施不足，應予有關人員以提出意見之機會，並將其認為必要之文件及資訊轉發之。

如有需要，其應規定適當矯正措施。

任何機關拒絕實施此類矯正措施均屬犯罪。

133.　如任何服務或民政機關為實現本法及法規目標採取之措施達到辦事處要求，辦事處得因其請求，免其適用本法任何規定。

134.　（*廢止*）。

第五章

企業法語化

135.　本章規定適用於一切企業，包含公用事業企業。

136.　企業僱用勞工人數在百人以上者，須設組成人數在六人以上之法語化委員會。

法語化委員會應分析企業之語言情況，並報告企業管理人員，以轉達辦事處。如有需要，委員會應為企業擬定法語化計畫並監管其實施。企業經核發法語化證書後，委員會應保證企業各級仍依第 141 條規定普遍使用法語。

法語化委員會得設次級委員會協助執行作業。

法語化委員會應舉行會議，每六個月至少一次。

137.　法語化委員會及各次級委員會，成員中企業勞工代表人數不得少於二分之一。

前項代表應由代表過半數勞工之員工工會指定，或如數間員工工會共同代表過半數勞工時，由各工會協議指定。如無協議或有其他情形，代表應由企業全體勞工依企業管理人員所定方式及條件選舉產生。

指定勞工代表之任期不應超過二年。但代表得連任之。

137.1. 法語化委員會或次級委員會之勞工代表，得於出席委員會或次級委員會會議及執行任何委員會或次級委員會作業必須時缺勤，而不損失工資。其應視為在工作之中，並應在此期間依正常比率獲得薪酬。

在任何情形下，僱主均不得僅以勞工參加委員會或次級委員會會議或作業為由，向該勞工支付薪酬或予以解僱、資遣、降級或調動。

因第二項禁止行為而受損害之勞工，得依情形行使第 45 條第二項或第三項所定權利。

138.　企業應向辦事處提供法語化委員會及各次級委員會之成員名單，及該名單之任何變更。

138.1.　（*刪除*）。

139.　六個月內僱用人數達五十人或以上之企業，須於該期間結束後六個月內向辦事處登記。為此，企業應通知辦事處其僱用之人數，並向其提供有關其法律地位與職能結構及其活動性質之一般資訊。

辦事處應向企業核發登記證書。

登記證書核發之日起六個月內，企業應將其語言情況分析送交辦事處。

140.　如辦事處審查企業語言情況分析後，認定企業各級依第 141 條規定普遍使用法語，應核發法語化證書。

但如辦事處認定企業各級未普遍使用法語，應通知企業須採取法語化計畫。於適用第 139 條規定之企業，辦事處得另令其成立由四人或六人組成之法語化委員會；於此情形下，第 136 條至第 138 條規定經必要修正後適用之。

法語化計畫應於收受通知之日起六個月內送交辦公室。該計畫須由辦公室核定。

141.　法語化計畫之目的為以下列方式推動企業各級普遍使用法語：

(1) 管理人員、專業協會成員及其他人員之官方語言知識；
(2) 必要時，於包含董事會在內之企業各級增加精通法語者之人數，以推廣法語使用；
(3) 以法語為工作語言及內部通訊語言；
(4) 於企業工作文件中使用法語，尤其於手冊及目錄中；
(5) 與民政機關、客戶、供應商、公眾及股東溝通時使用法語，後一種情形下，企業為《證券法》（第 V-1.1 章）所稱閉鎖性公司者除外；
(6) 使用法語用詞；
(7) 於公共標誌與海報及商業廣告中使用法語；
(8) 招收、升遷及調動之適當政策；
(9) 於資訊科技中使用法語。

142.　法語化計畫須考量：
(1) 臨近退休或長期於企業服務者之情形；
(2) 企業與外部之關係；
(3) 活動延伸至魁北克以外之企業於魁北克所設總部及研究中心之特殊情形；
(4) 生產有語言內容文化產品之企業中，其工作與該語言內容直接相關生產單位之具體情形；
(5) 企業營業項目。

143.　辦公室核定企業法語化計畫後，應出具該計畫之實施證明。
　　企業須遵循計畫要素及階段，並向其人員通報其實施情形。
　　企業另須向辦事處提出計畫實施情形報告，企業僱用人數少於百人者，為每二十四個月報告一次，企業僱用人數超過百人者，為每十二個月一次。

144.　於總部及研究中心實施法語化計畫者，得經與辦事處特別協議，許可以法語外之語言為業務語言。此類協議效期不超過五年，得延長之。
　　政府應以法規規定總部或研究中心得為此類協議之一方之情形、條件及依據規定。該法規得規定須依此類協議特定條款處理之事項。
　　於該協議仍具效力時，總部或研究中心視為遵循本章規定。
　　144.1.（刪除）。

145.　企業已完成法語化計畫之實施，且辦事處認定企業各級依第 141 條規定普遍使用法語者，辦事處應核發法語化證書。

146.　企業持有辦事處所發法語化證書者，均須保證企業各級仍依第 141 條規定普遍使用法語。
　　企業應每三年向辦事處報告企業法語使用之進展。

147.　企業未履行或不再履行本法或其下規定之義務者，辦事處得拒絕、中止或撤消其法語化計畫之實施證明或法語化證書。
　　作成決定前，辦事處得聽取任何利害關係人對有關企業情形之意見。

148.　政府應以法規規定有關核發、中止或撤消法語化計畫實施證明或法語化證書之程序。此類程序得因政府所設企業類別而異。
　　政府亦應以法規規定利害關係人依第 147 條第 2 項規定發表意見之程序。

149.　（刪除）。

150.　（刪除）。

151.　辦事處得經主管本法之部長核定，於《魁北克政府公報》為通知，要求僱用人數在五十人以下之企業分析其語言情況，並準備及實施法語化計畫。
　　企業遵循本法或其下規定之特定條款需要一定時間者，得請求辦事處協助並與後者為特別協議。於

該協議範圍內，辦事處得於其規定期限內免除企業適用本法或其下規定之任何條款。

辦事處應每年向部長報告企業採取措施及所授豁免情形。

151.1. 企業未遵循第 136 條至第 146 條及第 151 條規定有關其適用法語化流程之義務者，均屬犯罪，應受第 205 條規定之處罰。

152.（廢止）。

153. 辦事處得於其所定期限內，豁免企業適用本法任何規定或下列規定：

(a) 核發登記證書或法語化證書者，或

(b) 企業正實施辦事處所核定法語化計畫者。

辦公室應通知部長其授予之任何豁免。

154. 本章所定一般資訊、語言狀況分析與報告須以辦事處表格及問卷繳交。

154.1.（刪除）。

155.（刪除）。

155.1.（刪除）。

155.2.（刪除）。

155.3.（刪除）。

155.4.（刪除）。

156.（刪除）。

第三編

魁北克法語辦事處

第一章

建立

157. 茲特設一機構，稱「魁北克法語辦事處」。

158. 辦事處總部應設於魁北克或蒙特婁，地點由政府訂定。

總部地址及其任何變更通知應公布於《魁北克政府公報》。

辦事處應於魁北克及蒙特婁各設一辦公室，並得於魁北克他處設辦公室。

第二章

使命及職權

159. 辦事處負責制定及執行魁北克有關民政機關與企之業語言官方化、用詞及法語化政策。

辦事處亦負責保障本法受到遵循。

160. 辦事處應監督魁北克之語言情況，且應每五年至少向部長報告一次，尤其是法語之使用與地位，及各語言族群之行為與態度相關事宜。

161. 辦事處應保證法語為民政與企業工作、通訊、商務及業務之標準日常語言。除其他事項外，辦事處得採取任何適當措施以推廣法語。

辦事處應協助定義及訂定本法所定法語化計畫並監督其實施。

162. 辦事處得協助與通知民政機關、半公共機構、企業、協會及自然人，以矯正與豐富魁北克之口語及書面法語。

辦事處亦得收受各方有關法語素質或適用本法所遇問題之意見及建議，並向部長報告之。

163. 辦事處應訂定本法適用所需之研究計畫。其得進行或委託研究計畫所定之研究。

164. 辦事處得與任何個人或機構訂定協議或參與聯合計畫。

　　辦事處得依適用法規，與魁北克政府以外之政府、該政府之部門或機構、國際組織或該組織之機構訂定協議。

第二章之一

　　組織

　　第一節

　　一般規定

165.　辦事處應置成員八人。

　　下列辦事處成員應由政府任命：

　　(1) 董事和處長一人，任期不超過五年；及

　　(2) 人員六人，任期不超過五年。

　　主管執行語言政策之助理副部長應為辦事處之無表決權常任成員；助理副部長得任命職務代理人。

　　非常任成員於任期屆滿時，應繼續任職至撤換或重新任命。

　　165.1.　辦事處會議法定人數為過半數成員。

　　165.2.　會議應由處長主持，表決可否同數時，應由其取決之。

　　165.3.　辦事處得於魁北克任何地點舉行會議。辦事處成員得以電話或其他通訊設備參加會議，該設備應使與會者均能聽取各方聲音。

　　165.4.　處長於辦事處內部章程與政策範圍內負責管理及行政工作。

　　依第 38 條第 1 項與第 40 條、第 131 條至第 133 條、第 139 條、第 143 條及第 151 條規定，賦予辦事處之職權及職能，由處長行使，其應定期向辦事處報告。

　　辦事處得委由處長行使任何其他職權或職能。

　　165.5.　如處長不能出席或不能視事，應由部長指定另一辦事處成員代行其職權。

　　165.6.　處長執行職務應為全職。政府應規定處長薪酬、工作福利及其他工作條件。

　　辦事處其他成員不得支領薪酬，屬政府得規定情形、條件及範圍者除外。但其有權於政府規定條件及範圍內，報銷其於執行職務過程所生之合理費用。

　　165.7.　辦公室工作人員應依《公共服務法》（第 F-3.1.1 章）任命。

　　165.8.　辦事處及其成員、工作人員或其委員會成員，均不得因在行使職權時善意之公務行為而受起訴。

　　165.9.　辦事處得訂定內部章程。.

　　辦公室尤得設立常設或臨時委員會，定義其職權及職責，並決定其組成及運作模式。

　　委員會得經部長授權，全部或部分由非辦事處成員之人組成。

　　委員會成員不得支領薪酬，屬政府得規定情形、條件及範圍者除外。但其有權於政府規定條件及範圍內，報銷其於執行職務過程所生之合理費用。

　　辦事處亦得一般授權辦事處成員或工作人員擔任調解員，依第 47 條規定促進各方協議。

　　165.10.　經辦事處核定之辦事處會議紀錄，及辦事處所生或構成其紀錄一部分之文件及副本，經處長或經後者授權之工作人員簽署或證明者，為真實文件。

　　165.11.　辦事處應於每年 8 月 31 日前，向部長提出其前一財政年度活動之報告。

　　部長應於收受報告後 30 日內將報告送交國民議會，如議會休會，應於復會後 30 日內送交。

　　第二節

　　語言官方化委員會及語言情況監察委員會

　　165.12.　茲特於辦事處內設委員會，稱「語言官方化委員會」及「語言情況監察委員會」。

　　各委員會應因請求或主動於其指定領域內向辦事處提出建議及提案。

　　165.13.　各委員會應置下列辦事處任命成員五人：

　　(1) 委員會主席一人，自辦事處成員中選出，其辦事處成員任期尚未屆滿；

(2) 秘書一人，自辦事處工作人員中選出，任期不超過四年；及

(3) 非為辦事處成員或工作人員者三人，任期不超過四年。.

語言官方化委員會應含法國語言學專家至少二人，語言情況監察委員會應含人口學或社會語言學專家至少二人。

委員會成員於任期屆滿時，應繼續任職至撤換或重新任命。

165.14.　委員會成員不得支領薪酬，屬政府得規定情形、條件及範圍者除外。但其有權於政府規定條件及範圍內，報銷其於執行職務過程所生之合理費用。

165.15.　委員會應依辦事處內部章程所定規則運作。

第三編之一

檢查及調查

166.　辦事處得因本憲章之目的為檢查及調查。

167.　辦事處應主動或於申訴提出後採取行動。

如有申訴提出，處長得單獨行使辦事處職權。

168.　申訴均須以書面提出；其須闡明其依據理由並陳述申訴人身分。辦事處應協助申訴人作成申訴。

169.　申訴如顯無依據或出於惡意，辦事處應拒絕採取行動。

如申訴人有適當救濟管道，或如辦事處認定情況不能證明其介入正當性，辦事處得拒絕採取行動。

辦事處如拒絕採取行動，應將其決定通知申訴人，並說明其依據理由。如有可循之救濟管道，辦事處應通知投訴人。

170.　（廢止）。

171.　辦事處得一般或特別指定任何人員為調查或檢查。

172.　辦事處有依《公共調查委員會法》（第 C-37 章）任命委員之職權及豁免權，但下令拘押之權力除外。

辦事處於必要時得將該職權及豁免權授予其指定之人。

173.　不得因執行職務時善意之行為或不作為，對為檢查或調查之人提起訴訟。

174.　因本法之目的為檢查者，得於合理之工作時間內，進入任何對公眾開放之地點。於檢查過程中，該人員尤其得檢查任何產品或文件、複製及要求任何相關資訊。

該人員須因任何利害關係人之請求，表明身分並出示證明其能力之證書。

175.　辦事處得因本章之目的，要求某人於規定時間內轉發任何相關文件或資訊。

176.　任何人不得以任何方式妨礙辦事處或辦事處指定人員執行職務時之行為、隱瞞資訊或虛偽陳述以誤導辦事處或該人員，或拒絕提供辦事處或該人有權取得之任何資訊或文件。

177.　如辦事處認定有違反本憲章或其規定之規定者，應於指定時間內正式通知犯罪嫌疑人遵循規定。如犯罪嫌疑人不遵循規定，辦事處應將之轉送刑事檢控專員，以便其得於需要時提起適當刑事訴訟。

如有違反第 78.1 條、第 78.2 條、第 78.3 條或第 176 條者，辦事處應將之直接轉送刑事檢控專員，而無需事先正式通知。

第四章

廢止，2002, c. 28, s. 30.

178.　（廢止）。

179. （*廢止*）。

180. （*廢止*）。

181. （*廢止*）。

182. （*廢止*）。

183. （*廢止*）。

184. （*廢止*）。

第四編

法語高級理事會

185. 茲特設一理事會，稱「法語高級理事會」。

186. 理事會總部應設於魁北克，地點由政府訂定。

　　總部地址及其任何變更及其任何變更通知應公布於《魁北克政府公報》。

187. 理事會之任務為就有關魁北克法語之任何事宜向主管本法部長提供建議。

　　以此身分，理事會應：

　　(1) 就部長向其提出之任何事宜向部長提出建議；

　　(2) 提請部長注意任何其認定政府須注意之事項。

188. 執行任務時，理事會得：

　　(1) 接收及聽取個人或團體之意見；

　　(2) 進行或委託其認為必要之研究。

　　理事會亦得向公眾通報有關魁北克法語之任何事宜。

189. 理事會應置成員八人。

　　理事會成員應由政府任命如下：

　　(1) 主席一人，任期不超過五年；及

　　(2) 人員七人，政府得商其認定為消費者、教育界、文化社群、工會及管理人員代表之機構後選出，任期不超過五年。

　　任期屆滿時，成員應繼續任職至撤換或重新任命。

190. 理事會會議法定人數為過半數成員。

　　會議應由主席主持，表決可否同數時，應由其取決之。

191. 理事會得於魁北克任何地點舉行會議。

　　理事會成員得以電話或其他通訊設備參加會議，該設備應使與會者均能聽取各方聲音。

192. 主席負責理事會之管理及行政工作。

193. 如主席不能出席或不能視事，應由部長指定另一理事會成員代行其職權。

194. 主席執行職務應為全職。政府應規定主席薪酬、工作福利及其他工作條件。

　　理事會其他成員不得支領薪酬，屬政府得規定情形、條件及範圍者除外。但其有權於政府規定條件及範圍內，報銷其於執行職務時所生之合理費用。

195. 理事會工作人員應依《公共服務法》（第 F-3.1.1 章）任命。

196. 理事會得對其內部管理訂定規定。

　　理事會得設委員會協助其執行職權及職責。

　　委員會得經部長授權，全部或部分由非理事會成員之人組成。

　　委員會成員不得支領薪酬，屬政府得規定情形、條件及範圍者除外。但其有權於政府規定條件及

範圍內，報銷其於執行職務過程所生之合理費用。

197. 經理事會核定之理事會會議紀錄，及理事會所生或構成其紀錄一部分之文件及副本，經主席或經後者授權之工作人員簽署或證明者，為真實文件。

197.1.（刪除）。

198. 理事會應於每年 8 月 31 日前，向部長提出其前一財政年度活動之報告。

部長應於收受報告後 30 日內將報告送交國民議會，如議會休會，應於復會後 30 日內送交。

199.（刪除）。

200.（刪除）。

201.（刪除）。

202.（刪除）。

203.（刪除）。

204.（刪除）。

第五編

刑罰規定及其他懲處措施

205. 違反本法規定或政府依本法通過之法規者，即屬犯罪，應：

(a) 為自然人者，處罰款 600 至 6,000 元；

(b) 為法人者，處罰款 1,500 至 20,000 元。

為慣犯者，罰款加倍。

決定罰款金額時，法官除其他事項外，亦考量犯罪人犯罪所獲收入及其他利益，與犯罪所致之任何損害及社會經濟後果。

此外，判處本法所定犯罪者，已處以最高罰款，法官亦得因檢察官連同犯罪陳述提出之申請，於其他處罰外，對犯罪人處以相當於其犯罪實現或獲得之經濟收益之罰款。

205.1. 違反第 51 條至第 54 條規定，以有償或免費方式經銷、零售販賣、出租、為販賣之要約或出租，或以他法營銷下列物品，或抱持此目的之人，

(1) 產品其上、其容器或包裝上，或其隨附文件或物品上之文字，包含使用說明及保證書，不符本憲章規定者，

(2) 電腦軟體，含遊戲軟體及作業系統，或遊戲或玩具，不符本憲章規定者，或

(3) 出版品不符本憲章規定者，即屬犯罪，應處第 205 條所定罰款。

經營場所向公眾展示不符第 51 條規定之菜單或酒單者，亦屬犯罪，應處第 205 條所定罰款。

於第 52.1 條及第 54 條規定或依第 54.1 條規定所定之例外情形，其舉證責任在於主張例外情形之人。

206.（廢止）。

207. 檢察總長、刑事檢控專員或前二者授權之人，應依本法提起刑事訴訟。檢察總長應提起執行本法所需之所有其他程序。

208. 具民事管轄權之法院，均得因檢察總長之申請，下令於判決後八日內移除或銷毀不符本法之任何海報、標誌、廣告、廣告牌或照明標誌，其費用由被告承擔。

該申請得針對廣告裝置之所有者，或針對放置海報、標誌、廣告、廣告牌或照明標誌者，或令其放置之人。

208.1. 判決違反第 78.1 條或第 78.2 條者，均取消其擔任學校服務中心董事會成員或學校董事會專員之資格。資格取消期限為自有罪判決確定之日起五年。

208.2. 學校機構僱用人員違反第 78.1 條或第 78.2 條規定判決有罪確定者，刑事檢控專員應以書面通知學校機構。經通知後，學校機構應無薪停職該人員六個月。

208.3. 幫助他人實行本法或法規所定犯罪而為或不為某事，或建議、鼓勵或煽惑他人犯此類之罪者，亦屬犯罪。

208.4. 於有關本法或法規所定犯罪之刑事訴訟，證明犯罪由任何一方之代理人、受託人或僱員實施之證據，即足以證明該犯罪為該方所實行，除非該方證明其已為盡職調查且採取所有必要預防措施，以確保遵循本法及法規。

208.5. 本法或法規所定犯罪之刑事訴訟，應於自犯罪之日起二年內提起之。

雖有第一項規定，但第 78.1 條或第 78.2 條所定犯罪之刑事訴訟，其期限為自檢察官知悉犯罪發生之日起一年。但如自犯罪之日起已逾五年者，不得起訴。

第六編

過渡性及其他規定

209. 第 11 條規定應自 1979 年 1 月 3 日起發生效力，且不影響於該日期未確定之案件。

第 13 條規定應自 1980 年 1 月 3 日起發生效力，且不影響於該日期未確定之案件。

第 34 條、第 58 條及第 208 條規定應自 1978 年 7 月 3 日起發生效力，但須遵循第 211 條規定。

210. 1974 年 7 月 31 日前所立廣告牌或照明標誌之所有者，須於第 58 條規定生效後遵循之。

211. 於雙語公共標誌遵循《官方語言法》（1974 年，第 6 章）第 35 條規定者，均須於 1981 年 9 月 1 日前為必要變更，尤應變更其廣告牌及照明標誌，以符本法。

212. 政府應委任一名部長實施本法。該部長應對於魁北克法語辦事處工作人員及法語高級理事會工作人員行使部門現任部長之職權。

委任法語部長負責實施本法。

2020 年 6 月 22 日第 657-2020 號樞密令，（2020）152 GO 2（法語），2935。

213. 本法適用於政府。

214. （本條規定自 1987 年 4 月 17 日起停止生效）。

附表

A. 民政機關

1. 政府及政府部門。

2. 政府機構：

政府或部長依法任命多數成員之機構，其官員或僱員依《公共服務法》（第 F-3.1.1 章）任命，或至少其半數股本來自綜合收入基金，但衛生服務與社會服務、一般與職業學院及魁北克大學除外。

2.1（本項廢止）。

3. 市政及學校機構：

(a) 大都會區及交通管理機關：

魁北克大都會區與蒙特婁大都會區、魁北克交通局、蒙特婁交通局、烏塔韋交通局、拉瓦爾交通局及朗基爾交通局；

(b) 自治市、視為自治市之自治市鎮；

(b.1) 受自治市管轄，參與對其領土管理之機關；

(c) 學校機構：

學校服務中心、學校董事會及蒙特婁島學校稅務管理委員會。

4. 衛生服務及社會服務：

《衛生服務及社會服務法》(第 S-4.2 章)或《克里原住民衛生服務及社會服務法》(第 S-5 章)定義內之機構。

B.　半公共機構

1.　公共事業企業：

如非政府機構之電話、電報及電纜傳輸企業，航空、船舶、公共汽車及鐵路運輸企業，生產、運輸、分銷或販賣天然氣、水或電之企業，及交通委員會授權之企業。

2.　專業協會：

《專業法》(第 C-26 章)附表 I 所列之專業協會，或依該法設立之專業協會。

廢止時間表

依《法規合併法》(第 R-3 章)第 17 條規定，於 1977 年 12 月 31 日生效之 1977 年法規第 5 章，除第 224 條至第 229 條及第 232 條外，均已廢止，自修正法規第 C-11 章生效之日起生其效力。

依《法規合併法》(第 R-3 章)第 17 條規定，於 1979 年 6 月 1 日生效之 1977 年法規第 5 章第 11 條、第 34 條、第 58 條及第 208 條，自修正法規第 C-11 章更新至 1979 年 6 月 1 日起廢止。

西班牙加泰隆尼亞語言法

前言

一、加泰隆尼亞語之意義及現狀

　　加泰隆尼亞語是加泰隆尼亞國家形成及特徵之基本要素，是無論來自何方的公民溝通、融合及社會凝聚力之基本工具，也是加泰隆尼亞與其他加泰隆尼亞語地區之間的特殊紐帶，其形塑了一個語言社群，幾個世紀以來，以獨創方式為普世文化做出了寶貴貢獻。此外，還見證了加泰隆尼亞人民對自身土地及特有文化的忠誠。

　　最初於加泰隆尼亞境內發展，傳至其他地區─人們甚至法律賦予了其不同的名字─加泰隆尼亞語一直是該地的語言，也因而受到加泰隆尼亞歷史上某些事件的負面影響，使其處境岌岌可危。造成這種局面的有多種原因，如兩個半多世紀以來遭受的政治迫害及法律制裁、近數十年來發生人口變化的政治與社會經濟環境，此外還有與其他歐洲官方語言同樣有限的語言範圍，於通訊、資訊及文化產業正走向全球化的當今世界尤其如此。

　　因此，由於上述所有情形，加泰隆尼亞目前的社會語言情況非常複雜。民族語言並未完全獲得正常使用，且國際範圍內使用人數相對較少，又遇上了加泰隆尼亞境內許多公民的母語是其更偏好使用的卡斯提亞語，而由於這一點，他們常為豐富加泰隆尼亞文化本身做出重大貢獻，母語為他種語言之公民也有同樣的貢獻。故此，這種情況需要的語言政策，必須有效協助實現加泰隆尼亞本土語言的正常使用，而同時保證嚴格尊重所有公民的語言權利。

二、法律架構

　　加泰隆尼亞語現行法律架構由 1978 年西班牙憲法及 1979 年加泰隆尼亞自治法所規定。

　　前者承認西班牙國內人民的多樣性，於第 3 條陳述「卡斯提亞語為我國官方西班牙語言」，而作為官方語言，「所有西班牙人均負學習之義務及使用之權利」。此外，《憲法》規定「其他西班牙語言亦應依其法律規定於各自之自治區中為其官方語言」。

　　《自治法》第 3 條規定「1. 加泰隆尼亞語為加泰隆尼亞本土語言。2. 加泰隆尼亞語為加泰隆尼亞之官方語言，卡斯提語亦為西班牙全境之官方語言。3. 自治政府應保障兩種語言之正常及官方使用，應採取適當措施保證其為人學習，並創造條件，使之於加泰隆尼亞公民權利及義務為完全平等。4. 應教授阿蘭語 [3]，且視其為特別尊重及保護之對象」。

　　1983 年 4 月 18 日有關加泰隆尼亞語言正常化之第 7 號法令進一步拓展了上述法律條文，該法令於語言史上意義重大，象徵對加泰隆尼亞語的制裁結束；其十四年的實施使語言知識得以於多數人中傳播，社會各界一致同意之政策引向了語言正常使用的過程。

　　法令生效期間發生了重要變化：於技術領域，已普遍使用電腦及資訊網路；於文化及商業領域，建立了自由貿易，且已擴展至尤其是通訊及視聽領域之文化交流；於政治領域，一方面西班牙加入了現稱歐盟的歐洲經濟共同體，受多語言原則約束，另一方面，自治政府接管了《自治法》規定的許多權限；於社會及社會語言學領域，加泰隆尼亞語的語言能力已有普及─雖並未使公共使用也同樣增加─且移民流動的變化相當大。此外，一部分由於憲法法庭之判例，一部分由於加泰隆尼亞之立法及法釋義學研究，我國語言法有了長足的發展。最後，必須指出歐洲議會所通過各項決議之內容：1987 年 11 月 30 日有關歐洲共同體區域及少數民族語言文化之決議；1990 年 12 月 11 日有關共同體語言及加泰隆尼亞語情況之決議，及 1994 年 2 月 9 日有關歐洲共同體文化及語言少數民族之決議。此外，值得一提的是，歐洲理事會部長委員會於 1992 年 11 月 5 日以公約形式通過的《歐洲區域或少數民族語言憲章》，及 1996 年 6 月 6 日於巴塞隆納舉行之世界語言權利大會的《世界語言權利宣言》，其得到了眾議院及加泰隆尼亞議會一致支持。

三、立法目的

上述所有情形均促使了修正與更新 1983 年法令，更新當時達成之政治及社會協議，以便能鞏固該法於政府及教育領域推動之加泰隆尼亞語言正常化過程，使媒體及文化產業適應現今需求，並制定針對社會經濟領域之語言法規；這一切是為了於加泰隆尼亞語及其正常使用上能獲得完全語言能力，使該語言之社會使用具備新的推力。

1983 年法令之修正及更新亦須能重申於語言權利義務上實現完全平等的法律承諾，於學習及使用兩種官方語言之權利義務尤是，意即依現有法律架構，加泰隆尼亞公民必須學習加泰隆尼亞語及卡斯提亞語，並應有權使用之。

為繼續推動這一過程，更必須對國家及歐洲法律進行變更，並加強支持政策及相關預算規定。

四、本法內容及結構

本法表述人民本身語言及官方語言之法律概念。因此，加泰隆尼亞本土語言之概念適用於加泰隆尼亞語，加泰隆尼亞公務機關及機構承諾保護加泰隆尼亞語、以一般方式使用，及促進其於各層級之公共使用。官方語言概念適用於加泰隆尼亞語及卡斯提亞語，其所保障之所有公民主觀權利均有明確說明，即得以學習兩種語言、能於所有私人及公開活動中自由使用之，於與政府機關關係中以所選擇之語言接受服務，並逐步、漸進地與所有向公眾提供服務之社會代理人建立關係，且不因語言而受歧視。本法謹記上述原則，管理兩種官方語言於加泰隆尼亞之使用，並訂定措施以促進加泰隆尼亞語之使用，以實現其正常使用及推廣措施，而保證其於所有領域之存在。

於官方及行政領域，本法規定加泰隆尼亞政府及機構普遍使用加泰隆尼亞語，但不影響公民以其選擇之官方語言向其發言之權利，並聲明兩種官方語言之所有公共及私人文件均完全有效，於國家與司法機關及公共登記處在內之所有領域中，兩種官方語言完全無差別。

於教育，本法保證所有人群均能熟練使用兩種語言，同時保證學生不因語言而受歧視，亦不分為不同群體；以上所述均於維持 1983 年法令所適用聯合語言系統之同時，符合憲法法庭之判例。此外，本法亦訂定了推動加泰隆尼亞大學教育之措施。

於媒體領域，於自治政府職責範圍內，本法規定廣播電視中之加泰隆尼亞語使用，以保證廣播電視節目中使用加泰隆尼亞語，並訂定措施以推廣平面媒體。於文化產業上，本法維持並加強了《加泰隆尼亞語言正常化法》已訂定之電影、書籍、音樂及娛樂推廣措施，亦涵蓋了電腦科學、電訊網路及語言工程產品，其已成為處理各領域資訊之基礎。

於社會經濟領域，本法採取措施規範加泰隆尼亞語之存在，並推動其於因市場或其他原因而未獲充分保障之領域中的使用。因此，公營公司、執照持有者及公共服務機構應成為語言正常使用過程中之積極代理人，以保障消費者語言權利。目的為逐步實現兩種語言於經濟領域中之平等待遇，同時加泰隆尼亞所有公民均獲得完整加泰隆尼亞語知識，且一直是藉由自治政府訂定之社會協議。

最後，本法承認、保護並推動阿蘭谷中阿蘭語之教育及使用，其參照 1990 年 7 月 13 日有關阿蘭谷特殊待遇之第 16 號法令，並充分尊重阿蘭谷機構之權力。

本法向公民提供的是指導方針，僅規定了政府機關及特定公司於必要時之義務，因其活動性質為公共服務，且目的為保障公民語言權利。因此，惟公務員及上述公司於違反本法所定義務時，依現行部門法律，可能受到行政處罰。

就結構而言，本法由三十九條規定、八項增訂條款、三項暫行條款及三項最終條款組成。條文分為七章，各為一般原則（預備章）、機構使用（第一章）、地名及人名（第二章）、教育（第三章）、大眾媒體及文化產業（第四章）、社會經濟活動（第五章）及制度激勵（第六章）。其因而遵循 1983 年第 7 號法案之結構，但增訂了專門有關姓名及社會經濟活動之章節。

預備章 一般原則

第 1 條

立法目的

1. 本法目標為拓展《加泰隆尼亞自治法》第 3 條，以保護、促進及規範於所有領域中加泰隆尼亞語之使用，及於阿蘭谷中阿蘭語之使用，並保障加泰隆尼亞語與卡斯提亞語之正常及官方使用。
2. 本法主要目的為：
   a) 保護及推動公民使用加泰隆尼亞語。
   b) 有效使用加泰隆尼亞語及卡斯提亞語，不使任何公民受歧視。
   c) 推動加泰隆尼亞語於行政、教育、大眾媒體、文化產業及社會經濟領域之正常使用。
   d) 保證公民均能熟練使用加泰隆尼亞語。
3. 本法另一目的為於公民語言權利及義務上實現平等、推動任何必要行動、及消除目前造成困難之障礙。

第 2 條

加泰隆尼亞本土語言

1. 加泰隆尼亞語為加泰隆尼亞本土語言，且以其為民族之區別。
2. 作為加泰隆尼亞本土語言，加泰隆尼亞語是：
   a) 加泰隆尼亞一切機構之語言，特別是自治政府行政機關、地方機關、公營公司、一般公司與公共服務、機構媒體、教育及地名之語言。
   b) 於加泰隆尼亞之國家行政機關以其規定方式優先使用之語言，其他機構及一般向公眾提供服務之公司與實體亦同。
3. 第 2 項所定內容默示機構特別承諾，於不損害加泰隆尼亞語及卡斯提亞語之官方性質下，於公民中推廣知識及使用。

第 3 條

官方語言

1. 加泰隆尼亞語為加泰隆尼亞官方語言，卡斯提亞語亦同。
2. 加泰隆尼亞語及卡斯提亞語為官方語言，公民得於一切私人及公開活動中使用而不加區別，無有例外。以兩種官方語言之任何一種進行之法律程序，就其使用語言，具有完全有效性及效力。

第 4 條

語言權利

1. 依《自治法》第 3 條，及於自治政府以積極政策創造允許語言權利及義務完全平等環境之情形下，加泰隆尼亞人民均有權：
   a) 於兩種官方語言均能熟練使用。
   b) 以兩種官方語言之任何一種、以口語或書面形式，於其關係及私人與公開程序中表達意見。
   c) 依本法規定方式以兩種官方語言之任何一種接受服務。
   d) 於所有領域中自由使用兩種官方語言之任何一種。
   e) 不因其所用官方語言而受歧視。
2. 人民均得向法院及法庭提起訴訟，以獲得對其語言使用權之法律保護。
3. 人民均得向自治政府及保護官 [5] 請求其於職權範圍內採取行動，以特定方式保障語言權利。

第 5 條

自治政府政策指導原則

1. 自治政府應保障公民之語言權利、加泰隆尼亞語與卡斯提亞語之正常及官方使用、兩種語言於全體

人民之教育、於政府機關服務工作人員之語言能力，及公民於所有領域語言權利及義務上之完全平等。

2. 自治政府應採取必要措施及提供適足資源，以保障、保護及推動加泰隆尼亞語於所有領域之使用。

第 6 條

加泰隆尼亞語之統一

1. 加泰隆尼亞語為一項遺產，與構成同一語言社群之其他地區共享。自治政府應保證能保護加泰隆尼亞語之統一，並推動加泰隆尼亞語於國外之使用與傳播及各加泰隆尼亞語地區間之交流。

2. 依現行法律，加泰隆尼亞語研究院 [6] 負語言權威之責任。

第 7 條

阿蘭語之承認及保護 [因 2010 年 10 月 1 日第 35 號法律於奧克語即阿蘭谷之阿蘭語之限制規定，部分廢除]

阿蘭語為阿蘭谷本地之奧克語變體，其使用應遵循 1990 年 7 月 13 日第 16 號法令有關阿蘭谷之特殊待遇規定，另亦應遵循本法規定，且不得解釋為對阿蘭語之限制使用。

第一章 機構使用

第 8 條

法規之公布

1. 加泰隆尼亞議會所頒布法案，應以加泰隆尼亞語及卡斯提亞語同步公布於《加泰隆尼亞自治政府官方公報》[7] 。議會負責準備卡斯提亞語之官方版本。

2. 加泰隆尼亞自治政府、機關與機構及加泰隆尼亞地方機關之一般規定及規範性決議，於適當時，應以加泰隆尼亞語及卡斯提亞語同步公布於《加泰隆尼亞自治政府官方公報》。

第 9 條

加泰隆尼亞政府機關之語言

1. 加泰隆尼亞自治政府、地方機關與其他公營公司、機構，及其負責之持執照服務及公司，應於其內部程序及相互關係中使用加泰隆尼亞語。於向居於加泰隆尼亞語地區內之個人或公司之通訊及通知中，亦應正常使用之，但不損害公民請求收受為卡斯提亞語者之權利。

2. 自治政府應以法規規定於其管轄下所有機構之行政活動中加泰隆尼亞語之使用。

3. 地方公司及大學應依第 1 項規定，於各自職責範圍內規定加泰隆尼亞語之使用。其他公營公司均亦應同樣規定之。

第 10 條

行政程序

1. 於加泰隆尼亞自治政府機關、地方機關及其他公司所執行之行政程序中，應使用加泰隆尼亞語，但不得損害公民以卡斯提亞語提交文件、發表聲明及因其請求接受通知之權利。

2. 政府機關應以當事人請求之官方語言提供對其有影響事項之翻譯證明。翻譯請求不得對申請人造成任何障礙或費用，或任何程序延誤或程序及規定時間期限之暫停。

第 11 條

加泰隆尼亞服務工作人員之語言能力

1. 於加泰隆尼亞政府機關、公司或公共機構服務之工作人員，應充分適當掌握兩種官方語言，口語及書面溝通皆同，以便其得以適切履行指派職位之職責。

2. 為使第 1 項規定生效，自治政府應保證向於加泰隆尼亞自治政府、地方機關、公立大學及司法機關服務之工作人員教授加泰隆尼亞語，並推動再利用此類人員之措施。

3. 招聘任職於自治政府、地方機關及大學行政服務部門之工作人員時，包含約聘人員在內，其加泰隆

尼亞語之口語及書面能力應與該職位之職責相應，以符公共服務相關法律規定條文。

第 12 條

國家機關

1. 國家政府機關之**機構及實體**於加泰隆尼亞執行之口語或書面行政程序，以任何一種官方語言為之者，均為有效，無需翻譯。
2. 人民均有權自行選擇官方語言，以口語或書面形式，於加泰隆尼亞中與國家政府溝通及接受服務，且不得向人民要求提供任何形式之**翻譯**。

第 13 條

司法程序

1. 司法程序，以任何一種官方語言為之者，無論口語或書面形式，均為有效，無需翻譯。
2. 人民均有權自行選擇官方語言，以口語或書面形式，與司法機關溝通及接受服務，且不得向人民要求提供任何形式之**翻譯**。
3. 因其請求，人民均得以所要求官方語言接受對其有影響之裁定及判決程序證明，且不因語言延遲。
4. 第 1 項、第 2 項及第 3 項規定，於教會法庭及仲裁法庭亦適用之。
5. 於自治政府負責之司法機關服務工作人員安置規定中，第 11 條規定應依具體相關規定，於所定條件下適用之。

第 14 條

公文書

1. 以任何一種官方語言作成之公文書均應為有效。
2. 公文書應以授予人所選擇官方語言製作之，有多人者，以其協定之語言製作之。如未能就語言達成協議，契約或文書應以兩種官方語言製作之。
3. 製作文書前，應明確詢問授予人所選擇之語言；於任何情形下，選擇其一均不得導致文書製作及授權之延遲。如未選擇特定語言，應以加泰隆尼亞語製作文書。
4. 公共宣誓官應依相關人員請求之語言，以卡斯提亞語或加泰隆尼亞語提供副本及證明，且應依其職責於適當情形下提供文書及原始文本之**翻譯**。原文本及其副本經**翻譯**一事應於頁邊空白處及註腳中記錄之，但無須法律紀錄。
5. 公共宣誓官辦公室應有能力以兩種語言之任何一種服務公民，且須配有充分適足了解此兩種語言之工作人員，以履行其工作作業相關職責。

第 15 條

民商事文書

1. 語言選擇非為私文書之形式要件。故以兩者之任何一種語言作成之文書均應為有效，使用語言非加泰隆尼亞官方語言者，不損害民事、商業或訴訟法得規定之**翻譯**。
2. 私文書，無論其為契約與否，亦不論其性質，以加泰隆尼亞兩種官方語言之任何一種作成者，均應為有效，且於加泰隆尼亞境內之法庭內外均無需翻譯即為完成。
3. 第 2 項所稱文書應以雙方所協定官方語言製作之。但如為定型化契約、規範契約、具標準條款之契約或具一般條件之契約，則應以消費者所選擇語言製作之，且應以加泰隆尼亞語及卡斯提亞語之單獨副本供客戶立即使用。
4. 各種證券，包含代表貿易公司股份之證券，均應以兩種官方語言之任何一種製作者為有效。
5. 金融實體向其客戶提供之支票、本票、收據及其他文件，應至少以加泰隆尼亞語製作之。

第 16 條

集體談判協議

1. 集體談判協議應以兩種官方語言之任何一種製作者為有效。

2. 集體談判協議應以各方所協定官方語言製作之，或如未能就語言達成協議，應以兩種官方語言分別製作二份單獨副本。

第 17 條

公共登記處

1. 登記項目以兩種官方語言之任何一種為記錄者，均應為有效。
2. 所有加泰隆尼亞之公共登記處，除僅具行政性質之登記處外，其登記項目應以製作文件或聲明所用官方語言記錄之。文件為雙語者，登記項目應使用向登記處提交文件者所選之語言。
3. 登記官應以請求所用之官方語言核發證明。
4. 登記處應有能力以兩種官方語言之任何一種向公民提供服務，且應有語言能力充分適足之工作人員履行其工作職位之職責。
5. 登記處應保證當事方所請求之任何官方語言登記項目，其無論口語或書面翻譯，均即時且準確。
6. 登記處供公眾使用之表格及其他印刷資料，至少應以加泰隆尼亞語製作之。

第二章 名稱

第 18 條

地名

1. 加泰隆尼亞地名之加泰隆尼亞語版本為唯一官方地名，以符加泰隆尼亞語研究院之語言規範，但應為阿蘭語之阿蘭谷地名除外。
2. 有關自治市及市鎮 [8] 名稱之決定由地方政府立法機關主管。
3. 各城市街道及村莊之名稱由地方議會負責決定，而加泰隆尼亞其他地名之決定，包含城際道路，則由此類地名主管自治政府負責之。
4. 第 2 項及第 3 項所稱之名稱為一切用途之法定名稱，其標誌亦應相應書寫之。自治政府於一切情形下遵從已成為國內法一部分之國際法規，應規定加泰隆尼亞語於公共標誌之正常使用。

第 19 條

人名

1. 加泰隆尼亞公民有權使用依規定正確書寫之名字及姓氏，並在其姓氏之間使用連接詞「i」。
2. 利害關係人得安排於民事登記處以加泰隆尼亞語之法規正確方式記錄其名字及姓氏，無論最初登記之日期，向負責人簡單聲明及提出正確語言格式認證文件，以法規應規定方式為之。
3. 對於阿蘭語之語言規範，本規定於阿蘭語姓名適用之。

第三章 教育

第 20 條

教育語言

1. 加泰隆尼亞語為加泰隆尼亞本地語言，亦為各級各類學校之教育語言。
2. 各級教育機構應以加泰隆尼亞語為其內外部之教育及行政活動中正常表達之工具。

第 21 條

非大學教育

1. 加泰隆尼亞語應正常使用為非大學教育之教育學習載體。
2. 兒童有權以其常用語言接受初步教育，無論其為加泰隆尼亞語或卡斯提亞語。政府應保障此一權利，且應提供適當資源使之生效。父母或監護人得因請求代表其子女行使此權利。
3. 課程綱要應保障加泰隆尼亞語及卡斯提亞語之教學，使所有兒童，無論其開始受教育時之常用語言為何，於義務教育結束時均能正常、正確使用兩種官方語言。

4. 於後義務教育中，教育主管機關應推動課程發展教學政策，以保證兩種語言之能力及使用得到完善，使青少年均從教育中獲得預期之工具及文化知識。

5. 學生於中心或團體班中，均不得依其常用語言分開之。

6. 學生未認證具適當程度之加泰隆尼亞語與卡斯提亞語口語及書面知識者，不得向其頒發中等教育畢業證書。

7. 於自治政府所定情形下，對於任何於全部或部分教育期間獲免學習加泰隆尼亞語之學生，或於加泰隆尼亞以外地區受義務教育之學生，不得要求提供加泰隆尼亞語能力證明。

8. 學生遲於平常時間進入加泰隆尼亞教育體系者，應獲得加泰隆尼亞語教學之特殊及額外支持。

第 22 條

大學教育

1. 於高等教育學院及大學中，教職人員及學生有權以自行選擇之官方語言，以口語及書面形式表達意見。

2. 自治政府、大學及高等教育學院，應於各自職責範圍內採取適當措施，保障與推動加泰隆尼亞語於所有教學、非教學及研究領域之使用，包含博士學位論文及正式專業考試。

3. 大學應提供課程及其他適合資源，使學生與教職人員得提升對加泰隆尼亞語之理解及知識。

4. 如有必要，大學得對國際承諾相關活動中之語言使用訂定具體標準。

第 23 條

常設訓練及特殊待遇

1. 常設成人訓練課程之課程綱要，應包含加泰隆尼亞語及卡斯提亞語課程。

2. 語言專業之教育學院，應提供兩種官方語言之教學。

3. 自治政府主管之特殊教育機構，不教授語言者，應向知識不足之學生提供加泰隆尼亞語課程。

第 24 條

教職人員

1. 加泰隆尼亞教育機構中各級非大學教育之教職人員，均應了解兩種官方語言，且應有能力於其教學中使用之。

2. 師資訓練學院及課程之課程綱要，應依各教學專業之要求，以使學生完整掌握兩種官方語言之能力而訂定之。

3. 加泰隆尼亞大學院校之教職人員，應依教學需求，對兩種官方語言具充分了解。本規定不適用於訪問教師等相類情形。大學應負責訂定落實本規定之機制及有關時間期限。

第四章 大眾媒體及文化產業

第 25 條

公共廣播及電視媒體

1. 加泰隆尼亞自治政府及地方機關主管之廣播電視節目，其所用正常語言應為加泰隆尼亞語。於此情形，地方機關主管之媒體得考量其受眾特徵。

2. 於不損害第 26 條第 1 項及第 5 項規定之實施下，本條第 1 項所稱媒體應推廣加泰隆尼亞之文化表現形式，以加泰隆尼亞語製作者尤是。

3. 加泰隆尼亞廣播電視公司應保證以阿蘭語向阿蘭谷定期播送廣播及電視節目。

4. 自治政府應採取措施，協助於加泰隆尼亞地區良好接收以加泰隆尼亞語播送之其他地區電視電臺。

第 26 條

經許可營業之廣播電視媒體節目

1. 於不損害 1996 年 7 月 5 日第 8 號法令之適用範圍內，對於有線視聽節目之規定，該法所稱組織應

保證本身及其他電視服務製作之各類節目，其播放時間至少半數為加泰隆尼亞語。

2. 第 1 項規定於加泰隆尼亞領土內私營電視執照持有人亦適用之。

3. 自治政府發給執照之廣播節目，應保證節目時間至少半數為加泰隆尼亞語，但自治政府得依其聽眾特性，以法規調整該比例。

4. 自治政府應以加泰隆尼亞語使用比例超過規定最低限度為發給表面波電視電臺執照、有線及無線廣播提供電視節目之標準。

5. 廣播電視公司應保障其音樂節目有適足之加泰隆尼亞藝術家所作歌曲，且歌曲至少四分之一以加泰隆尼亞語或阿蘭語演唱之。

6. 本條所稱廣播公司及向阿蘭谷廣播或提供節目者，應保證其廣播中阿蘭語之顯著存在。

第 27 條

平面媒體

1. 於自治政府及地方機關出版之平面新聞雜誌中，通常使用之語言應為加泰隆尼亞語。

2. 於加泰隆尼亞通行之雜誌，全部或大部分以加泰隆尼亞語編寫者，自治政府應推廣及補助之。

3. 市政或地方性質之雜誌，全部或大部分以加泰隆尼亞語編寫者，自治政府及地方機關應推廣及得補助之。

4. 第 2 項及第 3 項所稱補助之授予，應依加泰隆尼亞語傳播、商業化及使用之客觀標準，於預算規定範圍內，且於議會或地方機關委員會之控制下為之。

第 28 條

文化產業及娛樂事業

1. 自治政府應幫助、鼓勵及推動：

　　a) 加泰隆尼亞語之文學及科學產出，於加泰隆尼亞語地區內外散布與自加泰隆尼亞語譯為其他語言之文學科學作品，及自其他語言譯為加泰隆尼亞語之作品。

　　b) 加泰隆尼亞語書籍雜誌之出版、散布及傳播。

　　c) 加泰隆尼亞語電影之製作，以其他語言所作電影之加泰隆尼亞語配音及字幕，及此類產品任何形式之散布及放映。

　　d) 加泰隆尼亞語錄音及影音素材之製作、散布及發行。

　　e) 加泰隆尼亞語娛樂節目之製作及演出。

　　f) 以加泰隆尼亞語演唱音樂之創作、演出及製作。

　　g) 針對盲人設計之加泰隆尼亞語書面及聲音資料之製作、出版及散布，及向該部門提供之加泰隆尼亞語基本文化產品。

　　h) 一切其他加泰隆尼亞語公共文化活動。

2. 保障文化產業及其他領域中加泰隆尼亞語之使用所採取之一切措施，均應依客觀標準，不受歧視，且合於預算規定範圍。

3. 電影產品以非原本語言配音或字幕發行與放映者，對其放映及發行，自治政府得以法規規定語言配額，以保證現有電影中加泰隆尼亞語之顯著存在。對電影產品所定之配額，無論為加泰隆尼亞語配音或字幕，均不得超過年度發行或放映電影總數之一半，且應基於客觀標準。相關規定應於 1994 年 6 月 8 日第 17 號國家法令之範圍內頒布，其針對保護及推廣電影，且遵循所規定之待遇。

第 29 條

語言及電腦產業

自治政府應以適足措施協助、鼓勵及推廣：

　　a) 與語言產業有關之各類加泰隆尼亞語產品，如語音辨識系統、自動翻譯等科技進步可行成果，其研究、生產及行銷。

　　b) 加泰隆尼亞語之電腦軟體、電腦遊戲、數位及多媒體產品，及於適合時譯為加泰隆尼亞語之該類

產品，其生產、散布及行銷。

c) 加泰隆尼亞語之車載資通訊網路產品及資訊。

第五章 社會經濟活動

第 30 條

公開公司

1. 自治政府及地方機關之公開公司，及管理或經營許可服務之持照公司，於其內部章程及文件，與其標誌、說明書、所生產或提供產品或服務之標籤及包裝上，應正常使用加泰隆尼亞語。

2. 第 1 項所稱公司，其向居於加泰隆尼亞語地區之個人發出通知及通訊，包含發票及其他業務文件時，應正常使用加泰隆尼亞語，但不損害公民以卡斯提亞語收受之權利—或於適當時，因請求以加泰隆尼亞語為之。

第 31 條

公共服務公司

1. 公司及公共或私人實體，提供運輸、供應、通訊等公共服務者，於其標誌及擴音器宣傳中應至少使用加泰隆尼亞語。

2. 第 1 項所稱公司及實體，向居於加泰隆尼亞之個人發出書面通訊及通知，包含發票及其他業務文件時，應至少使用加泰隆尼亞語，但不損害公民請求以卡斯提亞語收受之權利。

3. 第 2 項有關發票及其他業務文件之規定，其解釋應不損害國家於其直接提供或由其所屬公司及實體提供前項服務時，組織前項服務之責任。

第 32 條

提供公眾服務

1. 公司及機構涉及產品販賣與提供服務，而於加泰隆尼亞開展活動者，應於消費者以加泰隆尼亞之任何一種官方語言表達意見時，有能力向消費者提供服務。

2. 自治政府應以適當措施推動於第 1 項所稱活動中更廣為使用加泰隆尼亞語。

3. 含一般資訊之常設標誌及海報，及向公眾開放機構之使用者及消費者提供服務之文件，應至少以加泰隆尼亞語製作之。本規定不適用於商標、商業名稱或受工業財產權立法保護之標誌。

第 33 條

合約或補助公司

公司與自治政府或加泰隆尼亞地方機關訂定契約或合作協議者，或受益於其協助或補助者，於其針對公眾之標誌、公告及文件中，至少於後者與協助或協議之對象有關時，應至少使用加泰隆尼亞語。

第 34 條

使用者及消費者資訊

1. 資訊陳述於加泰隆尼亞散布產品之標籤、包裝及說明書上者，得為加泰隆尼亞語、卡斯提亞語或任何其他歐盟語言。

2. 受益於原產地認證、地區認證及品質認證之加泰隆尼亞產品，及於加泰隆尼亞領土範圍內散布之手工藝品，其標籤所述之強制性資料及自願附加資訊，應必須至少為加泰隆尼亞語。

3. 自治政府應以法規規定向特定行業消費者及使用者提供之資訊，於加泰隆尼亞領土範圍內散布之工商業產品，尤其包裝食品、危險有毒產品及煙草製品，其標籤及使用說明書亦同，以保證依本法、歐盟規則及其他法律條例，加泰隆尼亞語之存在逐步增加。

第 35 條

廣告

1. 自治政府及地方機關、其公開公司及執照持有者，與其他加泰隆尼亞機構及公法公司，其於加泰隆

尼亞領土範圍內所為之機構廣告，應一般使用加泰隆尼亞語。

2. 自治政府及地方機關應以適當措施支持、鼓勵及推動於廣告，尤其於公共道路上者，使用加泰隆尼亞語，以使之成為該行業正常使用語言。

第 36 條

專業及勞工活動

1. 自治政府及專業聯合會應推動於其專業活動中使用加泰隆尼亞語。

2. 自治政府應鼓勵及推動於工作中心、勞資關係，與集體談判協議、公司協議及勞動契約中使用加泰隆尼亞語，且應直接推動工會及商業組織之參與，以實現該目的。

3. 集體談判協議及公司協議，得包含旨在促進員工了解加泰隆尼亞語，並保障其於工作中心與勞動契約、工資單及所有其他文件之使用之語言條款。自治政府應鼓勵於集體談判協議中納入此類條款。

4. 常設標誌及含文字資訊，為供工作中心工作人員使用，且於工作中心之設置為強制性者，應至少使用加泰隆尼亞語。

第六章 制度激勵

第 37 條

推廣措施

1. 自治政府應支持、鼓勵及推動於勞動、專業、商業、廣告、文化、社會、體育、休閒及其他活動中使用加泰隆尼亞語。

2. 自治政府及地方機關，於各自職責範圍內，應推廣加泰隆尼亞語之公共形象及使用，且得向與加泰隆尼亞語正常使用及推廣有關之行動提供稅務減免。

第 38 條

支援中心

1. 自治政府應與地方機關協議，建立並補助致力於推動加泰隆尼亞語知識、使用及傳播之中心，於社會語言情況需要之處尤是。語言推廣聯盟為訂定地區語言推廣政策之機構，應負責此類支援中心。

2. 第 1 項所定之中心應有充足人力物力以履行其職責。

第 39 條

規劃措施

1. 自治政府應利用由定期計畫組成之通用語言計畫工具，以針對各種情形確定最適合之目標及措施，並評估結果。計畫機制應會同各涉及主體及群體訂定之，且應考量參與、簡化及有效之原則。

2. 自治政府應製作加泰隆尼亞之社會語言地圖，其應每五年接受一次審查，以依實際情況調整語言政策行動，同時評估所採取行動之後果。

3. 自治政府應每年向議會通報語言政策行動，與第 1 項及第 2 項所稱機制範圍內取得之成果。

增訂條款

一

與其他機構及實體之合作

1. 於不損害本法之適用下，與歐盟、國家政府、司法權總委員會，及國家、歐洲或歐洲或國際範圍內公私營公司之合作內，尤其於服務、廣播及電視領域中者，自治政府應保持注意，以實現加泰隆尼亞語之普及使用。

2. 自治政府應注意於全國、跨歐洲及國際媒體中有加泰隆尼亞語之適足存在。

二

三

外部投射

1. 自治政府應注意加泰隆尼亞文化及語言於語言領域外之發展，主要是於學術及研究領域，與歐盟機構及其政策中。自治政府得參與加泰隆尼亞語地區之共同組織，以實現該目標。
2. 依 1996 年 12 月 27 日第 18 號法令有關國外加泰隆尼亞語社群關係之規定，自治政府應使國外加泰隆尼亞語社群得以傳播及學習加泰隆尼亞語。

四

加泰隆尼亞語姓名正規拼寫法

第 19 條所定，以正確格式替換不正確書寫或拼寫之名稱，應依 1977 年 1 月 4 日第 17 號國家法令第 2 條所定程序管理，其涉及改革《民事登記法》第 54 條或得替代之同等法規。

五

履行保證

本法不考量對公民之處罰。但：

    a) 違反第 26 條規定應視為違反執照之基本條件，故應適用規範有線廣播視聽節目之 1996 年 7 月 5 日第 8 號法令所定處罰、1987 年 12 月 18 日第 31 號國家法令之遠距通訊條例，及 1994 年 7 月 12 日第 25 號法令，其將第 89/552 /EEC 號指令納入西班牙法律條例。

    b) 有關公司及實體，違反第 15 條、第 30 條、第 31 條及第 32.3 條規定者，應視為對服務使用者及消費者意願之無理拒絕，故應適用 1990 年 1 月 8 日第 1 號法令有關市場紀律及消費者與使用者保護之規定。

六

經濟規定

自治政府於預算中，應訂定相關規定，以利用充分方法及資源，開展因實施本法而生之活動及措施，且對於多語言教育制度、兩種官方語言之政府機關，及受限地區語言之文化分布，應特別注意其成本，另亦應考量地域及部門分布之客觀需求。

七

注意及鼓勵職責

自治政府應注意，使國家其他公共機關之法規與行政行為尊重憲法與法定條例之原則及本法，且對於國家法規妨礙加泰隆尼亞語於任何領域之使用，或限制公民之完全語言平等者，應鼓勵立法修正之。

八

公務員規則

本法規定，依公務員監督規範，對於政府機關服務之工作人員具約束力。

九

正式書面及口語翻譯 [依 2017 年 3 月 28 日第 5 號法案第 224 條規定，增訂有關稅務、行政、金融及公共部門措施，與對大型商業場所、停留於觀光場所、放射性物質、含糖飲料及二氧化碳排放之稅務訂定與監管措施之規定]

1. 正式宣誓之口筆譯，自他種語言至加泰隆尼亞語與奧克語及反之者，須由指派或具資格之人員為之。
2. 於加泰隆尼亞語與奧克語之宣誓口筆譯，其資格種類及規定須以政令為之。於奧克語，擬定政令時須諮詢阿蘭總委員會。
3. 宣誓筆譯及口譯之合格人員須簽名蓋章，以證明口筆譯之真實性及準確性。

暫行條款

一

語言使用規定

第 9.3 條所定語言使用規定，應於本法施行後二年內核定之。

二

公司適應

1. 受本法影響之公司及實體，其應有二年時間以適應第 15 條及第五章之規定。對於獨立經營者，該
期限為五年。
2. 於五年內或較遲之期限屆滿前，第 34 條所稱產品或服務，得於不符標籤語言規定之情形下，**繼續**
提供市場。

三

廣播電視電臺

第 25 條及第 26 條規定，應適用於本法施行後，由自治政府負責授權，發給或換發執照之電臺。

最終條款

一

1987 年 4 月 15 日第 8 號法令修正

1. 1987 年 4 月 15 日第 8 號市政及地方處理法第 5 條已修正，其內容應為如下：

「*第 5 條*

1. 加泰隆尼亞語為加泰隆尼亞地方機關之本身語言，故應為其活動中正常及普遍使用之語言。
2. 所有公民均有權選擇與地方機關交流所用之官方語言，後者有相應義務依 1998 年 1 月 7 日第 1 號
法令所定有關語言政策之規定，以其所擇語言服務之。」

2. 1987 年 4 月 15 日第 8 號市政及地方處理法第 294.2 條已修正，其內容應為如下：

「*第 294.2 條*

地方機關應依其公務人員任用計畫，以下列方式招聘工作人員：公開公告及應聘制度、國家考試及免
費國家考試應聘制度，其應保障平等、擇優、能力及公告原則。於招聘過程中，應認證加泰隆尼亞語
之語言能力，而阿蘭谷之地方機關亦應認證阿蘭語，該能力於口語及書面程度上，均適合所任工作職
位之職責。」

3. 1987 年 4 月 15 日第 8 號市政及地方處理法第 310.2 條已修正，其內容應為如下：

「*第 310.2 條*

加泰隆尼亞地方機關，對職務於全國內有效之地方機關公務人員，於其工作職位之應聘條件公告中，
應列明口語及書面語言能力要求。」

二

法規制定

自治政府應獲授權以施行制定及適用本法必要之法規規定。

三

法規替代及有效性

1. 1983 年 4 月 18 日有關加泰隆尼亞語言正常化之第 7 號法令，已由本法條文取代，但無礙不相矛盾
內容成為加泰隆尼亞法律傳統之一部分。
2. 因制定 1983 年第 7 號法令而生之一切不反對本法之條文均應為有效，但不損害得為之任何法規修
正。
3. 1993 年 3 月 5 日第 3 號《消費者法》條文及因制定該法而通過且不反對本法之規定，均應為有效。

威爾斯語 2050
百萬人說威爾斯語

威爾斯語 2050：百萬人說威爾斯語

適用對象

威爾斯政府部門；威爾斯公務機關；威爾斯第三部門機構；威爾斯私部門公司；威爾斯教育組織；提倡使用威爾斯語之組織；家庭、兒少及社群相關組織；其他利害關係人。

所需行動

令利害關係人得知策略內容並據此採取行動。

概述

本文件為威爾斯部長提倡與促進使用威爾斯語之策略，係根據《2006 威爾斯政府法》第 78 節擬成。本策略取代〈活語言：讓威爾斯語活下去—— 2012-17 威爾斯語策略〉，並關聯至政策聲明〈活語言：讓威爾斯語活下去——繼續前進〉。〈威爾斯語 2050 策略〉闡明威爾斯政府為達 2050 年百萬人說威爾斯語目標之長期方針。

詳細資訊

本文件相關疑問請洽：
威爾斯政府威爾斯語司
Cathays Park
Cardiff
CF10 3NQ
E-mail: Cymraeg@gov.wales

副本

本文件可於威爾斯政府官網 gov.wales 下載。

相關文件

〈2016-2021 帶領威爾斯向前〉（2016）、〈活語言：讓威爾斯語活下去—— 2012-17 威爾斯語策略〉（2012）、〈活語言：讓威爾斯語活下去——繼續前進〉（2014）、〈2011 威爾斯語（威爾斯）辦法〉、〈全威爾斯語教育策略〉（2010）
本文件亦提供威爾斯語版本。

目錄

部長的話

願景

　　　　2050 年百萬人說威爾斯語

　　　　實現願景

　　　　背景

　　　　國家策略

　　　　長期策略

　　　　策略目標

　　　　達成目標

　　　　落實策略

概念基礎與原則

　　　生命歷程方法

達百萬人

　　　語言技能習得

　　　推估與達百萬人軌跡

　　　作為軌跡基礎之假設

　　　語言使用

三大策略主題

主題 1：增加說威爾斯語者人數

　　　1.　家庭中的語言傳播

　　　2.　幼兒教育

　　　3.　義務教育

　　　4.　後義務教育

　　　5.　教育人力、資源與認證

主題 2：增加使用威爾斯語

　　　6.　職場

　　　7.　服務

　　　8.　社會上使用威爾斯語

主題 3：打造有利條件——基礎設施與背景環境

　　　9.　社群與經濟

　　　10. 文化與媒體

　　　11. 威爾斯與國際

　　　12. 數位科技

　　　13. 語言基礎設施

　　　14. 語言規劃

　　　15. 評估與研究

結論

參考文獻

部長的話

2050 年百萬人說威爾斯語

威爾斯語是威爾斯的國寶之一。威爾斯語幫助我們界定何謂威爾斯人,以及威爾斯這個國家。威爾斯政府企圖在 2050 年達到百萬人能說會道威爾斯語的目標。此企圖確實是相當大的挑戰,但如果想為後代保留威爾斯語的活力,那麼我們相信這項挑戰是值得的,也是必要的。

本策略的由來,是 1967 年第一部《威爾斯語言法》已歷五十載歲月。如今時代變遷,而威爾斯語仍在威爾斯立法裡高居神聖地位。

2011 年人口普查結果出爐,我們也藉此機會坦誠交流和重新評估對威爾斯語的未來抱持的想法。當變則變,我們的策略必須推陳出新,在規劃的作法上加以系統化,而且必須加強合作,以維護威爾斯語應有的經典傳承。

我們非常清楚,以政府身分而言,我們有責任為這項工作確立方向和扮演領導角色。威爾斯政府現在和將來都會致力完成這項任務。然而同樣重要的是,以國家身分而言,我們是該一肩扛起這項挑戰。政府無法強硬要求家長和照顧者一定要和兒童使用威爾斯語、兒童遊戲玩樂時一定要使用威爾斯語、或民眾一定要在社會上使用威爾斯語。然而我們能努力做到的,是提供適當條件來增加說威爾斯語者人數和增加使用威爾斯語。

對我們的願景而言,教育至關重要,但我們應當確保接受教育體系洗禮的年輕人,在各種場合皆能順暢自如、滿懷自信地使用威爾斯語。無庸置疑,數位科技將會是教育相關願景裡的核心要角,能夠協助職場邁向雙語化,並支援社會用途。

本文整體要旨在於,我們需達到威爾斯語已內化至日常生活各種層面的地步。要實現這樣的理想,全國民眾都必須共襄盛舉——無論是能夠流利口說威爾斯語者、會說但不願說威爾斯語者、學過威爾斯語的新使用者、以及自認不會說威爾斯語者。大家都能盡一份心力,我們也希望大家踴躍參與,一同實現願景。

我們提高期望,並立下極具企圖心的願景,相信如此將有機會改變威爾斯語的未來命運。讓我們一起推動威爾斯語發展茁壯,利用無分男女老少皆能通曉的活語言,來打造真正雙語的威爾斯國度。

Rt. Hon Carwyn Jones AM
第一部長

Alun Davies AM
終生學習與威爾斯語部長

願景

2050 年百萬人說威爾斯語

2050 年：威爾斯語蓬勃發展，會說威爾斯語者人數達到一百萬，生活所有層面皆能使用威爾斯語。對於不會說威爾斯語者而言，他們對威爾斯語懷有好感和歸屬感，並且認同威爾斯語對威爾斯文化、社會和經濟的貢獻。

實現願景

欲實現「2050 年百萬人說威爾斯語」的願景，挑戰在於必須發起既廣泛且深度的改變。我們需突破界限，並且大破大立以促進更多人學習與使用威爾斯語。這項策略將以既有基礎為根據，憑藉其移動至語言歷程的下一階段。我們定出實現願景的三大策略主題：
1. 增加說威爾斯語者人數
2. 增加使用威爾斯語
3. 打造有利條件——基礎設施與背景環境
為實現願景，我們將依照三大主題採取行動，且也應了解三者間的互依關係。

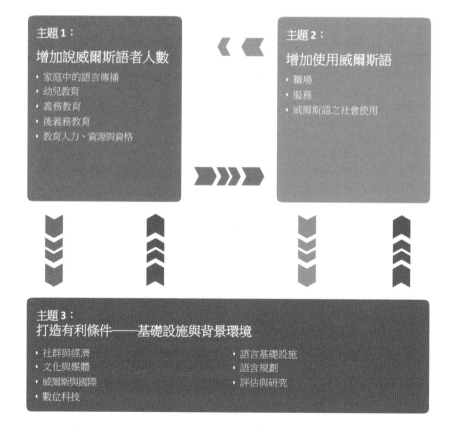

背景

本策略並非首開先河者。過去二十五年來，在政府對威爾斯語的支援下，已取得重大進展。

威爾斯語現具備官方地位；相關立法已完成，令說威爾斯語者有權利接受威爾斯語服務，且政府已指派威爾斯語長官負責監督上述權利之實施。《2015 後代福祉法》規定，服務範圍涵蓋全威爾斯的特定公務機關應致力達成七項福祉目標，其中一項為「文化活力充沛、威爾斯語蓬勃發展的威爾斯」；至於規劃提供全威爾斯語教育的制度亦有法定基礎。威爾斯政府有義務提倡與促進使用威爾斯語，努力達成福祉目標。

2016 年 9 月，我們發布威爾斯政府接下來五年的計畫〈2016-2021 帶領威爾斯向前〉，闡述政府推動改善威爾斯經濟與公共服務的方案，打造繁榮穩定、健全活躍、積極進取、聯合團結的威爾斯。〈2016-2021 帶領威爾斯向前〉列出政府在實現上述改善方面的優先事項，這些辦法充滿企圖心，旨在為處於人生各階段的眾人帶來改變。

我們在本策略中表明宏大企圖，希望擴大威爾斯語的使用層面，並增加說威爾斯語者的人數。我們亦許下承諾，將致力達成 2050 年百萬人說威爾斯語的目標，以及持續投資以鼓勵更多人在日常生活使用與講說威爾斯語。

提出〈2016-2021 帶領威爾斯向前〉計畫的同時，我們亦發表福祉目的，闡明如何利用《2015 後代福祉法（威爾斯）》來訂定政府方案和盡力協助達成全國共通的七項福祉目標。

國家策略

本策略是為全威爾斯所制定，期盼全國上下共同推動百萬人說威爾斯語的願景。會說威爾斯語者的人數有機會增加，尤其是在人口密度高但說威爾斯語者比例低的地區。另一方面，我們必須確保威爾斯語社群的未來活力，這些地方有助增加威爾斯語在生活各層面的使用。

我們期許能在全國各處維護有助學習和使用威爾斯語技能的有利情勢。我們希望增加威爾斯語在家庭中的傳播，及早教導每位孩童學習威爾斯語，擁有可供所有人學習威爾斯語技能的教育體系，以及職場更加重視威爾斯語技能。另一方面，我們將致力支援民眾能夠在社會上、工作上和獲取服務時使用威爾斯語。

這表示必須根據威爾斯各區域本身的語言組成來加以考量，詳加規劃以取得地方上的適當平衡。舉例而言，威爾斯語社群的挑戰在於必須確保民眾擁有能夠滿足職涯發展和家庭生計的優質工作，如此一來民眾才會續留或返回社群。至於其他地區，提倡職場與商場上使用威爾斯語的重要性將與日俱增。

數位革命橫跨本策略的三大主題，而威爾斯語必須是數位革命裡的一環。我們必須確保本策略的實施初期具備威爾斯語優良科技，以支援威爾斯語在教育、職場和社會上的使用。

說威爾斯語者（三歲以上）比例，依 LSOA（低尺度高層級輸出區域）劃分，2011 年

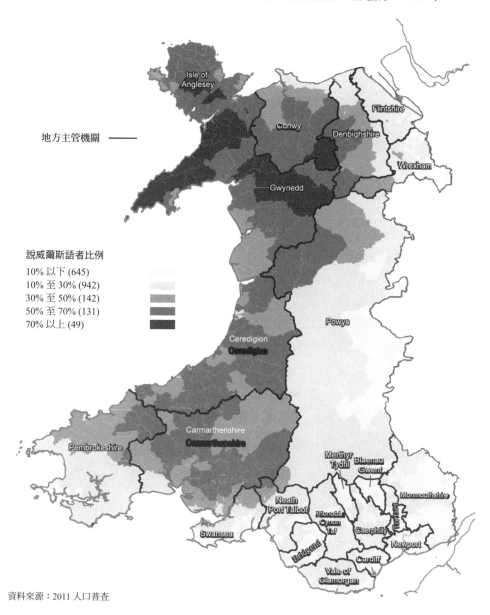

地方主管機關 ——————

說威爾斯語者比例
10% 以下 (645)
10% 至 30% (942)
30% 至 50% (142)
50% 至 70% (131)
70% 以上 (49)

資料來源：2011 人口普查

193.12-13
地理與科技
© 皇家版權與資料庫權利 2013。保留一切權利。
威爾斯政府。執照號碼 100021874。

Llywodraeth Cymru
Welsh Government

說威爾斯語者比例變化情形，依 LSOA 劃分，2001 年至 2011 年 (a)

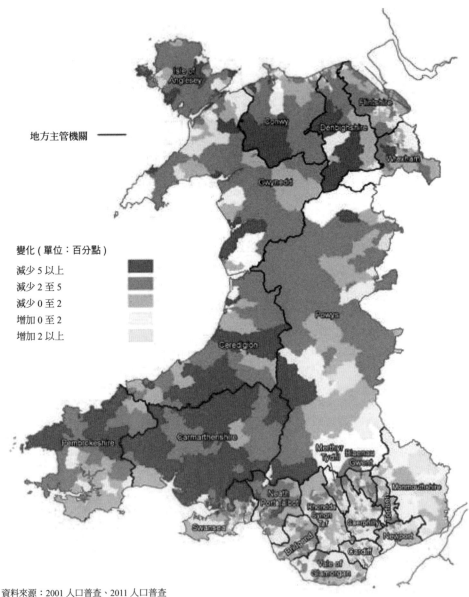

地方主管機關 ────

變化（單位：百分點）

減少 5 以上
減少 2 至 5
減少 0 至 2
增加 0 至 2
增加 2 以上

資料來源：2001 人口普查、2011 人口普查

(a) 僅呈現 2001 年至 2011 年間未改變之 LSOA

193.12-13
地理與科技
© 皇家版權與資料庫權利 2013。保留一切權利。
威爾斯政府。執照號碼 100021874。

Llywodraeth Cymru
Welsh Government

威爾斯語社群數量，2011 年

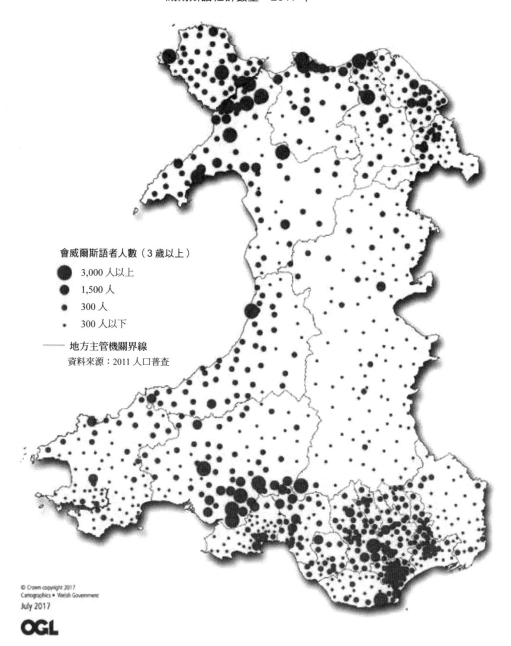

會威爾斯語者人數（3 歲以上）

- 3,000 人以上
- 1,500 人
- 300 人
- 300 人以下

—— 地方主管機關界線
資料來源：2011 人口普查

© Crown copyright 2017
Cartographics • Welsh Government
July 2017

OGL

長期策略

設定長期目標，代表著要達到增加說威爾斯語者人數的理想，所需採取的行動並非一夕可成：語言規劃是件漫長艱辛的工作。長期的規劃讓我們得以思考更遠大的布局，並著重於最能影響未來三十年語言走向的策略變革。

然而，增加說威爾斯語者人數固然是一項長期願景，而且每十年才會有意義地進行來測量此種人數，但我們現在仍需奮起行動，奠定基礎。這些行動必須能夠呈現出企圖心的規模。

本策略最初數年將聚焦於奠定基礎，以利長期而言增加說威爾斯語者的人數。

策略目標

除了達成 2050 年百萬人說威爾斯語的目標，我們也清楚還需以威爾斯語的使用來衡量本策略的成功與否。本策略首要目標如下：

- 2050 年，說威爾斯語者人數達到一百萬。
- 2050 年，每日說威爾斯語且會說不只少數字詞的說威爾斯語者，人口比例從 10%（2013-15 年）增加至 20%。

2050 年百萬人說威爾斯語的目標，必然會帶出一個問題：「說者」的定義是什麼；亦即，一個人必須精通威爾斯語到何種程度，才能將其視為「說威爾斯語者」。我們首先會看人口普查數據，人口普查會請受訪者自評威爾斯語技能。根據最近期的 2011 年人口普查，威爾斯有 562,000 名說威爾斯語者。[1]

諸多因素可能足以影響個體如何評估自身和其他家庭成員的語言技能（例如，他們的語言參考點，或他們如何根據所認識他人的語言技能來衡量自身能力，或他們的動機或渴望在多大程度上激發其重視自身的威爾斯語技能）。透過本策略，我們期望打造有利條件，讓威爾斯全體國民皆能接觸運用威爾斯語，以及讓每位說威爾斯語者（無論能力等級為何）都能夠選擇使用自身的威爾斯語技能，並得到鼓勵和支援，在包容、正向的環境裡，依照個人意願來進一步精進語言技能。

達成目標

為達成目標，我們將推動下列重大變革。實施的成功，必須仰賴諸多組織協力合作。

- 加快腳步擴展全威爾斯語幼教服務，目標未來十年內增開 150 所托兒所，幫助順利銜接至全威爾斯語教育。
- 提高各年級接受全威爾斯語教育者的比例，目標 2031 年從 22%（根據 2015/16 年威爾斯語七歲學生 7,700 人）增加至 30%（約為各年級 10,500 人），2050 年增加至 40%（約為各年級 14,000 人）。
- 改革對所有學生教導威爾斯語的作法，目標 2050 年至少有 70% 學生在離校時自稱會說威爾斯語。
- 增加能教導威爾斯語的小學教師數量，目標 2031 年從 2,900 人增加至 3,900 人，2050 年增加至 5,200 人；增加能教導威爾斯語的中學教師數量，目標 2031 年從 500 人增加至 900 人，2050 年增加至 1,200 人；增加能全威爾斯語教學的中學教師數量，目標 2031 年從 1,800 人增加至 3,200 人，2050 年增加至 4,200 人。
- 改革十六歲後學生的全威爾斯語與雙語教育和技能，確保青年有機會繼續深造雙語技能，以促進經濟繁榮。
- 檢討鞏固威爾斯語地位的立法，確保相關法律有建立堅實基礎來提倡和促進使用威爾斯語。

---

1 人口普查詢問威爾斯受訪者是否聽懂威爾斯語、是否會說威爾斯語、是否會讀威爾斯語或、是否會寫威爾斯語（或是否不具備威爾斯語能力）。

- 確保威爾斯政府以身作則，政府職員身體力行提倡和促進多加使用威爾斯語。
- 制定經濟發展方面的區域新重點，讓威爾斯各區皆能享有經濟繁榮之福，並支援各區建立自身特有的身分認同。
- 特別著力於語言科技，令威爾斯語數位版圖煥然一新。
- 制定增進理解雙語化的國家計畫。

落實策略

為實現願景，我們將：
- 發揮強大領導力並善用自身影響力，幫助威爾斯語發展；
- 提供財務支援，提倡與促進使用威爾斯語；
- 立法為威爾斯語建立堅強的基礎設施；
- 政府以身作則使用與接觸威爾斯語。

策略的成功實施，需在下列各方面達到適當平衡：以正向、包容的方式提倡與促進使用威爾斯語；推動改善威爾斯語服務的系統性規劃；健全的監管架構。

我們將定期發布工作計畫，詳述應採取何種行動以達成目標。第一期 2017–21 年的工作計畫將隨本策略一併發布。

我們將持續監督評量本策略的實施情形，以確保落實執行所需的重大變革。我們將利用「威爾斯國家指標」的指標 36 和 37，來追蹤國家福祉目標和本策略二大整體目標的進度。此兩項指標為：
- 福祉指標 36：每日說威爾斯語且會說不只少數字詞的說威爾斯語者比例。
- 福祉指標 37：會說威爾斯語者比例。

本策略實施時將遵守若干基本原則。後續數頁將概述該原則。

概念基礎與原則

為實現 2050 年百萬人說威爾斯語和增加使用威爾斯語技能的願景，現在和未來需採取一致行動，以達成下列目標：
- 增加說威爾斯語者人數
- 增加並擴大說威爾斯語者使用語言技能的機會
- 打造人人有意願使用威爾斯語的環境。

語言使用和語言行為，有著各式各樣互依的因素為條件。語言學家 Joshua Fishman 提出的語言復興理論模型，以及此後用來證明語言行為多面向本質的研究行動，提供基礎幫助我們理解語言使用動力學（Grin 與 Moring 2002；Darquennes 2007）[2]。Miquel Strubell（Strubell 2011）提出凱瑟琳輪模型來展示下列因素間的相互關係：
- 語言學習
- 語言中的貨品與勞務供給與需求
- 語言中的貨品與勞務消費
- 語言效用的觀感
- 學習與使用語言的動機

Strubell 提出的根本原則為，語言活力取決於帶動語言成長的諸多互依因素間的互動情形。凱瑟

---

2 見〈威爾斯語言策略評估架構〉（http://gov.wales/statistics-and-research/welsh-language-strategy-evaluation/?skip=1&lang=en）

琳輪用來呈現這些因素之間的相互依賴關係。雖然此類圖示型態的模型有其限制，但 Strubell 的凱瑟琳輪仍可當作有助益的起點，讓我們由此為威爾斯語建立永續長久的基礎設施。

　　另一方面，要制定並實施 2050 年威爾斯語願景的策略，必須了解當今的說威爾斯語者如何使用威爾斯語，也必須考量其未來可能會如何使用威爾斯語。我們必須準備好適度調整語言規劃政策的作法，以反映出社會、經濟和政治上的變化，這些變化目前塑造、也會在未來繼續塑造當代威爾斯的樣貌。我們無法詳細掌握人民在 2050 年確切的生活型態，但近幾十年觀察的發展很可能繼續扭轉我們的日常生活。我們目睹了全球化、運輸、以及更多樣化的概念詮釋如家庭單位和「社群」，是如何帶動深遠的變化。我們也目睹了科技進展如何造就辦公與人際溝通的全新方式。同時，這些變化並未取代地理界定的社群、基於親自溝通而成立的社會網絡的重要性，也未取代家人身為家庭生活重心的關鍵角色。

　　因此我們在制定威爾斯語長期計畫時，主旨是確保語言規劃的目的和作法，能夠呈現出我們理解說威爾斯語者在彼此互動連通的廣大脈絡裡如何使用語言。

　　近二十年來，社會語言學研究逐漸聚焦於說某語言者在界線往往不固定的各種網絡和環境裡，如何使用自身的語言資源，和如何定義自身的語言認同（Heller 2011、Pennycook 2010；Pietikäinen 2013；Martin-Jones 與 Martin 2017）。此種詮釋將說者視為多種不同語言資源的使用者，以及將說者視為在各種說者網絡與社群裡的參與者，使得我們所期望威爾斯語成為活躍語言的願景方面浮現許多問題；所謂的活躍語言，是能夠同等通行於關係緊密的鄉村社群、都市環境裡的分散社會網絡、和跨越地理空間的虛擬社群。

　　將說者視為在各種網絡裡的參與者，也會使得我們對於諸如「社群」和「鄰里」等概念的理解產生問題。我們的說威爾斯語者人數持續成長的願景，認可由地區和親自互動所界定的社群與社會網絡能帶來的重要貢獻。我們認可並重視這些社群在提供使用威爾斯語的社會環境方面發揮的作用。然而，協助維持說威爾斯語者人口密度高的地理社群的活力，是複雜局面裡的一項重要因子。民眾依憑多種不同的社會因素過各自生活，而目前趨勢也會將民眾推往多種方向。

　　由於每日互動的界定型態不斷改變，而且策略實施期間這些型態很可能還會繼續變化，因此必須確保我們也會繼續拓展對於「社群」、實踐社群和說者網絡的組成所應有的理解。我們預期，民眾花大量時間待的地方，包括職場、社團、新社交場合和各種線上網絡，重要性將日益增加。我們的語言規劃必須足夠穩健靈活，才能因應上述趨勢。

　　說威爾斯語者人口密度高的地區，依然是願景裡的重點。威爾斯有些地區具備有助增加說威爾斯

語者的最有利情勢：住在一處地理區域裡的說某語言者人數愈多，他們每日溝通時使用該語言的機率也會愈高。威爾斯還有一些地區擁有最多的流利說威爾斯語者。

上述地區的特點是本質上屬於鄉村，經濟目前主要仰賴公部門、農業和觀光，城鎮是提供各種服務和就業領域的中心。

這些社群面臨的挑戰無法輕易解決。不過我們明白，語言規劃和經濟發展必須雙管齊下，才能打造在經濟和語言上皆確實可行的說威爾斯語社群。

說威爾斯語者比例較低的幾處地區，近年來隨著全威爾斯語教育的成長，以及民眾從鄉村移動至城市、從北部和西部移動至東南部的趨勢，可以觀察出說威爾斯語者的人數上升。此現象促成威爾斯語在部分地區的強化，將威爾斯語能力引進職場和南部經濟，而威爾斯南部本身正逐漸提高威爾斯語的地位。

比起說威爾斯語者比例較高的地區，上述地區較不常聽見威爾斯語，因此這些地區的挑戰便是增加民眾在日常生活使用威爾斯語的機會。

生命歷程方法

本策略認可家庭語言傳播對威爾斯語未來活力帶來的重要貢獻。然而，我們也承認單靠提高家庭語言傳播率，仍無法確保能讓說威爾斯語者人數增加至指定規模。在家庭以外場域習得說威爾斯語能力者，對本策略的成功亦能產生卓著貢獻。本策略一項關鍵目標，是為各年齡的新學生打造適合條件來發展和使用語言技能，從幼兒經各階段義務教育和十六歲後教育，直到成人，皆有機會學習威爾斯語。

近期以新進說某語言者為主題的研究，提供了寶貴的見解，讓我們更加了解透過教育或某種學習形式、而非透過在家庭或社群接觸來習得語言者的經歷和軌跡（O'Rourke、Pujolar 等人 2015）。具體而言，「mudes」的概念，亦即「對語言行為的適應」，是很有用的基礎，可助理解人們如何在一生中發展自身的語言技能和實務（Pujolar and Puigdevall 2015）。本策略的重點，在於個體習得或學習威爾斯語的機會，以及使用威爾斯語的機會，是如何逐漸建構出一種敘事。我們亦應謹記，個體的語言歷程未必遵循系統性的線性模式，而且這些歷程會和各種社會因素交織互聯。

本策略聚焦於隨時間的經驗累積，以及聚焦於個體軌跡與形塑這些軌跡的社會脈絡之間的關聯，此種取向運用了以生命歷程方法為主的原則。儘管生命歷程模型多應用於公衛、老化和社經結果等領域（Billari 2001；Ben-Shlomo 與 Kuh 2002；Mayer 2009），但其基本概念在許多方面仍與語言規劃政策相應。下列生命歷程方法的元素尤其相關：

- 歷史與地理背景環境對民眾經驗與機會的影響
- 找出關鍵「過渡期」
- 知悉不同個體有各種不同回應情勢的作法
- 個體和其家庭間、以及個體和其關係網絡間的相互關聯
- 過去如何形塑未來（即長期觀點）以及經驗的累積效應
- 個體作為積極參與者，能夠做出決定和選擇，並能為自身行動設定目標。

生命歷程方法另一值得關注的特點，是和風險元素有關之處——可能是「臨界點」，特定風險過了臨界點恐接著導致負面變化降臨；抑或是個體長久以來遭遇風險的經歷，這些結果的累積效應恐導致負面狀況或後果。

在習得、使用和與他人分享威爾斯語的脈絡中，必須精心加以規劃，才能確保具備盡可能最理想的條件，以實現下列成果：

● 支援初始發展自身威爾斯語技能的說者——在家、透過教育體系或生涯稍後的學習
● 協助說者能夠並願意持續使用威爾斯語——與家人、在社群和社會網絡、與同事、以及在獲取服務時使用
● 找出哪些情勢和因素最有可能減弱說者與威爾斯語的接觸，或讓說者不那麼願意使用威爾斯語
● 令說者有能力做出有助其在未來使用威爾斯語的決定。

身為政府，我們的挑戰在於必須深入理解民眾使用威爾斯語的方式，要能影響民眾在人生關鍵時刻（例如離開教育體系進入職場，或初為人父人母）所做的決定，以及加速促成有利民眾更容易使用威爾斯語的情況和空間。

達百萬人

一旦達成 2050 年百萬人說威爾斯語的目標，將可翻轉 20 世紀說威爾斯語者人數下滑的趨勢：1911 年，威爾斯三歲以上說威爾斯語者近一百萬人（977,000 人）。

下方圖表為上世紀威爾斯語的演進情形。根據 2011 年人口普查數據，如欲達成百萬人說威爾斯語，則新進說威爾斯語者尚需約 438,000 人。這不僅代表必須採取行動以增加說威爾斯語者人數，還必須維持現有人數，畢竟死亡和移出將會影響說威爾斯語者人數。

圖表 1：三歲以上會說威爾斯語者人數，1911–2011 人口普查，附 2050 年期望目標[3]

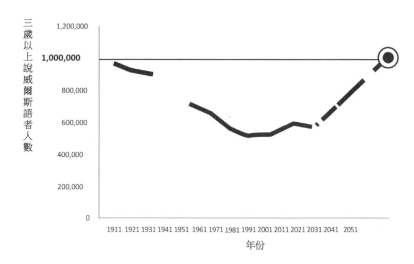

語言技能習得

　　欲達成 2050 年百萬人說威爾斯語的目標，代表必須進一步制定最有機會增加所需人數的方法。此種方法主要有二，一為將威爾斯語從某一代傳播至下一代，二為透過教育與訓練來發展並維持語言技能。

家庭中的語言傳播

　　2011 年人口普查顯示，在二名成人皆會說威爾斯語的伴侶家庭中，82% 的三至四歲兒童亦會說威爾斯語；在一名成人會說威爾斯語的伴侶家庭中，45% 的三至四歲兒童會說威爾斯語。鼓勵更多家長／照顧者將語言傳播給兒童，是本策略的重點優先任務。然而，藉由將威爾斯語從某一代傳播至下一代所能增加的說威爾斯語者人數，依然有限，因此教育便成為本策略的重要事項。

教育

　　為確保兒童能夠發展自身威爾斯語技能，並培育新的說威爾斯語者，全威爾斯語沉浸式教育是本策略的首要辦法。學校資料呈現就讀全威爾斯語學校的兒童人數。2015/16 年，在 35,000 名二年級學生當中，估計約 22%（7,700 人）會說威爾斯語（第一語言）。若此比例於 2050 年可提升至 40%，則將有約 14,000 名學生（根據 2015 年二年級學生世代之人數），多出約 6,300 人。由此可知，對於達成百萬人說威爾斯語的目標而言，維護教育體系的教學任務十分重要。另外亦可由此得知幼兒教育的重要性，幼教可作為及早接受沉浸式教育的據點，並藉由幼教來加強全威爾斯語教育的需求。Mudiad Meithrin 最新的學務資料（2015/16 年）顯示，就讀 Mudiad Meithrin 團體的兒童中，有 86% 升上全威爾斯語小學就讀。

　　我們希望所有學生皆有機會接受雙語教育。為達成百萬人說威爾斯語的目標，必須增加成功習得威爾斯語的全英語教育學生人數。

　　威爾斯語成人進修教育的重要性同樣不容忽視。根據 2015/16 學年資料，有 16,375 名成人正透

---

3 註：1941 年未舉辦人口普查。

過正規的成人威爾斯語教育管道來學習威爾斯語。我們需加倍努力以明確得知正在學習威爾斯語者、以及有自信使用威爾斯語者的人數，此方面將由國家威爾斯語學習中心負責處理。

推估與達百萬人軌跡

下方圖表 2 為 2017 年至 2050 年間威爾斯三歲以上說威爾斯語者人數的二種可能路徑。

● **推估**：根據延續 2011 年人口普查所見威爾斯語者趨勢和人口趨勢，政策未變動。
● **達百萬人軌跡**：根據為實現本策略願景所需採取的政策變動。

圖表 2：三歲以上說威爾斯語者人數之推估與軌跡，2011–2050

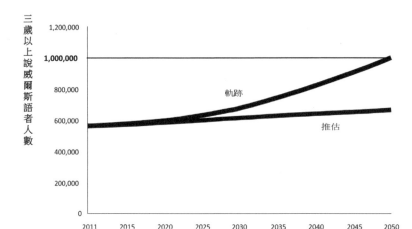

推估

較低線條是說威爾斯語者人數的推估，係根據人口推估和 2011 年人口普查資料。我們將人口普查視為威爾斯說威爾斯語者人數的可靠資料來源，並據此立下百萬人說威爾斯語的目標。然而國家統計局曾發起「人口普查轉型計畫」以補強 2021 年人口普查。威爾斯政府將持續藉助與國家統計局的密切關係來參與該計畫，讓本策略優先任務的其中之一能繼續作為威爾斯語方面穩健扎實的統計基礎。

推估所根據的情境，是威爾斯語政策版圖和威爾斯語教育將維持和現況一致。

推估是用來估計 2050 年說威爾斯語者的人數，以利大致理解如欲達成百萬人說威爾斯語目標，尚需增加多少名說威爾斯語者。一如任何推估，本推估應謹慎看待之，因為本推估是以一系列假設為根據，這些假設本身則是根據先前模式，而先前模式可能會隨時間變化。

達百萬人軌跡

較高線條是達百萬人的可能歷程，係根據本策略的政策意圖。

諸多因素會影響達百萬人的精準歷程，因此我們將不斷檢視進度，以便監督已取得的成果，必要時重新檢討軌跡。

第一個四年的成果極微。我們預期第一個十年結束時成果才會較可觀，此時已實現重大變革里程

碑的其中二項：擴展全威爾斯語幼教服務，增開 150 所托兒所；2031 年各年級接受全威爾斯語教育者的比例增加至 30%。

　　此軌跡運用了人口模型，並輸入有關教育成果、家庭中語言傳播、以及成人威爾斯語教育的不同假設，以得出達百萬人目標的一種可能軌跡。

　　建立未來人口變遷的模型相當複雜；建立政策變動對人口具體特性影響的模型，難度更高。是故，應據此考量得出為達百萬人目標所需遵循的大致軌跡。在此前提下，頁 395-396 表格列出 2017 年至 2050 年間定期期間距上的軌跡數據。

達百萬人歷程

整體目標：2050 年百萬人說威爾斯語

	2011	2017	2021
軌跡： 說威爾斯語者人數	562,000 人	570,000 人 * * 推估	600,000 人

如何實現

	2017	2021
提高語言傳播率		延續 2001 年至 2011 年人口普查所見之微幅增加趨勢
增加離校時會說威爾斯語之學生比例		引進新課程
增加全威爾斯語教育學生比例 目前比例係根據估計以威爾斯語為第一語言之七歲學生人數。 目標比例係根據假設此期間各年級學童人數將大致固定維持約 35,000 人	7,700 人 * （22%） * 2015/16 資料	8,400 人 （24%）
增加能教導威爾斯語或能全威爾斯語教學之教師人數	小學 * 2,900 人 中學 * 500 人能教導威爾斯語 1,800 人能全威爾斯語教學 * 2015/16 資料	小學 3,100 人 中學 600 人能教導威爾斯語 2,200 人能全威爾斯語教學
增加成為說威爾斯語者之成人人數		假設 2011 年後每年新增 1,000 人

增加使用威爾斯語之目標

					2017 〉	2021 〉
每日說威爾斯語且會說不只少數字詞之說威爾斯語者比例					10%* *2013–15 資料	11%

2026	2031	2036	2041	2046	2050
630,000	680,000	750,000	830,000	920,000	1,000,000

2026 〉	2031 〉	2036 〉	2041 〉	2046 〉	2050
傳播率漸增，2031–50 期間增幅加速					
	第一代學生修畢新課程，義務教育結束時，全部學生中有 55% 會說威爾斯語（約每年 19,000 名學生） 此後漸增至 2050 年比例達 70%				義務教育結束時，全部學生中有 70% 會說威爾斯語（約每年 25,000 名學生）
	各年級約 10,500 人（30%） 漸增至 2050 年比例達 40%				各年級約 14,000 人（40%）
	小學 3,900 人 中學 900 人能教導威爾斯語 3,200 人能全威爾斯語教學				小學 5,200 人 中學 1,200 人能教導威爾斯語 4,200 人能全威爾斯語教學
假設 2021 年起每年新增 2,000 人					

2026	2031	2036	2041	2046	2050
11%	12%	14%	16%	18%	20%

作為軌跡基礎之假設

2017–21

家庭中語言傳播：預期 2001 年至 2011 年傳播率微幅增加，且至 2021 年將持續增加。
教育：預期全威爾斯語教育學生比例、以及全英語教育學生語言成果方面的目前型態將相當保持固定不變。

2021–31

家庭中語言傳播：預期傳播率漸增，但幅度不大。
教育：預期全威爾斯語教育學生比例漸增，2031 年達 30%。此外，由於引進全威爾斯語新課程，已於教育體系中的學生擁有的威爾斯語技能，預期可在此期間內逐漸進步。
2021–31 年，首度有機會納入成人習得威爾斯語者的人數——此處之根據是假設 2021 年起報名初學者課程的任何人士皆是新增的說威爾斯語者，這些人並未在 2021 年人口普查時自稱具備威爾斯語能力。依照 2021 年人口普查，假設每年將新增 2,000 名透過成人威爾斯語教育而學會說威爾斯語者。

2031–50

家庭中語言傳播：由於更多人將因已引進的教育體系而會說威爾斯語，且更多人將因本策略所述的變革而使用威爾斯語，因此可假設傳播率會比上一個十年增加更快。
教育：此期間之初，修畢威爾斯語新課程的第一世代將滿 16 歲。預期全威爾斯語教育學生比例漸增，2050 年達 40%。

語言使用

　　軌跡呈現出達成 2050 年百萬人說威爾斯語目標的可能途徑。然而此類模型呈現不出未來語言使用方面的情境。威爾斯語言能力的相關資料固然重要，但我們還需確保在實施策略時亦有確實蒐集和監測語言使用的相關證據。如前所述，本策略的目標，是增加每日說威爾斯語且會說不只少數字詞的人口比例，2050 年從 10%（2013–15 年）提升至 20%。

　　本策略首先將運用〈2013–15 威爾斯語使用調查〉（威爾斯政府與威爾斯語長官 2015），此報告詳列會說威爾斯語之成人與青年的語言使用模式——說威爾斯語的通順程度、頻率、地點、時間及對象。

三大策略主題

本節簡述作為實現願景計畫之基礎的三大策略主題,以及各主題的目的。

如前所述,語言習得不僅和為了增加威爾斯語者人數而採取的行動息息相關,也與為了扎根語言實務和增加威爾斯語使用而採取的行動有密切關聯。為令背景環境促進實現上述目標,我們必須在基礎設施和背景環境方面打造有利條件。

三大主題相輔相成,各主題底下的諸多目的亦互為表裡。舉例而言,若只是增加接受全威爾斯語教育的學童人數,卻未為其提供機會和背景環境來運用習得的語言技能,將不足以達成目標。

因此我們在實施策略時所採取的多項介入措施,將有助實現一個以上的目標,且範圍涵蓋一個以上的主題。

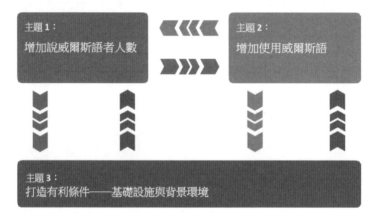

主題1:
增加說威爾斯語者人數

主題2:
增加使用威爾斯語

主題3:
打造有利條件——基礎設施與背景環境

2016 年針對策略草案所辦理的諮詢,有助我們擬定各主題底下的目的。接下來實施策略時,必須了解我們是從一個已有優勢的地位開始做起。本策略奠基於數十年來威爾斯的語言規劃行動。

本文後續篇幅,將詳盡介紹各主題及其目的,以及為實現各主題和目的所需推動的階段性變革。將於 2017–21 期間展開的分項工作計畫,則詳述目的實施方面的短期優先事項。

主題 1：
增加說威爾斯語者人數

> 目標：2050 年說威爾斯語者達百萬人

達成百萬人說威爾斯語目標的二項主要作法：

● 在家庭中將威爾斯語從一代傳播至下一代
● 透過從幼兒至成人的教育和訓練，發展並維持威爾斯語技能

　　本策略認同家庭中語言傳播對威爾斯語的未來活力貢獻極大。然因透過代間語言傳播所能增加的說威爾斯語者人數有限，故仍以教育和訓練體系作為新增說威爾斯語者人數的首要管道。

　　我們必須確保所有年齡層民眾皆有機會發展自身的威爾斯語技能，並在日常生活有自信地使用威爾斯語。

　　人口普查資料顯示，說威爾斯語者人數隨年齡遞增，直到 15 歲為止。16 歲至 25 歲間的說威爾斯語者人數漸減。因此本策略的主要目標之一，即是確保不會有太多青年在從義務教育升上擴充教育 / 高等教育時失去自身威爾斯語技能，並確保有更多青年在進入二十幾歲時能夠精通威爾斯語。

　　為加強透過教育體系增加說威爾斯語者人數的相關行動，多加培養能教導威爾斯語和能全威爾斯教學的人力實為一大重點。

> 目的：
> 1. 家庭中語言傳播：擴大支援家庭中的語言傳播，令兒童擁有學習威爾斯語的最佳起跑點。
> 2. 幼兒教育：擴展全威爾斯語幼教服務，以此作為進入全威爾斯語教育的銜接點。
> 3. 義務教育：辦理有助增加有自信說威爾斯語者人數的義務教育。
> 4. 後義務教育：辦理有助提升晉級率的後義務教育，且無論精通程度如何，人人皆可獲得支援以發展使用於社會和職場上的威爾斯語技能。
> 5. 教育人力、資源與資格：妥善規劃以大幅增加和改善下列項目：
>   – 能教導威爾斯語和能全威爾斯教學的教育訓練人力
>   – 支援增辦教育方面所需的資源和資格

　　為達成百萬人說威爾斯語目標，我們將推動下列重大變革。實施的成功，必須仰賴諸多組織協力合作。

● 加快腳步擴展全威爾斯語幼教服務，目標未來十年內增開 150 所托兒所，幫助順利銜接至全威爾斯語教育。
● 提高各年級接受全威爾斯語教育者的比例，目標 2031 年從 22%（根據 2015/16 年威爾斯語七歲學生 7,700 人）增加至 30%（約為各年級 10,500 人），2050 年增加至 40%（約為各年級 14,000 人）。
● 改革對所有學生教導威爾斯語的作法，目標 2050 年至少有 70% 學生在離校時自稱會說威爾斯語。
● 增加能教導威爾斯語的小學教師數量，目標 2031 年從 2,900 人增加至 3,900 人，2050 年增加至 5,200 人；增加能教導威爾斯語的中學教師數量，目標 2031 年從 500 人增加至 900 人，2050 年增加至 1,200 人；增加能全威爾斯語教學的中學教師數量，目標 2031 年從 1,800 人增加至 3,200 人，2050 年增加至 4,200 人。
● 改革十六歲後學生的全威爾斯語與雙語教育和技能，確保青年有機會繼續深造雙語技能，以促進經濟繁榮。

1. 家庭中的語言傳播

　　家長／照顧者在家庭中將威爾斯語傳播給兒童，能夠為兒童的語言發展奠定有益的基礎。

　　針對足以影響家庭中威爾斯語傳播和使用之因素的研究，其探討的面向諸如家長的威爾斯語能力、對威爾斯語和英語的態度所起的作用、以及在家中精通一或多種語言的實務要點。Gathercole 等人（2007）的研究發現，似乎最能顯著影響兒童所說語言和家長對兒童說的語言的因素，包括家長的語言背景和家長的威爾斯語能力（此項能力與許多因素高度相關，包括與朋友及親密的社交網絡使用威爾斯語）。這方面和本策略的主題 2 有明顯關聯，主題 2 討論的是在社會上打造機會讓成人和家庭能使用威爾斯語。近期發布的研究（威爾斯政府 2017b）指出，語言使用和語言傳播是個人的、複雜的議題，並指出說威爾斯語者對於使用威爾斯語所抱持的態度方針會如何逐漸改變。

　　〈2013–15 威爾斯語使用調查〉（威爾斯政府與威爾斯語官員 2015）的結果顯示，比起在學校學習說威爾斯語者，自幼在家學習威爾斯語者較有可能流利說威爾斯語。該調查亦顯示，流利說威爾斯語者比非流利者較常使用威爾斯語。該調查披露的另一項事實為，年輕的說威爾斯語者較有可能在學校而非在任何其他地方學習威爾斯語，而年長的說威爾斯語者較有可能自幼在家而非在任何其他地方學習威爾斯語。

　　目前不同家庭環境的傳播率各異，二名成人皆會說威爾斯語的伴侶家庭，傳播率 82%；一名成人會說威爾斯語的伴侶家庭，傳播率 45%；一名成人會說威爾斯語的單親家庭，傳播率 53%。我們將因應以上不同情形而調整介入措施。

　　任何政府都無法控制民眾在自家的行為，也無法強迫家長／照護者必須與兒童說威爾斯語。因此我們務必要鼓勵和支援家庭來與兒童說威爾斯語，向家長和準家長推廣威爾斯語機會的優勢，並確保家庭有機會學習威爾斯語。

　　上述訊息必須納入會與家長和準家長接觸的許多專業人士的工作當中，包括接生員、基層醫護以及向家庭提供資訊的服務，以便在育兒時期的關鍵時刻清晰、一致地描摹威爾斯語和雙語的願景。我們的目的，是讓支援新家長和準家長的專業人士深入體會家庭中語言傳播的重要性，期能將正面的語言實務深植於兒童與青年的內心，他們是未來世代的家長。

　　語言傳播的重要性始終是本策略的關鍵層面，且隨著我們發現透過教育體系習得威爾斯語的人數增加，於是在學校而非在家習得威爾斯語的比例變高，因此語言傳播方面的挑戰也會逐漸改變。我們必須據此調整政策。

我們的目的：**擴大支援家庭中的語言傳播，令兒童擁有學習威爾斯語的最佳起跑點。**

2. 幼兒教育

幼兒教育的長期目的，是達到五歲以下兒童有充分接觸威爾斯語的程度，讓兒童能夠展開旅程邁向流利使用威爾斯語。

過去四十年來，志願部門在 Mudiad Meithrin 的贊助下，持續提供威爾斯語托兒服務，令全威爾斯的兒童皆有機會接受全威爾斯語的幼兒保育和服務。

藉由幼兒保育和服務的正規化，以及威爾斯語的主流化，未來便有機會維持和強化全威爾斯語教育的角色，同時確保各個幼兒階段的兒童皆能進一步發展自身的威爾斯語技能，讓未來時代擁有更多契機。

除了發展各幼兒階段的威爾斯語使用，以及大幅提升全威爾斯語幼教的能力，我們還需確保家長／照護者和準家長清楚現有可得的幼教範圍，以便在知情狀況下為兒童的未來做出選擇。有關全威爾斯語托兒服務可得性的證據顯示，威爾斯部分地區未提供此種服務；證據亦顯示，用於評量全威爾斯語幼教需求的方法各有差異（拯救兒童 2015；威爾斯政府 2016a ；威爾斯政府 2016b ；威爾斯政府 2017a）。

若能令民眾熟知擴大全威爾斯語幼教的目標，以及確保民眾已深入理解針對弱勢兒童、家庭和社群的計畫範圍，將能相當有助於處理貧窮問題，並確保全威爾斯的兒童無論何種背景出身和居住於何處，皆有機會成為有自信的說威爾斯語者。

我們期望能夠加快腳步擴展全威爾斯語幼教服務，目標未來十年內增開 150 所托兒所，幫助順利銜接至全威爾斯語教育。

我們的目的：擴展全威爾斯語幼教服務，以此作為進入全威爾斯語教育的銜接點。

3. 義務教育

我們必須大幅增加義務教育中發展威爾斯語技能的學生人數，並確保每位學生發展的威爾斯語技能可達到有利其在日常生活中使用威爾斯語的標準。我們將在評量全威爾斯語教育的需求後，以系統性的方式積極主動增辦全威爾斯語教育。為達成說威爾斯語者人數大幅增加的目標，未來三十年內，尤其是接下來五至十年內，需採取一致行動來鞏固基礎。

　　威爾斯各地區之間、以及小學和中學之間的全威爾斯語和雙語教育模式，互有差異。其中許多差異反映大群體裡的語言使用模式，其他差異則反映政策實施作法之別。雖然教育體系需有充分彈性來因應威爾斯各地區的語言特性，但我們也務必要確保已基於清楚理解學生的語言成果來規劃和辦理教育。

　　為增加提供威爾斯小學與中學的威爾斯語教育，以培養有自信的說威爾斯語者，我們必須採行數項措施。由於預期人口未來不會大幅增加，因此並不需大量增設新校。故而地方主管機關面臨的挑戰，在於重新安排教育的提供，以創造更多全威爾斯語的場所，並逐漸確保將有更多所雙語學校提高威爾斯語課程的比例，為學生打下扎實的語言基礎。一旦地方主管機關有機會因地方發展計畫或大規模經濟發展而開設新校，我們會預期地方主管機關能夠推出強大的方案，清楚展現其提案如何符合我們增加說威爾斯語者人數的目的。

　　各個地方主管機關亦有機會透過提供特別教育給稍晚接觸全威爾斯語教育者，以建立全威爾斯語教育的銜接點，無論在小學或中學。多種模型已實施於威爾斯各地。我們必須加強了解何種模型最能有效提供教育，並採取行動以逐漸增加此種教育。

　　全英語教育界對於實現培養說威爾斯語者的目標功不可沒。為達成百萬人說威爾斯語的目標，我們必須在所有其他學校改革威爾斯語教學方式，期望 2050 年至少半數學生在離校時自稱會說威爾斯語。我們有意針對教導威爾斯語作為一種語言來制定單獨一貫課程，著重於主要將威爾斯語當作溝通工具來學習威爾斯語，尤其是口語溝通。

　　威爾斯所有學校將需逐漸為全體學生引進威爾斯語一貫課程，並在課程中安排習得威爾斯語技能。透過此作法，我們希望確保 2050 年至少 70% 的全體學生在離校時已發展自身的威爾斯語技能，而且在生活所有層面皆能有自信地使用威爾斯語。課程引進需要時間。成功與否取決於教育人力的技能培養，以及學生有無機會在課堂以外的大環境使用威爾斯語。

　　地方主管機關、校董和校長需發揮企圖心、支援和強大的領導力，以提高各年級接受全威爾斯語教育者的比例，目標 2050 年從 22%（根據 2015/16 年威爾斯語七歲學生 7,700 人）增加至 40%。我們將預期地方主管機關能夠擴大辦理現有的全威爾斯語教育，以及提升不同教育階段的晉級率。我們將同意地方主管機關的地方目標，助其達成各自目標。

　　我們亦需確保家長／照護者與學生能夠理解各種教育模型的語言成果，使其在知情狀況下，根據威爾斯語對日常生活及對職場的相關性來選擇教育途徑。

我們的目的：辦理有助增加能說威爾斯語者人數的義務教育。

---

4. 後義務教育

若要在義務教育階段當中對個體投資時間和金錢，則務必要確保青年會在教育歷程中持續發展自身語言技能，才能在有自信使用威爾斯語的情形下進入職場。

隨著更多組織承擔《威爾斯語標準》方面的義務，職場將需要更多雙語人力來讓這些組織能夠符合語言要求。因此具備雙語技能的青年預期將有更多職場機會。

過半數學生在 16 歲完成義務教育離校，絕大部分若非接受擴充教育或工作導向學習，即是直接進入職場。因此後義務教育與訓練提供者的角色十分重要，有助維持學生的威爾斯語技能，以滿足漸增的雙語人力需求。

在威爾斯政府支援下，擴充教育學院近年已採取行動，增加提供 16 歲以上的全威爾斯語或雙語教育與訓練。由於社群對語言的需求，部分學院比其他學院更積極規劃提供相關教育。但仍有機會大幅增加可供學生選擇的選項，此方面需要各所學院的策略規劃和協同合作。

工作導向學習界發現，近年來在自身學習計畫中安排雙語學習或使用些許威爾斯語的學生，人數持續但緩慢增加。

高等教育界正實施具體介入措施，清楚聚焦於發展全威爾斯語教育的需求。近年來透過全威爾斯語教育修習學分的學生數有所增加，但仍有機會繼續提升人數。

後義務教育界必須在擴充教育、高等教育和工作導向學習領域中改弦易轍，擴大提供全威爾斯語教育和雙語教育。此方面將需招募更多學生繼續以全威爾斯語教育來修習部分或全部課程，需確保教育人力具備全威爾斯語教學或雙語教學的必要技能，需確保更多職場能夠提供威爾斯語就業機會，並需確保組織擁有強大領導力來實現必要改革。

為鞏固上述行動，青年將需了解繼續發展自身威爾斯語技能對於準備進入職場可帶來的好處，以及了解經常使用威爾斯語以維持流利度和自信的重要性。

成人威爾斯語教育

成人威爾斯語教育界對於實現百萬人說威爾斯語的目標貢獻極大。成人威爾斯語教育讓各年齡層和各種能力等級的成人能夠增進自身的威爾斯語技能，能夠恢復學習或新開始學習威爾斯語，使其有自信地在職場、社會或家庭使用威爾斯語。

近年來成人威爾斯語教育界出現結構上的變化。目前有機會提供國家層級的成人威爾斯語教育，支援職場、家庭方面的課程，並有機會更有效使用可輔助學習的科技。

我們希望透過提供各種學習機會和不同學習方法，來確保學生能夠繼續發展自身的威爾斯語技能，有自信使用威爾斯語，並自認是說威爾斯語者（頁 405-406 之「教育人力、資源與認證」章節將深入探討此面向）。

我們的目的：辦理有助提升晉級率的後義務教育，且無論精通程度如何，人人皆可獲得支援以發展使用於社會和職場上的威爾斯語技能。

5. 教育人力、資源與認證

教育人力

為增加說威爾斯語者人數，教育體系完全仰賴人力：教師、支援人員、幼教人員、訓練師與講師。若希望說威爾斯語者和使用威爾斯語者的人數能夠增加到所需程度，第一項必要步驟將是奠定基礎以便充分供應適當場所的教師和教育從業人員，讓兒童和青年可接受全威爾斯語教育。打造出語言技能強健、能夠激勵鼓舞學生的教育人力，是本策略成功推行的關鍵重點。

我們最優先的任務，是提升教育體系的能力，以滿足擴辦全威爾斯語教育與訓練的需求，和滿足改善全英語學校威爾斯語教學方式的需求。就義務教育界而言，我們需進行人力規劃，以便培訓新教師、支援受訓的教師和教學助理，並針對現有人力來擴大休假方案和新增專業學習機會。就小學教師而言，我們需增加能教導威爾斯語的小學教師數量，目標 2031 年從 2,900 人增加至 3,900 人，2050 年增加至 5,200 人；增加能教導威爾斯語的中學教師數量，目標 2031 年從 500 人增加至 900 人，2050 年增加至 1,200 人；增加能全威爾斯語教學的中學教師數量，目標 2031 年從 1,800 人增加至 3,200 人，2050 年增加至 4,200 人。

幼教人員的威爾斯語與全威爾斯語訓練，將透過數項計畫來進行。由於增加全威爾斯語托兒服務是達成百萬人說威爾斯語目標不可或缺的一環，我們必須確保制定協調一致的計畫來培育此項重要人力。我們也必須大幅增加能全威爾斯語教學的 16 歲以上講師和訓練師人數。

我們將加強注重全威爾斯語和威爾斯語教育學與方法論上的訓練，以確保教育人力在增進技能和知識時，能夠得知關於有效沉浸式學習法和全威爾斯語與雙語教學的證據。

全威爾斯語教育的永續發展，必須要有各層級的高效能領導者大力提倡威爾斯語和影響廣大人力，如此將能回過頭來激勵兒童和青年欣賞和使用威爾斯語。

資源與認證

除應增加能全威爾斯語教學的教育能力，我們亦需在威爾斯語的資源和認證上，提升和擴大其範圍。

整體而言，在威爾斯政府的財政支援下，教育資源的品質和廣度近年已有增加和改善，足以支援課程和認證方面的學習和教學。證據顯示，多處地區仍需要多種教材，尤其是威爾斯語的數位與互動資源。我們亦得知由於延誤發布全威爾斯語資源，使得教育從業人員難以開辦課程。且教育界似乎不甚了解有何可用資源，以及這些資源在支援教學與學習上有何用途（威爾斯政府 2016a）。因此，我們將為威爾斯所有基礎設施規劃產出威爾斯語和英語課程的相關及時資源，並確保將這些資源廣泛推廣至相關受眾。

威爾斯 14 歲至 19 歲青年需要有意義的認證，令其能夠為社會帶來貢獻及滿足經濟需求。針對威爾斯 14 歲至 19 歲學生的認證體系，必須提供各種全威爾斯語的認證，並具備清楚的晉級途徑。此方

面需增加能全威爾斯語工作的評量者與協調者人數，並令認證頒授機構有義務以威爾斯語和英語提供必要的資源和評鑑。我們將支援認證頒授機構持續為學生擴大提供服務和選項。

　　欲制定威爾斯語學習方面的單獨一貫課程，還必須要求威爾斯語認證著重於口說和聽力，以及職場上的威爾斯語使用。我們亦需確保雙語和多語學生的技能（例如跨語言技能）獲得理解、發展和認同。我們將妥善規劃以確保上述技能在認證體系裡受到承認。

我們的目的：妥善規劃以大幅增加和改善下列項目：
* 能教導威爾斯語和能全威爾斯教學的教育訓練人力
* 支援增辦教育方面所需的資源與認證

主題 2：
增加使用威爾斯語

> 目標：2050 年，每日說威爾斯語且會說不只少數字詞的說威爾斯語者，人口比例從 10%（2013-15 年）增加至 20%。

　　朝向百萬人說威爾斯語的目標前進，是威爾斯語蓬勃發展願景的其中一項層面。然而蓬勃發展的威爾斯語，是指確實有在使用威爾斯語。我們希望威爾斯語的使用是日常生活中的例行事項，讓所有能力等級的說威爾斯語者皆能有自信地在正規和非正規的場合使用威爾斯語，並讓產品和服務主動提供威爾斯語版本。

　　我們的目的，是希望所有學生離校時已有能力在社會和職場上使用威爾斯語。為幫助實現教育投資的益處，我們需擁有可經常練習和使用威爾斯語的機會。〈2013–15 威爾斯語使用調查〉（威爾斯政府與威爾斯語官員 2015）顯示，威爾斯語使用流利度和使用頻率之間呈顯著關聯—— 84% 的流利說威爾斯語者每日說威爾斯語。

　　民眾需有機會在各種能夠反應生活眾多面向的情境裡使用威爾斯語，包括在家庭中、職場上、地方活動、或較廣大的興趣網絡和跨地域社群裡的機會。使用威爾斯語的機會和服務必須是主動提供，無需個體自行請求使用威爾斯語。最終願景是讓民眾能在各處皆有的各個機會中使用威爾斯語。

　　此方面需因人而異，了解不同民眾有不同需求。

　　例如新的說威爾斯語者，或是不具備威爾斯語技能並將兒童送往就讀全威爾斯語學校的家長 / 照護者，其需求皆有別於流利自信的說威爾斯語者。無論威爾斯語是在成長過程中耳濡目染、在學校學習或成人時習得，威爾斯語始終是大家的語言，而我們的介入措施將致力讓人人皆有機會使用威爾斯語。

　　隨著現代社會性質改變，我們將需善加理解民眾的生活方式，以及生活方式與語言實踐間的關聯。我們需評估地方社群 / 鄰里在何種程度上依然是個體語言實務的主要影響因素，並需做好準備，制定承認個體流動漸增的政策介入措施。

　　社群的語言組成，各地區互有差異，因而需視差異情形進行有目的性的規劃，以根據地方需求來支援威爾斯語。在部分社群，由於威爾斯語是日常慣用語言，因此每日互動中隨時皆有機會使用威爾斯語；至於其他社群，將需確保已有安排和促進說威爾斯語的機會。

　　增加使用威爾斯語行動的成功與否，端視下列各項因素的綜合表現：語言習得、自信與流利度、機會的品質、以及使用威爾斯語技能的渴望程度。本節接下來的篇幅，將說明我們在不同背景環境裡增加使用威爾斯語的願景。

> 目的：
> 6. 職場：各行各業職場增加使用威爾斯語。
> 7. 服務：擴大為說威爾斯語者提供的服務範圍，並增加威爾斯語服務的使用。
> 8. 社會上使用威爾斯語：藉助社會上使用威爾斯語的正規和非正規機會，深植正面的語言使用實務。

　　為達成每日說威爾斯語者人口比例 20% 的目標，我們將推動下列重大變革。

- 檢討鞏固威爾斯語地位的立法，確保相關法律有建立堅實基礎來提倡和促進使用威爾斯語。
- 確保威爾斯政府以身作則，政府職員身體力行提倡和促進多加使用威爾斯語。

6. 職場

　　職場是日常生活重要的組成，也在個體的語言發展上擔當重要場域。無論是流利的說威爾斯語者，沒有自信說威爾斯語並盼望增進技能者，還是新進說威爾斯語者，職場都提供了使用、練習和學習威爾斯語的機會。

　　目前立法已定出架構，確保《威爾斯語標準》規範所涵蓋的實體必須以雙語提供客戶直接服務。此方面需要相關實體提升規劃雙語職場的能力，並找出哪些職位亟需或重視威爾斯語技能。這些行動已因此為個體提供更多在職場上認可、增進或習得威爾斯語技能的機會。

　　部分實體已率先展開行動，並使用威爾斯語作為內部行政管理語言，繼而增加威爾斯語技能的需求和使用機會。身為威爾斯基層公部門服務的主要雇主，此方面的重點，將是在地方政府、醫療部門和社會照護部門中多加使用威爾斯語。

　　職場語言規劃的原則，並非僅關乎立法規範涵蓋的機構。我們希望相關工作可以在各行各業扎根，期能大幅增加個體在職場環境中使用威爾斯語技能的機會。

　　〈2013–15 威爾斯語使用調查〉（威爾斯政府與威爾斯語官員 2015）的證據顯示，較多的說威爾斯語者，是在雇主支援可在工作大部分層面使用威爾斯語的環境中，與同事使用威爾斯語。因此，各行各業需發揮強大而顯著的領導力，鞏固雙語成為職場的自然要件，如此不僅是為了確保遵守法規，更是為了確保將公司文化轉向至認可雙語職場的好處，亦即漸增的雙語人力能為經濟帶來貢獻。

　　我們需進一步建立和分享雙語技能屬於職場規劃一環的認知，包括預期特殊技能的供需、員工的招聘與留用、技能查核以及差距分析，以提升雙語職場。一份針對威爾斯八項行業 4,000 多個雇主的調查（威爾斯政府 2014）估計，所有員工當中，近四分之一員工具備些許威爾斯語技能，14% 員工有在工作上使用威爾斯語。

　　〈2015 雇主技能調查〉指出，所有技能差距當中，欠缺威爾斯語技能的問題占約五分之一（22%），威爾斯語書寫技能占 19%，威爾斯語口說技能占 15%。威爾斯語書寫技能的問題在技能短缺當中占 11%（英國就業與技能委員會 2015）。

　　因此，我們將加強重視職場，視職場為推廣和促進多加使用威爾斯語的策略據點。此方面將需為青年鋪設更順暢的路徑，令其可從教育體系晉升至重視雙語技能、認為雙語技能十分有助實現企業目標的職場。

　　我們將鼓勵推動眾多威爾斯語職場訓練，協助所有能力等級的說威爾斯語者提升自信，並確保其具備所需能力可在工作上使用威爾斯語技能。我們亦將聚焦於增進管理者、領導者和企業主的語言意

識。

　　若能更加理解和認識威爾斯語科技和資源所能創造的機會，亦將有助個體更有自信在工作上使用威爾斯語。我們將致力增加運用研發中的語言科技，以便所有能力等級的員工之間能夠更常使用雙語溝通，讓眾人更能便利使用威爾斯語。

　　我們將促進上述原則在各行各業的知識轉移，以增加個體在職場使用威爾斯語的機會，並支援領導者和管理者推動必要改革。

　　威爾斯政府身為威爾斯的重要雇主，我們將在此方面以身作則，政府職員身體力行提倡和促進多加使用威爾斯語。

我們的目的：各行各業職場增加使用威爾斯語。

7. 服務

　　我們希望擴大以威爾斯語提供的服務範圍，並希望增加威爾斯語服務的使用，無論該服務是由公部門、私部門或第三部門提供。

　　不同模型可用於提倡和促進提供雙語服務。在此架構中，部分組織必須接受《威爾斯語標準》的法規監督，增加提供威爾斯語服務；其他組織則受鼓勵自願提供雙語服務，且在作法上可尋求可用支援。

　　我們希望透過公部門、私部門及第三部門已奠定的基礎，推動增加提供雙語服務。為採取行動，我們承認不同組織在目前提供的雙語服務層級上有著不同的起始點。

　　個體在職場和個人生活中常與企業接洽，因此企業的重要性與日俱增，能夠為民眾提供使用威爾斯語的機會。站在企業角度，增加其提供的雙語客服，足以反映企業的在地服務有尊重社群及當地居民。

　　我們承認必須採取更多行動，令企業界更加知曉提供威爾斯語服務能夠為企業本身、進而為客戶帶來何種潛在好處和機會。此方面將需給予企業更明顯、更實用和更專屬的協助，並著重於例如規劃威爾斯語技能、藉由客服來提升其提供的雙語溝通等課題。

　　公部門、第三部門或私部門即使已具備使用威爾斯語的服務和機會，仍無法保證民眾將會善用這些服務和機會。關於說威爾斯語者使用雙語服務的證據顯示，威爾斯語服務的使用會受各種因素影

響，包括服務的便利度和能見度、說威爾斯語者對服務提供品質的觀感、以及行為選擇（公民諮詢局 2015）。〈2013–15 威爾斯語使用調查〉（威爾斯政府與威爾斯語官員 2015）顯示，僅過半數說威爾斯語者在接洽公務機關時至少有偶爾試圖使用威爾斯語；而比較不常說威爾斯語者，每日說威爾斯語者試圖使用威爾斯語的可能性多出一倍。在總是試圖於公務機關使用威爾斯語者當中，僅過半數認為其總是或幾乎總是成功使用威爾斯語。

關鍵重點在於，不應有任何不利於接受威爾斯語服務的阻礙，且威爾斯語服務應主動提供、廣泛提供，且威爾斯語服務品質應等同英語服務品質。

服務提供者除需投資威爾斯語服務並主動提供，亦需知曉如何促進多加使用威爾斯語服務。此方面需藉助智慧行銷，服務提供者應負責設計出符合客戶需求的服務。此種客戶導向方針將需採取新穎且不同的辦法，並且改變心態，以吸引和培養更大的威爾斯語服務客戶群。

我們必須加強理解有何方式可協助所有能力等級的說威爾斯語者，在不習慣使用威爾斯語的場合使用威爾斯語。如欲快速改變威爾斯語服務的提供作法，可透過協助服務提供者以最主動的態度來提供服務。此方面的行動將需令服務提供者得知行為經濟學的最新研究。

我們亦將與企業界和第三部門領導者合作，增進其理解並認識雙語化，以及如何將雙語化融入成為客服的重要成分。

達成此目標的關鍵層面，將是如上節所述之確保有策略地規劃職場人力的威爾斯語技能。

在醫療和社會照護部門的服務方面，「主動提供」原則尤其重要。在威爾斯，國民保健服務 NHS、社會服務和社會照護由近 200,000 名員工負責辦理，且單以 NHS 而言，病人每年與 NHS 的互動可達 2000 萬次。此方面所牽涉的挑戰程度不容小覷。然而，就員工人數以及與大眾高度互動而言，醫療和社會照護部門可望大力幫助實現我們的目的。

我們的目的：擴大為說威爾斯語者提供的服務範圍，並增加威爾斯語服務的使用。

8. 社會上使用威爾斯語

語言使用實務

語言使用實務必須自幼扎根。本策略之主題 1 已提及代間語言傳播是維持和增加說威爾斯語者人數的重要手段。若能促進家庭在社會上使用威爾斯語，將可強化威爾斯語在家庭中的使用，兒童也多出可將威爾斯語視為日常生活重要組成的背景環境。

透過在家庭中使用威爾斯語，正面的實務和態度深植可深植兒童心中，但許多兒童是在托兒所、幼教或小學初次接觸威爾斯語，因此上述環境對於習得穩健的語言實務而言無比重要。

為了確保學生，尤其是單獨透過或主要透過教育習得威爾斯語者，能夠在課堂以外的大環境發展和使用威爾斯語技能，其中必然面臨若干挑戰，而〈全威爾斯語教育策略〉的評估即有指出部分挑戰（威爾斯政府 2016a）。此方面需配合〈2013–15 威爾斯語使用調查〉（威爾斯政府與威爾斯語官員2015）的證據加以考量，該調查顯示，比起任何其他地方，年輕的說威爾斯語者較有可能在學校學習說威爾斯語；且比起與朋友或在家，較有可能總是在學校說威爾斯語。

因此，我們必須妥善規劃提供給兒童和青年的教育，不僅令其有機會使用或練習威爾斯語，亦應向其灌輸威爾斯語的正面態度，促進主動使用威爾斯語。長此以往將能收得益處，可讓兒童和青年了解威爾斯語並非只和學校有關，更帶有豐富的社會和文化境界。

青年（14–19）

針對威爾斯六處社群使用威爾斯語之研究（威爾斯政府 2015）整理的證據顯示，青少年晚期的青年在語言活動（例如運動、音樂、社交）方面缺乏選擇。我們認為此情形可能會妨礙青年進一步發展其於義務教育階段習得的語言技能。此情形亦恐會強化威爾斯語是課堂所用語言的觀感，而非社會、工作和就業上使用的語言。

除了必須如主題 1 所述，增辦以威爾斯語提供的擴充教育和高等教育，並提供威爾斯語學徒制的學習機會，還應讓青年在社會上有更多非正規機會來使用威爾斯語技能，親身當面或透過社群媒體進行皆可，此方面將是關鍵要務。我們亦需承認自身並不曉得所有解決方案，並承認需執行研究以探討何種因素驅動此年齡層的決策及其語言使用。

威爾斯語使用機會

以往我們一向認為，辦理或安排活動即可算是在社群環境提供使用威爾斯語的機會。儘管活動屬於其中一環，卻未能完全呈現民眾的生活方式。許多情形中，民眾往往過於忙碌或需優先處理其他要務，因而並無加入社團，亦無定期頻繁參與正規活動。此類個體較有可能在街坊、店家和利用服務時使用威爾斯語。

欲因應此項挑戰，代表將需根據威爾斯各地區的語言組成來考量各地區事務，並妥善規劃以便在地方上取得正規與非正規活動間的適當平衡，打造有利自然使用威爾斯語的背景環境，並採取行動讓威爾斯語正規化和提升威爾斯語的聲望。

此方面的要點之一，將是培養出理解語言規劃關鍵要點的卓越領導者，如此將可促使民眾和政府以外的組織（無論有無獲得政府資助）扮演獨立的催化劑。我們的目的是跳脫為每個組織和活動提供經費的作法，以支援能夠給予社群自主行動平臺的機會。

新進說威爾斯語者之機會

威爾斯語是屬於眾人的語言，眾人皆有潛力成為說威爾斯語者。成人才學習威爾斯語的新進說威爾斯語者，需有足夠機會來練習自身的威爾斯語技能和在社會上使用威爾斯語，方能達到流利程度。此類機會需動員既有的流利說威爾斯語者的參與，以其作為催化劑，促使新進說威爾斯語者在日常生活中使用威爾斯語。幾處社群蒐集而得的證據（威爾斯政府 2015）顯示，一些新進說威爾斯語者認為，說威爾斯語者若偏向與社群中的學生使用英語，會不利於新進說威爾斯語者練習技能和培養威爾斯語自信的機會。

因此，我們將制定各種介入措施，諸如向流利說威爾斯語者傳達訊息，告知與新進說威爾斯語者

對話時的重點行為，以及確保流利說威爾斯語者願意付出時間協助提升新進說威爾斯語者的自信，串連成人教育課程和社群中的非正規使用。

我們的目的：藉助社會上使用威爾斯語的正規和非正規機會，深植正面的語言使用實務。

主題 3：
打造有利條件──基礎設施與背景環境

　　前二項主題已說明為達成 2050 年增加說威爾斯語者人數之目標所應採取的行動，以及為達成增加使用威爾斯語之目標所需推動的變革。本主題將討論未來三十年應實現何種改變，以支援增加說威爾斯語者人數和增加使用威爾斯語的相關行動。本主題是關於打造適合的條件和環境，讓威爾斯語及說威爾斯語者能夠蓬勃發展。

　　如欲打造能讓說威爾斯語者續留或返回說威爾斯語社群的社會條件，經濟實為必要考量。我們雖無法控制足以影響經濟成長的每個因素，但我們仍有能力影響若干層面，包括：威爾斯語技能、威爾斯語聲望、公部門工作的地點、群集、確保威爾斯語在大型經濟發展中被視為重要技能、以及威爾斯語使用機會。

　　為促進說威爾斯語者人數的增加、提升說威爾斯語者的自信、以及令威爾斯語通用於各種環境，我們需動用數位資源、健全多元的媒體、盡力善用最新科技且反應靈活的現代化翻譯專業、以及語言資源（字典、術語學、語料庫）。以上所有要素反映並維護威爾斯語身為活語言的地位，並且對無論何種能力等級的說威爾斯語者而言皆至關重要。

　　欲成功實行策略，我們需將語言規劃的責任分攤至各種組織，如此可培養語言規劃方面的能力和專業，並增進對雙語化的理解。

　　為衡量介入措施成效和根據證據制定未來政策，我們務必要繼續發展威爾斯語的研究和評估計畫。我們將與威爾斯及外地的研究夥伴合作辦理此項任務。

　　我們的願景，是見到威爾斯語成為日常生活中的正規成分，眾人對威爾斯語有好感，且威爾斯語的使用漸增。我們希望威爾斯語能與威爾斯全體民眾切身相關，無論民眾說的是威爾斯語、英語亦或其他語言；我們也希望激發搬遷至威爾斯者尊重和欣賞威爾斯語。此方面需提升威爾斯語在全球的地位，並更加努力宣揚威爾斯語是我們當代文化中的關鍵組成。

目的：
9. 社群與經濟：支援說威爾斯語社群的社經基礎設施。
10. 文化與媒體：確保威爾斯語受到保護，成為當代文化中的必要成分。
11. 威爾斯與國際：確保威爾斯語是威爾斯相關行動的要角，以增進威爾斯與國際的關係，並使用威爾斯語來迎接並融入搬遷至威爾斯者。
12. 數位科技：確保威爾斯語是數位科技改革的核心重點，讓所有數位場域皆能使用威爾斯語。
13. 語言基礎設施：確保本策略實施時務必持續發展威爾斯語基礎設施（字典、術語學、翻譯專業）。
14. 語言規劃：在已深入理解雙語化及說威爾斯語者需求並有提供支援的情形下，於全國、區域和地方層級深耕語言規劃及推廣。
15. 評估與研究：持續以威爾斯語及說威爾斯語者之相關證據為基礎，藉此評估介入措施成效和制定威爾斯語政策。

　　為達成主題 3 的目標，我們將推動下列重大變革。
- 制定經濟發展方面的區域新重點，讓威爾斯各區皆能享有經濟繁榮之福，並支援各區建立自身特有的身分認同。
- 特別著力於語言科技，令威爾斯語數位版圖煥然一新。
- 制定增進理解雙語化的國家計畫。

9. 社群與經濟

建設可確保說威爾斯語社群扎根的經濟

維持與增長高密度說威爾斯語者社群的重要性備受關注，數個原因可說明此方面何以重要。說威爾斯語者社群裡，自稱流利說威爾斯語者的比例較高，最常使用威爾斯語的說威爾斯語者比例也較高。

各社群雖各有特色，但亦存在些許共同點，其中包括人口流動度高，年輕的說威爾斯語者遷出，遷入者則主要為年長人士。許多地區屬於鄉村，多半依賴農業、食品業和觀光業。這些地區也包含市集城鎮，以及高度仰賴公部門（如醫療服務與地方政府）的大學城。這些地區還包含小區塊的剝奪與鄉村貧窮，平均薪資在英國排名極低。

關於說威爾斯語社群的論述，經常著重於必須為未來世代保護這些社群，於是便出現不應讓這些社群接受改變和發展經濟的心態。雖能理解此種心態的緣由，然政府仍有責任在全威爾斯推動經濟發展和共創繁榮。在社會本質改變的同時，我們無法期待說威爾斯語社群依然保持原封不動。因此威爾斯政府完全認同在鄉村地區建設蓬勃永續經濟的重要性，包括前述之地區。

我們希望這些地區有優良的工作，令年輕人得以續留此地，或令原本因不同生涯規劃而離家的年輕人歸返，在此生活及成家。我們不僅需有能讓民眾續留此地和吸引其返鄉的就業機會，還需有可讓民眾願意轉職的美好職涯。

農業是此方面的關鍵之一。英國脫歐後，維護農業利益將成為我們的首要任務。另一關鍵是在說威爾斯語地區安排公部門工作，這些地區具備隨時可上工的雙語人力。我們亦希望確保這些地區和其他地區的說威爾斯語者獲得充分鼓勵而勇於創業。我們亦需深入探究以威爾斯語工作的合作事業是否可望為社群創造利益。

說威爾斯語地區有機會進一步運用威爾斯語和既有雙語人力所帶來的機會。威爾斯語對經濟的價值包括語言產業，例如教育、翻譯、語言規劃、諮詢服務、語料庫工作和語言科技，這些領域皆與威爾斯語有直接關聯。至於諸如文化、媒體和觀光業等其他領域，威爾斯語則可擔任提供服務時的要角。威爾斯語亦能提升地方感，許多品牌已將威爾斯語作為獨特賣點。

經濟發展與威爾斯語

在威爾斯這類開放市場經濟中，經濟的成長與發展會出現某種程度的分配不均。然而，政府有職責致力確保威爾斯各地區皆能受惠於經濟成長。為利達成此目標，我們將採取行動，為經濟發展創造區域層面的貢獻，扶持全國的經濟發展。為實現區域重點，我們將協助包括說威爾斯語社群在內的威爾斯各地區共享經濟繁榮之福，並讓威爾斯成為民眾想在此居住、工作、學習和投資的迷人所在。

土地使用規劃系統應在得知語言規劃相關原則的支援下，打造適合條件來開創蓬勃永續說威爾斯語的社群，以協助維持威爾斯語的活力。

特定社群中的經濟發展類型、規模和確切地點之相關決策，可能會影響語言使用，進而影響語言的永續性與活力。此方面需強化語言規劃與土地使用規劃間的關聯。

威爾斯政府主張，威爾斯語的考量應知會地方經濟發展計畫的準備流程，並應具備指南以協助此方面規劃的主管機關。根據《(威爾斯)規劃法2015》，目前所有層級的發展規劃，計畫中需納入評估其政策對威爾斯語的可能影響。

我們的目的：支援說威爾斯語社群的社經基礎設施。

10. 文化與媒體

文化

語言與文化之間有著諸多面向的複雜關係，威爾斯語亦然。文化是社會、身分認同和國族情感的必要成分。文化能夠賦權，有助提升自信、技能和就業能力，這些皆是本策略的關鍵要點。文化在威爾斯大眾生活中的重要性與日俱增，包括經濟、健康、教育和再生。我們需提倡並鞏固文化意識與語言意識，以促進繁榮。

威爾斯語是威爾斯文化裡的重要面向，我們有威爾斯語，才有威爾斯這個民族。威爾斯語亦擁有獨一無二的豐富文化，並具備多種表現形式。身為威爾斯人，我們需更努力在威爾斯國內外表揚此種參與式文化（「文化」一詞的威爾斯語為「diwylliant」）。

我們在有關加強深植語言意識以支援語言使用（主題2所述）的行動，不僅包括威爾斯語意識，還包含欣賞威爾斯的豐富多元文化，以涵蓋整體局面。我們亦希望在流行文化的所有藝術形式中，在文學、劇場、電影和電視上，能夠更普遍見到和聽到威爾斯語。由例如運動員、音樂家、演員及其他知名人士和組織擔任使用威爾斯語的楷模，有助提升威爾斯語作為活語言的地位。

　　文化界本身的角色相當重要，可協助辦理威爾斯語活動，以及籌備旨在推廣和促進認識威爾斯獨特文化的事件、產品與活動。文化界亦應確保威爾斯文化和威爾斯皆有融入重要場合，以此向國際展現威爾斯本色。

　　隨著說威爾斯語者人數增加，隨著我們迎接世界各地的人來到威爾斯，或許應提供更多機會，以便在愈趨多元文化的新環境中提倡使用威爾斯語。

　　觀光業是提升外界對威爾斯語觀感的重要助力，因為觀光業可以展現威爾斯的形象、語言和文化，對象不僅是國外人士，還包括威爾斯本國民眾。我們應清晰表達威爾斯獨具特色的語言和文化，除了要能打動民眾的心，也要吸引在威爾斯旅遊、求學和居住的人士。威爾斯語能讓旅客和投資人感覺此地與眾不同，至於推廣威爾斯語的全國活動，例如國家詩歌音樂藝術節（National Eisteddfod），則值得登上全球舞臺（亦可參見本書頁 417-418 之「威爾斯與國際」一節）。

出版與媒體

　　幾十年來，廣播媒體始終是國家復興語言的重要力量。威爾斯第四臺（S4C）和 BBC 威爾斯語廣播（BBC Radio Cymru）的威爾斯語節目，獲得活躍的獨立製作業的支援，包括 ITV 威爾斯。此方面務必持續進行，且務必增加提供此類節目，我們亦將盡全力支援和增進提供威爾斯語節目，即使節目可能於未來播出亦然。

　　基於印刷媒體界的式微，威爾斯公共廣播電視公司扮演的角色尤其關鍵。英國的報紙和廣播公司是威爾斯主要的媒體輸出，但皆極少報導威爾斯的生活和社會，包括威爾斯文化。威爾斯在英國媒體中的形象，需能更明顯呈現威爾斯的豐富多元文化，包括對威爾斯語的認識。

　　展望未來，我們的願景是見到有更多內容和更優質的節目是為威爾斯製作、在威爾斯製作，涵蓋威爾斯生活的所有層面，包括威爾斯的文化和遺產。過去幾年我們已建立重要的夥伴關係，並仍需擴大尋求和其他實體的合作。

我們的目的：確保威爾斯語受到保護，成為當代文化中的必要成分。

11. 威爾斯與國際

串連威爾斯與國際

　　在眾多發展悠久、歷經淬鍊、與時俱進的語言當中，威爾斯語也是其中一員。威爾斯語位居全球語言之列，並持續為英國、歐洲和世界的當代文化做出貢獻。

　　想要繼續支援威爾斯語的地位，就必須拓廣眼界，放眼全球，並認清世界各地無數人的日常生活使用的語言不只一種，並應知曉威爾斯語比許多其他語言處在更強健的狀態。

　　學習新語言能讓個體更開放接納其他文化，並藉此習得不同的經驗與技能，有助我們在本國及國外開創成就。在此脈絡下，威爾斯語增進我們的歸屬感，並幫助我們認識威爾斯和國際。無論民眾是否會說威爾斯語，若民眾能理解威爾斯語對國族認同的重要性，就會尊重威爾斯語，對威爾斯語投入情感，進而希望威爾斯語長久延續並蓬勃發展。

　　國際關係有助提升威爾斯語在國外的形象。此方面包括與國外的威爾斯語社群保持密切連結，例如巴塔哥尼亞地區的說威爾斯語社群 Y Wladfa，以及接觸已遷離威爾斯者，令其能繼續透過威爾斯語來協助社群和範圍更廣大的社會。我們亦應增進和其他語言的關係，尤其是使用少數民族語言的國家。身在威爾斯的我們，已從各國的語言規劃者借鏡學到經驗，並推出曾受他人採用的解決方案，此

種互惠合作將繼續維持。

向國際行銷威爾斯和威爾斯語

　　威爾斯深具觀光魅力。重大盛事上的強力對內投資，讓威爾斯有機會在世界舞臺上加強自身形象。我們的目的，是建立一個當代的、有吸引力的國家品牌，在英國和國際場合宣傳威爾斯，並且鼓勵威爾斯民眾帶著自信向前探索。此方面包括以威爾斯道地本色來迎接本國民眾與外地旅客，並宣揚威爾斯是雙語國家。「威爾斯品牌」（Brand Cymru）是國內外宣傳威爾斯時使用的統一品牌，我們將繼續確保威爾斯語是「威爾斯品牌」的亮眼主角。

迎接並融入搬遷至威爾斯者

　　語言是帶動融入的利器，在許多案例中，語言是此類融入計畫的要點。

　　藉由向全世界深植對威爾斯語的認識，威爾斯語亦有助我們迎接前來威爾斯居住的民眾，並使其融入成為威爾斯社會的一份子。

　　有鑑於國內人口遷移的影響，以及與搬遷至威爾斯者的溝通，於是我們在威爾斯語正規化和奠定對威爾斯語好感方面的願景顯得分外重要。此方面關鍵在於正面的論述和實質的支援，以確保民眾充分理解自身目前居住的社群。

　　國內人口遷移是威爾斯語的挑戰，但也是威爾斯語的契機，可藉此證明如何利用威爾斯語來接納多元文化和多樣性。此方面可透過學習威爾斯語的計畫或協助兒童與家庭的計畫來進行，以支援學習並引導民眾認識新社群。

　　另一重要作法，則是利用職場向移入者介紹威爾斯語，確保其知曉威爾斯語和威爾斯文化，並令其有機會學習與使用威爾斯語。

　　流利說威爾斯語者的態度和貢獻也值得重視。正如針對任何新進說某種語言者的計畫，我們也將需為流利說威爾斯語者制定相關計畫，鼓勵其參與非正規學習，幫助移入者學習威爾斯語，例如西班牙加泰隆尼亞的「語言志願服務」（Voluntariat per la Llengua）計畫。

我們的目的：確保威爾斯語是威爾斯相關行動的要角，以增進威爾斯與國際的關係，並使用威爾斯語來迎接並融入搬遷至威爾斯者。

12. 數位科技

數位科技扭轉了我們的生活方式，而且科技在未來本策略實施期間仍會不斷變革。雖無從得知未來科技的確切發展，但我們彼此溝通的方式顯然必將繼續改變。這對少數民族語言而言既是挑戰，亦是機會。

因此極重要的是，我們必須在科技發展上有所投資，以確保有辦法盡可能在眾多場合透過語音和鍵盤輸入來使用威爾斯語。未來我們應當側重於大舉投資語言科技基礎設施，例如威爾斯語語音轉文字技術和機器翻譯能力。

我們需在此方面加強鼓勵大企業更加活用威爾斯語和支援威爾斯語的發展。此願景的核心行動，還包括遊說跨國企業並和其密切合作，促使跨國企業考量威爾斯語及提供威爾斯語服務。

科技在我們的食衣住行育樂不可或缺，其重要性自不待言。例如在教育資源方面，必會納入數位資源這一塊；同樣地，有關可在職場上協助說威爾斯語者的資源，可在社會上使用威爾斯語的機會，以及威爾斯語服務與產品等方面，數位科技當然不容遺漏。而且正如任何威爾斯語的資源或服務，我們也需讓民眾能夠善用手邊可得的數位服務。

我們需確保任何重大科技發展皆務必提供威爾斯語服務；除此之外，我們亦相信威爾斯民眾可望率先享受雙語與多語科技的便利。我們將致力研擬投資語言科技的經濟方案，期能有助數位科技在威爾斯和國際的進展。

我們仍將重視與處於相似社經環境的語言合作，善用聯合創新的機會。

我們的目的：確保威爾斯語是數位科技改革的核心重點，讓所有數位場域皆能使用威爾斯語。

13. 語言基礎設施

為打造適合條件以增加說威爾斯語者和使用威爾斯語者的人數，我們需具備堅實的基礎設施，並需持續長期投資此類基礎設施，為未來扎穩根基。

語料庫、字典與術語學

活語言不斷演進，並能反映大環境。我們相信有必要維護現代的語言基礎設施，包括語料庫（亦即印刷文字或錄音的大規模收藏）、字典與術語學資源，以確保威爾斯語繼續保持最新狀態和跟上外界脈動。

語料庫對翻譯者、字典編輯者和術語學者的助益甚鉅，而語料庫也是語言軟體的關鍵工具，在科技界占有一席之地。語料庫地位雖如此重要，但以往語料庫在威爾斯並不如在其他國家受到同等關注，未來實有必要轉變此種情形。

字典編輯優質資源的重要性易遭低估。若能確保此類計畫的長期未來發展，將有助進一步實現威爾斯語的正面成果，提升威爾斯語知名度，並為威爾斯語學生和流利說威爾斯語者提供優質資源。

除語料庫計畫外，術語學的優質資源同樣相當重要，可促進威爾斯語在日常生活各層面的使用，包括諸如科技、法律和教育等專業領域。

翻譯專業

我們希望威爾斯語能夠盡量在生活諸多層面達到正規化，因而翻譯專業便顯得尤具策略重要性。舉例而言，隨著更多實體和機構出於自願或立法規定而提供威爾斯語服務，我們將需能隨時供應技能高超、品質優良的翻譯者與口譯者。

過去數年來，翻譯專業方面已有長足進展，而在威爾斯語漸趨正規化的情形下，威爾斯政府亦努力促進翻譯專業的發展，並針對未來有所調整。此方面將需持續確保能隨時供應具備現代技能的專業翻譯者和已畢業語言學者，輔以可支援專業標準和專業行為的穩健認證與法規制度。如此將能令尋求翻譯服務的企業與機構安心以對，並增長對翻譯流程的信心，以促進使用威爾斯語。

另一關鍵要點是為了因應威爾斯語使用情形日增，翻譯者的技能庫需加以拓展，語言學者所提供服務的範圍也應擴大。舉例而言，我們將需增加使用同步口譯，以促進社群和職場多加使用威爾斯語。

由於支援翻譯流程的科技日新月異，翻譯者的角色也應有所調整，例如翻譯記憶搭配合適機器翻譯的使用。威爾斯必須站在最新科技發展的最前線。另一方面，翻譯專業亦需隨著新起的技能需求和工作流程的調整需求而變通，與科技發展同步，而翻譯輸入十分有助品質保證流程，可確保翻譯輸出擁有最高品質。

隨著具備威爾斯語技能的人力增加，我們將需微調專業翻譯者的角色。雙語工作的成長，將能令翻譯服務著重於適切傳遞訊息，妥善應用專業語言技能，並可望提升翻譯服務的增值能力。

我們的目的：確保本策略實施時務必持續發展威爾斯語基礎設施（字典、術語、翻譯專業）。

14. 語言規劃

本策略所述的介入措施當中，許多皆有要求需理解各種層級的語言規劃。為在地方、區域和國家層級有效規劃和採取行動，我們需在適當場所安排創意十足、才華洋溢的人員，且人員應已理解語言規劃的理論與原則，以利推動策略。

多處不同場所已有語言規劃師的服務，例如各個公共機關、學術或民間機構。有些人可能並未自認是語言規劃師，但他們確實理解語言規劃，並擁有足以帶來改變的影響力。

領導者是此情境中的關鍵要角，能夠積極推動打造出在各種政治層級、社群內、公共服務、職場和經濟上鼓勵使用威爾斯語的環境。強大的領導力亦有助推動策略和締結新的夥伴關係。

有效的語言規劃，必須要能理解威爾斯各地區不同的風土民情，以據此規劃相應的介入措施。

我們已著手進行國家層級的語言規劃，並聚焦於特定地區。近期地方主管機關已根據《威爾斯語標準》對其施加的規定來制定威爾斯語策略。然而未來在區域層級仍有語言規劃的空間。如此將有助制定專屬的介入措施，例如著重在職場、職涯與經濟、職場威爾斯語訓練、以及說威爾斯語社群與地方經濟間的關係。

我們的目的：在已深入理解雙語化及說威爾斯語者需求並有提供支援的情形下，於全國、區域和地方層級深耕語言規劃及推廣。

15. 評估與研究

如欲實現本策略的目標，我們將需取得穩固的證據庫，並需盡力評估本策略相關計畫和介入措施的成效。我們將制定評估與研究計畫，作為上述事項的基礎。自〈威爾斯語策略評估架構〉（2013）

發布以來，我們便不斷尋找何種方式可衡量威爾斯語策略的成效，並將相關資料收入證據庫。我們將繼續執行此項工作，在規劃計畫的同時，亦應考量最適合用於評估計畫成效的方式。我們的研究計畫，亦將持續在威爾斯語和說威爾斯語者相關統計資料中找出差距並加以彌補。

　　我們希望加強理解說威爾斯語者一生中的語言經驗；為此，我們的研究計畫將格外重視蒐集和分析個體的長期資料。我們希望透過綜合探討量化和質化資料，以便更加理解說威爾斯語者在人生不同階段的語言經驗和語言實務，進而幫助我們制定有意義的穩健政策。我們亦將有必要確保持續蒐集說威爾斯語者使用威爾斯語方面的資訊，並鑽研如何透過〈威爾斯語使用調查〉來蒐集此資訊。

　　原始的評估架構致力確保我們的研究與評估方式，能夠呈現出我們對語言行為動力學和語言社會學的理解。我們將持續精進和增長此方面知識。

　　為達成此項目的，我們需與諸多機構組織合作，高等教育的角色更是關鍵。我們承認仍需加強能力和專業，以針對威爾斯語和透過威爾斯語進行研究。藉由夥伴關係的支援，並向其他組織告知相關機會的優點以鼓勵其強化研究基礎設施，我們希望如此將有助為未來培育專業人才與研究人員。

　　身為政府，我們所能發揮的重大貢獻，是提倡眾人理解證據與有效政策發展之間的關聯。我們將持續努力宣傳此種關聯性，鼓勵夥伴和政策制定者深入認識，並訪查研究的使用者。

我們的目的：持續以威爾斯語及說威爾斯語者之相關證據為基礎，藉此評估介入措施成效和制定威爾斯語政策。

結論

　　本策略所有層面皆著重於為達成 2050 年百萬人說威爾斯語目標所需的長期策略。我們完全了解如此是替自身立下艱鉅挑戰，然而在企圖心、意志和決心的驅動下，我們將堅定實現已確立的目標。

　　藉由確保在規劃和目標投資之間取得適當平衡，我們相信將可盼來微小卻重要的成果，這些成果將在前往 2050 年的路途中逐漸累積為豐碩收穫。

　　我們理解，本策略的初期成功，首先有賴政府的角色。我們需持續進行各項行動的規劃、投資和行銷，以便充分善用威爾斯語帶給社會和經濟的益處。

　　即使如此，單憑政府並無法肩負威爾斯語未來前景的責任。威爾斯語屬於威爾斯的每位公民，而個體要如何看待威爾斯的活遺產，終究仍視個體自身的選擇。政府的責任，就是確保個體在做出此種

選擇時，不至於因為個體在日常生活中見不到、聽不到和用不到威爾斯語的此類經驗而受影響。

政府策略無法強迫個體一定要使用威爾斯語。為了讓威爾斯語真正茁壯成長，我們期許每一位威爾斯人都能接納雙語威爾斯的理念。我們已向相關組織、社團和個體徵詢本策略實施方面的建議與意見，現在我們希望人人各盡其職，共助順利執行本策略。

我們將持續監督與評估本策略的實施情形。儘管我們定下的是長期願景，但仍需承認意料外的事件可能會在未來影響我們對威爾斯語圓滿狀態的預期。為減少出現此種狀況，我們需做好準備，願意隨時調整，如此將有助我們迅速因應策略性的變化，同時不必更動本策略所述的主要目標。一旦我們有能力增進和鞏固實施重大變革的作法，2050 年百萬人說威爾斯語的願景，定將更有機會成真。

參考文獻

Ben-Shlomo, Y. and Kuh, D. (2002) 'A life course approach to chronic disease epidemiology: Conceptual models, empirical challenges and interdisciplinary perspectives', *International Journal of Epidemiology*, 31, pp. 285-293.

Billari, F. C. (2001) 'The analysis of early life courses: Complex descriptions of the transition to adulthood', *Journal of Population Research*, 18: pp. 119-142.

Citizens Advice Bureau (2015) *English by default – understanding the use and non-use of Welsh language services*, Cardiff. www.citizensadvice.org.uk/about-us/policy/policy-research-topics/ citizens-advice-cymru-wales-policy-research/english-by-default understanding-the-use-and-non-use-of-welsh-language-services

Darquennes, J. (2007) 'Paths to Language Revitalization', *Contact Linguistics and Language Minorities* [Plurilingua], Volume XXX, pp. 61-76.

Gathercole, V. C. M. (ed.) (2007) *Language Transmission in Bilingual Families in Wales*, Cardiff: Welsh Language Board. http://vcmuellergathercole.weebly.com/uploads/1/8/6/9/18699458/2_ revised_ adroddiad_gathercole_saesnegggrev.pdf

Grin, F. and Moring, T. (2002) *Support for Minority Languages in Europe*. Report for DG Education and Culture, European Commission. http://europa.eu.int/comm/education/policies/lang/languages/langmin/ files/support.pdf

Heller, M. (2011) *Paths to Post-Nationalism: A Critical Ethnography of Language and Identity*, Oxford: Oxford University Press.

Martin-Jones, M. and Martin, D. (eds) (2017) *Researching Multingualism: Criticial and Ethnographic Perspectives*, Abingdon: Routledge.

Mayer, K. U. (2009) 'New Directions in Life Course Research', *Annual Review of Sociology*, Vol. 35: pp. 413-433.

O'Rourke, B., Pujolar, J. et al. (2015) 'New Speakers of Minority Languages: The Challenging Opportunity', *International Journal of the Sociology of Language*, 231 (Special Issue).

Pennycook, A. (2010) *Language as a Local Practice*, Abingdon: Routledge.

Pietikäinen, S. and Kelly-Holmes, H. (eds) (2013) *Multilingualism and the Periphery*, Oxford: Oxford University Press.

Pujolar, J. and Puigdevall, M. (2015) 'Linguistic mudes: how to become a new speaker in Catalonia', *International Journal of the Sociology of Language*, 231: pp. 167-187.

Save the Children (2015) *Ready to Read: Closing the gap in early language skills so that every child in Wales can read well*, London. www.savethechildren.org.uk/resources/online-library/ready-read-wales

Strubell, M. (2001) 'Catalan A Decade Later', in Fishman, J. A. (ed.), *Can Threatened Languages be Saved? Reversing Language Shift, Revisited: A 21st Century Perspective* (pp. 260-283). Clevedon, England: Multilingual Matters.

UK Commission for Employment and Skills (2015) *Employer Skills Survey.*

Welsh Government (2013) *Welsh Language Strategy Evaluation Framework*, Cardiff. http://gov.wales/statistics-and-research/welsh-language-strategy evaluation/?lang=en

Welsh Government (2014) *Welsh language skills needs in eight sectors*, Cardiff. http://gov.wales/statistics-and-research/welsh-language-skills-needs eight-sectors/?lang=en

Welsh Government (2015) *Welsh Language Use in the Community*, Cardiff. http://gov.wales/statistics-and-research/welsh-language-strategy evaluation/?lang=en

Welsh Government (2016a) *Evaluation of the Welsh-medium Education Strategy: Final Report*, Cardiff. http://gov.wales/statistics-and-research/welsh-medium-education strategy/?lang=en

Welsh Government (2016b) *Childcare in Further Education*, Cardiff. http://gov.wales/statistics-and-research/childcare-further education/?lang=en

Welsh Government (2017a) *Qualitative Research with Flying Start Families*, Cardiff. http://gov.wales/statistics-and-research/national-evaluation-flying start/?lang=en

Welsh Government (2017b) *Welsh Language Transmission and Use in Families. Research into conditions influencing Welsh language transmission and use in families*, Cardiff. http://gov.wales/statistics-and-research/welsh-language-transmission use-in-families/?skip=1&lang=en

Welsh Government and Welsh Language Commissioner (2015) *Welsh Language Use in Wales 2013–15*, Cardiff. http://gov.wales/statistics-and-research/welsh-language-use survey/?lang=en

歐洲條約彙編 - 第 148 號

歐洲區域或少數民族語言憲章

史特拉斯堡，1992 年 11 月 5 日

前言

簽署本協定之歐洲理事會會員國，

有鑑於歐洲理事會目標是使會員國間更加團結，尤其是為維護並實現為其共同遺產之理想及原則起見；

有鑑於保護歐洲部分有最終滅絕之危險的歷史區域或少數民族語言，有助維護並發展歐洲文化財富及傳統；

有鑑於在私人及公共生活中使用區域或少數民族語言為不可剝奪之權利，符合聯合國《公民與政治權利國際公約》體現之原則，亦符合歐洲理事會《保障人權與基本自由公約》之精神；

關注到歐安組織內部開展之工作，尤其是 1975 年赫爾辛基最終議定書及 1990 年哥本哈根會議文件；

強調跨文化及多語言之價值，並認為保護與鼓勵區域或少數民族語言不應損害官方語言及學習官方語言之必要性；

認識到於歐洲不同國家地區保護及推廣區域或少數民族語言，是對於國家主權與領土完整架構內基於民主及文化多樣性原則建設歐洲之重要貢獻；

考量到歐洲國家不同區域之具體情況及歷史傳統，

茲協定如下：

第一部分　總則

第 1 條 定義

於本憲章中：

　a 稱「區域或少數民族語言」者，謂下列語言：

　　i 傳統上由國民於該國特定領土內使用者，該類國民組成之群體人數少於該國其他人群；且

　　ii 不同於該國之官方語言；

　　其不包含該國官方語言之方言或移民之語言；

　b 稱「區域或少數民族語言使用地區」者，謂該語言為許多人表達方式之地理區域，其人數足證採納本憲章所定各種保護及推廣措施之正當；

　c 稱「非領土語言」者，謂與該國其他人群所用一種或多種語言不同，而為國民使用之語言，其雖傳統上於該國領土內使用，但不能辨別屬於該國特定區域。

第 2 條　承諾

1 各締約方承諾，於其領土內使用，且符合第 1 條定義之所有區域或少數民族語言，適用第二部分規定。

2 有關批准、接受或核定時指定之各種語言，依第 3 條，各締約方承諾，自《憲章》第三部分規定中選擇至少三十五項或款以為適用，其中至少包含自第 8 條及第 12 條中選擇之三條，與自第 9 條、第 10 條、第 11 條及第 13 條中各選擇之一條。

第 3 條　實際安排

1　各締約國應於其批准、接受或核定文書中，具體說明於各種區域或少數民族語言，或全部或部分領土較不廣為使用之官方語言，依第 2 條第 2 項所選條款應如何適用之。

2　任何締約方得於其後任何時間通知秘書長，其接受所批准、接受或核定文書中未指明之《憲章》任何其他條款規定所生之義務，或本條第 1 項將適用於他種區域或少數民族語言，或全部或部分領土較不廣為使用之官方語言。

3　前項所稱承諾應視為批准、接受或核定之整體一部分，自通知之日起具有同等效力。

第 4 條　現有保護制度

1　本憲章中任何內容均不得解釋為限制或減損《歐洲人權公約》所保障之任何權利。

2　本憲章規定不得影響任何有關區域或少數民族語言地位之更有利規定，或可能存在於締約方或由相關雙邊或多邊國際協定規定，而為少數民族之法律制度。

第 5 條　現有義務

本憲章中任何內容均不得解釋為暗示有權參與任何活動或為任何行動，而違反《聯合國憲章》宗旨或其他國際法義務，包含主權原則及國家領土完整。

第 6 條　資訊

締約方承諾，確保有關主管機關、組織及個人了解本憲章所定權利義務。

第二部分　依第 2 條第 1 項追求之目標及原則

第 7 條　目標及原則

1　對於區域或少數民族語言，於使用該類語言之領土內，依各語言之情況，締約方應基於下列目標與原則為其政策、立法及實踐，為下列措施：

　a　承認區域或少數民族語言為文化財富之表現形式；

　b　尊重各區域或少數民族語言之地理區域，以確保現有或新行政區劃不對推廣有關區域或少數民族語言構成障礙；

　c　需要採取果斷行動推廣區域或少數民族語言以保障之；

　d　促進及／或鼓勵於演講與寫作中、於公共及私人生活中使用區域或少數民族語言；

　e　於本憲章涵蓋領域內，維護及發展區域或少數民族語言使用群體與該國其他相同或類似形式語言使用群體間之聯繫，及建立與該國其他不同語言使用群體間之文化關係；

　f　於一切適當階段為區域或少數民族語言之教學研究提供適當形式及方法；

　g　提供設施，使生活於區域或少數民族語言使用區域者於其願意時能學習該語言；

　h　推動大學或同等機構對區域或少數民族語言之學習及研究；

　i　於本憲章涵蓋領域內，對於兩國或多國以相同或類似形式使用之區域或少數民族語言，推動適當類型之跨國交流。

2　締約方承諾，如尚未如此，消除有關區域或少數民族語言使用，意圖阻止或危及其維護或發展之任何不合理區別、排除、限制或偏好。採取有利於區域或少數民族語言之特別措施，目的為促進此類語言使用者與其他人群間之平等，或適當考量其具體情況，而不將其視為對更廣受使用語言之使用者之歧視行為。

3　締約方承諾，以適當措施推動該國所有語言群體間之相互理解，尤其是於其國內之教育與訓練目標中納入有關區域或少數民族語言之尊重、理解及容忍，並鼓勵大眾媒體追求相同目標。

4　締約方於訂定有關區域或少數民族語言之政策時，應考量該類語言使用群體所表達之需求及願望。於必要時，鼓勵其建立機構，以就有關區域或少數民族語言之所有事項向政府機關提出建議。

5　締約方承諾，非領土語言準用第 1 項至第 4 項所列原則。但對於有關語言，因實施本憲章而採取措

施之性質及範圍，應靈活訂定，同時謹記有關語言使用群體之需求及願望，尊重其傳統及特色。

第三部分　依第 2 條第 2 項承諾，推廣於公共生活中使用區域或少數民族語言之措施

第 8 條　教育

1 對於教育，締約方承諾，於該類語言使用領土內，依各語言之情況，且於不影響國家官方語言教學下，為下列措施：

a i 以相關區域或少數民族語言提供學前教育；或

　ii 以相關區域或少數民族語言提供主要部分之學前教育；或

　iii 至少於家人提出請求且人數充足之學生，適用第 i 目及第 ii 目所定措施之一；或

　iv 如公務主管機關於學前教育領域無直接權限，應支持及 / 或鼓勵實施第 i 目至第 iii 目所定措施；

b i 以相關區域或少數民族語言提供初等教育；或

　ii 以相關區域或少數民族語言提供主要部分之初等教育；或

　iii 於初等教育中提供相關區域或少數民族語言之教學，作為課程整體一部分；或

　iv 至少於家人提出請求且人數充足之學生，適用第 i 目至第 iii 目所定措施之一；

c i 以相關區域或少數民族語言提供中等教育；或

　ii 以相關區域或少數民族語言提供主要部分之中等教育；或

　iii 於中等教育中提供相關區域或少數民族語言之教學，作為課程整體一部分；或

　iv 至少於家人提出請求且人數充足之適當學生，或於適當時，適用第 i 目至第 iii 目所定措施之一；

d i 以相關區域或少數民族語言提供技術及職業教育；或

　ii 以相關區域或少數民族語言提供主要部分之技術及職業教育；或

　iii 於技術及職業教育中提供相關區域或少數民族語言之教學，作為課程整體一部分；或

　iv 至少於家人提出請求且人數充足之適當學生，或於適當時，適用第 i 目至第 iii 目所定措施之一；

e i 以區域或少數民族語言提供大學及其他高等教育；或

　ii 向此類語言作為大學及高等教育科目之學習提供便利；或

　iii 如因國家於高等教育機構之作用，第 i 目及第 ii 目不能適用，應鼓勵及 / 或允許以區域或少數民族語言提供大學或其他形式之高等教育，或將此類語言作為大學或高等教育科目學習之設施；

f i 安排提供主要或全部以區域或少數民族語言教學之成人及繼續教育課程；或

　ii 提供該類語言作為成人及繼續教育科目；或

　iii 如公務主管機關於成人教育領域無直接權限，應支持及 / 或鼓勵提供該類語言作為成人及繼續教育科目；

g 對保障區域或少數民族語言所反映歷史文化之教學做出安排；

h 向實施締約方所接受之第 a 款至第 g 款必須之教師提供基本及進階訓練；

　i 設立一間或多間監督機構，負責監督於建立或發展區域或少數民族語言教學所採取之措施及取得之進展，就其調查結果製作定期報告並公布之。

2 對於教育，及對於區域或少數民族語言傳統使用地區外之領土，締約方承諾，對區域或少數民族語言使用者人數足證合理者，於各適當教育階段允許、鼓勵，或提供區域或少數民族語言之教學或以之教學。

第 9 條　司法主管機關

1 締約方承諾，對於司法轄區中使用區域或少數民族語言之居民人數證明下列措施合理者，依各語言之情況，於法官不認為本項所定便利條件妨礙適當司法行政時，為下列措施：

a 於刑事訴訟中：

  i 規定法院應因當事人一方之請求，以區域或少數民族語言進行訴訟；及／或

  ii 保障被告有權使用本身區域或少數民族語言；及／或

  iii 規定請求及證據，無論為書面或口頭，不應僅因其以區域或少數民族語言提出，而認定為不可接受；及／或

  iv 因請求以相關區域或少數民族語言提供有關法律訴訟之文件，
    如有必要使用口譯及筆譯，有關人員不負擔額外費用；

b 於民事訴訟中：

  i 規定法院應因當事人一方之請求，以區域或少數民族語言進行訴訟；及／或

  ii 允許訴訟當事人於必須親自出庭時，得使用本身區域或少數民族語言，而不因此生額外費用；及／或

  iii 允許以區域或少數民族語言製作文書及證據，
    於必要時使用口譯及筆譯；

c 於法院有關行政事項之訴訟中：

  i 規定法院應因當事人一方之請求，以區域或少數民族語言進行訴訟；及／或

  ii 允許訴訟當事人於必須親自出庭時，得使用本身區域或少數民族語言，而不因此生額外費用；及／或

  iii 允許以區域或少數民族語言製作文書及證據，
    於必要時使用口譯及筆譯；

d 採取措施確保第 b 款與第 c 款之第 i 目及第 iii 目，及任何必要口譯與筆譯之使用不涉及有關人員之額外費用。

2 締約方承諾：

a 不僅因其以區域或少數民族語言製作，而否認於國內製作之法律文件之有效性；或

b 不僅因其以區域或少數民族語言製作，而否認於國內製作之法律文件於各方間之有效性，且規定於援引人向其告知文件內容之情形下，可對非此類語言使用者之利害關係第三方援引該類文件；或

c 不僅因其以區域或少數民族語言製作，而否認於國內製作之法律文件於各方間之有效性。

3 締約方承諾，以區域或少數民族語言提供最重要之國家法律文本，及尤其與此類語言使用者有關者，除非另有規定。

第 10 條　行政主管機關及公共服務

1 對於國家行政區中使用區域或少數民族語言之居民人數證明下列措施合理者，依各語言情況，締約方承諾，於合理可行之範圍內，為下列措施：

a i 保證行政主管機關使用區域或少數民族語言；或

  ii 保證其中與公眾接觸之公務員，於與以該類語言向其提出請求者之關係中，使用區域或少數民族語言；或

  iii 保證區域或少數民族語言使用者得以此類語言提出口頭或書面請求且以之獲回覆；或

  iv 保證區域或少數民族語言使用者得以此類語言提出口頭或書面請求；或

  v 保證區域或少數民族語言使用者得以此類語言有效提出文書；

b 以區域或少數民族語言或雙語向民眾提供廣為使用之行政文件及表格；

c 允許行政主管機關以區域或少數民族語言製作文件。

2 對於地方及區域主管機關，其領土上使用區域或少數民族語言之居民人數足證下列規定措施合理者，締約方承諾，其允許及／或鼓勵為下列措施：

a 於區域或地方主管機關架構內使用區域或少數民族語言；

b 區域或少數民族語言使用者以此類語言提出口頭或書面請求之可能；
c 區域主管機關亦以相關區域或少數民族語言公布其官方文件；
d 地方主管機關亦以相關區域或少數民族語言公布其官方文件；
e 區域主管機關於其議會辯論中使用區域或少數民族語言，但不排除使用國家官方語言；
f 地方主管機關於其議會辯論中使用區域或少數民族語言，但不排除使用國家官方語言；
g 於必要時結合官方語言名稱使用或採用區域或少數民族語言之傳統正確形式地名。

3 對於行政主管機關或其代理人提供之公共服務，締約方承諾，於使用區域或少數民族語言之領土內，依各語言情況，且於合理可行之範圍內，為下列措施：
a 保證於提供服務時使用區域或少數民族語言；或
b 允許區域或少數民族語言使用者以此類語言提出請求且以之獲回覆；或
c 允許區域或少數民族語言使用者以此類語言提出請求。

4 締約方承諾，採取下列一款或多款措施，以實施所接受之第 1 項、第 2 項及第 3 項規定：
a 可能需要之筆譯或口譯；
b 對所需公務員及其他公共服務人員之招聘及必要時之訓練；
c 對於具區域或少數民族語言知識公共服務人員，於使用該語言之領土中任命者，盡力遵循其要求。

5 締約方承諾，因相關者之請求，允許以區域或少數民族語言使用或採用姓氏。

第 11 條　媒體

1 締約方承諾，對於使用此類語言之領土內之區域或少數民族語言使用者，依各語言情況，於公務機關直接或間接主管，而於該領域有權力或作用之範圍內，於尊重媒體獨立自主之原則下，為下列措施：
a 於廣播電視履行公共服務使命之範圍內：
　i 保證設立區域或少數民族語言之至少一家廣播電臺及至少一個電視頻道；或
　ii 鼓勵及／或促進設立區域或少數民族語言之至少一家廣播電臺及至少一個電視頻道；或
　iii 訂定適足規定，使廣播業者提供區域或少數民族語言之節目；
b i 鼓勵及／或促進設立區域或少數民族語言之至少一家廣播電臺；或
　ii 鼓勵及／或促進定期播送區域或少數民族語言之廣播節目；
c i 鼓勵及／或促進設立區域或少數民族語言之至少一個電視頻道；或
　ii 鼓勵及／或促進定期播送區域或少數民族語言之電視節目；
d 鼓勵及／或促進製作及發行區域或少數民族語言之視聽作品；
e i 鼓勵及／或促進設立及／或維護區域或少數民族語言之至少一家報紙；或
　ii 鼓勵及／或促進定期發表區域或少數民族語言之報紙文章；
f i 於法律規定向媒體提供一般經濟補助時，代使用區域或少數民族語言之媒體負擔額外費用；或
　ii 對於區域或少數民族語言之視聽產品，亦適用現有經濟補助措施；
g 支持對區域或少數民族語言媒體之記者及其他工作人員進行訓練。

2 締約方承諾，保證直接接收與區域或少數民族語言相同或相似語言之鄰國廣播電視節目之自由，且不反對轉播該語言之鄰國廣播電視節目。其亦承諾，保證與區域或少數民族語言相同或相似語言之平面媒體，其言論自由及資訊自由流通不受任何限制。前述自由之行使，因負有義務及責任，可能受種種形式、條件、限制或處罰約束，其為法律規定及民主社會所必需，因國家安全、領土完整或公共安全之利益，目的為防止混亂或犯罪、保護健康或道德、保護他人名譽或權利、防止秘密收受之資訊揭露，或維護司法權威及公正。

3 締約方承諾，於可能依法設立，負責保障媒體自由及多元化之機構內，保證區域或少數民族語言使用者之利益有所代表或納入考量。

第 12 條　文化活動及設施

1 對於文化活動及設施—尤其圖書館、影片圖書館、文化中心、博物館、檔案館、學院、劇院及電影院，與文學作品及電影製作、白話之文化表現形式、節日及文化產業，特別包含新技術之使用—締約方承諾，於使用該類語言之領土，於公務機關主管範圍內，其於該領域有權力或作用為下列措施：

　a 鼓勵區域或少數民族語言特有之表達形式及倡議類型，及培育接觸以此類語言所作作品之不同方法；

　b 協助與開發翻譯、配音、後期配音及字幕活動，以培育由其他語言接觸以區域或少數民族語言所作作品之不同方法；

　c 協助與開發翻譯、配音、後期配音及字幕活動，以培育由區域或少數民族語言接觸以其他語言所作作品之管道；

　d 保證負責組織或支持各類文化活動之機構適當考量將區域或少數民族語言與文化之知識及使用納入其發起或支持之事業；

　e 推動措施，保證負責組織或支持各類文化活動之機構，能支配完全掌握有關區域或少數民族語言以及其他人群語言之工作人員；

　f 鼓勵特定區域或少數民族語言使用者之代表直接參與設施提供及文化活動規劃；

　g 鼓勵及／或促進設立一間或多間機構，負責蒐集、保存副本、展示或出版以區域或少數民族語言所作之作品；

　h 於必要時，建立及／或推動並資助翻譯及術語學研究服務，目的尤其為維護及發展各區域或少數民族語言之適當行政、商業、經濟、社會、技術或法律用詞。

2 對於區域或少數民族語言傳統使用領土以外之領土，締約方承諾，向區域或少數民族語言使用者人數足證合理者，依前項規定允許、鼓勵及／或提供適當文化活動及設施。

3 締約方承諾，於海外推行其文化政策時，對區域或少數民族語言及其所反映之文化為適當規定。

第 13 條　經濟及社會生活

1 對於經濟及社會活動，締約方承諾，於全國範圍內，為下列措施：

　a 刪除其立法中任何無正當理由禁止或限制於有關經濟或社會生活之文書中使用區域或少數民族語言之規定，尤其是勞動契約，及產品或裝置使用說明等技術文件；

　b 禁止於公司內部章程及私人文書中插入任何排除或限制區域或少數民族語言使用之條款，至少對於相同語言使用者之間如此；

　c 反對旨在阻止與經濟或社會活動有關之區域或少數民族語言使用之習慣；

　d 促進及／或鼓勵以前款規定外之方式使用區域或少數民族語言。

2 對於經濟及社會活動，締約方承諾，於公務機關主管範圍內，於使用區域或少數民族語言之領土內，且於合理可行之範圍內，為下列措施：

　a 於其金融及銀行法規中納入規定，允許以符合商業慣例之程序，於製作付款委託書（支票、匯票等）或其他財務文件時使用區域或少數民族語言，或於適當情形下保證實施該類規定；

　b 於其直接控制之經濟及社會部門（公部門），組織活動以推動使用區域或少數民族語言；

　c 保證醫院、養老院或收容所等社會照護設施，能以本身語言接收及治療因健康狀況不佳、年老或其他原因而需照護之區域或少數民族語言使用者；

　d 以適當方式保證安全指示亦以區域或少數民族語言製作之；

　e 安排公務主管機關所提供之消費者權利相關資訊以區域或少數民族語言提供之。

第 14 條　跨境交流

締約方承諾：

　a 適用現有雙邊及多邊協定，其對以相同或類似形式使用同一語言之國家具有約束力，或於必要時

　　尋求締結該類協定，以此培育有關國家中相同語言使用者於文化、教育、資訊、職業訓練及終身教育領域之聯繫；

b 因區域或少數民族語言之利益，促進及 / 或推動跨境協作，於領土內以相同或類似形式使用相同語言之區域或地方機關之間尤是。

第四部分　《憲章》適用

第 15 條　定期報告

1 締約方應以部長委員會所定形式，向歐洲理事會秘書長定期報告有關其依本憲章第二部分所採取之政策，及因適用其已接受之第三部分規定而採取之措施。初次報告應於《憲章》對有關締約方生效後一年內呈交，其他報告應於初次報告後每三年呈交一次。

2 締約方應公開其報告。

第 16 條　報告審查

1 依第 15 條呈交歐洲理事會秘書長之報告，應由依第 17 條組成之專家委員會審查。

2 於締約方合法設立之機構或協會，得請求專家委員會注意締約方依本憲章第三部分所為承諾之 相關事宜。於會商有關締約方後，專家委員會得考量下列第 3 項所定準備之資訊。此類機構或協會可進一步提出有關締約方依第二部分所採取政策之聲明。

3 基於第 1 項所定報告及第 2 項所稱資訊，專家委員會應對部長委員會準備報告。該報告應附有要求締約方提出之意見，且得由部長委員會公布之。

4 第 3 項所定報告應尤其包含專家委員會向部長委員會提出之提案，以便後者準備可能須向一或多締約方提出之建議。

5 歐洲理事會秘書長應每二年向議會大會就憲章適用情形提出詳細報告。

第 17 條　專家委員會

1 專家委員會應由每個締約方之一名成員組成，其由部長委員會自於《憲章》處理事務中具有最高誠信及公認能力之個人名單中任命，且應由有關締約方提名之。

2 委員會成員任期應為六年，且應有連任資格。不能完成任期之委員，應依第 1 項所定程序予以替換，且接替成員應補足其前任之任期。

3 專家委員會應採用議事規定。其秘書服務應由歐洲理事會秘書長提供。

第五部分　最終條款

第 18 條

本憲章應開放供歐洲理事會成員國簽署。其得為批准、接受或核定。批准書、接受書或核定書應交存於歐洲理事會秘書長處。

第 19 條

1 本憲章應於自歐洲理事會五個會員國依第 18 條規定表示同意受本憲章約束之日起三個月屆滿後下月首日生其效力。

2 對於隨後表示同意受其約束之任何會員國，《憲章》應於自批准書、接受書或核定書交存之日起三個月屆滿後下月首日生其效力。

第 20 條

1 本憲章生效後，歐洲理事會部長委員會得邀請任何非歐洲理事會會員之國家加入本憲章。

2 對於任何加入國，《憲章》應於加入書交存歐洲理事會秘書長處之日起三個月屆滿後下月首日生其效力。

第 21 條

1 任何國家於簽署時或於交存其批准書、接受書、核定書或加入書時，均得對本憲章第 7 條第 2 項至第 5 項提出一項或多項保留。不得為其他保留。

2 任何締約國依前項規定為保留者，得以通知歐洲理事會秘書長之方式全部或部分撤回保留。撤回應於秘書長收受該通知之日生效。

第 22 條

1 任何締約方得隨時以通知歐洲理事會秘書長之方式退出本憲章。

2 該類退出應於自秘書長收受通知之日起六個月屆滿後下月首日生效。

第 23 條

於下列事項，歐洲理事會秘書長應通知理事會會員國及任何已加入本憲章之國家：

  a 任何簽署；

  b 任何批准、接受、核定或加入文書之交存；

  c 本憲章依第 19 條及第 20 條生效之任何日期；

  d 適用第 3 條第 2 項規定時收受之任何通知；

  e 有關本憲章之任何其他行為、通知或通訊。

下列簽署人經正式授權，已簽署本憲章，以資證明。

1992 年 11 月 5 日，於史特拉斯堡完成，英語及法語兩種文本具有同等效力，正本一份，應保存於歐洲理事會之檔案中。歐洲理事會秘書長應將核證無誤副本送交歐洲理事會各會員國及任何受邀加入本憲章之國家。

薩米語言法
（1086/2003）

第一章 — 總則

第 1 節 — *本法宗旨*

本法宗旨係確保薩米人有關維護並發展自身語言與文化之憲法權利。

本法條款載明薩米人有權利於法院及其他公共機關使用自身語言，並載明機關有義務行使與提倡薩米人之語言權利。

本法目標係確保薩米人無論使用何種語言，皆有權利獲得公平審判與接受良好行政服務，並確保薩米人於無須特地指明上述權利之情形下，仍能享有語言權利。

第 2 節 — *適用範圍*

下列公共機關應遵守本法條款：

（1）Enontekiö、Inari、Sodankylä 及 Utsjoki 之市政機關，以及上述一或多個機關隸屬之聯合市政機關；

（2）管轄權全部或部分涵蓋上述機關之法院以及國家區域與地方主管機關；

（3）Lapland 省政府及其附設機關；

（4）薩米議會、薩米事務顧問委員會與《斯科爾特法》（253/ 1995）第 42 節所述之村莊會議；

（5）政府法務總長與國會監察使；

（6）消費者監察使與消費者陳訴委員會、平等監察使與平等委員會、資料保護監察使與資料保護委員會、少數族裔監察使；

（7）社會保險機構與農民社會保險機構；及

（8）審理針對不滿上述行政機關決定所提上訴之國家行政機關。

本法亦適用於管轄權涵蓋全部或一部薩米人原鄉之國家主管機關與畜牧合作社、以及馴鹿牧民協會中依《馴鹿畜牧法》（848/ 1990）與《馴鹿畜牧命令》（883/ 1990）規定之行政程序。

第 17 與 18 節條款載明本法對於國營企業、公司與私人實體之適用；第 30 節條款載明本法對於教會主管機關之適用。

薩米原鄉適用之特別條款載於第三章。

第 3 節 — *定義*

基於本法之目的：

（1）「薩米語」係指伊納里薩米人、斯科爾特薩米人或北薩米人之語言，視使用之語言或主要目標族群而定；

（2）「薩米人」係指（974/ 1995；laki saamelaiskäräjistä）第 3 節所述之薩米人個體；

（3）「薩米原鄉」係指《薩米議會法》第 4 節所述之薩米原鄉；及

（4）「主管機關」係指法院和另外公共機關、畜牧合作社和馴鹿牧民協會，如第 2 節第 1、2 款所述。

第二章 — 語言權利

第4節 — *薩米人於主管機關使用薩米語之權利*

薩米人於本法所述之任何主管機關,有權利就其本身事項或其聽審之事項使用薩米語。

主管機關不得假借薩米人知曉其他語言如芬蘭語或瑞典語為理由,限制或拒絕行使本法載明之語言權利。

第5節 — *法人於主管機關之語言權利*

紀錄語言為薩米語之公司行號和基金會,有權利於主管機關使用其語言;適合情形下,第4節所規定薩米人使用薩米語之權利適用本權利。

相應而言,教學語言為薩米語之教育機構有權利使用薩米語,如第1款規定。

第6節 — *代表機關之使用薩米語*

Enontekiö、Inari、Sodankylä 及 Utsjoki 市政代表機關之薩米人成員,有權利於會議及會議紀錄附加之書面陳述中使用薩米語。本條款適用於國家級理事會、委員會、工作組及薩米原鄉相應多成員組織之薩米人成員,且若討論之事務特別關乎薩米人,則亦適用於薩米原鄉以外之多成員組織之薩米人成員。相應而言,參與馴鹿牧民協會或其委員會會議之薩米人,有權利於會議中使用薩米語。

如有必要,應於本節前述會議安排口譯。

第7節 — *人口登記宣稱薩米語為母語之權利*

符合《自治市居住法》(201/1994)規定之芬蘭薩米人居民,有權利基於人口登記目的宣稱薩米語為其母語。

第8節 — *官方溝通*

主管機關亦應於其向大眾發布之溝通內容使用薩米語。

薩米原鄉之官方廣告、通知與宣傳,及向大眾發布之其他資訊,以及供大眾使用之標示與表格,其說明文字,應以薩米語製作和發布。

惟由地方法院、法官、國家地方法院、同級部會、國家地方獨立局處、或任一該局處之官員針對有關個別利益之事項而發布之官方廣告,通知和公告,若明顯無使用薩米語之必要,則得斟酌單獨使用芬蘭語。

第2節第1、2款所述機關以外之國家主管機關,如本節第1款所述之廣告、通知、宣傳、發布資訊及表格及其說明文字,若內容主要關乎薩米人,或除此以外具有針對薩米人之特別理由,則亦應以薩米語製作和發布。

為選舉與公投製作之通知卡片不得以薩米語製作,惟薩米議會法第24節所述之卡片除外。

第9節 — *法律、其他法令、立法提案與報告*

主要關乎薩米人之法律,以及其他此種法令、條約,及芬蘭法典公布之其他文書與通知,應由政府或相關部會決定亦發布薩米語翻譯版本。本條款適用於部會或另外國家主管機關系列文件公布之命令、指南、決定與通知。

部會或國家級委員會、工作組或相應組織製作與發布之立法提案與報告或其摘要,若內容主要關乎薩米人之法律,或除此以外具有針對薩米人之特別理由,則應由部會決定亦發布薩米語版本。

第10節 — *主管機關使用薩米語為辦公語言*

活動單獨關乎薩米人之主管機關,辦公語言得併用薩米語與芬蘭語。

第三章 — 適用薩米原鄉之條款

第 11 節 — *特別義務*

上文第 2 節第 1 款所述之主管機關，其位於薩米原鄉之辦公室和其他場所亦應遵守第 12 至 16 節之條款。

第 12 節 — *於主管機關使用薩米語之權利*

薩米人於主管機關洽公時，有權利自行選擇使用薩米語或芬蘭語。《語言法》（423/2003）條款載明使用瑞典語之權利。

薩米原鄉以外之國家主管機關，若該機關負責審理針對不滿薩米原鄉內部決定所提之上訴，則薩米人亦享有前述權利。

第 13 節 — *以薩米語接收含決定之文件或其他文件之權利*

某事項所關係之薩米人一方，若該事項關乎其自身權利、利益或義務，則應依請求以薩米語發布傳票申請書、判決書、決定、紀錄或另外文件，惟文件明顯無關事項解決方案時除外。若該事項之薩米人一方就該事項接洽主管機關時，使用薩米語書寫及交談，則應於上述相同範圍內及相同條件下以薩米語發布含決定之文件，無須另行對此提出請求。

惟該事項若涉及多方，且各方並無全體一致使用薩米語，則含決定之文件應僅以薩米語官方翻譯版本之形式發布。

第 14 節 — *薩米語知識與資格要求*

主管機關招聘人員時，應留意各辦公室或其他場所之員工亦能以薩米語服務客戶。此外，主管機關應提供訓練或採取其他辦法，以確保員工具備辦理主管機關職務所必要之薩米語知識。

除非下開資格要求已列於法律或依法通過之條款，否則薩米語知識得透過法律、或依法透過政府命令或相關部門法令，將其規定為國家主管機關員工之資格，並如《自治市法》（365/1995）規定為市政主管機關員工之資格。若相關辦公室、職位或職務並無規定薩米語知識之資格要求，則亦應將薩米語知識視為特殊專長。

適合情形下，《公務機關員工語言知識要求法》（424/ 2003）之條款適用於薩米語資格要求。薩米語知識之驗證，可參考《語言公開測驗法》（668/ 1994）所述測驗之成果、學習歷程中通過之測驗、或高等教育機構學習之成果。

第 15 節 — *主管機關使用薩米語之義務*

主管機關在其寄發依法應向某方或某人告知未決事項或事項將成未決之公告、傳票及信函中，無論程序使用何種語言，若已知或可合理查明接收者之語言，則文件內容應使用接收者之語言，或併用芬蘭語與薩米語。

主管機關回覆以薩米語寫成之書面溝通訊息時，應使用薩米語回覆，毋需另行請求。

主管機關除此之外亦應於其活動中提倡使用薩米語。

第 16 節 — *市政文件使用薩米語*

自治市若去年一月一日時薩米語人口比例占該市人口逾三分之一，則市政機關亦應於紀錄及其他未向私人單位發布、但屬普遍關注性質之文件中使用薩米語。其他自治市之市政機關在視為必要之範圍內，亦應於此種文件中使用薩米語。

第 17 節 — *國營企業與國營或市營公司*

國營企業或由國家或第 2 節第 1 款第 1 項所述一或多個自治市行使職權之服務業公司，於薩米原鄉應提供本法所述之語言服務，亦應以薩米語向大眾提供資訊，其程度應切合活動之性質與脈絡，且整體評估而言其作法不可對企業或公司不合理。本法針對主管機關之規定，亦適用於辦理主管機關職務之國營企業。

第 18 節 — *私人實體提供語言服務之義務*

若公共行政職務依法或根據法律受指派予私人實體，則於薩米原鄉執行職務時，本法針對主管機關之規定適用於該私人實體。若該職務於薩米原鄉之受指派者，係由主管機關之決定或其他辦法所確定，或由受指派者與主管機關簽署之契約所確定，則主管機關應確保該職務執行時有提供本法規定之語言服務。於薩米原鄉指派予私人實體之任務非屬公共行政職務時，若有將本法規定之服務標準定為必要條件，則主管機關亦應確保該職務執行時有提供本法規定之語言服務。

第四章 — 口譯與翻譯權利

第 19 節 — *口譯權利*

符合本法規定之事項使用薩米語進行口頭審理時，該事項應指派予通曉薩米語之官員。若主管機關未有通曉薩米語之官員可承接該事項，則主管機關應免費安排口譯，或自行負責口譯事宜。

第 20 節 — *翻譯含決定之文件或其他文件之權利*

行政事項、行政司法程序事項或刑事事項之傳票申請書、判決書、決定、紀錄或另外文件，已以芬蘭語或瑞典語所擬之，若該事項關乎薩米人一方之權利、利益或義務，則主管機關應依請求為薩米人一方免費提供該文件之薩米語官方翻譯版本，惟文件明顯無關事項解決方案時除外。翻譯版本應附加於含決定之文件或其他文件。

若官方翻譯版本經指出翻譯錯誤，除非顯無修正之必要，否則主管機關應修正該錯誤。此種情形中，修正後之文件應免費提供予薩米人一方。

第 21 節 — *向薩米語司取得翻譯之權利*

符合本法規定之主管機關，且該機關將發布含決定之文件作為薩米語官方翻譯版本或薩米語原文版本，除非可從其他來源便利獲取翻譯，否則該機關有權利向薩米語司取得翻譯。針對該文件提出之薩米語文件，主管機關有相應之權利可取得其芬蘭語翻譯版本。

第 22 節 — *翻譯與口譯費用責任*

若國家主管機關欲向一方發放或發布含決定之文件或其他文件作為薩米語原文版本或薩米語翻譯版本，或欲使用口譯，則國家應負擔文件撰寫或翻譯之費用，或口譯費用。

自治市、聯合市政機關、教區及堂區應負擔第 4–6、12、13、15、16、30 節所述含決定之文件或其他文件撰寫或翻譯之費用，以及口譯費用。

第 23 節 — *客戶出資翻譯*

若客戶遞交薩米語文件予國家主管機關、自治市或聯合市政機關、或教會主管機關，即使客戶並無權利於主管機關使用薩米語，上述主管機關於必要時仍應接收客戶意見，後由客戶出資將該文件翻譯為主管機關所使用語言。

第五章 — 語言權利提倡辦法

第 24 節 — *主管機關保障語言權利之義務*

主管機關應於其活動及自身方面，確保本法保證之語言權利在實務上獲得保障落實。主管機關應向大眾明示其亦有提供薩米語服務。

主管機關得提供優於本法規定之語言服務。

第 25 節 — *進修薩米語之帶薪假及工作自由*

第 2 節第 1 款所述國家主管機關之官員，其管轄權全部處於薩米原鄉內部者，若於該主管機

關任期屆滿一年，則該官員有權利獲帶薪假以進修辦公所需之薩米語知識。該主管機關員工有相應之工作自由權利以進修薩米語。

任職於第 2 節第 1 款所述自治市或聯合市政機關、或任職於第 2 節第 1 款第 2、3 項所述國家主管機關之員工，其管轄權一部處於薩米原鄉內部者，以及任職於馴鹿牧民協會之員工，若任期屆滿一年，則該員工得獲帶薪假及工作自由以進修辦公所需之薩米語知識。帶薪假或工作自由之其他條件，得由政府命令訂定之。

休假或工作自由得訂定如下條件：官員與主管機關簽訂契約，令該官員休假或留職停薪結束後將於薩米原鄉內部之主管機關續任指定期間。任期得寫明於契約內，令該官員若於契約期間內離職或基於疾病以外之個人因素告知即將離職，則該官員至多應賠償語言進修直接費用之數額予主管機關。

第 26 節 — *薩米語司*

薩米議會應置薩米語司負責翻譯及本法規定之其他任務；薩米語司據點應位於薩米原鄉內部。

有關薩米語司之詳細規定，應由政府命令發布。

第 27 節 — *薩米語顧問*

Lapland 省政府與薩米原鄉之國家區域與地方主管機關得置薩米語顧問。顧問應免費向客戶提供服務。

第 28 節 — *督導與監督*

各主管機關負責督導本法於其所轄範圍內之施行情形。

薩米議會負責監督本法施行情形，且得就語言立法相關問題提出建議，並採取行動以糾正其所觀察之瑕疵。。

第 29 節 — *報告*

議會各任期中，薩米議會指派之薩米語司及薩米語委員會應針對下列事項發布報告：薩米語立法實施情形、薩米語權利行使情形、語言條件制定情形，詳細內容由政府命令訂定之。

《語言法》包含有關語言立法實施情形之政府報告規定。

第六章 — 其他規定

第 30 節 — *教會主管機關*

本法針對於國家主管機關使用薩米語之條款，亦適用於 Oulu 教區之教區辦公室、以及全部或一部處於薩米原鄉之堂區辦公室各方之語言，以及含決定之文件及其他文件所使用語言，惟該事項依《教會法》（1054/1993）認定屬教會內部事務者除外；以及適用於 Oulu 東正教教區辦事處。

本法第 1、4、5、8、20、24 節規定，相應適用於 Enontekiö、Inari、Utsjoki 及 Sodankylä 之福音路德教區，惟該事項依《教會法》認定屬教會內部事務者除外；以及適用於 Lapland 東正教堂區。

第 31 節 — *國家經費*

國家預算應撥付金額供國家支援自治市、教區、薩米原鄉內之畜牧合作社、及第 18 節所述私人實體，以支付施行本法之特定額外費用。

第 32 節 — *若干行政脈絡中之薩米語地位*

單獨規定適用於薩米人以母語接受小學與初中教育之權利，適用於以薩米語提供指導，及適用於以薩米語作為教學語言、學科語言與學位語言之地位。

《兒童日托法》（36/1973）條款載明薩米人以母語接受日托之權利。

第 2 節第 1 款所述主管機關施行《病人地位與權利法》（785/1992）與《社會福利地位與權利法》（812/2000）之時，應遵守本法條款。

第 33 節 — *詳細條款*

有關本法實施之詳細條款，應由政府命令發布之。

第七章 — 生效與過渡條款

第 34 節 — *生效*

本法於 2004 年 1 月 1 日生效；本法之生效，廢止《薩米語使用於主管機關法》（516/1991），如之後所修訂。

為利本法實施之必要辦法，得於本法生效前採行。

本法應公布於《芬蘭法典》，亦應翻譯為伊納里薩米語、斯科爾特薩米語或北薩米語。

第 35 節 — *過渡條款*

其他法律或命令提及已廢止之《薩米語使用於主管機關法》者，於本法生效後應視為提及本法。

除非主管機關以其他方式就各方權利與利益作成決定，否則先前立法之條款繼續適用於本法生效前成為未決之事項。

Government.no
薩米法

1987 年 6 月 12 日第 56 號關於薩米議會與其他薩米法律事項之法律（薩米法）
法律 | 日期：2007 年 5 月 29 日 | 地方政府與區域發展部
（http://www.regjeringen.no/en/dep/kdd/id504/）

第一章　總則

§ 1-1. 本法宗旨
本法宗旨係促進挪威薩米人保障並發展自身語言、文化及生活方式。

§ 1-2. 薩米議會
薩米人將成立全國性質之薩米議會，由薩米人於薩米人族群選出。

§ 1-3. 薩米議會年度報告
薩米議會年度報告將呈交國王。

§ 1-4. 國家財務責任
郡與自治市針對薩米議會選舉所產生之特定費用，由國家負擔。
國王將發布有關第 1 項條款實施之法規。

§ 1-5. 薩米語
薩米語與挪威語具同等價值。兩者應根據第三章條款獲授予同等地位。

§ 1-6. 薩米旗幟
薩米旗幟為 1986 年 8 月 15 日第 13 屆挪威薩米大會採用之旗幟。
薩米議會得發布法規以規定薩米旗幟使用辦法之詳細規則。

第二章　薩米議會

§ 2-1. 薩米議會業務與權限
薩米議會之業務，為議會認定對薩米人特別有影響之任何事項。
薩米議會得針對其業務範圍內任何事項自行提出與發揚意見。薩米議會亦得自行將事項轉知公務機關與私人機構等。
供薩米人用途之年度財務預算分配，薩米議會得授權管理之。本部將制定薩米議會財務管理之規則。
薩米議會有權決定上述事項於何種時機遵循本法其他條款，或另行制定規則。

§ 2-2. 徵詢薩米議會意見
其他公務機關應於針對薩米議會業務範圍內任何事項作成決定前，令薩米議會有發表意見之機會。

§ 2-3. 選舉方式、選舉時間與議會任期
薩米議會採直接選舉方式選出。
若選區之提名候選人超過一名，則選舉採比例代表制。其他情形之選舉採多數決。
薩米議會選舉與挪威國會選舉同日舉行。
薩米議會任期四年，自選舉該年十月一日起算。

§ 2-4. 選區與席次分配

薩米議會之選舉，將自下列選區選出三名議員併候補議員：

1. Varanger（South Varanger、Nesseby、Vadsø、Vardø 與 Båtsfjord 自治市）
2. Tana（Tana、Berlevåg 與 Gamvik 自治市）
3. Karasjok（Karasjok 自治市）
4. Kautokeino（Kautokeino 自治市）
5. Porsanger（Porsanger、Lebesby、Nordkapp 與 Måsøy 自治市）
6. Alta/Kvalsund（Kvalsund、Hammerfest、Sørøysund、Alta、Hasvik 與 Loppa 自治市）
7. Nord-Troms（Kvænangen、Nordreisa、Skjervøy、Kåfjord、Storfjord 與 Lyngen 自治市）
8. Midt-Troms（Karlsøy、Tromsø、Balsfjord、Målselv、Bardu、Lenvik、Berg、Torsken 與 Tranøy 自治市）
9. Sør-Troms（Sørreisa、Dyrøy、Salangen、Lavangen、Gratangen、Skånland、Ibestad、Harstad、Bjarkøy 與 Kvæfjord 自治市）
10. Nordre Nordland（Andøy、Øksnes、Bø、Sortland、Hadsel、Vågan、Vestvågøy、Flakstad、Moskenes、Værøy、Røst、Lødingen、Tjeldsund、Evenes 與 Narvik 自治市）
11. Midtre Nordland（Ballangen、Tysfjord、Hamarøy、Steigen、Sørfold、Bodø、Fauske、Skjerstad、Saltdal、Gildeskål、Beiarn 與 Meløy 自治市）
12. 南薩米區（Nordland 郡自 Rana 與 Rødøy 及以南 [包含兩者] 之自治市、Nord-Trøndelag 與 Sør-Trøndelag 兩郡、Hedmark 郡之 Engerdal 自治市）
13. 南 挪 威（Møre og Romsdal、Sogn og Fjordane、Hordaland、Rogaland、Vest-Agder、Aust-Agder、Telemark、Buskerud、Vestfold、Akershus、Østfold、Oppland、Hedmark [Engerdal 自治市除外] 與 Oslo 各郡）。

§ 2-5. 選舉權利

凡選區中有權利於地方政府選舉投票者，以及投票日於選區納入薩米選民登記者（見 § 2-6），皆有權利於薩米議會選舉中投票。

§ 2-6. 薩米選民登記

凡宣稱自認為薩米人者，以及符合下列任一條件者：

a. 以薩米語為母語；或
b. 父母、祖父母或曾祖父母有人以薩米語為母語；或
c. 身為已完成或曾完成薩米選民登記者之子女

得於本身居住之自治市要求另行登記納入薩米選民。

薩米選民登記係根據自治市之國民人口登記、前次選舉所登記之薩米選民、以及議會任期當中收到之選民納入或除籍要求。

一旦於薩米選民登記中納為薩米選民者，該人得登記於國民人口登記。上述登記內容僅能由負責舉行薩米議會選舉之主管機關查閱，或經本部同意後查閱。

薩米選民登記得採電子方式保存。

§ 2-7. 選舉資格與候選人提名權利

凡於選區納入薩米選民登記者，皆有資格參與薩米議會選舉。參選者亦應於投票日於國民人口登記中納入選區居民。惟薩米議會之行政人員無資格參與選舉。

凡於選區納入薩米選民登記者，皆有權利於選區提名候選人。候選人提名名單應由至少 15 名有提名權利之薩米人連署。

社團、黨派或類似協會得向薩米議會申請登記為特定黨名。登記之要求應由至少 200 名有資格於薩米議會選舉中投票及提名候選人者連署支持。國王得就登記之條件與程序制定詳細條款。

§2-8. 接受選舉之義務、豁免理由與出席會議之義務

凡有資格參與薩米議會選舉者，除非具備本節第二款之豁免理由，否則皆有接受選舉之義務。

凡有下列情形者，得行使聲稱豁免選舉之權利：

a. 截至選舉該年底已屆六十歲；或

b. 前四年已擔任薩米議會議員；或

c. 向選區之薩米選舉委員會證明，自身於履行薩米議會議員義務方面將有極大困難。

凡獲選為薩米議會議員者，或獲選為薩米議會指派機構之成員者，除非具備無法出席之合理理由，否則皆有義務出席薩米議會或各機構之會議。

員工於薩米議會或於指派為成員之機構所應負義務之要求範圍內，有請假之資格。

§2-9. 議會任內之豁免與請辭

履行自身公事義務時將有極大困難之薩米議會議員，得申請由薩米議會於指定期間或剩餘任期內減輕自身公事。

依《憲法》第53條喪失投票權利之議員，或加入薩米議會行政人員之議員，其剩餘任期應請辭薩米議會。

§2-10. 選舉主管機關

薩米議會為薩米議會選舉之最高選舉主管機關。

§2-11. 補充選舉條款

國王得頒布有關薩米議會選舉之補充條款。

§2-12. 薩米議會之行政、組織與程序

薩米議會自有行政組織。行政人員由薩米議會指派。

適合情形下，薩米議會員工應遵守適用於公務員之立法。

薩米議會得成立任何其認為適合之理事會、政務會或委員會，且除非另有規定，否則薩米議會得授權予上述組織。

第2-9、2-10、2-14節所述之決策權不可轉讓授權。

理事會、政務會或委員會作成之個別決定，於符合《公共行政法》條款之情形下，得向薩米議會或由薩米議會指派之任何特別申訴委員會申訴之。

§2-13. 會議語言

薩米議會會議中，所有人士有權利依個人意願使用薩米語或挪威語。

§2-14. 程序規則

薩米議會將頒布有關薩米議會召集與議程之規則。

§2-15. 薩米議會全職議員有資格領取符合另外退休金計畫規定之退休金。國王得頒布法規以規定薩米議會其他議員亦有資格領取退休金。

國王得就退休金權利之估算與退休金計畫之實施，頒布詳細法規。

第三章　薩米語

§3-1. 定義

下列定義應適用於本章：

1.「薩米語行政區」係指 Karasjok、Kautokeino、Nesseby、Porsanger、Tana 和 Kåfjord 自治市。

2.「公務機關」係指任何國家或自治市機關。

3.「行政區地方公務機關」係指管轄權涵蓋薩米語行政區之自治市或一部自治市之任何自治市、郡或

國家機關。

4.「行政區區域公務機關」係指管轄權涵蓋全部或一部薩米語行政區一個以上自治市、惟未涵蓋全郡之任何郡或國家機關。

§3-2. 規則翻譯：通告與表單

特別關乎全部或一部薩米人之法令規章,應翻譯為薩米語。

公務機關特別針對行政區全部或一部人口發布之通告,應同時採用薩米語與挪威語。

有關行政區地方或區域公務機關使用之表單,應同時提供薩米語與挪威語版本。國王將就本條款之實施頒布詳細規則。

§3-3. 取得薩米語回復之權利

凡向行政區地方公務機關提出申請者,有資格取得薩米語之回覆。惟倘若向上述機關辦公室以外處所辦公之官員提出口頭申請,則本條款不適用之.。

凡向行政區區域公務機關提出書面申請者,有資格取得薩米語之書面回覆。特殊情形中,國王得例外處理特定之區域公務機關。

§3-4. 司法體系使用薩米語之延伸權利

若法院之管轄權涵蓋全部或一部行政區,則亦應適用下列有關薩米語使用之規定:

1. 任何人皆有權利遞交以薩米語寫成之含附件書面訴狀、書面證據或其他書面申請。若法院欲將申請文件遞送對造,則法院應確保文件需翻譯為挪威語。於對造同意下,得省略翻譯程序。

2. 若法定合法程序允許以口頭申請代替書面申請,則任何人皆有權利以薩米語向法院提出口頭申請。若法院有義務將申請事宜作成書面紀錄,則提出申請者得要求該紀錄以薩米語寫成。此種要求不妨礙任何時間限制。第 1 款第二、三句相應適用之。

3. 任何人皆有權利於法院開庭時講說薩米語。若有不諳薩米語者出席訴訟程序,應採用由法院指派或准許之口譯。

4. 經當事人任一方之請求,法院庭長得決定訴訟程序使用之語言應為薩米語。第 3 款第二句相應適用之。

5. 若訴訟程序使用之語言為薩米語,法院庭長得決定法院紀錄亦應採用薩米語。法院將確保該紀錄需翻譯為挪威語。

6. 一旦當事人任一方提出要求,法院將確保以挪威語寫成之法院紀錄需翻譯為薩米語。此種要求不妨礙任何時間限制。

管轄權涵蓋全部或一部行政區之警察與檢察主管機關,亦應遵守下列有關薩米語使用之規定:

1. 任何人皆有權利於機關辦公室接受訊問時講說薩米語。

2. 任何人於口頭上提出正式投訴或發出尋求司法救濟之口頭通知時,皆有權利講說薩米語。

Troms 與 Finnmark 之監獄機關,亦應遵守下列有關薩米語使用之規定:

1. 第 3-5 節相應適用於監獄受刑人。

2. 監獄受刑人有資格以薩米語彼此交談及與親戚交談。

3. 監獄受刑人向監獄主管機關發出尋求司法救濟之口頭通知時,有資格講說薩米語。

§3-5. 公衛與社會部門使用薩米語之延伸權利

凡於行政區欲使用薩米語以維護自身有關地方與區域公衛與社會機構方面之利益者,皆有資格以薩米語接受服務。

§3-6. 個別教會服務

凡於行政區之挪威會眾教會者,皆有資格以薩米語接受個別教會服務。

§3-7. 進修請假權利

行政區之地方或區域公務機關若需具備薩米語知識，則機關員工有資格請帶薪假。本權利得訂定條件，令員工完訓後需於上述機關服務指定期間。國王得就本條款之實施頒布詳細規則。

§3-8. 薩米語受教權利

任何人皆有權利以薩米語接受教育。國王得就本條款之實施頒布詳細規則。

有關小學與中學以薩米語及透過薩米語施教方面，應適用《小學與初中教育法》及《高中教育法》之條款及據其規定之條款。

§3-9. 市政管理之薩米語

市議會得決定薩米語於全部或一部市政管理中應與挪威語具同等地位。

§3-10. 條款範圍延伸

本章條款限於行政區地方或區域公務機關者，國王得決定其全部或一部亦應適用於代表國家或自治市作成決定之其他公務機關或私法人。

§3-11. 申訴

若公務機關未遵守本章條款，該情事之直接相關人士得向當事機關之直屬上級機關提出申訴。當申訴情事關乎自治市或郡機關時，郡長為接受申訴之對象。

職務對全部或一部薩米人口具特殊重要性之全國性薩米組織及國家公務機關，於上述情事有權利提出申訴。相同權利適用於無個別人士特別受影響之情形。

§3-12. 薩米語委員會

薩米語委員會已成立。薩米議會負責指派該會之委員，並決定委員長與副委員長人選。

國王將就薩米語委員會之成分、組織、任期、職務等頒布詳細規則。

第四章　過渡條款與生效

§4-1. 過渡條款

薩米議會為挪威薩米議會之進一步發展。薩米議會將承接挪威薩米議會之全部職務、權利與義務。

國王將頒布有關薩米議會召集與議程之規則。上述規則應適用至薩米議會已根據第 2-14 節制定自身程序規則為止。

§4-2. 生效

本法於國王決定之日期生效。

地方政府與區域發展部

主題

| 法律與命令 | | 薩米人 |

 Government.no

地方政府與區域發展部網頁負責單位：
編輯：Kjersti Bjørgo
網頁編輯：Henrik Enevold

電話：+47 22 24 90 90
E-mail: postmottak@kmd.dep.no
本部聯絡窗口：Depkatalog
識別編號：972 417 858

薩米語法律：瑞典

瑞典法典編號：2009:600
部會／局處：文化部
標題：語言法（2009:600）
頒布日期：2009 年 5 月 28 日

本法內容與宗旨

第 1 節

本法條款規定瑞典語、國家少數民族語言與瑞典手語。本法條款亦規定公部門有責任確保個體可取用語言，以及規定公部門及國際場合之語言使用。

第 2 節

本法宗旨係明定瑞典語及其他語言於瑞典社會之地位與用途。本法亦旨在保護瑞典語與瑞典之語言多樣性，以及保護個體可取用語言。

第 3 節

若其他法令之條款殊異於本法，則該條款適用之。

瑞典語

第 4 節

瑞典語為瑞典之主要語言。

第 5 節

瑞典語為主要語言，通行於社會，瑞典每位居民皆可取用瑞典語，且瑞典語可使用於社會所有領域。

第 6 節

公部門有使用與發展瑞典語之特殊責任。

國家少數民族語言

第 7 節

國家少數民族語言為芬蘭語、意第緒語、梅安語（托爾訥河谷芬蘭語）、羅曼尼奇布語與薩米語。

第 8 節

公部門有保護與提倡國家少數民族語言之特殊責任。

瑞典手語

第 9 節

公部門有保護與提倡瑞典手語之特殊責任。

公部門之語言使用

第 10 節

法院、行政主管機關及於公部門辦公之其他機關之語言為瑞典語。
其他立法之條款規定使用國家少數民族語言及其他北日耳曼語之權利。
另有條款規定法院與行政主管機關使用口譯員及翻譯文件之義務。

第 11 節

公部門之語言應具素養、簡潔及可理解。

第 12 節

政府機關有特殊責任，應確保其各專業領域之瑞典專有名詞易於理解，並確保使用與發展此類專有名詞。

國際場合之瑞典語

第 13 節

瑞典語為瑞典於國際場合之官方語言。

瑞典語作為歐盟官方語言之地位應受維護。

個人所選擇使用之語言

第 14 節

瑞典全體居民皆有機會學習、發展與使用瑞典語。此外，

1. 身分為國家少數民族者，有機會學習、發展與使用少數民族語言；且

2. 聽障人士或因其他理由需要手語者，有機會學習、發展與使用瑞典手語。

母語非屬第一項所述任一語言者，有機會發展與使用其母語。

第 15 節

公部門有責任依照第 14 節規定確保個人所選擇使用之語言。

勃蘭登堡邦索勃人權利組織法（索勃人法 -SWG）

1994 年 7 月 7 日（GVBl.I/94，【第 21 號】，第 294 頁）
最近一次根據本法第 2 條修改，日期為 2018 年 10 月 15 日（GVBl.I/18，【第 23 號】）

目錄

前言
第 1 條 民族身分權
第 2 條 索勃民族
第 3 條 索勃人傳統居住區
第 4 條 索勃民族旗幟
第 4a 條 索勃人社團和協會聯合會和社團上訴權
第 5 條 邦議會索勃人事務理事會
第 5a 條 邦政府索勃人事務專員
第 5b 條 邦政府報告
第 6 條 社區索勃人事務專員
第 7 條 文化
第 8 條 語言
第 9 條 研究與學術
第 10 條 教育
第 11 條 傳統居住區內的雙語標識
第 12 條 媒體
第 13 條 跨邦合作
第 13a 條 支出補償
第 13b 條 法規授權
第 13c 條 臨時條例
第 14 條 公布
附件：本法生效時索勃人傳統居住區的鄉鎮和鄉鎮區域

前言

索勃人從幾世紀前就開始在勞席茨地區聚居，雖然在歷史上曾多次被嘗試同化，但索勃人的語言和文化仍保留至今。應遵從索勃人的意願，在未來繼續保護和加強其民族特徵，

- 促進傳統居住區位於勃蘭登堡邦和薩克森邦的索勃人的民族團結，
- 鑒於德意志聯邦共和國是索勃人的祖國，需要承認索勃人平等的公民地位，並致力於保護、支援和發展其語言和文化，
- 勃蘭登堡邦在保護、繼承、維護和支持索勃人民族身分方面負有重要責任，
- 需要與薩克森邦開展緊密合作，
- 保護和加強勞席茨地區獨一無二的德意志 - 索勃雙元文化特徵，
- 索勃人的民族身分權和維護少數民族權利的完整性是人權和自由權的一部分。
- 德意志聯邦共和國作出了一系列旨在保護和支持國內少數民族的國際承諾，主要包括《歐盟基本權利憲章》《歐盟反歧視指令》《保護少數民族框架公約》和《歐洲區域或少數民族語言憲章》。
- 根據《基本法》第 3 條、《統一條約》第 35 條第 14 號議定書注釋，以及《勃蘭登堡邦憲法》第 25 條，邦議會通過了以下法律：

第 1 條
民族身分權

（1）在勃蘭登堡邦生活的索勃民族居民是享有平等權利的本國人民的組成部分。

（2）索勃民族和每個索勃人都有權自由表達、維護和發展他們的民族、文化和語言特徵，不應違反其意願嘗試進行任何同化。

（3）索勃民族和每個索勃人都有權保護、繼承和維護他們的民族特徵。勃蘭登堡邦以及位於索勃人傳統居住區內的鄉鎮和鄉鎮社團需保護該權利，並為索勃居民保護和發展其語言、傳統和文化遺產提供支援。需有效確保索勃人的政治參與權。

第 2 條
索勃民族

任何承認自身為索勃人的公民均屬於索勃民族。這種認同是自由的，不得對其進行質疑或核查。不得因這種認同對該公民進行歧視。

第 3 條
索勃人傳統居住區

（1）需確保索勃民族保護、繼承和維護他們的傳統居住區的權利。在制定邦和社區政策時需要考慮索勃人傳統居住區（以下簡稱「傳統居住區」）的特殊性和索勃人的權益。

（2）本法意義上的傳統居住區包括Cottbus/Chóśebuz縣級市，以及 Dahme-Spreewald 縣、Oberspreewald-Lausitz 縣和 Spree-Neiße/Sprjewja-Nysa 縣的鄉鎮和鄉鎮區域，在這些地區有持續到現在的索勃民族語言或文化傳統。具體而言，在 2014 年 2 月 11 日《勃蘭登堡邦索勃人權利法修訂案》（GVBl. I 第 7 號）生效時，傳統居住區包括本法附件中所列的鄉鎮和區域。

（3）鄉鎮所屬關係的變化不會造成其脫離傳統居住區範圍。當鄉鎮合併時，曾屬於傳統居住區的鄉鎮變更為歸屬於傳統居住區的鄉鎮區域。若由於開發礦產原因需要將傳統居住區內的鄉鎮或區域居民遷移，且根據《勃蘭登堡邦褐煤支持法》第 3 條無法在傳統居住區內找到合適的遷移地點，則需要將新的遷移地點歸入傳統居住區範圍內。

（4）傳統居住區確定了實施保護和支援索勃民族特徵的區域措施的地理範圍。在個別情況下，負責索勃人事務的部門可在徵求各地區和邦議會索勃人事務理事會意見後，根據鄉鎮申請暫時豁免區域措施。根據第 13c 條第 1 款規定，豁免期限不得超過傳統居住區設立後的 4 年。

第 4 條
索勃民族旗幟

索勃民族旗幟由藍、紅、白三種顏色組成。該旗幟可與國家標誌同等使用。

第 4a 條
索勃人社團和協會聯合會和社團上訴權

（1）索勃民族和索勃人的權益在鄉鎮和社區層面可由獲得批准的索勃人社團和協會聯合會代表。

（2）索勃人社團和協會聯合會由負責索勃人事務的部門徵求邦議會索勃人事務理事會意見後批准，根據章程，該聯合會

　　1. 不僅要暫時支持索勃民族的權益，

　　2. 還要在獲得批准後至少存續 3 年時間，並在此期間承擔第（1）項規定的職責，

　　3. 提供符合實際的履行任務的保證；在審批時需要考慮社團當前工作的類型和範圍、成員範圍、民主的內部結構和社團的運作能力，

　　4. 此外，根據《法人所得稅法》第 5 條第 1 款第 9 項規定，由於此類社團屬於公益性質，因此免除法人所得稅。

（3）若邦或地方政府採取的措施或其不作為違反了邦關於索勃民族或索勃人權利的法律法規，則根據

第 2 款規定獲得批准的聯合會可在不損害自身權利的情況下，對邦或地方政府採取的措施或其不作為提出上訴。若一位索勃人自身通過訴訟或本可以通過訴訟追求自身的權利，則根據第 1 句規定的上訴是不可受理的。

第 5 條
邦議會索勃人事務理事會

（1）索勃人事務理事會在每一屆邦議會任期內選舉產生。委員會由 5 名成員組成。根據第 2 款選出的委員會成員由邦議會主席任命。在組成新一屆索勃人事務理事會前由當前理事會履行相應職責。

（2）由根據第 4a 條組建的聯合會開展一次自由、平等、不記名的理事會成員直接選舉，並任命一個選舉委員會，該選舉委員會需從其成員中推選一名選舉負責人。按照《勃蘭登堡邦選舉法》規定，所有在本邦擁有選舉權的索勃人均可參與選舉。滿足第 2 句規定的前提是已申請在選民登記表中登記。聯合會需按照第 4a 條規定在一個辦事處內共同設立一個選舉登記處。在章程中規定以索勃人事務為主要工作目標的協會和社團可將候選人申請遞交給選舉負責人。所有已在邦議會索勃人事務理事會的選民登記表中登記，且已滿 18 歲的索勃人均可被推選。已在選民登記表中登記的選民可通過郵寄選舉的方式投票。選舉結果由選舉委員會確定。得票最多的前 5 位候選人當選。若出現得票數相同的情況，則由選舉負責人抽籤決定。準備和開展選舉的必要支出由勃蘭登堡邦承擔。邦政府中負責內政事務的成員有權在徵求索勃人事務理事會的意見並與邦議會主委員會進行協商後，通過法律法規管理成立選舉機構、選舉資格、選民登記表、確定選舉日期、根據第 5 句規定的候選人資格、選舉準備和實施、根據第 11 句規定的支出補償等具體事項。

（3）索勃人事務理事會向邦議會提供諮詢建議。其職責是在所有關於索勃人權利的諮詢事務中維護索勃人的權益。邦議會將聽取該理事會的意見。在進行相應諮詢事務時，理事會成員在各委員會中進行諮詢投票。具體事項由邦議會議事規則規定。

（4）理事會成員自願行使其職權。他們可獲得工作津貼。具體事項由邦議會主席指導方針規定。第 2 句中的津貼也包括在勃蘭登堡邦外出差的差旅費，只要出差目的與理事會在國家或歐盟層面的工作相關。

第 5a 條
邦政府索勃人事務專員

邦政府將任命一位元索勃人事務專員。他 / 她將在所有關於索勃人問題上支持各部門間的協調合作。

第 5b 條
邦政府報告

邦政府需在任期中期時向邦議會提交一份關於邦內索勃民族情況的報告，報告需根據關於保護索勃語言和文化的國際義務擬定。報告應包括現狀描述，分析索勃語言和文化支援政策的有效性，並闡述邦政府的相關計畫。

第 6 條
社區索勃人事務專員

（1）每個傳統居住區內的縣和 Cottbus/Chóśebuz 縣級市都應設立一個專門的索勃人事務專員全職崗位，並在社區自治權範圍內採取保護索勃人權益的其他相關措施。

（2）傳統居住區內的各政府部門、自治市、鄉鎮和社區團體均應在社區自治權範圍內任命一名索勃人事務專員，或採取保護索勃人權益的其他相關措施。

（3）索勃人事務專員代表索勃人的利益。他 / 她是索勃人的對口連絡人，致力於促進索勃人和非索勃人的繁榮共存。各縣的專員還將為鄉鎮、社區團體和各政府部門的索勃人事務提供支援。專員辦公地點設在各行政部門辦公地。專員需遵守《勃蘭登堡邦市政憲法》第 19 條第 2、3 款規定。《勃蘭登堡邦社區共同體工作法》的相關規定不受影響。

第 7 條
文化

（1）勃蘭登堡邦將保護和支持索勃文化。其主要通過加入與索勃民族相關的基金會履行支持索勃文化的義務。

（2）傳統居住區內的鄉鎮和社區團體將在其文化工作中融入索勃文化。其將支持索勃藝術和習俗，促進當地居民尊重索勃傳統，以包容、相互尊重的方式共存。

第 8 條
語言

（1）勃蘭登堡邦將索勃語言——特別是低地索勃語——視為本邦精神和文化遺產之一，並鼓勵使用這一語言。公民可自由使用這一語言。在公共場合說寫索勃語是受到保護和支持的。

（2）任何傳統居住區內的居民都有權在邦立機構和受其監管的法人主體、公益性機構和基金會，以及在鄉鎮和社區團體的辦公場所使用低地索勃語。若居民行使了這一權利，則應產生與使用德語同樣的效果。使用低地索勃語提出的問題和要求可用低地索勃語回答和決定。不得因此向居民收取費用或進行其它歧視性行為。

第 9 條
研究與學術

勃蘭登堡邦支持針對低地索勃語地區及索勃歷史和文化的研究和學術。將在這一地區與薩克森邦開展緊密合作。

第 10 條
教育

（1）在父母願意的情況下，應向傳統居住區內的兒童和青少年提供學習低地索勃語的機會。傳統居住區內的幼兒園和中小學有義務及時告知父母和學生學習低地索勃語的機會。

（2）傳統居住區內的幼兒園和中小學應在其遊戲設計和教育工作中根據學生年齡段加入不同的索勃歷史和文化知識。

（3）勃蘭登堡邦將與薩克森邦合作培養能夠教授低地索勃語和雙語課程的教師，以滿足第 1 款中提出的教育目標。這需要保證提供合適的語言實踐和教學法培訓，以及低地索勃人的語言、文學、歷史和文化知識教育。

（4）勃蘭登堡邦將為幼兒園教師提供低地索勃語的培訓、進修和繼續教育。

（5）還將保證在教師的培訓、進修和繼續教育中提供關於索勃歷史和文化的知識教育。積極宣傳上述培訓、進修和繼續教育課程。

（6）在將低地索勃語作為教學語言的中小學需配備掌握低地索勃語的師資力量。

（7）將通過提供成人繼續教育課程保護和傳承索勃語言和文化。

（8）勃蘭登堡邦致力於在為公職人員提供的培訓和繼續教育課程中考慮索勃人的利益，並加入低地索勃語知識的學習內容，同時積極宣傳這些課程。

第 11 條
傳統居住區內的雙語標識

（1）傳統居住區內的公共建築和設施、街道、小徑、廣場、橋樑和路標，以及指向這些地區的路牌均需用德語和低地索勃語兩種語言表示。

（2）勃蘭登堡邦致力於將傳統居住區內的其他建築也用德語和低地索勃語雙語標識，只要這些建築具有公共作用。

第 12 條
媒體

（1）在公共媒體節目中適當考慮索勃文化和語言。
（2）勃蘭登堡邦致力於讓私營媒體也考慮索勃文化和語言。

第 13 條
跨邦合作

勃蘭登堡邦支持下勞席茨和上勞席茨的索勃人開展文化交流。為實現這一目標，勃蘭登堡邦將與薩克森邦緊密合作。這包括兩邦共同資助開展索勃語言、文化和歷史保護和研究的機構，以及提供索勃文化教學的相關機構的活動。勃蘭登堡邦支援索勃協會和機構與其他聯邦和國家開展合作。

第 13a 條
支出補償

勃蘭登堡邦將為傳統居住區內的鄉鎮和社區團體開展本法中的各項活動成本提供財政補償。補償費用包括：

    1. 設置索勃人事務全職專員（第 6 條第 1 款）的費用；
    2. 使用低地索勃語（第 8 條）的行政費用；
    3. 在公共建築和設施、道路、廣場、橋樑和路標使用雙語標識的費用（第 11 條）。

根據第 1 句和第 2 句提供的補償金是為了履行本法規定的任務。補償金額根據額外費用確定。

第 13b 條
法規授權

（1）邦政府中負責內政事務的成員有權在與邦議會中負責內政事務的委員會和索勃人事務理事會進行協商後，通過法律法規管理第 8 條具體事項的實施。
（2）邦政府中負責中小學和幼兒園的成員有權在與邦議會中負責中小學和幼兒園的委員會以及索勃人事務理事會進行協商後，通過法律法規管理第 10 條的具體事項。
（3）邦政府中負責交通的成員有權在與邦議會中負責交通的委員會以及索勃人事務理事會進行協商後，通過法律法規管理第 11 條的具體事項。
（4）邦政府中負責索勃人事務的成員有權在與邦議會中負責索勃人事務的委員會以及索勃人事務理事會進行協商後，通過法律法規管理關於建立根據第 13a 條審查和支付成本相關費用的流程的具體事項。

針對過去財政年度的記錄允許對下一年進行預測的情況，法規允許確定一個基於人員費和材料費的年度總費用，並根據申請批准補償一年的額外費用。在 2014 年 2 月 11 日《勃蘭登堡邦索勃人權利法修訂案》（GVBl. I 第 7 號）生效後的前兩個完整財政年度後，應對成本補償額度進行整體評估。

第 13c 條
臨時條例

（1）負責索勃人事務的部門可根據鄉鎮或索勃人事務理事會的申請，在與邦議會主委員會進行協商後修改傳統居住區範圍。在徵求各鄉鎮、縣、獲得批准的索勃人聯合會以及索勃人事務理事會的意見後可作出該決定。若負責部門在審查申請後確定，申請地區沒有達到本法規定的從屬傳統居住區的前提條件，則需將相關情況上報給邦議會。根據第 1 句規定提出申請的時限為本法生效後的 24 個月內。
（2）邦政府中負責索勃人事務的成員有權在與邦議會總委員會以及索勃人事務理事會進行協商後，通過法律法規管理根據第 1 款規定的申請流程和申請審查的具體事項。

第 14 條
公布

本法使用德語和低地索勃語公布。

附件

本法生效時索勃人傳統居住區的鄉鎮和鄉鎮區域

1. Briesen / Brjazyna
2. Burg (Spreewald) / Bórkowy (Błota)
3. Byhleguhre-Byhlen / Běła Góra-Bělin
4. Cottbus / Chóśebuz
5. Dissen-Striesow / Dešno-Strjažow
6. Drachhausen / Hochoza
7. Drebkau / Drjowk
8. Drehnow / Drjenow
9. Felixsee - Ortsteil Bloischdorf / Feliksowy jazor - wejsny źěl Błobošojce
10. Forst (Lausitz) - Ortsteil Horno / Barść (Łužyca) - měsćański źěl Rogow
11. Guhrow / Góry
12. Heinersbrück / Móst
13. Hornow-Wadelsdorf / Lěśće-Zakrjejc
14. Jänschwalde / Janšojce
15. Kolkwitz / Gołkojce
16. Lübbenau / Spreewald / Lubnjow / Błota
17. Neu Zauche / Nowa Niwa
18. Peitz / Picnjo
19. Schmogrow-Fehrow / Smogorjow-Prjawoz
20. Spremberg / Grodk
21. Straupitz / Tšupc
22. Tauer / Turjej
23. Teichland / Gatojce
24. Turnow-Preilack / Turnow-Pśiłuk
25. Vetschau / Spreewald / Wětošow/Błota
26. Werben / Wjerbno
27. Welzow - Ortsteil Proschim / Wjelcej - měsćański źěl Prožym
28. Wiesengrund - Ortsteil Mattendorf / Łukojce - wejsny źěl Matyjojce

---

編者注：
所附檔包含自 2019 年 1 月 1 日起開始實施的《索勃人法》的索勃語翻譯。這是由 BRAVORS 編輯部作為服務提供的非官方文本，不是官方公布的法律條文。
非官方索勃人法文本

薩克森自由邦
憲法

1992 年 5 月 27 日
薩克森邦議會於 1992 年 5 月 26 日的立憲大會上通過以下憲法：

序言
在麥森邊區、
薩克森邦和下西里西亞地區的歷史傳承下，在薩克森歷史憲法的支撐下，
薩克森自由邦的人民挺過了國家社會主義和共產主義暴政的苦難歷史，
銘記著其犯下的歷史罪惡，
以服務正義、和平和保護創造力的意願為指引，
並感恩於 1989 年 10 月的和平解放，
薩克森邦制定了本憲法。

第 1 章
薩克森邦的基礎

第 1 條
【憲法原則】

[1] 薩克森自由邦是德意志聯邦共和國的一個聯邦。[2] 它是一個民主的社會法治邦，致力於保護自然生存基礎和文化。

第 2 條
【首府、邦色、邦徽】

（1）薩克森邦首府是德勒斯登。

（2）邦色是白色和綠色。

（3）[1] 邦徽是一個被黑色和金色分成 9 塊的傾斜的綠色花環。[2] 具體事項由一部法律規定。

（4）在索勃人居住區除邦色和邦徽外也可同等使用索勃人的顏色和徽章，在邦內的西里西亞地區也可使用西里西亞人的顏色和徽章。

第 3 條
【自由邦權力的行使和分配】

（1）[1] 所有自由邦權力來自人民。[2] 它既由人民在選舉和投票中行使，也通過專門的立法、行政和司法機構行使。

（2）[1] 立法權由邦議會或直接由人民行使。[2] 行政權由邦政府和行政部門行使。[3] 司法權由獨立的法官行使。

（3）立法權受憲法規章約束，行政和司法權受法律法規約束。

第 4 條
【選舉和投票原則】

（1）所有根據憲法由人民進行的選舉和投票都應是面向全體、直接、自由、平等和不記名的。

（2）所有在邦內居住或長期停留，並在選舉或投票日當天年滿 18 歲的公民都擁有選舉和投票權。

（3）[1] 具體事項由法律規定。[2] 其中，只有在本邦停留的時間達到特定時長的公民，以及雖擁有多處住

所，但主要居住地位於邦內的公民，才擁有選舉和投票權。

第 5 條
【自由邦公民、少數民族】

（1）[1]薩克森邦公民包括德意志族、索勃民族和其他民族的居民。[2]薩克森邦承認其擁有故鄉的權利。

（2）薩克森邦將確保和保護德國籍少數民族和種族維護其身分以及傳承其語言、宗教、文化和風俗的權利。

（3）薩克森邦尊重在本邦合法居留的外國少數民族的權益。

第 6 條
【索勃人】

（1）[1]在本邦生活的索勃民族居民是本邦公民的平等組成部分。[2]薩克森邦將確保和保護他們維護其身分以及傳承其語言、宗教、文化和風俗的權利，特別是通過中小學、學前班和文化機構。

（2）[1]在邦和地方規劃中要考慮索勃人民的生活需求。[2]需保護索勃民族居住地的德意志——索勃文化特徵。

（3）薩克森邦致力於促進索勃人的合作，特別是在上勞席茨和下勞席茨地區。

第 7 條
【將體面的生活作為自由邦目標】

（1）薩克森邦認可每個人都應享有體面生活的權利，特別是工作權、舒適居住權、體面生活權、社會保障權和教育權。

（2）薩克森邦致力於履行集體義務，為老人和殘疾人提供支援，並為他們提供平等的生活條件。

第 8 條
【促進男女平等】

促進男女在法律和事實上的平等是薩克森邦的一大責任。

第 9 條
【兒童和青少年保護】

（1）薩克森邦致力於保護每一位兒童在心理、精神和身體方面健康成長的權利。

（2）讓青少年遠離品德、精神和身體上的危險。

（3）薩克森邦支持針對兒童和青少年的預防性健康防護，以及建立護理設施。

第 10 條
【保護自然生存基礎】

（1）[1]保護作為生存基礎的環境是薩克森邦和所有本邦居民的義務，也是為了下一代需要承擔的責任。[2]薩克森邦將保護土地、天空、水域、動植物，以及包括不斷擴大的居住區在內的全部領土。[3]它致力於實現原材料的節約利用和回收，以及能源和水資源的節約使用。

（2）[1]獲得批准的環保社團擁有根據法律規定參與與環境相關的行政程式的權利。[2]它們可在環境問題上提起法律訴訟；具體事項由一部法律規定。

（3）[1]薩克森邦將保護公民享受自然美景和在大自然中放鬆的權利，只要其與第 1 款中的目標不衝突。[2]這就是說要讓公眾能夠接觸高山、森林、田野、湖泊和河流。

第 11 條
【支持文化、藝術、科學和體育】

（1）薩克森邦支持文化、藝術和科學創造及體育活動，以及這些領域間的交流。

（2）[1]所有公民都有權參與各類文化和體育活動。[2]為實現這一目標需建立面向公眾開放的博物館、圖書館、檔案館、紀念館、劇院、體育館、音樂和其他文化設施，以及大學、獨立學院、中小學和

其他教育設施。

（3）[1]紀念碑和其他文化產品受到薩克森邦的保護和維護。[2]薩克森邦致力於確保它們在本地留存。

第 12 條
【跨境地區合作】

薩克森邦支援跨境地區合作，以擴展鄰國關係，促進歐洲共同發展和世界的和平發展。

第 13 條
【達成自由邦目標的義務】

薩克森邦有義務根據其能力追求本憲法中規定的目標，並採取行動為之努力。

第 2 章
基本權利

第 14 條
【公民尊嚴】

（1）[1]公民尊嚴不可侵犯。[2]尊重和保護公民尊嚴是所有自由邦權力機關的義務。

（2）公民尊嚴的不可侵犯性是所有基本權利的基礎。

第 15 條
【全面的行動自由】

每位公民都享有自由發展其個性的權利，只要這不違反其他權利，且不與憲法規定或道德準則相抵觸。

第 16 條
【生命權、身體完整權和人身自由權】

（1）[1]每位公民都享有生命權和身體完整權。[2]人身自由權不可侵犯。[3]只有基於一部法律才可對這幾項權利進行干涉。

（2）任何人都不得遭受殘酷、非人道或有辱人格的待遇或處罰，也不得在未經本人自願和明確同意情況下對其進行科學或其他實驗。

第 17 條
【剝奪自由的法律基礎】

（1）[1]只有基於一部正式法律才能按照其規定的方式限制公民的自由。[2]且必須立刻告知該公民限制其自由的原因。

（2）[1]只有法官才可作出允許和延長剝奪自由的決定。[2]任何非基於司法命令剝奪自由的情況必須及時獲得司法決定。[3]員警根據自身的權利將人拘留的時間不得長於其被捕當天結束。[4]具體事項由一部法律規定。

（3）[1]任何因有刑事犯罪嫌疑被暫時逮捕的公民最遲要在被捕後的第二天被帶見法官，法官要告知嫌疑人逮捕的原因，對其進行審訊並給與其提出抗辯的機會。[2]法官必須立即開具一份寫有原因的書面逮捕令，或要求釋放。

（4）任何關於允許或延長剝奪自由的司法決定都需立即通知被拘留人的一位受託人或家庭成員。

第 18 條
【平等原則】

（1）法律面前人人平等。

（2）男女平等。

（3）任何人都不得因其性別、出身、種族、語言、家鄉和籍貫、信仰、宗教或政治傾向受到歧視或優

待。

第 19 條
【信仰、良心和宗教自由】

（1）信仰自由、良心自由以及宗教和世界觀自由不可侵犯。

（2）應保證宗教活動不受干擾。

第 20 條
【觀點、新聞和廣播自由】

（1）[1]任何公民都有以口頭、書面和圖畫形式自由表達和傳播其觀點的權利，並有權不受阻礙地從所有開放來源獲取資訊。[2]應保證新聞自由和通過廣播和電影報導的自由。[3]不應對其進行審查。

（2）在不損害私營廣播經營權的條件下，應保證公共廣播的存在和發展。

（3）這幾項權利受到一般法律規定、保護青少年的法律規定，以及個人榮譽權的限制。

第 21 條
【藝術和科學自由】

[1]藝術、科研和學術是自由的。[2]學術自由不得違反對憲法的忠誠。

第 22 條
【保護婚姻和家庭】

（1）婚姻和家庭是薩克森邦特別保護的重點。

（2）任何在家中撫養孩子或照顧有需要的人的公民都應該得到支援和救濟。

（3）[1]照顧和培養孩子是父母天然的權利，同時也是他們應盡的義務。[2]薩克森邦關注他們的行為。

（4）只有當法定監護人不作為或孩子因為其它原因將被拋棄時，才可基於一部法律違背法定監護人意願讓孩子與家人分開。

（5）任何母親都有權獲得社區的保護和照顧。

第 23 條
【集會自由】

（1）任何人都有權在未報備或未獲得允許的情況下進行和平、無武器的集會。

（2）室外集會的權利可通過法律或基於一部法律進行限制。

第 24 條
【結社自由】

（1）所有公民都有權建立社團。

（2）禁止成立目標或活動違反刑法、憲法規定或國際共識的社團。

第 25 條
【結盟自由】

[1]應保證所有公民和職業為維護和促進工作和經濟條件建立社團的權利。[2]任何想要限制或阻礙行使本項權利的協議都是無效的；且這樣的行為是違法的。

第 26 條
【企業和服務機構中的共決】

[1]在薩克森邦的企業、服務機構和公共機構內部需設立代表職工的組織。[2]職工按照法律規定享有共決權。

第 27 條
【信件、郵件和通訊保密】

（1）信件、郵件和通訊保密不可侵犯。

（2）[1]僅可基於一部法律設置限制。[2]若限制措施是為了保護自由民主的基本秩序或聯邦的安全，則該法律可規定不必告知相關人員，且可由人民代表機構指定的機關和輔助機關代替法律程式開展審查工作。[3]在這種情況下，若限制措施的目標風險可被排除，則需告知相關人員進行限制措施的情況。

第 28 條
【職業自由】

（1）[1]只要不違反聯邦法規，公民可自由選擇職業和工作地。[2]職業選擇可通過法律或基於一部法律進行管理。

（2）有償童工是絕對禁止的。

（3）不得強制任何人從事特定工作，傳統一般性的、面向所有人的公共服務義務除外。

第 29 條
【培訓和教育自由】

（1）所有公民都有權自由選擇教育地點。

（2）所有公民都有權獲得進入公立教育機構的平等機會。

第 30 條
【住宅不可侵犯性】

（1）住宅是不可侵犯的。

（2）只有法官可對住宅進行搜查，在迫在眉睫的危險情況下也可由法律規定的其他機關執行，但僅可按照規定的方式進行。

（3）此外，只有在抵禦一個共同風險或一位公民的生命危險，以及基於一部法律預防針對公共安全和秩序的緊急危險，特別是消除空間緊缺、抗擊流行病的風險或保護處於危險中的青少年時，才可進行干涉或限制。

第 31 條
【財產和繼承權】

（1）[1]應保護財產和繼承權。[2]內容和限制由法律規定。

（2）[1]財產負有義務。[2]它的使用應同時服務大眾的利益，特別是要保護自然生存基礎。

第 32 條
【徵用、轉移為公有資產】

（1）[1]徵用只可用於大眾利益。[2]它可通過法律或基於一部法律實施，該法需規定補償的方式和額度。

（2）土地、自然資源和生產資料可以社會化為目的通過法律轉移為公有財產或其他形式的公有資產，該法需規定補償的方式和額度。

（3）補償額度需在公平考慮大眾和參與者利益的情況下確定。

第 33 條
【資料保護權】

[1]任何公民都有權自主決定其個人資料的採集、使用和轉遞。[2]在沒有獲得公民自願且明確的同意時，不得採集、保存、使用和轉遞個人資料。[3]本項權利僅可通過法律或基於一部法律進行干涉。

第 34 條
【環境資料的查詢】

任何個人都有權查詢與自身生活區域相關的自然環境資料，只要這些資料是由薩克森邦採集或保存的，且不違反聯邦法規、協力廠商受法律保護的權益或多數人的利益。

第 35 條
【請願權】

[1]任何個人都有權自己或與他人一起向主管部門和人民代表機構遞交書面請求或申訴。[2]這需要在合理期限內回復。

第 36 條
【自由邦權力與基本權利的關係】

本憲法中提出的基本權利直接適用於立法、行政和司法。

第 37 條
【基本權利的限制】

（1）[1]若本憲法中的一項基本權利可被法律或基於一部法律被限制，則該法必須適用於一般情況，而不僅適用於特殊情況。[2]此外該法必須在條款中提出該基本權利。
（2）在任何情況下都不得觸及基本權利的內涵。
（3）基本權利同樣適用位於德意志聯邦共和國內的法人主體，只要它們在本質上適用這些權利。

第 38 條
【法律途徑保證】

[1]任何人的權利被公共部門損害均可訴諸法律。[2]只要沒有給出適用其他途徑的理由，則均適用普通法律途徑。[3]第 27 條第 2 款第 2 句不受影響。

第 3 章
邦議會

第 39 條
【職能、自由議員】

（1）邦議會是選舉產生的人民代表機構。
（2）邦議會行使立法權，按照本憲法規定監督行政權的行使，也是政治決策的場所。
（3）[1]議員代表全體人民的利益。[2]他們只遵循自己的良知，不受任務和命令約束。

第 40 條
【議會反對派】

[1]建立和運用議會反對派對自由民主至關重要。[2]邦議會中非政府的組成部分在議會和社會上擁有機會平等權。

第 41 條
【選舉制度、選舉權】

（1）[1]邦議會通常由 120 位議員組成。[2]他們是通過一項基於個人選舉制和比例代表原則的程式被推選出來的。
（2）[1]所有符合條件的選民都可參與選舉。[2]只有在本邦達到特定停留時長的公民才擁有選舉權。
（3）具體事項由一部法律規定。

第 42 條
【競選資格、議員權利】

（1）想要競選邦議會席位的公民可要求獲得必要的假期以準備競選。

（2）[1] 不得阻礙任何人接受和行使議員職務。[2] 不允許以這一理由辭退或解除服務或勞動關係。

（3）[1] 議員可要求獲得合理的、能夠保障其獨立性的補償。[2] 他們在薩克森邦內部享有免費使用所有公共交通工具的權利。

（4）具體事項由一部法律規定。

第 43 條
【獲得和失去議員資格】

（1）[1] 被推選為議員的人在選舉被接受後即獲得議員資格，但邦議會議員的法律地位不會在新一屆邦議會召開會議前獲得。[2] 可拒絕接受選舉。

（2）[1] 議員可隨時放棄議員資格。[2] 這需要向邦議會主席提交書面聲明。[3] 該聲明不可撤回。

（3）當議員失去選舉權時，其議員資格也同時解除。

第 44 條
【任期、會議、召集】

（1）[1] 邦議會每五年選舉一次。[2] 其任期結束於新一屆邦議會召開會議時。[3] 這也適用於邦議會解散的情況。

（2）新一屆選舉必須在任期結束前進行，在邦議會解散的情況下則需要在 60 天內進行。

（3）[1] 新一屆邦議會需要在選舉結束後 30 天內召開會議。[2] 第一次會議由前一任主席召集，並在選出新任邦議會主席前主持會議。

（4）[1] 邦議會決定其會議的結束和再次召開時間。[2] 主席可提前召集邦議會。[3] 且當至少四分之一的邦議會成員或邦政府要求時，主席有義務這樣做。

第 45 條
【選舉審查】

（1）[1] 選舉審查是邦議會的責任。[2] 它還可決定是否取消一位成員的議員資格。

（2）成員可針對該決定向憲法法院提起上訴。

（3）具體事項由一部法律規定。

第 46 條
【議事規則、黨團】

（1）邦議會制定了一部議事規則。

（2）其中包括議員組成黨團的相關規定。

（3）不得限制無黨團議員的權利。

（4）更改議事規則需要至少三分之二的多數議員同意。

第 47 條
【主席】

（1）邦議會需選舉出主席及其副職和書記，主席、副主席以及其他成員共同組成主席團。

（2）主席根據議事規則主持議會協商。

（3）[1] 主席在邦議會大樓內行使住所權和員警權力。[2] 未經他的同意不得在邦議會房間內進行任何搜查或扣押。

（4）[1] 主席根據預演算法規定管理邦議會的經濟事務。[2] 他在邦議會管理中代表薩克森邦的利益。[3] 他有權雇傭和解雇職員和工人，也有權在與主席團商議後聘任和解聘邦議會公職人員。4 主席是聯

邦議會公職人員、職員和工人的最高領導。

第 48 條
【議會協商、決議、決議文本】

（1）[1]邦議會的協商過程是公開的。[2]當至少 12 位議員或一位邦政府成員提出申請，且獲得至少三分之二的在場議員通過時，邦議會也可不公開該過程。[3]該申請需要在非公開會議上審議。

（2）邦議會具有決議權，除非主席根據邦議會的一位元成員在投票開始前提出的申請，確定在場議員人數少於一半。

（3）[1]只要憲法沒有其他規定，邦議會根據多數票作出決議。[2]對於邦議會進行的選舉，議事規則可允許例外。

（4）任何人不得對邦議會及其委員會召開的公開會議的真實報告負責。

第 49 條
【邦政府的參與】

（1）邦議會及其委員會可要求邦政府任何一位成員在場。

（2）[1]邦政府成員及其專員可參加邦議會及其委員會的會議，必須在任何時候聽取他們的意見。[2]他們需遵從主席和委員會主席的執法權。

（3）[1]對於調查委員會為收集證據以外目的召開的非公開會議，聯邦政府成員及其專員僅可在被邀請的條件下參加。[2]他們的意見可被聽取。[3]在任何條件下，調查委員會都應給予邦政府針對取證結果提出意見的機會[4]關於邦政府成員及其專員參加調查委員會會議權利的其他限制由法律規定。

第 50 條
【邦政府的資訊彙報義務】

邦政府有義務向邦議會彙報自身的行動，只要這是履行其職責所必需的。

第 51 條
【議員的提問和諮詢權】

（1）[1]邦政府或它在邦議會及其委員會中的成員必須盡可能及時、完整地回復各議員提出的問題或議會質詢。[2]邦政府在各委員會中的專員也承擔同樣的義務。

（2）若提出的問題觸及邦政府自身行政責任的核心領域，或回復該問題將違反法律規定、損害協力廠商權利或多數人的保密權益，則邦政府可拒絕回答。

（3）具體事項由邦議會議事規則規定。

第 52 條
【委員會】

（1）[1]邦議會設立了一些常設委員會。[2]議事規則規定了其職責、組成和工作方式。

（2）[1]邦議會可根據至少 12 位元議員或一個黨團的申請批准成立臨時委員會。[2]各委員會的主題和目標將在決議中確定。

（3）委員會可公開開會。

第 53 條
【請願委員會】

（1）邦議會設立一個請願委員會處理收到的請求和申訴。

（2）根據邦議會議事規則，請求和申訴也可遞交到其他委員會。

（3）請願委員會的權利，特別是進入公共機構和提交文書的權利，由法律規定。

第 54 條
【調查委員會】

（1）[1]邦議會有權，且在至少五分之一的成員提出申請的情況下有義務組建調查委員會。[2]調查的對象由決議確定。[3]不得違背申請人意願更改少數申請中提及的調查對象。

（2）[1]委員會將在公開聽證會上收集它或申請人認為必要的證據。[2]當委員會至少三分之二的在場成員提出要求時，可不公開聽證過程。

（3）當至少五分之一的委員會成員提出申請時，可進行證據收集。

（4）在至少五分之一的調查委員會成員的要求下，邦政府有義務提交卷宗並授權他們的公職人員作證，只要這不觸及邦政府自身行政責任的核心領域，或不違反法律規定、損害協力廠商權利或多數人的保密權益。

（5）法院和行政機關有義務提供法律和行政協助。

（6）[1]關於調查委員會的組建、權利和程式的具體事項由法律規定[2]信件、郵件和通訊保密不受影響。

（7）[1]調查委員會的決議和結果不受司法審查。[2]但法院可自由評價和評估作為調查基礎的事實。

第 55 條
【議員的追認權和豁免權】

（1）[1]議員不得在任何時間因其投票或因其在邦議會或行使議員權利時的表達遭到法院或官方的起訴，也不得以其他方式在邦議會外承擔責任。[2]這不適用於誹謗性的侮辱。

（2）[1]議員只有在獲得邦議會同意的情況下才能因其可能受到法律懲罰的行為被調查、逮捕或拘留，除非他們在犯罪過程中或第二天被逮捕。[2]在需要對議員進行任何其他形式的人身自由限制時都需要徵求邦議會同意。

（3）任何針對議員的刑事訴訟以及任何拘留或對其人身自由的其他限制，都必須根據邦議會的要求在任期內或更短的時間內暫停。

第 56 條
【議員拒絕作證的權利】

（1）議員可拒絕為把他們實質上視為議員而傾訴事實的人，以及為事實本身作證。

（2）議員在行使議員權利時要求合作的人可以拒絕就他們在這種合作中完成的任務作證。

（3）在拒絕作證權的範圍內，不允許進行搜查和沒收檔及其他資訊載體。

第 57 條
【資料保護專員】

[1]為了維護資料保護權，以及在行使議會控制權時提供支援，邦議會需任命一個資料保護專員。[2]具體事項由一部法律規定。

第 58 條
【解散邦議會】

邦議會可在至少三分之二成員的同意下自行解散。

第 4 章
邦政府

第 59 條
【地位和職責、組成、工作範圍】

（1）[1]邦政府是最高行政機關。[2]它由薩克森邦領導和管理。[3]根據憲法規定，它是立法機關的一部分。

（2）[1]邦政府由總理和邦務部長組成。[2]邦政府的其他成員還包括邦務秘書。

（3）[1]邦政府決定其成員的工作範圍。[2]總理可自行接管一個工作範圍。

第 60 條
【邦政府的組建】

（1）總理由邦議會根據成員的多數票選出，投票採取不記名、不交換意見的方式。

（2）若第 1 款中的選舉無法成功，則在進一步選舉中獲得多數票的人勝出。

（3）若沒有在新一屆邦議會組建後或總理職務完成後的 4 個月內選出新的總理，則邦議會將解散。

（4）[1] 總理可任命和解雇邦務部長和邦務秘書。[2] 他也可任命其副職。

第 61 條
【就職宣誓】

[1] 邦政府成員在上任時要在邦議會前進行就職宣誓。[2] 他要宣讀：「我發誓，我要將我的力量奉獻給人民的利益，增加他們的福祉，讓他們免受傷害，維護和保衛憲法和法律，認真履行我的義務，為所有人伸張正義。」[3] 在誓詞中也可加入一句保證——「所以上帝是會真正幫助我的」。

第 62 條
【邦政府成員的法律地位、不相容性】

（1）邦政府成員的職位待遇，特別是工資和養老金由法律規定。

（2）[1] 邦政府成員不得從事任何其他的有償職務、職業和工作。[2] 他們不得進入任何私營企業的監事會或董事會。[3] 自由邦在其中擁有多數影響力的企業除外。[4] 根據第 3 句規定，邦政府在承擔任何一項功能時都需通知邦議會。[5] 邦政府可在邦議會同意下准許其他例外。

第 63 條
【政策能力、部門主權】

（1）總理確定政策指導方針並為此負責。

（2）在政策指導方針框架內各邦務部長自行領導其工作職責範圍內的事務。

第 64 條
【管轄權、議事規則】

（1）邦政府主要負責制定法律草案；決定自由邦在聯邦參議院上的投票，以及憲法或法律規定的事務；協調涉及多個部門工作範圍的想法分歧，以及決定具有根本性或深遠意義的問題。

（2）邦政府制定了一部議事規則。

第 65 條
【代表自由邦、締結自由邦條約】

（1）總理對外代表薩克森邦。

（2）自由邦條約的締結需要獲得邦政府和邦議會的同意。

第 66 條
【任命權】

[1] 總理可任命和解雇自由邦法官和公職人員。[2] 本項權利可通過法律或基於一部法律轉交給其他自由邦機關。

第 67 條
【赦免權】

（1）[1] 總理可行使赦免權。[2] 只要不是在複雜情況下，他可以在邦政府同意下將本項權利轉交給其他自由邦機關。

（2）普遍性的減輕處罰和普遍撤銷未決刑事訴訟只能通過法律宣布。

第 68 條
【辭職、就職期結束、代理政府】

（1）邦政府及其所有成員可在任何時間宣布辭職。

（2）總理和其他邦政府成員的職務在新一屆邦議會組建後結束，邦務部長和邦務秘書的職務也隨總理任期結束而解除。

（3）在邦政府成員辭職或以其他形式結束任期的情況下，成員需要在將職務交接給繼任者前繼續履行職務。

第 69 條
【建設性不信任投票】

（1）邦議會只可通過一種方式罷免總理，即議會多數成員推選出一位繼任者。

（2）在提出罷免申請和進行選舉之間至少要有 3 天時間。

第 5 章
立法

第 70 條
【立法倡議、立法決議】

（1）法律草案由邦政府、邦議會集體或由公民通過公民動議提出。

（2）法律由邦議會或直接由公民通過全民公投通過。

第 71 條
【公民動議】

（1）[1]所有在邦內擁有投票權的公民都有權發起一項公民動議。[2]它必須獲得至少 40000 名擁有投票權的公民的簽名支持。[3]它必須基於一份合理的法律草案。

（2）[1]公民動議需提交給邦議會主席。[2]他需在徵求邦政府意見後及時作出是否受理的決定。[3]若他認為該公民動議違憲，則由憲法法院根據他的申請作出決定。4 在作出反對決定之前，不得將該公民動議按不可受理處理。

（3）邦議會主席將公開已受理的公民動議，並闡述理由。

（4）邦議會將為申請人提供聽證機會。

第 72 條
【關於舉行公民表決的提議、全民公投】

（1）[1]若邦議會在 6 個月內仍未同意未經修改的公民動議，則申請人可發起一項關於舉行公民表決的提議，以針對該申請進行一次全民公投。[2]申請人可將一份根據公民動議修改的法律草案作為關於舉行公民表決的提議的基礎。[3]這種情況適用第 71 條第 2 款。

（2）[1]進行一次全民公投需要獲得至少 450000 名、但不超過 15% 的有投票權公民在提議上的簽名支持。[2]需提供至少 6 個月的時間爭取支援。[3]邦議會可在全民公投中加入自己的法律草案。

（3）[1]在成功通過提議和舉行全民公投之間要有 3-6 個月的時間，以向公眾提供關於公投目標的資訊並發起討論。[2]這一期限僅可在徵求申請人同意後縮短或延長。

（4）[1]全民公投時需要投「是」或「否」。[2]有效投票的多數選擇決定結果。

第 73 條
【不受理公民動議、關於舉行公民表決的提議和全民公投，覆議】

（1）關於納稅、薪資和預算法律的公民動議、舉行公民表決的提議和全民公投不被受理。

（2）由全民公投否決的公民動議最早可在本屆邦議會任期結束後再次發起。

（3）關於公民動議、舉行公民表決的提議和全民公投的具體事項由一部法律規定，其中包括了對組織

關於舉行公民表決的提議的費用的補償要求，以及一次適當投票活動的要求。

第 74 條
【修憲】

（1）[1] 憲法僅可通過法律修改，該法律需明確改變或補充憲法文本。[2] 修改不得違反本憲法第 1、3、14 和 36 條的基本原則。[3] 憲法法院根據邦政府或至少四分之一邦議會成員的申請作出是否受理修憲申請的決定。

（2）一部修憲法的通過需要獲得至少三分之二邦議會成員的同意。

（3）[1] 當超過一半的邦議會成員申請時，憲法可通過全民公投修改。[2] 它也可根據第 72 條通過一次全民公投修改。[3] 當多數具有投票權的公民同意時，修憲法可通過。

第 75 條
【法規、行政法規】

（1）[1] 發布法規的權力僅可通過法律授予。[2] 其中需要規定授權的內容、目的和範圍。[3] 規定中需要明確法律依據。

（2）只要法律沒有其他規定，執行法律所必需的一般性行政法規由邦政府發布。

第 76 條
【法律法規的簽發、頒布、生效日期】

（1）[1] 根據憲法通過的法律在總理和主管邦務部長會簽後由邦議會主席簽發，並由總理於一個月內在薩克森自由邦法律法規公報上頒布。[2] 當邦議會認為其具有急迫性時，法律必須立即簽發和頒布。

（2）法規由其發布機構簽發，邦政府法規由總理和主管邦務部長簽發，且只要法律沒有其他規定，法規需要在薩克森自由邦法律法規公報上頒布。

（3）[1] 法律和法規需要規定其生效日期。[2] 若沒有相關規定，則法律法規將在法律法規公報上發布後的第 14 天結束後生效。

第 6 章
司法

第 77 條
【法院、法官獨立性、榮譽法官】

（1）司法權由憲法法院和法院以人民的名義行使，憲法法院和法院根據聯邦和自由邦法律設立。

（2）法官是獨立的，只受法律約束。

（3）在司法機構中，從公民中選出的女性和男性共同協作。

第 78 條
【法定法官、聽證權】

（1）[1] 不得剝奪任何人的法定法官。[2] 不允許設立例外法庭。

（2）任何人都有在法院的聽證權。

（3）[1] 任何人都有權獲得公平、順暢和公開的審判，並享有辯護權。[2] 僅可根據法律規定不公開審判。

第 79 條
【法官的法律地位】

（1）[1] 只有根據司法判決並以法律規定的理由和形式，才能違背長期聘用的全職法官的意願，在任期結束前將其解雇、長期或臨時解除其職務、將其調至其他崗位、要求其退休。[2] 法律可規定年齡限制，終身聘用的法官在達到該限制時即可退休。[3] 當法院所在的地點和區域發生變化時，可將法官調至其他法院或解除其職務，但必須保持全額工資。

（2）此外，法官的任命、就職宣誓和法律地位由法律規定。

（3）法律可規定，法官的任命和聘用需有法官選拔委員會的參與。

第 80 條
【指控法官】

（1）[1] 當一名法官在職或非在職時違反了聯邦或自由邦的憲法規定，則聯邦憲法法院可根據邦議會申請將該法官調至其他崗位或要求其退休。[2] 在故意違反的情況下可予以解雇。

（2）[1] 指控申請必須由至少三分之一的邦議會成員提出。[2] 指控需要得到至少三分之二的在場邦議會成員的同意才可通過，同時同意的人數要超過成員總人數的一半。

第 81 條
【憲法法院的職責和組成】

（1）憲法法院負責

　　1. 在最高邦立機關或其他通過憲法或邦議會或邦政府議事規則賦予相應職權的主體提出申請時，針對最高邦立機關或其他主體關於法律和義務範圍的爭端給出憲法解釋；

　　2. 在至少四分之一的邦議會成員或邦政府提出申請時，針對他們對邦法與本憲法一致性的質疑或意見分歧給出憲法解釋；

　　3. 在法院根據《基本法》第 100 條第 1 款中止訴訟程式後，裁決邦法與本憲法的一致性問題；

　　4. 在個人在本憲法中提出的基本權利（第 4、14-38、41、78、91、102、105、107 條）受到公權機關的侵害後提出憲法申訴時，裁決該申訴；

　　5. 決定本憲法賦予它的其他事項；

　　6. 決定法律賦予它的事項。

（2）憲法法院由 5 名職業法官和 4 名其他成員組成。

（3）[1] 憲法法院成員根據邦議會三分之二以上成員的同意選出，任期為 9 年。[2] 由一名職業法官擔任院長。[3] 成員不得在聯邦或邦的議會、參議院或政府中任職。

（4）[1] 具體事項由一部法律規定。[2] 此外還規定，憲法法院的選舉每 3 年舉行一次，憲法法院第一次選舉任命的成員任期和由於一名法官提前辭職而補選的成員任期由第 3 款單獨規定。

第 7 章
行政

第 82 條
【行政主體】

（1）[1] 行政權由邦政府及其下屬機構以及自治主體行使。[2] 它代表共同利益並為人民服務。

（2）[1] 自治主體包括鄉鎮、縣和其他社區團體。[2] 將確保其在法律範圍內自主管理自身事務的權利。

（3）根據法律規定，其他公法主體、慈善組織和基金會也是自治主體。

第 83 條
【行政組織】

（1）[1] 邦立行政機關的設立、空間布局和職責由法律規定。[2] 可由下級行政機關以可靠合理方式完成的任務可交由這些機關執行。

（2）[1] 邦立機關設立的具體事宜由邦政府負責。[2] 邦政府可授權給總理。

（3）[1] 自由邦不設立任何具有員警權利的秘密情報機關。[2] 情報資源的使用需經過由人民代表機構指定的機關和輔助機關審查，只要其不需經過司法監督。[3] 具體事項由法律規定。

第 84 條
【社區自治】

（1）[1]鄉鎮在其區域是公共責任的承擔主體，法律規定由其他主體承擔的特定公共責任除外。[2]社區團體在其責任範圍內也享有同等地位。

（2）在通過法律或法規管理涉及鄉鎮和社區團體的一般性問題前，需要及時聽取鄉鎮和社區團體或它們組成的聯盟的意見。

第 85 條
【任務移交、額外工作補償】

（1）[1]可通過法律將一些特定任務移交給社區自治主體完成。[2]這些任務可由社區自治主體以可靠合理的方式完成。[3]該法律必須規定費用的支付問題。

（2）[1]若移交的任務將給社區自治主體帶來額外工作，則需給予合理的補償。[2]這也適用於自願工作轉為義務工作，以及薩克森自由邦通過或基於一部法律完成移交或現有的工作後直接造成了額外的財政支出的情況。

（3）在移交公共任務方面，自由邦可保留根據更詳細的法律規定發布指令的權利。

第 86 條
【自治主體代表機構】

（1）[1]在鄉鎮和縣，公民必須選出一個代表機構。[2]在小鄉鎮，可在選出的代表機構處召開鄉鎮大會。

（2）鄉鎮的居民可參與自治，特別是通過接受榮譽職務。

（3）具體事項由一部法律規定。

第 87 條
【財政、財政補貼】

（1）自由邦致力於讓社區自治主體能夠完成其職責。

（2）鄉鎮和縣有權根據法律徵收自己的稅款和其他費用。

（3）鄉鎮和縣須考慮自由邦的職責，在跨鄉鎮財政補貼的框架內分享自由邦的稅收。

（4）具體事項由一部法律規定。

第 88 條
【自治主體的區域變動】

（1）鄉鎮和縣的區域可為公共利益改變。

（2）[1]在區域內的鄉鎮協商一致並獲得自由邦批准後，鄉鎮區域可通過法律或基於一部法律改變。[2]違背鄉鎮意願拆分鄉鎮需要依據一部法律執行。[3]在改變鄉鎮區域前，必須聽取受到直接影響地區的居民的意見。

（3）[1]縣域可通過法律或基於一部法律改變。[2]縣的拆分需要依據一部法律執行。

（4）具體事項由一部法律規定。

第 89 條
【社區監督】

（1）自由邦將監督鄉鎮、縣和其他社區團體行政管理的合法性。

（2）法律可規定，承擔債務義務和擔保、出售資產需經受委託監督的機關批准，該機關從有序經濟管理的角度出發，可給予或不予批准。

第 90 條
【社區憲法申訴】

社區自治主體可向憲法法院提出申訴，聲明一部法律違反了第 82 條第 2 款或第 84-89 條的規定。

第 91 條
【公共職務、獲得公職】

（1）主權權利的行使是一項永久性任務，通常會移交給具有公法職務和忠誠關係的公職人員執行。

（2）所有公民都可根據其適合性、能力和專業表現平等地獲得任何公職。

第 92 條
【行使職權、公職人員的就職宣誓】

（1）自由邦和自治主體的公職人員服務於全體人民，而不是某個黨派或其他組織，他們行使職權和履行職責時不分黨派、不看個人，只從事實出發。

（2）[1]每名公職人員都要宣讀以下誓詞：「我發誓，我將盡我所能履行我的職責，重視和保衛憲法和法律，為所有人伸張正義。」[2]在誓詞中也可加入一句保證──「所以上帝是會真正幫助我的」。

第 8 章
財政

第 93 條
【預算計畫、預演算法】

（1）[1]自由邦的所有收入和支出均需在預算計畫中體現；對於邦屬企業和專項資金只需記錄其流入和流出的情況。[2]預算計畫的收入和支出需配平。

（2）[1]為一個或多個會計年度制定的預算計畫通過預演算法確定，其中後者需要按年度分隔。[2]預算的確定需在會計年度開始前完成，對於多個會計年度的預算則需在第一個會計年度開始前確定。

（3）[1]預演算法中只可包括關於自由邦收入和支出，以及該法生效時限的條例。[2]預演算法可規定，其條例在下一部預演算法頒布後失效或根據第 95 條獲得授權後更晚失效。

（4）債務必須記錄在預算計畫的附錄中。

第 94 條
【預算計畫的意義和影響】

（1）1 預算計畫確定和滿足財政需求，這些支出預計是在預算計畫覆蓋的時間範圍內履行邦政府職責所必需的。[2]預算計畫是預算和經濟管理的基礎。

（2）在制定和執行預算計畫時，需要考慮總體經濟平衡的要求、經濟節儉原則以及社會平衡原則。

（3）預算計畫授權行政機關進行支出和承擔責任。

（4）預算計畫不會產生或消除任何權利或責任。2

第 95 條
【借貸、承擔擔保】

（1）進行借貸及承擔擔保或其他保證等需要在未來年份進行支出的行為需要法律授權。

（2）[1]預算計畫需在沒有借貸的條件下配平。[2]借貸的禁令也適用於薩克森自由邦在法律上非獨立的專項資金。[3]2010 年 12 月 31 日通過的借貸授權在未被收回前不受影響。

（3）根據第 85 條和第 87 條規定，社區自治主體的權利不受借貸禁令的影響。

（4）[1]若經濟發展至少偏離過去 4 年平均稅收收入（正常情況）的 3%，則可不遵守第 2 款的規定。[2]借貸僅限於將稅收缺口擴大到前四年平均稅收的 99%。[3]在滿足第 6 款的前提條件下可擴大到超過 99%。4 根據該條款，額外稅收將用於償還債務。

（5）[1]在自由邦無法控制且自由邦的財政狀況被嚴重破壞的自然災害或非正常緊急狀況下，可不遵守第 2 款規定。[2]進行借貸需要同時制定一個償還計畫。

（6）[1]由邦議會確定例外情況。[2]在第 4 款的情況下邦議會根據半數以上成員的意見作出決定；在第 5 款或第 4 款中將稅收缺口擴大到 99% 以上的情況下，邦議會根據三分之二以上成員意見作出決定。[3]

在這些特殊情況下需要最晚在 8 年內償還所有債務。

（7）[1] 薩克森自由邦為邦內未來的養老金領取者在退休時領取養老金和津貼預備了足夠的準備金。[2] 這筆資金與一般的邦預算分開記錄，並專款專用。[3] 在提取該資金時，需要考慮節省資金的數額與現有養老金和津貼義務數額的關係。

（8）具體事項由一部法律規定。[3]

第 96 條
【超支和計畫外支出】

[1] 超支和計畫外的支出和義務需要獲得邦財政部長的同意。[2] 其只可用於滿足不可預見和不可避免的需求。[3] 事後需要補上邦議會的批准。4 具體事項由法律規定。

第 97 條
【增加支出和減少收入】

（1）[1] 邦議會關於增加預算計畫確定的預算或增加新支出的決議需獲得邦政府同意。[2] 這也同樣適用於關於減少收入的邦議會決議。[3] 必須保證能夠滿足需求。

（2）[1] 邦政府可根據第 1 款規定要求邦議會暫停決議過程。[2] 在這種情況下，邦政府需在 6 個星期內向邦議會提交一份意見聲明。

第 98 條
【臨時預算管理】

（1）若在一年結束時既沒有確定下一年度的預算計畫，也沒有通過緊急預演算法，則邦政府可在法律規定範圍內執行以下支出：

    1. 維持法定設施和實施法定措施的必要支出；

    2. 履行自由邦法定義務的必要支出；

    3. 繼續進行建造、採購以及其他工作或保證以此為目的的津貼的必要支出，只要這些工作已在上一年度的預算計畫中得到批准。

（2）[1] 若根據特別法律或流動資金儲備的稅收、費用和其他來源的收入無法抵補第 1 款中提到的支出，則邦政府可籌措有序預算管理所需的貸款。[2] 貸款額度不得超過上一年度預算計畫總金額的四分之一。

第 99 條
【公布帳目】

為減輕邦政府的責任，邦財政部長每年需要向邦議會公開自由邦所有的收入和支出，以及財產和債務的變動。

第 100 條
【審計、審計署】

（1）[1] 自由邦的帳目和整體預算和經濟管理由審計署審計。[2] 審計署是獨立的邦立機關。

（2）[1] 其成員包括主席、副主席和審計部門負責人。[2] 他們具有與法官同等的獨立性。

（3）[1] 審計署主席由邦議會在總理的推薦下根據三分之二以上多數票選出。[2] 副主席由總理根據審計署主席的建議，經邦議會同意後任命。

（4）審計署每年直接向邦議會彙報，並同時告知邦政府。

（5）具體事項由一部法律規定。

第 9 章
教育

第 101 條
【撫育和教育原則】

（1）應教導年輕人敬畏生命、博愛、維護和平、保護環境、熱愛家園、具有道德和政治責任感、公平處事並尊重他人的信念、具備專業技能、參與社會活動並樹立自由民主的態度。

（2）[1] 教育和學校系統的基礎是父母決定其子女的撫育和教育的天然權利。[2] 這在提供不同學校的入學資格時需要尤其注意。

第 102 條
【學校系統、教材自由】

（1）[1] 薩克森邦保證學校教育的權利。[2] 其會提供義務教育。

（2）年輕人的教育由公立和私立中小學負責。

（3）[1] 應保證私人主體建立中小學的權利。[2] 若此類中小學承擔與公立中小學相同的職責，則需要獲得自由邦的批准。[3] 只有在此類中小學的教學目標和設施以及教師的學術教育水準不弱於公立中小學，且不根據父母財產狀況招生的條件下，才會獲得批准。[4] 若不足以確保教師的經濟和法律地位，則不予批准。

（4）[1] 公立中小學的課程和教材是免費的。[2] 若要求與公立中小學承擔相同職責的私立中小學也做到同樣免費，則需要提供財政補貼。

（5）具體事項由一部法律規定。

第 103 條
【學校監督】

（1）整個學校系統受自由邦監督。

（2）可在學校監督機構建立志願性的顧問委員會。

（3）獲得公共承認資格的考試必須在主管的邦立機關或自由邦授權的機構的監督下進行。

第 104 條
【學校內部的共決】

（1）家長和學生有權通過推選出的代表參與塑造學校的生活和工作。

（2）具體事項由一部法律規定。

第 105 條
【倫理和宗教課程】

（1）[1] 倫理和宗教課程屬於中小學的必修科目，宗教和非宗教中小學除外。[2] 在學生達到加入宗教的法定年齡前，
由父母決定他們的孩子學習哪些科目。

（2）[1] 宗教課程根據教會和宗教團體的基本原則教授，不受自由邦的一般監督。[2] 教授宗教課程的教師需要獲得教會和宗教團體的授權。[3] 教會和宗教團體有權在與邦立監督機構協商後監督宗教課程的教學。

（3）不得違背任何教師的意願，要求其教授宗教課程。

第 106 條
【職業教育】

[1] 職業教育在實踐教育基地和職業學校開展。[2] 薩克森邦支援職業學校系統。

第 107 條
【獨立學院自由】

（1）獨立學院可自由開展研究和教學。
（2）[1] 獨立學院有權在法律和經自由邦批准的章程範圍內進行符合其特色的自主管理，不受自由邦的監督。[2] 獨立學院學生也可參與自主管理。
（3）獨立學院通過行使建議權參與教職工的聘用。
（4）[1] 允許開辦私立獨立學院。[2] 具體事項由一部法律規定。

第 108 條
【成人教育】

（1）成人教育是受到支持的。
（2）成人教育機構可由自由邦、自治主體和私人主體設立。

第 10 章
教會和宗教團體

第 109 條
【教會的作用、執事工作、威瑪教會條款】

（1）承認教會和宗教團體對保護和加強人生的宗教和道德基礎的重要作用。
（2）[1] 教會和宗教團體是獨立於薩克森邦的。[2] 它們可在適用於所有人的法律範圍內不受自由邦干預地履行其職責。[3] 此外，教會和宗教團體與自由邦的關係由條約規定。
（3）應確保教會和宗教團體的執事和慈善工作。
（4）德意志國於 1919 年 8 月 11 日頒布的憲法中的第 136、137、138、139、141 條規定是本憲法的組成部分。

第 110 條
【宗教或私立公益性設施】

（1）教會和宗教團體以公共利益為目的設立公益性設施或機構的，有權要求自由邦根據法律規定給予合理的成本補償。
（2）具有相同職責並開展相同工作的私人主體也有同樣的權利。

第 111 條
【宗教學／神學和宗教教育教職】

（1）[1] 教會和宗教團體有權成立自己的教學機構，以培養牧師和教會工作者。2 若其符合中小學和獨立學院法律規定，則它們與邦立教學機構具有同等地位。
（2）[1] 神學和宗教教育學教職的授予需與教會協商。[2] 其它協商不受影響。

第 112 條
【自由邦對教會的補貼】

（1）應保證自由邦對教會基於法律、條約或合法頭銜的補貼。
（2）[1] 教會和宗教團體的文物建築是全體公民的文化遺產，不受財產權影響。[2] 教會和宗教團體有權根據法律規定要求自由邦為它們維護建築的花費提供補償。

第 11 章
過渡和最終規定

第 113 條
【緊急狀態、緊急議會】

（1）[1] 若自由邦的存在、自由民主的基本秩序或居民的生存必需品供應面臨危險，或在自然災害或重大事故造成的緊急狀態下，邦議會無法立即召開大會，則由一個所有邦議會黨團共同組成的邦議會委員會作為緊急議會行使邦議會的權利。[2] 此類委員會通過的法律不可更改憲法。[3] 它也無權罷免總理。

（2）[1] 當自由邦的存在或自由民主的基本秩序面臨危險時，則停止舉行由公民開展的選舉和投票。[2] 停止舉行選舉和投票的決議由邦議會根據三分之二多數成員同意作出。[3] 若邦議會無法立即召開大會，則由第 1 款中提到的委員會根據三分之二多數成員同意作出。[4] 被推遲的選舉和投票應在邦議會確定危險解除後的 6 個月內進行。有關人員和機構的任期延長至新一屆選舉日結束。

（3）關於邦議會無法立即召開大會的決議由邦議會主席作出。

（4）[1] 在第 1 款的情況下，若法律無法及時在自由邦法律法規公報上公布，則以其他方式公布。[2] 在情況允許後，需要將該法律補登進法律法規公報。

（5）當第 1 款中提到的委員會在下一次邦議會大會結束後的 4 個星期內提出申請時，邦議會可廢除該委員會作出的決議。

第 114 條
【反對權】

在沒有其他補救辦法的情況下，全體公民均有權反對想要廢除憲法規定的人。

第 115 條
【公民的定義】

本憲法中公民的定義根據《基本法》第 116 條第 1 款確定。

第 116 條
【賠償】

公民在如今的薩克森自由邦地區或作為該地區的居民，由於自身的政治、宗教、世界觀、種族、祖先來源、國籍、社會地位、身體殘疾、同性戀傾向或其他原因遭到國家社會主義或共產主義暴政迫害的，有權根據法律規定要求賠償。

第 117 條
【彌補歷史】

薩克森邦將盡其所能，消除歷史上個人和社會失敗的原因，減輕侵犯人類尊嚴的後果，並加強過上自決和負責任生活的能力。

第 118 章
【控告議員和部長】

（1）若一名邦議會或邦政府成員涉嫌在選舉前
　　1. 違反人道或法治國家基本原則，特別是侵犯 1966 年 12 月 19 日簽署的《公民和政治權利國際公約》維護的人權，或侵犯 1948 年 12 月 10 日發布的《人權宣言》中提出的基本權利，
　　2. 或曾在前德意志民主共和國（DDR）的安全部／國家安全局任職，
　　並因此不再適合長期擔任議員或邦政府成員，則邦議會可向憲法法院提出指控以取消其議員或公職資格。

（2）[1] 提出指控的申請需要獲得至少三分之一的邦議會成員同意。[2] 指控需要得到至少三分之二的在場

邦議會成員的同意才可通過，同時同意的人數要超過成員總人數的一半。

（3）具體事項由一部法律規定，其中也可規定取消獲得養老金的權利。

第 119 條
【公務部門的就業和繼續就業】

[1] 公務部門的就業和繼續就業適用《德國統一條約》（統一條約）中的規定。[2] 曾有以下行為的主體不可擔任公職：

　　1. 違反人道或法治國家基本原則，特別是侵犯 1966 年 12 月 19 日簽署的《公民和政治權利國際公約》維護的人權，或侵犯 1948 年 12 月 10 日發布的《人權宣言》中提出的基本權利，

　　2. 或曾在前德意志民主共和國（DDR）的安全部／國家安全局任職，

他們在公務部門的任職是不可接受的。

第 120 條
【邦法的持續適用性】

（1）薩克森自由邦地區的邦法保持有效，只要其與本憲法不衝突。

（2）第 81 條第 1 款第 2、3 項和第 90 條意義上的邦法也包括本憲法生效前已有的法律法規。

第 121 條
【薩克森科學院】

自由邦支持位於萊比錫的薩克森科學院。

第 122 條
【接受、頒布、生效】

（1）本憲法的通過需要獲得三分之二以上邦議會成員的同意。

（2）它由邦議會主席簽發，並由總理在薩克森自由邦法律法規公報上公布。

（3）本憲法在頒布後當天生效。[4]

第 109 條第 4 款附錄：

第 136 條
威瑪憲法

（1）公民和國民權利不受宗教自由權的制約和限制。

（2）享受公民和國民權利以及擔任公職與宗教信仰無關。

（3）[1] 無權要求任何人公布自身的宗教信仰。[2] 只有在與權利和義務相關或法定統計調查需要時，有關部門才有權詢問公民所屬的宗教團體。

（4）不得強迫任何人進行教會活動或儀式、參加宗教活動或進行宗教宣誓。

第 137 條
威瑪憲法

（1）不存在任何國教。

（2）[1] 應保證創建宗教團體的自由。[2] 在共和國區域內結成宗教團體不受任何限制。

（3）[1] 每個宗教團體都可在適用於所有人的法律限制內自行規定和管理自己的事務。[2] 其可在沒有邦和鄉鎮參與的條件下分配職務。

（4）宗教團體可根據民法的一般規定獲得立法能力。

（5）[1] 宗教團體可一直保持公法法人身分，只要它當前具有此身分。[2] 如果其他宗教團體的章程和成員人數能夠保證其長期存在，則可提出申請獲得同樣的權利。[3] 若多個此類公法宗教團體結成一個聯合體，則該聯合體也具有公法法人身分。

（6）具有公法法人身分的宗教團體有權按照邦法規定根據民事稅表徵收稅款。

（7）以培養共同世界觀為主要職責的協會具有與宗教團體同等的權利。

（8）若執行這些規定需要其他規定支援，則由各邦制定。

第 138 條
威瑪憲法

（1）[1] 國家基於法律、條約或特殊合法頭銜向宗教團體支付的補貼通過邦法批准。[2] 共和國為此制定了原則。

（2）應保證宗教團體和宗教協會對其用於文化、教育和慈善目的的機構、基金會和其他資產的財產權及其他權利。

第 139 條
威瑪憲法

法律保護將星期日和國家承認的節日作為休息日和精神提升日。

第 141 條
威瑪憲法

[1] 只要軍隊、醫院、懲教機構或其他公共機構需要敬拜和牧靈，則需允許宗教團體進行宗教活動，但不得強迫。

[2] 以上憲法在此簽發。

德勒斯登，1992 年 5 月 27 日

Erich Iltgen

薩克森邦議會主席

邦立憲大會

本憲法將在薩克森邦律法規公報上公布。德勒斯登，1992 年 5 月 27 日

Kurt Biedenkopf 教授／博士 薩克森自由邦總理

---

1 根據 2013 年 7 月 11 日的法律（SächsGVBl. S. 502）重新表述第 85 條第 2 款。

2 根據 2013 年 7 月 11 日的法律（SächsGVBl. S. 502）重新表述第 94 條第 2 款。

3 根據 2013 年 7 月 11 日的法律（SächsGVBl. S. 502）重新表述第 95 條。

4 頒布於 1992 年 6 月 5 日。

修訂條例

2013 年 7 月 11 日《薩克森自由邦修憲法》（SächsGVBl. S. 502）

日本阿伊努語法律

二〇一九年（平成三十一年）法律第十六號
　　實現尊重阿伊努族人自豪感之社會所需適用措施推動法
目次
　　第一章　總則（第一條─第六條）
　　第二章　基本方針等事項（第七條、第八條）
　　第三章　民族共生象徵空間組成設施之管理措施（第九條）
　　第四章　推動阿伊努族適用措施地區計畫之認定等事項（第十條─第十四條）
　　第五章　獲認定之推動阿伊努族適用措施地區計畫所定事業適用之特別措施（第十五條─第十九條）
　　第六章　獲指定法人（第二十條─第三十一條）
　　第七章　阿伊努族政策推動總部（第三十二條─第四十一條）
　　第八章　雜則（第四十二條─第四十五條）
　　附則
　　　第一章　總則
（目的）
第一條　本法之目的係鑑於日本群島北部周邊所處情況，尤其北海道原住民族阿伊努族人自豪感根源，亦即阿伊努族傳統與阿伊努族文化（以下稱「阿伊努族傳統等」）面臨之處境，以及近年來主要與原住民族有關之國際情勢，爰規範推動阿伊努族適用措施之基本理念、國家等組織擔負之責任義務、由政府擬定基本方針、民族共生象徵空間組成設施之管理措施、由市町村（含特別區以下亦同）擬定推動阿伊努族適用措施地區計畫、以及由內閣總理大臣認定該計畫、獲認定之推動阿伊努族適用措施地區計畫所定事業適用之特別措施、設置阿伊努族政策推動總部等作為，以實現阿伊努族人能夠本著民族自豪感生活及尊重其自豪感之社會，藉此有助實現全體國民相互尊重個人之人格與特質而共生之社會。
（定義）
第二條　本法之「阿伊努族文化」意指阿伊努族語、阿伊努族傳承之生活型態、音樂、舞蹈、工藝等文化成果以及由此發展而出之文化成果。
2　本法之「阿伊努族適用措施」意指有助振興愛奴文化及推廣與宣導教育阿伊努族傳統等知識（以下稱「振興阿伊努族文化等作為」），以及為使阿伊努族人本著民族自豪感生活之振興阿伊努族文化等作為之環境整備適用措施。
3　本法之「民族共生象徵空間組成設施」意指組成民族共生象徵空間（指作為振興阿伊努族文化等作為之據點，設於國土交通省法規命令與文部科學省法規命令規定處所之國有財產法（一九四八年（昭和二十三年）法律第七十三號）第三條第二項規定之行政財產）之設施
（含其占地），且定於國土交通省法規命令與文部科學省法規命令者。
（基本理念）
第三條　為使阿伊努族人自豪感受到尊重，推動阿伊努族適用措施須以增進國民對阿伊努族人自豪感根源之阿伊努族傳統等，以及包含我國在內國際社會面臨之多元民族共生及多元文化發展重要課題之了解為宗旨。
2　為使阿伊努族人能本著民族自豪感生活，推動阿伊努族適用措施須同時顧及對阿伊努族人自主意志之尊重。
3　國家、地方自治團體等相關單位等須相互密切合作，並以阿伊努族人生活範圍遍及日本全國而不限於北海道為前提，基於全國觀點推動阿伊努族適用措施。

第四條 任何人均不得對阿伊努族人,以其為阿伊努族之理由而有歧視、侵害其權利、利益之行為。

(國家及地方自治團體之責任義務)

第五條 國家及地方自治團體負有責任及義務依循前二條所定之基本理念,擬定及實際執行阿伊努族適用措施。

2 國家及地方自治團體須努力採行培養阿伊努族文化傳承者之適當措施。

3 國家及地方自治團體須透過教育活動、宣傳活動等活動,增進國民對阿伊努族之了解。

4 國家須努力推動有助振興阿伊努族文化等作為之調查研究,同時致力採行提供必要建言等措施,以推動由地方自治團體實際執行之阿伊努族適用措施。

(國民之努力)

第六條 國民應努力協助實現阿伊努族人能夠本著民族自豪感生活,同時讓阿伊努族人之自豪感受到尊重之社會。

　　第二章　基本方針等事項

(基本方針)

第七條 政府須制定綜合且有效推動阿伊努族適用措施所需之基本方針(以下稱「基本方針」)。

2 基本方針應制定下列事項:

　一 阿伊努族適用措施之意義及目標事項

　二 政府應實際執行之阿伊努族適用措施之基本方針

　三 民族共生象徵空間組成設施之管理基本事項

　四 第十條第一項所定推動阿伊努族適用措施地區計畫,獲得同條第九項認定之基本事項。

　五 前揭各款規定事項除外,推動阿伊努族適用措施所需之必要事項。

3 內閣總理大臣須要求內閣會議決定通過阿伊努族政策推動總部擬定之基本方針草案。

4 內閣總理大臣如於前項規定之內閣會議作出決定,須即刻公布基本方針。

5 政府須於情勢變化而有必要時,變更基本方針。

6 第三項及第四項規定,於變更基本方針時準用之。

(都道府縣方針)

第八條 都道府縣知事應根據基本方針,努力制定於其都道府縣區域內推動阿伊努族適用措施所需之方針(以下於本條及第十條簡稱「都道府縣方針」)。

2 都道府縣方針應約略制定下列事項:

　一 阿伊努族適用措施之目標事項

　二 該都道府縣應實際執行之阿伊努族適用措施之方針

　三 前二款規定事項除外,推動阿伊努族適用措施所需之必要事項。

3 都道府縣知事擬於都道府縣方針內,制定與其他地方自治團體有關係之事項時,須事先聽取該地方自治團體首長對該事項之意見。

4 都道府縣知事如已制定都道府縣方針,除努力即刻公布該方針外,亦須即刻通知相關市町村長。

5 前二項規定,於變更都道府縣方針時準用之。

　　第三章　民族共生象徵空間組成設施管理措施

第九條 國土交通大臣及文部科學大臣已依第二十條第一項規定為指定時,應委託該獲指定人(於次項簡稱「獲指定法人」)管理民族共生象徵空間組成設施。

2 依前項規定受託管理設施之獲指定法人,為支應其受託執行之民族共生象徵空間組成設施管理所需費用,得收取民族共生象徵空間組成設施之入場門票費等費用(於第二十二條第二項簡稱「入場門票費等費用」)。

3 除前項規定事項除外,執行第一項規定委託之必要事項由內閣法規命令定之。

　　第四章　推動阿伊努族適用措施地區計畫之認定等事項

(推動阿伊努族適用措施地區計畫之認定)

第十條 市町村得單獨或共同根據基本方針（轄區涵蓋該市町村之都道府縣知事已制定都道府縣方針時，則為市町村得根據基本方針同時審酌該都道府縣方針），依內閣府法規命令，擬定在該市町村區域內推動阿伊努族適用措施所需之計畫（以下簡稱「推動阿伊努族適用措施地區計畫」），再向內閣總理大臣申請認定。

2 推動阿伊努族適用措施地區計畫應記載下列事項：
　一 阿伊努族適用措施地區計畫之目標
　二 下列推動阿伊努族適用措施之必要事業相關事項：
　　Ａ 有助保存或傳承阿伊努族文化之事業
　　Ｂ 有助促進民眾了解阿伊努族傳統等之事業
　　Ｃ 有助振興觀光等振興產業之事業
　　Ｄ 有助促進地區內或地區之間交流或國際交流之事業
　　Ｅ 其他由內閣府法規命令規定之事業
　三 計畫期間
　四 其他由內閣府法規命令規定之事項

3 市町村欲擬定推動阿伊努族適用措施地區計畫時，須聽取該計畫中擬記載之前項第二款規定事業實際執行人之意見。

4 第二項第二款（不含第Ｄ目）所定事業之事項中，得記載於國有林地（指國有林地管理經營法（一九五一年（昭和二十六年）法律第二百四十六號）第二條第一項規定之國有林地，於第十六條第一項亦同）採集供舉行阿伊努族傳承之儀等振興阿伊努族文化等作為利用之林業產物。

5 除前項規定事項外，第二項第二款（不含第Ｄ目）規定事業之事項中，得記載為保存或傳承阿伊努族傳承之儀式或漁法（以下於本項簡稱「儀式等做法」）、或者推廣及宣導教育儀式等做法之知識，得於內陸水域（指漁業法（一九四九年（昭和二十四年）法律第二百六十七號）第六十條第五項第五款規定之內陸水域）從事捕撈供上述目的使用鮭魚之事業（以下於本條及第十七條簡稱「內陸水域鮭魚捕撈事業」）事項。此時應以內陸水域鮭魚捕撈事業為單位，記載各內陸水域鮭魚捕撈事業之實際執行區域。

6 除前二項規定事項外，第二項第二款（以第Ｃ目相關部分為限）規定事業之事項中，得記載使用包含該市町村之地區名稱或簡稱在內之商標、或者拓展預期將使用該商標之商品或服務需求之事業（以下於本項及第十八條簡稱「拓展商品等需求之事業」）事項。此時應以拓展商品等需求之事業為單位，記載各該商品等需求事業之目標及實際執行期間。

7 擬實際執行第二項第二款第Ａ目至第Ｅ目當中任一事業者，得向該市町村提議擬定推動阿伊努族適用措施地區計畫。此時，提議人須根據基本方針，擬定並出示與該提議相關之推動阿伊努族適用措施地區計畫草案。

8 受理前項規定提議之市町村須即刻通知該提議人，其是否將依提議擬定推動愛奴執行措施地區計畫。此時，該市町村如不擬定推動阿伊努族適用措施之地區計畫，須明示其理由。

9 內閣總理大臣接獲依第一項規定提出之認定申請時，如判定該推動阿伊努族適用措施地區計畫符合下列基準，應予認定該計畫：
　一 符合基本方針。
　二 一般認為實際執行該推動阿伊努族適用措施之地區計畫，將對推動該地區之阿伊努族適用措施相當有貢獻。
　三 該計畫可望順利確實際執行。

10 內閣總理大臣作成前項認定之際，得於其判定為必要時，請求阿伊努族政策推動總部提供意見。

11 內閣總理大臣擬作成第九項之認定時，須通知擬定該推動阿伊努族適用措施之地區計畫且申請認定之市町村所屬都道府縣知事。此時，都道府縣知事如已制定都道府縣方針，得向內閣總理大臣表明其對第九項認定之意見。

12推動阿伊努族適用措施地區計畫如已記載特定事項相關事項（指第四項至第六項當中任一規定事項，以下亦同），內閣總理大臣擬作成第九項之認定時，須取得該特定事項相關事項之相關中央行政機關首長（以下稱「相關中央行政機關首長」）對該特定事項相關事項之同意。

13推動阿伊努族適用措施地區計畫如已記載內陸水域鮭魚捕撈事業之事項，內閣總理大臣擬作成第九項之認定時，須聽取擬定該推動阿伊努族適用措施地區計畫且申請認定之市町村（該計畫如由市町村共同擬定時，係以轄區涵蓋該內陸水域鮭魚捕撈事業實際執行區域之市町村為限）所屬都道府縣知事之同意。

14內閣總理大臣作成第九項之認定時，須即刻公告其內容。

（獲認定之推動阿伊努族適用措施地區計畫之變更）

第十一條 市町村擬變更（不含內閣府法規命令規定之輕微變更）已獲前條第九項認定之推動阿伊努族適用措施地區計畫時，須取得內閣總理大臣之認定。

2 前條第三項至第十四項之規定，於變更已獲同條第九項認定之推動阿伊努族適用措施地區計畫時準用之。

（要求提供報告）

第十二條 內閣總理大臣得要求獲第十條第九項認定（含前條第一項變更之認定）之市町村（以下稱「認定市町村」），報告其獲第十條第九項認定之推動阿伊努族適用措施地區計畫（已獲前條第一項變更之認定時，則為變更後計畫，以下稱「獲認定之推動阿伊努族適用措施地區計畫」）實際執行情形。

2 獲認定之推動阿伊努族適用措施地區計畫如記載特定事業相關事項，中央相關行政機關首長得要求該獲認定之市町村報告該特定事業相關事項實際執行情形。

（要求採行措施）

第十三條 為使獲認定之推動阿伊努族適用措施地區計畫正確適當實際執行，內閣總理大臣得於其判定為必要時，要求獲認定之市町村採行實際執行該獲認定之推動阿伊努族適用措施之地區計畫所需措施。

2 獲認定之推動阿伊努族適用措施地區計畫如記載特定事業相關事項，為使該特定事業相關事項正確適當實際執行，中央相關行政機關首長得於其判定為必要時，要求該獲認定之市町村採行實際執行該特定事業相關事項之必要措施。

（撤銷認定）

第十四條 內閣總理大臣如判定獲認定之推動阿伊努族適用措施地區計畫不符合第十條第九項各款規定之一，得撤銷該認定。此時，獲認定之推動阿伊努族適用措施地區計畫如有記載特定事業相關事項，內閣總理大臣須預先通知中央相關行政機關首長。

2 接獲前項通知之中央相關行政機關，得向內閣總理大臣陳述其對依同項規定撤銷認定之意見。

3 除前項規定情形外，獲認定之推動阿伊努族適用措施地區計畫如有記載特定事業相關事項，中央相關行政機關亦得向內閣總理大臣陳述其對依第一項規定撤銷認定之意見。

4 第十條第十四項規定，於依第一項規定撤銷認定時準用之。

第五章　獲認定之推動阿伊努族適用措施地區計畫所定事業適用之特別措施（第十五條—第十九條）

（交付金之發放等事項）

第十五條 國家得依內閣府法規命令規定，於預算範圍內發放交付金予獲認定之市町村，支應其實際執行獲認定之推動阿伊努族適用措施地區計畫所定事業（以第十條第二項第二款規定事業為限）之所需經費。

2 對以前項交付金支應實施之事業所需費用，不予依其他法令規定由國家負擔或發放補助或交付金，不受其他法令規定之拘束。

3 除前二項規定事項外，第一項交付金發放之必要事項，以內閣府法規命令定之。

（於國有林地內設定共用林地）

第十六條 農林水產大臣判定為使土地獲得高度利用，有必要調節國有林地經營與獲認定之市町村（限於擬定獲認定之推動阿伊努族適用措施之地區計畫之市町村，且該計畫已記載第十條第四項規定事項，以下於本項亦同）居民使用時，得依契約讓該獲認定之市町村之居民或於該獲認定之市町村內一定區域內擁有住所者取得權利，使其有權共同使用第十條第四項規定記載事項相關之國有林地，於該國有林地採集舉行阿伊努族傳承儀式等振興阿伊努族文化等作為所需利用之林業產物。

2 前項契約視同國有林地經營管理法第十八條第三項規定之共用林地契約，適用該法第五章（不含第十八條第一項及第二項）規定。適用時，第十八條第三項本文之「第一項」改為「實現尊重阿伊努族人自豪感之社會所需適用措施推動法（二〇一九年（平成三十一年）法律第十六號）第十六條第一項」，「市町村」改為「獲認定之市町村（指國有林地經營管理法第十二條第一項規定之獲認定之市町村，以下亦同）」，同項但書及同法第十九條第五款、第二十二條第一項及第二十四條之「市町村」改為「獲認定之市町村」，同法第十八條第四項之「第一項」及同法第二十一條之二之「第十八條」改為「實現尊重阿伊努族人自豪感之社會所需適用措施推動法第十六條第一項」。

（漁業法及水產資源保護法規定許可適用上之注意、處理）

第十七條 為實際執行獲認定之推動阿伊努族適用措施地區計畫記載之內陸水域鮭魚捕撈事業，需取得漁業法第一百十九條第一項、第二項或水產資源保護法（一九五一年（昭和二十六年）法律第三百十三號）第四條第一項所定農林水產省法規命令或都道府縣規則規定之許可時，農林水產大臣或都道府縣知事如接獲許可之申請，應予妥適注意、處理，使該內陸水域鮭魚捕撈事業順利實際執行。

（商標法之特例）

第十八條 獲認定之推動阿伊努族適用措施地區計畫記載之拓展商品等需求之事業，限於該拓展商品等需求之事業實際執行期間（於次項及第三項簡稱「實際執行期間」）內，適用次項至第六項規定。

2 獲認定之推動阿伊努族適用措施地區計畫記載拓展商品等需求之事業，其相關商品或服務之相關地區團體商標之商標註冊（商標法（一九五九（昭和三十四年）法律第一百二十七號）第七條之二第一項所定地區團體商標之商標註冊，以下於本項及次項亦同）申請案，應繳納商標法第四十條第一項、第二項、第四十一條之二第一項或第七項註冊費者如為該商品或服務相關之拓展商品等需求之事業實際執行主體，特許廳廳長得依內閣法規命令減收或免收該註冊費（以於實際執行期間內取得地區團體商標之商標註冊申請案，或者於實際執行期間內辦理地區團體商標之延展註冊申請案為限）。此時適用商標法第十八條第二項及第二十三條第一項與第二項規定，該規定之「如已繳納」改為「如已繳納或已免收」。

3 獲認定之推動阿伊努族適用措施地區計畫記載之拓展商品等需求之事業，其相關商品或服務相關地區團體商標之商標註冊申請案，擬取得該地區團體商標之商標註冊者如為該商品或服務相關之拓展商品等需求之事業實際執行主體，特許廳廳長得依內閣法規命令減收或免收商依標法第七十六條第二項規定應繳納之商標註冊申請手續費（以於實際執行期間內申請商標註冊之申請案為限）。

4 商標權如屬共有，其共有人包含依本條第二項規定享有註冊費減收或免收（以下於本項簡稱「減免」）者，且共有持分確定時，商標法第四十條第一項、第二項、第四十一條之二第一項或第七項之註冊費，係以前揭規定之註冊費金額（共有人如屬獲減免者，則為其獲減免後之金額）乘以各共有人持分比率再加總算出之金額為準，繳費義務人須繳納此金額，不受商標法第四十條第一項、第二項、第四十一條之二第一項或第七項規定拘束。

5 因申請商標註冊而產生之權利如屬共有，其共有人包含依第三項規定享有商標註冊申請手續費減收或免收（以下於本項簡稱「減免」）者，且共有持分確定時，該共有人申請註冊自身商標而產生之權利，依商標法第七十六條第二項規定應繳納之商標註冊申請手續費，係以前揭規定之商標註冊申請手續費金額（共有人如屬獲減免者，則為其獲減免後之金額）乘以各共有人持分比率再加總算出之金額為準，繳費義務人須繳納此金額，不受商標法第七十六條第二項規定拘束。

6 依前二項規定算出之註冊費或手續費金額，如有未滿 10 日圓之尾數，即無條件捨去該尾數。

（地方債適用上之注意、處理）

第十九條 獲認定之市町村發行地方債，以支應其根據獲認定之推動阿伊努族適用措施地區計畫實際執行事業需要之經費，國家應予特別注意、處理，使該獲認定之市町村得於其財政狀況允許範圍內發行地方債，以及在國家之資金狀態允許範圍內憑財政融資資金買入該市町村發行之地方債。

第六章 獲指定法人

（指定等作為）

第二十條 國土交通大臣及文部科學大臣得依申請指定經判定有能力正確適當且確實執行次條規定業務，且其設立目的為從事振興阿伊努族文化等作為之一般社團法人或一般財團法人，執行次條規定業務；全國獲指定之法人團體數量，以一為限。

2 前項申請者如有下列各款情形之一，國土交通大臣及文部科學大臣不得為前項進行指定：

一 遭依本法處罰金刑，且自執行完畢之日或不再受執行之日起未逾兩年。

二 遭依第三十條第一項規定撤銷指定，且自撤銷之日起未逾兩年。

三 其幹部當中有人符合下列情形之一：

A 遭處禁錮以上刑罰或依本法規定遭處罰金刑，且自執行完畢之日或不再受執行之日起未逾兩年。

B 遭依第二十七條第二項規定命令解任，且自解任之日起未逾兩年。

3 國土交通大臣及文部科學大臣已依第一項規定作成指定時，須公告獲指定者（以下稱「獲指定法人」）之名稱、地址及其辦公室所在地。

4 獲指定法人擬變更其名稱、地址及其辦公室所在地時，須預先向國土交通大臣及文部科學大臣申報。

5 國土交通大臣及文部科學大臣接獲前項規定之申報時，須公告該申報相關事項。

（業務）

第二十一條 指定法人應執行下列業務：

一 接受第九條第一項規定委託，管理民族共生象徵空間組成設施。

二 培養阿伊努族文化傳承者等從事振興阿伊努族文化之業務。

三 從事阿伊努族傳統等之宣傳活動等阿伊努族傳統等知識之推廣及宣導教育。

四 從事有助振興阿伊努族文化等作為之調查研究。

五 對從事振興阿伊努族文化、推廣及宣導教育阿伊努族傳統等知識或有助振興阿伊努族文化等作為之調查研究者，提供建言、獎助等支援。

六 從事前揭各款業務之外，其他為振興阿伊努族文化等作為之必要業務。

（民族共生象徵空間組成設施管理業務規程）

第二十二條 獲指定法人須訂定前條第一款所列業務（以下稱「民族共生象徵空間組成設施管理業務」）相關規程（以下稱「民族共生象徵空間組成設施管理業務規程」），並取得國土交通大臣及文部科學大臣認可，擬變更該規程時亦同。

2 民族共生象徵空間組成設施管理業務規程須規定民族共生象徵空間組成設施管理業務之執行方式、民族共生象徵空間組成設施之入場門票費等費用等國土交通省法規命令與文部科學省法規命令規定事項。

3 國土交通大臣及文部科學大臣如判定已依第一項獲認可之民族共生象徵空間組成設施管理業務規程，對正確適當且確實實際執行民族共生象徵空間組成設施管理業務已屬不當時，得命令獲指定法人應變更該規程。

（事業計畫等事項）

第二十三條 獲指定法人須於每事業年度擬定事業計畫書及收支預算書，並在該事業年度開始前（如屬獲第二十條第一項所定指定之日所屬事業年度，係於獲指定後即刻）取得國土交通大臣及文部科

學大臣認可，擬變更該規程時亦同。

2　獲指定法人須於每事業年度擬定事業報告書及收支決算書，於該事業年度結束後三個月內提交國土交通大臣及文部科學大臣。

（區分會計）

第二十四條　獲指定法人須依國土交通省法規命令與文部科學省法規命令規定，將民族共生象徵空間組成設施管理業務相關之會計，與民族共生象徵空間組成設施管理業務以外業務相關之會計區分再予整理。

（國家派遣職員之特例）

第二十五條　國家公務員法（一九四七年（昭和二十二年）法律第一百二十號）第一百零六條之二第三項規定之合併計算退休金之法人，包含獲指定法人。

2　國家派遣職員（指屬於國家公務員法第二條規定一般職之職員，因配合任命權人或受任命權人委任者之請求，成為獲指定法人之職員（毋須擔任全職職務者除外，且以從事第二十一條規定業務者為限，以下於本項亦同）而離職，後續成為該獲指定法人之職員，並持續以該獲指定法人之職員身分在職之情形下，該獲指定法人之職員，於次項亦同）適用國家公務員退休金法（一九五三年（昭和二十八年）法律第一百八十二號）第七條之二及第二十條第三項規定時，視同該法第七條之二第一項規定之公庫等職員。

3　獲指定法人或國家派遣職員適用國家公務員互助會法（一九五八年（昭和三十三年）法律第一百二十八號）第一百二十四條之二規定時，分別適同同條第一項規定之公庫等或公庫等職員。

（職員派遣等作為適用上之注意、處理）

第二十六條　除前條規定事項外，為使獲指定法人正確適當且確實貫徹第二十一條所定業務，國家應於其判定為必要時努力派遣職員，或者對其判定為適當之人力支援給予必要之注意、處理。

（幹部之選任及解任）

第二十七條　獲指定法人選任及解任其從事第二十一條規定業務之幹部須獲國土交通大臣及文部科學大臣認可，始生效力。

2　獲指定法人從事第二十一條規定業務之幹部，有違反本法或本法規定之命令、依本法或命令作成之處分或民族共生象徵空間組成設施管理業務規程之行為、有與第二十一條規定業務有關之顯著不當行為、或獲指定法人因該幹部在任而有第二十條第二項第三款規定情形時，國土交通大臣及文部科學大臣得令命該獲指定法人解任該幹部。

（要求提交報告及到場檢查）

第二十八條　國土交通大臣及文部科學大臣得於本法施行之必要限度內，要求獲指定法人提交其業務相關報告，或者指派職員前往該獲指定法人之辦公室，檢查其業務狀況或帳冊、文件等物品或詢問其相關人等。

2　依前項規定到場檢查之職員須攜帶顯示其身分之證明文件，於相關人等提出請求時出示該證明文件。

3　依第一項規定到場檢查之權限，不得解釋允許實施犯罪搜索之權限。

（監督命令）

第二十九條　為施行本法，國土交通大臣及文部科學大臣得於其判定為必要時，向獲指定法人下達與第二一條規定業務有關之監督必要命令。

（撤銷指定等處分）

第三十條　獲指定法人如有下列各款情形之一，國土交通大臣及文部科學大臣得撤銷依第二十條第一項規定所為之指定：

一　違反本法或本法規定之命令。

二　已成為恐有無法正確適當確實執行第二十一條規定業務之虞者。

三　執行民族共生象徵空間組成設施管理業務，未遵循已依第二十二條第一項規定獲認可之民族共

生象徵空間組成設施管理業務規程。

四 已違反第二十二條第三項、第二十七條第二項或前條規定之命令。

五 無正當理由而未執行民族共生象徵空間組成設施管理業務。

2 國土交通大臣及文部科學大臣依前項規定撤銷第二十條第一項規定之指定時，須公告之。

（撤銷指定時之過渡措施）

第三十一條 國土交通大臣及文部科學大臣如依前條第一項規定撤銷第二十條第一項規定之指定，於
撤銷後重新指定新獲指定法人時，遭撤銷指定之原獲指定法人之民族共生象徵空間組成設施管理業
務相關財產，將歸屬新獲指定法人。

2 除前項規定事項外，依前條第一項規定撤銷第二十條第一項規定之指定時，民族共生象徵空間組成
設施管理業務相關財產之管理或其他所需過渡措施（含罰則相關之過渡措施），得於一般判斷為合
理之必要範圍內，以內閣法規命令定之。

第七章 阿伊努族政策推動總部

（設置）

第三十二條 為綜合有效推動阿伊努族適用措施，於內閣設阿伊努族政策推動總部（以下稱「總部」）。

（所掌事務）

第三十三條 總部職掌下列事務：

一 擬定基本方針草案。

二 推動實際執行基本方針。

三 除前二款所列事務外，與規劃及研擬以及綜合調節阿伊努族適用措施之重要事項相關之事務。

（組織組成）

第三十四條 總部係由阿伊努族政策推動總部長、阿伊努族政策推動副總部長及阿伊努族政策推動總
部成員組成。

（阿伊努族政策推動總部長）

第三十五條 總部之首長為阿伊努族政策推動總部長（以下稱「總部長」），由內閣官房長官擔任。

2 總部長統籌總部之事務，並指揮監督總部之職員。

（阿伊努族政策推動副總部長）

第三十六條 總部置阿伊努族政策推動副總部長（於次項及次條第二項簡稱「副總部長」），由內閣成
員擔任。

2 副總部長輔佐總部長之職務。

（阿伊努族政策推動總部成員）

第三十七條 總部置阿伊努族政策推動總部成員（於次項簡稱「總部成員」）。

2 總部成員由下列人員（不含第一款至第八款所列人員當中，擔任副總部長之人員）擔任：

一 法務大臣

二 外務大臣

三 文部科學大臣

四 厚生勞動大臣

五 農林水產大臣

六 經濟產業大臣

七 國土交通大臣

八 環境大臣

九 除前揭各款所列人員外，由內閣總理大臣從擔任總部長及副總部長以外之內閣成員中，指定其
判定為貫徹執行總部所掌事務之特別必要人員。

（提交資料等協助）

第三十八條 總部為貫徹執行其所掌事務得於其判定為必要時，請求相關行政機關、地方自治團體、

獨立行政法人（指獨立行政法人通則法（一九九九年（平成十一年）法律第一百零三號）第二條第一項規定之獨立行政法人）及地方獨立行政法人（指地方獨立行政法人法（二〇〇三年（平成十五年）法律第一百十八號）第二條第一項規定之地方獨立行政法人）首長，以及特殊法人（指依法律直接設立之法人或依特別法律以特別設立行為設立之法人，且適用總務省設置法（一九九九年（平成十一年）法律第九十一號）第四條第一項第八款規定者）之代表人，提交資料、表明意見、說明意見或其他必要配合行為。

2 總部為貫徹執行其所掌事務而認為有特別必要時，得委託前項規定以外人員提供必要協助。

（事務）

第三十九條 總部之事務由內閣官房處理，且由內閣官房副長官補銜命掌理之。

（主管大臣）

第四十條 總部相關事項依內閣法（一九四七年（昭和二十二年）法律第五號）規定，由內閣總理大臣擔任主管大臣。

（授權訂定內閣法規命令）

第四十一條 除本法規定事項外，總部之必要事項由內閣法規命令定之。

第八章 雜則

（權限委任）

第四十二條 本法規定之國土交通大臣權限，得依國土交通省法規命令規定，將其中局部權限委任北海道開發局長。

2 第十六條規定之農林水產大臣權限，得依農林水產省法規命令規定，將其中局部權限委任森林管理局長。

3 依前項規定委任森林管理局長之權限，得依農林水產省法規命令規定，再委任森林管理署長。

（授權訂定法規命令）

第四十三條 除本法規定事項外，為實際執行本法之必要事項由法規命令定之。

（罰則）

第四十四條 未依第二十八條第一項規定提交報告或為虛偽不實之報告，又或拒絕、妨礙或規避同項規定之檢查，抑或對同項規定之提問不予陳述或為虛偽不實之陳述者，處以三十萬日圓以下罰金。

2 法人之代表人、法人或自然人之代理人、受僱人等員工，如有與該法人或自然人之業務有關且違反前項規定之行為，除處罰該行為人外，亦對該法人或自然人處同項之刑罰。

第四十五條 違反第二十九條規定命令者，處五十萬日圓以下罰鍰。

附則 節錄

（施行期日）

第一條 本法自公布之日起算未逾一個月範圍內，由內閣法規命令規定之日起施行。但附則第四條及第八條規定，自公布之日起施行。

（廢止振興阿伊努族文化及推廣與宣導教育阿伊努族傳統等知識之法律）

第二條 廢止振興阿伊努族文化及推廣與宣導教育阿伊努族傳統等知識法（一九九七年（平成九年）法律第五十二號）。

（配合振興阿伊努族文化及推廣與宣導教育阿伊努族傳統等知識法廢止之過渡措施）

第三條 於前條規定施行前已有之行為，仍適用舊法之罰則。

（準備行為）

第四條 擬依第二十條第一項規定獲指定者，得於本法施行前提出申請。

（授權訂定內閣法規命令）

第八條 除附則第三條及第四條規定事項外，本法施行之必要過渡措施由內閣法規命令定之。

（研議）

第九條 政府應於本法施行逾五年後，研議本法施行情形，且於認為必要時根據研議結果採行所需措

　施。

附則（二○一八年（平成三十年）十二月十四日法律第九十五號）節錄

（施行期日）

第一條 本法自公布之日起算未逾一個月範圍內，由內閣法規命令規定之日起施行。

附則（二○二一年（令和三年）五月十九日法律第三十六號）節錄

（施行期日）

第一條 本法自二○二一年（令和三年）九月一日起施行。

（罰則適用之過渡措施）

第五十九條 於本法施行前已有之行為，仍適用舊法之罰則。

附錄
研討會精彩相片錦集

2018 臺灣客語及少數族群語言復振國際研討會

研討會與會者全體大合照。

研討會與會講者及貴賓大合照。

客家委員會李永得（時任主委）與國立中央大學周景揚校長於研討會開場進行
致詞。

索勃學校協會主席 Ludmila Budar 女士與國立政治大學語言學研究所戴智偉副
教授兼所長進行國外經驗分享交流。

挪威薩米大學 Pigga Keskitalo 教授與北海道大學阿伊努‧原住民研究中心丹菊逸治副教授進行國外經驗分享交流。

向與會嘉賓介紹傳統文化。

邀請國際講者至桃園市復興區義盛國小觀摩原住民族族　原住民族族語教學課程後合
語教學課程。　影留念。

國際講者體驗傳統廟宇文化。　國際講者體驗傳統糕點。

2021 臺灣客語及少數族群語言政策國際研討會

與會嘉賓進行合照。

與會者全體大合照。

客家委員會楊長鎮主委與國立中央大學周景揚校長參與開幕並進行致詞。

專業客華語口譯老師於研討會現場進行雙向同步口譯。

與會者專注參與的神情。

紐西蘭毛利電視臺臺長 Shane Taurima 先生研討會連線畫面。

歐洲語言平等網絡秘書長 Davyth Hicks 博士研討會連線畫面。

威爾斯語言部門（Prosiect 2050）領導人 Jeremy Evas 博士研討會連線畫面。

國立中央大學客家學院周錦宏院長主持研討會場次。

國立中央大學客家學院王保鍵教授接受電視臺採訪。

客語及少數族
群語言政策

國家圖書館出版品預行編目（CIP）資料

客語及少數族群語言政策 / 周錦宏, 王保鍵, 蔡芬芳
主編. -- 初版. -- 高雄市：巨流圖書股份有限公司,
2022.09
　　面；　公分

ISBN 978-957-732-671-3（平裝）

1.CST: 客語 2.CST: 少數民族語言 3.CST: 語言政策
4.CST: 文集

802.507　　　　　　　　　　　　　　111013818

主　　　　編　周錦宏、王保鍵、蔡芬芳
責 任 編 輯　張如芷
封 面 設 計　曹淨雯

發 　行 　人　楊曉華
總 　編 　輯　蔡國彬

出　　　　版　巨流圖書股份有限公司
　　　　　　　802019 高雄市苓雅區五福一路 57 號 2 樓之 2
　　　　　　　電話：07-2265267
　　　　　　　傳真：07-2264697
　　　　　　　e-mail：chuliu@liwen.com.tw
　　　　　　　網址：http://www.liwen.com.tw

編 　輯 　部　100003 臺北市中正區重慶南路一段 57 號 10 樓之 12
　　　　　　　電話：02-29222396
　　　　　　　傳真：02-29220464
劃 撥 帳 號　01002323 巨流圖書股份有限公司
購 書 專 線　07-2265267 轉 236

法 律 顧 問　林廷隆律師
　　　　　　　電話：02-29658212

出 版 登 記 證　局版臺業字第 1045 號

ISBN / 978-957-732-671-3（平裝）
初版一刷・2022 年 9 月

定價：650 元